PARADISE REGAINED,

SAMSON AGONISTES,

AND THE
COMPLETE SHORTER POEMS

"He had auburn hair. His complexion exceeding fair—he was so fair that they called him *the Lady of Christ's College*" (see Aubrey, p. xxvii).

JOHN MILTON

PARADISE REGAINED,

SAMSON AGONISTES,

AND THE
COMPLETE SHORTER POEMS

Edited by William Kerrigan,
John Rumrich,
and Stephen M. Fallon

MODERN LIBRARY

NEW YORK

2012 Modern Library Paperback Edition

Published in the United States by Modern Library,
an imprint of The Random House Publishing Group,
a division of Random House, Inc., New York.

MODERN LIBRARY and the TORCHBEARER Design are registered
trademarks of Random House, Inc.

Originally published as part of *The Complete Poetry and Essential Prose of
John Milton* in hardcover in the United States by Modern Library,
an imprint of The Random House Publishing Group,
a division of Random House, Inc., in 2007.

Grateful acknowledgment is made to the Harry Ransom Humanities
Research Center, the University of Texas at Austin, for permission to
publish the following material: "Paradise regain'd: A poem. In IV books.
To which is added Samson Agonistes" PR 3563 1671; "Facsimile of the
manuscript of Milton's Minor poems, preserved in the library of Tr"
Aj M642 + B648w; and "Poems of Mr. John Milton: both English and
Latin, compos'd at several times" PR 3550 C23. Used by permission.

Illustration credits can be found on page ix.

ISBN 978-0-8129-8371-5
eBook ISBN 978-0-679-64558-0

www.modernlibrary.com

Contents

ENGLISH POEMS

BOOK OF MISCELLANEOUS POEMS

LATE MASTERPIECES

List of Illustrations

All illustrations are used with permission.

REFERENCES AND ABBREVIATIONS

Most of the many editions, books, and articles cited in the notes and headnotes can be found, alphabetized by author, in the "Works Cited" bibliography at the end of this volume. Where an author's surname is given without a date, it means that only one of this author's works has been cited in the edition. Where a name is coupled with a date, it means that at least two works by this author have been cited, or that there are two or more authors with this surname. Multiple entries in "Works Cited" are arranged chronologically.

We use these abbreviations for works by John Milton:

1637	*A Masque Presented at Ludlow Castle (1637)*.
1645	*Poems of Mr. John Milton* (1645).
1667	*Paradise Lost. A Poem Written in Ten Books* (1667).
1671	*Paradise Regained. A Poem in IV Books. To which is added Samson Agonistes* (1671).
1674	*Paradise Lost. A Poem in Twelve Books. The Second Edition . . .* (1674).
BMS	Bridgewater manuscript of *Masque*.
CMS	Manuscript of poems by Milton at Trinity College, Cambridge.
MLM	*The Complete Poetry and Essential Prose of John Milton,* ed. William Kerrigan, John Rumrich, and Stephen M. Fallon. Modern Library edition: New York, 2007.
Yale	*Complete Prose Works of John Milton,* ed. Don M. Wolfe et al. (8 vols., Yale Univ. Press, 1953–80).
Apology	*An Apology for Smectymnuus*
Areop	*Areopagitica*
CD	*Christian Doctrine*
Damon	*Epitaph for Damon*
DDD	*The Doctrine and Discipline of Divorce*
Eikon	*Eikonoklastes*
El	*Elegy*
Il Pens	*Il Penseroso*
L'All	*L'Allegro*
Lyc	*Lycidas*

Masque   *A Masque Presented at Ludlow Castle.*
Nat Ode   *Nativity Ode*
Of Ed   *Of Education*
Of Ref   *Of Reformation*
PL   *Paradise Lost*
PR   *Paradise Regained*
Pro   *Prolusion*
RCG   *The Reason of Church Government Urged Against Prelaty*
REW   *The Ready and Easy Way to Establish a Free Commonwealth*
SA   *Samson Agonistes*
Son   *Sonnet*
1Def   *Pro Populo Anglicano Defensio (First Defense of the English People)*
2Def   *Defensio Secunda (Second Defense of the English People)*
TKM   *The Tenure of Kings and Magistrates*

Citations to Milton's prose refer either to the *MLM* or, for passages not included in the Modern Library Milton, to the volume and page number of the Yale edition.

We use the following abbreviations for works by Shakespeare:

AWW   *All's Well That Ends Well*
ANT   *Antony and Cleopatra*
AYL   *As You Like It*
COR   *Coriolanus*
CYM   *Cymbeline*
HAM   *Hamlet*
1H4   *The First Part of King Henry the Fourth*
2H4   *The Second Part of King Henry the Fourth*
H5   *King Henry the Fifth*
LR   *King Lear*
R3   *King Richard the Third*
JC   *Julius Caesar*
LLL   *Love's Labor's Lost*
MAC   *Macbeth*
MM   *Measure for Measure*
MV   *The Merchant of Venice*
MND   *A Midsummer Night's Dream*
ADO   *Much Ado About Nothing*
OTH   *Othello*
PER   *Pericles*
LUC   *The Rape of Lucrece*
ROM   *Romeo and Juliet*
TMP   *The Tempest*
TIM   *Timon of Athens*

TRO *Troilus and Cressida*
TN *Twelfth Night*
VEN *Venus and Adonis*
WT *The Winter's Tale*

Unless otherwise indicated, we quote the Bible from the AV (King James Version), and use standard abbreviations when referring to its books; we sometimes cite *Geneva* (*The Geneva Bible,* 1588). Classical works are cited with standard abbreviations, such as, prominently, *Il.* and *Od.* for Homer's *Iliad* and *Odyssey, Ec.* and *Aen.* for Vergil's *Eclogues* and *Aeneid,* and *Her.* and *Met.* for Ovid's *Heroides* and *Metamorphoses.*

We use these abbreviations for works by the following authors:

Torquato Tasso, *GL Gerusalemme Liberata*
Ludovico Ariosto, *OF Orlando Furioso*
Edmund Spenser, *SC, FQ The Shepheardes Calender, The Faerie Queene*

A CHRONOLOGY OF MILTON'S LIFE

1608　(December 9) John Milton born on Bread Street in London.

1615　(November 24?) Brother Christopher born.

1620　(?) Enters St. Paul's School under the headmastership of Alexander Gill, Sr. Begins his friendship with Charles Diodati. Thomas Young tutors Milton at home.

1625　(February 12) Admitted to Christ's College, Cambridge.

1629　(March 26) Receives his B.A. degree. In December writes *On the Morning of Christ's Nativity.*

1632　(July 3) Receives his M.A. degree. Retires to his father's country house at Hammersmith for continued study.

1634　(September 29) *A Masque* performed at Ludlow Castle in Wales.

1635 or 36　Moves with his parents to Horton.

1637　*A Masque* published (dated 1637 but possibly published in 1638). Mother, Sara, dies in Horton on April 3. *Lycidas* written in November and published the next year.

1638–9　Milton tours the Continent from April or May 1638 to July or August 1639. Charles Diodati dies in August 1638.

1639　Settles in London, where he makes his living as a tutor.

1641　Earliest antiprelatical tracts—*Of Reformation* (May), *Of Prelatical Episcopacy* (June or July), *Animadversions on the Remonstrant's Defense* (July)—published.

1642　Publishes *The Reason of Church Government* (January or February) and *An Apology for Smectymnuus* (April). Marries Mary Powell in June or July. In August she leaves him and the Civil War begins.

1643　*The Doctrine and Discipline of Divorce* published in August.

1644　The second edition of *The Doctrine and Discipline of Divorce* published in February; *Of Education* in June; *The Judgment of Martin Bucer* in August; *Areopagitica* in November.

1645　Two more divorce pamphlets, *Tetrachordon* and *Colasterion,* published in March. Reconciles with Mary in July or August and moves to a larger house in Barbican in September.

1646　*Poems of Mr. John Milton* published in January, dated 1645. Daughter Anne born July 29.

1647   (March 13) On or about this date his father dies, leaving Milton the Bread Street house and a moderate estate. (September–October) Moves to a smaller house in High Holborn.

1648   (October 25) Daughter Mary born.

1649   (January 30) Charles I executed. *Eikon Basilike* published a week later. (February 13) *The Tenure of Kings and Magistrates* published, with a second edition in September. (March 15) Appointed Secretary for Foreign Tongues and ordered to answer *Eikon Basilike*. (May 11) Salmasius's *Defensio Regia* arrives in England. (October 6) *Eikonoklastes* published, answering *Eikon Basilike*.

1651   (February 24) The *Pro Populo Anglicano Defensio* (*A Defense of the English People*) published, answering Salmasius. (March 16) Son John born.

1652   (February or March) Total blindness descends. Daughter Deborah born May 2. Wife Mary dies on May 5. Son John dies in June.

1653   Duties as Secretary for Foreign Tongues are reduced by the addition of an assistant. Cromwell installed as Protector in December.

1654   *Defensio Secunda* (*Second Defense of the English People*) published in May.

1655   Milton is pensioned in April and though he continues to work for the Protectorate, devotes more time to private studies. *Pro Se Defensio* (*Defense of Himself*) published in August.

1656   (November 12) Marries Katharine Woodcock.

1657   (October 19) Daughter Katharine born.

1658   Probably begins work on *Paradise Lost*. Wife Katharine dies on February 3. Daughter Katharine dies on March 17. Cromwell dies in September, succeeded by his son Richard.

1659   *A Treatise of Civil Power* published in February. Richard Cromwell resigns in May. *Considerations Touching the Likeliest Means to Remove Hirelings out of the Church* published in August.

1660   *The Ready and Easy Way to Establish a Free Commonwealth* published in February, with a second edition in April. Charles II proclaimed king in May. Milton arrested and imprisoned between September and November and released in December.

1663   (February 24) Marries Elizabeth Minshull. Moves to a house in Artillery Walk, near Bunhill Fields.

1665   Around June, moves to Chalfont St. Giles to avoid the London plague.

1667   (October or November) *Paradise Lost* published as a poem in ten books.

1670   (around November 1) *History of Britain* published.

1671   *Paradise Regained* and *Samson Agonistes* published.

1672   *Artis Logicae* (*The Art of Logic*) published.

1673   *Of True Religion* published. An enlarged edition of *Poems* published, also including *Of Education*.

1674   *Epistolae Familiarum* (*Familiar Letters*) published, including his *Prolusions*. *Paradise Lost. A Poem in Twelve Books* published around July 1. Milton dies November 9 or 10 and is buried in St. Giles, Cripplegate.

MINUTES OF THE LIFE OF
MR. JOHN MILTON

John Aubrey

There are several seventeenth-century Milton biographers, including the anonymous biographer (most likely Milton's friend Cyriack Skinner), the Oxford historian Anthony à Wood, Milton's nephew and former student Edward Phillips, and the deist John Toland. One can find their works in Helen Darbishire's *The Early Lives of Milton* (1932), which attributes the anonymous biography to Edward Phillips's brother, John. We choose to print the biographical notes gathered by the antiquarian John Aubrey, which are notable for their author's extraordinary attention to personal details and efforts to verify his information by consulting those who knew Milton well, including the poet's widow, his brother, and some of his friends.

Aubrey's manuscript notes are loosely organized, partly chronologically and partly by the person interviewed. Our text follows the chronologically arranged version established by Andrew Clark (2:62–72). Those wanting to identify the sources of individual comments may consult Clark's edition or Darbishire's. We have reproduced Clark's interpolated headings, but we have in some places made different choices in our inclusions and exclusions. We have also modernized the text, changing punctuation and spelling. Aubrey's notes are peppered with ellipses, where he leaves blanks to be filled in should further information appear. Bracketed ellipses in our text indicate places where we omit material found in Clark's edition; otherwise the ellipses are Aubrey's.

[HIS PARENTAGE]

His mother was a Bradshaw.

Mr. John Milton was of an Oxfordshire family.

His grandfather, . . . , (a Roman Catholic), of Holton, in Oxfordshire, near Shotover.

His father was brought up in the University of Oxon, at Christ Church, and his grandfather disinherited him because he kept not to the Catholic religion (he found a Bible in English in his chamber). So thereupon he came to London, and became a scrivener (brought up by a friend of his; was not an apprentice) and got a plentiful estate by it, and left it off many years before he died. He was an ingenious man; delighted in music; composed many songs now in print, especially that of *Oriana.*[1]

I have been told that the father composed a song of fourscore parts for the Landgrave of Hesse, for which [his] highness sent a medal of gold, or a noble present. He died about 1647; buried in Cripplegate church, from his house in the Barbican.

[HIS BIRTH]

His son John was born in Bread Street, in London, at the Spread Eagle, which was his house (he had also in that street another house, the Rose, and other houses in other places).

He was born Anno Domini . . . the . . . day of . . . , about . . . o'clock in the . . .

(John Milton was born the 9th of December, 1608, *die Veneris,*[2] half an hour after 6 in the morning.)

[HIS PRECOCITY]

Anno Domini 1619, he was ten years old, as by his picture; and was then a poet.

[SCHOOL, COLLEGE, AND TRAVEL]

His schoolmaster then was a Puritan, in Essex, who cut his hair short.

He went to school to old Mr. Gill, at Paul's School. Went at his own charge only to Christ's College in Cambridge at fifteen, where he stayed eight years at least. Then he traveled into France and Italy (had Sir H. Wotton's commendatory letters). At Geneva he contracted a great friendship with the learned Dr. Diodati of Geneva (*vide* his poems). He was acquainted with Sir Henry Wotton, ambassador at Venice, who delighted in his company. He was several years <*Quaere,* how many? *Resp.,* two years> beyond sea, and returned to England just upon the breaking out of the civil wars.

From his brother, Christopher Milton: When he went to school, when he was very young, he studied very hard and sat up very late, commonly till twelve or

1. *Oriana:* Milton's father contributed a song, "Fair Orian," to *The Triumphs of Oriana* (1601), a volume of songs dedicated to Queen Elizabeth I.
2. *die Veneris:* Venus's Day, i.e., Friday.

one o'clock at night, and his father ordered the maid to sit up for him; and in those years (10) composed many copies of verses which might well become a riper age. And was a very hard student in the university, and performed all his exercises there with very good applause. His first tutor there was Mr. Chapell; from whom receiving some unkindness <whipped him>; he was afterwards (though it seemed contrary to the rules of the college) transferred to the tuition of one Mr. Tovell,[3] who died parson of Lutterworth.

He went to travel about the year 1638 and was abroad about a year's space, chiefly in Italy.

[RETURN TO ENGLAND]

Immediately after his return he took a lodging at Mr. Russell's, a tailor, in St. Bride's churchyard, and took into his tuition his [Milton's] sister's two sons, Edward and John Phillips, the first 10, the other 9 years of age; and in a year's time made them capable of interpreting a Latin author at sight, etc., and within three years they went through the best of Latin and Greek poets: Lucretius and Manilius <and with him the use of the globes and some rudiments of arithmetic and geometry> of the Latins; Hesiod, Aratus, Dionysius Afer, Oppian, Apollonii *Argonautica,* and Quintus Calaber. Cato, Varro, and Columella *De re rustica* were the very first authors they learned. As he was severe on the one hand, so he was most familiar and free in his conversation to those to whom most sour in his way of education. N.B. he made his nephews songsters, and sing, from the time they were with him.

[FIRST WIFE AND CHILDREN]

He married his first wife, Mary Powell of Fosthill,[4] at Shotover, in Oxonshire, Anno Domini . . . ; by whom he had four children. [He] hath two daughters living: Deborah was his amanuensis (he taught her Latin, and to read Greeke to him when he had lost his eyesight, which was anno Domini . . .).

[SEPARATION FROM HIS FIRST WIFE]

She went from him to her mother's at . . . in the king's quarters, near Oxford, anno Domini . . . ; and wrote the *Triplechord* about divorce.[5]

Two opinions do not well on the same bolster. She was a . . . Royalist, and went to her mother to the King's quarters, near Oxford. I have perhaps so much charity to her that she might not wrong his bed: but what man, especially con-

---

3. I.e., Nathaniel Tovey.
4. I.e., Forest Hill.
5. **Triplechord** *about divorce:* most likely *Tetrachordon* (four strings).

templative, would like to have a young wife environed and stormed by the sons of Mars, and those of the enemy party?

His first wife (Mrs. Powell, a Royalist) was brought up and lived where there was a great deal of company and merriment <dancing, etc.>. And when she came to live with her husband, at Mr. Russell's in St. Bride's churchyard, she found it very solitary; no company came to her; oftentimes heard his nephews beaten and cry. This life was irksome to her, and so she went to her parents at Fosthill. He sent for her, after some time; and I think his servant was evilly entreated: but as for manner of wronging his bed, I never heard the least suspicions; nor had he, of that, any jealousy.

[SECOND WIFE]

He had a middle wife, whose name was Katharine Woodcock. No child living by her.

[THIRD WIFE]

He married his second [sic] wife, Elizabeth Minshull, anno . . . (the year before the sickness): a gentle person, a peaceful and agreeable humor.

[HIS PUBLIC EMPLOYMENT]

He was Latin secretary to the Parliament.

[HIS BLINDNESS]

His sight began to fail him at first upon his writing against Salmasius, and before 'twas full completed one eye absolutely failed. Upon the writing of other books after that, his other eye decayed.

His eyesight was decaying about 20 years before his death. His father read without spectacles at 84. His mother had very weak eyes, and used spectacles presently after she was thirty years old.

[WRITINGS AFTER HIS BLINDNESS]

After he was blind he wrote these following books, viz.: *Paradise Lost, Paradise Regained, Grammar, Dictionary* (imperfect).

I heard that after he was blind that he was writing a Latin dictionary (in the hands of Moses Pitt). *Vidua affirmat*[6] she gave all his papers (among which this

---

6. **Vidua affirmat:** His widow maintains.

dictionary, imperfect) to his nephew, a sister's son, that he brought up, . . . Phillips, who lives near the Maypole in the Strand. She has a great many letters by her from learned men, his acquaintance, both of England and beyond the sea.

[HIS LATER RESIDENCES]

He lived in several places, e.g., Holborn near Kingsgate. He died in Bunhill, opposite the Artillery-garden wall.

[HIS DEATH AND BURIAL]

He died of the gout, struck in the 9th or 10th of November, 1674, as appears by his apothecary's book.

He lies buried in St. Giles Cripplegate, upper end of the chancel at the right hand, *vide* his gravestone. Memorandum: his stone is now removed, for about two years since (now 1681) the two steps to the communion table were raised. I guess John Speed[7] and he lie together.

[PERSONAL CHARACTERISTICS]

His harmonical and ingenious soul did lodge in a beautiful and well-proportioned body—*"In toto nusquam corpore menda fuit,"* Ovid.[8]

He was a spare man. He was scarce so tall as I am, [. . .] of middle stature.

He had auburn hair. His complexion exceeding fair—he was so fair that they called him *the Lady of Christ's College.* Oval face. His eye a dark gray.

He had a delicate tuneable voice, and had good skill. His father instructed him. He had an organ in his house; he played on that most.

Of a very cheerful humor. He would be cheerful even in his gout-fits, and sing.

He was very healthy and free from all diseases: seldom took any physic (only sometimes he took manna):[9] only towards his latter end he was visited with the gout, spring and fall.

He had a very good memory; but I believe that his excellent method of thinking and disposing did much to help his memory.

7. *John Speed:* author of *The History of Great Britain,* he is buried in St. Giles, as is John Foxe, author of *The Book of Martyrs* and *Acts and Monuments.*
8. 1 *Amores* 5.18: "There was not a blemish on her body."
9. **manna:** a mild laxative.

He pronounced the letter R <*littera canina*[10]> very hard (a certain sign of a satirical wit—from John Dryden.).

[PORTRAITS OF HIM]

Write his name in red letters on his pictures, with his widow, to preserve.[11]

His widow has his picture, drawn very well and like, when a Cambridge-scholar, which ought to be engraven; for the pictures before his books are not *at all* like him.

[HIS HABITS]

His exercise was chiefly walking.

He was an early riser <*scil.* at 4 a clock *mane*[12]>; yea, after he lost his sight. He had a man read to him. The first thing he read was the Hebrew bible, and that was at 4 h. *manè*, 1/2 h. plus. Then he contemplated.

At 7 his man came to him again, and then read to him again and wrote till dinner; the writing was as much as the reading. His (2nd) daughter, Deborah, could read to him in Latin, Italian and French, and Greek. [She] married in Dublin to one Mr. Clarke <sells silk, etc.>; very like her father. The other sister is Mary, more like her mother.

After dinner he used to walk 3 or 4 hours at a time (he always had a garden where he lived); went to bed about 9.

Temperate man, rarely drank between meals.

Extreme pleasant in his conversation and at dinner, supper, etc; but satirical.

[NOTES ABOUT SOME OF HIS WORKS]

From Mr. E. Phillips:—All the time of writing his *Paradise Lost,* his vein began at the autumnal equinoctial, and ceased at the vernal or thereabouts (I believe about May); and this was 4 or 5 years of his doing it. He began about 2 years before the king came in, and finished about three years after the king's restoration.[13]

In the 4th book of *Paradise Lost* there are about six verses of Satan's exclamation to the sun, which Mr. E. Phillips remembers about 15 or 16 years before ever

---

10. **littera canina:** dog letter, so called because making a continuous *r* sound resembles a dog's growl when threatening attack.
11. A note to himself.
12. **Scil. . . . manè:** It is well known (*scilicet*) . . . in the morning.
13. I.e., Milton composed his epic between 1658 and 1663.

his poem was thought of, which verses were intended for the beginning of a tragedy which he had designed, but was diverted from it by other business.

Whatever he wrote against monarchy was out of no animosity to the king's person, or out of any faction or interest, but out of a pure zeal to the liberty of mankind, which he thought would be greater under a free state than under a monarchial government. His being so conversant in Livy and the Roman authors, and the greatness he saw done by the Roman commonwealth, and the virtue of their great commanders induced him to.

From Mr. Abraham Hill:—Memorandum: his sharp writing against Alexander More, of Holland, upon a mistake, notwithstanding he had given him by the ambassador all satisfaction to the contrary: viz. that the book called *Clamor* was writ by Peter du Moulin. Well, that was all one; he having writ it,[14] it should go into the world; one of them was as bad as the other.

Memorandum:—Mr. Theodore Haak. Regiae Societatis Socius, hath translated half his *Paradise Lost* into High Dutch in such blank verse, which is very well liked of by Germanus Fabricius, Professor at Heidelberg, who sent to Mr. Haak a letter upon this translation: *"incredibile est quantum nos omnes affecerit gravitas styli, et copia lectissimorum verborum,"*[15] etc.—*vide* the letter.

Mr. John Milton made two admirable panegyrics, as to sublimity of wit, one on Oliver Cromwell, and the other on Thomas, Lord Fairfax, both which his nephew Mr. Phillips hath. But he hath hung back these two years, as to imparting copies to me for the collection of mine […]. Were they made in commendation of the devil, 'twere all one to me: 'tis the ὕψος[16] that I look after. I have been told that 'tis beyond Waller's or anything in that kind.[17][…]

[HIS ACQUAINTANCE]

He was visited much by learned [men]; more than he did desire.

He was mightily importuned to go into France and Italy. Foreigners came much to see him, and much admired him, and offered to him great preferments to come over to them; and the only inducement of several foreigners that came over into England was chiefly to see Oliver Protector and Mr. John Milton; and would see the house and chamber where he was born. He was much more admired abroad than at home.

14. Milton published his *Second Defense of the English People* (1654), with its attack on More as the author of the *Cry of the King's Blood* (*Regii Sanguinis Clamor*), even after learning that another had written the book.
15. "It is incredible how much the dignity of his style and his most excellent diction have affected all of us."
16. ὕψος: loftiness, altitude.
17. We omit here a catalog of Milton's works.

His familiar learned acquaintance were Mr. Andrew Marvell, Mr. Skinner, Dr. Pagett, M.D.

Mr. . . . [Cyriack] Skinner, who was his disciple.

John Dryden, Esq., Poet Laureate, who very much admires him, and went to him to have leave to put his *Paradise Lost* into a drama in rhyme. Mr. Milton received him civilly, and told him *he would give him leave to tag his verses.*[18]

His widow assures me that Mr. T. Hobbes was not one of his acquaintance, that her husband did not like him at all, but he would acknowledge him to be a man of great parts, and a learned man. Their interests and tenets did run counter to each other, *vide* Mr. Hobbes' *Behemoth*.

18. **tag his verses:** the ends of laces hanging from clothing could be "tagged," or fitted with metal ornaments. Tagging is here a metaphor for placing rhyming words at the ends of poetic lines, as Dryden did when he transformed the blank verse of *Paradise Lost* (1667) into the heroic couplets of his opera *The State of Innocence* (composed 1674; published 1677).

"Anno Domini 1619, he was ten years old, as by his picture; and was then a poet."

A Chronology of Milton's Poetry

Title of Poem	Composition	Earliest Print Publication
A Paraphrase on Psalm 114	1624	1645, 1673
Psalm 136	1624	1645, 1673
Apologus de Rustico et Hero	1624?*	1673
Carmina Elegiaca	1624?*	1876
Ignavus satrapam	1624?*	1876
Philosophus ad regem	1624?*	1645, 1673
Elegia prima	1626 (early April?)	1645, 1673
Elegia tertia, In Obitum Praesulis Wintoniensis	1626 ("Autumn 1626")	1645, 1673
Elegia secunda, In Obitum Praeconis Adademici	1626 ("Autumn 1626")	1645, 1673
In Obitum Praesulis Eliensis	1626 ("Autumn 1626")	1645, 1673
In Obitum Procancellarii Medici	1626 ("Autumn 1626")	1645, 1673
In Proditionem Bombardicam	1626?**	1645, 1673
In eandem	1626?** (post Mar. 1625 b/c ref to KJ I's death)	1645, 1673
In eandem	1626?**	1645, 1673
In eandem	1626?**	1645, 1673
In inventorem Bombardae	1626?**	1645, 1673
In quintum Novembris	1626 (Nov.)	1645, 1673
Elegia quarta	1627 (btwn Mar. 11 & Apr. 28)	1645, 1673
Elegia septima	1627 (May?)	1645, 1673 [1628—poem to Alexander Gill, Jr.?]
On the Death of a Fair Infant Dying of a Cough	1628 (Jan.–April)	1673
De Idea Platonica	1628 (June)? 1631?	1645, 1673
At a Vacation Exercise in the College	1628 (near July 4 or as late as Oct.)	1673
Elegia quinta	1629 (spring)	1645, 1673
Song. On May Morning	1629 (or 1630 or early 1631) (spring)	1645, 1673

TITLE OF POEM	COMPOSITION	EARLIEST PRINT PUBLICATION
Sonnet 1 ("O Nightingale")	1629 (or 1630) (spring)	1645, 1673
Sonnet 2 ("Enchanting lady")	1629 (Michaelmas term)?	1645, 1673
Sonnet 3 ("As on a rugged hill")	1629 (Michaelmas term)?	1645, 1673
Canzone ("Ladies and young men in love")	1629 (Michaelmas term)?	1645, 1673
Sonnet 4 ("Diodati—and I will tell you")	1629 (Michaelmas term)?	1645, 1673
Sonnet 5 ("Surely, my lady, your beautiful eyes")	1629 (Michaelmas term)?	1645, 1673
Sonnet 6 ("A young, quiet, naïve lover")	1629 (Michaelmas term)?	1645, 1673
The Fifth Ode of Horace. Book I.	1629 (late)? (Campbell: "wholly undatable")	1673
On the Morning of Christ's Nativity	1629 (Dec. 25)	1645, 1673
Elegia sexta	1629 (late Dec.)	1645, 1673
The Passion	1630? (Mar. 26, Good Friday)	1645, 1673
On Shakespeare	1630	1632, 1645, 1664, 1673
On the University Carrier	1631 (soon after Jan. 1)	1645, 1658, 1673
Another on the Same	1631 (soon after Jan. 1)	1640, 1657, 1645, 1658, 1673
Epitaph on the Marchioness of Winchester	1631 (Easter term)	1645, 1673
Naturam non pati senium	1631? (June 1631, per Shawcross; also 1628–32)	1645, 1673
L'Allegro	1631? (summer 1631, per Oras)	1645, 1673
Il Penseroso	1631? (summer 1631, per Oras)	1645, 1673
Ad Patrem	1631? (per Bush; Shawcross: 1638; also 1632–45)	1645, 1673
Sonnet 7 ("How soon hath time")	1631 (Dec.)	1645, 1673
Elegiac couplet on Ariosto	1632?	1931-38 ?
Arcades	1632 (late summer)	1645, 1673
At a Solemn Musick	1632?	1645, 1673
On Time	1632–33? (Shawcross: 1637)	1645, 1673
Upon the Circumcision	1633?	1645, 1673
A Masque Presented at Ludlow Castle	1634 (Sept.)	1637, 1645, 1673
Psalm 114	1634 (Nov.)	1645, 1673
Haec ego mente (appended to *Elegia septima*)	1635? (Carey: "must . . . be post-1628")	1645, 1673
Lycidas	1637 (Nov.)	1638, 1645, 1673
Fix here ye	1638 (Apr.?)	1876
Ad Salsillum poetam Romanum	1638 (Oct.–Nov.?)	1645, 1673

Title of Poem	Composition	Earliest Print Publication
Mansus	1638 (Dec.) or 1639 (Jan.–Feb.)	1645, 1673
Ad Leonoram Romae canentem	1639 (Feb.) or 1638 (Oct.–Nov.)	1645, 1673
Ad eandem ("The poet Torquato")	1639 (Feb.) or 1638 (Oct.–Nov.)	1645, 1673
Ad eandem ("Why, credulous Naples")	1639 (Feb.) or 1638 (Oct.–Nov.)	1645, 1673
Epitaphium Damonis	1639 (autumn)	1640, 1645, 1673
Translations from *Of Reformation*	1641 (Jan.–May)	1641 (May)
Translation from *Reason of Church-Government*	1641–42 (Aug. 4–Jan. 1)	1642 (late Jan. or Feb.)
Translations from *Apology against a Pamphlet*	1642 (Apr.)	1642 (Apr.)
Sonnet 8 ("Captain, or Colonel")	1642 (Nov.?)	1645, 1673
Sonnet 10 ("Daughter to that good Earle")	1642–45	1645, 1673
Sonnet 9 ("Lady, that in the prime")	1643–45	1645, 1673
Translation from *Areopagitica*'s title page	1644 (Nov.)	1644 (Nov. 23)
Translation from *Tetrachordon*	1645 (Feb.)	1645 (Mar. 4)
In Effigiei ejus Sculptorem	1645	1645, 1673
Sonnet 13 ("Harry, whose tuneful")	1646 (Feb. 9)	1648, 1673
Sonnet 12 ("I did but prompt the age")	1646	1673
On the New Forcers of Conscience	1646 (Shawcross: early 1647)	1673
Sonnet 14 ("When Faith and Love")	1646 (Dec.)	1673
Ad Joannem Rousium	1647 (Jan. 23)	1673
Sonnet 11 ("A book was writ of late")	1647?	1673
Psalms 80-88	1648 (Apr.)	1673
Sonnet 15 ("Fairfax, whose name in arms")	1648 (btwn July 8 & Aug. 17)	1694
Translation from *Tenure of Kings & Magistrates*	1649 (Feb.)	1649 (Feb. 13)
Translations from *History of Britain*	1649 (Feb.–Mar.)	1670
Verse from *Pro Populo Anglicano Defensio*	1650	1651 (Feb. 24)
Sonnet 16 ("Cromwell, our chief of men")	1652 (May)	1694
Sonnet 17 ("Vane, young in years")	1652 (June–July)	1662, 1694
Psalms 1-8	1653 (Aug. 8–14)	1673
Verses from *Defensio Secunda*	1653–54	1654 (May 30)
Sonnet 18 ("Avenge O Lord")	1655 (shortly after June 20)	1673
Sonnet 19 ("When I consider")	1655 (btwn July & Oct.)°	1673
Sonnet 20 ("Lawrence of virtuous")	1655 (Oct.–Nov.?)	1673
Sonnet 21 ("Cyriack, whose grandsire")	1655 (Oct.–Dec.?)	1673
Sonnet 22 ("Cyriack, this three years' day")	1655 (Oct.–Dec.?)	1694
Sonnet 23 ("Methought I saw")	1652? 1658?	1673

Title of Poem	Composition	Earliest Print Publication
Paradise Lost	1640s?, 1658–63? (per Aubrey)	1667 (Aug.?), 1674 (July 6?)
Paradise Regained	1665 (Aug.)–1670?	1671
Samson Agonistes	1660s?	1671

* = composed during Milton's school days   ** = evidently composed for academic celebrations of Guy Fawkes Day   ° = also dated as early as 1651 or 1652

A NOTE ON THE TEXT

Paradise Regained and *Samson Agonistes* were first printed in tandem. Although the book was licensed on July 2, 1670, and entered into the *Stationers' Register* on September 10, 1670, all known copies bear the date 1671. The book, postdated, was probably issued in 1670 (Knoppers xcviii–xcviv, 1). Its publication occurred about midway between the first edition (1667) and the second edition (1674) of *Paradise Lost*. The back of this haphazardly printed volume contains a list of errata for each poem and ten lines omitted (whether a late revision or a printing error, we have no way of knowing) from *Samson Agonistes*.

Both poems appear on the title page, but whereas one is a bit oversold, the other is distinctly undersold. *Paradise Regained* was the featured attraction, set in large letters at the top of the title page. The name of the brief epic, whatever else Milton may have had in mind, encouraged browsers in London bookstalls to believe, somewhat misleadingly, that this new work was a sequel to *Paradise Lost*. *Samson Agonistes*, set in smaller print at the bottom of the title page, is introduced a line earlier by the words "To which is added." The title page's treatment of *Samson* seems to a modern reader breathtakingly casual: this has to rank among the most consequential afterthoughts in English publishing.

Since there are no surviving manuscripts of *Paradise Regained* or *Samson Agonistes*, our text for these two poems derives primarily from their first edition. All subsequent printings took place after Milton's death in 1674. The second edition of 1680 introduced numerous variants, most of which reappeared in the third edition of 1688. It is a measure of the unreliability of the second and third editions that neither corrected the errors listed at the end of the first. In fact, the texts of *Paradise Regained* and *Samson Agonistes* were not emended in the manner specified by the 1671 printing until the variorum of Thomas Newton (1752; reissued 1753). The two poems continued to be published together in early editions, and the tradition persists to this day, as our own volume attests. Controversies about dating the composition of the works, especially the vexed case of *Samson Agonistes*, are discussed in our headnotes.

Texts for the main body of Milton's shorter poems, including those in Italian, Latin, and Greek, are based on *Poems of Mr. John Milton* (1645) and the revised and enlarged second edition of this book in 1673. We have also consulted

PARADISE
REGAIN'D.
A
POEM.

In IV *BOOKS*.

To which is added

SAMSON AGONISTES.

The Author

JOHN MILTON.

LONDON,

Printed by *J. M.* for *John Starkey* at the
Mitre in *Fleetstreet*, near *Temple-Bar*.
MDCLXXI.

the holograph drafts and transcriptions of those shorter poems found in the Cambridge Manuscript (also called the Trinity Manuscript). Unique problems with the texts of *A Masque* and "Lycidas" are considered in the headnotes to those works. In general, we have drawn on clarifying moments in the early printed versions and the manuscripts, when they exist, without feeling bound to the old editorial idea of a singular "copy text." The virtues of an eclectic approach to editing Milton have been ably set forth by John Creaser (1983, 1984).

Milton's shorter poems are organized in a manner unique to this edition. Numerous editors have tried to retain the order in which these poems appeared in Milton's 1645 *Poems,* finding a way to tip in works that first appeared in his 1673 *Poems,* translations found in his prose works, or pieces never published during his lifetime but discovered subsequently by scholars. Others try to present all the minor poems in their probable order of composition. The result in both cases is chaotic to the modern eye. Poems in different languages jostle against each other. Some works, particularly the shortest of the minor poems, seem to get lost in the mix, and even if all the poems in an edition have been numbered sequentially, remain difficult to locate without consulting a table of contents that is itself difficult to locate.

No doubt this teeming profusion is revealing. It shows that the young Milton did in fact move from language to language, genre to genre, turning the different aspects of his education into different expressions of his developing literary ambitions. But we think that little will be lost in the way of revelation by reconfiguring the minor poems, while something will be gained in the way of clarity and ease of use. We have therefore divided them into three groups. "English Poems," much the largest one, contains all the poems Milton wrote in English, including classical and biblical translations, with the exception of his sonnets. A second group, "English and Italian Sonnets," includes the poems entitled "Sonnets" and numbered in both the 1645 and 1673 editions. The sonnets group has the further justification that its poems should for some purposes be studied together, given their power and originality in the history of this important poetic form. A final category, "Latin and Greek Poems," contains all the poems written in those languages; the English prose translations accompanying these pieces are the work of Gordon Braden, and were commissioned for this edition. Within each section the works have been placed in their probable order of composition. "A Chronology of Milton's Poems," prepared by Stephen B. Dobranski, allows readers to determine at a glance the likely time frame for the composition of any poem printed in this edition. Our headnotes and annotations, first published in 2007, have been revised and updated for this printing.

We have sought to ease the journey of modern readers. Most of Milton's capitalization, italics, and contractions have been removed. Quotation marks came into vogue some years after the death of Milton, and do not appear in early manuscripts or editions of his works. We have added them. His spelling has been modernized and Americanized; "musick" becomes "music," and "vigour" becomes "vigor." But there are important exceptions to these preferences. Our efforts at modernization have been checked by a desire to preserve whenever possible the sound, rhythm, and texture of his poems. We have therefore left archaic words and some original spellings intact; "enow" does not become "enough," and "highth" does not become "height." In cases where Milton's contractions indicate that a syllable voiced in the modern pronunciation of a word is to be elided, as with "flow'ry" in l. 84 of "At a Vacation Exercise" or "Heav'nly" in l. 15 of "On the Morning of Christ's Nativity," we have left them alone. Sometimes the final *-ed* in words like "fixed" is not voiced, as in lines 70 and 141 of the *Nativity Ode*. Where *-ed* is a voiced syllable, as in l. 4 of "Il Penseroso," we have placed an accent mark slanting down from left to right.

Punctuation offers the most troubling questions for modernizers. For punctuation, or "pointing" as it was called in Milton's day, serves two purposes at least. It displays the logic of the syntax, aiding a reader in the basic chore of construing sense. But especially in a poetic text, and most especially in poetic texts of the seventeenth century, punctuation also indicates rhythmic pauses. It is generally assumed, perhaps without much evidence, that a semicolon points to a longer pause than a comma, a colon to a longer pause than a semicolon, and a period to the most pronounced pause of all. Milton's punctuation is difficult to update for modern readers in both of its functions. With regard to construing sense, his syntax does not come packaged in the modern unit of the sentence. His clauses twist and turn, sending out tendrils of sense both forwards and backwards. Linking verb with subject is sometimes a puzzling chore, as it is in reading Latin. His pronouns are often hard to track down to single antecedents. Perhaps, in some instances, ambiguity rather than clarity was the author's intention. On the rhythmic side, many of the commas and semicolons that look superfluous by modern standards could well indicate the sound-patterns of his verse. But in poetry, as in good prose, sound-patterns are, above and beyond their inherent beauty, meaning-patterns. Countless works of literary criticism have demonstrated that sound effects in literary language contribute to meaning, and we see no reason to doubt these results. Milton, moreover, is widely judged to be a master of this aspect of literary craftsmanship.

Given these concerns, we have sought within a general framework of modernization to respect the punctuation schemes developed by Milton and his publishers. We remove a number of commas. Some are changed to semicolons and periods for the sake of readability. But in places where marking the rhythm seems paramount, we reproduce either closely or entirely the pointing of the early texts.

The addition of quotation marks at times restrains the growth of ambiguity in a reader's mind, particularly in the case of "Lycidas," where the various speeches reported in the course of the poem could be punctuated differently than they have been in our text of the poem. Some readers find these multiplying uncertainties both needless and overvalued. Some prefer being suspended in the free-form possibilities of the original pointing. But whatever benefits may stem from preserving this feature of Milton's early texts are in our view outweighed by the crowning benefit of making this difficult author as readable as possible for modern students. Like all editions, ours is only a beginning. Old spelling texts with old-style punctuation are readily available, and should a reader become particularly fascinated with a specific passage or work, we strongly recommend that these versions be consulted.

ENGLISH POEMS

PSALM 114

The 1645 *Poems* informed its readers that "this and the following Psalm were done by the author at fifteen years old." They could well have been school exercises, as is usually assumed, but Milton's father's combination of faith and musical skill expressed itself in a keen appreciation for the Psalter. Milton Sr. in fact contributed six settings to Thomas Ravenscroft's *The Whole Book of Psalms* (1621). These translations are his son's earliest surviving English compositions.

When the blest seed of Terah's faithful son,
After long toil their liberty had won,
And passed from Pharian fields to Canaan land,
Led by the strength of the Almighty's hand,
5 Jehovah's wonders were in Israel shown,
His praise and glory was in Israel known.
That saw the troubled sea, and shivering fled,
And sought to hide his froth-becurlèd head
Low in the earth; Jordan's clear streams recoil,
10 As a faint host that hath received the foil.
The high, huge-bellied mountains skip like rams
Amongst their ewes, the little hills like lambs.
Why fled the ocean? And why skipped the mountains?
Why turnèd Jordan toward his crystal fountains?
15 Shake earth, and at the presence be aghast
Of him that ever was, and ay shall last,
That glassy floods from rugged rocks can crush,
And make soft rills from fiery flint-stones gush.

1. **faithful son:** Abraham.
3. **Pharian:** Egyptian.
10. **foil:** defeat.

PSALM 136

Let us with a gladsome mind
Praise the Lord, for he is kind,
    For his mercies ay endure,
    Ever faithful, ever sure.

5   Let us blaze his name abroad,
For of gods he is the God;
    For, &c.

O let us his praises tell,
10   Who doth the wrathful tyrants quell.
    For, &c.

Who with his miracles doth make
Amazèd heav'n and earth to shake.
15   For, &c.

Who by his wisdom did create
The painted heav'ns so full of state.
    For, &c.
20

Who did the solid earth ordain
To rise above the wat'ry plain.
    For, &c.

25 Who by his all-commanding might,
Did fill the new-made world with light.
    For, &c.

And caused the golden-tressèd sun,
30 All the day long his course to run.
    For, &c.

The hornèd moon to shine by night,
Amongst her spangled sisters bright.
35 For, &c.

---

10. **Who:** 1673. 1645 has *that* here and in lines 13, 17,
   21, and 25. In each case we follow 1673.

He with his thunder-clasping hand,
Smote the first-born of Egypt land.
    For, &c.

40

And in despite of Pharaoh fell,
He brought from thence his Israel.
    For, &c.

45   The ruddy waves he cleft in twain,
Of the Erythraean main.
    For, &c.

The floods stood still like walls of glass,
50   While the Hebrew bands did pass.
    For, &c.

But full soon they did devour
The tawny king with all his power.
55   For, &c.

His chosen people he did bless
In the wasteful wilderness.
    For, &c.

60

In bloody battle he brought down
Kings of prowess and renown.
    For, &c.

65   He foiled bold Seon and his host,
That ruled the Amorean coast.
    For, &c.

And large-limbed Og he did subdue,
70   With all his over-hardy crew.
    For, &c.

And to his servant Israel
He gave their land therein to dwell.
75   For, &c.

---

46. **Erythraean:** adjective from the Greek for "red," applied by Herodotus 1.180; 2.8, 158 to the Red Sea.
65. **Seon:** Sihon, King of the Amorites (Num. 21.21–32).
66. **Amorean:** Amorite.
69. **Og:** giant King of Bashan, slain by Moses (Num. 21.33–35).
73. **his servant Israel:** Jacob.

He hath with a piteous eye
Beheld us in our misery.
    For, &c.
80
And freed us from the slavery
Of the invading enemy.
    For, &c.

85   All living creatures he doth feed,
And with full hand supplies their need.
    For, &c.

Let us therefore warble forth
90   His mighty majesty and worth.
    For, &c.

That his mansion hath on high
Above the reach of mortal eye.
95   For his mercies ay endure,
    Ever faithful, ever sure.

ON THE DEATH OF A FAIR INFANT
DYING OF A COUGH

This work belongs to a group of English lyrics that first appeared in the 1673 *Poems*. Based on the testimony of Milton's nephew Edward Phillips (Darbishire 1932, 62), the subject of the poem has generally been thought to have been Anne Phillips (b. January 1626 and d. January 1628), Milton's niece, and the mother addressed in the last stanza his sister Anne Phillips. Carey argues against these identifications, primarily on the grounds that Milton was nineteen and could not have written the elegy, as he claims to have, *Anno aetatis 17* (at the age of seventeen). The alternative is that Milton, whether unconsciously or not, backdated the poem (LeComte 7–8). Others of Carey's arguments seem tendentious. He takes "Summer's chief honor if thou hadst outlasted/Bleak Winter's force that made thy blossom dry" to assert that the child did not outlive a single winter (and therefore could not have been little Anne Phillips, who lived two years), whereas in fact the lines declare that the child did not outlive the winter in which she contracted the cough "that made thy blossom dry," and are therefore consistent with the Anne Phillips hypothesis.

    In Stanza 5 the poem erupts with questions that always haunt tragic deaths.

Why did God permit this infant to die? "Could Heav'n for pity thee so strictly doom?" These painful questions open up the large subject of theodicy, the justification of God's ways to men, that will occupy the argumentative center of *Paradise Lost.* In this early lyric, perhaps his first original poem in English, Milton tries to lay doubts to rest by finding a providential scheme within which the infant's death can be seen as a divine attempt to bring Earth and Heaven closer together or improve the lot of mankind.

The poem ends with a prophecy that we take literally: "This if thou do he will an offspring give,/That till the world's last end shall make thy name to live." Hoping to make "offspring" metaphorical, modern editors often cite God's promise to the eunuchs in Isaiah 56.5: "Even unto them will I give . . . a name better than of sons and daughters: I will give them an everlasting name, that shall not be cut off." So Milton's "offspring" becomes salvation and eternal bliss, matters that render trivial all parental concern with earthly offspring. But Milton does not say that the fame of the offspring is eternal. Quite the opposite, he says that it will last until the end of the world. Recourse to Isaiah in interpreting "Fair Infant" probably does not occur before 1921 (Hughes et al. 2:135). Proponents clearly hope that the biblical passage can fend off the apparent sense of Milton's lines, which in turn is thought to suppose a Milton so fame-crazed that he would console a patient sister with the promise of another child with a glorious future. But that is precisely what he has done. Milton's sister was indeed pregnant at the time of the fair infant's death, and she gave birth to Elizabeth Phillips in April 1628.

～⁘～

ANNO AETATIS 17

I

O fairest flower no sooner blown but blasted,
Soft silken primrose fading timelessly,
Summer's chief honor if thou hadst outlasted
Bleak Winter's force that made thy blossom dry;
5   For he being amorous on that lovely dye
       That did thy cheek envermeil, thought to kiss
   But killed alas, and then bewailed his fatal bliss.

1–2. **O fairest . . . fading:** The opening echoes *The Passionate Pilgrim* 10.1–2: "Sweet rose, fair flower, untimely plucked, soon faded,/Plucked in the bud and faded in the spring!" This work was ascribed to Shakespeare in 1599 and 1640, but we now believe that Shakespeare wrote only five of its twenty sonnets. The author of the one echoed by Milton is unknown.

1. **blown:** bloomed.

2. **timelessly:** unseasonably, not in due time.

3. **chief honor:** that for which Summer would be honored.

5. **amorous on:** in love with.

6. **envermeil:** tinge with vermilion.

6–7. **thought to kiss/But killed:** Shakespeare also conjoins *kiss* and *kill* in *VEN* 1110 and *OTH* 5.2.356–57.

II

For since grim Aquilo his charioteer
By boist'rous rape th' Athenian damsel got,
10   He thought it touched his deity full near,
If likewise he some fair one wedded not,
Thereby to wipe away th' infamous blot
    Of long-uncoupled bed, and childless eld,
Which 'mongst the wanton gods a foul reproach was held.

III

15   So mounting up in icy-pearlèd car,
Through middle empire of the freezing air
He wandered long, till thee he spied from far;
There ended was his quest, there ceased his care.
Down he descended from his snow-soft chair,
20   But all unwares with his cold-kind embrace
Unhoused thy virgin soul from her fair biding place.

IV

Yet art thou not inglorious in thy fate;
For so Apollo, with unweeting hand
Whilom did slay his dearly-lovèd mate,
25   Young Hyacinth born on Eurotas' strand,
Young Hyacinth the pride of Spartan land;
    But then transformed him to a purple flower:
Alack that so to change thee Winter had no power.

8–9. In Ovid, Boreas, the north wind, also called
Aquilo, snatches away Orithyia, daughter of the
king of Athens (*Met.* 6.682–710). Milton makes
Aquilo into Winter's charioteer, and his *boist'rous
rape* into the incitement of Winter's lust.

13. **eld:** old age.

15. **icy-pearlèd car:** chariot decorated with hail-
stones.

16. **middle empire:** the middle of the three tradi-
tional regions of air.

19. **snow-soft chair:** another description of the
chariot of line 15, now seemingly cushioned
with snow.

20. **cold-kind embrace:** an embrace kind in its in-
tention but chilling in its consequences.

23–27. Apollo accidentally killed his beloved Hy-
acinthus with a discus and made a brightly col-
ored (*purpureus*) flower spring from his blood
(Ovid, *Met.* 10.162–216). At least one commenta-
tor (Servius; see Allen 49) blamed Boreas
(Aquilo) for the accident.

23. **unweeting:** a variant of *unwitting*.

25. **born . . . strand:** Hyacinthus was born in
Sparta, which is situated on the river Eurotas.

V

Yet can I not persuade me thou art dead
30   Or that thy corse corrupts in earth's dark womb,
Or that thy beauties lie in wormy bed,
Hid from the world in a low delvèd tomb;
Could Heav'n for pity thee so strictly doom?
    O no! For something in thy face did shine
35   Above mortality that showed thou wast divine.

VI

Resolve me then O soul most surely blest
(If so it be that thou these plaints dost hear),
Tell me bright spirit where'er thou hoverest,
Whether above that high first-moving sphere
40   Or in the Elysian fields (if such there were).
    O say me true if thou wert mortal wight,
And why from us so quickly thou didst take thy flight.

VII

Wert thou some star which from the ruined roof
Of shaked Olympus by mischance didst fall;
45   Which careful Jove in nature's true behoof
Took up, and in fit place did reinstall?
Or did of late Earth's sons besiege the wall
    Of sheeny Heav'n, and thou some goddess fled
Amongst us here below to hide thy nectared head?

36. **Resolve me:** Answer my questions, solve my problems (*OED* 3.11b).

39. **first-moving sphere:** the *primum mobile*, the outermost sphere of the Ptolemaic universe.

40. **Elysian fields:** home of the blessed dead in Homer (*Od.* 4.561–69) and Plato (*Phaedo* 112E).

45. **behoof:** benefit.

47. **Earth's sons:** the Giants, who warred against the gods (Hesiod, *Theog.* 183–85).

VIII

50   Or wert thou that just maid who once before
      Forsook the hated earth, O tell me sooth,
      And cam'st again to visit us once more?
      Or wert thou that sweet smiling youth?
      Or that crowned matron, sage white-robèd Truth?
55   Or any other of that Heav'nly brood
      Let down in cloudy throne to do the world some good?

IX

      Or wert thou of the golden-wingèd host,
      Who having clad thyself in human weed,
      To earth from thy prefixèd seat didst post,
60   And after short abode fly back with speed,
      As if to show what creatures Heav'n doth breed,
         Thereby to set the hearts of men on fire
      To scorn the sordid world, and unto Heav'n aspire?

X

      But O why didst thou not stay here below
65   To bless us with thy Heav'n-loved innocence,
      To slake his wrath whom sin hath made our foe,
      To turn swift-rushing black perdition hence,
      Or drive away the slaughtering pestilence,
         To stand 'twixt us and our deservèd smart?
70   But thou canst best perform that office where thou art.

50. **that just maid:** Astraea, goddess of Justice, who fled the earth when corruption followed the golden age. See *Nat Ode* 141–46.

53. Something apparently dropped out of this line when the poem was first printed, in 1673. It is missing a metrical foot, and the *youth* lacks his allegorical identity. Words such as *Mercy* and *Virtue* have been inserted between *thou* and *that*, which saves the meter; but these allegorical figures are never male, and *youth* in Milton always refers to a male.

54. **white-robèd Truth:** See Cesare Ripa, *Iconologia* 530.

57. **golden-wingèd host:** the angels.

59. **prefixèd:** preordained.

66. **his:** God's.

68. **pestilence:** There was a major outbreak of plague in 1625–26. Milton could be assuming that the birth of Anne Phillips *did* drive away that plague. She will be an even more effective advocate in Heaven.

XI

Then thou the mother of so sweet a child
Her false imagined loss cease to lament,
And wisely learn to curb thy sorrows wild;
Think what a present thou to God hast sent,
75   And render him with patience what he lent;
     This if thou do he will an offspring give,
That till the world's last end shall make thy name to live.

---

71. **Then thou:** The address has shifted from the dead child to its mother.

75. **render:** give back; **lent:** The idea that life is lent to us by God and in the end must be paid back was commonplace (see Jonson, "On My First Son" 3–5, "On My First Daughter" 2–4).

76–77. See headnote.

AT A VACATION EXERCISE

At some point during the summer vacation months (July through October) of 1628, Milton presided over festive exercises at Christ's College. In keeping with the traditions behind such saturnalian occasions, he first of all delivered the two raucous Latin orations that constitute Prolusion 6. The speeches were peppered with boisterous jokes about gender, sex, farts, and the like. Then the master of ceremonies broke into these pentameter English couplets. Milton's opening address to the English language, including his dismissal of the stylistic tastes of "late fantastics" (l. 20), is playful. With "Yet I had rather, if I were to choose" (l. 29), the tone shifts from schoolboy fun to personal yearnings serious enough to be already drafting at age nineteen a life plan dedicated to their realization: for a noble epic subject, an answerable style, a unique access to the divine secrets of the universe, and an enraptured audience. After exhibiting his literary dreams, Milton returns via a beautiful imitation of Horace (see 53–58n) to the business at hand, which is to play out the role of mocking the "Ens," or Father of the concepts of Aristotelian logic, first adopted in the earlier Latin segment of the college entertainment. In graver minds, however, the hall must have kept on shimmering with the revelation of what this amusing student, if he were to choose, would rather be doing.

The work was first printed in 1673.

ANNO AETATIS 19

The Latin speeches ended, the English thus began.

Hail native language, that by sinews weak
Didst move my first endeavoring tongue to speak,
And mad'st imperfect words with childish trips,
Half unpronounced, slide through my infant lips,
5   Driving dumb silence from the portal door,
Where he had mutely sat two years before:
Here I salute thee and thy pardon ask,
That now I use thee in my latter task:
Small loss it is that thence can come unto thee,
10   I know my tongue but little grace can do thee:
Thou need'st not be ambitious to be first,
Believe me I have thither packed the worst:
And, if it happen as I did forecast,
The daintiest dishes shall be served up last.
15   I pray thee then, deny me not thy aid
For this same small neglect that I have made:
But haste thee straight to do me once a pleasure,
And from thy wardrobe bring thy chiefest treasure;
Not those new-fangled toys, and trimming slight
20   Which takes our late fantastics with delight,
But cull those richest robes, and gay'st attire
Which deepest spirits, and choicest wits desire:
I have some naked thoughts that rove about
And loudly knock to have their passage out;
25   And weary of their place do only stay
Till thou hast decked them in thy best array;
That so they may without suspect or fears
Fly swiftly to this fair assembly's ears;
Yet I had rather, if I were to choose,
30   Thy service in some graver subject use,

12. **thither:** in the Latin oration that preceded these English couplets.

19. **new-fangled toys:** idle fancies, appealing in their novelty.

20. **takes:** captivates, puts a spell upon; **late fantastics:** in the immediate context, showy dressers; but since dressing throughout lines 18–26 refers metaphorically to adopting a poetic style or manner, the *late* (recent) *fantastics* apparently names a modish school of writers given to fanciful notions. Some have taken Milton to be criticizing the metaphysical manner, but he might just as well be tweaking a form of expression cultivated by some of his fellow students.

27. **suspect:** suspicion.

29–52. Here Milton digresses from the academic conviviality of the immediate occasion to reveal his literary ambitions.

Such as may make thee search thy coffers round,
Before thou clothe my fancy in fit sound:
Such where the deep transported mind may soar
Above the wheeling poles, and at Heav'n's door
35 Look in, and see each blissful deity
How he before the thunderous throne doth lie,
Listening to what unshorn Apollo sings
To th' touch of golden wires, while Hebe brings
Immortal nectar to her kingly sire:
40 Then passing through the spheres of watchful fire,
And misty regions of wide air next under,
And hills of snow and lofts of pilèd thunder,
May tell at length how green-eyed Neptune raves,
In Heav'n's defiance mustering all his waves;
45 Then sing of secret things that came to pass
When beldam Nature in her cradle was;
And last of kings and queens and heroes old,
Such as the wise Demodocus once told
In solemn songs at King Alcinous' feast,
50 While sad Ulysses' soul and all the rest
Are held with his melodious harmony
In willing chains and sweet captivity.
But fie my wand'ring Muse, how thou dost stray!
Expectance calls thee now another way;
55 Thou know'st it must be now thy only bent
To keep in compass of thy predicament:
Then quick about thy purposed business come,
That to the next I may resign my room.

Then ENS *is represented as Father of the Predicaments, his ten sons, whereof
the eldest stood for* SUBSTANCE *with his Canons, which* ENS *thus
speaking, explains.*

32. **fancy:** invention.
33. **deep:** high (Lat. *altus* means both "high" and
"deep").
34. **the wheeling poles:** the spheres of the Ptole-
maic universe.
37. **unshorn:** stock epithet for Apollo.
38. **Hebe:** goddess of youth, daughter of Zeus.
40. **spheres of watchful fire:** The celestial
spheres were manned by watchful angels.
42. **lofts:** layers or stages of air; **pilèd:** stockpiled.
48. **Demodocus:** minstrel who sang of the fall of
Troy at the court of Alcinous (*Od.* 8.487–543)
and brought tears to the eyes of Odysseus.

53. Milton's abrupt return to the occasion echoes
Horace's rejection of epic Trojan tales (*Quo,
Musa, tendis?*) in *Odes* 3.3.70.
53–58. Milton in the role of Ens or Father on this
occasion must now introduce by name his ten
Sons, the "categories" Aristotle defined in his
Categories. The Muse's *bent* (aim) must be to
keep within the *compass* (limits) of her *predica-
ment,* or present situation. In scholastic logic
based on Aristotle, the grammatical "accidents"
that befell a "substance" or particular entity
were called "predicaments."

Good luck befriend thee son; for at thy birth
60   The fairy ladies danced upon the hearth;
Thy drowsy nurse hath sworn she did them spy
Come tripping to the room where thou didst lie;
And sweetly singing round about thy bed
Strew all their blessings on thy sleeping head.
65   She heard them give thee this, that thou shouldst still
From eyes of mortals walk invisible;
Yet there is something that doth force my fear,
For once it was my dismal hap to hear
A sibyl old, bow-bent with crookèd age,
70   That far events full wisely could presage,
And in time's long and dark prospective glass
Foresaw what future days should bring to pass.
"Your Son," said she, "(nor can you it prevent)
Shall subject be to many an accident.
75   O'er all his brethren he shall reign as king,
Yet every one shall make him underling,
And those that cannot live from him asunder
Ungratefully shall strive to keep him under;
In worth and excellence he shall outgo them,
80   Yet being above them, he shall be below them;
From others he shall stand in need of nothing,
Yet on his brothers shall depend for clothing.
To find a foe it shall not be his hap,
And Peace shall lull him in her flow'ry lap;
85   Yet shall he live in strife, and at his door
Devouring War shall never cease to roar:
Yea, it shall be his natural property
To harbor those that are at enmity."
What power, what force, what mighty spell, if not
90   Your learned hands, can loose this Gordian knot?

*The next, QUANTITY and QUALITY, spoke in prose, then RELATION
was called by his name.*

---

66. **walk invisible:** Because substance is an abstraction known only through particular accidents, Milton jokingly suggests that his personified Substance received at birth the gift of invisibility.

71. **time's . . . glass:** a crystal in which future events can be seen.

87–88. Cp. Aristotle, *Categories* 5.4a: "But what is most characteristic of substance appears to be this: that, although it remains, notwithstanding, numerically one and the same, it is capable of being the recipient of contrary qualifications."

90. **loose this Gordian knot:** overcome the paradoxes of Aristotle's logic. The knot to which the proverb alludes was originally tied by Gordius. The oracle declared that whoever untied it would rule Asia. Alexander cut it.

Rivers arise; whether thou be the son
Of utmost Tweed, or Ouse, or gulfy Dun,
Or Trent, who like some Earth-born giant spreads
His thirty arms along th' indented meads,
95　Or sullen Mole that runneth underneath,
Or Severn swift, guilty of maiden's death,
Or rocky Avon, or of sedgy Lea,
Or coaly Tyne, or ancient hallowed Dee,
Or Humber loud that keeps the Scythian's name,
100　Or Medway smooth, or royal-towered Thame.

The rest was prose.

91. **Rivers arise:** Two brothers named Rivers (George and Nizel) had been admitted to Christ's College in 1628. One of them played Relation, and is here *called by his name*. Milton proceeds to burlesque the catalogues of rivers found in Spenser (*FQ* 4.11.24–47) and often in Drayton's *Polyolbion*.

92. **gulfy:** full of eddies.
95. **sullen:** flowing sluggishly.
99. The name of the river *Humber* supposedly came from a Scythian invader who drowned in it after being defeated by Locrine.

SONG: ON MAY MORNING

Dates from 1629 to 1631 have been proposed for this poem in the absence of any evidence. Whenever Milton wrote this aubade or dawn song, it is a small gem. It hearkens back to Elizabethan songs such as Thomas Nashe's "Spring, the sweet spring" (the opening poem in Francis Turner Palgrave's famous anthology *The Golden Treasury*) and Shakespeare's "It was a lover and his lass" (from *AYL* 5.3). Like his predecessors, and it must be said, without a hint of what is popularly known as Puritanism, Milton joins in the ritual dance of the year's renewal, the return of flowers, the reaffirmation of "Mirth and youth, and warm desire." The lyric is an "early song," sung on the dawn of a May morning with the early charm of the English Renaissance song still blossoming in its shifting meters and exuberant enjambments.

As he often does, Milton saves the most remarkable effect for the end. We "wish thee long" when of course May is never long enough, and our annual wishes are doomed to disappointment. The message of the final words rolls back retrospectively through the entire poem, and we behold a second time, under the sign of "gone too soon," the dawn of a May morning. The effect anticipates what the mature poet will achieve with the endless spring of Paradise: represent it responsively and thoroughly while all the while making us ever more hopelessly aware of its having been lost too soon.

Now the bright morning Star, day's harbinger,
Comes dancing from the East, and leads with her
The flow'ry May, who from her green lap throws
The yellow cowslip, and the pale primrose.
5   Hail bounteous May that dost inspire
Mirth and youth, and warm desire;
Woods and groves are of thy dressing,
Hill and dale doth boast thy blessing.
Thus we salute thee with our early song,
10 And welcome thee, and wish thee long.

1. **morning Star:** Venus.

3. Milton's flower-throwing *May* recalls Spenser's   "faire May . . . throwing flowers out of her lap around" (*FQ* 7.7.34).

THE FIFTH ODE OF HORACE, LIB. I

This famous translation appeared for the first time in the 1673 *Poems.* Proponents of a late date, noting likenesses between the translation and Milton's mature style, suppose that he was deliberately studying Horace in an attempt to perfect his own literary gifts. But the fact that we have no other examples of such studious translations (unless we imagine that Milton was primarily tinkering with his style in the Psalm paraphrases) argues for an earlier date, perhaps 1629, on the assumption that the poem grew out of an academic exercise. It was not unusual for teachers to have their students compete in translating or adapting a classical work. By the eighteenth century, the practice extended to Milton's works. Thomas Warton in his 1785 edition notes that "Mr. Benson [presumably William Benson (1682–1754), who erected the Milton monument in Westminster Abbey] gave medals as prizes for the best verses that were produced on Milton at all our great schools."

The Horace translation was in fact immensely popular in the eighteenth century. "From 1700 to 1837," Raymond Havens reports, "no fewer than eighty-three poems, and probably many more, were written in Milton's Horatian stanza, which thus had a vogue almost as great, in proportion to the length and importance of the poem, as any of his own verse-forms enjoyed" (560). The best-known of the imitations is Collins's *Ode to Evening,* and the influence of Milton's unrhymed lines of shifting length can still be heard in such Victorian pieces as Tennyson's "Tears, idle tears" and Arnold's *Philomela.*

It is doubtful that Milton himself would have considered this vogue a sign of artistic health. The words of the headnote, "as near as the language will permit," indicate his awareness that this version of a Horatian ode is not a manifesto or an exemplar but a tour de force, a fantastic one-off. For the language does not permit. English word order cannot approach the free arrangements possible in an inflected language. Nor can Latin quantitative measures be imposed but for an enchanted moment on the accentual-syllabic system native to English. The poem affords us a brief look at an ideal English classicism that never happened. "Milton's youthful version of the Pyrrha Ode . . . is the only English translation in which it is really possible to perceive something of what makes the original what it is: the inimitable combination of difficulty and ease, artifice and grace, gravity and lightness" (Leishman, 52–53).

QUIS MULTA GRACILIS TE PUER IN ROSA

Rendered almost word for word without rhyme according to the Latin measure, as near as the language will permit.

What slender youth bedewed with liquid odors
    Courts thee on roses in some pleasant cave,
        Pyrrha? For whom bind'st thou
        In wreaths thy golden hair,
5   Plain in thy neatness? O how oft shall he
    On faith and changèd gods complain: and seas
        Rough with black winds and storms
        Unwonted shall admire:
    Who now enjoys thee credulous, all gold,
10 Who always vacant, always amiable
        Hopes thee, of flattering gales
        Unmindful? Hapless they
    To whom thou untried seem'st fair. Me in my vowed
    Picture the sacred wall declares t' have hung
15   My dank and dropping weeds
        To the stern god of sea.

5. **Plain in thy neatness:** Milton's restrained rendition of Horace's famously rich *simplex munditie* (or *simplex munditiis,* as modern editions read). The phrase has been taken as a comment on Horace's own poetic art but in context asserts that *Pyrrha* is ordinarily plain in adorning herself, which makes the wreaths of her current hairdo all the more suggestive of a new love interest.

8. **shall admire:** shall wonder at (in surprise).

9. **all gold:** entirely pure, gold through and through (not just in the tresses).

10. **vacant:** without other lovers; **amiable:** lovable.

11. **flattering:** treacherous, deceitful.

13–16. **Me . . . sea:** *Vota* or "vows" were prayers to the gods to avert some danger, accompanied by the promise of a thanksgiving offering should the danger pass. They were often commemorated by placing a votive tablet containing an inscription or a picture summarizing the vow on the wall of the temple. Horace's thankful speaker, having escaped metaphorical shipwreck (ill-fated love) through the favor of Neptune, has pictured himself hanging clothes still wet from the sea on the walls of Neptune's temple.

ON THE MORNING OF CHRIST'S NATIVITY

Though by no means the earliest of Milton's poems, the *Nativity Ode*, as it is commonly called, was printed first in both the 1645 and 1673 *Poems*, as if its author (or its publisher, or both) were entirely confident of the work's power. Here the mature poet presents his calling card. For the first time we see him shift from a personal voice seeking inspiration in the opening four stanzas to a communal voice performing our human part in the celestial harmonies that accompany the Incarnation, and defining with authoritative ease the proportions of joy and sorrow, wonder and apprehension, pride and shame, appropriate to this watershed moment. Other Nativity odes of the period dwelled on the paradox of an eternal God become a mortal child; Milton does that briefly in Stanza 2 of his induction. Other Nativity odes dwelled as modern Christmas cards do on the tender love passing back and forth between Mary and the infant Jesus; Milton touches on this theme in his final stanza. What Milton's poem has, in place of the conventional themes that consumed other lyrics on this topic, is a sense of the meaning of the Nativity within the full scope of Christian history, and an interest in the relationship between Christianity and the various cultures, religions, and artistic traditions found in the world at its advent.

Two of the most influential treatments of the ode are Arthur Barker's account of its structure (1940–41) and Rosemond Tuve's study of its imagery (37–72). See also the important recent studies by C.W.R.D. Moseley (99–114), David Quint, and Mary Oates O'Reilly.

Composed 1629

I

This is the month, and this the happy morn
Wherein the Son of Heav'n's eternal King,
Of wedded maid, and virgin mother born,
Our great redemption from above did bring;
5   For so the holy sages once did sing,
        That he our deadly forfeit should release,
        And with his Father work us a perpetual peace.

---

1. **this the happy morn:** Milton told Diodati that he began the poem on Christmas morning 1629. See *El 6* 88.

5. **holy sages:** Hebrew prophets.

6. **deadly forfeit:** sin and its penalty, death.

II

That glorious form, that light unsufferable,
And that far-beaming blaze of majesty,
10 Wherewith he wont at Heav'n's high council table,
To sit the midst of trinal unity,
He laid aside; and here with us to be,
    Forsook the courts of everlasting day,
And chose with us a darksome house of mortal clay.

III

15 Say Heav'nly Muse, shall not thy sacred vein
Afford a present to the infant God?
Hast thou no verse, no hymn, or solemn strain,
To welcome him to this his new abode,
Now while the heav'n by the sun's team untrod,
20   Hath took no print of the approaching light,
And all the spangled host keep watch in squadrons bright?

IV

See how from far upon the eastern road
The star-led wizards haste with odors sweet:
O run, prevent them with thy humble ode,
25 And lay it lowly at his blessèd feet;
Have thou the honor first, thy Lord to greet,
    And join thy voice unto the angel choir,
From out his secret altar touched with hallowed fire.

---

8. **unsufferable:** unbearable.

10. **wont:** was accustomed.

14. **house of mortal clay:** the human body. Cp. *Passion* 15–17.

15. **Heav'nly Muse:** Milton's first reference in a poem to the source of inspiration he would later invoke in *PL* 1.6. One of her names (*PL* 7.1–2) is Urania, the classical Muse of astronomy, but elevated to the Christian or Heavenly Muse in du Bartas's *La Muse Chrestiene* (1574). **sacred vein:** aptitude for religious verse.

19. **Now:** referring to the first Christmas morning, to which the poet has been imaginatively transported. On the complex time schemes and shifting verb tenses of the poem, see Nelson 32–33, 41–52, and Tayler 1979, 34–40.

22. **eastern road:** leading from the East (i.e., Asia) to Bethlehem.

23. **star-led wizards:** the Magi (Matt. 2); **odors:** spices (the frankincense and myrrh of Matt. 2.11).

24. **prevent:** come before. Milton implores the Muse to complete his poem-present, begun on Christmas morning (see III), before January 6, when the Epiphany (the manifestation of Jesus to the Gentiles, represented by the Magi) is traditionally celebrated. Given the poem's time play, Milton may be asking that his verses arrive in Bethlehem before the Magi.

28. An inverted line: the voice (27) is touched with hallowed fire from out the secret (*retired, set apart*) altar. In Isa. 6.6–7 an angel touches the prophet's lips with a burning coal from God's altar. Cp. *RCG* (*MLM* 843).

The Hymn

I

It was the winter wild,
30   While the Heav'n-born-child,
      All meanly wrapped in the rude manger lies;
   Nature in awe to him
   Had doffed her gaudy trim
      With her great master so to sympathize:
35   It was no season then for her
   To wanton with the sun her lusty paramour.

II

Only with speeches fair
   She woos the gentle air
      To hide her guilty front with innocent snow,
40   And on her naked shame,
   Pollute with sinful blame,
      The saintly veil of maiden white to throw,
   Confounded, that her maker's eyes
   Should look so near upon her foul deformities.

34. **so to sympathize:** be in accord with (by divesting herself of her glory).
35. **season:** both "time of year" and "proper occasion."

39. **front:** face.
41. **Pollute:** tainted by the Fall and its consequences; **blame:** culpability, not reproof.
43. **Confounded:** ashamed.

III

45 But he her fears to cease,
Sent down the meek-eyed Peace;
      She crowned with olive green, came softly sliding
Down through the turning sphere
His ready harbinger,
50   With turtle wing the amorous clouds dividing,
And waving wide her myrtle wand,
She strikes a universal peace through sea and land.

IV

No war, or battle's sound
Was heard the world around:
55   The idle spear and shield were high up hung,
The hookèd chariot stood
Unstained with hostile blood,
      The trumpet spake not to the armèd throng,
And kings sat still with awful eye,
60 As if they surely knew their sov'reign Lord was by.

V

But peaceful was the night
Wherein the Prince of Light
      His reign of peace upon the earth began:
The Winds with wonder whist,
65 Smoothly the waters kissed,
      Whispering new joys to the mild Ocean,
Who now hath quite forgot to rave,
While birds of calm sit brooding on the charmèd wave.

---

45. **cease:** end.
46. **meek-eyed:** gently, mercifully gazing (as opposed to the judgmental look Nature feared); **Peace:** Descending as in a court masque, with her emblematic olive crown and myrtle wand, Peace personifies the *pax romana*, during which Jesus was born, and prefigures the *perpetual peace* (7) to come at the end of time.
48. **turning sphere:** In the Ptolemaic universe, the outermost sphere imparts motion to the others while our planet rests at the stationary center (cp. Plato, *Phaedrus* 247b; Vergil, *Aen.* 6.797).
49. **harbinger:** forerunner.

50. **turtle:** turtledove; **amorous clouds:** surrounding and clinging to *Peace* as if in love with her.
51. **myrtle:** plant sacred to Venus.
56. **hookèd:** Chariots are "armed with hooks" (scythes) in 2 Macc. 13.2.
59. **awful:** filled with awe.
64. **whist:** hushed, silent.
68. **birds of calm:** halcyons (kingfishers). The ancients (Aristotle, *History of the Animals* 5.8) believed that calm seas always prevailed during the two midwinter weeks when the halcyons were brooding on their floating nests, laying eggs. **charmèd:** under a spell.

VI

The Stars with deep amaze
70 Stand fixed in steadfast gaze,
        Bending one way their precious influence,
    And will not take their flight,
    For all the morning light,
        Or Lucifer that often warned them thence;
75 But in their glimmering orbs did glow,
    Until their Lord himself bespake, and bid them go.

VII

And though the shady gloom
Had given day her room,
    The Sun himself withheld his wonted speed,
80 And hid his head for shame,
    As his inferior flame,
        The new-enlightened world no more should need;
    He saw a greater sun appear
    Than his bright throne, or burning axletree could bear.

VIII

85 The shepherds on the lawn,
    Or ere the point of dawn,
        Sat simply chatting in a rustic row;
    Full little thought they then,
    That the mighty Pan
90   Was kindly come to live with them below;
    Perhaps their loves, or else their sheep,
    Was all that did their silly thoughts so busy keep.

---

71. *Influence* is the astrological term for an ethereal liquid sent from the stars to the earth for good or ill (La Primaudaye 135–39). Here all the stars direct their influence (benign, presumably) toward Bethlehem. Cp. *PL* 9.105–7.

73. **For all:** in spite of.

74. **Lucifer:** the morning star. Venus is "otherwise called Hesperus and Vesper and Lucifer, both because he seemeth to be one of the brightest stars, and also first riseth and setteth last" (E.K.'s gloss on "December," in Spenser, *SC*).

75. **orbs:** the concentric hollow spheres that in the Ptolemaic scheme carry the stars and planets around the earth.

81. **As:** as if, or because.

83. **greater sun:** Christ. See Mal. 4.2; *PL* 5.171–72.

84. **throne:** described by Ovid in *Met.* 2.24; **axletree:** the axle of the sun's chariot.

86. **Or ere:** before; **point of dawn:** daybreak.

89. **mighty Pan:** Spenser also called Christ "mighty Pan" in *SC*, "May" 54, and E.K.'s gloss on the passage retells from Plutarch the story of how, at the time of the Crucifixion, a voice in the Mediterranean cried out that great Pan was dead (*The Obsolescence of Oracles* 418).

92. **silly:** simple, harmless.

IX

When such music sweet
Their hearts and ears did greet,
95   As never was by mortal finger strook,
Divinely-warbled voice
Answering the stringèd noise,
    As all their souls in blissful rapture took:
The Air such pleasure loath to lose,
100 With thousand echoes still prolongs each Heav'nly close.

X

Nature that heard such sound
Beneath the hollow round
    Of Cynthia's seat, the airy region thrilling,
Now was almost won
105 To think her part was done,
    And that her reign had here its last fulfilling;
She knew such harmony alone
Could hold all Heav'n and Earth in happier union.

XI

At last surrounds their sight
110 A globe of circular light,
    That with long beams the shame-faced Night arrayed;
The helmèd Cherubim
And sworded Seraphim,
    Are seen in glittering ranks with wings displayed,
115 Harping in loud and solemn choir,
With unexpressive notes to Heav'n's new-born heir.

98. **took:** captivated, put under a spell.
100. **close:** conclusion of a musical phrase, theme, or movement.
102–3. **hollow . . . seat:** the sphere of the moon; **airy region thrilling:** piercing the air between the moon and the earth.
104. **won:** persuaded.

110. **globe:** The Latin *globus* can mean both "troop" and "sphere." Both meanings are appropriate here as the globe of light gradually reveals *glittering ranks* (114) of angels.
114. **displayed:** unfolded.
116. **unexpressive:** indescribable.

XII

Such music (as 'tis said)
Before was never made,
    But when of old the sons of morning sung,
120 While the Creator great
His constellations set,
    And the well-balanced world on hinges hung,
    And cast the dark foundations deep,
And bid the welt'ring waves their oozy channel keep.

XIII

125 Ring out ye crystal spheres,
Once bless our human ears,
    (If ye have power to touch our senses so)
And let your silver chime
Move in melodious time,
130   And let the bass of heav'n's deep organ blow,
    And with your ninefold harmony
Make up full consort to th' angelic symphony.

---

119. **when of old:** See Job 38.4–7.

122. **well-balanced world:** Cp. *PL* 7.242: "And Earth self-balanced on her center hung"; **hinges:** supports; in this case probably the two poles of the axis about which the earth revolves. This line comes at the poem's midpoint.

124. **welt'ring:** tumbling; **oozy:** slimy, muddy.

125. **ye crystal spheres:** Each of the planetary spheres was believed to produce a unique note of the overall "music of the spheres," normally inaudible on the fallen Earth. Here Milton imagines that vast music joining in the higher harmony of the *angelic symphony* (132).

126. **Once:** only.

130. **the bass:** The lowest note of the celestial music is that of the Earth (with the likely implication that this bass note has been silent or out of tune since the Fall).

131. **ninefold:** Cp. the "nine enfolded spheres" of *Arcades* 64, while in *PL* 3.481–83 there are ten spheres. It is likely that Milton prefers nine spheres in this instance because they correlate with the nine orders of angels.

132. **full consort to:** full harmony with (there being a sphere answerable to every order of angel); **symphony:** harmony (not the modern sense of a particular form of musical composition).

XIV

For if such holy song
Enwrap our fancy long,
135   Time will run back, and fetch the age of gold,
And speckled Vanity
Will sicken soon and die,
    And lep'rous Sin will melt from earthly mold,
And Hell itself will pass away,
140   And leave her dolorous mansions to the peering day.

XV

Yea Truth and Justice then
Will down return to men,
    Orbed in a rainbow; and, like glories wearing,
Mercy will sit between,
145   Throned in celestial sheen,
    With radiant feet the tissued clouds down steering,
And Heav'n as at some festival,
Will open wide the gates of her high palace hall.

XVI

But wisest Fate says no,
150   This must not yet be so,
    The babe lies yet in smiling infancy,
That on the bitter cross
Must redeem our loss;
    So both himself and us to glorify:
155   Yet first to those ychained in sleep,
    The wakeful trump of doom must thunder through the deep.

135. **age of gold:** Christian interpretation of Vergil's *Ec.* 4 led to an association between the Nativity and the restoration of Saturn's age of gold.

136. **speckled:** spotted.

138. **mold:** the material (earth and clay) from which man was made.

140. **peering:** Opinion is divided between "just now appearing" and "overlooking, prying."

141–48. In classical terms, the return of Justice (Astraea) will reinaugurate the golden age (135n). Peace (45–52), Truth, Justice, and Mercy are the four daughters of God. They often debate the fate of fallen man, then achieve recon-

ciliation through their unanimous approval of Christ's sacrifice. See also *Eikon* in Yale 3:583–84.

143–44. The 1645 version is "Th' enamelled arras of the rainbow wearing,/And Mercy set between." Mercy set between recalls Christ's position in *the midst of trinal unity* (11).

146. **tissued:** woven with gold or silver threads. Mercy's descent on a cloud again suggests (see 46n) the machinery of court masques.

148. **gates:** See Ps. 24.7.

155. **ychained:** a Spenserian archaism; **sleep:** death.

156. **wakeful:** arousing.

XVII

With such a horrid clang
As on Mount Sinai rang
　　While the red fire, and smold'ring clouds out brake:
160　The agèd earth aghast
With terror of that blast,
　　Shall from the surface to the center shake;
　　When at the world's last session,
　　The dreadful judge in middle air shall spread his throne.

XVIII

165　And then at last our bliss
Full and perfect is,
　　But now begins; for from this happy day
Th' old Dragon under ground
In straiter limits bound,
170　　Not half so far casts his usurpèd sway,
　　And wroth to see his kingdom fail,
　　Swinges the scaly horror of his folded tail.

157. **clang:** the sound of a trumpet.
158. **As on Mount Sinai:** God appears on Sinai "in thunders and lightnings ... and the voice of the trumpet exceeding loud" (Exod. 19.16). The *As* joining these two events has providential force, since the fearful appearance on Sinai typologically foreshadows the Last Judgment.
161. **that blast:** the thundering *trump of doom* (156).
163. **session:** the sitting of a court of justice.

164. **middle air:** the clouds in which Christ will return (Dan. 7.13; Matt. 24.30). Clouds inhabit the middle of the three traditional regions of air (Svendsen 1969, 88).
168. **old Dragon:** Rev. 20.2: "The dragon, that old serpent, which is the devil."
171. **wroth:** stirred to wrath.
172. **Swinges:** lashes.

XIX

The Oracles are dumb,
No voice or hideous hum
175   Runs through the archèd roof in words deceiving.
Apollo from his shrine
Can no more divine,
    With hollow shriek the steep of Delphos leaving.
No nightly trance, or breathèd spell,
180   Inspires the pale-eyed priest from the prophetic cell.

XX

The lonely mountains o'er,
And the resounding shore,
    A voice of weeping heard, and loud lament;
From haunted spring, and dale
185   Edged with poplar pale,
    The parting Genius is with sighing sent;
With flow'r-inwoven tresses torn,
The Nymphs in twilight shade of tangled thickets mourn.

XXI

In consecrated earth,
190   And on the holy hearth,
    The Lars and Lemures moan with midnight plaint;
In urns, and altars round,
A drear and dying sound
    Affrights the flamens at their service quaint;
195   And the chill marble seems to sweat,
    While each peculiar power forgoes his wonted seat.

173–236. Christ's expulsion of the pagan gods was a familiar topos—see Tuve 66n for theological versions. In *PL* 1.373–521, the pagan gods are identified with fallen angels.
173. **Oracles are dumb:** The chief source for the belief that pagan oracles ceased to speak at Christ's birth is Plutarch's *The Obsolescence of Oracles.* See also Sir Thomas Browne, *Pseudodoxia Epidemica* 7.12.
175. **words deceiving:** See *PR* 1.430–31.
178. **Delphos:** Delphi.
179. **nightly:** by night, nocturnal (not "occurring every night"); **breathèd spell:** Lucan reports

that a vapor in the cave at Delphi produced the ability to prophesy (*Pharsalia* 5.82–85).
186. **Genius:** classical god of a locale.
187. **flow'r-inwoven tresses torn:** The garlands are signs of joy and celebration, now turned to devastation by the birth of Christ. Tearing of the hair is a gesture of lamentation (Ezra 9.3).
191. **Lars:** *lares,* Roman household gods whose worship took place in a separate apartment called *lararia* or hearth; **Lemures:** Roman spirits of dead bad men, supposed to wander at night and trouble the living.
194. **flamens:** priests; **quaint:** elaborate.
195. **seems to sweat:** a dire sign.

XXII

Peor and Baälim
Forsake their temples dim,
    With that twice-battered god of Palestine,
200 And moonèd Ashtaroth,
Heav'n's queen and mother both,
    Now sits not girt with tapers' holy shine;
The Libyc Hammon shrinks his horn;
In vain the Tyrian maids their wounded Thammuz mourn.

XXIII

205 And sullen Moloch fled,
Hath left in shadows dread,
    His burning idol all of blackest hue;
In vain with cymbals' ring,
They call the grisly king,
210   In dismal dance about the furnace blue;
The brutish gods of Nile as fast,
Isis and Orus, and the dog Anubis haste.

197. **Peor and Baälim:** Peor was a local (Moabite) manifestation of Baäl (pl. Baälim), originally a Phoenician sun god whose worship became widespread and diverse in the ancient Middle East. Cp. Num. 25.3, 5.18; Deut. 3.29; *PL* 1.406–17n.

199. **twice-battered god:** Dagon. The Philistines twice set his image beside the Ark. The first morning he had fallen on his face, and the second his head and the palms of his hands were cut off (1 Sam. 5.2–4). Cp. *PL* 1.457–66.

200. **moonèd Ashtaroth:** Ashtareth is the Hebrew name for the Syrian Astarte, a fertility goddess associated with the moon. As with Baälim, Milton uses the plural Ashtaroth to indicate her various local manifestations.

203. **Libyc Hammon:** the Egyptian god Ammon, represented as a ram with massive horns; **shrinks his horn:** draws in his horn; hence,

withdraws from a position of prominence (*OED* 13).

204. **Tyrian:** Phoenician; **Thammuz:** The Phoenician original of the Greek Adonis was annually slain by a wild boar and then resurrected: but not this year. See Ezek. 8.14.

205. **sullen:** baleful; **Moloch:** an Ammonite brass idol in whose flames the Hebrews sacrificed their children while priests drowned out the screams with trumpets and timbrels.

211. **brutish:** worshiped as animal forms.

212. **Isis . . . Orus . . . Anubis:** *Isis,* sister and wife of Osiris, was the Egyptian moon goddess. Horus (*Orus*), sometimes identified with the sun, was her child. The jackal-headed *Anubis* was the offspring of Osiris and Nephthys, another of his sisters.

XXIV

Nor is Osiris seen
In Memphian grove, or green,
215   Trampling the unshow'red grass with lowings loud:
Nor can he be at rest
Within his sacred chest,
    Naught but profoundest Hell can be his shroud;
In vain with timbrelled anthems dark
220 The sable-stolèd sorcerers bear his worshipped ark.

XXV

He feels from Judah's land
The dreaded infant's hand,
    The rays of Bethlehem blind his dusky eyn;
Nor all the gods beside,
225 Longer dare abide,
    Not Typhon huge ending in snaky twine:
Our babe to show his Godhead true,
Can in his swaddling bands control the damnèd crew.

213. **Osiris:** the chief Egyptian god, worshiped in the form of a black bull (hence his *lowings loud,* 215).

215. **unshow'red:** not rained on.

217. **sacred chest:** Set, the Egyptian god of darkness, imprisoned Osiris in a chest, and threw it into the Nile.

218. **shroud:** place of retreat.

219. **timbrelled:** accompanied by tambourines.

220. **sable-stolèd:** black robed; **worshipped ark:** Herodotus 2.63: "The image of the god [Osiris], in a little wooden gilt casket, is carried . . . from the temple by the priests."

221. **Judah's land:** where Bethlehem lies—Isa. 19.17:

"The land of Judah shall be a terror unto Egypt."

226. **Typhon:** The last-mentioned of the Egyptian gods has a *snaky twine* because the Egyptian Set, brother and enemy to Osiris, was confused with the Greek Typhon, a monster human above the waist but with great coils of twisted serpents below it.

227–28. Just as the break between Christian and pagan seems absolute, Milton compares the victorious Christ child to the infant Hercules, who strangled two serpents sent by Juno to kill him. On Hercules as a pagan type of Christ, see Hughes 1953, 106, and Allen 129–30.

XXVI

So when the Sun in bed,
230 Curtained with cloudy red,
      Pillows his chin upon an orient wave,
The flocking shadows pale,
Troop to th' infernal jail,
      Each fettered ghost slips to his several grave,
235 And the yellow-skirted fays
Fly after the Night-steeds, leaving their moon-loved maze.

XXVII

But see the virgin blest,
Hath laid her babe to rest.
      Time is our tedious song should here have ending:
240 Heav'n's youngest teemèd star,
Hath fixed her polished car,
      Her sleeping Lord with handmaid lamp attending:
And all about the courtly stable,
Bright-harnessed angels sit in order serviceable.

231. **orient:** eastern, bright.

232–34. It was a popular belief that ghosts and other spirits fled the dawn. See Shakespeare, *HAM* 1.1.152, 1.5.89–91, and *MND* 3.2.379–84.

234. **fettered ghost:** dead soul whose earthly interests tie it to this world. Cp. *Masque* 470–75.

235. **fays:** fairies. Milton seems to be the first to make them *yellow-skirted*.

236. **Night-steeds:** horses that draw the chariot of Night; **moon-loved maze:** "fairy rings," the markings left by their circle dance; the dance is *moon-loved* because loved by the moon, or loved by fairies when the moon shines, or both.

239. **our tedious song:** It was conventional modesty for a poet to refer to his work (usually toward the end of it) as *tedious*. See Gascoigne, "Gascoigne's woodmanship" 150; Browne, *Britannia's Pastorals* 2.3.482.

240. **youngest teemèd:** latest born.

241. **fixed:** "The star, which they saw in the east, went before them, till it came and stood over where the young child was" (Matt. 2.9).

244. **Bright-harnessed:** clad in bright armor; **serviceable:** ready to serve.

THE PASSION

The opening of this poem clearly alludes to *On the Morning of Christ's Nativity*, which was begun at Christmas 1629. So *The Passion* was probably written in 1630, perhaps at Easter time. The poems on the birth and death of Christ also seem related to *Upon the Circumcision*, in that all three take as their subjects a liturgical moment from the life of Christ and both *The Passion* and *Upon the Circumcision* refer to the *Nativity Ode*.

The most interesting thing about this lyric is the fact that Milton could not finish it, and marked the impasse with a prose postscript in which the subject of Christ's Passion is declared to be "above the years he had when he wrote it." Milton might at the time have been singling out the Passion for another treatment in the future, but as it happened his major work on the life of Christ, *Paradise Regained,* focused on the temptation in the wilderness.

The eight emphatic lines on the Crucifixion in *Paradise Lost* (12.412–19) were the best he had to offer on that topic. Unlike Richard Crashaw or even George Herbert, Milton never warmed to the subject of Christ's blood. His religious poetry (with the partial exception of *Upon the Circumcision*) is notably distant from the Eucharist. Unlike the *Nativity Ode, The Passion* does not find typological energy in its segment of Christ's life. The lyric moves in space, from landscape to landscape, but not in melodious time.

—————

I

Erewhile of music, and ethereal mirth,
Wherewith the stage of air and earth did ring,
And joyous news of Heav'nly infant's birth,
My muse with angels did divide to sing;
5   But headlong joy is ever on the wing,
In wintry solstice like the shortened light
Soon swallowed up in dark and long out-living night.

II

For now to sorrow must I tune my song,
And set my harp to notes of saddest woe,
10   Which on our dearest Lord did seize ere long,
Dangers, and snares, and wrongs, and worse than so,
Which he for us did freely undergo.
Most perfect hero, tried in heaviest plight
Of labors huge and hard, too hard for human wight.

---

4. **divide:** meaning both "share" (with the angels) and "perform divisions" (musical variations on a theme).

6. Like the shortened daylight at the winter solstice.

13. **Most perfect hero:** Hercules is a type or prefiguration of Christ. See *Nat Ode* 227–28n.

III

15 He sov'reign priest, stooping his regal head
That dropped with odorous oil down his fair eyes,
Poor fleshly tabernacle enterèd,
His starry front low-roofed beneath the skies;
O what a mask was there, what a disguise!
20   Yet more; the stroke of death he must abide,
Then lies him meekly down fast by his brethren's side.

IV

These latter scenes confine my roving verse,
To this horizon is my Phoebus bound,
His Godlike acts, and his temptations fierce,
25 And former sufferings other where are found;
Loud o'er the rest Cremona's trump doth sound;
      Me softer airs befit, and softer strings
Of lute, or viol still, more apt for mournful things.

V

Befriend me Night, best patroness of Grief,
30 Over the pole thy thickest mantle throw,
And work my flattered fancy to belief,
That heav'n and earth are colored with my woe;
My sorrows are too dark for day to know:
      The leaves should all be black whereon I write,
35 And letters where my tears have washed a wannish white.

---

15. **sov'reign priest:** Two of Christ's three offices are King and Priest (*CD* 1.15).

16. **dropped with odorous oil:** The name Christ means "anointed" in Greek.

17. **fleshly tabernacle:** For the body as tabernacle, see 2 Cor. 5.1, 2 Pet. 1.13–14.

26. **Cremona's trump:** Milton expresses admiration for the Neo-Latin *Christiad* (1535) of Marco Girolamo Vida, a native of Cremona.

28. **still:** quiet.

30. **pole:** sky.

34–35. Though editors often maintain otherwise, we have no seventeenth-century elegies printed on black pages with white letters. But elegies were often printed with a band of black on the edge of the page. Milton, Carey suggests, wishes that his pages were *all* (entirely) black.

VI

See see the chariot, and those rushing wheels
That whirled the prophet up at Chebar flood;
My spirit some transporting cherub feels,
To bear me where the towers of Salem stood,
40   Once glorious towers, now sunk in guiltless blood;
     There doth my soul in holy vision sit
In pensive trance, and anguish, and ecstatic fit.

VII

Mine eye hath found that sad sepulchral rock
That was the casket of Heav'n's richest store,
45   And here though grief my feeble hands uplock,
Yet on the softened quarry would I score
My plaining verse as lively as before;
     For sure so well instructed are my tears,
That they would fitly fall in ordered characters.

VIII

50   Or should I thence, hurried on viewless wing,
Take up a weeping on the mountains wild,
The gentle neighborhood of grove and spring
Would soon unbosom all their echoes mild,
And I (for grief is easily beguiled)
55   Might think th' infection of my sorrows loud,
Had got a race of mourners on some pregnant cloud.

This subject the author finding to be above the
years he had when he wrote it, and nothing
satisfied with what was begun, left it unfinished.

---

37. **the prophet:** Ezekiel. He saw the chariot of God borne by cherubim near the river Chebar (Ezek. 1 and 10).
39. **Salem:** Jerusalem.
42. **ecstatic:** outside the body.
43. **that sad sepulchral rock:** the Holy Sepulchre in Jerusalem (Mark 15.46).
44. **casket:** treasure chest.

47. **plaining:** mourning; **lively:** vividly, feelingly.
49. **in ordered characters:** in letters (*characters*) so ordered as to spell the words of my poem.
50. **viewless:** invisible.
56. **got:** begot. Milton glances at the myth of Ixion. He tried to rape Hera, but she substituted a cloud for herself, and on that cloud Ixion begot a race of centaurs (Pindar, *Pyth.* 2.21–24).

ON SHAKESPEARE

This poem is dated 1630 in the 1645 *Poems,* but if actually written that early, was not published until the Second Folio of 1632, where it appeared anonymously under the title "An Epitaph on the Admirable Dramatic Poet W. Shakespeare." We know nothing of the circumstances linking Milton to the makers of the Second Folio.

It is satisfying in several ways that this should be the first printed of Milton's English poems. The great poet of the age to come begins his career by honoring the great poet of the age just past. He does so by calling attention early on to the extraordinary fame, the amazing hold on living memory, that is to this day such a remarkable aspect of the Shakespeare phenomenon.

What needs my Shakespeare for his honored bones,
The labor of an age in pilèd stones,
Or that his hallowed relics should be hid
Under a star-ypointing pyramid?
5   Dear son of Memory, great heir of Fame,
What need'st thou such weak witness of thy name?
Thou in our wonder and astonishment
Hast built thyself a livelong monument.
For whilst to th' shame of slow-endeavoring art,
10   Thy easy numbers flow, and that each heart
Hath from the leaves of thy unvalued book
Those Delphic lines with deep impression took,
Then thou our fancy of itself bereaving,
Dost make us marble with too much conceiving;
15   And so sepulchered in such pomp dost lie,
That kings for such a tomb would wish to die.

1–2. It seems likely that the idea of the Folio as a monument (though hardly original) derives in this case from poems affixed to the First Folio, especially Ben Jonson's *To the Memory of . . . Shakespeare* 22–24.

3. **hallowed relics:** Shakespeare's (metaphorical) sainthood is implied.

4. **star-ypointing:** pointing to the stars. An archaism popularized by Spenser, the *y*-prefix is a metrically handy vestige of Middle English. Usually joined to past participles (cp. *Nat Ode* 155, *L'All* 12), here it is used with the present. The bibliographical record suggests that this ungrammatical combination of past and present tenses was intended.

5. **Dear son of Memory:** the parentage of the muses, daughters of Mnemosyne (Memory), is here transferred to Shakespeare.

8. **livelong:** durable. The 1632 Folio reads "lasting." The usage is unique and seems designed to stress Shakespeare's *living* presence.

10. **numbers:** rhythmic verses. As Heming and Condell remarked in their preface to the First Folio, "His mind and hand went together. And what he thought, he uttered with that easiness, that we have scarce received from him a blot in his papers." Cp. "inspires/Easy my unpremeditated verse" (*PL* 9.23–24). *That* substitutes for *whilst* (9).

11. **unvalued:** The primary sense is "invaluable," but "not regarded as valuable" lurks in the background (it was so used by Shakespeare).

12. **Delphic:** Apollo, the god of poetry, had his oracle at Delphi.

14. **make us marble:** Cp. *Il Pens* 42n. It is not the book that entombs Shakespeare but its en-

ON THE UNIVERSITY CARRIER

Who sickened in the time of his vacancy,
being forbid to go to London, by reason
of the plague.

Thomas Hobson drove a weekly coach from Cambridge to the Bull Inn, Bishopgate Street, in London, and also rented horses. He must have been a notable figure in the university, since his death on New Year's Day of 1631 inspired a number of poems, including two by Milton himself. The carrier's insistence that customers take the mount standing nearest the stable door or go without is said to have originated the proverbial phrase "Hobson's choice" (the title of a memorable 1954 David Lean film). The phrase, as a contributor to *Spectator* 509 put it, "became a proverb, when what ought to be your election was forced upon you" (Newton 1:47).

The plague of 1630 closed the university, resulting in a suspension of Hobson's routine. Though he escaped the plague, his vacation led to a decline and eventually, so it was thought, to his death.

Here lies old Hobson, Death hath broke his girt,
And here alas, hath laid him in the dirt;
Or else the ways being foul, twenty to one,
He's here stuck in a slough, and overthrown.
5   'Twas such a shifter, that if truth were known,
Death was half glad when he had got him down;
For he had any time this ten years full,
Dodged with him, betwixt Cambridge and the Bull.
And surely, Death could never have prevailed,
10 Had not his weekly course of carriage failed;
But lately finding him so long at home,
And thinking now his journey's end was come,
And that he had ta'en up his latest inn,
In the kind office of a chamberlain
15 Showed him his room where he must lodge that night,
Pulled off his boots, and took away the light:
If any ask for him, it shall be said,
"Hobson has supped, and 's newly gone to bed."

tranced readers; **conceiving:** both "taking into the mind, becoming possessed" and "imagining, forming mental representations."
1. **girt:** girth or saddle belt.
5. **'Twas:** he was; **shifter:** trickster.

7. **he:** probably Hobson, but possibly Death.
8. **Dodged with him:** shifted position so as to baffle him; **the Bull:** Bull Inn (see headnote).
14. **chamberlain:** the attendant at an inn in charge of the bedchambers.

ANOTHER ON THE SAME

Strenuous, repetitive wit is familiar enough in Donne, Jonson, Herrick, Lovelace, and other seventeenth-century writers. But the second Hobson epigram is the only example of this period style in Milton's work. The quick spurt of higher wit at the end of the poem, where the account of Hobson's work suddenly merges with Milton's own artistic work and the poem itself passes away, anticipates the far more sublime passage merging poet and poem in the epilogue to *Lycidas*.

◦◦◦◦

> Here lieth one who did most truly prove,
> That he could never die while he could move,
> So hung his destiny never to rot
> While he might still jog on, and keep his trot,
> 5   Made of sphere-metal, never to decay
> Until his revolution was at stay.
> Time numbers motion, yet (without a crime
> 'Gainst old truth) motion numbered out his time;
> And like an engine moved with wheel and weight,
> 10   His principles being ceased, he ended straight;
> Rest that gives all men life, gave him his death,
> And too much breathing put him out of breath;
> Nor were it contradiction to affirm
> Too long vacation hastened on his term.
> 15   Merely to drive the time away he sickened,
> Fainted, and died, nor would with ale be quickened;
> "Nay," quoth he, on his swooning bed outstretched,
> "If I may not carry, sure I'll ne'er be fetched,
> But vow though the cross doctors all stood hearers,
> 20   For one carrier put down to make six bearers."
> Ease was his chief disease, and to judge right,

---

5. **sphere-metal:** The celestial spheres were thought to have been made of an indestructible material (Aristotle, *On the Heavens* 1.3).

6. **at stay:** at a standstill.

7. **Time numbers motion:** Aristotle defines time as the measure of motion (*Physics* 4.11–12).

8. **motion . . . time:** But in the case of Hobson, motion measured time (since his time was up when he stopped moving).

9. **engine:** machine (specifically, a clock).

10. **principles:** forces that achieve a regular result; **straight:** immediately.

14. **term:** end, but punning on "university term."

15. **drive the time away:** banish the time; but the idle carrier also desires employment, and in this sense would *drive the time away*.

18. A play on the phrase "fetch and carry," with *fetched* meaning "restored to consciousness."

19. **cross doctors:** the university professors who oppose Hobson's crossings to London.

20. **put down:** both "removed from office" and "killed"; **bearers:** both "carriers" and "pallbearers."

He died for heaviness that his cart went light,
His leisure told him that his time was come,
And lack of load made his life burdensome,
25   That even to his last breath (there be that say't)
As he were pressed to death, he cried, "More weight."
But had his doings lasted as they were,
He had been an immortal carrier.
Obedient to the moon he spent his date
30   In course reciprocal, and had his fate
Linked to the mutual flowing of the seas,
Yet (strange to think) his wain was his increase:
His letters are delivered all and gone,
Only remains this superscription.

22. **heaviness:** sadness.
26. **pressed to death:** a mode of execution used on prisoners who would not plead. They were put beneath boards on which rocks were placed and might cry out for more weight (a quicker death).
29–30. **Obedient . . . reciprocal:** Like the tides, he went back and forth each month (between Cambridge and London) in obedience to the moon.
32. **wain:** wagon, with a pun on *wane*, meaning "decrease, waste."
34. **this superscription:** the address on a letter and the inscription on a gravestone. Milton alludes to the poem itself, which is just now, in its final line, *delivered all and gone.*

AN EPITAPH ON THE MARCHIONESS OF WINCHESTER

Jane Savage married Lord John Paulet, the Marquis of Winchester, in 1622. She died at the age of twenty-three, soon after giving birth to a stillborn son on April 15, 1631; the cause of death was apparently an infection spread from a lanced abscess in her cheek. Other poems for the Marchioness survive, and lines 53–60 suggest that a volume by Cambridge elegists was at least planned. We know of nothing to connect Milton to this Roman Catholic family, though there is some evidence that Jane at the end of her life was inclining toward Protestantism (R. F. Williams 2:106). The suffering and frequent death of women in childbirth impressed Milton from an early age as a heavy instance of the "woe" (*PL* 1.3) rooted in our fallen condition (Louis Schwartz 2009).

In its tetrameter couplets, mixing regular with "headless" or trochaic lines, and in its confident classicism, the poem recalls Ben Jonson. But the climactic allusion to the biblical figure of Rachel has the same easy inventiveness with which the Jonsonian tradition approaches classical materials, and is therefore pure Milton.

This rich marble doth inter
The honored wife of Winchester,
A viscount's daughter, an earl's heir,
Besides what her virtues fair
5   Added to her noble birth,
More than she could own from earth.
Summers three times eight save one
She had told, alas too soon,
After so short time of breath,
10 To house with darkness, and with death.
Yet had the number of her days
Been as complete as was her praise,
Nature and fate had had no strife
In giving limit to her life.
15 Her high birth, and her graces sweet,
Quickly found a lover meet;
The virgin choir for her request
The god that sits at marriage feast;
He at their invoking came
20 But with a scarce-well-lighted flame;
And in his garland as he stood,
Ye might discern a cypress bud.
Once had the early matrons run
To greet her of a lovely son,
25 And now with second hope she goes,
And calls Lucina to her throes;
But whether by mischance or blame
Atropos for Lucina came;
And with remorseless cruelty,
30 Spoiled at once both fruit and tree:
The hapless babe before his birth
Had burial, yet not laid in earth,
And the languished mother's womb
Was not long a living tomb.

11–14. If her life had been as long as her praise were full, then the natures of those who mourn her would not feel cheated by fate.

16. In 1622, at the age of fourteen, she married John Paulet.

17. **request:** invoke.

18. **god:** Hymen.

20. Hymen's torch also sputtered at the ill-fated wedding of Orpheus and Eurydice (Ovid, *Met.* 10.6–7).

22. **cypress:** a tree long associated with mourning.

23. **early matrons:** timely midwives.

24. **greet her of:** congratulate her on; **son:** Charles, born 1629.

25. **second hope:** hope of a second child.

26. **Lucina:** Roman goddess of childbirth.

28. **Atropos:** The last of the three Fates; she cuts the thread of life.

31–32. **before his birth/Had burial:** Before she died, Jane delivered a stillborn boy.

35 So have I seen some tender slip
     Saved with care from winter's nip,
     The pride of her carnation train,
     Plucked up by some unheedy swain,
     Who only thought to crop the flow'r
40 New shot up from vernal show'r;
     But the fair blossom hangs the head
     Sideways as on a dying bed,
     And those pearls of dew she wears,
     Prove to be presaging tears
45 Which the sad morn had let fall
     On her hast'ning funeral.
     Gentle lady, may thy grave
     Peace and quiet ever have;
     After this thy travail sore
50 Sweet rest seize thee evermore,
     That to give the world increase,
     Shortened hast thy own life's lease;
     Here, besides the sorrowing
     That thy noble house doth bring,
55 Here be tears of perfect moan
     Wept for thee in Helicon,
     And some flowers, and some bays,
     For thy hearse to strew the ways,
     Sent thee from the banks of Came,
60 Devoted to thy virtuous name;
     Whilst thou bright saint high sit'st in glory,
     Next her much like to thee in story,
     That fair Syrian shepherdess,
     Who after years of barrenness,
65 The highly favored Joseph bore
     To him that served for her before,
     And at her next birth much like thee,
     Through pangs fled to felicity,
     Far within the bosom bright

---

35. **slip:** a shoot or sprig of a plant. In the forthcoming simile, the *slip* is Jane, the *unheedy swain* is death, and the *flow'r* is her stillborn son.

44. **presaging tears:** tears wept in advance of the fact of death, as if in premonition.

49. **travail:** labor, including the pain of childbirth.

50. **seize thee:** establish you in a place of dignity. *Sweet rest* is personified.

54. **bring:** bring forth.

56. **Helicon:** a mountain sacred to the Muses; some take it as a reference to Cambridge.

59. **Came:** the river Cam, which flows through Cambridge.

63. **Syrian shepherdess:** Rachel, Jacob's wife, who bore Joseph, then died giving birth to a second son, Benjamin.

66. **him:** Jacob; Gen. 29.20: "And Jacob served seven years for Rachel."

70 Of blazing majesty and light;
    There with thee, new welcome saint,
    Like fortunes may her soul acquaint,
    With thee there clad in radiant sheen,
    No marchioness, but now a queen.

73. **With thee there:** The reversal of *There with
thee* (71) is an early appearance of one of Mil-
ton's trademark effects.

L'ALLEGRO and IL PENSEROSO

The companion poems, as *L'Allegro* (Ital. for "the joyful man") and *Il Penseroso*
(Ital. for "the pensive man") are termed, do not appear in the Trinity College
manuscript and are therefore difficult to date. Their rustic settings suggest the
years following Cambridge, when Milton lived in his father's country homes at
Hammersmith (1632–35) and Horton (1635–38), but they could just as well have
been written earlier, during a normal college vacation.

The poems were widely and almost studiously imitated during the eigh-
teenth century (Havens 236–75) and, at least in the academic study of Milton, re-
tain their prestige today, despite the fact that the artful echoing between and
within the poems, combined with their prosodic exuberance, apparently places
them at some distance from theoretical concerns prominent in contemporary
literary criticism. But absence can itself become a topic. Annabel Patterson
(1988), with Raymond Williams in mind, observes that the ideal landscapes of the
poems have been censored of any indications of real work. Marshall Grossman
helps to fill in the picture by noting an anxiety over living off the labor of others.
Ken Hiltner, taking issue with political readings based on elements missing from
the pastoral form, defends the surface integrity of the poems (90–1).

Are the poems complementary or disjunctive? It belongs to their art that
they are both. On the one hand, the goddess scornfully dismissed at the begin-
ning of each poem is not the goddess celebrated in the other poem but her
pathological antitype. The poems do not expressly reject each other. On the
other hand, both speakers are trying to seal pacts with their respective god-
desses. If Mirth can provide the bounties sought by the happy man, he declares,
"Mirth with thee, I mean to live," and the pensive man adopts the same formula
in his closing address to Melancholy. Each, should his terms be met, has a com-
mitment to devote his life to his respective goddess. There is no hint that they
are simply shopping around for the best deal and after their evocations of an
ideal day will find out what's on offer from rival goddesses.

It seems clear that the pensive man wants more than the companion speaker,
though this observation should not be taken to suggest that the happy man does
not want a very great deal. Specifically, he wants a sure antidote to eating cares,

a place in a literary tradition that includes Jonson and Shakespeare, and access to a music more powerful than that of Orpheus. But the pensive man wants liberty of contemplation, the high magic of the Platonic and Hermetic traditions, the genres of tragedy and epic, the narrative enchantment of Chaucer, mysterious dreams, a religious music able to bring all Heaven before his eyes, time to acquire universal knowledge, and in the end "something like prophetic strain." Mirth's gifts would make any wise man happy. The gifts of Melancholy are those of a life of planned accomplishment similar to Milton's.

L'ALLEGRO

  Hence loathèd Melancholy,
   Of Cerberus, and blackest Midnight born,
  In Stygian cave forlorn
  'Mongst horrid shapes, and shrieks, and sights unholy,
5 Find out some uncouth cell,
   Where brooding Darkness spreads his jealous wings,
  And the night-raven sings;
   There under ebon shades, and low-browed rocks,
  As ragged as thy locks,
10 In dark Cimmerian desert ever dwell.
  But come thou goddess fair and free,
  In Heav'n yclept Euphrosyne,
  And by men, heart-easing Mirth,
  Whom lovely Venus at a birth
15 With two sister Graces more
  To ivy-crownèd Bacchus bore;
  Or whether (as some sager sing)
  The frolic wind that breathes the spring,

1. **loathèd Melancholy:** Melancholy entered the Renaissance in two main traditions. In Galenic medicine it was a pathological condition caused by excessive black bile. But Aristotle remarked briefly that all extraordinary men in the arts and sciences were melancholic, thus associating melancholy with genius (see Wittkower and Wittkower 102). The *loathèd Melancholy* dismissed here is the Galenic kind, not the *divinest* variety of the companion poem.

2. An invented genealogy. Erebus is the traditional husband of Night; Milton mates her with *Cerberus,* the hound of Hades, whose name means "heart-devouring."

3. According to Vergil, *Aen.* 6.418, Cerberus lived in a cave near the river Styx.

5. **uncouth:** desolate.

7. **night-raven:** a bird, perhaps an owl or night heron, associated with evil omens.

8. **shades:** trees.

9. **ragged:** rugged.

10. **Cimmerian:** Cimmerians live in perpetual darkness (Homer, *Od.* 11.13–19).

11. **fair and free:** a common romance formula, also found in Jonson's *Epigram 76;* **free:** of gentle birth and breeding.

12. **yclept:** called; **Euphrosyne:** Mirth, one of the three sister Graces. The other two were Aglais (Brilliance) and Thalia (Bloom).

14. **at a birth:** at one birth.

17. **some sager sing:** Milton invents this genealogy.

Zephyr with Aurora playing,
20   As he met her once a-Maying,
There on beds of violets blue,
And fresh-blown roses washed in dew,
Filled her with thee a daughter fair,
So buxom, blithe, and debonair.
25   Haste thee nymph, and bring with thee
Jest and youthful Jollity,
Quips and Cranks, and wanton Wiles,
Nods, and Becks, and wreathèd Smiles,
Such as hang on Hebe's cheek,
30   And love to live in dimple sleek;
Sport that wrinkled Care derides,
And Laughter holding both his sides.
Come, and trip it as ye go
On the light fantastic toe,
35   And in thy right hand lead with thee,
The mountain nymph, sweet Liberty;
And if I give thee honor due,
Mirth, admit me of thy crew
To live with her, and live with thee,
40   In unreprovèd pleasures free;
To hear the lark begin his flight,
And singing startle the dull night,
From his watch-tower in the skies,
Till the dappled dawn doth rise;
45   Then to come in spite of sorrow,
And at my window bid good morrow,
Through the sweet-briar, or the vine,
Or the twisted eglantine.

20. **a-Maying:** a reference to the May Day observances condemned by some Puritans.

24. **buxom, blithe, and debonair:** The three adjectives were often connected, as in Thomas Randolph's "A bowl of wine is wondrous boon cheer/To make one blithe, buxom, and debonair" (*Aristippus* 18); **buxom:** unresisting, yielding; **blithe:** happy; **debonair:** good-looking, affable, and in this case literally *de bon air,* given that the father is a wind.

27. **Quips:** sharp remarks; **Cranks:** jokes where a word (*heart-easing,* say) is twisted to resemble another of diverse meaning (*heart-eating*).

28. **Nods:** gestures of salutation; **Becks:** A beck is probably an upward movement of the head ("come on") corresponding to a beckoning by hand.

29. **Hebe:** goddess of youth.

33. **trip it:** dance.

34. **fantastic:** whimsical, fancifully conceived (transferred from the dance to the foot or *toe* of the dancer). In the form of "trip the light fantastic," this has become one of Milton's gifts to the proverb hoard of our language, but while *trip* may continue to suggest dancing to some users, *light fantastic* has become vaguely attached to neon lights or dramatically lit nightclubs, and *toe,* initially left out in tribute to the familiarity of the line, has been forgotten.

40. **unreprovèd:** blameless.

45. **Then to come:** Some think that the lark comes to the speaker's window, but most modern editions favor L'Allegro; **in spite of:** in defiance of.

48. **eglantine:** another name for sweetbriar.

While the cock with lively din,
50 Scatters the rear of darkness thin,
And to the stack, or the barn door,
Stoutly struts his dames before,
Oft list'ning how the hounds and horn,
Cheerly rouse the slumb'ring morn,
55 From the side of some hoar hill,
Through the high wood echoing shrill.
Some time walking not unseen
By hedge-row elms, on hillocks green,
Right against the eastern gate,
60 Where the great sun begins his state,
Robed in flames, and amber light,
The clouds in thousand liveries dight.
While the plowman near at hand,
Whistles o'er the furrowed land,
65 And the milkmaid singeth blithe,
And the mower whets his scythe,
And every shepherd tells his tale
Under the hawthorn in the dale.
Straight mine eye hath caught new pleasures
70 Whilst the landscape round it measures,
Russet lawns, and fallows gray,
Where the nibbling flocks do stray,
Mountains on whose barren breast
The laboring clouds do often rest:
75 Meadows trim with daisies pied,
Shallow brooks, and rivers wide.
Towers, and battlements it sees
Bosomed high in tufted trees,
Where perhaps some beauty lies,

---

50. **Scatters the rear:** The image is of an army in retreat, its back part being scattered by pursuing forces.

55. **hoar:** probably just a color word, denoting the frost-colored mists covering the hills in summertime.

57. **Some time walking:** "In those vernal seasons of the year, when the air is calm and pleasant, it were an injury and sullenness against nature not to go out, and see her riches, and partake in her rejoicing with heaven and earth" (*Of Ed,* in *MLM* 980).

60. **state:** royal progress (as when the monarch goes on a journey of state).

62. **dight:** clothed.

67. **tells his tale:** Editors have long argued about whether this means "counts his sheep" or "tells his story (of love)." Given the time of day, the first seems likelier.

71. **Russet lawns:** unplowed lands whose grasses have been turned reddish brown by the sun; **fallows:** plowed but unseeded lands.

75. **pied:** variegated.

78. **tufted:** growing in clusters.

79. **lies:** dwells.

80   The cynosure of neighboring eyes.
        Hard by, a cottage chimney smokes,
        From betwixt two agèd oaks,
        Where Corydon and Thyrsis met,
        Are at their savory dinner set
85   Of herbs, and other country messes,
        Which the neat-handed Phyllis dresses;
        And then in haste her bower she leaves,
        With Thestylis to bind the sheaves;
        Or if the earlier season lead
90   To the tanned haycock in the mead,
        Sometimes with secure delight
        The upland hamlets will invite,
        When the merry bells ring round,
        And the jocund rebecks sound
95   To many a youth, and many a maid,
        Dancing in the checkered shade;
        And young and old come forth to play
        On a sunshine holiday,
        Till the livelong daylight fail,
100   Then to the spicy nut-brown ale,
        With stories told of many a feat,
        How fairy Mab the junkets ate;
        She was pinched, and pulled she said,
        And he by friar's lantern led,
105   Tells how the drudging goblin sweat,
        To earn his cream-bowl duly set,
        When in one night, ere glimpse of morn,
        His shadowy flail hath threshed the corn
        That ten day-laborers could not end,

---

80. **cynosure:** that which serves to direct. Mariners steered by the polestar (Cynosure). So the beautiful lady is the constant referent by means of which men plot their courses.

83. **Corydon and Thyrsis:** common names in Renaissance pastoral.

91. **secure:** carefree.

94. **rebecks:** fiddles.

102. **Mab:** queen of the fairies, famously described by Shakespeare's Mercutio (*ROM* 1.4.54–95); **junkets:** cream cheeses or other dishes made with cream.

103. **She:** woman relating her tale of the supernatural to the group, just as, in the next line, *he* is a man telling his; **pinched:** Mab "pinches coun-

try wenches,/If they rub not clean their benches" (Jonson, *The Satyr* 58–59).

104. **friar's lantern:** unexplained. Milton seems to have in mind misleading lights such as the jack-o'-lantern or will-o'-the-wisp, but editors have yet to find one connected to a friar.

105. **drudging goblin:** Hobgoblin, a.k.a. Robin Goodfellow or Puck, takes up the drudgery of country maids in Jonson's *Love Restored* 59.

106. **cream-bowl:** conventional reward for a *drudging goblin.*

109. **end:** put in a barn. In one night the hobgoblin threshes more corn than ten men could *end* in a day.

110   Then lies him down the lubber fiend,
      And stretched out all the chimney's length,
      Basks at the fire his hairy strength;
      And crop-full out of doors he flings,
      Ere the first cock his matin rings.
115   Thus done the tales, to bed they creep,
      By whispering winds soon lulled asleep.
      Towered cities please us then,
      And the busy hum of men,
      Where throngs of knights and barons bold,
120   In weeds of peace high triumphs hold,
      With store of ladies, whose bright eyes
      Rain influence, and judge the prize
      Of wit, or arms, while both contend
      To win her grace, whom all commend.
125   There let Hymen oft appear
      In saffron robe, with taper clear,
      And pomp, and feast, and revelry,
      With mask, and antique pageantry,
      Such sights as youthful poets dream
130   On summer eves by haunted stream.
      Then to the well-trod stage anon,
      If Jonson's learned sock be on,
      Or sweetest Shakespeare, Fancy's child,
      Warble his native wood-notes wild.
135   And ever against eating cares,
      Lap me in soft Lydian airs,
      Married to immortal verse
      Such as the meeting soul may pierce

110. **lubber:** an inferior household servant, a drudge.

111. **chimney's:** fireplace's.

113. **crop-full:** completely full.

120. **weeds of peace:** courtly garments.

121. **store of:** plenty of.

122. **Rain influence:** Astrologically, *influence* is a tenuous but efficacious liquid supposed to flow from the stars. In love poetry, the lady's eyes were often compared to stars; hence the eyes of these ladies are said to *rain influence* on those whom they favor with a glance.

125. **Hymen:** marriage god, as usual wearing a *saffron robe* and carrying a torch (*taper*).

131. **anon:** instantly.

132. **learned sock:** The *sock* or low-heeled slipper of the Greek comic actor here stands for comedy itself. Jonson was (and wanted to be thought) a particularly learned playwright, the opposite of the warbling Shakespeare.

135. **eating cares:** translates Horace's *curas edacis* (*Odes* 2.11.18).

136. **Lap me:** enfold me, as in a garment; **soft Lydian airs:** Plato condemns effeminate Lydian music in favor of the martial Phrygian and solemn Dorian modes (*Rep.* 3.398–99). On Milton's unusual endorsement of it, see Hughes 1925.

137. **Married:** The marriage of music and verse was a poetic commonplace, as Warton demonstrated. Cp. *Solemn Music* 2–3.

138. **meeting:** coming forward in response or welcome (in this particular case, *meeting* in the sense of "anticipating harmony").

In notes, with many a winding bout
140 Of linkèd sweetness long drawn out,
    With wanton heed, and giddy cunning,
    The melting voice through mazes running;
    Untwisting all the chains that tie
    The hidden soul of harmony;
145 That Orpheus' self may heave his head
    From golden slumber on a bed
    Of heaped Elysian flow'rs, and hear
    Such strains as would have won the ear
    Of Pluto, to have quite set free
150 His half-regained Eurydice.
    These delights, if thou canst give,
    Mirth with thee, I mean to live.

139. **bout:** a movement turning or circling back on itself.

141. **wanton heed, and giddy cunning:** "The adjectives describe the appearance, the nouns the reality" (R. C. Browne).

145. **Orpheus' self:** Orpheus himself. To regain his dead wife, Eurydice, he sang for Proserpine and Pluto; **heave:** lift with effort.

147. **Elysian:** According to Ovid (*Met.* 11.61–66), Orpheus was reunited with Eurydice in the Elysian fields after his death at the hands of the Maenads, but there is no reference to her presence here.

147–50. **and hear . . . Eurydice:** The strains that Orpheus now hears would have convinced Pluto *to have quite set free* his captive—that is, released Eurydice without the condition (a fatal one in the event) that Orpheus could not look back at her as they walked out of Hades. Had Orpheus commanded this music, Eurydice would have been *entirely* regained.

151–52. Milton evokes the close of Marlowe's much-imitated "The Passionate Shepherd to His Love": "If these delights thy mind may move,/Then live with me, and be my love."

IL PENSEROSO

Hence vain deluding joys,
    The brood of Folly without father bred,
How little you bestead,
    Or fill the fixèd mind with all your toys;
5 Dwell in some idle brain,
    And fancies fond with gaudy shapes possess,
As thick and numberless
    As the gay motes that people the sunbeams,

1. **joys:** The poem begins, like *L'Allegro*, with a judgmental dismissal of a parody of the opposite goddess.

2. **without father bred:** either raised without a father, hence by implication bastards, or conceived without a father, hence unnatural.

3. **bestead:** help.

6. **fancies fond:** foolish fancies.

Or likest hovering dreams,
10   The fickle pensioners of Morpheus' train.
But hail thou goddess, sage and holy,
Hail divinest Melancholy,
Whose saintly visage is too bright
To hit the sense of human sight;
15   And therefore to our weaker view,
O'erlaid with black, staid Wisdom's hue.
Black, but such as in esteem,
Prince Memnon's sister might beseem,
Or that starred Ethiop queen that strove
20   To set her beauty's praise above
The sea nymphs, and their powers offended.
Yet thou art higher far descended,
Thee bright-haired Vesta long of yore,
To solitary Saturn bore;
25   His daughter she (in Saturn's reign,
Such mixture was not held a stain);
Oft in glimmering bow'rs, and glades
He met her, and in secret shades
Of woody Ida's inmost grove,
30   While yet there was no fear of Jove.
Come pensive nun, devout and pure,
Sober, steadfast, and demure,
All in a robe of darkest grain,
Flowing with majestic train,
35   And sable stole of cypress lawn,
Over thy decent shoulders drawn.
Come, but keep thy wonted state,

10. **pensioners:** attendants or dependents; *Morpheus:* son of Sleep and god of dreams.

11–55. The welcome to Melancholy, with her genealogy and her companions, parallels *L'All* 11–36. For the identity of this Melancholy, see *L'All* in.

14. **hit:** suit, agree with.

18. **Memnon's sister:** Memnon, the handsome dark-hued King of Ethiopia, fought for the Trojans and was slain by Achilles. Eventually tradition gave him a beautiful sister, as in Lydgate's *Troy Book* 5.2887–906.

19. **starred Ethiop queen:** A second ideal of black beauty is Cassiopea, who boasted that she was more beautiful than the Nereids. She is *starred* because after her death Neptune transformed her into a constellation.

23. **Vesta:** daughter of Saturn, goddess of flocks and herbs and households, and devoted to virginity. Milton invented the idea of Vesta as Melancholy's mother.

24. **Saturn:** This god had long been associated with the melancholic or saturnine temperament. See Klibansky et al.

27. **glimmering bow'rs:** retreats overarched with trees, through which light glimmers.

28–30. Eventually, knowing that one of his sons was destined to usurp his throne, a fearful Saturn ate his children; the siring of Melancholy took place before that fear.

33. **grain:** hue.

35. **sable stole:** long black robe; **cypress lawn:** fine linen.

36. **decent:** comely, handsome.

With even step, and musing gait,
And looks commercing with the skies,
40 Thy rapt soul sitting in thine eyes:
There held in holy passion still,
Forget thyself to marble, till
With a sad leaden downward cast,
Thou fix them on the earth as fast.

45 And join with thee calm Peace, and Quiet,
Spare Fast, that oft with gods doth diet,
And hears the Muses in a ring,
Ay round about Jove's altar sing.
And add to these retired Leisure,
50 That in trim gardens takes his pleasure;
But first, and chiefest, with thee bring,
Him that yon soars on golden wing,
Guiding the fiery-wheelèd throne,
The Cherub Contemplation,
55 And the mute Silence hist along,
'Less Philomel will deign a song,
In her sweetest, saddest plight,
Smoothing the rugged brow of Night,
While Cynthia checks her dragon yoke,
60 Gently o'er th' accustomed oak;
Sweet bird that shunn'st the noise of folly,
Most musical, most melancholy!
Thee chantress oft the woods among,
I woo to hear thy evensong;
65 And missing thee, I walk unseen
On the dry smooth-shaven green,
To behold the wand'ring moon,
Riding near her highest noon,
Like one that had been led astray
70 Through the heav'n's wide pathless way;
And oft, as if her head she bowed,

---

39. **commercing:** communicating.
42. **Forget thyself to marble:** become so entranced that your body is like a statue. Cp. *On Shakespeare* 14.
43. **sad:** serious (not "sorrowful"); **leaden:** Astrology associated lead with saturnine influences; **cast:** expression.
44. **fast:** fixedly.
48. **Ay:** continually. Muses dance around Jove's altar in Hesiod, *Theog.* 1–10.
53. **fiery-wheelèd throne:** Cp. God's chariot

(Ezek. 1 and 10), which also appears in *The Passion* 36–40.
54. **Cherub Contemplation:** According to traditional angelology, the cherubim contemplate God. *Cherub* is the singular of cherubim.
55. **hist along:** summoned without noise.
56. **Philomel:** the nightingale. See *Masque* 234n; **deign:** grant.
59. **Cynthia:** goddess of the moon, associated with Hecate and her dragon-drawn chariot.

Stooping through a fleecy cloud.
Oft on a plat of rising ground,
I hear the far-off curfew sound,
75   Over some wide-watered shore,
Swinging slow with sullen roar;
Or if the air will not permit,
Some still removèd place will fit,
Where glowing embers through the room
80   Teach light to counterfeit a gloom,
Far from all resort of mirth,
Save the cricket on the hearth,
Or the bellman's drowsy charm,
To bless the doors from nightly harm:
85   Or let my lamp at midnight hour,
Be seen in some high lonely tow'r,
Where I may oft outwatch the Bear,
With thrice-great Hermes, or unsphere
The spirit of Plato to unfold
90   What worlds, or what vast regions hold
The immortal mind that hath forsook
Her mansion in this fleshly nook:
And of those daemons that are found
In fire, air, flood, or under ground,
95   Whose power hath a true consent
With planet, or with element.
Sometime let gorgeous Tragedy
In sceptered pall come sweeping by,
Presenting Thebes, or Pelops' line,
100   Or the tale of Troy divine.

73. **plat:** plot, a small piece of land.
74. **curfew:** bell rung (usually at 9:00 P.M.) as a sign to put out fires.
83. **bellman:** night watchman calling the hours; Herrick's "The Bell-man" provides examples of his charms.
87. **outwatch the Bear:** Since Ursa Major (*the Bear*) never sets but simply disappears in the morning sky, the phrase means "stay awake all night."
88. **thrice-great Hermes:** Hermes Trismegistus, alleged author of the *Corpus Hermeticum,* for centuries wrongly supposed to be the earliest work of Western philosophy. In Hermes one could read of spells for summoning the dead. See Milton's *Of the Platonic Idea* 33; **unsphere:** call down from the planetary sphere (where it now resides).

93. **daemons:** In Hermeticism, spiritual beings corresponding to the four elements inhabit the entire cosmos. For the Christian Platonist Marsilio Ficino, the Greek-Platonic notion of daemons or attendant spirits was equivalent to angels (*Commentary on Plato's Symposium,* 110–13).
95. **consent:** accord.
98. **pall:** robe (Lat. *palla*) symbolic of tragedy.
99. **Thebes:** Aeschylus, Sophocles, and Euripides all set tragedies in Thebes; **Pelops' line:** The descendants of Pelops included tragic characters such as Atreus, Thyestes, Agamemnon, Orestes, Electra, and Iphigenia.
100. **tale of Troy divine:** Sophocles and Euripides set tragedies in Troy. Homer calls the city "divine" in *Od.* 11.86, 17.293.

Or what (though rare) of later age,
Ennobled hath the buskined stage.
But, O sad virgin, that thy power
Might raise Musaeus from his bower,
105   Or bid the soul of Orpheus sing
Such notes as warbled to the string,
Drew iron tears down Pluto's cheek,
And made Hell grant what love did seek.
Or call up him that left half-told
110   The story of Cambuscan bold,
Of Camball, and of Algarsife,
And who had Canace to wife,
That owned the virtuous ring and glass,
And of the wondrous horse of brass,
115   On which the Tartar king did ride;
And if aught else, great bards beside,
In sage and solemn tunes have sung,
Of tourneys and of trophies hung;
Of forests, and enchantments drear,
120   Where more is meant than meets the ear.
Thus, Night, oft see me in thy pale career,
Till civil-suited Morn appear,
Not tricked and frounced as she was wont,
With the Attic boy to hunt,
125   But kerchiefed in a comely cloud,
While rocking winds are piping loud,
Or ushered with a shower still,
When the gust hath blown his fill,
Ending on the rustling leaves,

102. **buskined:** dressed for the performance of tragedies in the "buskin," a high boot worn by Greek tragic actors, as opposed to the "sock" of comic actors (see *L'All* 132n).

104. **Musaeus:** a mythical early poet sometimes said to be the son of Orpheus.

105–8. Whereas the Orphic music requested at the end of *L'Allegro* (see 147–50n) is higher than that sung by Orpheus himself, the magus of *Il Penseroso* would hear the exact song Orpheus performed.

109. **him:** Chaucer, who left his *Squire's Tale* unfinished. The tale mixes Arabic settings with Western chivalry.

112. The line echoes Spenser's continuation of the *Squire's Tale* in *FQ* 4.3.52; **to wife:** as wife.

113. **virtuous:** endowed with magical power.

114. **wondrous horse of brass:** The brass horse was *wondrous* in being able to bear its rider any distance within twenty-four hours.

120. **more ... than meets the ear:** allegorical writing, such as Spenser practiced. *Meets* is likely intended to remind us of "the meeting soul" of *L'Allegro* 138, where the harmonies of the music are fully realized through the ear.

121. **pale career:** moonlit course.

122. **civil-suited:** soberly dressed. Cp. Shakespeare, *ROM* 3.2.10–11: "civil Night,/Thou sober-suited matron."

123. **tricked and frounced:** adorned and with curled hair.

124. **Attic boy:** Aurora or Morning loved the young Cephalus, an ardent hunter (Ovid, *Met.* 7.690–865).

127. **still:** quiet.

130 With minute drops from off the eaves.
And when the Sun begins to fling
His flaring beams, me goddess bring
To archèd walks of twilight groves,
And shadows brown that Sylvan loves
135 Of pine, or monumental oak,
Where the rude axe with heavèd stroke,
Was never heard the nymphs to daunt,
Or fright them from their hallowed haunt.
There in close covert by some brook,
140 Where no profaner eye may look,
Hide me from Day's garish eye,
While the bee with honeyed thigh,
That at her flow'ry work doth sing,
And the waters murmuring
145 With such consort as they keep,
Entice the dewy-feathered Sleep;
And let some strange mysterious dream
Wave at his wings in airy stream,
Of lively portraiture displayed,
150 Softly on my eyelids laid.
And as I wake, sweet music breathe
Above, about, or underneath,
Sent by some spirit to mortals good,
Or th' unseen Genius of the wood.
155 But let my due feet never fail,
To walk the studious cloister's pale,
And love the high embowèd roof,
With antique pillars' massy proof,
And storied windows richly dight,
160 Casting a dim religious light.
There let the pealing organ blow,
To the full-voiced choir below,

---

130. **minute:** small.
134. **Sylvan:** Roman god of the woods, subsequently identified with Pan.
139. **close covert:** a secret retreat inside dense growth.
141. **garish:** excessively bright.
145. **consort:** musical harmony.
148. **Wave at his wings:** Milton is describing a dream that begins, in the waking state, as a stream of moving images (*lively portraiture*) borne on the wings of Sleep.
154. **Genius of the wood:** See *Arcades* 62–78.

156. **pale:** enclosure.
157. **embowèd:** vaulted.
158. **massy proof:** proven strong in their massiveness (i.e., able to uphold the heavy roof).
159. **storied:** ornamented with biblical stories; **dight:** decorated.
160. **dim religious light:** Cp. Donne, *A Hymn to Christ:* "Churches are best for prayer that have least light"; also the dim churches of More's *Utopia,* built that way because "overmuch light doth disperse men's cogitations" (230).

In service high, and anthems clear,
As may with sweetness, through mine ear,
165 Dissolve me into ecstasies,
And bring all Heav'n before mine eyes.
And may at last my weary age
Find out the peaceful hermitage,
The hairy gown and mossy cell,
170 Where I may sit and rightly spell,
Of every star that heav'n doth show,
And every herb that sips the dew;
Till old experience do attain
To something like prophetic strain.
175 These pleasures Melancholy give,
And I with thee will choose to live.

164. **As:** such as.
165. **Dissolve me into ecstasies:** "separate my
soul from my body."
169. **hairy gown:** traditional garb of the ascetic.
170. **spell:** learn.
171–72. The shift from *star* to *herb* recalls the down-
ward course of Melancholy's stare in 39–44.

173. **old experience:** long study.
174. **strain:** melody, whether of song or poetry
(*OED* 3.12, 12b). Cp. *Lyc* 87: "That strain I heard
was of a higher mood."
175–76. See *L'All* 151–52 n.

ARCADES

Arcades, probably the opening of a larger entertainment, was performed in
honor of Alice, Dowager Countess of Derby, at some point in the early 1630s.
Then in her seventies, she was a veteran of early Stuart masquing, having per-
formed in Jonson's *Masque of Blackness* (1605) and *Masque of Beauty* (1607), and
having been the main presence in John Marston's *The . . . Lord and Lady of Hunt-
ingdon's Entertainment of their right Noble Mother Alice* (1607, but not published until
1801). Milton would have been particularly aware that his beloved Spenser had
dedicated *Tears of the Muses* (1591) to her, represented her under the name
"Amaryllis" in *Colin Clouts Come Home Again* (1595), and in both works boasted of
being her kin (she was born Alice Spenser). So Milton was not just augmenting
a literary fame first spread by Spenser, although that aspect of the piece was no
doubt gratifying. He was also honoring Spenser's blood.

Alice married Sir Thomas Egerton, Lord Keeper, in 1600, and his son Sir
John subsequently wed her daughter. In 1617 Sir John Egerton was created the
first Earl of Bridgewater, and was appointed Lord Lieutenant of Wales in 1631.
Milton's *A Masque (Comus)* celebrates Egerton's assumption of his duties in
Wales.

Henry Lawes, a family friend to the musically minded Miltons, was music tutor to the earl's children. It seems a reasonable conjecture that he was responsible on this occasion for steering the Bridgewater family toward a young and unknown poet, just as he was responsible for the more important commission to write *A Masque.*

Milton compliments Alice more extravagantly than Spenser. He does not praise her more outrageously than Marston; no one could. But Milton, while submitting to the conventions of the masque, is far more loyal than Marston to a much older literary genre: pastoral. He can imagine no higher praise for a great figure like Countess Alice than to enshrine her as the supreme rural queen in Arcadia, held in awe by the genius of the woods and sought by a pilgrim band of nymphs and shepherds.

Part of an entertainment presented to the
Countess Dowager of Darby at Harefield, by some
noble persons of her family, who appear on the
scene in pastoral habit, moving toward the seat of
state, with this song.

1. *Song*

Look nymphs, and shepherds look,
What sudden blaze of majesty
Is that which we from hence descry
Too divine to be mistook:
5   This, this is she
To whom our vows and wishes bend,
Here our solemn search hath end.

Fame that her high worth to raise,
Seemed erst so lavish and profuse,
10   We may justly now accuse
Of detraction from her praise;
      Less than half we find expressed,
      Envy bid conceal the rest.

Title. **Arcades:** Arcadians. Arcadia is a Greek valley long associated with the pastoral genre. In the Renaissance, both Sannazaro and Sidney set pastoral fictions there.
6. **vows:** prayers, promises made to gods.
8–13. The passage alludes to poetic praises of the countess once written by Spenser and others but today reduced to a trickle.
8. **raise:** extol, exalt.
9. **erst:** formerly.
12. **Less than half:** Cp. the Queen of Sheba to Solomon: "Behold, the half was not told me" (1 Kings 10.7).

Mark what radiant state she spreads,
15 In circle round her shining throne,
Shooting her beams like silver threads:
This, this is she alone,
    Sitting like a goddess bright,
    In the center of her light.

20 Might she the wise Latona be,
Or the towered Cybele,
Mother of a hundred gods;
Juno dares not give her odds;
    Who had thought this clime had held
25 A deity so unparalleled?

As they come forward, the Genius of the Wood appears, and turning toward
them, speaks.

Genius. Stay gentle swains, for though in this disguise,
I see bright honor sparkle through your eyes;
Of famous Arcady ye are, and sprung
Of that renownèd flood, so often sung,
30 Divine Alpheus, who by secret sluice,
Stole under seas to meet his Arethuse;
And ye the breathing roses of the wood,
Fair silver-buskined Nymphs as great and good,
I know this quest of yours, and free intent
35 Was all in honor and devotion meant
To the great mistress of yon princely shrine,
Whom with low reverence I adore as mine,
And with all helpful service will comply
To further this night's glad solemnity;
40 And lead ye where ye may more near behold
What shallow-searching Fame hath left untold;

14. **radiant state:** The word *state* could refer to splendor befitting the great, or a raised chair beneath a canopy, or the canopy alone. The third meaning best suits the context.
20. **Latona:** mother of Apollo and Diana.
21. **Cybele:** Phrygian goddess identified with Rhea and Ops, the wife of Saturn and mother of Jove, Juno, and other deities. Vergil describes her wearing a towered crown and clutching a hundred of her grandchildren (*Aen.* 6.784–87).
23. **give her odds:** offer to compete with her on terms that favor the countess.
30. **secret sluice:** hidden channel.

31. **Arethuse:** nymph devoted to Diana, who turned *Arethuse* into a stream to help her flee the river god *Alpheus.* Arethuse flowed under the sea to the island of Ortygia in Syracuse, Sicily. Alpheus pursued her there, and their waters mingled in a fountain.
32. **breathing:** fragrant.
33. **silver-buskined:** clad in high silver boots.
34. **free:** noble, generous.
37. **low reverence:** deep bow.
39. **solemnity:** festive ceremony.
41. **shallow-searching:** looking superficially. Cp. the attack on fame in 8–13.

Which I full oft amidst these shades alone
Have sat to wonder at, and gaze upon:
For know by lot from Jove I am the pow'r
45 Of this fair wood, and live in oaken bow'r,
To nurse the saplings tall, and curl the grove
With ringlets quaint, and wanton windings wove.
And all my plants I save from nightly ill,
Of noisome winds, and blasting vapors chill.
50 And from the boughs brush off the evil dew,
And heal the harms of thwarting thunder blue,
Or what the cross dire-looking planet smites,
Or hurtful worm with cankered venom bites.
When evening gray doth rise, I fetch my round
55 Over the mount, and all this hallowed ground,
And early ere the odorous breath of morn
Awakes the slumb'ring leaves, or tasseled horn
Shakes the high thicket, haste I all about,
Number my ranks, and visit every sprout
60 With puissant words, and murmurs made to bless;
But else in deep of night when drowsiness
Hath locked up mortal sense, then listen I
To the celestial sirens' harmony,
That sit upon the nine enfolded spheres,
65 And sing to those that hold the vital shears,
And turn the adamantine spindle round,
On which the fate of gods and men is wound.
Such sweet compulsion doth in music lie,
To lull the daughters of Necessity,
70 And keep unsteady Nature to her law,
And the low world in measured motion draw

---

49. **blasting:** withering.
50. **evil dew:** mildew.
51. **thwarting thunder blue:** *Thunder* here stands for *lightning.* Its blue light is *thwarting,* cutting across the sky.
52. **cross dire-looking planet:** Saturn, *cross* (adverse) because *dire-looking* (of evil aspect in an astrological sense).
53. **worm with cankered venom:** The term *cankerworm* was applied to caterpillars and insect larvae that eat leaves and buds. Cp. *Lyc* 45.
54. **fetch my round:** make my customary circuit.
57. **tasseled horn:** ornamented hunting horn.
59. **Number my ranks:** count my trees in their rows (like soldiers in a formation).

60. **puissant . . . bless:** potent magic charms and blessings.
63. **celestial sirens' harmony:** In Plato's *Rep.* 10.616–17, each of the celestial spheres has a siren who sings one note; together these notes make up the music of the spheres.
65. **those that hold the vital shears:** In Plato (see 63n) the celestial spheres are threaded on the spindle of Necessity. Her daughters, the three Fates, sit around her and turn the spindle. In this line Milton imagines that all three of the Fates wield the *shears* that cut life's thread (technically, that is the job of Atropos). *Vital* here means "fatal to life."
71. **measured:** rhythmical.

After the heavenly tune, which none can hear
Of human mold with gross unpurgèd ear;
And yet such music worthiest were to blaze
75   The peerless height of her immortal praise,
Whose luster leads us, and for her most fit,
If my inferior hand or voice could hit
Inimitable sounds; yet as we go,
Whate'er the skill of lesser gods can show,
80   I will assay, her worth to celebrate,
And so attend ye toward her glittering state;
Where ye may all that are of noble stem
Approach, and kiss her sacred vesture's hem.

2. *Song*

O'er the smooth enameled green
85   Where no print of step hath been,
        Follow me as I sing,
        And touch the warbled string.
Under the shady roof
Of branching elm star-proof,
90   Follow me,
I will bring you where she sits,
Clad in splendor as befits
        Her deity.
Such a rural queen
95   All Arcadia hath not seen.

3. *Song*

Nymphs and shepherds dance no more
    By sandy Ladon's lilied banks.
On old Lycaeus or Cyllene hoar,
    Trip no more in twilight ranks;
100   Though Erymanth your loss deplore,

---

72. **none can hear:** Cp. *Nat Ode* 125n, and *Pro 2* (Yale 1:238).

73. **mold:** the earth from which our bodies are formed.

74. **blaze:** proclaim.

77. **hit:** imitate perfectly.

80. **assay:** attempt.

81. **state:** chair of state.

84. **enameled:** adorned with many colors (referring here to flowers of many colors).

89. **star-proof:** admitting no starlight, with perhaps the astrological sense of "admitting no malign celestial influences."

97. **Ladon:** a river in Arcadia that empties into the Alpheus (see 31n).

98–102. *Lycaeus, Cyllene, Erymanth,* and *Maenalus* are all mountains in Arcadia.

A better soil shall give ye thanks.
From the stony Maenalus,
Bring your flocks, and live with us;
Here ye shall have greater grace,
105 To serve the Lady of this place.
Though Syrinx your Pan's mistress were,
Yet Syrinx well might wait on her.
Such a rural queen
All Arcadia hath not seen.

106. **Syrinx:** A nymph pursued by Pan. She ran
into the river Ladon and became a reed.

AT A SOLEMN MUSIC

Some poems in the Trinity College manuscript appear as fair copies. Others
seem to have been composed in the manuscript itself. *At a Solemn Music* belongs
to this second category, as there are four distinct drafts, the first one written on
the reverse of the leaf containing the end of *Arcades* and the last a fair copy. It
seems a safe bet that the poem was begun soon after *Arcades*. The pastoral enter-
tainment cannot be securely dated, though 1632 seems likely (Campbell 47).

The title means "At a Sacred Concert." Listening appreciatively to a piece of
vocal music inspires a lofty meditation on the place of music in the universe
and its history. Leo Spitzer's *Classical and Christian Ideas of World Harmony*, a clas-
sic of intellectual history, explores the traditions behind the poem and also con-
tains a discussion of it (see as well Heninger).

Blest pair of sirens, pledges of Heav'n's joy,
Sphere-borne harmonious sisters, Voice and Verse,
Wed your divine sounds, and mixed power employ
Dead things with inbreathed sense able to pierce,
5 And to our high-raised fantasy present
That undisturbèd song of pure concent,
Ay sung before the sapphire-colored throne
To him that sits thereon

1. **sirens:** Plato identified celestial music with the
songs of eight sirens (*Rep.* 10.616–17). Cp. *Arcades*
63–64; **pledges:** both "offspring" and "assurances."
4. The songs of Orpheus had this power, as in *PL*
7.34–36. Cp. *Masque* 561–62.

6. **concent:** concord.
7. **Ay:** forever; **sapphire-colored throne:** God's
throne; see Ezek. 1.26.

With saintly shout, and solemn jubilee,
10 Where the bright Seraphim in burning row
Their loud uplifted angel trumpets blow,
And the Cherubic host in thousand choirs
Touch their immortal harps of golden wires,
With those just spirits that wear victorious palms,
15 Hymns devout and holy psalms
Singing everlastingly;
That we on earth with undiscording voice
May rightly answer that melodious noise;
As once we did, till disproportioned sin
20 Jarred against nature's chime, and with harsh din
Broke the fair music that all creatures made
To their great Lord, whose love their motion swayed
In perfect diapason, whilst they stood
In first obedience, and their state of good.
25 O may we soon again renew that song,
And keep in tune with Heav'n, till God ere long
To his celestial consort us unite,
To live with him, and sing in endless morn of light.

9. **jubilee:** joyful shouting. The Hebrew Jubilee was a ritual emancipation of slaves celebrated every fifty years. Christians considered it a type of the Atonement.

14. **those just spirits:** justified spirits, the saints. Cp. Rev. 7.9: "a great multitude . . . clothed in white robes, and palms in their hands."

17. **undiscording:** Milton's coinage suggests not mere concord, but a concord won from a constant victory over discord.

19. **disproportioned:** disharmonious.

23. **diapason:** complete concord.

27. **consort:** harmony of voices, company of musicians.

ON TIME

Editors generally date this poem in the early 1630s. In the Trinity College manuscript, a phrase is written beneath the title "On Time." All that is legible today is the words "set on a clock case," which have been scored out. The manuscript was ill-handled for many years, and by the time it was photographed for facsimile reproduction in 1899, a strip of paper had been pasted over the top left side of this page (fol. 8). On the basis of eighteenth- and nineteenth-century transcriptions, we know that originally something was written before "set"—probably "to be." But we do not know whether the author considered "to be set on a clock case," before he struck it out, as a subtitle or an alternative title. Presumably the word *set* indicates that the poem is to be glued onto the clock case, perhaps to the back of the case's door.

The clock Milton has in mind is the one modern horologists call a "lantern clock." It was the earliest household clock manufactured in England. Made of brass, it sat on a wall shelf. The two ends of a line threaded in the mechanism of the clock hung through a hole in the shelf. A lead weight was affixed to the short end of the line, and its subsequent graduated descent drove the mechanism. After about thirty hours, the weight had to be transferred to the other side (now the short side) of the line. A lantern clock had one dial for marking hours and a twelve-hour face. In the 1630s, when Milton wrote this poem, England stood on the brink of an industrial boom in clockmaking that would last through the next century and well into the nineteenth. English makers would capture much of the European market from their main competitors in Germany, and the excellent design and accuracy of the English clock would become a matter of considerable national pride. The long good time of this British industry could be said to have begun when, in 1631, a royal patent was granted to the London Guild of Clockmakers. Milton's lyric enters the history of British clocks on the threshold of a major economic triumph.

Fly envious Time, till thou run out thy race,
Call on the lazy leaden-stepping hours,
Whose speed is but the heavy plummet's pace;
And glut thyself with what thy womb devours,
5   Which is no more than what is false and vain,
And merely mortal dross;
So little is our loss,
So little is thy gain.
For when as each thing bad thou hast entombed,
10   And last of all, thy greedy self consumed,
Then long eternity shall greet our bliss
With an individual kiss;
And joy shall overtake us as a flood,
When everything that is sincerely good

1. **envious:** The adjective was conventionally attached to personified *Time,* but in this poem the malice is specific: Time envies man because Time has no stake in Eternity, no share in the Christian promise of salvation.
2. **leaden-stepping:** The mechanisms of early lantern clocks were driven by the graduated falling of lead-weighted cords.
3. **plummet:** the lead weight referred to in 2n.
4. **womb:** stomach.
7–8. Milton returned to the end-words of these lines for the titles of *Paradise Lost* and *Paradise Regained.*

9. **when as:** when. The *when*s of lines 9, 14, and 19 refer, as it were, to the first moment after time, to eternity in its sudden newness.
12. **individual kiss:** an indivisible and therefore unending kiss; but the word *individual* was just acquiring its modern sense of "peculiar to a particular person," and Milton might be suggesting that the joy of salvation will be felt by the individual soul not (as in Averroism) by a collective world-soul. A professor at Milton's college, Henry More, was for a time an Averroist (Nicolson 1960, 299–300).
14. **sincerely:** wholly.

15   And perfectly divine,
     With Truth, and Peace, and Love shall ever shine
     About the supreme throne
     Of him, t' whose happy-making sight alone,
     When once our Heav'nly-guided soul shall climb,
20   Then all this earthy grossness quit,
     Attired with stars, we shall forever sit,
         Triumphing over Death, and Chance, and thee, O Time.

18. **happy-making sight:** anglicizes the theological term "beatific vision."

20. **quit:** left behind.

21. **Attired with stars:** Cp. Rev. 12.1: "upon her head a crown of twelve stars."

22. **Chance:** The defeat of chance is a common motive in Christian thought. See Boethius, *The Consolation of Philosophy*, 5.1 and *passim.*

UPON THE CIRCUMCISION

Though often dated in 1633, this poem's evident connection with both the *Nativity Ode* and *The Passion* may argue for an earlier composition. If it were the last written of the three, *Upon the Circumcision* could be viewed as literary redemption for the failure of *The Passion*. Here Milton *is* able to deal with the death of Christ, but at a temporal distance made possible by traditional typology. The first blood of the circumcision prefigures the sacrifice of the Crucifixion; Milton's climactic association of the wound of the circumcision knife with the spear wound after Christ's death on the Cross belongs to the design of Christian history. The struggle between love and law announced in the center of the poem suggests Paul, and the "circumcision" of the "heart" (the poem's final word) was indeed a favorite theme of the Apostle (see 28n).

Ye flaming Powers, and wingèd warriors bright,
That erst with music, and triumphant song
First heard by happy watchful shepherds' ear,
So sweetly sung your joy the clouds along
5   Through the soft silence of the list'ning night;
Now mourn, and if sad share with us to bear
Your fiery essence can distill no tear,
Burn in your sighs, and borrow

1. **Powers:** one of the nine orders of angels in Pseudo-Dionysius, but here naming all angels.

2. **erst:** formerly, alluding like the opening of *The Passion* to the *Nat Ode*.

6–9. Milton suggests that the angels, if they cannot ordinarily cry, could burn, and with this sunlike heat draw up to Heaven the seas of tears wept on Earth.

Seas wept from our deep sorrow;
10   He who with all Heav'n's heraldry whilere
Entered the world, now bleeds to give us ease;
Alas, how soon our sin
    Sore doth begin
      His infancy to seize!
15   O more exceeding love or law more just?
Just law indeed, but more exceeding love!
For we by rightful doom remédiless
Were lost in death, till he that dwelt above
High throned in secret bliss, for us frail dust
20   Emptied his glory, ev'n to nakedness;
And that great cov'nant which we still transgress
Entirely satisfied,
And the full wrath beside
Of vengeful Justice bore for our excess,
25   And seals obedience first with wounding smart
This day: but O ere long
    Huge pangs and strong
      Will pierce more near his heart.

10. **Heav'n's heraldry:** heraldic pomp (of the Nativity); **whilere:** a while back.

11. **now bleeds:** at the circumcision.

12–14. The shrinking lines imitate the seizing.

12. **our sin:** the Fall, which makes Christ's sacrifice necessary.

15–16. Christ's sacrifice is the defeat of law (the law demanding our death), symbolized by the circumcision knife, by love (forgiveness), symbolized by his blood.

21. **that great cov'nant:** the Mosaic Law.

22. Cp. *PL* 3.212: "The rigid satisfaction, death for death."

24. **excess:** violation of the law.

28. **Will pierce:** alluding to the spear thrust into

Christ's side (John 19.34). The first blood of the circumcision is a type or prefiguration of the Crucifixion. Herbert connected that final wound with the birth of Eve from the side of Adam and the origin of the Eucharist: "They will pierce my side . . . /That as sin came, so sacraments might flow" ("The Sacrifice" 246–47); **heart:** See Paul's discussion of the circumcision of the heart in Rom. 2.28–29, 3.30, 4.9–17; Col. 2.11–14; et cetera.

A MASQUE PRESENTED
AT LUDLOW CASTLE, 1634 [COMUS]

This work is commonly known under the title *Comus*, which it was given when revised for the stage in the eighteenth century. In its three printings during Milton's lifetime, it was uniformly entitled *A Masque Presented at Ludlow Castle*.

The masque was performed on Michaelmas night (September 29) 1634 in the great hall at Ludlow Castle in Shropshire to celebrate the first visit of the Earl of Bridgewater, recently appointed Lord President of the Council of Wales and

Lord Lieutenant of the Welsh and border counties, to the territory he was now to administer. It is misleading to speak of roles and parts with regard to the court masque of the seventeenth century, since these were not off-the-rack characters open to any actor or actress but tailor-made for specific people. The Lady was Bridgewater's daughter, Alice Egerton, age fifteen; the Elder and Younger Brothers were Bridgewater's sons John, Viscount Brackley, age eleven, and Lord Thomas Egerton, age nine. It may help to explain how *A Masque* could be at once a public performance and a personal statement to note that the masquing family (older sister and two younger brothers) mirrors, with Milton in the role of the Older Brother, the poet's own family (an older sister, Ann, a younger brother, Christopher).

The Attendant Spirit was the music tutor of the Egerton children, Henry Lawes, a man with a great deal of experience in this dramatic genre (see the headnotes to *Arcades* and *Sonnet 13*). He wrote the songs for *Masque,* and supervised its anonymous publication in 1637. The Earl of Bridgewater was the stepson and son-in-law of the Countess Dowager of Derby, for whom Milton had devised *Arcades,* which had also been staged by Lawes. It seems likely that the success of *Arcades* encouraged Lawes to commission a second, more ambitious work from the young Milton.

Besides the versions printed in 1637, 1645, and 1673, there are two significant manuscripts. Milton seems to have made his initial entries in the Trinity College manuscript (*CMS*) in 1632 and continued to revise the work throughout his lifetime. Several fair copies are believed to have been made at various stages of the *CMS* text, and there is now good reason to think (Sprott; Gaskell; Brown) that the other significant manuscript, the so-called Bridgewater manuscript (*BMS*) kept among the papers of the Egerton family, is one of those copies, a rather poor one done by a scribe perhaps as early as 1634. But the *BMS* was once considered the acting text used in 1634, and quite possibly in the hand of Henry Lawes. This mistaken conception of the *BMS* figures in a good bit of now dubious theorizing about the political, psychological, or philosophical meaning of supposed revisions to the performance version of *A Masque.*

The anonymous 1637 edition is prefaced by a letter from Henry Lawes to the work's Elder Brother, John Egerton. Lawes reveals that, although he has had many requests for copies of the masque, a burden this publication intends to shed, the entertainment is "not openly acknowledged by the author." It would seem that only a reluctant author, and not Lawes, could have chosen the odd Vergilian epigraph (*Ec.* 2.58–59) for the 1637 *Masque: Eheu quid volui misero mihi: floribus austrum Perditus* ("Did I mean my own destruction when I let the south wind blow upon my flowers?"). Whatever was meant by this strangely apprehensive epigraph, Milton seems entirely proud of the work by 1645, where *A Masque* is placed last among the English poems, prefaced by the Lawes letter from 1637 and a second letter from the poet and diplomat Sir Henry Wotton, thanking Milton for sending him "a dainty piece of entertainment." The letters are absent in 1673, no doubt because Milton had outgrown this simplistic technique for courting prestige.

The history of the court masque has been studied by Enid Welsford, John Demaray, and Cedric Brown. A new slant on the genre, aimed at linking aesthetic and political analysis, emerged in Stephen Orgel's *The Illusion of Power* (1975), one of the founding studies of the so-called New Historicism, whose influence can be felt in the treatment of masques in Graham Parry's *The Golden Age Restor'd: The Culture of the Stuart Court, 1603–42* (1981) and Jonathan Goldberg's *James I and the Politics of Literature* (1983). But histories of masquing of any kind tend to illuminate Milton's sharp differences with standard procedures. Ben Jonson introduced the character of Comus to the English masque tradition in *Pleasure Reconciled with Virtue* (performed in 1618 but not printed until 1640). Jonson's Comus was a god of gluttony, patron of meat and drink, and was whisked away by Hercules in the first antimasque; he bears little if any relation to Milton's wily sorcerer. The Circe episode of the *Odyssey* was a popular source of plot devices ("hinges," as Jonson called them) in the masque tradition. William Browne's *Inner Temple Masque* and Aurelian Townshend's *Tempe Restored* are the two examples most frequently mentioned by critics and editors, though again, it is immediately clear that neither work has, or even aspires to, the philosophical concentration of *Masque*. Among stage plays, George Peele's *An Old Wives' Tale* is credited with the plot of two brothers having to rescue a sister from an evil enchanter. There are also intriguing connections with John Fletcher's *The Faithful Shepherdess*, which contains an ardent defense of chastity against its enemies, and a villain who defends unchastity by reference to nature's foison. Finally, the Shakespearean vigor of phrase and figure in *A Masque* has often been noted (Leavis).

Explanations for the peculiarities of the work, especially its interest in chastity, have been sought in topical events. Barbara Breasted and Rosemary Mundhenk pointed to the sexual outrages committed by the Second Earl of Castlehaven, who was the brother-in-law of Bridgewater's wife. He was tried and executed in 1631 for a number of sexual crimes involving his wife and his servants. Leah Marcus pled for the importance of the illiterate serving maid Margery Evans, who had perhaps been raped and wrongfully jailed in 1631, and whose appeal came under the jurisdiction of the Earl of Bridgewater. These attempts to situate *Masque* in its historical milieu suggest that its elevated conception of chastity was meant to dissociate the Egerton family from scandal and can be thought of as emanating, not from anything unusual or interesting in the soul of Milton, but rather from the immediate concerns of his patrons. Such arguments can never be what they most want to be—a bulwark against the possibility of psychological explanation. For even if we suppose that "base the entertainment on chastity" was part of Milton's commission, there is no reason why something in his soul might not have responded, "That's no problem, believe me."

⌒⌒

THE PERSONS

    The Attendant Spirit, afterwards in the habit of Thyrsis
    Comus, with his crew
    The Lady
    1. Brother
    2. Brother
    Sabrina the Nymph.

    The chief persons which presented were
    The Lord Brackley,
    Mr. Thomas Egerton his brother,
    The Lady Alice Egerton.

    The first scene discovers a wild wood.

    The Attendant Spirit descends or enters.

    Before the starry threshold of Jove's court
    My mansion is, where those immortal shapes
    Of bright aërial spirits live enspherèd
    In regions mild of calm and serene air,
5   Above the smoke and stir of this dim spot,
    Which men call earth, and with low-thoughted care
    Confined and pestered in this pinfold here,
    Strive to keep up a frail and feverish being
    Unmindful of the crown that Virtue gives
10 After this mortal change, to her true servants
    Amongst the enthroned gods on sainted seats.
    Yet some there be that by due steps aspire

[Stage direction]: The printed versions of 1637, 1645, and 1673 have "Attendant Spirit," while *CMS* and *BMS* have "a guardian spirit, or daemon."

3. enspherèd: in their allotted sphere, like the spirit of Plato in *Il Pens* 88–89.

5. smoke and stir: the corrupt atmosphere (*rank vapors* in 17) of this place and the pointless strife of most of its inhabitants (*Strive* in 8); the quasi-hendiadys evokes Shakespeare (see Wright 1981).

6. men call earth: Socrates says that the earth we take for granted is a misty hollow, whereas the true earth's surface lies among the stars (Plato, *Phaedo* 109–11).

7. pestered: crowded; restrained, by shackles or a tether; pinfold: holding pen for animals.

10. mortal change: death, the change from mortal existence. Cp. *immortal change* (841).

To lay their just hands on that golden key
That opes the palace of eternity:
15 To such my errand is, and but for such,
I would not soil these pure ambrosial weeds
With the rank vapors of this sin-worn mold.
     But to my task. Neptune, besides the sway
Of every salt flood, and each ebbing stream,
20 Took in by lot 'twixt high and nether Jove
Imperial rule of all the sea-girt isles
That like to rich and various gems inlay
The unadornèd bosom of the deep,
Which he to grace his tributary gods
25 By course commits to several government,
And gives them leave to wear their sapphire crowns,
And wield their little tridents; but this isle,
The greatest and the best of all the main,
He quarters to his blue-haired deities,
30 And all this tract that fronts the falling sun
A noble peer of mickle trust and power
Has in his charge, with tempered awe to guide
An old and haughty nation proud in arms:
Where his fair offspring nursed in princely lore
35 Are coming to attend their father's state,
And new-entrusted scepter, but their way
Lies through the perplexed paths of this drear wood,
The nodding horror of whose shady brows
Threats the forlorn and wand'ring passenger.
40 And here their tender age might suffer peril,
But that by quick command from sov'reign Jove
I was dispatched for their defense and guard;
And listen why, for I will tell ye now
What never yet was heard in tale or song
45 From old or modern bard in hall or bow'r.

---

13. **golden key:** Cp. the "golden key" of *Lyc* III, which also opens the gates of Heaven.

16. **weeds:** clothes, specifically the *sky robes* of l. 83.

17. **sin-worn mold:** could be either the pestilent earth or the pestilent body. From which side of his garments is the soiling expected?

18. **sway:** rule.

20. **Took ... Jove:** After Saturn's overthrow, Neptune and his brothers, Jove and Pluto (*nether Jove*), divided the universe by casting lots (*Il.* 15.187–93).

27. **this isle:** Britain.

29. **quarters:** assigns.

30. **this tract:** Wales and the Welsh Marches.

31. **noble peer:** the Earl of Bridgewater; **mickle:** great.

33. **nation:** Wales.

35. **state:** throne (cp. "seat of state" in the headnote of *Arcades*).

37. **perplexed:** entangled; **wood:** Cp. Dante, *Inf.* 1–3, and Spenser, *FQ* 1.1.7–10.

38. **nodding:** The *shady brows* of the forest bend over or droop.

45. **hall or bow'r:** rooms in a castle: the common *hall* where feasts were hosted, and the *bower* or bedroom.

Bacchus that first from out the purple grape
Crushed the sweet poison of misusèd wine,
After the Tuscan mariners transformed,
Coasting the Tyrrhene shore, as the winds listed,
50 On Circe's island fell (who knows not Circe
The daughter of the Sun? Whose charmèd cup
Whoever tasted, lost his upright shape,
And downward fell into a groveling swine).
This nymph that gazed upon his clust'ring locks,
55 With ivy berries wreathed, and his blithe youth,
Had by him, ere he parted thence, a son
Much like his father, but his mother more,
Whom therefore she brought up and Comus named,
Who ripe and frolic of his full-grown age,
60 Roving the Celtic and Iberian fields,
At last betakes him to this ominous wood,
And in thick shelter of black shades embowered,
Excels his mother at her mighty art,
Off'ring to every weary traveler,
65 His orient liquor in a crystal glass,
To quench the drought of Phoebus, which as they taste
(For most do taste through fond intemperate thirst)
Soon as the potion works, their human count'nance,
Th' express resemblance of the gods, is changed
70 Into some brutish form of wolf, or bear,
Or ounce, or tiger, hog, or bearded goat,
All other parts remaining as they were;
And they, so perfect is their misery,

48. **the Tuscan mariners transformed:** Bacchus transformed his abductors into dolphins (Ovid, *Met.* 3.582-691).

49. **Tyrrhene shore:** coast of Italy facing Sardinia and Corsica.

51. **daughter of the Sun:** as Circe is said to be in Homer (*Od.* 10.135–38); **charmèd cup:** The Circe of Homer and Ovid does offer men a cup, but her wand effects their metamorphosis into animals (*Od.* 10.233–39; *Met.* 14.277–80); the expanded role of the cup in Milton suggests temptation and moral choice.

55. **ivy berries:** Bacchus is often represented with a crown woven of grapevine and ivy.

56. **a son:** Comus, from the Greek *komos* or "revelry," was a minor deity in classical culture, associated with the marriage ceremony and drunkenness; he appears as a belly god in Jon-

son's mask *Pleasure Reconciled to Virtue* (1618). Milton here invents his parentage.

59. **frolic of his full-grown age:** sportive with his mature powers.

60. **Celtic, and Iberian:** French and Spanish.

65. **orient:** bright.

66. **drought of Phoebus:** thirst brought on by the sun.

66–77. Milton's account differs from Homer's in the following particulars: the potion, not the wand, effects the change; only the head is changed; the victims are not transformed into swine only but into various beasts; they do not realize their change (in Homer they yearn to be men again); they forget their friends and their birthplace.

67. **fond:** foolish.

71. **ounce:** lynx.

73. **perfect:** complete.

Not once perceive their foul disfigurement,
75 But boast themselves more comely than before,
And all their friends and native home forget
To roll with pleasure in a sensual sty.
Therefore when any favored of high Jove
Chances to pass through this advent'rous glade,
80 Swift as the sparkle of a glancing star,
I shoot from Heav'n to give him safe convoy,
As now I do: but first I must put off
These my sky robes spun out of Iris' woof,
And take the weeds and likeness of a swain
85 That to the service of this house belongs,
Who with his soft pipe and smooth-dittied song,
Well knows to still the wild winds when they roar,
And hush the waving woods, nor of less faith,
And in this office of his mountain watch,
90 Likeliest, and nearest to the present aid
Of this occasion. But I hear the tread
Of hateful steps, I must be viewless now.

Comus enters with a charming-rod in one hand, his glass in the other, with
him a rout of monsters headed like sundry sorts of wild beasts, but otherwise
like men and women. Their apparel glistering, they come in making a riotous
and unruly noise, with torches in their hands.

Comus.
The star that bids the shepherd fold,
Now the top of heav'n doth hold,
95 And the gilded car of day,
His glowing axle doth allay
In the steep Atlantic stream,
And the slope sun his upward beam
Shoots against the dusky pole,
100 Pacing toward the other goal

79. **advent'rous:** dangerous.

83. **Iris' woof:** rainbow-colored thread.

84. **weeds:** clothes; **swain:** shepherd.

84–88. A compliment to Henry Lawes, put somewhat awkwardly into his own mouth (he played the Attendant Spirit).

87. **knows to:** knows how to.

88. **nor of less faith:** "nor is his loyalty less than his musical skill."

90. **Likeliest:** fittest (to aid).

90–91. **nearest . . . occasion:** help closest to the situation.

92. **viewless:** invisible.

93. **star:** Hesperus, the evening star; **fold:** pen their sheep.

95. **gilded car of day:** the chariot of the sun.

96. **allay:** cool.

97. **steep:** swift-flowing.

98. **slope sun:** descending, so that only its *upward beam* is still visible.

99. **dusky pole:** northern sky.

Of his chamber in the east.
Meanwhile welcome joy, and feast,
Midnight shout, and revelry,
Tipsy dance, and jollity.
105 Braid your locks with rosy twine,
Dropping odors, dropping wine.
Rigor now is gone to bed,
And Advice with scrupulous head,
Strict Age, and sour Severity,
110 With their grave saws in slumber lie.
We that are of purer fire
Imitate the starry choir,
Who in their nightly watchful spheres,
Lead in swift round the months and years.
115 The sounds and seas with all their finny drove
Now to the moon in wavering morris move,
And on the tawny sands and shelves,
Trip the pert fairies and the dapper elves;
By dimpled brook and fountain brim,
120 The wood-nymphs decked with daisies trim
Their merry wakes and pastimes keep:
What hath night to do with sleep?
Night hath better sweets to prove,
Venus now wakes, and wakens Love.
125 Come let us our rites begin,
'Tis only daylight that makes sin,
Which these dun shades will ne'er report.
Hail goddess of nocturnal sport,
Dark-veiled Cotytto, t' whom the secret flame
130 Of midnight torches burns; mysterious dame
That ne'er art called, but when the dragon womb

---

105. **rosy twine:** roses twisted together.
110. **saws:** maxims; dictates.
111. **purer fire:** It was a commonplace that men were composed of the four elements. Comus asserts that the fire in their makeup is of the *purer* kind found in the stars, and that this affinity makes their dance like the stars' movements.
113. **watchful spheres:** Angelic intelligences were thought to guide or watch over the planetary spheres.
115. **sounds and seas:** straits and open seas.
116. **morris:** folk dance associated with May Day ceremonies. It used pantomime to tell elaborate stories, and its performers wore bells on their

costumes. Will Kemp, Shakespeare's clown, once morrised for nine days in journeying from London to Norwich (Lee and Onions 2:238–40).
117. **shelves:** sandbanks.
118. **Trip:** dance; **pert:** brisk.
121. **wakes:** nocturnal revels.
129. **Cotytto:** Roman authors associated this Thracian goddess with licentious rites performed at night (Juvenal 2.91–92; Horace, *Epod.* 17.56–57).
131. **dragon womb:** Renaissance commentators assumed that the dragon-drawn chariot of *Met.* 7.218–19 belonged to Hecate, daughter of Night (Harding 50), patroness of witchcraft, and companion to Milton's Cotytto.

Of Stygian darkness spits her thickest gloom,
And makes one blot of all the air,
Stay thy cloudy ebon chair,
135 Wherein thou rid'st with Hecat', and befriend
Us thy vowed priests, till utmost end
Of all thy dues be done, and none left out,
Ere the blabbing eastern scout,
The nice Morn on th' Indian steep
140 From her cabined loophole peep,
And to the tell-tale Sun descry
Our concealed solemnity.
Come, knit hands, and beat the ground,
In a light fantastic round.

The Measure

145 Break off, break off, I feel the different pace
Of some chaste footing near about this ground.
Run to your shrouds, within these brakes and trees;
Our number may affright: some virgin sure
(For so I can distinguish by mine art)
150 Benighted in these woods. Now to my charms,
And to my wily trains; I shall ere long
Be well stocked with as fair a herd as grazed
About my mother Circe. Thus I hurl
My dazzling spells into the spongy air,
155 Of power to cheat the eye with blear illusion,
And give it false presentments, lest the place
And my quaint habits breed astonishment,
And put the damsel to suspicious flight,
Which must not be, for that's against my course;
160 I under fair pretence of friendly ends,
And well-placed words of glozing courtesy

138. **blabbing eastern scout:** the sun, a *blabbing* tattletale because it makes ill deeds visible to others.

139. **nice:** modest, fastidious; but as Carey points out, the classical Aurora was hardly that, and Comus may be mocking her hypocrisy; **Indian steep:** mountains (Leonard thinks the Himalayas) in the eastern land of India.

140. **cabined loophole:** a small window, such as a porthole.

142. **concealed solemnity:** secret rites.

144. **light fantastic round:** a nimble ring dance

that will seem to bring grotesque fancies to life. Cp. *L'All* 34.

[Stage direction] Measure: song and dance.

147. **shrouds:** hiding places.

151. **trains:** allurements.

153–54. **hurl . . . air:** At this point Comus throws some sort of sparkle dust into the air, which is *spongy* because it takes in and retains the effect.

155. **blear:** dim, misty.

156. **false presentments:** illusions.

157. **quaint habits:** curious clothes.

161. **glozing:** flattering.

Baited with reasons not unplausible
Wind me into the easy-hearted man,
And hug him into snares. When once her eye
165 Hath met the virtue of this magic dust,
I shall appear some harmless villager
Whom thrift keeps up about his country gear;
But here she comes, I fairly step aside
And hearken, if I may her business hear.

The Lady enters.

170 *Lady.* This way the noise was, if mine ear be true,
My best guide now; methought it was the sound
Of riot and ill-managed merriment,
Such as the jocund flute or gamesome pipe
Stirs up among the loose unlettered hinds,
175 When for their teeming flocks and granges full
In wanton dance they praise the bounteous Pan,
And thank the gods amiss. I should be loath
To meet the rudeness and swilled insolence
Of such late wassailers; yet O where else
180 Shall I inform my unacquainted feet
In the blind mazes of this tangled wood?
My brothers when they saw me wearied out
With this long way, resolving here to lodge
Under the spreading favor of these pines,
185 Stepped as they said to the next thicket side
To bring me berries, or such cooling fruit
As the kind hospitable woods provide.
They left me then, when the gray-hooded Ev'n
Like a sad votarist in palmer's weed
190 Rose from the hindmost wheels of Phoebus' wain.
But where they are, and why they came not back,

163. **Wind me:** insinuate myself; **easy-hearted:** gullible, trusting.
165. **virtue:** efficacy.
166–69. Here we compromise between 1673 and the two earlier versions of 1637 and 1645. Our l. 167, present in the early texts, dropped out in 1673, which also printed our ll. 168–69 in the reverse order. We keep the earlier line and the earlier order of 168–69, but emend l. 169 from its initial form ("And hearken, if I may, her business here") to the version established in the 1673 Errata.
168. **fairly:** quietly.
174. **loose unlettered hinds:** lewd, illiterate farmhands.
175. **teeming:** multiplying; **granges:** barns.
176. **Pan:** Greek god of woods and shepherds.
177. **amiss:** in the wrong way.
178. **swilled:** drunken.
179. **wassailers:** revelers.
180. **inform:** find guidance for.
189. **votarist:** one bound by a vow (here a vow of pilgrimage); **palmer's weed:** pilgrim's clothes.
190. **wain:** chariot.

Is now the labor of my thoughts; 'tis likeliest
They had engaged their wand'ring steps too far,
And envious darkness, ere they could return,
195   Had stole them from me, else O thievish Night
Why shouldst thou, but for some felonious end,
In thy dark lantern thus close up the stars,
That Nature hung in heav'n, and filled their lamps
With everlasting oil, to give due light
200   To the misled and lonely traveler?
This is the place, as well as I may guess,
Whence even now the tumult of loud mirth
Was rife, and perfect in my listening ear,
Yet naught but single darkness do I find.
205   What might this be? A thousand fantasies
Begin to throng into my memory
Of calling shapes, and beck'ning shadows dire,
And airy tongues, that syllable men's names
On sands, and shores, and desert wildernesses.
210   These thoughts may startle well, but not astound
The virtuous mind, that ever walks attended
By a strong siding champion Conscience.——
O welcome pure-eyed Faith, white-handed Hope,
Thou hovering angel girt with golden wings,
215   And thou unblemished form of Chastity,
I see ye visibly, and now believe
That he, the Supreme Good, t' whom all things ill
Are but as slavish officers of vengeance,
Would send a glist'ring guardian if need were
220   To keep my life and honor unassailed.
Was I deceived, or did a sable cloud
Turn forth her silver lining on the night?
I did not err, there does a sable cloud
Turn forth her silver lining on the night,
225   And casts a gleam over this tufted grove.

---

193. **engaged:** pledged.
194. **envious:** malicious.
197. **dark lantern:** a lantern with a gate to shut up its light. What in this production will count as starlight (221–25) may at this point be shuttered in a dark lantern. See 331n.
203. **rife:** loud; **perfect in:** perfectly clear to.
204. **single:** total.
207–9. **calling shapes . . . wildernesses:** Sources have been adduced, but Milton was drawing on motifs common in travel literature and folklore.

212. **siding champion:** a champion that takes one's side.
215. **unblemished form of Chastity:** The Lady places Chastity of some sort after Faith and Hope, where St. Paul leads one to expect Charity (1 Cor. 13.13). Does *unblemished* modify *form*, suggesting that the Lady sees the essence or idea of Chastity? Or does it modify *form of Chastity*, suggesting that another form of it is blemished?
221–25. The repetition of the interrogative as a declarative is an effect borrowed from Ovid, *Fasti* 5.549.

I cannot hallo to my brothers, but
Such noise as I can make to be heard farthest
I'll venture, for my new enlivened spirits
Prompt me; and they perhaps are not far off.

Song

230 Sweet Echo, sweetest Nymph that liv'st unseen
        Within thy airy shell
    By slow Meander's margent green,
    And in the violet-embroidered vale
        Where the love-lorn nightingale
235 Nightly to thee her sad song mourneth well.
    Canst thou not tell me of a gentle pair
        That likest thy Narcissus are?
            O if thou have
        Hid them in some flow'ry cave,
240   Tell me but where,
        Sweet queen of parley, daughter of the sphere.
    So may'st thou be translated to the skies,
    And give resounding grace to all heav'n's harmonies.

    Comus. Can any mortal mixture of earth's mold
245 Breathe such divine enchanting ravishment?
    Sure something holy lodges in that breast,
    And with these raptures moves the vocal air
    To testify his hidden residence;
    How sweetly did they float upon the wings
250 Of silence, through the empty-vaulted night
    At every fall smoothing the raven down
    Of darkness till it smiled: I have oft heard

---

230. **Echo:** Because Echo chattered while Zeus dallied with other women, Hera condemned her never to say anything except what had just been said to her. She became one of the lovers of Narcissus.

231. **airy shell:** the arched sky.

232. **Meander:** winding river in Asia Minor, perhaps as classical code for the Severn; **margent:** bank.

234. **love-lorn:** The term, which Milton was among the first to use, originally meant not "abandoned by one's love" but "ruined by one's love," as Philomela was ruined by Tereus.

236–37. Are the brothers like *Narcissus* in being youthful and attractive or because, like *Narcissus* and his image, they resemble each other and are inseparable?

241. **parley:** conversation; **daughter of the sphere:** born in the mortal, sublunary sphere.

242. **translated:** taken to Heaven.

243. **resounding grace:** a perfect term for what Echo might add to heavenly harmonies; the phrase occurs in "the only Alexandrine in *Comus,* mimicking the lengthening of heaven's song by Echo" (Carey).

248. **his:** its, referring to *something holy* in line 246.

249. **they:** referring to *these raptures* in line 247.

251. **fall:** cadence.

My mother Circe with the Sirens three,
Amidst the flow'ry-kirtled Naiades
255 Culling their potent herbs and baleful drugs,
Who as they sung, would take the prisoned soul,
And lap it in Elysium; Scylla wept,
And chid her barking waves into attention,
And fell Charybdis murmured soft applause:
260 Yet they in pleasing slumber lulled the sense,
And in sweet madness robbed it of itself,
But such a sacred and home-felt delight,
Such sober certainty of waking bliss
I never heard till now. I'll speak to her
265 And she shall be my queen. Hail, foreign wonder!
Whom certain these rough shades did never breed,
Unless the goddess that in rural shrine
Dwell'st here with Pan or Sylvan, by blest song
Forbidding every bleak unkindly fog
270 To touch the prosperous growth of this tall wood.
Lady. Nay gentle shepherd, ill is lost that praise
That is addressed to unattending ears;
Not any boast of skill, but extreme shift
How to regain my severed company
275 Compelled me to awake the courteous Echo
To give me answer from her mossy couch.
Comus. What chance good Lady hath bereft you thus?
Lady. Dim darkness and this leafy labyrinth.
Comus. Could that divide you from near-ushering guides?
280 *Lady.* They left me weary on a grassy turf.
Comus. By falsehood, or discourtesy, or why?
Lady. To seek i' the valley some cool friendly spring.
Comus. And left your fair side all unguarded, Lady?
Lady. They were but twain, and purposed quick return.

---

253. **Sirens three:** the sea nymphs whose song led sailors to their doom (*Od.* 12.166–200). There is no classical precedent for associating them with Circe, but they appear as Circe's attendants in William Browne's *Inner Temple Mask*, 1–96.

254. **flow'ry-kirtled:** wearing skirts of flowers; **Naiades:** nymphs of rivers and springs, four of whom serve Circe in *Od.* 10.348–51.

255. **potent herbs:** In Vergil, *Aen.* 7.19, Circe uses *potentibus herbis* to transform men into beasts.

256–59. In Ovid, *Met.* 14.8–74, *Circe* transforms the nymph *Scylla* into first a monster, then the treacherous rock facing *Charybdis*. Here both become the enchanted audience of Circe's song.

257. **lap it in Elysium:** wrap the soul in bliss.

261. **robbed it of itself:** rendered it unconscious.

262. **home-felt:** heartfelt.

267. **Unless the goddess:** i.e., unless you are the goddess.

268. **Sylvan:** Sylvanus, god of the woods, sometimes identified with *Pan*.

272. **unattending:** inattentive.

273. **extreme shift:** "my last chance, given the circumstances."

277–90. The passage is an example of stichomythia, or dialogue in single lines, a common device in Greek and Renaissance drama.

285   *Comus.* Perhaps forestalling night prevented them.
     Lady. How easy my misfortune is to hit!
     Comus. Imports their loss, beside the present need?
     Lady. No less than if I should my brothers lose.
     Comus. Were they of manly prime or youthful bloom?
290   *Lady.* As smooth as Hebe's their unrazored lips.
     Comus. Two such I saw, what time the labored ox
     In his loose traces from the furrow came,
     And the swinked hedger at his supper sat;
     I saw them under a green mantling vine
295   That crawls along the side of yon small hill,
     Plucking ripe clusters from the tender shoots;
     Their port was more than human, as they stood;
     I took it for a fairy visïon
     Of some gay creatures of the element
300   That in the colors of the rainbow live
     And play i' th' plighted clouds. I was awestruck,
     And as I passed, I worshipped; if those you seek,
     It were a journey like the path to Heav'n
     To help you find them.
     Lady.   Gentle villager
305   What readiest way would bring me to that place?
     Comus. Due west it rises from this shrubby point.
     Lady. To find out that, good shepherd, I suppose,
     In such a scant allowance of starlight,
     Would overtask the best land-pilot's art,
310   Without the sure guess of well-practiced feet.
     Comus. I know each lane, and every alley green,
     Dingle, or bushy dell of this wild wood,
     And every bosky bourn from side to side
     My daily walks and ancient neighborhood,
315   And if your stray attendance be yet lodged,
     Or shroud within these limits, I shall know
     Ere morrow wake, or the low-roosted lark
     From her thatched pallet rouse; if otherwise
     I can conduct you, Lady, to a low

285. **prevented:** anticipated.
286. **hit:** guess.
290. **Hebe:** the goddess of youth.
291. **what time:** at the time when.
292. **traces:** straps.
293. **swinked hedger:** workman tired (*swinked*) from cutting hedges.
294. **mantling:** spreading.
297. **port:** deportment, bearing.
299. **element:** sky.
301. **plighted:** folded.
311. **alley:** path.
312. **Dingle:** wooded hollow.
313. **bosky bourn:** bushy stream.
315. **stray attendance:** missing attendants.
316. **shroud:** seek shelter.
318. **if otherwise:** if you prefer.

320 But loyal cottage, where you may be safe
Till further quest.
Lady.   Shepherd I take thy word,
And trust thy honest offered courtesy,
Which oft is sooner found in lowly sheds
With smoky rafters, than in tap'stry halls
325 And courts of princes, where it first was named
And yet is most pretended: in a place
Less warranted than this, or less secure
I cannot be, that I should fear to change it.
Eye me blest Providence, and square my trial
330 To my proportioned strength. Shepherd lead on.—

The two brothers

Elder brother. Unmuffle ye faint stars, and thou fair moon
That wont'st to love the traveler's benison,
Stoop thy pale visage through an amber cloud,
And disinherit Chaos, that reigns here
335 In double night of darkness and of shades;
Or if your influence be quite dammed up
With black usurping mists, some gentle taper,
Though a rush candle from the wicker hole
Of some clay habitation, visit us
340 With thy long leveled rule of streaming light,
And thou shalt be our star of Arcady,
Or Tyrian Cynosure.
Second brother.   Or if our eyes
Be barred that happiness, might we but hear
The folded flocks penned in their wattled cotes,

322–26. **And trust . . . pretended:** The sentiment appears in Ariosto, *OF* 14.62, but near replicas abound. "Full of courtesy, full of craft" was a proverb of the day (Tilley C732).

327. **warranted:** protected against danger.

329. **square:** bring into alignment with (my allotted strength).

331. **Unmuffle:** remove the covering of darkness; perhaps the line triggers a stage effect, such as the uncovering of lit tapers or the opening of dark lanterns (see 197n).

332. **wont'st:** is accustomed to; **benison:** blessing.

334. **disinherit:** dispossess; **Chaos:** Night and Chaos are paired also in *PL* 2.894–97.

335. **shades:** trees.

336. **influence:** Astrologers taught that an ethereal liquid or *influence* flowed from the stars to affect human destiny.

338. **rush candle:** pith of a rush plant dipped in tallow; its light was feeble; **wicker hole:** window made of plaited twigs.

341. **star of Arcady:** The Elder Brother alludes to Ovid's myth (*Met.* 2.409–531) of Callisto, princess of Arcadia, who was raped by Jove and bore a child, Arcas, whom Juno changed into the constellation Ursa Major (*star of Arcady*). Greek sailors steered by it.

342. **Tyrian Cynosure:** Ursa Minor, by which Phoenician (*Tyrian*) sailors steered.

344. **wattled cotes:** animal pens made of stakes interlaced with branches and twigs.

345   Or sound of pastoral reed with oaten stops,
      Or whistle from the lodge, or village cock
      Count the night watches to his feathery dames,
      'Twould be some solace yet, some little cheering
      In this close dungeon of innumerous boughs.
350   But O that hapless virgin our lost sister,
      Where may she wander now, whither betake her
      From the chill dew, amongst rude burs and thistles?
      Perhaps some cold bank is her bolster now
      Or 'gainst the rugged bark of some broad elm
355   Leans her unpillowed head fraught with sad fears.
      What if in wild amazement and affright,
      Or while we speak within the direful grasp
      Of savage hunger, or of savage heat?
      Elder brother. Peace brother, be not over-exquisite
360   To cast the fashion of uncertain evils;
      For grant they be so, while they rest unknown,
      What need a man forestall his date of grief,
      And run to meet what he would most avoid?
      Or if they be but false alarms of fear,
365   How bitter is such self-delusïon?
      I do not think my sister so to seek,
      Or so unprincipled in virtue's book,
      And the sweet peace that goodness bosoms ever,
      As that the single want of light and noise
370   (Not being in danger, as I trust she is not)
      Could stir the constant mood of her calm thoughts,
      And put them into misbecoming plight.
      Virtue could see to do what Virtue would
      By her own radiant light, though sun and moon
375   Were in the flat sea sunk. And Wisdom's self

---

345. **pastoral reed:** the shepherd's pipe, made of oat straw; **stops:** finger holes.

349. **close:** confined.

356. **amazement:** frenzy.

357–65. This passage from the printed texts appears in neither of the manuscripts, which have in its place the following lines: "So fares as did forsaken Proserpine/When the big rolling flakes of pitchy clouds/And darkness wound her in."

358. of the hunger of savage beasts or the lust of savage men.

359. **over-exquisite:** excessively precise.

360. **cast:** forecast (as in "casting a horoscope"); **fashion:** form.

361. **be so:** be evils.

362. **forestall:** introduce before the proper time. A proverb of the day was "He that seeks trouble never misses it" (Tilley T532).

366. **so to seek:** so without resources, so much at a loss.

367. **unprincipled:** uninstructed.

368. **bosoms:** encloses in its bosom.

369. **single:** mere.

372. **misbecoming:** unbecoming.

373–74. **Virtue . . . light:** Editors cite Jonson (*Pleasure Reconciled to Virtue* 339–42) and Spenser (*FQ* 1.1.12), but the phrasing (albeit not the sense) is closer to Shakespeare's "Lovers can see to do their amorous rites/By their own beauties" (*ROM* 3.2.8–9).

375. **Wisdom's self:** Wisdom herself.

Oft seeks to sweet retired solitude,
Where with her best nurse Contemplatïon
She plumes her feathers, and lets grow her wings
That in the various bustle of resort
380 Were all to-ruffled, and sometimes impaired.
He that has light within his own clear breast
May sit i' th' center, and enjoy bright day,
But he that hides a dark soul and foul thoughts
Benighted walks under the midday sun;
385 Himself is his own dungeon.
Second brother.   'Tis most true
That musing Meditation most affects
The pensive secrecy of desert cell,
Far from the cheerful haunt of men and herds,
And sits as safe as in a senate-house;
390 For who would rob a hermit of his weeds,
His few books, or his beads, or maple dish,
Or do his gray hairs any violence?
But beauty like the fair Hesperian tree
Laden with blooming gold, had need the guard
395 Of dragon watch with unenchanted eye,
To save her blossoms, and defend her fruit
From the rash hand of bold incontinence.
You may as well spread out the unsunned heaps
Of miser's treasure by an outlaw's den,
400 And tell me it is safe, as bid me hope
Danger will wink on opportunity,
And let a single helpless maiden pass
Uninjured in this wild surrounding waste.
Of night or loneliness it recks me not,
405 I fear the dread events that dog them both,
Lest some ill-greeting touch attempt the person
Of our unownèd sister.
Elder brother.   I do not, brother,
Infer, as if I thought my sister's state

376. **seeks to:** repairs to.
380. **all to-ruffled:** very much ruffled.
382. **center:** center of the earth.
386. **affects:** is drawn to, has affection for.
387. **secrecy:** seclusion.
389. **senate-house:** the safest of places, being both public and the center of law and order.
390. **weeds:** clothes.
391. **beads:** rosary.
393. **Hesperian tree:** The tree bearing golden ap-
ples was guarded by the Hesperides (three daughters of Hesperus) and by a dragon.
401. **wink on:** overlook.
404. **it recks me not:** I don't care (whether we are talking about the effects of night or loneliness).
406. **ill-greeting:** greeting with evil intent; **touch:** sexual touch; **attempt:** try to ravish.
407. **unownèd:** lost.
408. **Infer, as if I thought:** argue as one who thought.

Secure without all doubt, or controversy:
410 Yet where an equal poise of hope and fear
Does arbitrate th' event, my nature is
That I incline to hope, rather than fear,
And gladly banish squint suspicïon.
My sister is not so defenseless left
415 As you imagine; she has a hidden strength
Which you remember not.
Second brother. What hidden strength,
Unless the strength of Heav'n, if you mean that?
Elder brother. I mean that too, but yet a hidden strength
Which if Heav'n gave it, may be termed her own:
420 'Tis chastity, my brother, chastity:
She that has that, is clad in complete steel,
And like a quivered nymph with arrows keen
May trace huge forests, and unharbored heaths,
Infamous hills, and sandy perilous wilds,
425 Where through the sacred rays of chastity,
No savage fierce, bandit, or mountaineer
Will dare to soil her virgin purity:
Yea there, where very desolation dwells
By grots and caverns shagged with horrid shades,
430 She may pass on with unblenched majesty,
Be it not done in pride, or in presumption.
Some say no evil thing that walks by night
In fog, or fire, by lake, or moorish fen,
Blue meager hag, or stubborn unlaid ghost,
435 That breaks his magic chains at curfew time,
No goblin, or swart fairy of the mine,
Hath hurtful power o'er true virginity.
Do ye believe me yet, or shall I call
Antiquity from the old schools of Greece
440 To testify the arms of chastity?

---

409. **without:** beyond.
413. **squint:** looking obliquely: a behavior thought to characterize suspicious people.
419. **if:** even if.
422. **quivered nymph:** a nymph devoted to Diana, and therefore to both archery and chastity.
423. **trace:** walk through.
426. **bandit:** from the Italian *bandito*, meaning originally "someone placed under the ban of excommunication"; **mountaineer:** mountain savage.

429. **shagged:** covered with shrubs; **horrid:** bristling.
430. **unblenched:** unfaltering.
432. Evoking *HAM* 1.1.120–23: "Some say . . . no spirit dare stir abroad."
434. **Blue:** livid; **meager:** emaciated.
435. **curfew time:** when the evening bell was rung (usually 9:00 P.M.).
436. **swart:** black.
439. **old schools:** the various schools of ancient philosophy.

Hence had the huntress Dian her dread bow,
Fair silver-shafted queen forever chaste,
Wherewith she tamed the brinded lioness
And spotted mountain pard, but set at naught
445 The frivolous bolt of Cupid; gods and men
Feared her stern frown, and she was queen o' th' woods.
What was that snaky-headed Gorgon shield
That wise Minerva wore, unconquered virgin,
Wherewith she freezed her foes to congealed stone,
450 But rigid looks of chaste austerity,
And noble grace that dashed brute violence
With sudden adoration and blank awe?
So dear to Heav'n is saintly chastity,
That when a soul is found sincerely so,
455 A thousand liveried angels lackey her,
Driving far off each thing of sin and guilt,
And in clear dream and solemn vision
Tell her of things that no gross ear can hear,
Till oft converse with Heav'nly habitants
460 Begin to cast a beam on th' outward shape,
The unpolluted temple of the mind,
And turns it by degrees to the soul's essence,
Till all be made immortal: but when lust
By unchaste looks, loose gestures, and foul talk,
465 But most by lewd and lavish act of sin,
Lets in defilement to the inward parts,
The soul grows clotted by contagion,
Embodies and imbrutes, till she quite lose

443. **brinded:** tawny.
444. **pard:** panther or leopard.
445. **bolt:** arrow.
447–48. **that snaky-headed . . . wore:** *Minerva,* who changed Medusa's hair to snakes because Neptune violated her in Minerva's temple, wore the image of that snaky head on her shield. Like Medusa herself, the image turned opponents to stone. Ironically, the Lady, rather than an opponent of chastity, will become paralyzed in Milton's masque.
452. **blank:** rendering powerless.
455. Cp. the *thousand fantasies* of line 205.
458. **no gross ear can hear:** Cp. *Arcades* 72–73.
459–63. **Till . . . immortal:** The rather uncommon idea of body being gradually transformed into spirit or soul also appears in *PL* 5.497–500. This notion is mostly found among occultists influenced by Neoplatonism and Hermeticism; see,

for example, George Rust, *A Letter of Resolution Concerning Origen.*
459. **oft converse:** frequent spiritual intercourse, possibly including conversation. Cp. *PL* 7.9.
460–61. **outward shape . . . mind:** The temple of the mind is a virgin (*unpolluted*) body.
462. **it:** the outward shape, the body.
463. **all:** the entirety of the person, body and soul. Despite the body-soul dualism implicit in its emphasis on chastity, *A Masque* also yearns for a Hebraic sense of their indivisibility. These contrary impulses will settle into the mature monism or animate materialism of *PL* 5.469–503 (S. Fallon 1991, 83).
465–75. Milton follows Plato's *Phaedo* 81 in this account of lewd souls becoming embodied (the opposite of chastity's transformation of body into soul).
465. **lavish:** lascivious.

The divine property of her first being.

470 Such are those thick and gloomy shadows damp
Oft seen in charnel vaults, and sepulchers
Lingering, and sitting by a new-made grave,
As loath to leave the body that it loved,
And linked itself by carnal sensualty

475 To a degenerate and degraded state.
Second brother. How charming is divine philosophy!
Not harsh and crabbèd as dull fools suppose,
But musical as is Apollo's lute,
And a perpetual feast of nectared sweets,

480 Where no crude surfeit reigns.
Elder brother.   List, list, I hear
Some far-off hallo break the silent air.
Second brother. Methought so too; what should it be?
Elder brother.   For certain
Either someone like us night-foundered here,
Or else some neighbor woodman, or at worst,

485 Some roving robber calling to his fellows.
Second brother. Heav'n keep my sister. Again, again, and near.
Best draw, and stand upon our guard.
Elder brother.   I'll hallo;
If he be friendly he comes well, if not,
Defense is a good cause, and Heav'n be for us.

The Attendant Spirit habited like a shepherd

490 That hallo I should know, what are you? Speak;
Come not too near, you fall on iron stakes else.
Spirit. What voice is that, my young lord? Speak again.
Second brother. O brother, 'tis my father's shepherd sure.
Elder brother. Thyrsis? Whose artful strains have oft delayed

495 The huddling brook to hear his madrigal,
And sweetened every muskrose of the dale,

---

469. **property:** essential character.

470–75. Milton adapts Plato's *Phaedo* 81.

474. **sensualty:** Though our text is modernized, we prefer *sensualty*, found in the *CMS* and 1645, to the unmetrical *sensuality*, found in the *BMS*, 1637, and 1673.

478. **musical as is Apollo's lute:** Cp. Shakespeare, *LLL* 4.3.339–40: "Sweet and musical/As bright Apollo's lute."

480. **crude:** indigestible.

483. **night-foundered:** engulfed in night.

[**Stage direction**] **habited:** dressed.

491. **iron stakes:** swords.

494. **Thyrsis:** The name of the singer of Theocritus's first eclogue and one of the competing singers in Vergil, *Ec.* 7, hence an embodiment of pastoral tradition. Milton speaks of himself as Thyrsis in *Damon*. There follows a second compliment to the musical talents of Henry Lawes (see 84–88).

495. **huddling:** crowding together, presumably to hear Thyrsis's song.

How cam'st thou here good swain? Hath any ram
Slipped from the fold, or young kid lost his dam,
Or straggling wether the pent flock forsook?
500 How couldst thou find this dark sequestered nook?
Spirit. O my loved master's heir, and his next joy,
I came not here on such a trivial toy
As a strayed ewe, or to pursue the stealth
Of pilfering wolf; not all the fleecy wealth
505 That doth enrich these downs, is worth a thought
To this my errand, and the care it brought.
But O my virgin Lady, where is she?
How chance she is not in your company?
Elder brother. To tell thee sadly shepherd, without blame,
510 Or our neglect, we lost her as we came.
Spirit. Ay me unhappy! Then my fears are true.
Elder brother. What fears good Thyrsis? Prithee briefly show.
Spirit. I'll tell ye. 'Tis not vain or fabulous
(Though so esteemed by shallow ignorance)
515 What the sage poets taught by th' Heav'nly Muse,
Storied of old in high immortal verse
Of dire Chimeras and enchanted isles,
And rifted rocks whose entrance leads to Hell,
For such there be, but unbelief is blind.
520   Within the navel of this hideous wood,
Immured in cypress shades a sorcerer dwells
Of Bacchus and of Circe born, great Comus,
Deep skilled in all his mother's witcheries,
And here to every thirsty wanderer,
525 By sly enticement gives his baneful cup,
With many murmurs mixed, whose pleasing poison
The visage quite transforms of him that drinks,
And the inglorious likeness of a beast
Fixes instead, unmolding reason's mintage
530 Charactered in the face; this have I learnt
Tending my flocks hard by i' th' hilly crofts

---

499. **wether:** castrated ram.
501. **next:** nearest.
502. **toy:** trifle.
506. **To this:** compared to this.
508. **How chance:** how does it chance that.
515. **sage poets . . . Muse:** The sage poets are not
   necessarily Christian, for Milton believed that
   poetic "abilities, wheresoever they be found,
   are the inspired gift of God" (*MLM* 841). He

probably had in mind Homer, Vergil, Tasso,
Ariosto, and Spenser.
516. **Storied:** narrated.
517. **Chimeras:** monsters composed of lion, goat,
   and dragon parts.
518. **rifted:** split.
520. **navel:** center.
530. **Charactered:** engraved, like a face on a coin.
531. **crofts:** pieces of enclosed ground used for
   pasture or tillage.

That brow this bottom glade, whence night by night
He and his monstrous rout are heard to howl
Like stabled wolves, or tigers at their prey,
535   Doing abhorrèd rites to Hecate
In their obscurèd haunts of inmost bow'rs.
Yet have they many baits, and guileful spells
T' inveigle and invite th' unwary sense
Of them that pass unweeting by the way.
540   This evening late, by then the chewing flocks
Had ta'en their supper on the savory herb
Of knot-grass dew-besprent, and were in fold,
I sat me down to watch upon a bank
With ivy canopied, and interwove
545   With flaunting honeysuckle, and began
Wrapped in a pleasing fit of melancholy
To meditate my rural minstrelsy
Till fancy had her fill; but ere a close
The wonted roar was up amidst the woods,
550   And filled the air with barbarous dissonance,
At which I ceased, and listened them a while,
Till an unusual stop of sudden silence
Gave respite to the drowsy-frighted steeds
That draw the litter of close-curtained Sleep;
555   At last a soft and solemn breathing sound
Rose like a steam of rich distilled perfumes,
And stole upon the air, that even Silence
Was took ere she was ware, and wished she might
Deny her nature, and be never more
560   Still to be so displaced. I was all ear,
And took in strains that might create a soul
Under the ribs of Death. But O ere long
Too well I did perceive it was the voice

532. **brow:** make a brow in relation to, overlook.
534. **stabled wolves:** a crux: "wolves put in a sta-
ble" seems a surreal picture, though it has
Vergilian precedent (*Aen.* 7.15–20); "wolves hav-
ing broken into the fold" is of a piece with
"tigers at their prey," but *stabled* must be
wrenched to produce this sense; appealing to
"stabled" in *PL* 11.752, some have suggested
"wolves in their lairs." Like Hughes et al.
2:921–22, we prefer the first suggestion.
539. **unweeting:** unaware.
542. **knot-grass:** applied to various plants with
knotty stems; **dew-besprent:** sprinkled with
dew.

545. **flaunting:** waving gaily.
547. **meditate:** practice.
548. **ere a close:** before the conclusion of a single
musical phrase or cadence.
550. **barbarous dissonance:** Cp. *PL* 7.32.
552. **stop of sudden silence:** referring to the sud-
den breaking off of the dance (145).
553. **drowsy-frighted:** drowsy but frightened;
some editors, on the sole authority of *CMS,*
print "drowsy-flighted."
554. **litter:** chariot.
555. **sound:** the Lady's song.
558. **took:** charmed.

Of my most honored Lady, your dear sister.
565 Amazed I stood, harrowed with grief and fear,
And "O poor hapless nightingale," thought I,
"How sweet thou sing'st, how near the deadly snare!"
Then down the lawns I ran with headlong haste
Through paths and turnings often trod by day,
570 Till guided by mine ear I found the place
Where that damned wizard hid in sly disguise
(For so by certain signs I knew) had met
Already, ere my best speed could prevent,
The aidless innocent Lady his wished prey,
575 Who gently asked if he had seen such two,
Supposing him some neighbor villager;
Longer I durst not stay, but soon I guessed
Ye were the two she meant; with that I sprung
Into swift flight, till I had found you here,
580 But further know I not.
Second brother.   O night and shades,
How are ye joined with Hell in triple knot
Against th' unarmèd weakness of one virgin
Alone and helpless! Is this the confidence
You gave me brother?
Elder brother.   Yes, and keep it still,
585 Lean on it safely; not a period
Shall be unsaid for me: against the threats
Of malice or of sorcery, or that power
Which erring men call chance, this I hold firm,
Virtue may be assailed, but never hurt,
590 Surprised by unjust force, but not enthralled,
Yea even that which mischief meant most harm,
Shall in the happy trial prove most glory.
But evil on itself shall back recoil,
And mix no more with goodness, when at last
595 Gathered like scum, and settled to itself,
It shall be in eternal restless change

---

566. **hapless nightingale:** The Lady's song alluded to Philomela (234n). She sang, the Attendant Spirit implies, better than she knew.
585. **period:** sentence.
586. **for me:** for my part.
587. **that power:** Since the Elder Brother is swearing against this power, perhaps against the threats of this power, it seems unlikely that he alludes to providence, as Hughes et al. maintain. Perhaps he means "whatever gods there

may be (behind the illusion of chance) that have been thought to say something contrary to what I am about to profess."
589–90. The Elder Brother has seemed to be saying, unrealistically, that virtue could repel or prevent physical assault. He now declares more convincingly that virtue cannot be destroyed by physical assault.
594. **when:** till.

Self-fed and self-consumed; if this fail,
The pillared firmament is rottenness,
And earth's base built on stubble. But come let's on.
600 Against th' opposing will and arm of Heav'n
May never this just sword be lifted up.
But, for that damned magician, let him be girt
With all the grisly legions that troop
Under the sooty flag of Acheron,
605 Harpies and Hydras, or all the monstrous forms
'Twixt Africa and Ind, I'll find him out,
And force him to restore his purchase back,
Or drag him by the curls to a foul death,
Cursed as his life.
Spirit.　　　　　Alas good vent'rous youth,
610 I love thy courage yet, and bold emprise,
But here thy sword can do thee little stead;
Far other arms and other weapons must
Be those that quell the might of Hellish charms;
He with his bare wand can unthread thy joints,
615 And crumble all thy sinews.
Elder brother.　　　　　Why prithee shepherd
How durst thou then thyself approach so near
As to make this relation?
Spirit.　　　　　Care and utmost shifts
How to secure the Lady from surprisal
Brought to my mind a certain shepherd lad
620 Of small regard to see to, yet well skilled
In every virtuous plant and healing herb

597. **Self-fed and self-consumed:** as indeed evil is in *PL* 2.798–800; 10.629–37; **if this fail:** if what I have said prove false.

598–99. **The pillared firmament . . . stubble:** The created universe is imagined as a building with a foundation (*earth's base*) on which pillars (see Job 26.11) support the dome of the sky. If evil should prove to belong to the design of creation, then the pillars would be rotten, the foundation resting on flimsy *stubble* (short stalks left after harvest).

604. **Acheron:** one of the four rivers of Hades (cp. *PL* 2.578).

605. **Harpies and Hydras:** *Harpies* were rapacious birds with women's faces; the *Hydra,* eventually slain by Hercules, was a water serpent with heads that multiplied when cut off.

606. **Ind:** India.

607. **purchase:** ill-gotten prizes.

610. **emprise:** either "undertaking" (what he has just vowed to do) or "enterprise" (general spiritedness).

611. **stead:** service.

614. **bare:** mere; **unthread:** dislocate, take out of their sockets.

615. **crumble:** shrivel up.

617. **relation:** report; **shifts:** plans in exigent circumstances.

619. **shepherd lad:** almost certainly Milton himself, as the poet memorializes his friendship with Lawes.

620. **Of small regard to see to:** is "characteristic in its proud modesty, corresponding to the 'uncouth swain' of *Lycidas*" (B. A. Wright). The knowledge of plants and herbs (see *Il Pens* 172) has poetic utility here, in the flower catalog of *Lycidas,* and in Milton's epic account of the Garden of Eden.

That spreads her verdant leaf to the morning ray.
He loved me well, and oft would beg me sing,
Which when I did, he on the tender grass
625 Would sit, and hearken even to ecstasy,
And in requital ope his leathern scrip,
And show me simples of a thousand names
Telling their strange and vigorous faculties;
Amongst the rest a small unsightly root,
630 But of divine effect, he culled me out;
The leaf was darkish, and had prickles on it,
But in another country, as he said,
Bore a bright golden flower, but not in this soil:
Unknown, and like esteemed, and the dull swain
635 Treads on it daily with his clouted shoon,
And yet more med'cinal is it than that Moly
That Hermes once to wise Ulysses gave;
He called it Haemony, and gave it me,
And bade me keep it as of sov'reign use
640 'Gainst all enchantments, mildew blast, or damp
Or ghastly Furies' apparition;
I pursed it up, but little reck'ning made,
Till now that this extremity compelled;
But now I find it true, for by this means
645 I knew the foul enchanter though disguised,
Entered the very lime-twigs of his spells,
And yet came off: if you have this about you
(As I will give you when we go) you may
Boldly assault the necromancer's hall;
650 Where if he be, with dauntless hardihood,
And brandished blade rush on him, break his glass,
And shed the luscious liquor on the ground,
But seize his wand; though he and his cursed crew
Fierce sign of battle make, and menace high,

---

626. **scrip:** small bag carried by shepherds.
627. **simples:** medicinal herbs; **thousand names:**
    Cp. lines 205, 455.
635. **clouted:** patched, mended.
636. **Moly:** Hermes gave this plant, which has a
    white flower and black root, to Odysseus to
    protect him against Circe's spells. Commenta-
    tors often supposed it to represent temperance
    or education.
638. **Haemony:** Milton invented this herb, and no
    one is sure what, beyond competing with
    Homer, he had in mind. The term might derive

from Haemonia (Thessaly, associated with
magic), or *haimonios* (Gk. for "bloodred"), which
sometimes leads interpreters to the blood of
Christ. Hanford and B. A. Wright (1938) saw it
as a symbol of Milton's youthful Christian-
Platonic philosophy. Others take it as a symbol
of Christian grace.
640. **blast:** infection; mildew was thought to be se-
    riously malignant; **damp:** noxious vapor.
642. **little reck'ning made:** took little heed.
646. **lime-twigs:** traps, alluding to the practice of
    catching birds by spreading lime on branches.

655 Or like the sons of Vulcan vomit smoke,
Yet will they soon retire, if he but shrink.
Elder brother. Thyrsis, lead on apace, I'll follow thee,
And some good angel bear a shield before us.

*The scene changes to a stately palace, set out with all manner of deliciousness:
soft music, tables spread with all dainties. Comus appears with his rabble, and
the Lady set in an enchanted chair, to whom he offers his glass, which she puts
by, and goes about to rise.*

Comus. Nay, Lady, sit; if I but wave this wand,
660 Your nerves are all chained up in alabaster,
And you a statue; or as Daphne was
Root-bound, that fled Apollo.
Lady.   Fool, do not boast;
Thou canst not touch the freedom of my mind
With all thy charms, although this corporal rind
665 Thou hast immanacled, while Heav'n sees good.
Comus. Why are you vexed Lady? Why do you frown?
Here dwell no frowns, nor anger, from these gates
Sorrow flies far: see, here be all the pleasures
That fancy can beget on youthful thoughts
670 When the fresh blood grows lively, and returns
Brisk as the April buds in primrose season.
And first behold this cordial julep here
That flames and dances in his crystal bounds
With spirits of balm and fragrant syrups mixed.
675 Not that Nepenthes which the wife of Thone
In Egypt gave to Jove-born Helena
Is of such power to stir up joy as this,
To life so friendly, or so cool to thirst.
Why should you be so cruel to yourself,
680 And to those dainty limbs which Nature lent

[Stage direction] puts by: refuses; **goes about:**
attempts.
660. **nerves:** sinews.
661. *Daphne* was turned into a laurel as she ran
away from a lustful Apollo (Ovid, *Met.*
1.545–52). But this metamorphosis saved her
from a sexual predator, and it is therefore
somewhat odd that Comus would threaten the
Lady with Daphne's fate. The Apollo-Daphne
myth was central to the tradition of Petrarchan
love poetry.
663. "Though his body be thrown into fetters, no

bondage can enchain his soul," as Cicero (*On
the Chief Good and Evil* 3.22) and others have ob-
served. The issue is not rape. As the Lady real-
izes, Comus wants her to consent, in a free
mental act, to his seduction. Cp. line 1019.
672. **julep:** sweet drink.
674. **balm:** aromatic fragrance.
675–76. Helen slips *Nepenthes,* a potion for dis-
pelling grief given her by the Egyptian wife of
Thone, into Menelaus's drink (Homer, *Od.*
4.219–32).
679. Cp. *SA* 784.

For gentle usage and soft delicacy?
But you invert the cov'nants of her trust,
And harshly deal like an ill borrower
With that which you received on other terms,
685   Scorning the unexempt condition
By which all mortal frailty must subsist,
Refreshment after toil, ease after pain,
That have been tired all day without repast,
And timely rest have wanted; but fair virgin
690   This will restore all soon.
      Lady.   'Twill not false traitor,
'Twill not restore the truth and honesty
That thou hast banished from thy tongue with lies.
Was this the cottage and the safe abode
Thou told'st me of? What grim aspects are these,
695   These ugly-headed monsters? Mercy guard me!
Hence with thy brewed enchantments, foul deceiver.
Hast thou betrayed my credulous innocence
With vizored falsehood and base forgery,
And wouldst thou seek again to trap me here
700   With lickerish baits fit to ensnare a brute?
Were it a draft for Juno when she banquets,
I would not taste thy treasonous offer; none
But such as are good men can give good things,
And that which is not good, is not delicious
705   To a well-governed and wise appetite.
      Comus. O foolishness of men! that lend their ears
To those budge doctors of the Stoic fur,
And fetch their precepts from the Cynic tub,
Praising the lean and sallow Abstinence.
710   Wherefore did Nature pour her bounties forth,

---

681. **usage:** active use, as opposed to mere hoarding.

682. **the cov'nants of her trust:** the particular clauses of the agreement governing Nature's loan. The financial metaphors throughout this passage suggest a libertine parody of the parable of the talents in Matt. 25. See Hoxby 17–24.

685. **unexempt condition:** condition from which no one is exempt.

694. **aspects:** countenances.

698. **vizored:** hidden, as the face is hidden by a visor.

700. **lickerish:** pleasant to the taste; the word also means "lustful."

703. "A bad man's gifts convey no benefit" (Euripides, *Medea* 618).

707. **budge doctors:** pompous academics, with *budge* referring to a fur worn on academic gowns; **Stoic:** the school of Stoic philosophers opposed luxury and hedonism.

708. **Cynic tub:** the school of Cynicism opposed not only riches but the ordinary pleasures of life. Diogenes the Cynic for a time resided in a tub.

710–36. Most of the sources adduced by scholars pertain to the idea that beauty must be seen, not the argument about Nature's abundance. The nurse in Seneca's *Hippolytus* 469–81, maintaining that without copulation Nature would

With such a full and unwithdrawing hand,
Covering the earth with odors, fruits, and flocks,
Thronging the seas with spawn innumerable,
But all to please and sate the curious taste?
715　And set to work millions of spinning worms,
That in their green shops weave the smooth-haired silk
To deck her sons, and that no corner might
Be vacant of her plenty, in her own loins
She hutched th' all-worshipped ore and precious gems
720　To store her children with; if all the world
Should in a pet of temperance feed on pulse,
Drink the clear stream, and nothing wear but frieze,
Th' All-giver would be unthanked, would be unpraised,
Not half his riches known, and yet despised,
725　And we should serve him as a grudging master,
As a penurious niggard of his wealth,
And live like Nature's bastards, not her sons,
Who would be quite surcharged with her own weight,
And strangled with her waste fertility;
730　Th' earth cumbered, and the winged air darked with plumes,
The herds would over-multitude their lords,
The sea o'erfraught would swell, and th' unsought diamonds
Would so emblaze the forehead of the deep,
And so bestud with stars, that they below
735　Would grow inured to light, and come at last
To gaze upon the sun with shameless brows.
List, Lady, be not coy, and be not cozened
With that same vaunted name Virginity:

---

be empty, anticipates the argument in reverse. The closest analogue is Colax's penultimate speech in Thomas Randolph's *The Muses' Looking-Glass* 2.3 (see Smith 1922).

714. **sate:** satisfy entirely; **curious:** fastidious, but with a suggestion of searching out all possibilities, however rare or perverse.

716. **green shops:** green workshops (in mulberry trees).

719. **hutched:** stored in a coffer.

721. **a pet of:** a foolish craze for; **pulse:** food consisting of vegetables that are also seeds (beans, lentils, et cetera); Daniel and his companions favored this diet at the court of Nebuchadnezzar (Dan. 1.8–16).

722. **frieze:** coarse woolen cloth.

727. **like Nature's bastards:** like illegitimate children who make no claim to their parent's property.

728. **surcharged:** overloaded.

729. **strangled:** suffocated.

732–36. The *deep* is the central portion of the earth, and its *forehead* is the part of the deep closest to the surface. To inhabitants of the deep, gems shining in the forehead appear like stars, and if left unmined would eventually lure them to the surface.

737–54. On the idea that beauty should be public and mutual, not solitary, see Sidney, *Arcadia* 3.10; Daniel, *Complaint of Rosamond* 512–32; Drayton, *England's Heroical Epistles,* "King John to Matilda," 119–56; and Carew, "To A.L. Persuasions to Love": "That rich treasure/Of rare beauty . . ./Was Bestowed on you by Nature/To be enjoyed, and 'twere a sin/There to be scarce, where she hath been/So prodigal of her best graces" (8–13).

738. **vaunted:** boasted or bragged of, highly prized.

Beauty is Nature's coin, must not be hoarded,
740 But must be current, and the good thereof
Consists in mutual and partaken bliss,
Unsavory in th' enjoyment of itself.
If you let slip time, like a neglected rose
It withers on the stalk with languished head.
745 Beauty is Nature's brag and must be shown
In courts, at feasts, and high solemnities
Where most may wonder at the workmanship;
It is for homely features to keep home,
They had their name thence; coarse complexïons
750 And cheeks of sorry grain will serve to ply
The sampler, and to tease the housewife's wool.
What need a vermeil-tinctured lip for that,
Love-darting eyes, or tresses like the morn?
There was another meaning in these gifts,
755 Think what, and be advised, you are but young yet.
Lady. I had not thought to have unlocked my lips
In this unhallowed air, but that this juggler
Would think to charm my judgment, as mine eyes,
Obtruding false rules pranked in reason's garb.
760 I hate when Vice can bolt her arguments
And Virtue has no tongue to check her pride:
Impostor, do not charge most innocent Nature,
As if she would her children should be riotous
With her abundance; she good cateress
765 Means her provision only to the good
That live according to her sober laws,
And holy dictate of spare Temperance:
If every just man that now pines with want
Had but a moderate and beseeming share
770 Of that which lewdly-pampered Luxury
Now heaps upon some few with vast excess,
Nature's full blessings would be well dispensed

Marlowe, *Hero and Leander*, 1.209: "This idol which you term virginity."

740. **current:** in circulation (referring to *Nature's coin*).

745. **brag:** show, display.

750. **grain:** color; **ply:** work at.

751. **tease:** comb out in preparation for spinning.

752. **vermeil:** vermilion.

757. **juggler:** sorcerer, trickster.

759. **pranked:** dressed up.

760. **bolt:** sift, pick (from the bolting or sifting of the meal from the bran in milling).

768–74. Cp. *LR* 3.4.28–35, 4.1.68–72: "Let the superfluous and lust-dieted man/That slaves your ordinance, that will not see/Because he does not feel, feel now your power quickly;/So distribution should undo excess,/And each man have enough."

In unsuperfluous even proportion,
And she no whit encumbered with her store;
775   And then the Giver would be better thanked,
His praise due paid, for swinish gluttony
Ne'er looks to Heav'n amidst his gorgeous feast,
But with besotted base ingratitude
Crams, and blasphemes his feeder. Shall I go on?
780   Or have I said enough? To him that dares
Arm his profane tongue with contemptuous words
Against the sun-clad power of Chastity,
Fain would I something say, yet to what end?
Thou has nor ear nor soul to apprehend
785   The sublime notion and high mystery
That must be uttered to unfold the sage
And serious doctrine of Virginity,
And thou art worthy that thou shouldst not know
More happiness than this thy present lot.
790   Enjoy your dear wit and gay rhetoric
That hath so well been taught her dazzling fence,
Thou art not fit to hear thyself convinced;
Yet should I try, the uncontrollèd worth
Of this pure cause would kindle my rapt spirits
795   To such a flame of sacred vehemence
That dumb things would be moved to sympathize,
And the brute earth would lend her nerves and shake,
Till all thy magic structures reared so high
Were shattered into heaps o'er thy false head.
800   *Comus.* She fables not, I feel that I do fear
Her words set off by some superior power;
And though not mortal, yet a cold shudd'ring dew
Dips me all o'er, as when the wrath of Jove

778. **besotted:** morally stupefied.

779–806. **Shall I . . . more strongly:** Though missing from the two manuscripts, this passage appears in all three of the texts (1637, 1645, 1673) published in Milton's lifetime.

785. **high mystery:** religious truth known only through divine revelation.

786–87. **sage/And serious:** Milton refers to "our sage and serious poet Spenser" in *Areop* (p. 939).

787. **Virginity:** As Leonard notes, "virginity" in Protestant thought could include chaste marriage; see Calvin, *Institutes* 4.12.28: "The second kind of virginity is the chaste love of marriage." But the Lady gives no indication that she is using the word as a synonym for "chastity in

general," and Comus has accused her of being deceived by that "vaunted name Virginity."

790. **gay:** showy, specious.

791. **fence:** skill in verbal fencing.

793. **uncontrollèd:** unchecked; indisputable.

796. **dumb things:** creatures without the power of speech.

797. Horace, *Odes* 1.34.9, feels a thunderbolt strike so magnificently that it shakes his skepticism about the gods.

803. **Dips me:** suffuses me with moisture; **Jove:** He defeated Saturn and the Titans with thunderbolts, then imprisoned the Titans in *Erebus* (the dark underworld).

Speaks thunder and the chains of Erebus
805 To some of Saturn's crew. I must dissemble,
And try her yet more strongly. Come, no more,
This is mere moral babble, and direct
Against the canon laws of our foundation;
I must not suffer this, yet 'tis but the lees
810 And settlings of a melancholy blood;
But this will cure all straight, one sip of this
Will bathe the drooping spirits in delight
Beyond the bliss of dreams. Be wise, and taste.—

*The brothers rush in with swords drawn, wrest his glass out of his hand, and
break it against the ground; his rout make sign of resistance, but are all
driven in; the Attendant Spirit comes in.*

Spirit. What, have you let the false enchanter scape?
815 O ye mistook, ye should have snatched his wand
And bound him fast; without his rod reversed,
And backward mutters of dissevering power,
We cannot free the Lady that sits here
In stony fetters fixed, and motionless;
820 Yet stay, be not disturbed, now I bethink me,
Some other means I have which may be used,
Which once of Meliboeus old I learnt,
The soothest shepherd that e'er piped on plains.
There is a gentle nymph not far from hence,
825 That with moist curb sways the smooth Severn stream,
Sabrina is her name, a virgin pure;

804. **thunder and the chains of Erebus:** an exam-
ple of zeugma, the double use of a verb: Jove
"speaks" in the thunder, and "speaks the sen-
tence of" Erebus on the defeated Titans.
808. **canon laws:** rules, but also glancing at the
church's Canon Law; **foundation:** institution
such as a church or college.
810. **melancholy blood:** The heaviest, darkest
human blood is saturated with the melancholic
humor, which is the cause of madness.
816. **rod reversed:** Circe reverses her wand to free
Odysseus's men (Ovid, *Met.* 14.300). Sandys 1632
identified the wand with "sinister persuasions
to pleasure" and the reversed wand with "disci-
pline, and a view of their own deformity" (481).
817. **backward mutters:** spells muttered backward
to free the Lady. Spenser's Britomart forces an
enchanter to reverse his incantation and so re-
lease Amoret (*FQ* 3.12.36).

822. **Meliboeus:** He is a character in Vergil's first
eclogue. Most editors suppose him to represent
Spenser, the author to whom Milton is first of
all indebted for his knowledge of Sabrina's
story (*FQ* 2.10.14–19).
823. **soothest:** most truthful.
824–41. In the oldest source, Geoffrey of Mon-
mouth's *History of Britain* 2.4–5, which Milton
follows closely when retelling the story in his
own *History of Britain* (Yale 5:18), *Sabrina* is the
adulterous child of *Locrine* and Estrildis. *Guen-
dolen,* his previous wife and queen, defeats and
kills Locrine in battle, and for revenge throws
Estrildis and Sabrina into the stream, which she
names Sabrina (in time altered to *Severn*). Like
Drayton, Milton has Sabrina transformed into a
goddess by *Nereus*'s daughters (*Polyoblion* 5.1–30).
825. **sways:** rules.

Whilom she was the daughter of Locrine,
That had the scepter from his father Brute.
She guiltless damsel, flying the mad pursuit
830 Of her engagèd stepdame Guendolen,
Commended her fair innocence to the flood
That stayed her flight with his cross-flowing course;
The water nymphs that in the bottom played
Held up their pearlèd wrists and took her in,
835 Bearing her straight to agèd Nereus' hall,
Who piteous of her woes, reared her lank head,
And gave her to his daughters to imbathe
In nectared lavers strewed with asphodel,
And through the porch and inlet of each sense
840 Dropped in ambrosial oils till she revived,
And underwent a quick immortal change,
Made goddess of the river; still she retains
Her maiden gentleness, and oft at eve
Visits the herds along the twilight meadows,
845 Helping all urchin blasts and ill-luck signs
That the shrewd meddling elf delights to make,
Which she with precious vialed liquors heals.
For which the shepherds at their festivals
Carol her goodness loud in rustic lays,
850 And throw sweet garland wreaths into her stream
Of pansies, pinks, and gaudy daffodils.
And, as the old swain said, she can unlock
The clasping charm, and thaw the numbing spell,
If she be right invoked in warbled song,
855 For maidenhood she loves, and will be swift
To aid a virgin, such as was herself
In hard-besetting need; this will I try,
And add the power of some adjuring verse.

---

831. **Commended her fair innocence:** There is no suggestion of Sabrina's suicide in Geoffrey of Monmouth (824–41n). Milton also stresses her virginity.

834. **pearlèd wrists:** Water nymphs favor pearl adornments, as is clear from a stage direction in Ben Jonson's *Mask of Blackness:* his water nymphs wear on "the front, ear, necks and wrists, ornament of the most choice and orient pearl."

835. **Nereus:** a sea god who fathered fifty Nereids.

838. **lavers:** basins; **asphodel:** the immortal flower that grows in Homer's Elysian fields (*Od.* 11.539).

845. **Helping all urchin blasts:** remedying infections caused by ill spirits.

846. **shrewd:** mischievous.

852. **old swain:** Meliboeus.

853. **clasping charm . . . spell:** Leonard suggests that a distinction is intended between the *clasping charm,* which simply holds the Lady to the chair, and the more serious *numbing spell,* which renders her speechless and unconscious.

858. **adjuring:** entreating.

Song

Sabrina fair,
860   Listen where thou art sitting
Under the glassy, cool, translucent wave,
    In twisted braids of lilies knitting
The loose train of thy amber-dropping hair;
    Listen for dear honor's sake,
865   Goddess of the silver lake,
        Listen and save.

Listen and appear to us
In name of great Oceanus,
By th' earth-shaking Neptune's mace,
870   And Tethys' grave majestic pace,
By hoary Nereus' wrinkled look,
And the Carpathian wizard's hook,
By scaly Triton's winding shell,
And old sooth-saying Glaucus' spell,
875   By Leucothea's lovely hands,
And her son that rules the strands,
By Thetis' tinsel-slippered feet,
And the songs of Sirens sweet,
By dead Parthenope's dear tomb,

863. **amber-dropping:** *Amber* in this context could be either a color word or an odor word (a shortened form of *ambergris*—the morbid intestinal secretion of a whale, but nonetheless a valued source of perfumes).

864. **honor's sake:** Female honor in this period almost always centers on chastity. In the seventeenth century, this concept gradually came under attack by male poets (Donne, Carew, Rochester) and even by a female poet (Aphra Behn).

865. **lake:** Vergil terms the Tiber a *lacus* in *Aen.* 8.66, 74.

867–89. These lines contain the *adjuring verse* mentioned in line 858.

868. **Oceanus:** father of all rivers.

869. **earth-shaking:** Homeric epithet for Poseidon/ *Neptune,* god of the sea and earthquakes; **mace:** trident.

870. **Tethys:** wife of Oceanus and mother of rivers.

871. **Nereus:** See 835n.

872. **Carpathian wizard:** Proteus, who lived in the Carpathian Sea, was the shepherd of Neptune's seals.

873. **Triton:** Neptune's herald, bearing a conch shell; **winding:** sounding, trumpeting.

874. **Glaucus:** a fisherman who became a sea god when he ate a magical herb (Ovid, *Met.* 13.904–68).

875. **Leucothea:** After leaping from a cliff to avoid the wrathful Juno, Ino was made the sea god *Leucothea* by Neptune (Ovid, *Met.* 4.512–42).

876. **her son:** Melicertes, whom Ino (see previous note) was holding when she jumped into the sea. Neptune turned him into Palaemon, god of harbors.

877. **Thetis:** a Nereid described by Homer as "silver-footed" (*Il.* 18.127), the mother of Achilles.

878. Even though the sweetness of their song is emphasized, it is odd that this catalog of benign sea deities should arrive at the *Sirens,* companions of Circe who lured sailors to their deaths (see 252–57).

879. **Parthenope:** a Siren who drowned herself when Odysseus escaped; she is supposed to be buried in Naples (Ovid, *Met.* 14.101).

880 And fair Ligea's golden comb,
    Wherewith she sits on diamond rocks
    Sleeking her soft alluring locks,
    By all the nymphs that nightly dance
    Upon thy streams with wily glance,
885 Rise, rise, and heave thy rosy head
    From thy coral-paven bed,
    And bridle in thy headlong wave,
    Till thou our summons answered have.
           Listen and save.

Sabrina rises, attended by water-nymphs, and sings.

890   By the rushy-fringèd bank,
    Where grows the willow and the osier dank,
      My sliding chariot stays,
    Thick set with agate, and the azurn sheen
    Of turkis blue, and emerald green
895   That in the channel strays,
    Whilst from off the waters fleet
    Thus I set my printless feet
    O'er the cowslip's velvet head,
      That bends not as I tread;
900 Gentle swain, at thy request
      I am here.

    Spirit. Goddess dear
    We implore thy powerful hand
    To undo the charmèd band
905 Of true virgin here distressed,
    Through the force, and through the wile
    Of unblest enchanter vile.
    Sabrina. Shepherd 'tis my office best
    To help ensnarèd chastity;
910 Brightest Lady look on me,
    Thus I sprinkle on thy breast
    Drops that from my fountain pure,
    I have kept of precious cure;

---

880. **Ligea:** another of the Sirens: Vergil described her shining tresses (*Georg.* 4.336).

893. **azurn:** azure.

894. **turkis:** turquoise.

897. **printless feet:** feet that leave no footprints; cp. Shakespeare, *TMP* 5.1.34.

904. **charmèd band:** bonds secured by a magical charm.

906. **force . . . wile:** On force and fraud as the two great instruments of achievement, see Machiavelli, *Discourses* 2.13.

Thrice upon thy finger's tip,
915 Thrice upon thy rubied lip,
Next this marble venomed seat
Smeared with gums of glutinous heat
I touch with chaste palms moist and cold,
Now the spell hath lost his hold;
920 And I must haste ere morning hour
To wait in Amphitrite's bower.

Sabrina descends, and the Lady rises out of her seat.

Spirit. Virgin, daughter of Locrine
Sprung of old Anchises' line,
May thy brimmèd waves for this
925 Their full tribute never miss
From a thousand petty rills,
That tumble down the snowy hills:
Summer drought, or singèd air
Never scorch thy tresses fair,
930 Nor wet October's torrent flood
Thy molten crystal fill with mud;
May thy billows roll ashore
The beryl and the golden ore;
May thy lofty head be crowned
935 With many a tower and terrace round,
And here and there thy banks upon
With groves of myrrh and cinnamon.
Come Lady while Heaven lends us grace,
Let us fly this cursèd place,
940 Lest the sorcerer us entice
With some other new device.
Not a waste or needless sound
Till we come to holier ground.
I shall be your faithful guide
945 Through this gloomy covert wide,
And not many furlongs thence
Is your father's residence,
Where this night are met in state

917. **glutinous:** sticky, gluey; critics often hear sexual undertones (Flosdorf 4–5; Kerrigan 1983, 45–48; Marcus 1983, 317).
918. **cold:** in antithesis to the heat of the previous line, and implying "chaste."
921. **Amphitrite:** wife of Neptune.

923. **Anchises' line:** the line of Trojan kings of Britain descended from Anchises, father of Aeneas; see Geoffrey of Monmouth, *History of Britain.*
924. **brimmèd:** full to the river's brim.
928. **singèd:** scorching.

Many a friend to gratulate
950   His wishèd presence, and beside
      All the swains that there abide,
      With jigs and rural dance resort;
      We shall catch them at their sport,
      And our sudden coming there
955   Will double all their mirth and cheer;
      Come let us haste, the stars grow high,
      But Night sits monarch yet in the mid sky.

The scene changes, presenting Ludlow Town and the President's castle. Then come in country dancers, after them the Attendant Spirit with the two brothers and the Lady.

Song

Spirit. Back, shepherds, back, enough your play,
      Till next sunshine holiday,
960   Here be without duck or nod
      Other trippings to be trod
      Of lighter toes, and such court guise
      As Mercury did first devise
      With the mincing Dryades
965   On the lawns and on the leas.

This second song presents them to their father and mother.

      Noble Lord, and Lady bright,
      I have brought ye new delight,
      Here behold so goodly grown
      Three fair branches of your own;
970   Heav'n hath timely tried their youth,
      Their faith, their patience, and their truth.

949. **gratulate:** welcome.

959. **sunshine holiday:** Cp. *L'All* 98.

960. **duck or nod:** awkward curtsy or bow.

961. **trippings:** dances.

962. **guise:** manner; the Attendant Spirit is contrasting the country dancers who have just performed with the court dancers about to perform.

963. **Mercury:** Though not the inventor of dance, he figured prominently in court masques, and his appearance here is doubly appropriate owing to his gift of Moly to Odysseus.

964. **mincing:** Quoted by the *OED* as an instance of "mincing" 1.b, "behaving in an affectedly dainty manner," but Demaray explains that "mince" is also "a dancing term that meant doubling the time to make twice as many steps to a musical measure" (118). While this meaning is not recorded in the *OED*, see Shakespeare, *MV* 3.4.67: "I'll . . . turn two mincing steps into a manly stride"; **Dryades:** forest nymphs.

970. **timely:** early.

970–71. The meter, the phrasing, the rhyme are all suggestive of Jonson (see *His Excuse for Loving*).

And sent them here through hard assays
With a crown of deathless praise,
　　To triumph in victorious dance
975 O'er sensual folly and intemperance.

The dances ended, the Spirit epilogizes.

Spirit. To the ocean now I fly,
And those happy climes that lie
Where day never shuts his eye,
Up in the broad fields of the sky:
980 There I suck the liquid air
All amidst the gardens fair
Of Hesperus, and his daughters three
That sing about the golden tree:
Along the crispèd shades and bow'rs
985 Revels the spruce and jocund Spring;
The Graces and the rosy-bosomed Hours,
Thither all their bounties bring,
There eternal Summer dwells,
And west winds with musky wing
990 About the cedarn alleys fling
Nard and Cassia's balmy smells.
Iris there with humid bow
Waters the odorous banks that blow
Flowers of more mingled hue
995 Than her purfled scarf can show,
And drenches with Elysian dew
(List mortals, if your ears be true)
Beds of hyacinth and roses

---

972. **assays:** trials.
976. **ocean:** In Plato (*Phaedo* 112e) the river Ocean lies on the genuine surface of the earth, which is among the stars.
980. **liquid:** clear, bright.
982–83. Hesiod, *Theog.* 215, says that the Hesperides "tend the fair apples beyond glorious Okeanos."
984. **crispèd shades:** leafy boughs *crisped* or curled by both leaves and shadows.
985. **spruce:** lively.
986. **Graces:** three goddesses who attended Venus and were in the Renaissance associated with a wide range of bounties; **Hours:** three goddesses who preside over the seasons. Graces and Hours dance together in *PL* 4.267.
988. In 1637, 1645, and *CMS*, this line began with "That," meaning "so that." But the word is canceled by the errata of 1673 (the last text Milton corrected).
990. **cedarn:** composed of cedars.
991. **Nard and Cassia:** fragrant plants.
992. **Iris:** goddess of the rainbow.
993. **blow:** bring into bloom.
995. **purfled:** variegated.
997. Cp. *PL* 7.30–31, where Milton also expresses his literary aspiration while dividing his audience into high and low, worthy and unworthy.

Where young Adonis oft reposes,
1000 Waxing well of his deep wound
In slumber soft, and on the ground
Sadly sits th' Assyrian queen;
But far above in spangled sheen
Celestial Cupid, her famed son, advanced,
1005 Holds his dear Psyche sweet entranced
After her wand'ring labors long,
Till free consent the gods among
Make her his eternal bride,
And from her fair unspotted side
1010 Two blissful twins are to be born,
Youth and Joy; so Jove hath sworn.
    But now my task is smoothly done,
I can fly, or I can run
Quickly to the green earth's end,
1015 Where the bowed welkin slow doth bend,
And from thence can soar as soon
To the corners of the moon.
    Mortals that would follow me,
Love Virtue, she alone is free;
1020 She can teach ye how to climb
Higher than the sphery chime;
Or if Virtue feeble were,
Heav'n itself would stoop to her.

---

999. **Adonis:** Loved by Venus, he was killed by a boar, then brought back to life in the Garden of Adonis. Spenser's famous version of the Garden of Adonis (*FQ* 3.6.46–48) is set on this earth. Milton translates the locale to the heavens and fuses it with the garden of the Hesperides.

1000. **Waxing:** growing.

1002. Venus and Adonis make love in Spenser's garden but not in Milton's. Although recovery appears imminent, Venus is sad.

1004–8. Apuleius, *The Golden Ass* 4.28–6.24, tells the story of Cupid's love for the mortal Psyche (Gk. for "soul"). She underwent many trials before Venus allowed her to marry her son. See Milton's allusion to her in *Areop* (*MLM* 938).

1004. **Celestial Cupid:** His double nature (son of Venus, yet residing on a celestial plane higher than hers) reminds some readers of Christ; **advanced:** raised, elevated.

1011. **Youth and Joy:** In Apuleius Psyche gives birth to Voluptas, in Spenser to Pleasure. Mil-

ton invents the twins and one of their identities (Joy was obviously suggested by Voluptas and Pleasure). Cp. Milton's *Apology* (*MLM* 851): "The first and chiefest office of love begins and ends in the soul, producing those happy twins of her divine generation, knowledge and virtue."

1015. **bowed welkin:** either "arched vault of the sky" or "the vault of the sky arched by a rainbow"; **slow doth bend:** Beheld from the western boundary of the earth, the sky seems in its vastness to bend slowly.

1017. **corners of the moon:** horns of the moon.

1021. Above the spheres of the Ptolemaic universe and the music they make, which is to say, in Heaven.

1023. **stoop:** bow down, descend, with the paradoxical connotations of humbling oneself (*OED* 2a) and being condescending (*OED* 2c). In 1639 Milton, traveling abroad, copied the final two lines in the album of the Cerdogni family of Geneva.

LYCIDAS

The year 1637 must have seemed more than usually marked by death to the twenty-eight-year-old Milton. His mother, Sara, died on April 3. Soon thereafter the plague came to Horton, where Milton was living with his father, and lasted through August. Ben Jonson, intestate and apparently senile, died on August 6, and three days later was buried, amid a large party of mourners, under the pavement in the north aisle of Westminister Abbey. There were plans for a monument, but life moves on, and they came to nothing. On August 10, Edward King, a Fellow of Christ's College, Cambridge, preparing himself to become an Anglican clergyman, set sail from Chester Bay to visit his family in Ireland. While the vessel was coasting along the shores of northern Wales, it struck a rock. The only surviving account tells us that King was thrown onto his knees by the force of the collision and stayed there, praying, as the ship went down.

A volume of memorial elegies was planned by King's Cambridge friends. We have no evidence that Milton was a close acquaintance, but at such times the entire university community conventionally shared the grief. Milton was asked to contribute late in the death-packed year of 1637. In the Trinity College manuscript, *Lycidas* is dated "Novemb: 1637," the same month in which Milton was planning to take rooms in London. *Justa Eduardo King* (Obsequies for Edward King) was published in Cambridge at the University Press early in 1638. It was a twinned or double book, not unlike Milton's 1645 and 1673 *Poems,* in that it contained two title pages followed by separately paginated sections in different languages. The first, in Latin, introduced twenty-three elegies in Latin and Greek. The second and English title page, headed "Obsequies to the memory of Mr. Edward King," announced thirteen English poems. The last of these, and the final poem in the volume, was Milton's *Lycidas,* printed without a headnote and signed with his initials.

It is one of the most famous, most powerful, and most studied poems in English literature. Two anthologies provide good starting places for beginners. Scott Elledge's *Milton's "Lycidas": Edited to Serve as an Introduction to Criticism* is particularly focused on the tradition behind the poem and the precise sense of its words. C. A. Patrides's *Milton's Lycidas: The Tradition and the Poem* is more expansive and contains some of the best essays on the work written in the twentieth century, as well as a valuable review of the history of *Lycidas* criticism by M. H. Abrams (216–35).

In the end, Lycidas is appointed "genius of the shore," in which office he shall be good "to all that wander in that perilous flood." As an enduring presence in the minds of its readers, the poem *Lycidas* has often served as spiritual companion and guardian. On Ralph Waldo Emerson's first voyage to Europe, his ship encountered a fierce Atlantic storm, and for three days passengers lived in fear of drowning at sea. Emerson calmed himself by retrieving *Lycidas* from memory, "clause by clause, here a verse and there a word, as Isis in the fable the broken body of Osiris" (R. D. Richardson 131). The meaning of the poem, and the meaning of teaching the poem, are the twinned subjects of a remarkable short story, "Wash Far Away," by the poet and scholar John Berryman (1976).

The headnote was added in 1645. At that time, as Milton looked back on his pastoral elegy, he felt that the words of denunciation he had penned in 1637 for St. Peter (130–31) had prophesied the overthrow of the Anglican establishment.

In this monody the author bewails a learned friend, unfortunately drowned in his passage from Chester on the Irish Seas, 1637. And by occasion foretells the ruin of our corrupted clergy, then in their height.

Yet once more, O ye laurels, and once more
Ye myrtles brown, with ivy never sere,
I come to pluck your berries harsh and crude,
And with forced fingers rude,
5   Shatter your leaves before the mellowing year.
Bitter constraint, and sad occasion dear,
Compels me to disturb your season due:
For Lycidas is dead, dead ere his prime,
Young Lycidas, and hath not left his peer:
10 Who would not sing for Lycidas? He knew
Himself to sing, and build the lofty rhyme.
He must not float upon his wat'ry bier

Headnote: The headnote was added in 1645. The *CMS* has only the first sentence; **monody:** in Greek literature, a dirge performed by a single voice; **by occasion:** A main difference between Protestant and Catholic meditation in Milton's day is that the latter concentrated on preset subjects, while the former was prompted by events and was therefore "by occasion" (see the full title of Donne's *The Anatomy of the World* and Huntley 123).

1. **Yet once more:** Heb. 12.26–27, alluding to Hag. 2.6–7: "Yet once more I shake not the earth only, but also heaven. And this word, Yet once more, signifieth the removing of those things that are shaken, as of things that are made, that those things which cannot be shaken may remain." On the biographical and generic senses of the apocalyptic opening, see Tayler 1979, 48–50. **laurels:** the crown of the poet was traditionally woven of laurels, sacred to Apollo.

2. **myrtles:** sacred to Venus and symbolic of love or love poetry; **ivy:** sacred to Bacchus and sometimes symbolic of learning or immortality; **never sere:** evergreen.

3. **crude:** unripe.

4. **rude:** ungentle (*forced*) or unskilled.

5. **Shatter:** scatter, destroy.

6. **occasion:** see note to headnote; **dear:** heartfelt.

8. **Lycidas:** a reasonably common name in classical pastoral. See Theocritus 7 and 27.42; Bion 2, 6; Vergil, *Ec.* 7.67, 9, and also Milton's *Damon* 132. Herrick's *Hesperides* contains "An Eclogue or Pastoral between Endimion Porter and Lycidas Herrick." There appears to be no particular significance to Milton's choice of this name.

8–9. Cp. the repeated name in Spenser's *Astrophel*: "Young Astrophel, the pride of shepherds praise,/Young Astrophel, the rustic lasses love."

10. Cp. Vergil, *Ec.* 10.3: "Who would not sing for Gallus?"; **He knew:** he knew how.

11. **build:** a classical idiom, as in Horace, *Epod.* 1.3.24: "You build charming poetry"; **rhyme:** verse (not necessarily rhymed).

Unwept, and welter to the parching wind,
Without the meed of some melodious tear.
15   Begin then, sisters of the sacred well,
That from beneath the seat of Jove doth spring;
Begin, and somewhat loudly sweep the string.
Hence with denial vain, and coy excuse;
So may some gentle muse
20   With lucky words favor my destined urn,
And as he passes, turn
And bid fair peace be to my sable shroud.
For we were nursed upon the self-same hill,
Fed the same flock, by fountain, shade, and rill.
25   Together both, ere the high lawns appeared
Under the opening eyelids of the morn,
We drove afield, and both together heard
What time the grayfly winds her sultry horn,
Batt'ning our flocks with the fresh dews of night,
30   Oft till the star that rose, at evening, bright
Toward heav'n's descent had sloped his westering wheel.
Meanwhile the rural ditties were not mute,
Tempered to th' oaten flute,
Rough satyrs danced, and fauns with cloven heel
35   From the glad sound would not be absent long,

13. **welter:** roll to and fro.

14. **meed:** merited honor; **melodious tear:** poetic elegy. Collections of elegies issued by the universities were often entitled *Lacrymae* (Lat.: "tears").

15. **Begin then:** a formula for prompting the Muses found in Theocritus 1.64, the refrain of Moschus's *Lament for Bion*, and Vergil, *Ec.* 10.6; **well:** a spring, probably Aganippe on Mount Helicon, near the altar to Zeus, though sometimes explained as the Pierian spring, birthplace of the Muses, on Mount Olympus. Either could be referred to as the *seat of Jove*.

18. **coy:** shyly reserved or retiring.

19. **So:** on condition that I sing for Lycidas; **muse:** poet.

20. **lucky:** presaging good luck (by wishing me well); **urn:** grave.

21. The comma in this line is found in *Justa Eduardo King*. See Creaser 2010, p. 81.

22. **sable:** black.

23. **self-same hill:** probably Christ's College, Cambridge, which both Milton and King attended.

25. **lawns:** glades, the open spaces between woods.

26. **opening:** The 1638 edition read "glimmering"; **eyelids of the morn:** See Job 41.18.

28. **What time:** at the time when; **grayfly:** used of various insects; **winds:** blows; **sultry horn:** the metaphorical instrument by means of which grayflies hum in the midday heat. Browne discusses the question in *Pseudodoxia Epidemica* 3.27.10.

29. **Batt'ning:** fattening.

30. **star:** Hesperus, the evening star, whose appearance signals the shepherd to fold his flocks, as in *Masque* 93.

31. **westering:** Hesperus appears to set in the west.

32. **ditties:** In Milton's day the word *ditty* could refer to any kind of song and lacked the modern connotation of triviality.

33. **Tempered to:** attuned to; **oaten flute:** Pipes made from oat straw were traditional instruments of pastoral music.

34. **satyrs . . . fauns:** Greek *satyrs* had a human form, save for pointed ears and a tail. They were later identified with *fauns*, half human and half goat (*with cloven heel*).

And old Damaetas loved to hear our song.
　　But O the heavy change, now thou art gone,
Now thou art gone, and never must return!
Thee shepherd, thee the woods, and desert caves,
40　With wild thyme and the gadding vine o'ergrown,
And all their echoes mourn.
The willows, and the hazel copses green,
Shall now no more be seen,
Fanning their joyous leaves to thy soft lays.
45　As killing as the canker to the rose,
Or taint-worm to the weanling herds that graze,
Or frost to flowers, that their gay wardrobe wear,
When first the whitethorn blows;
Such, Lycidas, thy loss to shepherd's ear.
50　　Where were ye nymphs when the remorseless deep
Closed o'er the head of your loved Lycidas?
For neither were ye playing on the steep,
Where your old bards, the famous Druids lie,
Nor on the shaggy top of Mona high,
55　Nor yet where Deva spreads her wizard stream:
Ay me, I fondly dream!
Had ye been there—for what could that have done?
What could the Muse herself that Orpheus bore,
The Muse herself, for her enchanting son
60　Whom universal Nature did lament,

---

36. **Damaetas:** a traditional pastoral name. Milton may have had a specific tutor in mind; William Chappell and Joseph Mede are the two most popular candidates.

39–44. In Moschus's *Lament for Bion,* the orchards and groves bewail his loss; see also Ovid on the death of Orpheus (*Met.* 11.44–46).

40. **gadding:** wandering.

45. **canker:** a name given to caterpillars and insect larvae that harmed the leaves and buds of plants.

46. **taint-worm:** possibly "husk," a parasite fatal to newly weaned sheep.

48. **whitethorn:** hawthorn.

50. **Where were ye nymphs:** Speakers in Theocritus (1.66–69) and Vergil (*Ec.* 10.9–12) also interrogate nymphs.

52. **steep:** This might refer to a mountain in Wales but probably alludes to an island, though which one the author had in mind remains unclear. Bardsey, whose name proclaims an association with bards, seems the best candidate, though it

is not near the island of *Mona.* Milton may have been misled on Mona's proximity to Bardsey by an ambiguous Latin sentence in Camden's *Britannia.* See Hughes et al. 2:655 for details.

53. For a similar reference to the Druids as poets, see *Manso* 43.

54. **Mona:** Anglesey; Drayton, *Polyolbion* 9.425–29, remembering Tacitus, said that this island was once covered with sacred oaks (*shaggy*).

55. **Deva:** the river Dee, *wizard* because associated with magicians and divination.

56. **fondly:** foolishly; **dream:** give voice to the foolish thought "If only the Muses had been here."

58–63. The Muse is Calliope, inspirer of epic poetry. Her son Orpheus, still in love with Eurydice, was torn to pieces by the resentful Maenads, females devoted to Bacchus. All *Nature did lament* as his head, still singing, floated down the river Hebrus into the Aegean Sea, arriving finally at the island of Lesbos (Ovid, *Met.* 9.1–66; Vergil, *Georg.* 4.485–527). Cp. *PL* 7.32–38.

When by the rout that made the hideous roar,
His gory visage down the stream was sent,
Down the swift Hebrus to the Lesbian shore.
Alas! What boots it with uncessant care
65   To tend the homely slighted shepherd's trade,
And strictly meditate the thankless muse?
Were it not better done as others use,
To sport with Amaryllis in the shade,
Or with the tangles of Neaera's hair?
70   Fame is the spur that the clear spirit doth raise
(That last infirmity of noble mind)
To scorn delights, and live laborious days;
But the fair guerdon when we hope to find,
And think to burst out into sudden blaze,
75   Comes the blind Fury with th' abhorrèd shears,
And slits the thin-spun life. "But not the praise,"
Phoebus replied, and touched my trembling ears.
"Fame is no plant that grows on mortal soil,

---

61. **rout:** band (with negative connotation, as here).

64. **What boots it:** Of what advantage or profit is it?

65. **homely:** humble; **slighted:** treated with indifference or disdain; **shepherd's trade:** writing poetry.

66. **strictly:** rigorously (note *with uncessant care* in l. 64); **meditate the thankless muse:** compose poetry at the bidding of a muse who cannot protect me from death; the idiom "meditate the Muse" is found in Vergil, *Ec.* 1.2. Some editors take *thankless* to refer to an ungrateful public.

67. **use:** are accustomed to doing.

68. **Amaryllis:** Amaryllis, though she appears in Theocritus, is particularly associated with Vergil; see especially *Ec.* 2.14–16, since Milton evokes its phrasing.

69. **Neaera:** She appears in classical literature, and her hair was ever worthy of comment, but Milton almost certainly has in mind the Neaera of the sixteenth-century Dutch Neo-Latin lyricist Johannes Secundus (*Basia* 7, 8).

70. **Fame is the spur:** This declaration has become proverbial and is the title of a 1947 British film of a novel by the same name; **clear:** noble, pure (from Lat. *clarus*).

71. **That last infirmity of noble mind:** Milton is here imitating a classical maxim found in numerous writers, including Tacitus 4.6: "Even in the case of wise men the desire for glory is last cut off." Milton's contemporary Owen

Felltham put it this way in *Of Fame:* "Desire of glory is the last garment that even wise men lay aside. For this we may trust Tacitus" (*Resolves* 47).

73. **guerdon:** reward (fame, in this case).

74. **sudden blaze:** flash of glory; *blaze* could mean "to make public." Cp. *PL* 10.453; *PR* 3.47.

75. **blind Fury with th' abhorrèd shears:** Atropos, the third of the Fates, is here represented as a *Fury,* normally thought of as an agent of vengeance, and as *blind,* not a usual attribute of either Fates or Furies. Death is fierce and purposeless.

76. **slits:** cuts (not lengthwise).

77. **touched my trembling ears:** echoing Vergil, *Ec.* 6.3–4, where the poet is probably alluding to Callimachus, *Aetia,* Fragment 1. The gesture both warns the poet to stop and reminds him of something he has forgotten. Also, in ancient Rome, witnesses were summoned by a touch on the ear. Masson's suggestion that a person's ears were thought to tingle when someone else was talking about him is probably irrelevant, since *trembling* is most likely a transferred epithet and refers to the trembling of the poet's ears *after* they have been touched by *Phoebus* Apollo. Apollo as the god of poetry appropriately concludes the first and classical section of the poem, in which shepherding represents writing poetry.

      Nor in the glistering foil
80   Set off to th' world, nor in broad rumor lies,
      But lives and spreads aloft by those pure eyes,
      And perfect witness of all-judging Jove;
      As he pronounces lastly on each deed,
      Of so much fame in Heav'n expect thy meed."
85   O fountain Arethuse, and thou honored flood,
      Smooth-sliding Mincius, crowned with vocal reeds,
      That strain I heard was of a higher mood:
      But now my oat proceeds,
      And listens to the herald of the sea
90   That came in Neptune's plea.
      He asked the waves, and asked the felon winds,
      "What hard mishap hath doomed this gentle swain?"
      And questioned every gust of rugged wings
      That blows from off each beakèd promontory:
95   They knew not of his story,
      And sage Hippotades their answer brings,
      That not a blast was from his dungeon strayed;
      The air was calm, and on the level brine,
      Sleek Panope with all her sisters played.
100   It was that fatal and perfidious bark
      Built in th' eclipse, and rigged with curses dark,
      That sunk so low that sacred head of thine.
        Next Camus, reverend sire, went footing slow,

---

79. **glistering foil:** thin leaf of gold or silver placed under a precious stone to enhance its brilliance.

80. **nor in broad rumor lies:** Cp. Pope, *Essay on Man:* "What's fame, a fancied life in other's breath?"

84. **meed:** reward (lifting the idea of fame as *guerdon* from earth to Heaven). See 14n.

85–87. The poem returns to pastoral after the "higher mood" of Phoebus's speech. *Arethuse,* invoked by Theocritus (1.117), represents Greek pastoral, while the river *Mincius,* celebrated by Vergil, represents Roman pastoral. The river god Alpheus pursued the nymph Arethusa, who turned into a river herself; they ran untainted through the sea and emerged, mingling, in the Sicilian spring named Arethusa.

87. **mood:** musical mode.

88. **oat:** pipe made from oat straw, whose song is symbolic of pastoral verse.

89–131. A procession of mourners is conventional in pastoral elegy. See Milton's *Damon* 69–90.

89. **herald:** Triton, Neptune's son.

90. **in Neptune's plea:** to plead Neptune's innocence of the charge of responsibility for Lycidas's (King's) death by calling a number of witnesses.

91. **felon:** wild, with also the sense of "criminal," in that the winds are at this point presumed to be guilty of Lycidas's death.

93–94. **beakèd promontory** and **rugged wings** is a classic example of transferred epithet: *beakèd* belongs with *wings* and *promontory* with *rugged.*

96. **Hippotades:** Aeolus, son of Hippotes and god of winds, who kept them imprisoned in a cavern (Vergil, *Aen.* 1.52–63).

99. **Panope:** one of the fifty Nereids (sea nymphs).

103. **Camus:** the god of the river Cam, representing Cambridge University; **footing slow:** The Cam does move slowly, but a fanciful pun on the derivation of *pedant* from the Italian *pedare* ("to foot it") has been suggested. A personification of Camus appears prominently in Phineas Fletcher's *Piscatory Eclogues.*

His mantle hairy, and his bonnet sedge,
105 Inwrought with figures dim, and on the edge
Like to that sanguine flower inscribed with woe.
"Ah! Who hath reft," quoth he, "my dearest pledge?"
Last came, and last did go,
The pilot of the Galilean lake;
110 Two massy keys he bore of metals twain
(The golden opes, the iron shuts amain).
He shook his mitred locks, and stern bespake,
"How well could I have spared for thee, young swain,
Enow of such as for their bellies' sake,
115 Creep and intrude, and climb into the fold?
Of other care they little reck'ning make,
Than how to scramble at the shearers' feast,
And shove away the worthy bidden guest.
Blind mouths! that scarce themselves know how to hold
120 A sheep-hook, or have learned aught else the least
That to the faithful herdman's art belongs!
What recks it them? What need they? They are sped;
And when they list, their lean and flashy songs
Grate on their scrannel pipes of wretched straw;

104. **hairy:** Academic gowns were fur-trimmed; **sedge:** a name applied to various plants growing near water. Crowns of sedge were conventional for river gods in masques.
105. **Inwrought:** worked in, sewn in.
106. **sanguine flower:** the hyacinth, on whose leaves Apollo inscribed AIAI ("Alas, alas"), because the plant sprang from the blood of his beloved Hyacinthus. See *Fair Infant* 23–27.
107. **reft:** taken; **pledge:** child. Cp. *PL* 2.818.
109. **pilot:** St. Peter, the fisherman of Galilee and founder of the Christian Church, to whom Jesus said he would give "the keys of the kingdom of Heaven" (Matt. 16), to bind and to loose. King had intended to take holy orders. For the two keys, see also *PL* 3.484–85 and *Areop* (p. 934).
111. **amain:** vehemently.
112. **mitred:** As the first bishop of the Christian Church, St. Peter wears a miter.
113. **for:** instead of; **swain:** shepherd.
113–29. This attack on ecclesiastical corruption resembles numerous passages from the Bible (Ezek. 34, John 10, 1 Peter 4) and Christian literature (Dante, *Par.* 27.55–57; Petrarch, *Ec.* 6 and 7; Spenser, *SC*, "May" and "September").
114. **Enow:** the plural of *enough*.
115. **climb:** John 10.1: "He that entereth not by the

door into the sheepfold, but climbeth up some other way."
117. **scramble:** contend with a crowd for a share of food, coin, wealth (*OED* 2); **shearers' feast:** festive supper given to the workers after sheep shearing (thus metaphorical here for the temporal rewards of the priesthood).
119. **Blind mouths:** Ruskin's famous comment still seems definitive: "A 'bishop' means 'a person who sees.' A 'pastor' means 'a person who feeds.' The most unbishoply character a man can have is therefore to be blind. The most unpastoral is, instead of feeding, to want to be fed—to be a mouth. Take the two reverses together, and you have 'blind mouths'" (*Sesame and Lilies* 1.22).
120. **or have learned aught else:** In his prose works, Milton often railed against the ignorance of the Anglican clergy. See *Apology* (Yale 1:933–35) and *Eikon* (Yale 3:437–38).
121. **faithful herdman's art:** the offices of the priesthood.
122. **What recks it them?:** What do they care?; **sped:** satisfied, well off.
123. **list:** please; **lean:** because yielding no sustenance; **flashy:** insipid, watery (not the modern "showy").
124. **scrannel:** thin, harsh-sounding.

125   The hungry sheep look up, and are not fed,
      But swoll'n with wind, and the rank mist they draw,
      Rot inwardly, and foul contagion spread:
      Besides what the grim wolf with privy paw
      Daily devours apace, and nothing said.
130   But that two-handed engine at the door,
      Stands ready to smite once, and smite no more."
         Return Alpheus, the dread voice is past
      That shrunk thy streams; return Sicilian muse,
      And call the vales, and bid them hither cast
135   Their bells, and flow'rets of a thousand hues.
      Ye valleys low, where the mild whispers use
      Of shades and wanton winds, and gushing brooks,
      On whose fresh lap the swart star sparely looks,
      Throw hither all your quaint enameled eyes,
140   That on the green turf suck the honeyed showers,
      And purple all the ground with vernal flowers.
      Bring the rathe primrose that forsaken dies,
      The tufted crow-toe, and pale jessamine,
      The white pink, and the pansy freaked with jet,
145   The glowing violet,
      The musk-rose, and the well-attired woodbine,
      With cowslips wan that hang the pensive head,

---

125. "They [the prelates] have fed themselves, and not their flocks" (*Animad* in Yale 1:726).

126. **swoll'n with wind:** suffering from the disease of sheep rot. Cp. the similar metaphor for the effects on the laity of ecclesiastical corruption in Petrarch, *Ec.* 6.21–31, 7.19–27, 9, and Dante, *Par.* 29.106–7; **draw:** inhale.

128. **grim wolf:** the Roman Catholic Church, especially the Jesuits, since the coat of arms of their founder, St. Ignatius, featured two gray wolves. Milton seems to be deploring the secret conversion of high-placed Anglicans to the old faith; **privy:** secret.

130. **two-handed engine:** The most famous crux in Milton. The phrasing (*smite once, and . . . no more*) recalls the opening lines (*Yet once more . . . and once more*) but with the shift from repetition to apocalyptic finality that St. Paul found in the very meaning of "Yet once more" (see 1n). Most interpretations go awry in at least one particular, such as Kelly and Bray's identification of the two-handed engine with a printing press, which cannot explain credibly why a press would smite once only. Perhaps the most convincing of the many attempts to solve the crux is Tayler's identification of the two-handed engine with St.

Peter's keys (1979, 234–36). **at the door:** ready to hand, soon to strike. Cp. Matt. 24.33.

132. **Alpheus:** See 85–87n.

135. **bells:** bell-shaped flowers.

136. **use:** haunt, habitually resort.

137. **shades:** tree-shaded places (B. A. Wright); **wanton:** unrestrained (blowing where they list).

138. **whose:** referring back to the *valleys low;* **swart star:** Sirius, the Dog Star, which rises during the hot "dog days" of summer. The star is *swart,* darkened by heat.

139. **quaint:** attractively adorned; **enameled:** many-colored.

141. **purple:** make bright.

142. **rathe:** early.

142–50. There are two versions of this passage in *CMS,* one of which is nearly identical to the printed text. The other, which has psychological interest, begins: "Bring the rathe primrose that unwedded dies/Colouring the pale cheek of unenjoyed love." Cp. Shakespeare, *WT* 4.4.122–24.

143. **tufted:** growing in clusters; **crow-toe:** wild hyacinth; **jessamine:** jasmine.

144. **freaked:** flecked or streaked.

146. **woodbine:** honeysuckle.

147. **wan:** pale.

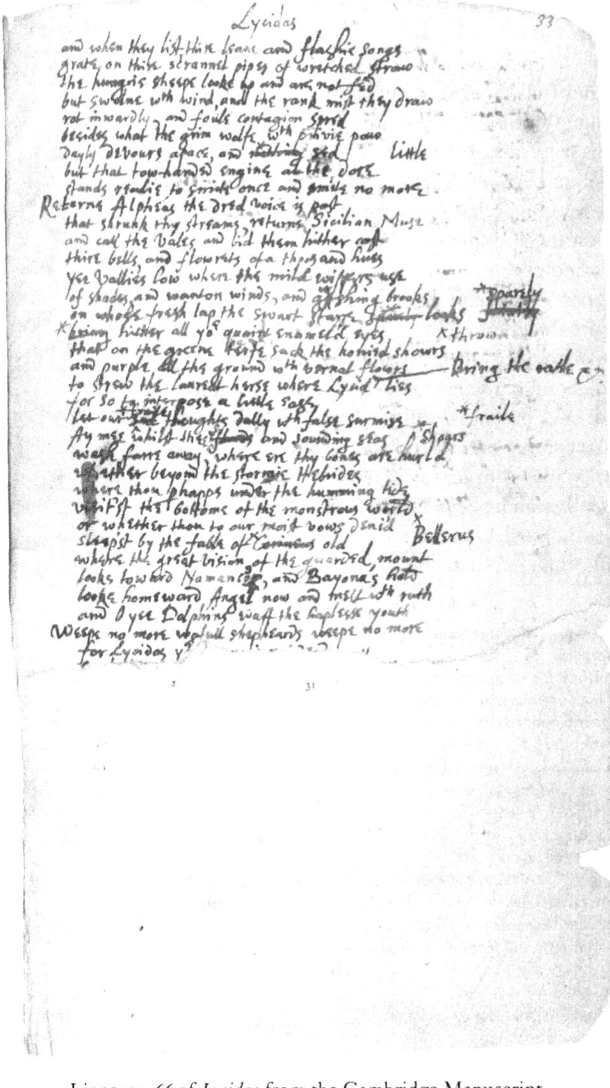

Lines 123–66 of *Lycidas,* from the Cambridge Manuscript.

And every flower that sad embroidery wears:
Bid amaranthus all his beauty shed,
150 And daffadillies fill their cups with tears,
To strew the laureate hearse where Lycid lies.
For so to interpose a little ease,
Let our frail thoughts dally with false surmise.
Ay me! Whilst thee the shores, and sounding seas
155 Wash far away, where'er thy bones are hurled,
Whether beyond the stormy Hebrides,
Where thou perhaps under the whelming tide
Visit'st the bottom of the monstrous world;
Or whether thou to our moist vows denied,
160 Sleep'st by the fable of Bellerus old,
Where the great vision of the guarded mount
Looks toward Namancos and Bayona's hold;
Look homeward angel now, and melt with ruth.
And, O ye dolphins, waft the hapless youth.
165   Weep no more, woeful shepherds, weep no more,
For Lycidas your sorrow is not dead,
Sunk though he be beneath the wat'ry floor,
So sinks the day-star in the ocean bed,
And yet anon repairs his drooping head,

---

148. **sad:** sober-colored; **embroidery:** markings on the flowers.

149. **amaranthus:** the name (from Gk. for "unfading") of both a genus of ornamental plants and an imaginary immortal flower (cp. *PL* 3.353–57).

151. **laureate:** decked with the laurels (both wreaths and poems) invoked in the poem's opening line. Memorial stanzas were sometimes attached to a hearse.

152–62. T. S. Eliot wrote of this passage that "for the single grandeur of sound, there is nothing finer in poetry" (*On Poetry and Poets*, 164).

153. **false surmise:** That the body of Lycidas lies on a laureate hearse is one false surmise; according to Brooks and Hardy (183), the ritual of strewing apparently sympathetic (but actually indifferent) flowers is another.

157. **whelming:** *CMS* and 1638 have "humming."

158. **bottom . . . world:** the bottom of the sea, a realm of monsters.

159. **moist vows:** tearful funeral rites.

160. **fable of Bellerus:** The hero or giant Bellerus seems to have been invented by Milton in order to make *Bellerium*, as Land's End is known in Latin, eponymous.

161. **great vision . . . mount:** According to Camden's *Britannia*, the archangel Michael ap-

peared to monks on St. Michael's Mount. A section of the rock is called "St. Michael's Chair."

162. **Namancos and Bayona's hold:** the district of Namancos and the stronghold of Bayona in Spain, one of England's traditional enemies. Camden remarked that "there is no other place in this island [save Land's End] that looks towards Spain" (B. A. Wright).

163. **Look homeward angel:** Michael is asked to turn his gaze away from Spain to the Irish Sea, which somewhere contains the body of Lycidas.

164. **ye dolphins:** Dolphins are invoked to minister to the body primarily because they had performed this service for the poet Arion (Herodotus 1.24) and the infant Melicertes (Ovid, *Met.* 4.481–54). They have also served as symbols of the resurrection; **waft:** convey from sea to land.

165. The repeated *no more . . . no more* continues the pattern established in the opening lines and line 131, and shifts from apocalyptic finality (see 130n) to the certitude of faith, which ends mourning.

166. **your sorrow:** the object of your sorrow.

168. **day-star:** the sun.

170 And tricks his beams, and with new-spangled ore,
     Flames in the forehead of the morning sky:
     So Lycidas sunk low, but mounted high,
     Through the dear might of him that walked the waves,
     Where other groves, and other streams along,
175 With nectar pure his oozy locks he laves,
     And hears the unexpressive nuptial song,
     In the blest kingdoms meek of joy and love.
     There entertain him all the saints above,
     In solemn troops, and sweet societies
180 That sing, and singing in their glory move,
     And wipe the tears for ever from his eyes.
     Now, Lycidas, the shepherds weep no more;
     Henceforth thou art the genius of the shore,
     In thy large recompense, and shalt be good
185 To all that wander in that perilous flood.
         Thus sang the uncouth swain to th' oaks and rills,
     While the still Morn went out with sandals gray;
     He touched the tender stops of various quills,
     With eager thought warbling his Doric lay:
190 And now the sun had stretched out all the hills,
     And now was dropped into the western bay;

---

170. **tricks:** dresses anew; **ore:** gold.

171. **forehead:** forefront. Shakespeare has "the forehead of the morning" in *COR* 2.1.57.

173. **him that walked the waves:** "A designation of our Saviour, by a miracle [Matt. 14.25–31] which bears an immediate reference to the subject of the poem" (Warton).

174. **groves, and other streams:** Cp. Rev. 22.1–2.

175. **nectar:** the drink of the gods; **oozy:** still wet from the sea; **laves:** washes.

176. **unexpressive:** inexpressible; **nuptial song:** the song sung at the nuptials of the lamb in Rev. 19.5.

178. **the saints above:** The word *saints* can mean "all of the redeemed in Heaven," but Milton also used it to refer to angels.

181. Cp. Rev. 21.4: "And God shall wipe away all tears from their eyes" (also Isa. 25.8). Milton transfers the action from God to the saints.

183. **genius:** the guardian spirit of a locality. A sudden shift from Christian to classical, as Milton again refuses to sever the two cultural traditions.

184. **thy large recompense:** God's generous recompense to Lycidas for his early and terrifying death.

185. The poet himself has been among the first to benefit from the offices of Lycidas.

186–93. The epilogue has the form of an *ottava rima* stanza (eight iambic pentameter lines rhyming abababcc).

186. **uncouth:** unknown, unskilled; **oaks and rills:** The pastoral community of shepherds, the processions of gods and goddesses, the divine speakers—all suddenly disappear. The poem was sung to an empty landscape.

188. **tender:** either frail or responsive; **stops:** finger holes; **various quills:** the hollow reeds of the shepherd's pipes, *various* because of the mixture of styles in the poem.

189. **With eager thought:** eager, that is, after the hesitant beginning; **Doric:** The earliest pastoral poets (Theocritus, Moschus, and Bion) wrote in the Doric dialect.

190. "The setting sun had stretched out the shadows of the hills."

At last he rose, and twitched his mantle blue:
Tomorrow to fresh woods, and pastures new.

192. **he:** For a moment *he* is ambiguously both the poet and the sun. The ambiguity is not dispelled by *twitched his mantle blue,* which could refer in some fashion to the morning sky. **twitched:** pulled up around his shoulders (in preparing to depart); **blue:** Literary shepherds mostly wore gray mantles, but blue ones were not unknown (William Browne, *Shepherd's Pipe* 2.37–38).

193. **fresh woods, and pastures new:** These could refer in general to changes in the future (editors often mention Milton's forthcoming journey to the continent), or to the landscape of Heaven that awaits the faithful. Poetically and autobiographically, they could also refer to the epic poem customarily undertaken after the completion of the young poet's pastoral songs.

PSALMS 80–88

Milton's headnote expresses a pronounced concern with the literalness of these efforts. Deviations from that standard must wear italics. As first printed in 1673, the translations also had marginal notes giving sometimes the Hebrew, sometimes a full English version of the Hebrew, at a few of the places where Milton expanded or paraphrased the original. This fussiness over what is and what is not in the Bible relates these Psalm translations to seventeenth-century controversies over the metrical Psalter. In 1647 the Westminster Assembly appointed a committee to revise the Francis Rous Psalter of 1641. For practical purposes they divided the Psalms into four groups, the third of which began, suggestively, with Psalm 80, just like Milton's group (Hunter 1961). Other political contexts have been explored (Boddy; Hill 1993, 381–82).

The translations were given a date of April 1648 in the second edition of the *Poems.* Our notes make some use of Milton's original marginalia.

Nine of the Psalms done into meter, wherein all but what is in a different character, are the very words of the text, translated from the original.

Psalm 80

1) Thou shepherd that dost Israel *keep*
  Give ear *in time of need,*
Who leadest like a flock of sheep
  Thy lovèd Joseph's seed,
5 That sitt'st between the Cherubs *bright*
  Between their wings outspread
Shine forth, *and from thy cloud give light,*
  And on our foes thy dread.

2) In Ephraim's view and Benjamin's,
10   And in Manasseh's sight
Awake thy strength, come, and *be seen*
          To save us *by thy might.*
3) Turn us again, *thy grace divine*
          To us O God *vouchsafe;*
15 Cause thou thy face on us to shine
          And then we shall be safe.
4) Lord God of Hosts, how long wilt thou,
          How long wilt thou declare
Thy smoking wrath *and angry brow*
20   Against thy people's prayer?
5) Thou feed'st them with the bread of tears,
          Their bread with tears they eat,
And mak'st them largely drink the tears
          Wherewith their cheeks are wet.
25 6) A strife thou mak'st us *and a prey*
          To every neighbor foe;
Among themselves they laugh, they play,
          And flouts at us they throw.
7) Return us, *and thy grace divine,*
30   O God of Hosts *vouchsafe;*
Cause thou thy face on us to shine,
          And then we shall be safe.
8) A vine from Egypt thou hast brought,
          Thy free love made it thine,
35 And drov'st out nations *proud and haught*
          To plant this *lovely* vine.
9) Thou didst prepare for it a place
          And root it deep and fast
That it *began to grow apace,*
40   *And* filled the land *at last.*
10) With her *green* shade *that* covered *all,*
          The hills were *overspread;*
Her boughs *as high as* cedars tall
          Advanced their lofty head.
45 11) Her branches *on the western side*
          Down to the sea she sent,
And *upward* to that river *wide*
          Her other branches *went.*

---

11. **Awake:** *Gnorera* means "arouse."
19. **smoking wrath:** *Gnashanta* means "you are smoking."

23. **largely:** *Shalish* means "third of a measure."
27–28. **laugh ... throw:** *Jilgnagu* means "mock."

12) Why hast thou laid her hedges low
50 And broken down her fence,
That all may pluck her, as they go,
   With rudest violence?
13) The *tuskèd* boar out of the wood
   Upturns it by the roots,
55 Wild beasts there browse, and make their food
   Her grapes and tender shoots.
14) Return now, God of Hosts, look down
   From Heav'n, thy seat divine,
Behold *us, but without a frown,*
60 And visit this *thy* vine.
15) Visit this vine, which thy right hand
   Hath set, and planted *long,*
And the young branch, that for thyself
   Thou hast made firm and strong.
65 16) But now it is consumed with fire,
   And cut *with axes* down;
They perish at thy dreadful ire,
   At thy rebuke and frown.
17) Upon the man of thy right hand
70 Let thy *good* hand be *laid,*
Upon the Son of Man, whom thou
   Strong for thyself hast made.
18) So shall we not go back from thee
   To ways of sin and shame,
75 Quicken us thou, then *gladly* we
   Shall call upon thy name.
Return us, *and thy grace divine*
   Lord God of Hosts *vouchsafe,*
Cause thou thy face on us to shine,
80 And then we shall be safe.

Psalm 81

1) To God our strength sing loud, *and clear*
   Sing loud to God *our King,*
To Jacob's God, *that all may hear*
   Loud acclamations ring.
5 2) Prepare a hymn, prepare a song,
   The timbrel hither bring;
The *cheerful* psalt'ry bring along
   And harp *with* pleasant *string;*
3) Blow, *as is wont,* in the new moon

10 With trumpets' *lofty sound,*
 Th' appointed time, the day whereon
  Our solemn feast *comes round.*
 4) This was a statute *giv'n of old*
  For Israel *to observe,*
15 A law of Jacob's God, *to hold*
  From whence they might not swerve.
 5) This he a testimony ordained
  In Joseph, *not to change,*
 When as he passed through Egypt land;
20 The tongue I heard, was strange.
 6) From burden, *and from slavish toil*
  I set his shoulder free;
 His hands from pots, *and miry soil*
  Delivered were *by me.*
25 7) When trouble did thee sore assail,
  On me then didst thou call,
 And I to free thee *did not fail,*
  And led thee out of thrall.
 I answered thee in thunder deep
30 With clouds encompassed round;
 I tried thee at the water *steep*
  Of Meriba *renowned.*
 8) Hear O my people, *hearken well,*
  I testify to thee
35 *Thou ancient stock* of Israel,
  If thou wilt list to me,
 9) Throughout the land of thy abode
  No alien god shall be,
 Nor shalt thou to a foreign god
40 In honor bend thy knee.
 10) I am the Lord thy God which brought
  Thee out of Egypt land;
 Ask large enough, and I, *besought,*
  Will grant thy full demand.
45 11) And yet my people would not *hear,*
  Nor hearken to my voice;
 And Israel *whom I loved so dear*
  Misliked me for his choice.
 12) Then did I leave them to their will
50 And to their wand'ring mind;

---

29. **in thunder deep:** *Besether ragnam* means "in the
secret place of thunder."

Their own conceits they followed still,
    Their own devices blind.
13) O that my people would *be wise*
    To serve me *all their days,*
55 And O that Israel would *advise*
    To walk my *righteous* ways.
14) Then would I soon bring down their foes
    That now so proudly rise,
And turn my hand against *all those*
60   *That are* their enemies.
15) Who hate the Lord should *then be fain*
    To bow to him and bend,
But *they, his people, should remain,*
    Their time should have no end.
65 16) And we would feed them *from the shock*
    With flour of finest wheat,
And satisfy them from the rock
    With honey *for their meat.*

Psalm 82

1) God in the great assembly stands
    Of kings and lordly states,
Among the gods on both his hands
    He judges and debates.
5 2) How long will ye pervert the right
    With judgment false and wrong,
Favoring the wicked *by your might,*
    Who thence grow bold and strong?
3) Regard the weak and fatherless,
10   Despatch the poor man's cause,
And raise the man in deep distress
    By just and equal laws.
4) Defend the poor and desolate,
    And rescue from the hands
15 Of wicked men the low estate
    Of him *that help demands.*
5) They know not nor will understand,
    In darkness they walk on;

1. **great assembly:** *Bagnadath-el* means "assembly of God."

3. **Among . . . hands:** *Bekerev* means "in the midst of."

5–6. **pervert . . . wrong:** *Tishphetu gnavel* means "judge falsely."

9–10. **Regard . . . cause:** *Shiphtu-dal* means "judge the poor."

The earth's foundations are all moved
20   And out of order gone.
        6) I said that ye were gods, yea all
            The sons of God most high,
        7) But ye shall die like men, and fall
            As other princes *die*.
25   8) Rise God, judge thou the earth *in might*,
            This *wicked* earth redress,
        For thou art he who shalt by right
            The nations all possess.

19–20. **moved . . . gone:** *Jimmotu* means "moved."   25–26. **judge . . . redress:** *Shophta* means "judge."

Psalm 83

        1) Be not thou silent *now at length*,
            O God hold not thy peace,
        Sit not thou still O God of *strength*,
            We cry and do not cease.
5   2) For lo thy *furious* foes *now* swell
            And storm outrageously,
        And they that hate thee *proud and fell*
            Exalt their heads full high.
        3) Against thy people they contrive
10   Their plots and counsels deep;
        Them to ensnare they chiefly strive
            Whom thou dost hide and keep.
        4) "Come let us cut them off," say they,
            "Till they no nation be,
15   That Israel's name forever may
            Be lost in memory."
        5) For they consult with all their might,
            And all as one in mind
        Themselves against thee they unite
20   And in firm union bind.
        6) The tents of Edom, and the brood
            Of *scornful* Ishmael,
        Moab, with them of Hagar's blood

5–6. **swell . . . outrageously:** *Jehemajun* means "are in tumult."

9–10. **contrive . . . counsels:** *Jagnarimu Sod* means "deliberate cunningly."

11. **Them to ensnare:** *Jithjagnatsu gnal* means "conspire against."

12. **Whom . . . keep:** *Tsephuneca* means "your hidden things."

17. **with all their might:** *Lev jachdau* means "together with one heart."

  That in the desert dwell,
25 7) Gebal and Ammon *there conspire,*
  And *hateful* Amalek,
  The Philistines, and they of Tyre
   Whose bounds the sea doth check.
  8) With them *great* Ashur also bands
30 *And doth confirm the knot;*
  All these have lent their armèd hands
   To aid the sons of Lot.
  9) Do to them as to Midian *bold*
   That wasted all the coast,
35 To Sisera, and as *is told*
   Thou didst to Jabin's *host,*
  When at the brook of Kishon *old*
   They were repulsed and slain,
  10) At Endor quite cut off, and rolled
40 As dung upon the plain.
  11) As Zeb and Oreb evil sped
   So let their princes speed;
  As Zeba, and Zalmunna *bled*
   So let their princes *bleed.*
45 12) *For they amidst their pride* have said,
   "By right now shall we seize
  God's houses, and *will now invade*
   Their stately palaces."
  13) My God, O make them as a wheel,
50 *No quiet let them find,*
  Giddy and *restless* let *them reel*
   Like stubble from the wind.
  14) As *when* an *aged* wood takes fire
   Which on a sudden strays,
55 The *greedy* flame runs higher and higher
   Till all the mountains blaze;
  15) So with thy whirlwind them pursue,
   And with thy tempest chase;
  16) And till they yield thee honor due,
60 Lord fill with shame their face.
  17) Ashamed and troubled let them be,
   Troubled and shamed forever,
  Ever confounded, and so die

47–48. **God's houses . . . stately palaces:** Milton's
note asserts that the Hebrew *Neoth Elihim* can
mean both English phrases.

With shame, *and 'scape it never.*
65 18) Then shall they know that thou whose name
        Jehovah is alone,
    Art the Most High, *and thou the same*
        O'er all the earth *art one.*

Psalm 84

1) How lovely are thy dwellings fair!
        O Lord of Hosts, how dear
    The *pleasant* tabernacles are!
        Where thou dost dwell so near.
5   2) My soul doth long and almost die
        Thy courts O Lord to see;
    My heart and flesh aloud do cry,
        O living God, for thee.
    3) There ev'n the sparrow *freed from wrong*
10   Hath found a house of *rest;*
    The swallow there, to lay her young
        Hath built her *brooding* nest;
    Ev'n *by* thy altars Lord of Hosts
        They find their safe abode,
15 *And home they fly from round the coasts*
        Toward thee, my King, my God.
    4) Happy, who in thy house reside
        Where thee they ever praise;
    5) Happy, whose strength in thee doth bide,
20   And in their hearts thy ways.
    6) They pass through Baca's *thirsty* vale,
        That dry and barren ground,
    As through a fruitful wat'ry dale
        Where springs and show'rs abound.
25 7) They journey on from strength to strength
        With joy and gladsome cheer
    Till all before *our* God at *length*
        In Sion do appear.
    8) Lord God of Hosts hear *now* my prayer,
30   O Jacob's God give ear;
    9) Thou God our shield look on the face
        Of thy anointed *dear.*
    10) For one day in thy courts *to be*
        Is better, *and more blest*
35 Than *in the joys of vanity,*
        A thousand days *at best.*

I in the temple of my God
   Had rather keep a door,
Than dwell in tents, *and rich abode*
40   With sin *for evermore.*
  11) For God the Lord both sun and shield
     Gives grace and glory *bright;*
No good from them shall be withheld
   Whose ways are just and right.
45 12) Lord *God* of Hosts *that reign'st on high,*
     That man is *truly* blest,
Who *only* on thee doth rely,
   And in thee only rest.

Psalm 85

  1) Thy land to favor graciously
     Thou hast not Lord been slack;
Thou hast from *hard* captivity
   Returnèd Jacob back.
5   2) Th' iniquity thou didst forgive
     That wrought thy people woe,
And all their sin, *that did thee grieve*
   Hast hid *where none shall know.*
  3) Thine anger all thou hadst removed,
10   And *calmly* didst return
From thy fierce wrath which we had proved
   Far worse than fire to burn.
  4) God of our saving health and peace,
     Turn us, and us restore;
15 Thine indignation cause to cease
   Toward us, *and chide no more.*
  5) Wilt thou be angry without end,
     For ever angry thus?
Wilt thou thy frowning ire extend
20   From age to age on us?
  6) Wilt thou not turn, and *hear our voice*
     And us again revive,
That so thy people may rejoice
   By thee preserved alive?
25 7) Cause us to see thy goodness Lord,
     To us thy mercy show;
Thy saving health to us afford
   And life in us renew.
  8) *And now* what God the Lord will speak

30   I will *go straight and* hear,
     For to his people he speaks peace
         And to his saints *full dear;*
     To his dear saints he will speak peace,
         But let them never more
35   Return to folly, *but surcease*
         To trespass as before.
         9) Surely to such as do him fear
         Salvation is at hand,
     And Glory shall *ere long appear*
40   *To* dwell within our land.
         10) Mercy and Truth *that long were missed*
         Now *joyfully* are met;
     Sweet Peace and Righteousness have kissed
         And hand in hand are set.
45   11) Truth from the earth *like to a flow'r*
         Shall bud and blossom *then,*
     And Justice from her Heav'nly bower
         Look down *on mortal men.*
         12) The Lord will also then bestow
50   Whatever thing is good;
     Our land shall forth in plenty throw
         Her fruits *to be our food.*
         13) Before him Righteousness shall go
         His royal harbinger,
55   Then will he come, and not be slow;
         His footsteps cannot err.

Psalm 86

         1) Thy *gracious* ear, O Lord, incline,
         O hear me *I thee pray,*
     For I am poor, and almost pine
         With need, *and sad decay.*
5   2) Preserve my soul, for I have trod
         Thy ways, and love the just;
     Save thou thy servant O my God
         Who *still* in thee doth trust.
         3) Pity me Lord for daily thee
10   I call; 4) O make rejoice
     Thy servant's soul; for Lord to thee
         I lift my soul *and voice;*
         5) For thou art good, thou Lord art prone
         To pardon, thou to all

15   Art full of mercy, thou *alone*
        To them that on thee call.
    6) Unto my supplication Lord
        Give ear, and to the cry
    Of my *incessant* prayers afford
20   Thy hearing graciously.
    7) I in the day of my distress
        Will call on thee *for aid;*
    For thou wilt *grant* me *free access*
        And answer, *what I prayed.*
25 8) Like thee among the gods is none
        O Lord, nor any works
    Of all that other gods have done
        Like to thy *glorious* works.
    9) The nations all whom thou hast made
30   Shall come, *and all shall frame*
    To bow them low before thee Lord,
        And glorify thy name.
    10) For great thou art, and wonders great
        By thy strong hand are done;
35   Thou *in thy everlasting seat*
        Remainest God alone.
    11) Teach me O Lord thy way *most right;*
        I in thy truth will bide;
    To fear thy name my heart unite,
40   *So shall it never slide.*
    12) Thee will I praise O Lord my God
        Thee honor, and adore
    With my whole heart, and blaze abroad
        Thy name for evermore.
45 13) For great thy mercy is toward me,
        And thou hast freed my soul,
    Ev'n from the lowest Hell set free,
        From deepest darkness foul.
    14) O God the proud against me rise
50   And violent men are met
    To seek my life, and in their eyes
        No fear of thee have set.
    15) But thou Lord art the God most mild,
        Readiest thy grace to show,
55   Slow to be angry, and *art styled*
        Most merciful, most true.
    16) O turn to me *thy face at length,*
        And me have mercy on;

Unto thy servant give thy strength,
60   And save thy handmaid's son.
17) Some sign of good to me afford,
    And let my foes *then* see
And be ashamed, because thou Lord
    Dost help and comfort me.

Psalm 87

1) Among the holy mountains *high*
    Is his foundation fast;
There seated in his sanctuary,
    His temple there is placed.
5 2) Sion's *fair* gates the Lord loves more
    Than all the dwellings *fair*
Of Jacob's *land, though there be store,*
    And all within his care.
3) City of God, most glorious things
10 Of thee *abroad* are spoke;
4) I mention Egypt, *where proud kings*
    Did our forefathers yoke;
I mention Babel to my friends,
    Philistia *full of scorn,*
15 And Tyre with Ethiop's *utmost ends:*
    Lo this man there was born.
5) But *twice that praise shall in our ear*
    Be said of Sion *last:*
This and this man was born in her,
20 High God shall fix her fast.
6) The Lord shall write it in a scroll
    That ne'er shall be outworn,
When he the nations doth enroll,
    That this man there was born.
25 7) Both they who sing, and they who dance
    With sacred songs are there;
In thee *fresh brooks and soft streams glance*
    And all my fountains *clear.*

Psalm 88

1) Lord God that dost me save and keep,
    All day to thee I cry;
And all night long, before thee *weep*
    Before thee *prostrate lie.*

5   2) Into thy presence let my prayer
         With sighs devout ascend;
     And to my cries, that *ceaseless are,*
         Thine ear with favor bend.
     3) For cloyed with woes and trouble store
10   Surcharged my soul doth lie;
     My life *at death's uncheerful door*
         Unto the grave draws nigh.
     4) Reckoned I am with them that pass
         Down to the *dismal* pit;
15   I am a man, but weak alas
         And for that name unfit.
     5) From life discharged and parted quite
         Among the dead *to sleep,*
     And like the slain *in bloody fight*
20   That in the grave lie *deep,*
     Whom thou rememberest no more,
         Dost never more regard:
     Them from thy hand delivered o'er
         Death's hideous house hath barred.
25   6) Thou in the lowest pit *profound*
         Hast set me *all forlorn,*
     Where thickest darkness *hovers round,*
         In horrid deeps *to mourn.*
     7) Thy wrath *from which no shelter saves*
30   Full sore doth press on me;
     Thou break'st upon me all thy waves,
         And all thy waves break me.
     8) Thou dost my friends from me estrange,
         And mak'st me odious,
35   Me to them odious, *for they change,*
         And I here pent up thus.
     9) Through sorrow, and affliction great
         Mine eye grows dim and dead;
     Lord all the day I thee entreat,
40   My hands to thee I spread.
     10) Wilt thou do wonders on the dead,
         Shall the deceased arise
     And praise thee *from their loathsome bed*
         With pale and hollow eyes?
45   11) Shall they thy loving kindness tell

31–32. **Thou break'st . . . break me:** Although
Milton's note claims that either line 31 or line 32
would correctly translate the original, only the
first would.

On whom the grave *hath hold,*
Or they *who* in perdition *dwell*
        Thy faithfulness *unfold?*
    12) In darkness can thy mighty *hand*
50   *Or* wondrous acts be known,
    Thy justice in the *gloomy* land
        Of *dark* oblivion?
    13) But I to thee O Lord do cry
        Ere yet my life be spent,
55   And *up to thee* my prayer *doth hie*
        Each morn, and thee prevent.
    14) Why wilt thou Lord my soul forsake,
        And hide thy face from me,
    15) That am already bruised, and shake
60   With terror sent from thee;
    Bruised, and afflicted and *so low*
        As ready to expire,
    While I thy terrors undergo
        Astonished with thine ire.
65   16) Thy fierce wrath over me doth flow,
        Thy threat'nings cut me through.
    17) All day they round about me go,
        Like waves they me pursue.
    18) Lover and friend thou hast removed
70   And severed from me far.
    They *fly me now* whom I have loved,
        And as in darkness are.

59. **shake:** Milton seems not to have considered
    that the Hebrew word can also be taken to
    mean "youth."

PSALMS 1–8

Milton's headnotes give the precise date of each of these translations except for
the first.

There is more metrical variety here than in the group from 1648. These
translations also have a strikingly high percentage of run-on lines. Their rela-
tionship to political circumstances has been variously assessed (Fixler 182; Hill
383). Others (Studley, Rohr-Sauer) stress the fact that Milton had been blind for

only a year and a half in August 1653, and call attention in particular to the rendering of blindness in Psalm 6.

Psalm 1

Done into verse, 1653

Blest is the man who hath not walked astray
In counsel of the wicked, and i' th' way
Of sinners hath not stood, and in the seat
Of scorners hath not sat. But in the great
5 Jehovah's law is ever his delight,
And in his law he studies day and night.
He shall be as a tree which planted grows
By wat'ry streams, and in his season knows
To yield his fruit, and his leaf shall not fall,
10 And what he takes in hand shall prosper all.
Not so the wicked, but as chaff which fanned
The wind drives, so the wicked shall not stand
In judgment, or abide their trial then,
Nor sinners in th' assembly of just men.
15 For the Lord knows th' upright way of the just,
And the way of bad men to ruin must.

Psalm 2

Here Milton uses *terza rima,* Dante's measure, where propulsive force is customarily provided by rhyme, not syntax, because the second and unrhymed line of each tercet supplies the rhyme-sound for the next tercet. Lawrence Binyon, poet and translator of Dante, clearly felt a kind of formal violence in Milton's lawless, overflowing syntax: "In the *Divina Commedia* each tercet is a stanza complete in itself, and almost always closed by a full stop. . . . Milton, with his instinct for moving on in a continuous motion and making his pauses without reference to the stanza, largely annuls the value of the rhymes" (185).

Done August 8, 1653. Terzetti

Why do the Gentiles tumult, and the nations
    Muse a vain thing, the kings of th' earth upstand
    With power, and princes in their congregations
Lay deep their plots together through each land,
5   Against the Lord and his Messiah dear?
    Let us break off, say they, by strength of hand

Their bonds, and cast from us, no more to wear,
    Their twisted cords: he who in Heaven doth dwell
    Shall laugh, the Lord shall scoff them, then severe
10 Speak to them in his wrath, and in his fell
    And fierce ire trouble them; but I saith he
    Anointed have my king (though ye rebel)
On Sion my holy hill. A firm decree
    I will declare; the Lord to me hath said,
15   Thou art my Son, I have begotten thee
This day; ask of me, and the grant is made;
    As thy possession I on thee bestow
    Th' heathen, and as thy conquest to be swayed
Earth's utmost bounds: them shalt thou bring full low
20 With iron scepter bruised, and them disperse
    Like to a potter's vessel shivered so.
And now be wise at length ye kings averse,
    Be taught ye judges of the earth; with fear
    Jehovah serve, and let your joy converse
25 With trembling; kiss the Son lest he appear
    In anger and ye perish in the way,
    If once his wrath take fire like fuel sere.
Happy all those who have in him their stay.

Psalm 3

August 9, 1653
When he fled from Absalom

Lord how many are my foes,
    How many those
    That in arms against me rise.
    Many are they
5   That of my life distrustfully thus say,
"No help for him in God there lies."
But thou Lord art my shield, my glory;
    Thee through my story
    Th' exalter of my head I count;
10   Aloud I cried
    Unto Jehovah; he full soon replied
And heard me from his holy mount.
I lay and slept, I waked again,
    For my sustain
15   Was the Lord. Of many millions
    The populous rout

I fear not though encamping round about
They pitch against me their pavilions.
Rise Lord, save me my God for thou
20   Hast smote ere now
    On the cheek-bone all my foes,
        Of men abhorred
    Hast broke the teeth. This help was from the Lord;
Thy blessing on thy people flows.

Psalm 4

August 10, 1653

Answer me when I call,
God of my righteousness;
In straits and in distress
Thou didst me disenthrall
5   And set at large; now spare,
        Now pity me, and hear my earnest prayer.
Great ones how long will ye
My glory have in scorn,
How long be thus forborne
10 Still to love vanity,
    To love, to seek, to prize
        Things false and vain and nothing else but lies?
Yet know the Lord hath chose,
Chose to himself apart
15 The good and meek of heart
(For whom to choose he knows);
Jehovah from on high
        Will hear my voice what time to him I cry.
Be awed, and do not sin,
20 Speak to your hearts alone,
Upon your beds, each one,
And be at peace within.
Offer the offerings just
        Of righteousness and in Jehovah trust.
25 Many there be that say
Who yet will show us good?
Talking like this world's brood;
But Lord, thus let me pray,
On us lift up the light,
30   Lift up the favor of thy count'nance bright.
Into my heart more joy

And gladness thou hast put
Than when a year of glut
Their stores doth over-cloy
35 And from their plenteous grounds
     With vast increase their corn and wine abounds.
In peace at once will I
Both lay me down and sleep,
For thou alone dost keep
40 Me safe where'er I lie;
As in a rocky cell
     Thou Lord alone in safety mak'st me dwell.

Psalm 5

August 12, 1653

Jehovah to my words give ear,
    My meditation weigh,
The voice of my complaining hear,
My King and God, for unto thee I pray.
5 Jehovah thou my early voice
    Shalt in the morning hear;
I' th' morning I to thee with choice
Will rank my prayers, and watch till thou appear.
For thou art not a God that takes
10   In wickedness delight;
Evil with thee no biding makes;
Fools or mad men stand not within thy sight.
All workers of iniquity
    Thou hat'st; and them unblest
15 Thou wilt destroy that speak a lie;
The bloody and guileful man God doth detest.
But I will in thy mercies dear,
    Thy numerous mercies, go
Into thy house; I in thy fear
20 Will towards thy holy temple worship low.
Lord lead me in thy righteousness,
    Lead me because of those
That do observe if I transgress;
Set thy ways right before, where my step goes.
25 For in his falt'ring mouth unstable
    No word is firm or sooth;
Their inside, troubles miserable;
An open grave their throat, their tongue they smooth.

God, find them guilty, let them fall
30   By their own counsels quelled;
Push them in their rebellions all
Still on; for against thee they have rebelled;
        Then all who trust in thee shall bring
            Their joy, while thou from blame
35   Defend'st them; they shall ever sing
And shall triumph in thee, who love thy name.
        For thou Jehovah wilt be found
            To bless the just man still,
        As with a shield thou wilt surround
40 Him with thy lasting favor and good will.

Psalm 6

August 13, 1653

Lord in thine anger do not reprehend me,
    Nor in thy hot displeasure me correct;
Pity me Lord for I am much deject,
    Am very weak and faint; heal and amend me,
5   For all my bones, that even with anguish ache,
        Are troubled, yea my soul is troubled sore;
    And thou O Lord how long? Turn Lord, restore
        My soul, O save me for thy goodness' sake,
    For in death no remembrance is of thee;
10   Who in the grave can celebrate thy praise?
    Wearied I am with sighing out my days,
        Nightly my couch I make a kind of sea;
    My bed I water with my tears; mine eye
        Through grief consumes, is waxen old and dark
15 I' th' midst of all mine enemies that mark.
        Depart all ye that work iniquity.
    Depart from me, for the voice of my weeping
        The Lord hath heard, the Lord hath heard my prayer;
    My supplication with acceptance fair
20   The Lord will own, and have me in his keeping.
    Mine enemies shall all be blank and dashed
        With much confusion; then grow red with shame;
    They shall return in haste the way they came
        And in a moment shall be quite abashed.

Psalm 7

August 14, 1653
Upon the words of Chush the Benjamite against him

Lord my God to thee I fly;
Save me and secure me under
Thy protection while I cry,
Lest as a lion (and no wonder)
5   He haste to tear my soul asunder,
Tearing and no rescue nigh.

Lord my God if I have thought
Or done this, if wickedness
Be in my hands, if I have wrought
10   Ill to him that meant me peace,
Or to him have rendered less,
And not freed my foe for naught;

Let th' enemy pursue my soul
And overtake it, let him tread
15   My life down to the earth and roll
In the dust my glory dead,
In the dust and there outspread
Lodge it with dishonor foul.

Rise Jehovah in thine ire,
20   Rouse thyself amidst the rage
Of my foes that urge like fire;
And wake for me, their fury assuage;
Judgment here thou didst engage
And command which I desire.

25   So th' assemblies of each nation
Will surround thee, seeking right;
Thence to thy glorious habitation
Return on high and in their sight.
Jehovah judgeth most upright
30   All people from the world's foundation.

Judge me Lord, be judge in this
According to my righteousness
And the innocence which is
Upon me: cause at length to cease

35   Of evil men the wickedness
     And their power that do amiss.

     But the just establish fast,
     Since thou art the just God that tries
     Hearts and reins. On God is cast
40   My defense, and in him lies,
     In him who both just and wise
     Saves th' upright of heart at last.

     God is a just judge and severe,
     And God is every day offended;
45   If th' unjust will not forbear,
     His sword he whets, his bow hath bended
     Already, and for him intended
     The tools of death, that waits him near.

     (His arrows purposely made he
50   For them that persecute.) Behold
     He travails big with vanity,
     Trouble he hath conceived of old
     As in a womb, and from that mold
     Hath at length brought forth a lie.

55   He digged a pit, and delved it deep,
     And fell into the pit he made;
     His mischief that due course doth keep,
     Turns on his head, and his ill trade
     Of violence will undelayed
60   Fall on his crown with ruin steep.

     Then will I Jehovah's praise
     According to his justice raise,
     And sing the name and deity
     Of Jehovah the Most High.

Psalm 8

August 14, 1653

     O Jehovah our Lord how wondrous great
       And glorious is thy name through all the earth!
     So as above the heavens thy praise to set
       Out of the tender mouths of latest birth,

5   Out of the mouths of babes and sucklings thou
        Hast founded strength because of all thy foes
    To stint th' enemy, and slack th' avenger's brow
        That bends his rage thy providence to oppose.

    When I behold thy heavens, thy fingers' art,
10   The moon and stars which thou so bright hast set
    In the pure firmament, then saith my heart,
        O what is man that thou rememb'rest yet,

    And think'st upon him; or of man begot
        That him thou visit'st and of him art found?
15   Scarce to be less than gods, thou mad'st his lot,
        With honor and with state thou hast him crowned.

    O'er the works of thy hand thou mad'st him Lord,
        Thou hast put all under his lordly feet,
    All flocks, and herds, by thy commanding word,
20   All beasts that in the field or forest meet,

    Fowl of the heavens, and fish that through the wet
        Sea-paths in shoals do slide, and know no dearth.
    O Jehovah our Lord how wondrous great
        And glorious is thy name through all the earth.

"Fix here"

When Alfred Norwood found Milton's *Commonplace Book* in 1874, he also discovered this couplet written on the back of a letter from Henry Lawes.

    Fix here ye overdated spheres
    That wing the restless foot of time.

1. **overdated:** outdated, worn out.

TRANSLATIONS FROM THE PROSE WORKS

FROM *Of Reformation* (1641)

1)

Ah Constantine, of how much ill was cause
Not thy conversion, but those rich domains
That the first wealthy Pope received of thee.

Dante, *Inferno* 19.115–17

2)

Founded in chaste and humble poverty,
'Gainst them that raised thee dost thou lift thy horn?
Impudent whore, where hast thou placed thy hope?
In thy adulterers, or thy ill-got wealth?
Another Constantine comes not in haste.

Petrarch, *Rime* 138.9–13

3)

And to be short, at last his guide him brings
Into a goodly valley, where he sees
A mighty mass of things strangely confused,
Things that on earth were lost, or were abused.

Ariosto, *Orlando Furioso* 34.73

4)

Then passed he to a flow'ry mountain green,
Which onced smelt sweet, now stinks as odiously;
This was that gift (if you the truth will have)
That Constantine to good Sylvestro gave.

Ariosto, *Orlando Furioso* 34.80

FROM *The Reason of Church Government* (1641)

5)

When I die, let the earth be rolled in flames.

Dio, *Roman History* 58.23

FROM *An Apology for Smectymnuus* (1642)

6)

Laughing to teach the truth
What hinders? As some teachers give to boys
Junkets and knacks, that they may learn apace.

Horace, *Satires* 1.1.24–26

7)

Jesting decides great things
Stronglier, and better oft than earnest can.

Horace, *Satires* 1.10.14-15

8)

'Tis you that say it, not I; you do the deeds,
And your ungodly deeds find me the words.

Sophocles, *Electra* 624-25

FROM THE TITLE PAGE OF *Areopagitica* (1644)

9)

This is true liberty, when freeborn men
Having to advise the public may speak free,
Which he who can, and will, deserves high praise;
Who neither can nor will, may hold his peace;
What can be juster in a state than this?

Euripides, *Supplices* 438–41

FROM *Tetrachordon* (1645)

10)

Whom do we count a good man, whom but he
Who keeps the laws and statues of the Senate,
Who judges in great suits and controversies,
Whose witness and opinion wins the cause;
But his own house, and the whole neighborhood
Sees his foul inside through his whited skin.

Horace, *Epistles* 1.16.40–45

FROM *The Tenure of Kings and Magistrates* (1649)

11)

There can be slain
No sacrifice to God more acceptable
Than an unjust and wicked king.

Seneca, *Hercules Furens* 922–24

FROM *The History of Britain* (1670)

12)

Goddess of shades, and huntress, who at will
Walk'st on the rolling sphere, and through the deep,
On thy third reign the earth look now, and tell
What land, what seat of rest thou bidd'st me seek,
What certain seat, where I may worship thee
For ay, with temples vowed, and virgin choirs.

Geoffrey of Monmouth, *History* I.II

13)

Brutus far to the west, in th' ocean wide
Beyond the realm of Gaul, a land there lies,
Sea-girt it lies, where giants dwelt of old;
Now void, it fits thy people; thither bend
Thy course, there shalt thou find a lasting seat,
There to thy sons another Troy shall rise,
And kings be born of thee, whose dreaded might
Shall awe the world, and conquer nations bold.

Geoffrey of Monmouth, *History* I.II

14)

Low in a mead of kine under a thorn,
Of head bereft li'th poor Kenelm king-born.

Flores Historiarum for 821 C.E.

ENGLISH AND ITALIAN SONNETS

INTRODUCTION TO ENGLISH AND ITALIAN SONNETS

Milton wrote twenty-four sonnets. The impulse to isolate this group from his other minor poems can be traced back to the various numbering schemes found in both the manuscript and printed versions during Milton's lifetime. In the 1645 *Poems*, ten sonnets were numbered from 1 to 10. The 1673 edition added nine more, ending with number 19. In the Trinity College manuscript (*CMS*), three sonnets (18–20 in the present edition) and four lines of another (our 21) are missing, but the sonnets present in the manuscript are numbered through to 23, and there is even a marginal note after *Sonnet 12* indicating that *On the New Forcers of Conscience* was "to come in here." Milton's editors have chosen to use the *CMS* numbering so persistently that generations of readers have known individual poems by these numbers. Here we print the standard twenty-three, followed by the one maverick sonnet (*On the New Forcers*) that, despite the marginal note, never got to be one of that number.

It was of course conventional to number sonnets, since they often formed an aggregate unit, a "sequence," held together by a narrative and by persistent thematic concerns. Milton's sonnet group clearly does not aspire to this conventional sort of unity. Why, then, did he number them? He must in some measure have been calling attention to his career-long interest in the form, and even to the possibility that, should the poems be read as a group, he might be seen to have done something interesting or original with that form.

The interest came in two phases. A youthful period from 1629 to 1632 produced a fragmentary group of Italian poems. Milton wrote no other poems in this language; his main ambition in Italian was to explore, in the correct Tuscan dialect, the origins of the love sonnet: *Questa è lingua di cui si vanta Amore* ("This is the tongue in which Love glories" [*Canzone* 15]). For this edition, the Italian poems have been newly translated into English prose by Gordon Braden.

Milton followed these experiments with one strikingly powerful religious meditation, *Sonnet 7*. There had been other religious sonnets written in England, notably Donne's *La Corona* and several sets of *Holy Sonnets*, but nothing in Donne's Jesuit-influenced meditations on death and apocalypse anticipated Milton's effort to gather religious strength in contemplating the end of an apparently unpromising youth. At the time of *Sonnet 7*'s composition, in 1632, there was only one other English sonnet of comparable power on a comparable subject, George Herbert's "The Answer."

Milton's most distinctive contributions to the history of the English sonnet came in the second phase of his sonnet writing, which began in 1642 and perhaps continued (depending on the date of *Sonnet 23*) to 1658. These sonnets have real people in them, whereas love sonnets tend notoriously to drift away from actual human beings with genuine names into cloudy realms of myth and metaphor. In the manner of Tasso's *Heroic Sonnets*, Milton addressed poems to great men such as Fairfax and Cromwell, but more often he used the form to celebrate his male and female friendships. His adaptations of Horatian conventions of address leave the impression that the sonnets are commentaries on proper names, enumerating virtues that these names are widely held to possess. Although Ben Jonson did not write sonnets, his habit of beginning poems with names ("Camden, most reverend head," "Donne, the delight of Phoebus," "Roe, and my joy to name") must have been an influence. Thirteen of the sonnets, opening with the name or title of the addressee, might with an eye toward *Paradise Lost* be termed personal invocations.

Milton's mature sonnets are all in some fashion occasional. Though few in number, they capture a broad range of human experiences. They register quiet moments of unpretentious conversation (21) as well as moments of sublime political outrage (18). They contain the evolution of his political beliefs and his lofty disappointment with the public he was trying to sway as a pamphleteer. They represent the initial emotional turmoil of blindness (19), then return to the subject for a glimpse, rare in literature, of spiritual serenity (22), only to close with clear evidence that the loss of sight blended into his other grievings (23).

It was in fact the writing of sonnets that kept Milton's poetic talents well-honed during the years of political commitment and public service, when he was unable to begin something on the scale of *Paradise Lost.* They do not sound like anyone else's sonnets. Shakespeare is closer to Petrarch than Milton's mature sonnets are to either predecessor. Wordsworth made this point in his polemical sonnet "Scorn not the Sonnet." His history of the form associates it with a number of objects: it was a key to Shakespeare, a lute to Petrarch, a pipe to Tasso, a crown to Dante, a lamp to Spenser. We come at the end to Milton, who can be listed among the authors who made the form into a musical instrument, but one able to emit a louder and more soulful music than was previously known:

> and, when a damp
> Fell round the path of Milton, in his hand
> The Thing became a trumpet; whence he blew
> Soul-animating strains—alas, too few!

SONNET 1

The first six sonnets, dealing with love, are thought to be early and to have been composed in less than a year, probably in 1629. The vogue of the English love sonnet had ended over thirty years before. But Milton's initial approach to the form is in important ways Italianate. He never writes in the so-called Shakespearean pattern of three quatrains and a couplet, but always in the Italian or Petrarchan pattern of two quatrains (the octave) and two tercets (the sestet), with the quatrains always rhyming abba (not interlaced abab, as in Shakespeare) and with shifting rhyme schemes in the sestet.

"O Nightingale," though often compared with *Song: On May Morning,* lacks the communal voice of that finer lyric. Generically the poem is a complaint in which the speaker, having suffered failures in love, seeks to enlist curative forces to end his misery.

O Nightingale, that on yon bloomy spray
  Warblest at eve, when all the woods are still,
  Thou with fresh hope the lover's heart dost fill,
  While the jolly Hours lead on propitious May;
5 Thy liquid notes that close the eye of day,
  First heard before the shallow cuckoo's bill
  Portend success in love; O if Jove's will
  Have linked that amorous power to thy soft lay,
  Now timely sing, ere the rude bird of hate
10 Foretell my hopeless doom in some grove nigh:
  As thou from year to year hast sung too late
For my relief, yet hadst no reason why:
  Whether the Muse or Love call thee his mate,
  Both them I serve, and of their train am I.

4. **Hours:** the goddesses of the seasons, usually three in number (spring, summer, winter).

5–7. To hear a cuckoo (later the *bird of hate*) was a bad omen; to hear a nightingale was a good omen. "The nightingale and the cuckoo sing both in one month," warned a Renaissance proverb (Tilley N181).

6. **shallow:** shrill.

13. **mate:** This word "has the primary meaning 'companion' but in its context also carries an allusion to the vulgar idea of 'mating'" (Honigmann 87).

SONNET 2

The end of *Elegy 6* probably alludes to this little group of Italian pieces. Eschewing the latest styles in Italian love poetry, Milton returned to the literary mannerisms of Petrarch, Bembo, and Tasso. Whatever the motives behind these poems might have been, among them was the desire to achieve an authentic feel for the origins of the love sonnet.

Donna leggiadra il cui bel nome onora
L'erbosa val di Reno, e il nobil varco,
Ben è colui d'ogni valore scarco
Qual tuo spirto gentil non innamora,
5 Che dolcemente mostrasi di fuora
De' suoi atti soavi giammai parco,
E i don', che son d'amor saette ed arco,
Là onde l'alta tua virtù s'infiora.
Quando tu vaga parli, o lieta canti
10 Che mover possa duro alpestre legno,
Guardi ciascun agli occhi, ed agli orecchi
L'entrata, chi di te si trova indegno.
Grazia sola di sù gli vaglia, innanzi
Che'l disio amoroso al cuor s'invecchi.

Enchanting lady whose fair name[1] honors the grassy valley of the Reno and the noble crossing, he is indeed empty of all worth whom your gentle spirit does not enamor, which sweetly expresses itself, never grudging in its graceful actions nor in the favors which are Love's arrow and bow, there[8] where your lofty virtue is decked with flowers. When in beauty you speak or in happiness you sing with the power to move hard alpine timber,[10] let every man guard the entrance to his eyes and to his ears who finds himself unworthy of you. May grace alone from above help him before amorous desire ages itself in his heart.

1. Milton divulges the lady's name by referring to the region of Italy named Emilia, where the Reno river flows (Smart 137–44).
8. **Là:** in her eyes.
10. First the lady's song has the power of Orpheus, then it becomes Siren-like in testing the self-discipline of the unworthy.

SONNET 3

Qual in colle aspro, a l'imbrunir di sera,
L'avvezza giovinetta pastorella
Va bagnando l'erbetta strana e bella
Che mal si spande a disusata spera
5 Fuor di sua natia alma primavera,
Così Amor meco insù la lingua snella
Desta il fior novo di strania favella,

As on a rugged hill, at the darkening of evening, the experienced young shepherdess goes watering the strange and beautiful little plant which can scarcely spread its leaves in an unfamiliar place, far from its lifegiving native springtime, so on my agile

Mentre io di te, vezzosamente altera,
Canto, dal mio buon popol non inteso,
10   E'l bel Tamigi cangio col bel Arno.
Amor lo volse, ed io a l'altrui peso
Seppi ch'Amor cosa mai volse indarno.
Deh! Foss'il mio cuor lento e'l duro seno
A chi pianta dal ciel sì buon terreno.

10. Milton has exchanged the Thames for the Arno, which is to say, given up English for Tuscan Italian. On the preeminence of the Tuscan dialect, see Prince 4–13.

tongue Love awakens the new flower of a strange language while of you, charmingly proud, I sing, unintelligible to my own good people, and change the beautiful Thames for the beautiful Arno.[10] Love willed it, and I knew from the distress of others that Love never willed anything in vain. Ah, would that my slow heart and hard breast might be as good soil for Him who plants from Heaven!

CANZONE

Since the *canzone* normally had several stanzas, this single-stanza lyric is, strictly speaking, not a *canzone* but a *canzone* stanza. It is not a sonnet either, but we print it here in order not to separate it from the other Italian lyrics.

Ridonsi donne e giovani amorosi
M'accostandosi attorno, e perché scrivi,
Perché tu scrivi in lingua ignota e strana
Verseggiando d'amor, e come t'osi?
5   Dinne, se la tua speme sia mai vana,
E de' pensieri lo miglior t'arrivi;
Così mi van burlando, altri rivi,
Altri lidi t'aspettan, ed altre onde
Nelle cui verdi sponde
10   Spuntati ad or, ad or a la tua chioma
L'immortal guiderdon d'eterne frondi:
Perché alle spalle tue soverchia soma?
   Canzon dirotti, e tu per me rispondi:
Dice mia donna, e'l suo dir è il mio cuore,
15   Questa è lingua di cui si vanta Amore.

7. **altri rivi:** other languages.

Ladies and young men in love laugh, crowding around me. "And why do you write, and why do you write in an unknown and strange tongue, versifying about love, and how do you dare to? Tell us, so that your hope not be vain and the best of your wishes succeed." So they tease me: "Other streams,[7] other shores wait for you, and other waters by whose green side now and again there grows for your hair the immortal guerdon of eternal leaves. Why add a great load to your shoulders?" Canzone, I will tell you, and you answer for me. My Lady says—and her speaking is my heart—"This is the tongue in which Love glories."

SONNET 4

Diodati, e te'l dirò con maraviglia,
   Quel ritroso io ch'amor spreggiar solea
   E de' suoi lacci spesso mi ridea,
   Già caddi, ov' uom dabben talor s'impiglia.
5   Nè treccie d'oro, nè guancia vermiglia
   M'abbaglian sì, ma sotto nova idea
   Pellegrina bellezza che'l cuor bea,
   Portamenti alti onesti, e nelle ciglia
   Quel sereno fulgor d'amabil nero,
10   Parole adorne di lingua più d'una,
   E'l cantar che di mezzo l'emispero
   Traviar ben può la faticosa luna;
   E degli occhi suoi avventa sì gran fuoco
   Che l'incerar gli orecchi mi fia poco.

Diodati[1]—and I will tell you with amazement—such a coy one as I who used to scorn Love and often laughed at his snares, have now fallen where an honest man sometimes entangles himself. Neither golden tresses nor rosy cheeks dazzle me so, but a foreign beauty based on a new idea cheers my heart: a noble, modest bearing, and under her eyebrows such serene radiance of lovely blackness, speech adorned with more than one tongue, and singing which could well lead the weary moon astray from the middle of the sky, and from her eyes shoots such a great fire that it would do me little good to seal up my ears.[14]

1. **Diodati:** Charles Diodati, the friend whom Milton addressed in his first and sixth elegies, and whose death he commemorated in *Epitaph for Damon*.
14. Odysseus puts wax in the ears of his crew to prevent them from hearing of the song of the Sirens (*Od.* 12). In this case, wax would be useless because of the lady's visual power.

SONNET 5

Per certo i bei vostr' occhi, donna mia,
   Esser non può che non sian lo mio sole;
   Sì mi percuoton forte, come ei suole
   Per l'arene di Libia chi s'invia,
5   Mentre un caldo vapor (nè senti' pria)
   Da quel lato si spinge ove mi duole,
   Che forse amanti nelle lor parole
   Chiaman sospir; io non so che si sia:
   Parte rinchiusa e turbida si cela
10   Scossomi il petto, e poi n'uscendo poco
   Quivi d'attorno o s'agghiaccia, o s'ingiela;
   Ma quanto agli occhi giunge a trovar loco
   Tutte le notti a me suol far piovose
   Finché mia Alba rivien colma di rose.

Surely, my lady, your beautiful eyes cannot help but be my sun; they strike me as powerfully as he does someone who travels across the sands of Libya. At the same time a hot vapor[5] (I have not felt it before) bursts from that side where I hurt—perhaps what lovers in their language call a sigh; I do not know what it is. Part of it, pent up and stormy, hides itself, shaking my breast, and then a little of it escaping either chills or freezes round about. But as much of it as finds its way to my eyes makes all nights tearful until my Dawn returns, crowned with roses.

5. **caldo vapor:** hot vapors in the heart are especially prominent in troubadour love poetry (Klein 73–85).

SONNET 6

Giovane piano, e semplicetto amante	A young, quiet, naïve lover, since
Poiché fuggir me stesso in dubbio sono,	I am in doubt how to escape from
Madonna a voi del mio cuor l'umil dono	myself, I will, my lady, make you
Farò divoto; io certo a prove tante	the devout humble gift of my
5 L'ebbi fedele, intrepido, costante,	heart. With certainty in many
Di pensieri leggiadro, accorto, e buono;	tests I have found it faithful, fear-
Quando rugge il gran mondo, e scocca il tuono,	less, constant, graceful in its
S'arma di sé, e d'intero diamante,	thoughts, shrewd, and good;
Tanto del forse, e d'invidia sicuro,	when the whole world roars and
10 Di timori, e speranze al popol use	the thunder shakes, it arms itself
Quanto d'ingegno e d'alto valor vago,	with itself and with solid
E di cetra sonora, e delle Muse:	adamant, as safe from doubt and
Sol troverete in tal parte men duro	envy, from the fears and hopes of
Ove amor mise l'insanabil ago.	ordinary people, as it is avid for
	intelligence and true worth, and
	for the sounding lyre and for the
	Muses. You will find it less hard
	only where Love has set an in-
	curable sting.

SONNET 7

The *CMS* contains two drafts, likely dating from 1633, of a letter to an unknown friend. The friend (possibly Milton's former tutor Thomas Young) had apparently chided Milton for wasting time with his studies and admonished him to seek ordination immediately. In the first draft of his reply, Milton denied that he was wasting time and, in his defense, alluded to the parables of the talents (Matt. 25.14–30) and the vineyard (Matt. 20.1–16). "Yet that you may see that I am something suspicious of myself, and do take notice of a certain belatedness in me, I am the bolder to send you some of my nightward thoughts some while since (because they come in not altogether unfitly) made up in a Petrarchan stanza" (p. 771). Milton then quoted *Sonnet 7,* in which he does indeed "take notice of a certain belatedness in me." The poem was probably composed on or about Milton's twenty-third birthday (December 9, 1631).

The octave, with its realization that youth is gone and there's nothing to show for it, tacitly creates a desire to act. But the sestet, turning in a new direction announced by the opening word *Yet,* replaces this desire with patience and confidence. Apparent delay becomes appropriate preparation. Time the thief becomes Time the guide. If Milton has the grace to harmonize his actions with the will of Heaven, he is as timely-happy as a mortal can be. The temptation to act now, followed by the resolve not to act just yet, is central to both *Sonnet 19* and the portrayal of Christ in *Paradise Regained.*

The syntax evokes three quatrains and a couplet, superimposing the ghost of the English Shakespearean sonnet on Milton's "Petrarchan stanza."

How soon hath Time the subtle thief of youth,
  Stol'n on his wing my three and twentieth year!
  My hasting days fly on with full career,
  But my late spring no bud or blossom shew'th.
5 Perhaps my semblance might deceive the truth,
  That I to manhood am arrived so near,
  And inward ripeness doth much less appear,
  That some more timely-happy spirits endu'th.
  Yet be it less or more, or soon or slow,
10 It shall be still in strictest measure even
  To that same lot, however mean or high,
  Toward which Time leads me, and the will of Heaven;
  All is, if I have grace to use it so,
  As ever in my great Taskmaster's eye.

1. **subtle:** cunning, with the emphasis on how the theft is scarcely noticed until it is fully accomplished.
2. **on his wing:** by his act of flight. Wings were among Time's conventional attributes.
3. **full career:** full speed.
4. **bud or blossom:** A despairing phrase, since the speaker not only has no complete accomplishment (*blossom*) but also no nascent work-in-progress (*bud*). Buds, blossoms, and flowers were common metaphors for poems.
5. **semblance:** appearance. "Although I am past forty, there is scarcely anyone to whom I do

not seem younger by about ten years" (*2Def* in *MLM* 1080).
8. **timely-happy spirits:** men whose accomplishments are in harmony with their years; **endu'th:** endows.
9. **it:** inward ripeness.
10. **still:** always.
10–11. **even/To:** level with.
13–14. "All that I do in time is as though done in eternity, provided that I have the grace to act in accord with God's will."
14. **Taskmaster:** See the parable of the laborers in the vineyard (Matt. 20.1–16).

SONNET 8

In the *CMS* this sonnet has two titles, "On his door when the city expected an assault" (in the hand of a copyist, and struck out) and "When the assault was intended to the city" (in the poet's hand). While it was probably never actually tacked to Milton's door, the poem does have the form of an inscription addressed to the soldier of a conquering army who comes upon the door to Milton's home. That a poet can indeed create enduring fame and "spread thy name o'er lands and seas" is proven by the two examples of literary clemency in the sestet, both of which crossed from Greece to England centuries before and were obviously still remembered.

The assault in question was expected in 1642, when the retreat of the Parliamentary army left the road to London open to Royalist troops. In October 1642, Londoners worked feverishly digging trenches and barricading the streets in order to prevent invasion. On November 12, Charles I and his army advanced as far as Brentford but retreated in the face of the Parliamentary army of the Earl of Essex. Milton wrote the sonnet at some time during this period of anticipated attack.

Captain or colonel, or knight in arms,
  Whose chance on these defenseless doors may seize,
  If deed of honor did thee ever please,
  Guard them, and him within protect from harms;
5 He can requite thee, for he knows the charms
  That call fame on such gentle acts as these,
  And he can spread thy name o'er lands and seas,
  Whatever clime the sun's bright circle warms.
Lift not thy spear against the muses' bower:
10 The great Emathian conqueror bid spare
  The house of Pindarus, when temple and tower
Went to the ground: and the repeated air
  Of sad Electra's poet had the power
  To save th' Athenian walls from ruin bare.

1. **colonel:** a trisyllable, pronounced "coronel."
2. **defenseless doors:** Milton's lodging was outside the gates of the city.
3. I.e., if ever deed of honor did thee please.
10. **Emathian conqueror:** Alexander the Great. When his army sacked Thebes, he spared a house once occupied by Pindar (Plutarch, *Alexander* 11).
12–14. When an army of Spartans, Thebans, and

Corinthians had defeated Athens and were about to raze it to the ground, a man from Phocis sang the first Chorus from Euripides' *Electra*. All were moved to compassion and refused to destroy a city that had produced such a poet (Plutarch, *Lysander* 15).
12. **repeated air:** recited chorus (see previous note).

SONNET 9

Presumably, since this poem follows *Sonnet 8* in the *CMS*, it was written after 1642, but the lady has not been satisfactorily identified. Some (Honigmann, Miller) have supposed that she was Mary Powell herself, despite the fact that what little we know of her youthful character hardly suggests a woman who had turned her back on marriage and earthly pleasure.

Lady that in the prime of earliest youth,
 Wisely hast shunned the broad way and the green,
 And with those few art eminently seen,
 That labor up the hill of heav'nly truth,
5 The better part with Mary, and with Ruth,
 Chosen thou hast, and they that overween,
 And at thy growing virtues fret their spleen,
 No anger find in thee, but pity and ruth.
 Thy care is fixed, and zealously attends
10 To fill thy odorous lamp with deeds of light,
 And hope that reaps not shame. Therefore be sure
 Thou, when the bridegroom with his feastful friends
 Passes to bliss at the midhour of night,
 Hast gained thy entrance, virgin wise and pure.

1. **prime:** the "springtime" of human life.
2. **broad way:** "Broad is the way that leadeth to destruction" (Matt. 7.13); **and the green:** See Job 8.12–13 on the greenness of the paths of those who forget God.
4. **hill of heav'nly truth:** Cp. Donne, *Sat.* 3.79–81; and for the history of the trope, see Milgate 290–92.
5. **The better part:** While Martha bustled, Mary sat at the feet of Christ. After Martha complained, Christ said, "One thing is needful: and Mary hath chosen that good part" (Luke 10.39–42); **Ruth:** The widowed Ruth lived with her mother-in-law rather than seek a new husband (Ruth 1.14).
6. **overween:** presume (to criticize you).
11. **hope that reaps not shame:** Cp. Rom. 5.5 ("And hope maketh none ashamed") and 10.11 ("Whosoever believeth in him shall not be ashamed").
11–14. Cp. the parable of the wise and foolish virgins in Matt. 25.1–13.
12. **feastful:** festive.
14. **entrance:** Besides the parable of the virgins (see 11–14n), Milton glances at John 10.9: "I am the door: by me if any man enter in, he shall be saved."

SONNET 10

Edward Phillips relates that "Our Author, now as it were a single man again, made it his chief diversion now and then in an evening to visit the Lady Margaret Lee.... This lady being a woman of great wit and ingenuity, had a particular honor for him, and took much delight in his company, as likewise her husband Captain Hobson . . . and what esteem he at the same time had for her, appears by a sonnet he made in praise of her" (Darbishire 64). The allusion to Milton being "as it were a single man" dates his acquaintance with Lady Margaret and his composition of this sonnet somewhere between July 1642, when Mary Powell Milton left him to return to her family, and early summer 1645, when the couple reconciled.

The poem, a notable feat of technical virtuosity, places one coherent syntactical structure between the two appositives at its ends ("Daughter to that good

Earl . . . , honored Margaret"), meditating on a woman and her names in such a way that she is indeed related truly (as daughter to that good Earl) and then shown to possess his virtues (as honored Margaret).

⸺

Daughter to that good Earl, once President
  Of England's Council, and her Treasury,
  Who lived in both, unstained with gold or fee,
  And left them both, more in himself content,
5 Till the sad breaking of that Parliament
  Broke him, as that dishonest victory
  At Chaeronea, fatal to liberty,
  Killed with report that old man eloquent,
  Though later born, than to have known the days
10 Wherein your father flourished, yet by you
  Madam, methinks I see him living yet;
  So well your words his noble virtues praise,
    That all both judge you to relate them true,
    And to possess them, honored Margaret.

1. **good Earl:** Having studied law, James Ley held several high positions in the reign of James I and was named Lord High Treasurer in 1624. Charles I created him Earl of Marlborough. Resigning as Treasurer in 1628, he was appointed President of the Council.
5–6. Ley died on March 14, 1629, twelve days after Charles had unsuccessfully tried to adjourn an unruly Parliament.

6. **dishonest:** shameful.
7. **Chaeronea:** Milton remembers the story that the rhetorician Isocrates died of voluntary starvation after Philip of Macedon's defeat of Athenian and Theban forces at Chaeronea (Dionysius of Halicarnassus, *Commentaries on the Ancient Orators,* "Isocrates").
13. **all:** all that hear you.

SONNET 11

This poem was numbered 12 in the *CMS* but became *Sonnet 11* in the 1673 *Poems.* Some editions revert to the manuscript numbering. *Tetrachordon,* along with *Colasterion,* was published in March 1645. The phrase *of late* means "recently." Yet the publication must have been far enough in the past for the minor vogue of the book, "now seldom pored on," to have been exhausted.

⸺

A book was writ of late called *Tetrachordon;*
  And woven close, both matter, form and style;
  The subject new: it walked the town a while,
  Numb'ring good intellects; now seldom pored on.

5   Cries the stall-reader, "Bless us! What a word on
    A title page is this!" and some in file
    Stand spelling false, while one might walk to Mile-
    End Green. Why is it harder, sirs, than Gordon,
    Colkitto, or Macdonnel, or Galasp?
10 Those rugged names to our like mouths grow sleek
    That would have made Quintilian stare and gasp.
    Thy age, like ours, O soul of Sir John Cheke,
    Hated not learning worse than toad or asp,
    When thou taught'st Cambridge and King Edward Greek.

1. **Tetrachordon:** The title of Milton's divorce pamphlet, *Tetrachordon,* is an elaborate conceit summarizing the entire work. The Greek term alludes to a four-note scale, the notes in this case being the four main treatments of marriage in the Bible (Gen. 1.27–28, 2.18, 23–24; Deut. 24.1–5; Matt. 5.31–32, 19.3–11; 1 Cor. 7.10–16). The argument of the pamphlet tries to bring these disparate passages into harmony.

3. **walked the town:** Cp. Horace, *Epist.* 1.20, where the poet consigns his book to a doomed life of prostitution.

4. **Numb'ring good intellects:** both "attracting good intellects among its readers" and "determining the number of good intellects."

5. **stall-reader:** one who browses in the stall outside a bookshop.

6. **in file:** in a row (along the stall).

7. **spelling false:** misinterpreting.

7–8. **Mile-/End Green:** Mile-End, the first mile stone outside Aldgate, marked the eastern boundary of London.

8–9. *Gordon* perhaps refers to George, Lord Gordon; *Macdonnel* (MacDonald) and *Colkitto* (Coll Keitache, a nickname given one of the Mac-

Donalds) were Scottish officers serving in the Royalist army of the Earl of Montrose. *Galasp* is George Gillespie, a member of the Westminster Assembly.

10. **rugged:** hard to pronounce, ill-tuned; **like:** similarly ill-tuned; **sleek:** easy.

11. **Quintilian:** first-century Roman rhetorician whose *Institutes* 1.5.8 condemned barbarous (foreign) words.

12. **Sir John Cheke:** This English educator, the first Professor of Greek at Cambridge, tutored King Edward VI, whose name appears on the title page of *Tetrachordon* because Milton wanted to call attention to a congenial marriage law passed during "those best and purest times" of his reign (*MLM* 987).

12–14. Here Milton puts *like ours* where it may appear to mean "like our age hates learning." But he almost certainly meant to say that Cheke's age, unlike the current one, honored learning. A modern author with this sense in mind would have written "Thy age . . . hated not learning, like ours [like ours does], worse than toad or asp."

SONNET 12

Milton's second sonnet on his divorce tracts, probably written in 1646, makes it clear that his arguments fared no better with his contemporaries than the Greek title of *Tetrachordon.* For a year after its publication, *The Doctrine and Discipline of Divorce,* the first and most often printed of the divorce pamphlets, seems to have occasioned conversation rather than written responses. When the printed notices began to appear, in late 1644, they were mostly by Presbyterians, overwhelmingly negative, and virtually without exception exercises in ridicule rather than reasoned argument (Parker 1971, 17–24). Milton felt that he had become infamous without being given a fair hearing. In the grand ironic reversal of this sonnet, he turns his readers' hostile judgment of his book into an appallingly accurate judgment of themselves.

On the Same

I did but prompt the age to quit their clogs
  By the known rules of ancient liberty,
  When straight a barbarous noise environs me
  Of owls and cuckoos, asses, apes and dogs.
5 As when those hinds that were transformed to frogs
  Railed at Latona's twin-born progeny
  Which after held the sun and moon in fee.
  But this is got by casting pearl to hogs;
  That bawl for freedom in their senseless mood,
10 And still revolt when truth would set them free.
  License they mean when they cry liberty;
  For who loves that, must first be wise and good;
  But from that mark how far they rove we see
  For all this waste of wealth, and loss of blood.

1. **clogs:** weights or encumbrances put upon beasts to keep them from straying.
2. **known rules:** Mosaic divorce law.
3. **barbarous noise environs me:** Cp. *Lyc* 61; *PL* 7.36–37.
5–7. *Latona* with her twin children, Apollo and Diana, subsequently the deities of the sun and the moon, tried to drink at a pond. When peasants muddied the water, she transformed them into frogs (Ovid, *Met.* 6.317–81).
7. **in fee:** in absolute possession.
8. **this is got by:** this is what you get from; **casting pearl to hogs:** "Neither cast ye your pearls before swine, lest they trample them under their feet, and turn again and rend you" (Matt. 7.6).
10. The line has two senses: "And always revolt against the truth that would set them free" and "And always backslide into mental clogs rather

than accept the truth that would set them free" (Leonard).
11. **License:** licentiousness, with a possible pun on license to print.
12. "None can love freedom heartily but good men; the rest love not freedom but license" (*TKM* in *MLM* 1024).
13. **mark:** target (of first being wise and good? of loving true liberty?); **rove:** shoot arrows away from the mark.
14. **For all:** in spite of; **this waste . . . blood:** this expenditure of wealth and loss of life (in the Civil War). Milton rails against the Presbyterians for rendering the sacrifices of the Civil War pointless because they have not, as promised, produced liberty but instead renewed ancient habits of spiritual bondage.

SONNET 13

Milton's admiration for the person and art of Henry Lawes was not affected in the slightest by the musician's ardent royalism. Nor was Lawes himself affected in the slightest by the young poet's equally ardent Puritanism. From 1630 Lawes was a member of the King's Private Music, which involved composing, planning, directing, and performing in court entertainments. During these years he continued his role as music tutor to the children of the Egerton family, and it was in this capacity that he was responsible for commissioning the young and unknown Milton to write the words for *Arcades* and *A Masque*.

As a musician, Lawes did not actually create a new style in songs. His work belonged to a period style in the middle seventeenth century that reversed an older manner by allowing poetry some role in determining the music.

To Mr. H. Lawes, on his Airs

Harry, whose tuneful and well-measured song
   First taught our English music how to span
   Words with just note and accent, not to scan
   With Midas' ears, committing short and long,
5   Thy worth and skill exempts thee from the throng,
   With praise enough for Envy to look wan;
   To after-age thou shalt be writ the man
   That with smooth air couldst humor best our tongue.
Thou honor'st verse, and verse must lend her wing
10   To honor thee, the priest of Phoebus' choir
   That tun'st their happiest lines in hymn or story.
Dante shall give Fame leave to set thee higher
   Than his Casella, whom he wooed to sing
   Met in the milder shades of Purgatory.

2. **to span:** to measure, as with the hand; here referring to the words matched with notes of proper length and stress.

3. **to scan:** to determine the number and nature of poetic feet.

4. **With Midas' ears:** to scan improperly or tastelessly; Midas was given ass's ears as a punishment for preferring the music of Pan to that of Apollo (Ovid, *Met.* 11.146–79); **committing**

short and long: placing a long syllable in a short note, or vice versa.

5. **exempts thee:** singles thee out.

12–14. On the threshold of Purgatory, Dante greets the shade of his friend Casella, a Florentine musician, and asks for a song; Casella proceeds to sing Dante's *Amor che me la mente mi ragiona* (*Purg.* 2.76–117).

14. **milder shades:** The threshold was less dark than the rest of Purgatory.

SONNET 14

The first of the three drafts of this poem in the *CMS* bears the title "On the religious memory of Mrs. Catharine Thomason my Christian friend." Mrs. Thomason, who died in December 1646, was the wife of George Thomason, a bookseller whose extensive collection of Civil War pamphlets is now housed in the British Museum and contains over 22,000 items printed between 1640 and 1660. He was a Presbyterian whose sympathies, in the later 1640s, swung toward the king. His wife, Catharine, was the ward and niece of the bookseller to whom George was originally apprenticed. Her love for books and learning is evident from her husband's will, which disperses her library to her children (she left eight of them) in the hope that they "will remember to whom they [the books] did once belong" and "will make the better use of them for their precious and dear mother's sake" (Hughes et al. 2:407).

      When Faith and Love which parted from thee never,
        Had ripened thy just soul to dwell with God,
        Meekly thou didst resign this earthy load
        Of death, called life, which us from life doth sever.
5   Thy works and alms and all thy good endeavor
        Stayed not behind, nor in the grave were trod;
        But as Faith pointed with her golden rod,
        Followed thee up to joy and bliss forever.
      Love led them on, and Faith who knew them best
10   Thy handmaids, clad them o'er with purple beams
        And azure wings, that up they flew so dressed,
      And spake the truth of thee on glorious themes
        Before the Judge, who thenceforth bid thee rest
        And drink thy fill of pure immortal streams.

1. **Faith and Love:** "The parts of Christian doctrine are two: Faith, or knowledge of God, and Love, or the worship of God" (*CD* 1.1, in *MLM* 1145).
8. **Followed thee up:** Rev. 14.13: "Blessed are the dead which die in the Lord . . . their works do follow them."
9. **Faith who knew them best:** Faith who best knew them (works, alms, all good endeavor) to be.
13. **the Judge:** Christ.
14. Cp. Ps. 36.8–9; Rev. 22.1, 17.

SONNET 15

Though present in the *CMS*, the Fairfax sonnet did not appear in the 1645 or 1673 *Poems*. It was first printed in Edward Phillips's edition of the *Letters of State* in 1694.

General Thomas Fairfax of the Parliamentary army had won victory after victory over Royalist forces since 1643, and his siege on Colchester in June through August 1648 was no exception. But while Fairfax was occupied with Colchester, the Scottish army invaded England in July, inspiring the many local rebellions Milton refers to as "Hydra heads." It would seem that Milton has not yet heard of Cromwell's victories over the invaders (see *Sonnet 16*). His wish that Fairfax could turn his talents from defeating the enemy to reforming Parliament's own scandalous practices was in vain. Unable to support the beheading of Charles I backed by Cromwell and his army, Fairfax in 1650 retired from public life to his country estate, where the young Andrew Marvell would tutor his daughter Maria and write in his honor "Upon Appleton House, to my Lord Fairfax," one of the greatest poems of the century.

On the Lord General Fairfax, at the Siege of Colchester

Fairfax, whose name in arms through Europe rings
    Filling each mouth with envy, or with praise,
    And all her jealous monarchs with amaze,
    And rumors loud, that daunt remotest kings,
5   Thy firm unshaken virtue ever brings
    Victory home, though new rebellions raise
    Their Hydra heads, and the false North displays
    Her broken league, to imp their serpent wings,
    O yet a nobler task awaits thy hand;
10   For what can war, but endless war still breed,
    Till truth and right from violence be freed,
    And public faith cleared from the shameful brand

---

5. **virtue:** the sum of manly powers, including courage and moral worth.

7. **Hydra heads:** Whenever Hercules cut off one of Hydra's many heads, two grew in its place; **false North:** The Scots, having signed a treaty with Charles I, invaded England in July 1648.

8. **broken league:** The Scottish invasion was thought by its opponents (which included Milton) to be a violation of the Solemn League and Covenant; **imp:** engraft feathers to improve the wings' flight.

12. **public faith:** Honigmann shows that Parliament referred to the public funding of the Civil War as the "public faith." Loans were solicited, then not repaid (for a time Milton himself lost much of his fortune in this manner) and the funds subsequently mismanaged, such that the Parliamentary army was always being promised "public faith" compensation that never arrived in full. See the digression on the Long Parliament in the manuscript of *The History of Britain*, where Milton denounces the scheme (Yale 5:444).

Of public fraud. In vain doth valor bleed
While avarice and rapine share the land.

SONNET 16

Like *Sonnet 15*, this poem appears in the *CMS* but was first printed by Edward Phillips in his 1694 *Letters of State*. Cromwell was a member of the Parliamentary committee to which the title alludes. In May 1652, when Milton apparently wrote the poem, the committee was considering a proposal that Parliament establish a national church and pay its clergy; dissent would be tolerated so long as it respected fifteen fundamental doctrines. The chief proponent of the scheme was John Owen, who had served as Cromwell's chaplain. Milton, like Cromwell, favored a wider scope of toleration. In the sonnet Milton urges the Puritan leader to embrace the separation of church and state, refusing "to bind our souls with secular chains," and repudiate the "hireling wolves" of a state-funded clergy.

To the Lord General Cromwell, May 1652,
On the proposals of certain ministers at the Committee for
Propagation of the Gospel

Cromwell, our chief of men, who through a cloud
   Not of war only, but detractions rude,
   Guided by faith and matchless fortitude
   To peace and truth thy glorious way hast ploughed,
5   And on the neck of crownèd Fortune proud
   Hast reared God's trophies and his work pursued,
   While Darwen stream with blood of Scots imbrued,
   And Dunbar field resounds thy praises loud,
   And Worcester's laureate wreath; yet much remains
10   To conquer still; peace hath her victories
   No less renowned than war, new foes arise
   Threat'ning to bind our souls with secular chains:

1. **through a cloud:** Cp. Marvell's *Horatian Ode,* 13–16.
2. **detractions rude:** Milton catalogs some of them in *2Def* (Yale 4:662–66).
5. **neck of crownèd Fortune:** alluding to the beheading of Charles I in January 1649.
6. **reared God's trophies:** A *trophy* was originally a structure erected on the battlefield or in a public place.
7. **Darwen stream:** This stream is near the place where Cromwell routed the invading Scottish army in August 1648.
8. **Dunbar field:** Cromwell defeated the Scottish army here in September 1650.
9. **Worcester's laureate wreath:** Cromwell scored a decisive victory over Charles II at Worcester in September 1651 (on the anniversary of his victory at Dunbar).
11. **new foes:** proponents of government-enforced conformity to a national church.

Help us to save free conscience from the paw
Of hireling wolves whose Gospel is their maw.

14. **hireling wolves:** Milton's contemptuous phrase for mercenary clergymen paid by the government; cp. John 10.13. In the Bible, enemies of Christ and Christianity are often represented as wolves (Matt. 7.15; Acts 20.29). Cp. *Lyc* 113–22.

SONNET 17

Although it appears in the *CMS,* this poem was first published in George Sikes's *Life and Death of Sir Henry Vane* (1662).

The elder Vane, also named Henry (1589-1655), served Charles I as Privy Councillor (1630), Treasurer of the Household (1639), and Secretary of State (1640). But his son Vane the Younger (1613–62) was deeply sympathetic toward the Puritans. For a time he lived in New England, where he became Governor of the Massachusetts Bay Colony (1636–37). Returning to England, he was appointed Secretary of the Navy and opposed the court party in Parliament. When Milton addressed him in this sonnet, in 1652, he was a member of the Council of State considering the same proposals that Cromwell had been implored to reject in *Sonnet 16.* Milton praised him for understanding the separation of "spiritual power and civil," which is the basis of religious freedom.

The ideal alliance between Cromwell and Vane forged in *Sonnets 16* and *17* did not survive long in the realm of history. Vane deplored Cromwell's dissolution of the Long Parliament in 1653 and retired from public life during the Protectorate. Upon Cromwell's death, he tried unsuccessfully to prevent the return of Charles II. After a two-year imprisonment, Vane was tried for treason, convicted, and executed in 1662.

To Sir Henry Vane the Younger

Vane, young in years, but in sage counsel old,
  Than whom a better senator ne'er held
  The helm of Rome, when gowns not arms repelled
  The fierce Epirot and the African bold;
5 Whether to settle peace or to unfold
  The drift of hollow states, hard to be spelled,

3. **gowns not arms:** The *gowns* or togas of the senators represent civil as opposed to military power.
4. **fierce Epirot and the African bold:** Both Pyrrhus, King of Epirus, and Hannibal invaded Italy in the third century B.C.E. and inspired noble resistance in the Roman senate.
6. **drift:** scheme, plot; **hollow:** false, insincere; **spelled:** discovered.

Then to advise how war may best, upheld,
Move by her two main nerves, iron and gold,
In all her equipage; besides to know
10   Both spiritual power and civil, what each means,
What severs each, thou hast learnt, which few have done.
The bounds of either sword to thee we owe;
Therefore on thy firm hand religion leans
In peace, and reckons thee her eldest son.

---

8. **iron and gold:** In his *Commonplace Book,* Milton quoted Machiavelli's *Discourses* 2.10 on the sinews of war being steel rather than gold (Yale 1:498).

9. **equipage:** apparatus of war.

12. **bounds of either sword:** limits of the jurisdiction of the two swords, spiritual and civil (church and state).

14. **eldest son:** despite Vane being, as we are told in the opening words of the sonnet, *young in years.*

SONNET 18

This poem was occasioned by events that took place in the Italian Alps in April through May 1655.

The Vaudois or Waldensians, who traced their origins to the twelfth century and according to some retained an Apostolic purity in matters of worship, lived in Alpine villages in France and Italy. In Italy the sect had been granted the right to settle in the Piedmont Valley by the Duke of Savoy, but the Vaudois had infiltrated villages forbidden by the treaty. The duke dispatched an army. In April 1655 around 1,712 Vaudois were massacred with great ferocity—burned alive, impaled, mutilated, hurled from precipices. Some fled for France and died of exposure in the mountains. When their leaders called for support from Protestant states, England responded fervently. Cromwell commanded a general fast, raised thousands of pounds for the victims, formed an alliance, wrote to various European leaders, including the Duke of Savoy, sent an envoy (Sir Michael Morland) to the duke, and seriously considered sending an army. Milton wrote this sonnet.

On the Late Massacre in Piedmont

Avenge O Lord thy slaughtered saints, whose bones
Lie scattered on the Alpine mountains cold,
Ev'n them who kept thy truth so pure of old

---

1. **Avenge:** The word is being used with biblical force; see Rev. 6.9–10 and Luke 18.7–8.

When all our fathers worshipped stocks and stones,
5   Forget not: in thy book record their groans
Who were thy sheep and in their ancient fold
Slain by the bloody Piedmontese that rolled
Mother with infant down the rocks. Their moans
The vales redoubled to the hills, and they
10   To Heav'n. Their martyred blood and ashes sow
O'er all th' Italian fields where still doth sway
The triple tyrant: that from these may grow
A hundredfold, who having learnt thy way
Early may fly the Babylonian woe.

4. **stocks and stones:** a standard phrase (*OED* "stock," 1d); see Jer. 2.27, 3.9.

5. **thy book:** the book of human actions to be consulted on Judgment Day; see Rev. 5.1.

10–13. Editors often cite the old saying that "the blood of martyrs is the seed of faith."

12. **triple tyrant:** The pope wore a three-tiered miter.

13. **thy way:** the true faith.

14. Puritans identified the Church of Rome with the Babylon whose doom was prophesied in Rev. 17–18. There are also Old Testament prophecies of the destruction of Babylon, with warnings to flee before the calamity occurs (Jer. 50–51, Isa. 48).

SONNET 19

This poem presents several points of controversy.

What is its date? What is its mood? Some experts, thinking the poem to have been written soon after Milton's total loss of sight in 1652, stress the author's uncertainty over whether God will ever ask him to work again. The main spiritual task of the poem is Milton's need to resign himself to this uncertainty. Others would date the poem later, in 1655–56, on the assumption that the sonnets were numbered chronologically in the 1673 *Poems,* and *Sonnet 18* was pretty clearly written in 1655. But the sonnets are *not* placed in perfectly sequential order (Morse). It is moreover hard to believe that someone who had just published *A Second Defense* (1654) and the *Defense of Himself* (1655) would speak of himself as uselessly hoarding his one talent. The year 1652 is the more probable date of composition.

Why would Milton say, whether in 1652 or 1655–56, that blindness had come to him "Ere half my days"? The poet was, after all, forty-three in 1652. It has been suggested that his father, who died at eighty-four, encouraged a sanguine calculation of the time allotted him on this earth; but if Milton believed that he had not yet reached the halfway point in 1652, he must have been confident in outliving his father. We have no solution to this difficulty and would simply remark that Milton wanted to do a very great deal in this life.

What does the analogy at the end of the poem mean? In the sonnet as a whole, Milton defeats beforehand a threatened impatience. He imagines God come to assess his labors, finding that he has done nothing since his blindness, and chiding him for that inactivity. Milton imagines that he would in turn chide God Himself by asking, "Doth God exact day labor, light denied?" Milton calls this a "murmur," a complaint, and we therefore know its tone to be sarcastic. "God, are you really being Godlike in chiding me for my lack of labor? How can you expect me to work in the dark night of my blindness?" But patience overcomes this fantasized complaint, and in the process lays to rest the terrifying implications of the parable of the talents (see Haskin 29–53). God will not chide. God, unlike an earthly taskmaster, does not need our work or our talents. Acceptance of the will of God is itself service enough. Then Milton alludes to angels that "post," doing the bidding of God, as opposed to angels "who only stand and wait." Both serve God. *Wait* may mean "attend as a servant" but surely also has the common sense of "stay in expectation," waiting to be given a bidding to do, a job to complete. For the time being, waiting is God's bidding. But Milton, it once again seems appropriate to remark, wanted to do a very great deal in this life.

　　　　　　　　　　　　　⌒‿⌒‿⌒

When I consider how my light is spent,
　Ere half my days, in this dark world and wide,
　And that one talent which is death to hide,
　Lodged with me useless, though my soul more bent
5　To serve therewith my Maker, and present
　My true account, lest he returning chide,
　"Doth God exact day labor, light denied?"
　I fondly ask; but patience to prevent
　That murmur soon replies, "God doth not need
10　Either man's work or his own gifts; who best
　Bear his mild yoke, they serve him best; his state

---

1. **When I consider:** The opening is formulaic; cp. Shakespeare, *Sonnet 15:* "When I consider everything that grows."

3. **that one talent:** See the parable of the talents in Matt. 25.14–30. The man with one talent hid it and was punished by being cast into the outer darkness.

4. **useless:** not in use, with a glance at usury (see Matt. 25.27); **bent:** determined.

5. **therewith:** with my spent light and useless talent as the cause or occasion of this greater determination to serve (*OED* 3b).

6. **true account:** Cp. "my certain account" in *Apology* (Yale 1:869).

7. Cp. "I must work the works of him that sent me, while it is day: the night cometh when no man can work" (John 9.4). Cp. also the parable of the vineyard, where all the day laborers, no matter how long they work, receive the same wages (Matt. 20.1–16).

8. **fondly:** foolishly.

9. **murmur:** complaint.

11. **mild yoke:** "My yoke is easy" (Matt. 11.30).

Is kingly. Thousands at his bidding speed
And post o'er land and ocean without rest:
They also serve who only stand and wait."

12–14. In the traditional angelology of Pseudo-Dionysius and Aquinas, the five lower orders are sent out to execute God's will, while the four higher orders stand ever in God's presence and transmit his commands to the lower orders. But Milton seems not to have accepted this distinction. Leonard rightly notes that in *Paradise*

Lost all the angels, however exalted their rank, carry messages and perform tasks. The word *only* in line 14 implies that standing and waiting is not as dignified as posting *o'er land and ocean;* and *wait* may well imply that in the future a command will be given (see headnote).

SONNET 20

Phillips says that "young Lawrence (the son of him that was President of Oliver's Council), to whom there is a sonnet among the rest, in his printed poems," frequently visited Milton after his move to Petty France, Westminster, in 1651 (Darbishire 74).

The "virtuous father," Henry Lawrence (1600–64), entered public life in 1648, attaching himself to Cromwell. He sat in successive Parliaments, became Lord President of the Council of State, and served as Keeper of the Library at St. James House. He wrote several theological treatises. In *A Second Defense,* Milton calls him a man "of supreme genius, cultivated in the liberal arts" (p. 1105).

His son and Milton's friend, Edward Lawrence (1633–57), became a member of Parliament in 1656 and died the next year at the age of twenty-four. Milton may have tutored him. The idea of retiring inside during a long and dark winter to enjoy the classical pleasures of wine, music, poetry, and free conversation is a major motif in Royalist poets of the so-called Cavalier school, such as Lovelace ("The Grasshopper"), Cowley ("The Grasshopper," the essay "Of Liberty"), and Herrick ("To Live Merrily, and to Trust to Good Verses"). All of them were inspired by the work of Ben Jonson, as was the young Milton. Here the mature sonneteer appropriates this Jonsonian and ultimately Horatian genre in the service of a Puritan conviviality.

Lawrence of virtuous father virtuous son,
    Now that the fields are dank, and ways are mire,

1. **father:** Henry Lawrence, whom Cromwell appointed permanent chairman of the Council of State in January 1654. Carey notes the Horatian character of the first line's syntax. Cp. *Odes* 1.16.1:

O matre pulchra filia pulchrior ("O maiden fairer than thy mother fair").

Where shall we sometimes meet, and by the fire
Help waste a sullen day, what may be won
5   From the hard season gaining? Time will run
On smoother, till Favonius re-inspire
The frozen earth, and clothe in fresh attire
The lily and rose, that neither sowed nor spun.
What neat repast shall feast us, light and choice,
10   Of Attic taste, with wine, whence we may rise
To hear the lute well touched, or artful voice
Warble immortal notes and Tuscan air?
He who of those delights can judge, and spare
To interpose them oft, is not unwise.

4. **waste:** spend, pass.

5. **hard season:** winter.

6. **Favonius:** the west wind, Zephyrus.

8. **neither sowed nor spun:** See Matt. 6.28–29.

9. **neat:** simple and elegant.

10. **Of Attic taste:** such as would have been preferred or appreciated in Athens.

12. **Tuscan air:** Italian song; according to Phillips, Milton shipped home from Italy "a chest or two of choice music books of the best masters flourishing about that time in Italy" (Darbishire 59).

13. **spare:** A crux: Some take *spare* to mean "forbear," in which case Milton is telling Lawrence to have a restricted number of good times, while others think *spare* means "spare the time," in which case Milton is telling Lawrence to have all the good times he can manage. It seems ominous for the "spare the time" camp that no one has yet found an example of the use of *spare* in which the direct object (time) is understood and the verb is followed by an infinitive. But Bush defends "spare the time" nonetheless (Hughes et al., 2:475–76).

SONNET 21

This second sonnet on conviviality is addressed to Cyriack Skinner (1627–1700). Milton may have tutored him in the 1640s. According to Phillips, he was in the 1650s a frequent visitor to Milton's home (Darbishire 74). Skinner is now widely believed to be the so-called "anonymous biographer," author of a short life of Milton that is our main source for certain biographical details.

⁓

Cyriack, whose grandsire on the Royal Bench
Of British Themis, with no mean applause
Pronounced and in his volumes taught our laws,

1. **grandsire:** Skinner's maternal grandfather was Sir Edward Coke (1552–1634), a famous lawyer, scholar, and defender of Parliamentary rights who became Chief Justice of the King's Bench in 1613.

2. **Themis:** Roman goddess of Justice.

Which others at their bar so often wrench;
5   Today deep thoughts resolve with me to drench
In mirth, that after no repenting draws;
Let Euclid rest and Archimedes pause,
And what the Swede intend, and what the French.
To measure life learn thou betimes, and know
10 Toward solid good what leads the nearest way;
For other things mild Heav'n a time ordains,
And disapproves that care, though wise in show,
That with superfluous burden loads the day,
And when God sends a cheerful hour, refrains.

4. **others at their bar:** other judges in their courts.
5–6. "Resolve with me today to drench deep thoughts in mirth."
6. **no repenting draws:** Cp. Jonson, "Inviting a Friend to Supper," 39–41.
7. "Drop for now your study of geometry and physics."

8. **Swede:** may be Charles X, who invaded Poland in 1655; the French were at war with Spain in 1655.
9. **betimes:** while time remains.
11. **a time ordains:** See Eccles. 3.1: "To every thing there is a time, and a time to every purpose under heaven."

SONNET 22

In another sonnet addressed to Cyriack Skinner (see headnote to *Sonnet 21*), Milton revisits the subject of his blindness. The poem was perhaps written in 1655–56. His confidence in God's guidance is far more settled and serene here than in the turbulent *Sonnet 19*.

Cyriack, this three years' day these eyes, though clear
To outward view, of blemish or of spot,
Bereft of light their seeing have forgot,
Nor to their idle orbs doth sight appear
5   Of sun or moon or star throughout the year,
Or man or woman. Yet I argue not
Against Heaven's hand or will, nor bate a jot
Of heart or hope, but still bear up and steer

1. **this three years' day:** for the last three years.
1–2. **clear . . . spot:** When a political opponent charged him with being hideously ugly, Milton replied that in fact his blind eyes looked just like ordinary eyes (*MLM* 1079), and Skinner confirms the point (Darbishire 32).
4. **orbs:** eyeballs.

7. **hand or will:** executive powers or commands; **bate a jot:** endure the slightest reduction.
8. **bear up:** The primary sense (linking with *steer*) is nautical: put the helm "up" so as to bring the vessel into the direction of the wind. But "keep up my courage" is in the background.

Right onward. What supports me dost thou ask?
10   The conscience, friend, to have lost them overplied
        In liberty's defense, my noble task,
    Of which all Europe talks from side to side.
        This thought might lead me through the world's vain masque
        Content though blind, had I no better guide.

10. **conscience:** consciousness.
11. **In liberty's defense:** In January 1650, the Council of State ordered Milton to reply to Salmasius's *Defensio Regia*. He later said that his physicians had advised him that the task would result in blindness. Milton persisted, sacrificing his eyesight "for the greatest possible benefit to the state" (*MLM* 1082).

12. **all Europe talks:** Not quite, but the *First Defense* did achieve some European notoriety (see Parker 1971, 32–38).
13. **vain masque:** The idea of life as a staged drama was commonplace; Bacon's *Of Truth* takes note of "the masques and mummeries and triumphs of the world."

SONNET 23

It is regrettable that one of Milton's most moving lyrics, possibly the most moving, should be enveloped in an unpoetic atmosphere of puzzle solving and scholarly debate. But that is the situation. For two centuries editors had assumed that the "late espousèd saint" of this sonnet was Katharine Woodcock, Milton's second wife. Then in 1945, William R. Parker wrote the first of a number of pieces urging the claims of Mary Powell, Milton's first wife.

Many of the facts cut in two directions. For example, Mary died in May 1652, three days after giving birth to Deborah, her third daughter. Katharine died in February 1658. Although she had given birth to a daughter in October 1657 (who would outlive her by only six weeks), Katharine's death was due not to childbirth but to consumption. With regard to which dead wife is Milton most likely to have thought of the Old Testament ritual of purification after childbirth? Katharine died long after the time prescribed for this purification (eighty days if the child was a daughter) had expired, whereas Mary did not survive the purification period. Milton might have thought: "Katharine lived beyond the time of uncleanness yet was not returned to me, save in a dream." But he might equally well have thought: "Mary did not live through the time of uncleanness. Would that she had, and would that she had been returned to me, as she is in this dream." It is well to bear in mind, whatever one decides, that the poem's "purification in the Old Law" is metaphorical for the wife's return to her husband, again to be "mine," and in the larger design of the poem prepares for the higher purity of her mind in line 9.

Milton, entirely blind in 1652, never saw Katharine but enjoyed "full sight" of Mary for many years. Which wife is more likely to be veiled? Katharine, the wife he never saw? So many interpreters have decided. It may be significant that Admetus does not recognize Alcestis while she is veiled, whereas Milton, surely, is in no doubt over the identity of the veiled shade in his dream. Perhaps the veiled face symbolizes his blindness, the fact that in this life he could form no image of her face even if she were to return to him. In Heaven he will behold her without the "restraint" of blindness. Thus far the evidence favors Katharine. But what is implied and not implied by "such, as yet once more I trust to have/Full sight of her in Heaven without restraint"? The phrase "yet once more," which seems to allude in a personal and mysterious way to *Lycidas,* implies that the event in question will occur three times (once, once more, yet once more). Now the lines favor Mary Powell by suggesting that Milton has had "full sight" of her on this earth, in this dream (the veil not counting against "full sight"), and trusts to see her again in Heaven. But Katharine Woodcock is not entirely ruled out. The "yet" in "yet once more" could conceivably be an intensive, indicating that the event will happen twice (once, yet once more). Milton could be saying that he has full sight of Katharine in the dream (the subsequent detail of the veil again being regarded in the context of the dream's "day" as no compromise in "full sight") and will see her face-to-face in Heaven.

The poem achieves inner coherence no matter which woman a reader has in mind. It may point us toward the sonnet's emotional force to glance briefly at the way in which possession is drawn out in the course of the poem. "Methought": the dream vision was mine, entirely private, more so than I knew at the time. It was a vision of "my" late saint, and this blossoms into a still more emphatic "Mine" at the opening of line 5. He trusts "to have" full sight of her in Heaven. To "my fancied sight," the goodness in her face could not be plainer. Then at last she (in answer to the poet's desire?) inclines "to embrace me." But Milton awakes, she disappears, and in the end all of the poem's yearning mineness narrows to only the empty, sightless "my night." How fragile, how pregnant with despair, was that opening "Methought"!

But Gerald Hammond has recently suggested that the cruel twist of fate at the end of the poem can also be viewed as a display of mental strength. The dreamer appears to remain entirely passive. He confesses to no coaxing, no response; the veiled woman bends to embrace him. The speaker's one positive act is to awaken at just that moment. Could it be an escape? The embraces of a woman come back from the grave might restore to a man everything he has lost and most desires to have again, but they might also draw him into the dead world of the past. Perhaps Milton, in losing the image he thought was "mine," regains his life. Perhaps his awakening "is not passive, but an act of heroic resistance" (Hammond 216).

Methought I saw my late espousèd saint
Brought to me like Alcestis from the grave,
Whom Jove's great son to her glad husband gave,
Rescued from death by force though pale and faint.
5   Mine as whom washed from spot of child-bed taint
Purification in the Old Law did save,
And such, as yet once more I trust to have
Full sight of her in Heaven without restraint,
Came vested all in white, pure as her mind:
10   Her face was veiled, yet to my fancied sight,
Love, sweetness, goodness in her person shined
So clear, as in no face with more delight.
But O as to embrace me she inclined,
I waked, she fled, and day brought back my night.

---

1. **Methought I saw:** As in *Sonnet 19,* the opening is formulaic; see Ralegh's "Methought I saw the grave where Laura lay." **late espousèd saint:** Critics make a great deal of whether *late* modifies *espousèd,* which would make the phrase mean "recently married saint" and cast doubt on Mary Powell as the woman in question, or instead modifies *espousèd saint,* which would make the phrase mean "recently deceased wife." The first reading is strained.

2. **Alcestis:** In Euripides' *Alcestis,* Admetus can escape death by persuading someone to die in his place, and his wife, Alcestis, volunteers. Hercules rescues her from Death and returns her, pale, trembling, and veiled, to her husband.

5. **as whom:** as one whom.

5–6. God lays down the ritual prescriptions for purifying women immediately after childbirth

in Lev. 12. During this time, women would not be seen by their husbands.

7. **yet once more:** The opening phrase of *Lycidas.* See headnote.

8. **without restraint:** Hammond (217, 221–23) notes the erotic force of "restraint" in *PL* 8.628. The end of the purification ritual signaled a resumption of sexual relations.

9. **all in white:** Cp. Rev. 7.13–14, 19.8.

10. **Her face was veiled:** as was the face of Alcestis (see 2n), though Milton, unlike Admetus, immediately recognizes his wife.

13–14. Among the numerous classical precedents for this failed embrace are Aeneas's three attempts to clasp the shade of his wife (*Aen.* 2.789–95) and Achilles' attempt to embrace the dream image of Patroclus (*Il.* 23.99–107).

ON THE NEW FORCERS OF CONSCIENCE UNDER THE LONG PARLIAMENT

Milton entered the pamphlet wars of the 1640s as a supporter of the Presbyterians in their struggle against Anglican Prelacy. *An Apology for Smectymnuus* (1642) took up the cause of five Presbyterian ministers who, under the joint pseudonym SMECTYMNUUS, were engaged in disputes with Bishop Joseph Hall. But by the time *On the New Forcers of Conscience* was written, probably late in 1646, Milton was firmly allied with Independents in opposition to the Presbyterians, who in his mind had come to resemble the Anglican prelates they had originally sought to oust.

In 1643 the Long Parliament appointed the Westminster Assembly to reorganize the Anglican Church. Presbyterians enjoyed an overwhelming majority in the Assembly, and they are the "New Forcers of Conscience" to whom Milton's poem is addressed. They used their power to thwart the aims of the Independents in the Assembly, who preferred toleration and liberty of conscience to the advantages of compulsory conformity. Although Parliament in August 1646 accepted the Assembly's plan to ordain ministers by Presbyterian synods or classes (Milton's "classic hierarchy"), the poem supposes that the rampant abuses of the Presbyterians will soon lead to their comeuppance in Parliament.

The poem has the form of a *sonetto caudato* or "tailed sonnet." Rather than come to closure at line 14, it produces a half-line (tailed line) and a couplet, then a second half-line or tail, before delivering the pentameter couplet at the end. Italian poets had used the tailed sonnet for humorous and satirical subjects.

Because you have thrown off your prelate lord,
And with stiff vows renounced his liturgy
To seize the widowed whore Plurality
From them whose sin ye envied, not abhorred,
5   Dare ye for this adjure the civil sword
To force our consciences that Christ set free,
And ride us with a classic hierarchy
Taught ye by mere A.S. and Rutherford?
Men whose life, learning, faith and pure intent
10   Would have been held in high esteem with Paul
Must now be named and printed heretics
By shallow Edwards and Scotch What-d'ye-call:

1. **you:** The poem is addressed to Presbyterians in the Westminster Assembly; **thrown off your prelate lord:** Parliament had resolved to abolish episcopacy in 1643, though it was not formally outlawed until the decree of 1646.

2. **his liturgy:** Archbishop Laud's version of the *The Book of Common Prayer*, abolished in 1645.

3. **Plurality:** the practice of holding more than one ministerial living. Presbyterians criticized Anglicans for this abuse but were now guilty of it themselves.

4. **abhorred:** a play on *whore* found in *OTH* (4.2.161–62) and *MM* (3.1.101).

5. **for this:** for the widowed whore Plurality; **adjure:** charge, entreat.

6. **force . . . free:** Milton believed that compelled conformity to the national church was a violation of Christian liberty.

7. **ride us:** tyrannize over us; **classic hierarchy:** Parliament decreed that English congregations

were to be grouped in Presbyteries or "Classes" in the Scottish manner.

8. **A.S.:** Adam Stewart, a Scottish divine who wrote pamphlets (signed with his initials) attacking the Independents; **Rutherford:** Samuel Rutherford, another and more substantial opponent of independency who resided in London from 1643 to 1647 as a commissioner of the Church of Scotland to the Westminster Assembly.

12. **shallow Edwards:** Thomas Edwards, an English Presbyterian, was the University Preacher at Cambridge and author of *Gangraena* (1646), which listed among numerous heresies Milton's doctrine of divorce. **Scotch What-d'ye-call:** often assumed without real evidence to be Robert Baillie, a Scottish Commissioner on the Assembly whose *Dissausive from the Errors of the Time* (1645) also attacked Milton's views on divorce.

But we do hope to find out all your tricks,
Your plots and packings worse than those of Trent,
15   That so the Parliament
May with their wholesome and preventive shears
Clip your phylacteries, though balk your ears,
          And succor our just fears
When they shall read this clearly in your charge:
20   "New *Presbyter* is but old *Priest* writ large."

14. **packings:** corrupt manipulations of a delibera-
tive body. **Trent:** The Council of Trent was in-
tended to reform the doctrines of the Roman
Catholic Church in response to the Reforma-
tion. But it was manipulated by the papacy and
became a standard Protestant example of
Catholic hypocrisy and treachery.
17. **phylacteries:** ostentatious and hypocritical
signs of piety; **balk your ears:** intentionally
omit (to clip) your ears. Parliament will not
punish the hypocritical Presbyterians by cut-
ting off their ears, which is how William

Prynne (1600–69) was twice punished. He lost
most of his ears for supposedly slandering the
king and queen in *Histrio-Mastix* (1633), and
then the remnants of them for Presbyterian at-
tacks on the Anglican Church in 1637.
19. **they:** Parliament; **your charge:** the indictment
that will be brought against the Presbyterians.
20. Etymologically, *priest* is an abbreviated form of
presbyter (from Gk. for "elder" and "priest").
Hence "Priest" *writ large* (written out in full)
would be *presbyter*.

LATIN AND GREEK POEMS

CARMINA ELEGIACA [*Elegiac Verses*]

When A. I. Horwood discovered Milton's *Commonplace Book* in 1874, he also found a holograph page containing the poem *Ignavus satrapam* and a fragment of a Latin prose composition on early rising. The two poems are almost certainly early school exercises, possibly from 1624.

───·◦·───

Surge, age, surge, leves, iam convenit, excute somnos,
    Lux oritus, tepidi fulcra relinque tori.
Iam canit excubitor gallus, praenuntius ales
    Solis, et invigilans ad sua quemque vocat.
5   Flammiger Eois Titan caput exerit undis
    Et spargit nitidum laeta per arva iubar.
Daulias argutum modulatur ab ilice carmen
    Edit et excultos mitis alauda modos.
Iam rosa fragrantes spirat silvestris odores,
10 Iam redolent violae luxuriatque seges.
Ecce novo campos Zephyritis gramine vestit
    Fertilis, et vitreo rore madescit humus.
Segnes invenias molli vix talia lecto
    Cum premat imbellis lumina fessa sopor.
15 Illic languentes abrumpunt somnia somnos
    Et turbant animum tristia multa tuum;
Illic tabifici generantur semina morbi.
    Qui pote torpentem posse valere virum?
Surge, age, surge, leves, iam convenit, excute somnos,
20 Lux oritur, tepidi fulcra relinque tori.

5. **Titan:** the sun.
7. **Daulias:** the swallow.
11. **Zephyritis:** Zephyr's consort is Flora, goddess of spring.

Get up, go, get up, it's time now, throw off worthless sleep, the light is rising, leave the frame of your warm bed! The watchman rooster is already singing, the winged harbinger of the sun, and, wide awake, calls each to his own business. The flame-bearing Titan[5] lifts his head out of Dawn's waves and scatters gleaming light over the happy fields. The Daulian[7] sings a sharp song from the oak tree, and the gentle lark puts forth exquisite notes. Now the wild rose breathes out sweet odors, now the violets are fragrant and the wheat fields run riot. Look, fruitful Zephyritis[11] dresses the fields with new grass, and the earth is moist with glassy dew. Sluggard, you will hardly find such things in your soft bed while unwarlike sleep presses your tired eyes. There dreams interrupt your languid slumber, and many troubling things disturb your spirit; there the seeds of wasting diseases are born. How can a lazy man be healthy? Get up, go, get up, it's time now, throw off worthless sleep, the light is rising, leave the frame of your warm bed!

IGNAVUS SATRAPAM
[Kings should not oversleep]

Ignavus satrapam dedecet inclytum
Somnus qui populo multifido praeest.
Dum Dauni veteris filius armiger
Stratus purpureo procubuit [toro]
5   Audax Euryalus, Nisus et impiger
Invasere cati nocte sub horrida
Torpentes Rutilos castraque Volscia:
Hinc caedes oritur clamor et absonus.

Ignoble sleep is unfitting for a famous satrap who rules a nation of many parts. While the arms-bearing son of old Daunus[3] lay stretched on a bed[4] of purple, bold Euryalus and unsluggish Nisus, a shrewd pair, on a harsh night invaded the drowsy Rutilians and the Volscian camp. Whence arose slaughter and confused outcry.

3. The camp of Turnus is attacked in *Aen.* 9.176-449.
4. The word *toro* is a conjecture; the last word of the line is missing from the manuscript.

APOLOGUS DE RUSTICO ET HERO
[The Fable of the Peasant and the Lord]

This work first appeared at the end of the *Elegiarum Liber* in the *Poems* of 1673. It is almost universally considered an early school exercise. The fable appears in Aesop, but Milton's model is Mantuan, *Opera* (Paris, 1513), 194.

Rusticus ex malo sapidissima poma quotannis
   Legit, et urbano lecta dedit domino:
Hic incredibili fructus dulcedine captus
   Malum ipsam in proprias transtulit areolas.
5   Hactenus illa ferax, sed longo debilis aevo,
   Mota solo assueto, protinus aret iners.
Quod tandem ut patuit domino, spe lusus inani,
   Damnavit celeres in sua damna manus.
Atque ait, Heu quanto satius fuit illa coloni
10   (Parva licet) grato dona tulisse animo!
Possem ego avaritiam frenare, gulamque
   voracem:
Nunc periere mihi et fetus et ipsa parens.

A peasant picked very tasty fruit every year from an apple tree, and gave the choicest to his lord in the city; captivated by the fruit's incredible sweetness, he transplanted the tree itself into his own garden. Fruitful up to then, but weak from old age, when moved from its accustomed soil, it immediately withers and becomes barren. Then, when this became clear to the lord, fooled by vain hope, he cursed the quickness of his hands in his own undoing. And he said, "Alas, how much better it was to receive my tenant's gifts, small as they were, with a grateful spirit! Would that I could have restrained my greed and voracious gluttony; now I have lost both the offspring and the parent itself."

PHILOSOPHUS AD REGEM
[*A Philosopher to a King*]

These Greek verses were printed in the 1645 and 1673 *Poems*. Though we cannot supply a certain date, the work was probably a school exercise.

⁓

Philosophus ad regem quendam qui eum ignotum et insontem inter reos forte captum inscius damnaverat τὴν ἐπὶ θανάτῳ πορευόμενος, haec subito misit

᾿Ω ἄνα εἰ ὀλέσῃς με τὸν ἔννομον, οὐδέ τιν' ἀνδρῶν
Δεινὸν ὅλως δράσαντα, σοφώτατον ἴσθι κάρηνον
῾Ρηϊδίως ἀφέλοιο, τὸ δ' ὕστερον αὖθι νοήσεις,
Μαψιδίως δ' ἄρ' ἔπειτα τεὸν πρὸς θυμὸν ὀδύρῃ,
Τοιόν δ' ἐκ πόλιος περιώνυμον ἄλκαρ ὀλέσσας.

A philosopher being conveyed to his death suddenly sent this to a certain king who unknowingly had condemned him after he had been accidentally taken, unrecognized and innocent, in the company of criminals.

O master, if you destroy me, a law-abiding man who has done no harm at all to anyone, know that you blithely take off a head of great wisdom, but afterward you will quickly understand, and then you will vainly lament in your heart that you deprived the city of such a widely renowned guardian.

ELEGIARUM LIBER [*Book of Elegies*]

ELEGIA PRIMA AD CAROLUM DIODATUM
[*Elegy 1. To Charles Diodati*]

This poem, probably written in 1626, is addressed to Charles Diodati (1609–1638), the great friend of Milton's youth. They attended St. Paul's together. Diodati went up to Oxford in 1623, while Milton, for reasons that remain unclear, did not enter Cambridge until February 1625. It has often been supposed that in the passage in which Milton refers to himself as an "exile" (ll. 17–20) he is discussing an altercation with his tutor William Chappell that resulted in a suspension. But, as Carey rightly points out, the evidence is weak, and Milton's "exile" was probably a normal college vacation.

Tandem, care, tuae mihi pervenire tabellae,
   Pertulit et voces nuntia charta tuas,
Pertulit occidua Devae Cestrensis ab ora
   Vergivium prono qua petit amne salum.
5 Multum, crede, iuvat terras aluisse remotas
   Pectus amans nostri, tamque fidele caput,
Quodque mihi lepidum tellus longinqua sodalem
   Debet, at unde brevi reddere iussa velit.
Me tenet urbs reflua quam Thamesis alluit unda,
10 Meque nec invitum patria dulcis habet.
Iam nec arundiferum mihi cura revisere Camum,
   Nec dudum vetiti me laris angit amor.
Nuda nec arva placent, umbrasque negantia molles;

At last, dear friend, your tablets have reached me, and the paper messenger has brought your voice, brought it from the western bank of Chester's Dee, where it seeks the Irish Sea with a downward flow. Believe me, it is a great joy that faraway lands have nurtured a heart which loves us, and so faithful a head, and that a distant country owes me a charming companion but is willing to pay the debt quickly when ordered. The city which the Thames washes with retreating waves holds me, and my sweet homeland does not keep me against my will. Nor do I now have any interest in returning to the reedy Cam; nor does love of

Quam male Phoebicolis convenit ille locus!
15 Nec duri libet usque minas perferre magistri
    Caeteraque ingenio non subeunda meo.
    Si sit hoc exilium, patrios adiisses penates,
    Et vacuum curis otia grata sequi,
    Non ego vel profugi nomen sortemve recuso,
20 Laetus et exilii conditione fruor.
    O utinam vates nunquam graviora tulisset
    Ille Tomitano flebilis exul agro;
    Non tunc Ionio quicquam cessisset Homero
    Neve foret victo laus tibi prima Maro.
25 Tempora nam licet hic placidis dare libera
    Musis,
    Et totum rapiunt me mea vita libri.
    Excipit hinc fessum sinuosi pompa theatri,
    Et vocat ad plausus garrula scena suos.
    Seu catus auditur senior, seu prodigus haeres,
30 Seu procus, aut posita casside miles adest,
    Sive decennali foecundus lite patronus
    Detonat inculto barbara verba foro,
    Saepe vafer gnato succurrit servus amanti,
    Et nasum rigidi fallit ubique patris;
35 Saepe novos illic virgo mirata calores
    Quid sit amor nescit, dum quoque nescit,
    amat.
    Sive cruentatum furiosa Tragoedia sceptrum
    Quassat, et effusis crinibus ora rotat;
    Et dolet, et specto, iuvat et spectasse dolendo;
40 Interdum et lacrimis dulcis amaror inest:
    Seu puer infelix indelibata reliquit
    Gaudia, et abrupto flendus amore cadit;
    Seu ferus e tenebris iterat Styga criminis ultor,
    Conscia funereo pectora torre movens;

14. **Phoebicolis:** poets.
15. The stern tutor is usually identified as William
    Chappell. Aubrey (p. xix) is responsible for the
    familiar but dubious notion that Chappell
    whipped Milton.
21. **vates:** Ovid, whom Augustus exiled to Tomis
    on the Black Sea.
23. **Ionio:** Smyrna in Ionia was one of the cities
    that claimed to be the birthplace of Homer.

my recently forbidden hearth
god torment me; nor are bare
fields attractive, denying soft
shade. How badly that place suits
Phoebus's followers.[14] It is not
pleasing to keep bearing the
threats of a harsh master[15] and
other things intolerable to my
talent. If this is exile—to have re-
turned to my homeland gods and
pursue a welcome leisure free
from worries—I have not
shunned the name, nor do I
refuse the fate, and I am happy to
rejoice in the condition of exile.
Oh, would that bard[21] had never
borne anything worse, that tear-
ful exile in the fields of Tomis;
then he would not have yielded
to Ionic Homer,[23] nor would the
highest praise have been yours,
defeated Vergil. For here it is
possible to give free time to the
peaceful Muses, and my books
(my life) take me over com-
pletely. The spectacle of the
curved theater attracts one when
tired, and the chatty stage sum-
mons its applause. Sometimes a
crafty old man is being heard, or
a prodigal heir, or a wooer, or a
soldier with his helmet off is
there, or a lawyer rich from a ten-
year-old case declaims barbarous
words to an ignorant forum.
Often a clever slave helps out a
son in love, and fools the nose of
his stern father at every turn;
often then a virgin, surprised by
new passion, does not know what
love is, and loves even as she does
not know. Sometimes furious
Tragedy shakes a bloody scepter
and twists her face, her hair
streaming; and it is painful, and I
watch, and it is a joy to have
watched in pain. And sometimes
there is a sweet bitterness in
tears, as when an unhappy boy
abandoned unconsummated joys,
and falls to be wept over, his love
extinguished; or when from the
shadows a fierce avenger of crime

45   Seu maeret Pelopeia domus, seu nobilis Ili,
          Aut luit incestos aula Creontis avos.
      Sed neque sub tecto semper nec in urbe
          latemus,
      Irrita nec nobis tempora veris eunt.
      Nos quoque lucus habet vicina consitus ulmo
50   Atque suburbani nobilis umbra loci.
      Saepius hic blandas spirantia sidera flammas
      Virgineos videas praeteriisse choros.
      Ah quoties dignae stupui miracula formae
      Quae posset senium vel reparare Iovis;
55   Ah quoties vidi superantia lumina gemmas,
          Atque faces quotquot volvit uterque polus;
      Collaque bis vivi Pelopis quae brachia vincant,
          Quaeque fluit puro nectare tincta via,
      Et decus eximium frontis, tremulosque capillos,
60   Aurea quae fallax retia tendit Amor;
      Pellacesque genas, ad quas hyacinthia sordet
          Purpura, et ipse tui floris, Adoni, rubor.
      Cedite laudatae toties Heroides olim,
          Et quaecunque vagum cepit amica Iovem.
65   Cedite Achaemeniae turrita fronte puellae,
          Et quot Susa colunt, Memnoniamque Ninon.
      Vos etiam Danae fasces submittite Nymphae,
          Et vos Iliacae, Romuleaeque nurus;
      Nec Pompeianas Tarpeia Musa columnas
70   Iactet, et Ausoniis plena theatra stolis.
      Gloria Virginibus debetur prima Britannis;

45. **Pelopeia domus:** The descendants of Pelops (Atreus, Thyestes, Agamemnon, Orestes, Electra, Iphigenia) were destined for tragedy. Cp. *Il Pens* 99–100.

57. Pelops was killed by his father, Tantalus, and served to the gods. Demeter ate a part of his shoulder. When Pelops was restored to life, the gods gave him an ivory shoulder (Ovid, *Met.* 6.403–11).

58. **via:** the Milky Way.

62. **tui floris, Adoni:** Venus caused the anemone to grow from Adonis's blood.

63. Milton alludes to the heroines of Ovid's *Heroides*.

66. **Susa:** a major city in Persia.

69. **Tarpeia Musa:** Ovid, who lived near the Tarpeian rock. He thought Pompey's colonnade and the Roman theater were the best places to meet women (*Ars Amatoria* 1.67, 3.387).

recrosses the Styx, moving guilty hearts with his funereal torch; or when the house of Pelops[45] grieves, or that of noble Ilus, or Creon's palace atones for incestuous ancestors. But we do not always hide indoors or in the city, nor is springtime wasted on us. A grove nearby, thickly planted with elm, holds us, and the noble shade of a site just outside the city. Often here you can see groups of young girls pass by: stars breathing forth seductive flames. Ah, how many times I have been amazed at the miracles of a worthy figure which could reverse the old age of Jove! Ah, how many times I have seen eyes outshining jewels and all the torches which revolve around either pole! And necks which would outdo the shoulders of twice-living Pelops[57] and the path[58] that runs dyed with pure nectar; and an exceptionally beautiful forehead, and dancing hair which treacherous Love casts as a golden net; and enticing cheeks beside which the purple hyacinth seems dull, and even the blush of your flower,[62] Adonis! Surrender, you heroines praised so many times in the past,[63] and whatever mistress trapped fickle Jove! Surrender, you women of Persia with the towering headdresses, and all of you who inhabit Susa[66] and Memnon's Nineveh! And you Greek nymphs, put down your fasces, and you young women of Troy and of Rome. And let the Tarpeian Muse[69] not boast of Pompey's colonnade, and the theaters crowded with Italian gowns. The prime glory is owed to the virgins of Britain; foreign woman, let it be enough for you to come next. And you, city of

Extera sat tibi sit foemina posse sequi.
Tuque urbs Dardaniis Londinum structa colonis
Turrigerum late conspicienda caput,
75 Tu nimium felix intra tua moenia claudis
Quicquid formosi pendulus orbis habet.
Non tibi tot caelo scintillant astra sereno
Endymioneae turba ministra deae,
Quot tibi conspicuae formaque auroque puellae
80 Per media radiant turba videnda vias.
Creditur huc gemenis venisse invecta columbis
Alma pharetrigero milite cincta Venus,
Huic Cnidon, et riguas Simoentis flumine
valles,
Huic Paphon, et roseam posthabitura Cypron.
85 Ast ego, dum pueri sinit indulgentia caeci,
Moenia quam subito linquere fausta paro;
Et vitare procul malefidae infamia Circes
Atria, divini Molyos usus ope.
Stat quoque iuncosas Cami remeare paludes,
90 Atque iterum raucae murmur adire Scholae.
Interea fidi parvum cape munus amici,
Paucaque in alternos verba coacta modos.

London, built by Trojan settlers,[73] whose tower-bearing head can be seen from far around, you are too happy for enclosing within your walls whatever beauty the pendulous earth holds. There are not as many stars shining for you in the calm heavens—the crowd attending on Endymion's goddess—as there are girls brilliant with beauty and gold, a crowd to be seen shining throughout your streets. It is believed that nurturing Venus, surrounded by her quiver-bearing soldiery, came here, carried by her twin doves, thinking Cnidos and the valleys watered by the river Sinois inferior to this, and Paphos and rosy Cyprus. But I, while the indulgence of the blind boy permits, am preparing to leave these happy walls as soon as possible, and to leave far behind the infamous halls of faithless Circe, using the aid of divine moly.[88] I am set to return to the reedy marshes of the Cam, and again to join the tumult of the noisy university. In the meantime, take this small gift from a loyal friend, a few words forced into alternating meter.[92]

73. According to ancient legends popularized by Geoffrey of Monmouth, Britain was founded by a Trojan named Brutus, the great-grandson of Aeneas.

88. **Molyos:** The herb moly protects Homer's Odysseus against the charms of Circe (*Od.* 10.305).

92. **alternos ... modos:** The alternating pentameter and hexameter lines of the elegiac couplet.

ELEGIA SECUNDA. IN OBITUM
PRAECONIS ACADEMICI CANTABRIGIENSIS
[*Elegy 2. On the Death of the Beadle of Cambridge University*]

The subject of this elegy is Richard Ridding, for thirty years the Senior Esquire Bedell (hence Beadle) of the university. He resigned his post in September 1626 and died soon thereafter.

Milton dated the poem in his standard manner. The Latin tag means "At the age of seventeen."

ANNO AETATIS 17

Te, qui conspicuus baculo fulgente solebas
  Palladium toties ore ciere gregem,
Ultima praeconum praeconem te quoque saeva
  Mors rapit, officio nec favet ipsa suo.
5   Candidiora licet fuerint tibi tempora plumis
  Sub quibus accipimus delituisse Iovem,
O dignus tamen Haemonio iuvenescere succo,
  Dignus in Aesonios vivere posse dies,
Dignus quem Stygiis medica revocaret ab undis
10   Arte Coronides, saepe rogante dea.
Tu si iussus eras acies accire togatas,
  Et celer a Phoebo nuntius ire tuo,
Talis in Iliaca stabat Cyllenius aula
  Alipes, aetherea missus ab arce Patris.
15   Talis et Eurybates ante ora furentis Achillei
  Rettulit Atridae iussa severa ducis.
Magna sepulchrorum regina, satelles Averni
  Saeva nimis Musis, Palladi saeva nimis,
Quin illos rapias qui pondus inutile terrae?
20   Turba quidem est telis ista petenda tuis.
Vestibus hunc igitur pullis Academia luge,
  Et madeant lachrymis nigra feretra tuis.
Fundat et ipsa modos querebunda Elegeia
  tristes,
  Personet et totis naenia moesta scholis.

1. **baculo:** the beadle's mace, carried in academic ceremonies.
2. The university is filled with devotees of Pallas, goddess of wisdom and learning.
6. Jove raped Leda in the shape of a swan.
7–8. Medea revives Jason's father, Aeson, with drugs from Thessaly (Ovid, *Met.* 7.251–93).
9. Asclepius, who restored Hippolytus to life in Ovid's *Fasti* 6.743–56.
12. **Phoebo:** the vice-chancellor.
13. Mercury (called *Cyllenius* because born on Mount Cyllene) is sent by his father, Jupiter, to guide Priam to Achilles (*Il.* 23.336–467).
15. **Eurybates:** One of the heralds Agamemnon sends to seize the captive Briseis from Achilles (*Il.* 1.318–44).
17. Avernus is a lake near Venice close to the cave where Aeneas descended to the underworld (*Aen.* 6.106–7); it is used poetically as a name for the underworld.

AT AGE 17

You who, illustrious with your shining staff,[1] used to rouse the Palladian flock[2] so many times with your voice—cruel death, the ultimate herald, takes you, also a herald, and shows no favor to his own profession. Though your temples may have been whiter than the feathers under which we are told Jove hid himself,[6] O! worthy nevertheless to be made young again with Haemonian juice,[7] worthy to be able to live to Aeson's age, worthy for the son of Coronis to have recalled from the waters of Styx with his medical art, at the goddess's repeated request.[9] If you were ordered to assemble a betogaed line, and to go as a swift messenger from your Phoebus,[12] so stood winged Hermes[13] in the Trojan court, sent from the aerial citadel of his father, and so Eurybates[15] delivered to the face of enraged Achilles the stern orders of lord Atrides. Great queen of tombs, servant of Avernus,[17] too cruel to the Muses, too cruel to Pallas, why do you not take those who are a useless burden on the earth? There is a crowd of such at which to aim your weapons. Therefore, Academy, in dark clothing mourn this man, and let the black bier be wet with your tears; and let plaintive Elegy herself pour out sorrowful harmonies, and sad dirges resound in all the schools.

ELEGIA TERTIA, IN OBITUM
PRAESULIS WINTONIENSIS

[*Elegy 3. On the Death of the Bishop of Winchester*]

This poem was occasioned by the death of the famous Anglican divine Lancelot Andrewes on September 25, 1626. Andrewes was greatly admired by T. S. Eliot, the most important literary tastemaker of the twentieth century. According to Eliot, his sermons "rank with the finest English prose of their time, of any time," and the spiritual wisdom of Andrewes makes Donne the preacher seem "a little of the religious spellbinder" or "the sorcerer of emotional orgy" (1964, 299, 302). But Eliot was admittedly conservative in religious (and other) matters. In his third political pamphlet, *The Reason of Church Government* (1641), Milton devoted some irritable pages to Andrewes's "shallow reasonings" about prelacy (Yale 1:768–79).

ANNO AETATIS 17

Moestus eram, et tacitus nullo comitante
    sedebam,
Haerebantque animo tristia plura meo,
Protinus en subiit funestae cladis imago
Fecit in Angliaco quam Libitina solo;
5 Dum procerum ingressa est splendentes
    marmore turres
Dira sepulchrali mors metuenda face;
Pulsavitque auro gravidos et iaspide muros,
  Nec metuit satrapum sternere falce greges.
Tunc memini clarique ducis, fratrisque verendi
10 Intempestivis ossa cremata rogis.
Et memini Heroum quos vidit ad aethera raptos,
  Flevit et amissos Belgia tota duces.
At te praecipue luxi, dignissime praesul,
  Wintoniaeque olim gloria magna tuae;
15 Delicui fletu, et tristi sic ore querebar,

AT AGE 17

I was sad, and sat silent, with no companion, and many sorrows clung to my soul—then suddenly came a vision of the grim killing[3] which Libitina[4] had done on English soil, while dreadful death, fearsome with her sepulchral torch, entered the splendidly marble palaces of the great,[5] and beat down walls heavy with gold and jasper, and did not fear to cut down a flock of satraps with her scythe. Then I remembered the bones of a famous lord and his respected brother, burned on untimely pyres. And I remembered the heroes[11] whom all Belgia saw snatched up into the skies and mourned as lost leaders. But especially I mourned you, most worthy bishop, once the great glory of your Winchester; I melted with weeping, and thus complained in a sad voice: "Sav-

3. During 1625 over 35,000, about a sixth of the city's population, died of the plague in London and its environs (Wilson 1963, 174–75).
4. **Libitina:** goddess of corpses.
5. Horace's *Odes* 1.4.13–14 is the best-known version of this commonplace.
11. **Heroum:** Among the prominent Englishmen to die in the Low Countries were the earls of Oxford and Southampton, and Sir Horace Vere. Breda fell to the Spaniards in May 1625.

Mors fera, Tartareo diva secunda Iovi,
Nonne satis quod silva tuas persentiat iras,
Et quod in herbosos ius tibi detur agros,
Quodque afflata tuo marcescant lilia tabo,
20   Et crocus, et pulchrae Cypridi sacra rosa?
Nec sinis ut semper fluvio contermina quercus
Miretur lapsus praetereuntis aquae.
Et tibi succumbit liquido quae plurima caelo
Evehitur pennis quamlibet augur avis,
25   Et quae mille nigris errant animalia silvis,
Et quod alunt mutum Proteos antra pecus.
Invida, tanta tibi cum sit concessa potestas,
Quid iuvat humana tingere caede manus?
Nobileque in pectus certas acuisse sagittas,
30   Semideamque animam sede fugasse sua?
Talia dum lacrimans alto sub pectore volvo,
Roscidus occiduis Hesperus exit aquis,
Et Tartessiaco submerserat aequore currum
Phoebus ab eoo littore mensus iter.
35   Nec mora, membra cavo posui refovenda cubili;
Condiderant oculos noxque soporque meos,
Cum mihi visus eram lato spatiarier agro;
Heu nequit ingenium visa referre meum.
Illic punicea radiabant omnia luce,
40   Ut matutino cum iuga sole rubent.
Ac veluti cum pandit opes Thaumantia proles,
Vestitu nituit multicolore solum.
Non dea tam variis ornavit floribus hortos
Alcinoi, Zephyro Chloris amata levi.

16. **Tartareo . . . Iovi:** Pluto, the Jove of the underworld.
20. **Cypridi:** Venus, to whom Cyprus was sacred.
26. **Proteos:** Proteus herded Neptune's seals.
32. **Hesperus:** the evening star.
33. **Tartessiaco . . . aequore:** the Atlantic Ocean.
41. **Thaumantia proles:** Iris, goddess of the rainbow.
44. **Chloris:** the Roman goddess of flowers, whose name changed to Flora after Zephyrus wooed her (Ovid, *Fasti* 5.195-378).

age Death, goddess second only to Tartarean Jove,[16] is it not enough that the woods feel your anger, and that you are given power over grassy fields, and that lilies wither when breathed upon by your poison, and also the crocus and the rose, sacred to beautiful Cypris;[20] or that you do not allow the oak next to the river to watch forever the flow of the passing water? And whatever bird, although an augur, that is carried on its wings through the liquid heavens succumbs to you, and however many thousands of animals wander in the dark forests, and whatever silent herd the caves of Proteus nurture.[26] Invidious one, since so much power is granted you, why does it please you to stain your hands with human slaughter, and to have sharpened sure arrows against a noble breast, and to have driven a half-divine soul from its home?" While, weeping, I turn such things over in my heart, dewy Hesperus[32] leaves the western waters, and Phoebus, having marked his journey from the eastern shore, had submerged his chariot in the Tartessian sea.[33] Without delay, I laid my body that needed restoring on my hollow bed, and night and sleep had closed my eyes, when I seemed to be wandering in a large field—alas, my skill cannot relate what I saw. There everything shone with a red light, as when mountaintops blush with the morning sun; and as when Thaumas's daughter[41] opens up her riches, the earth gleamed in multicolored clothing. The goddess Chloris,[44] loved by gentle Zephyrus, did not ornament the gardens of Alcinous with such varied flowers. Silver rivers wash

45 Flumina vernantes lambunt argentea campos,
      Ditior Hesperio flavet arena Tago.
    Serpit odoriferas per opes levis aura Favoni,
      Aura sub innumeris humida nata rosis.
    Talis in extremis terrae Gangetidis oris
50   Luciferi regis fingitur esse domus.
    Ipse racemiferis dum densas vitibus umbras
      Et pellucentes miror ubique locos,
    Ecce mihi subito praesul Wintonius astat,
      Sidereum nitido fulsit in ore iubar;
55 Vestis ad auratos defluxit candida talos,
      Infula divinum cinxerat alba caput.
    Dumque senex tali incedit venerandus amictu,
      Intremuit laeto florea terra sono.
    Agmina gemmatis plaudunt caelestia pennis,
60   Pura triumphali personat aethra tuba.
    Quisque novum amplexu comitem cantuque
        salutat,
      Hosque aliquis placido misit ab ore sonos:
    Nate veni, et patrii felix cape gaudia regni,
      Semper ab hinc duro, nate, labore vaca.
65 Dixit, et aligerae tetigerunt nablia turmae,
      At mihi cum tenebris aurea pulsa quies.
    Flebam turbatos Cephaleia pellice somnos;
      Talia contingant somnia saepe mihi.

the springtime fields; the sand is more golden than Hesperian Tagus.[46] The gentle breeze of Favonius[47] steals through odor-bearing riches—a moist breeze born from innumerable roses. Such is imagined to be the home of King Lucifer on the far shores of the land of Ganges. While I gaze on the shadows dense with grape-bearing vines and shining spaces in all directions, lo! suddenly the Bishop of Winchester stands next to me. A starry brightness shone from his radiant face; his white clothing flowed down to his golden ankles, a white fillet girded his divine head. And as the reverend old man moved in such clothing, the flowery earth trembled with a happy sound. Heaven's host applauds with jeweled wings, the pure ether resounds with a triumphal trumpet. Each salutes the new comrade with embrace and song, and one with peaceful mouth uttered these sounds: "Come, son, and in happiness take the joys of the paternal kingdom; from now on, son, be forever free of hard labor."[64] He spoke, and the winged troop touched their harps; but my golden repose was dispersed with the shadows. I wept for the dreams disturbed by Cephalus's mistress;[67] may such dreams come to me often.[68]

46. **Tago:** the Tagus, a river in Spain known for its golden sand.
47. **Favoni:** Zephyrus, the west wind.
64. Cp. Rev. 14.13: "They may rest from their labors."
67. **Cephaleia pellice:** Aurora, goddess of the dawn.
68. **Talia . . . mihi:** Milton adapts the famous last line of Ovid's *Amores* 1.5, which commemorates a delightfully unexpected afternoon of love-making with Corinna.

ELEGIA QUARTA. AD THOMAM IUNIUM
PRAECEPTOREM SUUM, APUD MERCATORES
ANGLICOS HAMBURGAE AGENTES
PASTORIS MUNERE FUNGENTEM

[*Elegy 4. To Thomas Young, his tutor, at present performing
the office of chaplain among the English merchants living in Hamburg*]

The Scotsman Thomas Young (1587?–1655) tutored the young Milton for some
period between his arrival in London around 1618 and 1620, when he departed
for Hamburg and the eleven-year-old Milton moved on to St. Paul's grammar
school. Young returned to England in 1628 and received the vicarage of Stow-
market in Suffolk. His sympathies were deeply Presbyterian. In the early 1640s,
Young was one of the five authors comprehended in the joint pseudonym
Smectymnuus (his initials supplied the *ty* in the middle). He was appointed to
the Westminster Assembly in 1643 and to the Mastership of Jesus College, Cam-
bridge, in 1644. Young was ousted from the Cambridge post in 1650 for refusing
to accept the terms of the Engagement (a secret treaty between Charles I and
the Scottish Commissioners trading three years of Presbyterian government in
the English Church for a Scottish invasion of England) and returned to Stow-
market. It is hard to believe that Milton did not have his old friend and teacher
somewhere in mind when, in the digression on the Long Parliament in *The His-
tory of Britain,* he complained of avaricious divines who "accept besides one,
sometimes two or more of the best livings, collegiate masterships in the univer-
sities, rich lectures in the city, setting sail to all winds that might blow gain into
their covetous bosoms" (Yale 5:446).

Curre per immensum subito mea littera
  pontum;
  I, pete Teutonicos laeve per aequor agros;
Segnes rumpe moras, et nil, precor, obstet eunti,
Et festinantis nil remoretur iter.
5 Ipse ego Sicanio fraenantem carcere ventos
  Aeolon, et virides sollicitabo deos,
Caeruleamque suis comitatam Dorida nymphis,
  Ut tibi dent placidam per sua regna viam.
At tu, si poteris, celeres tibi sume iugales,

1. An imitation of Ovid's *Tristia* 3.7.1–2.
7. **Dorida:** wife of Nereus and mother of the fifty
  Nereids.

AT AGE 18

Run quickly, my letter, across the
huge ocean;[1] go, seek the Teu-
tonic fields across the smooth sea.
Break off lazy delays, and let
nothing, I pray, get in your way,
and let nothing slow your jour-
ney as you hurry. I myself will so-
licit Aeolus, who holds back the
winds in their Sicilian cave, and
the green gods, and cerulean
Doris[7] in company with her
nymphs, to give you a peaceful
path through their kingdom. And
you, if you can, take up that swift

10 Vecta quibus Colchis fugit ab ore viri;
  Aut queis Triptolemus Scythicas devenit in
   oras,
  Gratus Eleusina missus ab urbe puer.
  Atque ubi Germanas flavere videbis arenas,
  Ditis ad Hamburgae moenia flecte gradum,
15 Dicitur occiso quae ducere nomen ab Hama,
  Cimbrica quem fertur clava dedisse neci.
  Vivit ibi antiquae clarus pietatis honore
  Praesul Christicolas pascere doctus oves;
  Ille quidem est animae plusquam pars altera
   nostrae,
20 Dimidio vitae vivere cogor ego.
  Hei mihi quot pelagi, quot montes interiecti
  Me faciunt alia parte carere mei!
  Charior ille mihi quam tu doctissime Graium
  Cliniadi, pronepos qui Telamonis erat;
25 Quamque Stagirites generoso magnus alumno,
  Quem peperit Libyco Chaonis alma Iovi.
  Qualis Amyntorides, qualis Philyreius heros
  Myrmidonum regi, talis et ille mihi.
  Primus ego Aonios illo praeeunte recessus
30 Lustrabam, et bifidi sacra vireta iugi;
  Pieriosque hausi latices, Clioque favente,
  Castalio sparsi laeta ter ora mero.
  Flammeus at signum ter viderat arietis Aethon,

team with which the Colchian[10] fled the presence of her husband, or the one in which the gracious boy Triptolemus,[11] sent from the Eleusinian city, came to the Scythian shores. And when you see the golden sands of Germany, bend your course to the walls of wealthy Hamburg, which is said to have gotten its name from the death of Hama,[15] whom a Danish club is reported to have sent to death. There lives a pastor famous for honoring the ancient faith, learned in the tending of Christian sheep. He indeed is more than the other part of my soul;[19] I am forced to live half a life. Alas, how many seas, how many mountains in between make me lack my other part! He is dearer to me than you, most learned of the Greeks,[23] were to the son of Clinias, who was the descendant of Telamon; than the great Stagirite[25] to his noble alumnus, whom the kindly woman of Chaonia bore to Libyan Jove. As the son of Amyntor, as the Philyrean hero to the king of the Myrmidons, so also he to me. With him leading me, I first traveled the Aonian retreats and the sacred green precincts of the forked mountain[30] and drank the Pierian waters, and with Clio's[31] favor sprinkled my happy mouth three times with Castalian wine. But three times fiery Aethon[33]

10. **Colchis:** Medea, who fled in a dragon-drawn chariot after killing her children.

11. Triptolemus also drove a chariot drawn by dragons (Ovid, *Met.* 5.642–61).

15. **Hama:** There was a story that Hamburg took its name from the Saxon champion Hama, who was killed by a Danish giant on the spot where the city now stands.

19. Evoking Horace's farewell to Vergil, *animae dimidium meae* ("half of my own soul"), in *Odes* 1.3.8.

23. **doctissime Graium:** Socrates, whose friendship with Alcibiades is represented in Plato's *Symposium.*

25. **Stagirites:** Aristotle, a native of Stageira, tutored Alexander the Great, who according to Plutarch (*Alexander* 2–3) was sired by Jupiter Ammon in the form of a snake.

30. **bifidi . . . iugi:** Parnassus, sacred to Apollo and the Muses.

31. **Clio:** the Muse of history.

33. **Aethon:** one of the horses of the sun's chariot. The arithmetic of the passage has been much debated.

Induxitque auro lanea terga novo,
35   Bisque novo terram sparsisti Chlori senilem
     Gramine, bisque tuas abstulit Auster opes:
     Necdum eius licuit mihi lumina pascere vultu,
     Aut linguae dulces aure bibisse sonos.
     Vade igitur, cursuque Eurum praeverte
     sonorum;
40   Quam sit opus monitis res docet, ipsa vides.
     Invenies dulci cum coniuge forte sedentem,
     Mulcentem gremio pignora chara suo,
     Forsitan aut veterum praelarga volumina patrum
     Versantem, aut veri biblia sacra Dei;
45   Caelestive animas saturantem rore tenellas,
     Grande salutiferae religionis opus.
     Utque solet, multam sit dicere cura salutem,
     Dicere quam decuit, si modo adesset, herum.
     Haec quoque paulum oculos in humum defixa
     modestos,
50   Verba verecundo sis memor ore loqui:
     Haec tibi, si teneris vacat inter praelia Musis
     Mittit ab Angliaco littore fida manus.
     Accipe sinceram, quamvis sit sera, salutem;
     Fiat et hoc ipso gratior illa tibi.
55   Sera quidem, sed vera fuit, quam casta recepit
     Icaris a lento Penelopeia viro.
     Ast ego quid volui manifestum tollere crimen,
     Ipse quod ex omni parte levare nequit?
     Arguitur tardus merito, noxamque fatetur,
60   Et pudet officium deseruisse suum.
     Tu modo da veniam fasso, veniamque roganti;
     Crimina diminui, quae patuere, solent.
     Non ferus in pavidos rictus diducit hiantes,
     Vulnifico pronos nec rapit ungue leo.
65   Saepe sarissiferi crudelia pectora Thracis
     Supplicis ad moestas delicuere preces.
     Extensaeque manus avertunt fulminis ictus,
     Placat et iratos hostia parva deos.
     Iamque diu scripsisse tibi fuit impetus illi,
70   Neve moras ultra ducere passus Amor.
     Nam vaga Fama refert, heu nuntia vera
     malorum!
     In tibi finitimis bella tumere locis,

looked upon the sign of the Ram and covered its woolly back with new gold, and twice, Chloris, you sprinkled the aged earth with new grass, and twice Auster[36] took your riches away; and I have not yet been allowed to feast my eyes on his face, or to drink with my ear the sweet sounds of his tongue. Go, therefore, and outstrip loud Eurus[39] in your course; the situation shows, you yourself see how urgent my orders are. You will perhaps find him sitting with his sweet wife, caressing in his lap their dear love tokens; or perhaps going through the great volumes of the ancient fathers, or the Holy Bible of the true God; or watering tender souls with heavenly dew, the great task of the religion of salvation. As is the custom, take care to speak a hearty greeting, such as would have befitted your master, if only he were there. Briefly fixing your modest eyes on the ground, remember also to speak these words in a respectful voice: "A faithful hand sends you these from the English shore, if there is time for the soft Muses amid the battles.[51] Accept a sincere greeting, though it is late; and may it be for this very reason the more welcome to you. Late indeed, but true, was that which chaste Penelope, daughter of Icarius, received from her tardy husband.[56] But why did I want to excuse this manifest guilt, when he himself cannot in any way minimize it? He is rightly accused of delay, and confesses his guilt, and is ashamed to have failed his office. Forgive him now that he has confessed and begs for pardon; crimes tend to diminish when they are laid open. The wild beast does not spread its gaping jaws for those that tremble, and the lion does not seize with its wounding claw those that lie

36. **Auster:** the south wind.
39. **Eurum:** the east wind.
51. **praelia:** Hamburg was not attacked in the Thirty Years' War, though armies passed near it.
56. **lento Penelopeia viro:** Odysseus.

Teque tuamque urbem truculento milite cingi,
   Et iam Saxonicos arma parasse duces.
75 Te circum late campos populatur Enyo,
   Et sata carne virum iam cruor arva rigat.
Germanisque suum concessit Thracia Martem;
   Illuc Odrysios Mars pater egit equos.
Perpetuoque comans iam deflorescit oliva,
80   Fugit et aerisonam Diva perosa tubam,
Fugit io terris, et iam non ultima virgo
   Creditur ad superas iusta volasse domos.
Te tamen interea belli circumsonat horror,
   Vivis et ignoto solus inopsque solo;
85 Et, tibi quam patrii non exhibuere penates,
   Sede peregrina quaeris egenus opem.
Patria, dura parens, et saxis saevior albis
   Spumea quae pulsat littoris unda tui,
Siccine te decet innocuos exponere foetus,
90   Siccine in externam ferrea cogis humum,
Et sinis ut terris quaerant alimenta remotis
   Quos tibi prospiciens miserat ipse Deus,
Et qui laeta ferunt de caelo nuntia, quique
   Quae via post cineres ducat ad astra, docent?
95 Digna quidem Stygiis quae vivas clausa
      tenebris,
   Aeternaque animae digna perire fame!

74. **Saxonicos . . . duces:** probably Dukes Freder-
   ick, William, and Bernard, sons of Duke John of
   Saxe-Weimar.
75. **Enyo:** goddess of war.
80. **Diva:** Eirene, goddess of peace.
81. **virgo:** Astraea, goddess of justice, the last of the
   gods to leave earth (Ovid, *Met.* 1.149–50).

prone. The cruel hearts of the spear-bearing Thracians have often melted at the mournful prayers of a suppliant. Outstretched hands ward off the lightning bolt, and a small offering placates the angry gods. For a long time now he has had the urge to write you, nor did Love tolerate any further delay. For now busy Rumor reports—alas, true messenger of evils!—that wars arise in the areas near you, and you and your city are encircled by a fierce army, and the Saxon lords[74] have already prepared for war. Enyo[75] devastates the countryside widely about you, and even now blood waters fields sown with men's flesh. Thrace has surrendered its own Mars to the Germans, and Father Mars has driven Odrysian horses there. The ever leafy olive is withering now, and the goddess[80] who hates the brazen-sounding trumpet has fled—look, she has fled from the earth!—and now the just virgin[81] is not believed the last to have flown to heavenly homes. Meanwhile the horror of war sounds about you, and you live alone and impoverished in an unknown land, and in your need seek in a foreign home the sustenance which the Penates of your homeland did not provide you. Harsh parent homeland, and more cruel than the white rocks which the foaming waves of your shore batter, is it right for you to expose your innocent offspring this way? Is this how you, with a heart of iron, force them onto foreign soil, and allow them to seek sustenance in distant lands—those whom God Himself, out of care for you, had sent, and who carry the happy message from Heaven, and who teach the way that after ashes leads to the stars? You are worthy indeed to live shut up in Stygian shad-

Haud aliter vates terrae Thesbitidis olim
  Pressit inassueto devia tesqua pede,
Desertasque Arabum salebras, dum regis Achabi
100 Effugit atque tuas, Sidoni dira, manus.
Talis et horrisono laceratus membra flagello,
  Paulus ab Aemathia pellitur urbe Cilix;
Piscosaeque ipsum Gergessae civis Iesum
  Finibus ingratus iussit abire suis.
105 At tu sume animos, nec spes cadat anxia curis
  Nec tua concutiat decolor ossa metus.
Sis etenim quamvis fulgentibus obsitus armis,
  Intententque tibi millia tela necem,
At nullis vel inerme latus violabitur armis,
110 Deque tuo cuspis nulla cruore bibet.
Namque eris ipse Dei radiante sub aegide tutus;
  Ille tibi custos, et pugil ille tibi;
Ille Sionaeae qui tot sub moenibus arcis
  Assyrios fudit nocte silente viros;
115 Inque fugam vertit quos in Samaritidas oras,
  Misit ab antiquis prisca Damascus agris,
Terruit et densas pavido cum rege cohortes,
  Aere dum vacuo buccina clara sonat,
Cornea pulvereum dum verberat ungula
  campum,
120 Currus arenosam dum quatit actus humum,
  Auditurque hinnitus equorum ad bella
  ruentum,
  Et strepitus ferri, murmuraque alta virum.
Et tu (quod superest miseris) sperare memento,
  Et tua magnanimo pectore vince mala.
125 Nec dubites quandoque frui melioribus annis,
  Atque iterum patrios posse videre lares.

97. **vates terrae Thesbitidis:** Elijah, who fled
from Ahab.
102. Paul, born in Tarsus in Cilicia, was scourged
and imprisoned at Philippi in Macedonia.
103. See Matt. 8.28–34.
113. In 2 Kings 19.35–36, God destroys Sennacherib's
army before the walls of Jerusalem.
115. In 2 Kings 7.6–7, God scatters the army of King
Ben-hadad by causing them to hear the sounds
of a great enemy force.
119. A variation on a familiar Vergilian tag (*Aen.*
8.596).

ows, and worthy to die from the soul's eternal hunger! Not otherwise the Tishbite prophet[97] once walked with unaccustomed foot the desolate pathways and rough deserts of Arabia as he fled the hands of King Ahab and of you, dire woman of Sidon. And in the same way Paul of Cilicia, his limbs torn by the horrid-sounding lash, was driven from the Emathian city;[102] and the ungrateful citizenry of the fishing village of Gergessa ordered Jesus himself[103] to leave their territory. But summon your spirit, and do not let anxious hope yield to worries or discoloring fear shake your bones. For though you are surrounded by glittering weapons and a thousand spears threaten you with death, still your unarmed side will not be pierced by any weapon, and no spearhead drink your blood. For you yourself will be safe beneath God's radiant shield, He your guardian and He your fighter—He who in the silent night beneath the walls of Zion[113] routed so many men of Assyria, and turned to flight those whom age-old Damascus sent from her ancient fields against the land of the Samaritans,[115] and terrified the dense cohorts along with their trembling king, while the clear trumpet sounds in the empty air, while the horny hoof pounds the dusty plane,[119] while the driven chariot beats the sandy soil, and the neighing of horses is heard as they run to battle, and the clangor of iron, and the deep roaring of men. And you, remember what is left for the wretched—to hope; and conquer your misfortunes with your great heart. And do not let yourself doubt that someday you will enjoy better times, and you will again be able to see the Lares of your homeland."

ELEGIA QUINTA. IN ADVENTUM VERIS

[*Elegy 5. On the Arrival of Spring*]

Milton's version of this popular topos in Renaissance Latin verse is now considered one of the best of the period. The poem links the renewal of the year with the renewal of literature, and to enact that connection Milton produced what A. S. P. Woodhouse termed a "distillation of the whole body of classic myth relatable to love and the coming of spring" (1943, 72). In other words, the elegy is a pastiche, but a glorious one, packed with artifice of the highest order.

Jocularity and extravagant mythological invention are frequent sidekicks in the Latin poetry (Teskey). The same pairing is on display in *To His Father, Manso,* and *To John Rouse.*

ANNO AETATIS 20

In se perpetuo Tempus revolubile gyro
    Iam revocat Zephyros vere tepente, novos.
Induiturque brevem Tellus reparata iuventam,
    Iamque soluta gelu dulce virescit humus.
5 Fallor? an et nobis redeunt in carmina vires,
    Ingeniumque mihi munere veris adest?
Munere veris adest, iterumque vigescit ab illo
    (Quis putet?) atque aliquod iam sibi poscit opus.
Castalis ante oculos, bifidumque cacumen
    oberrat,
10 Et mihi Pyrenen somnia nocte ferunt.
Concitaque arcano fervent mihi pectora motu,
    Et furor, et sonitus me sacer intus agit.
Delius ipse venit, video Peneide lauro
    Implicitos crines, Delius ipse venit.
15 Iam mihi mens liquidi raptatur in ardua coeli,
    Perque vagas nubes corpore liber eo.
Perque umbras, perque antra feror, penetralia
    vatum,
    Et mihi fana patent interiora deum.
Intuiturque animus toto quid agatur Olympo,

AT AGE 20

Time, turning upon itself in an endless circle, now as the spring warms itself calls back fresh zephyrs, and restored Earth puts on brief youth, and now, freed from the cold, the soil grows pleasantly green. Am I wrong, or does power also return to our songs, and is inspiration at hand for me as the spring's gift? It is the spring's gift, and flourishes again because of it (who would have thought?) and now demands some task for itself. Castalia comes before my eyes, and the forked peak;[9] and at night dreams bring Pirene[10] to me. And my heart is struck and burns with a mysterious impulse, and fury and sacred sound rouse me inwardly. The Delian[13] himself comes, I see hair bound with Penean laurel, the Delian himself comes. Now my mind is rapt into the heights of the liquid heavens, and free of the body I go through the wandering clouds. Through the shadows I am carried, through the inmost caves of the poets, and the inmost shrines of the gods are open to me. The soul compre-

9. **Castalis . . . cacumen:** See *El 4* 30n.
10. **Pyrenen:** Pirene, a Corinthian fountain sprung from the hoof mark of Pegasus and sacred to the Muses.
13. **Delius:** Apollo (born on the island of Delos); **Peneide lauro:** Daphne, daughter of the river god Peneus, was changed into a laurel as she fled Apollo.

20 Nec fugiunt oculos Tartara caeca meos.
Quid tam grande sonat distento spiritus ore?
Quid parit haec rabies, quid sacer iste furor?
Ver mihi, quod dedit ingenium, cantabitur illo;
Profuerint isto reddita dona modo.
25 Iam, Philomela, tuos foliis adoperta novellis
Instituis modulos, dum silet omne nemus.
Urbe ego, tu silva, simul incipiamus utrique,
Et simul adventum veris uterque canat.
Veris io rediere vices; celebremus honores
30 Veris, et hoc subeat Musa perennis opus.
Iam sol Aethiopas fugiens Tithoniaque arva,
Flectit ad Arctoas aurea lora plagas.
Est breve noctis iter, brevis est mora noctis
    opacae,
Horrida cum tenebris exulat illa suis.
35 Iamque Lycaonius plaustrum caeleste Bootes
Non longa sequitur fessus ut ante via;
Nunc etiam solitas circum Iovis atria toto
Excubias agitant sidera rara polo.
Nam dolus, et caedes, et vis cum nocte recessit,
40 Neve giganteum dii timuere scelus.
Forte aliquis scopuli recubans in vertice pastor,
Roscida cum primo sole rubescit humus,
Hac, ait, hac certe caruisti nocte puella
Phoebe tua, celeres quae retineret equos.
45 Laeta suas repetit silvas, pharetramque resumit
Cynthia, Luciferas ut videt alta rotas,
Et tenues ponens radios gaudere videtur
Officium fieri tam breve fratris ope.

25. **Philomela:** the nightingale.

30. **perennis:** So 1673; 1645 reads *"quotannis."* Milton changed the word after his political opponent Salmasius, a famous classicist, noted the long last syllable in *"quotannis."*

31. The sun has left the Ethiopians (i.e., the equator) and the East (associated with Tithonus, husband of the dawn goddess) to move northward.

35. **Lycaonius:** northern.

40. **giganteum:** Giants attacked the gods during the Iron Age, after Justice had fled the earth (Ovid, *Met.* 1.151f).

46. **Cynthia:** Diana, the moon goddess.

hends what is happening anywhere on Olympus, nor does blind Tartarus escape my eyes. What grand thing does the spirit sing with a wide-open mouth? What does this madness, this sacred fury give birth to? The spring, which gave me this inspiration, will be sung by it; in this way the repaid gifts will show a profit. Now Philomela,[25] hidden in new foliage, you begin your music while the entire grove is silent. I in the city, you in the woods, let us both begin, and let each simultaneously sing the arrival of spring. The spring—hail!—has returned again, let us celebrate in honor of the spring, and let the perennial[30] Muse take on this task. Now the sun, fleeing from the Ethiopians and the Tithonian fields,[31] turns his golden reins toward the Arctic regions. Night's journey is brief, dark night's stay is brief; shuddering, she goes into exile with her shadows, and now Lycaonian[35] Bootes does not, as before, wearily follow the heavenly wagon in a long journey; now only a few stars in the whole sky keep their regular patrol around Jove's halls. For deceit and murder and violence have left with the night, nor have the gods feared the wickedness of the Giants.[40] Perhaps some shepherd, leaning against a rock's peak when the dewy earth reddens at the first sunlight, says, "This, certainly this night, Phoebus, you were missing the girl who would hold back your swift horses." Cynthia[46] happily returns to her forests and takes up her quiver when from on high she sees the light-bringing wheels, and as she puts down her own soft beams seems to rejoice that her task has become so short with the help of

Desere, Phoebus ait, thalamos Aurora seniles;
50   Quid iuvat effoeto procubuisse toro?
Te manet Aeolides viridi venator in herba,
   Surge, tuos ignes altus Hymettus habet.
Flava verecundo dea crimen in ore fatetur,
   Et matutinos ocyus urget equos.
55 Exuit invisam Tellus rediviva senectam,
   Et cupit amplexus Phoebe subire tuos;
Et cupit, et digna est, quid enim formosius illa,
   Pandit ut omniferos luxuriosa sinus,
Atque Arabum spirat messes, et ab ore venusto
60   Mitia cum Paphiis fundit amoma rosis.
Ecce coronatur sacro frons ardua luco,
   Cingit ut Idaeam pinea turris Opim;
Et vario madidos intexit flore capillos,
   Floribus et visa est posse placere suis.
65 Floribus effusos ut erat redimita capillos,
   Taenario placuit diva Sicana deo.
Aspice Phoebe tibi faciles hortantur amores,
   Mellitasque movent flamina verna preces.
Cinnamea Zephyrus leve plaudit odorifer ala,
70   Blanditiasque tibi ferre videntur aves.
Nec sine dote tuos temeraria quaerit amores
   Terra, nec optatos poscit egena toros;
Alma salutiferum medicos tibi gramen in usus
   Praebet, et hinc titulos adiuvat ipsa tuos.
75 Quod si te pretium, si te fulgentia tangunt
   Munera (muneribus saepe coemptus Amor)
Illa tibi ostentat quascunque sub aequore vasto,
   Et superiniectis montibus abdit opes.
Ah quoties cum tu clivoso fessus Olympo
80   In vespertinas praecipitaris aquas,

---

49. Aurora's husband, Tithonus, was given immortality by the gods but not eternal youth. He therefore suffered the afflictions of old age, including impotence.

62. **Idaeam pinea turris Opim:** Cybele, a Phrygian fertility goddess, was worshiped in Rome as Ops, goddess of plenty. Ida was covered with pines, her sacred tree. She wore a turreted headdress.

66. **diva Sicana:** Proserpina. Pluto ravishes her in Ovid, *Met.* 5.385–408.

her brother. "Aurora," says Phoebus, "leave the chamber of old age;[49] what is the point of lying in an exhausted bed? The hunter Aeolides waits for you in the green grass; rise, lofty Hymettus holds your passion." The golden-haired goddess professes her guilt with a shamefaced look, and drives the horses of the morning faster. Reborn Earth sheds her hated old age and yearns, Phoebus, for your embraces—and yearns and is worthy, for what is more beautiful than she, as, luxuriant, she bares her all-nurturing breasts and breathes the harvests of Arabia, and from her lovely mouth pour forth sweet spices together with Paphian roses? Look! her high forehead is crowned with a sacred grove, just as a tower of pines girds Idaean Ops;[62] and she weaves varied flowers into her wet hair, and seems to have the power of charming with her own flowers. When she had knit her flowing hair with flowers, the Sicilian goddess[66] charmed the Taenarian god. Look, Phoebus: easy loves call to you, and the vernal winds carry honeyed prayers. Fragrant Zephyrus lightly beats his cinnamon wings, and birds seem to bring entreaties to you. Nor does inconsiderate Earth seek your love without a dowry, nor does she sue in poverty for the union for which she hopes. Bountiful, she offers you health-bringing herbs for medical use, and in so doing she herself enhances your titles. If this reward, if these dazzling gifts move you (love is often purchased with gifts), she displays before you whatever riches she hides under the vast ocean and the piled up mountains. Ah, how many times, when, tired from the steeps of Olympus you plunge into the evening waters, she says, "Why, Phoebus, does

Cur te, inquit, cursu languentem Phoebe diurno
    Hesperiis recipit caerula mater aquis?
Quid tibi cum Tethy? Quid cum Tartesside
    lympha?
Dia quid immundo perluis ora salo?
85   Frigora Phoebe mea melius captabis in umbra;
    Huc ades, ardentes imbue rore comas.
Mollior egelida veniet tibi somnus in herba;
    Huc ades, et gremio lumina pone meo.
Quaque iaces circum mulcebit lene susurrans
90   Aura per humentes corpora fusa rosas.
Nec me (crede mihi) terrent Semeleia fata,
    Nec Phaetonteo fumidus axis equo;
Cum tu Phoebe tuo sapientius uteris igni,
    Huc ades et gremio lumina pone meo.
95   Sic Tellus lasciva suos suspirat amores;
    Matris in exemplum caetera turba ruunt.
Nunc etenim toto currit vagus orbe Cupido,
    Languentesque fovet solis ab ignes faces.
Insonuere novis lethalia cornua nervis,
100   Triste micant ferro tela corusca novo.
Iamque vel invictam tentat superasse Dianam,
    Quaeque sedet sacro Vesta pudica foco.
Ipsa senescentem reparat Venus annua formam,
    Atque iterum tepido creditur orta mari.
105   Marmoreas iuvenes clamant *Hymenaee* per
    urbes,
    Littus *io Hymen,* et cava saxa sonant.
Cultior ille venit tunicaque decentior apta;
    Puniceum redolet vestis odora crocum.
Egrediturque frequens ad amoeni gaudia veris
110   Virgineos auro cincta puella sinus.
Votum est cuique suum, votum est tamen
    omnibus unum,
    Ut sibi quem cupiat det Cytherea virum.

83. **Tethy:** Tethys, mother of rivers.
91. **Semeleia fata:** Semele, loved by Zeus, was persuaded by the jealous Hera to ask her lover to appear to her in his divine splendor. He did so, and Semele was consumed by fire (Ovid, *Met.* 3.253–315).
101. Diana, goddess of the moon, was patroness of virginity. Vesta was goddess of the household; her priestesses were Vestal virgins.
105. Hymen, god of marriage, appears in the refrains (*io Hymen Hymenaee* and *Hymen o Hymenaee, Hymen ades o Hymenaee!*) of two of Catullus's epithalamia.
112. **Cytherea:** Venus.

the blue mother receive you in the Hesperian waters when you are exhausted from your daily round? What is Tethys[83] to you? What is the water of Tartessus, that you should wash your divine face in the unclean sea? You will do better, Phoebus, seeking coolness in my shade; come here, soak your flaming hair in the dew. Softer sleep will come to you on the cold grass; come here, and place your eyes upon my breast. And where you lie, the air, whispering softly, will stroke the bodies stretched out on dewy roses. Trust me, the fate of Semele[91] does not frighten me, nor the chariot smoking from Phaethon's horses. Since you, Phoebus, use your fire more wisely, come here, and place your eyes upon my breast." Thus lascivious Earth breathes out her love; the rest of her company rush to their mother's example. For now fickle Cupid runs everywhere in the world, and rekindles his languishing torches with the fire of the sun. His lethal bow sounds with new strings, and his glittering darts shine grimly with new iron. And now he attempts to defeat unconquered Diana,[101] and chaste Vesta, who tends the holy fire. Each year Venus herself renews her aging beauty, and is believed to rise again from the warm sea. Through marble cities young men cry out, "Hymenaeus!"[105] and the shore and the hollow rocks sound, "Io Hymen!" Well-dressed he comes, and handsome in his well-fitting tunic; his perfumed clothing smells like red crocus. Many a girl, her virgin breasts bound with gold, comes out into the joys of the pleasant spring. Each has her own prayer, but it is the same prayer for all: that Cytherea[112] give each the man she desires. Now the shepherd also plays on

Nunc quoque septena modulatur arundine
    pastor,
Et sua quae iungat carmina Phyllis habet.
115 Navita nocturno placat sua sidera cantu,
    Delphinasque leves ad vada summa vocat.
Iupiter ipse alto cum coniuge ludit Olympo,
    Convocat et famulos ad sua festa deos.
Nunc etiam Satyri cum sera crepuscula
    surgunt,
120   Pervolitant celeri florea rura choro,
Silvanusque sua Cyparissi fronde revinctus,
    Semicaperque deus, semideusque caper.
Quaeque sub arboribus Dryades latuere vetustis
    Per iuga, per solos expatiantur agros.
125 Per sata luxuriat fruticetaque Maenalius Pan,
    Vix Cybele mater, vix sibi tuta Ceres;
Atque aliquam cupidus praedatur Oreada
    Faunus,
    Consulit in trepidos dum sibi nympha pedes,
Iamque latet, latitansque cupit male tecta videri,
130   Et fugit, et fugiens pervelit ipsa capi.
Dii quoque non dubitant caelo praeponere
    silvas,
    Et sua quisque sibi numina lucus habet.
Et sua quisque diu sibi numina lucus habeto,
    Nec vos arborea dii precor ite domo.
135 Te referant miseris te Iupiter aurea terris
    Saecla! Quid ad nimbos aspera tela redis?
Tu saltem lente rapidos age Phoebe iugales
    Qua potes, et sensim tempora veris eant.
Brumaque productas tarde ferat hispida noctes,
140   Ingruat et nostro serior umbra polo.

114. **Phyllis:** generic name in pastoral for a shep-
herdess.
116. Pliny (9.8.24–8) held that dolphins were sus-
ceptible to music.
121.. Silvanus, the wood god, loved the boy Cy-
parissus, who was transformed into a cypress
after dying of grief for a pet deer that Silvanus
killed.
125. **Maenalius Pan:** Maenalus was an Arcadian
mountain sacred to Pan.
126. **Cybele:** See 62n. Ceres was her daughter.
127. **Oreada:** An Oread was a mountain nymph;
Faunus: a Roman wood god.

his sevenfold pipe, and Phyllis[114] has her own songs to join to his. The sailor calms his stars with a nighttime song and calls the agile dolphins to the surface of the waves.[116] Jupiter himself sports with his wife on high Olympus and summons the attendant gods to his feast. And now satyrs, when the late dusk rises, fly over the flowery countryside in swift chorus, and Silvanus bound with his cypress leaves[121]—the half-goat god and the half-god goat. And the Dryads who hid in the ancient trees range through the peaks, through the lonely fields. Maenalian Pan[125] frolics through the crops and through the bushes; Mother Cybele, Ceres[126] herself are scarcely safe from him. And lusty Faunus[127] catches some Oread while the nymph trusts in her trembling feet, and now is hidden, and hiding, badly concealed, wishes to be seen, and flees, and, fleeing, herself wishes to be captured. The gods also do not hesitate to prefer the woods to the heavens, and each grove has its own deities. And long may each grove have its own deities; do not leave your arboreal home, gods, I pray. Let ages of gold bring you back, Jupiter, to the unhappy earth! Why return to the clouds, your harsh weapons? At least drive your swift team as slowly as you can, Phoebus, and let spring's time go gradually. And let rough winter slowly bring its drawn-out nights, and let a later shadow threaten our sky.

ELEGIA SEXTA. AD CAROLUM
DIODATUM RURI COMMORANTEM

[*Elegy 6. To Charles Diodati, staying in the country*]

This poem, concluding with a reference to the recent composition of the *Nativity Ode*, seems to have been written soon after Christmas 1629. Diodati had apparently sent Milton a letter in a classical language in which he apologized for his uninspired verses and playfully asked Milton for a sign of his affection. Critics often disagree over the tone of Milton's poetic reply. Some recognize a serious personal dedication in his account of the Pythagorean sacrifices required of the heroic poet. Others discern a jocularity running throughout the work, its opening hyperboles about elegiac verse yielding with no shift in tone to its concluding hyperboles about heroic verse.

❦

Qui cum idibus Decemb. scripsisset, et sua carmina excusari postulasset si solito minus essent bona, quod inter lautitias quibus erat ab amicis exceptus, haud satis felicem operam Musis dare se posse affirmabat, hunc habuit responsum.

Mitto tibi sanam non pleno ventre salutem,
  Qua tu distento forte carere potes.
At tua quid nostram prolectat Musa Camenam,
  Nec sinit optatas posse sequi tenebras?
5 Carmine scire velis quam te redamemque colamque,
  Crede mihi vix hoc carmine scire queas,
Nam neque noster amor modulis includitur arctis,
  Nec venit ad claudos integer ipse pedes.
Quam bene solennes epulas, hilaremque Decembrim,
10 Festaque coelifugam quae coluere Deum,
Deliciasque refers, hyberni gaudia ruris,
  Haustaque per lepidos Gallica musta focos.

Who, when he had written on the Ides of December and asked for his own poems to be excused if they were less good than usual, because, he claimed, with the entertainment in which he had been caught up by his friends, he was not able to give sufficiently fruitful attention to the Muses, received this reply.

I send you, on an empty stomach, a wish for health which you, with a full one, perhaps need. But why does your muse coax forth ours, and not allow her to pursue the shadows she hopes for? Should you want to learn in poetry how much I return your love and am devoted to you, believe me, you can scarcely learn it from this poem. For neither is our love encompassed by tight-fitting metrics nor, being healthy, does it come on limping feet.[8] How well you describe the solemn banquets, and the December cheer, and the feasts which honor the heaven-fleeing god, and the delights, the joys of the country in winter, and the Gallic must

8. **claudos integer ipse pedes:** The "limping feet" of the alternating hexameters and pentameters in elegy was Ovid's joke (*Tristia* 3.1.11–12).

Quid quereris refugam vino dapibusque poesin?
Carmen amat Bacchum, carmina Bacchus
amat.

15 Nec puduit Phoebum virides gestasse
corymbos,
Atque hederam lauro praeposuisse suae.
Saepius Aoniis clamavit collibus *Euoe*
Mista Thyoneo turba novena choro.
Naso Corallaeis mala carmina misit ab agris;

20 Non illic epulae non sata vitis erat.
Quid nisi vina, rosasque racemiferumque
Lyaeum
Cantavit brevibus Teia Musa modis?
Pindaricosque inflat numeros Teumesius Euan,
Et redolet sumptum pagina quaeque merum;

25 Dum gravis everso currus crepat axe supinus,
Et volat Eleo pulvere fuscus eques.
Quadrimoque madens Lyricen Romanus Iaccho
Dulce canit Glyceran, flavicomamque Chloen.
Iam quoque lauta tibi generoso mensa paratur,

30 Mentis alit vires, ingeniumque fovet.
Massica foecundam despumant pocula venam,
Fundis et ex ipso condita metra cado.
Addimus his artes, fusumque per intima
Phoebum
Corda; favent uni Bacchus, Apollo, Ceres.

35 Scilicet haud mirum tam dulcia carmina per te
Numine composito tres peperisse deos.
Nunc quoque Thressa tibi caelato barbitos auro

drunk in front of charming fire-
places. Why do you complain
that poetry is a fugitive from
wine and feasting?[13] Song loves
Bacchus, Bacchus loves songs.
Phoebus was not ashamed to
have worn green clusters of ivy
berries, or to prefer ivy to his
own laurel. The crowd of nine,
mixed with the Bacchic chorus,
often cried out "Euoe!"[17] in the
Aonian hills. Naso sent bad
poems from the fields of the
Coralli; there were no banquets
there, the vine was not culti-
vated.[20] What besides wine and
roses and cluster-bearing Lyaeus
did the muse of Teos[22] sing in his
brief measures? Boeotian Bac-
chus[23] filled the verses of Pindar,
and every page smells of the
wine he drank, while the heavy
chariot clatters upside down with
its axle in the air, and the horse-
man flies by, dark with the dust
of Elis. Drunk with four-year-
old wine, the Roman lyricist[27]
sings sweetly of Glycera and
golden-haired Chloe, and now a
sumptuous table with choice
appointments nourishes your
mind's strength, warms your wit.
Cups of Massic wine[31] foam out
a fertile vein, and you pour out
verses stored in the bottle itself.
We add artistic skill to these, and
Phoebus poured through the in-
nermost heart; Bacchus, Apollo,
Ceres show their favor in unison.
Surely it is no wonder that three
gods, with their combined divin-
ity, have given birth to such sweet
songs through you. Now too the
Thracian lyre[37] with its golden
decoration, softly plucked with a

13. A distinction between poetic inspiration by
God (or a god) and poetic inspiration by wine
(*must* is new wine) was not uncommon in Re-
naissance literature.

17. **Euoe:** the cry of Bacchic revelers; **turba
novena:** the nine Muses.

20. In exile on the Black Sea, Ovid wrote *Tristia,
Ex Ponto,* and *Ibis.* The Coralli were a local tribe
of Geats who had little interest in his poetry.
(They didn't drink wine either.)

22. **Teia Musa:** the legendery poet Anacreon.

23. **Teumesius Euan:** Bacchus. Milton is referring
to Pindar's celebration of chariot races in the
Olympic games (*Olymp.* 2–4).

27. **Lyricen Romanus:** Horace. Glycera and
Chloe both appear as love interests in his *Odes.*

31. **Massica:** Mount Massicus was famous for its
wine (Horace, *Odes* 1.1.19).

37. **Thressa tibi caelato barbitos:** The lyre is
Thracian because Orpheus was a "Thracian
bard" (*PL* 7.34).

Insonat arguta molliter icta manu;
Auditurque chelys suspensa tapetia circum,
40 Virgineos tremula quae regat arte pedes.
Illa tuas saltem teneant spectacula Musas,
Et revocent, quantum crapula pellit iners.
Crede mihi dum psallit ebur, comitataque
plectrum
Implet odoratos festa chorea tholos,
45 Percipies tacitum per pectora serpere Phoebum,
Quale repentinus permeat ossa calor;
Perque puellares oculos digitumque sonantem
Irruet in totos lapsa Thalia sinus.
Namque elegia levis multorum cura deorum
est,
50 Et vocat ad numeros quemlibet illa suos;
Liber adest elegis, Eratoque, Ceresque,
Venusque,
Et cum purpurea matre tenellus Amor.
Talibus inde licent convivia larga poetis,
Saepius et veteri commaduisse mero.
55 At qui bella refert, et adulto sub Iove caelum,
Heroasque pios, semideosque duces,
Et nunc sancta canit superum consulta deorum,
Nunc latrata fero regna profunda cane,
Ille quidem parce Samii pro more magistri
60 Vivat, et innocuos praebeat herba cibos;
Stet prope fagineo pellucida lympha catillo,
Sobriaque e puro pocula fonte bibat.
Additur huic scelerisque vacans et casta
iuventus,
Et rigidi mores, et sine labe manus.
65 Qualis veste nitens sacra, et lustralibus undis
Surgis ad infensos augur iture deos.
Hoc ritu vixisse ferunt post rapta sagacem
Lumina Tiresian, Ogygiumque Linon,
Et lare devoto profugum Calchanta, senemque

48. **Thalia:** Muse of lyric poetry, according to
Horace (*Odes* 4.6.25).
51. **Erato:** Muse of love poetry, according to Ovid
(*Ars Am.* 2.16).
58. **cane:** Cerberus, watchdog of Hades.
59. **Samii pro more magistri:** Pythagoras, who
lived by ascetic rules.
68. Milton invents the self-denials of these shad-
owy figures.

skillful hand, plays for you; and
amid hung tapestries the harp is
heard, which guides virginal feet
with its quivering art. Let those
sights, in any case, occupy your
muse, and recall whatever slug-
gish drunkenness drives away.
Believe me, when the ivory
plucks the strings and the festive
crowd, in time with the lyre, fills
the perfumed halls, you will feel
Phoebus creep quietly through
your heart, as a sudden warmth
spreads through your bones; and
by way of girlish eyes and the
sounding finger, gliding Thalia[48]
will overrun your entire breast.
For light Elegy is cared for by
many of the gods, and she calls
whomever she pleases to her
numbers; Liber is there in ele-
giacs, and Erato[51] and Ceres and
Venus, and tender little Love
with his rosy mother. So great
banquets are right for such poets,
and frequently getting drunk on
old wine; but he who tells of
wars, and of heaven under the
rule of Jove in his maturity,
and reverent heroes and semi-
divine leaders, and sings now of
the sacred deliberations of the
supreme gods, now of the deep
realm where the fierce dog
barks[58]—let him live sparingly,
like the master of Samos,[59] and
let plants provide him with
harmless food; let the clearest
water stand nearby in a beech-
wood vessel, and let him drink
sober drafts from a pure spring.
Add to this a youth free of crime
and chaste, and strict morals, and
a hand free from stain. In such a
manner do you, prophet, splen-
did in sacred clothing, with puri-
fying waters, rise to go before the
hostile gods. In this way they say
wise Tiresias lived after the loss
of his eyes, and Ogygian Linus,[68]
and Calchas in flight from his ac-
cursed home, and Orpheus in
old age, when the wild beasts

70   Orpheon edomitis sola per antra feris;
     Sic dapis exiguus, sic rivi potor Homerus
        Dulichium vexit per freta longa virum,
     Et per monstrificam Perseiae Phoebados aulam,
        Et vada femineis insidiosa sonis,
75   Perque tuas rex ime domos, ubi sanguine nigro
        Dicitur umbrarum detinuisse greges.
     Diis etenim sacer est vates, divumque sacerdos,
        Spirat et occultum pectus, et ora Iovem.
     At tu siquid agam scitabere (si modo saltem
80   Esse putas tanti noscere siquid agam)
     Paciferum canimus caelesti semine regem,
        Faustaque sacratis saecula pacta libris,
     Vagitumque Dei, et stabulantem paupere tecto
        Qui suprema suo cum patre regna colit.
85   Stelliparumque polum, modulantesque aethere
        turmas,
     Et subito elisos ad sua fana deos.
     Dona quidem dedimus Christi natalibus illa;
        Illa sub auroram lux mihi prima tulit.
     Te quoque pressa manent patriis meditata
        cicutis;
90   Tu mihi, cui recitem, iudicis instar eris.

71. Here Milton deliberately contradicts Horace,
    who said that no good poet was a water drinker
    (*Epist.* 1.19.1–6).
73. **Perseiae Phoebados:** Circe.
74. **femineis insidiosa sonis:** the song of the
    Sirens. Odysseus descends to Hades in *Od.* 11.
89. It is debated whether these lines continue to
    allude to the *Nat Ode* or might instead refer to
    other poems (Carey 1964; Hughes et al. 1:26).

had been tamed in the solitary caves. Like them, spare in his diet and drinking from the stream,[71] Homer brought the man of Dulichium through the wide seas, and through the monster-making halls of the daughter of Perse and Phoebus,[73] and the shallows treacherous with female sounds,[74] and through your house, infernal king, where he is said to have detained crowds of shadows with black blood. For a bard is sacred to the gods, and a priest to the gods, and both his hidden heart and his mouth breathe forth Jove. But if you would know what I am doing (if indeed you think it worthwhile to know what I am doing), we are singing the peace-bringing king of heavenly seed, and the happy ages promised in the sacred books, and the baby cries of God, and the stabling under a poor roof of him who inhabits the highest kingdom with his father, and the star-spawning sky, and the hosts making music in the air, and the gods suddenly shattered in their own shrines. These gifts indeed we have given for Christ's birthday; these the first light brought me at dawn. For you also[89] are waiting modest things composed on paternal pipes; you to whom I recite them will be as it were my judge.

ELEGIA SEPTIMA
[*Elegy 7*]

Whereas the other dated elegies make use of arabic numerals, this one is dated with an ordinal. *Anno aetatis undevigesimo* would usually mean "in the nineteenth year of his age," when he was eighteen, throughout most of 1627. But considering that *anno aetatis* in conjunction with an arabic numeral always means "at the age of . . ." in Milton, some scholars suppose that the author of *Elegy 7* was nineteen.

Assuming that the poem was written around May Day 1627, and is earlier than *Elegy 5* and *Elegy 6*, Milton might have removed it from its chronological position and placed it at the end of his little book of elegies because the poem makes the best fit with his retraction, *Haec ego mente.*

ANNO AETATIS UNDEVIGESIMO

Nondum blanda tuas leges Amathusia noram,
Et Paphio vacuum pectus ab igne fuit.
Saepe cupidineas, puerilia tela, sagittas,
Atque tuum sprevi maxime, numen, Amor.
5 Tu puer imbelles dixi transfige columbas;
Conveniunt tenero mollia bella duci:
Aut de passeribus tumidos age, parve,
triumphos;
Haec sunt militiae digna trophaea tuae.
In genus humanum quid inania dirigis arma?
10 Non valet in fortes ista pharetra viros.
Non tulit hoc Cyprius (neque enim Deus ullus
ad iras
Promptior), et duplici iam ferus igne calet.
Ver erat, et summae radians per culmina villae
Attulerat primam lux tibi Maie diem:
15 At mihi adhuc refugam quaerebant lumina
noctem,
Nec matutinum sustinuere iubar.
Astat Amor lecto, pictis Amor impiger alis;
Prodidit astantem mota pharetra Deum;
Prodidit et facies, et dulce minantis ocelli,

IN HIS NINETEENTH YEAR

I did not yet know your laws, enticing Amathusia,[1] and my heart was empty of Paphian[2] fire. Often I have scorned Cupid's arrows—childish weapons—and your divinity, Love. "Boy," I said, "shoot down harmless doves; soft wars are right for a tender general. Or stage pompous triumphs over sparrows, little one; these are trophies worthy of your campaign. Why attack the human race with useless armaments? That quiver has no power against real men." The Cyprian boy[11] did not tolerate this (for no god is quicker to anger) and now burns in his rage with redoubled fire. It was spring, and the light shining on the top of the farmhouse brought your first day, May. But my eyes still sought fleeing night and did not bear the morning light. Love stood next to the bed, restless Love with colored wings. The moving quiver gave him away as he stood there; and his face gave him away, and his sweetly menacing eyes, and all those things

1. **Amathusia:** Venus, here named after her shrine at Amathus on Cyprus.
2. **Paphio:** Venus had a temple at Paphos on Cyprus.
11. **Cyprius:** Cupid, whose mother, Venus, was called "Cypris" from her associations with Cyprus (see 1n, 2n).

20   Et quicquid puero dignum et Amore fuit.
      Talis in aeterno iuvenis Sigeius Olympo
      Miscet amatori pocula plena Iovi;
      Aut qui formosas pellexit ad oscula nymphas
      Thiodamantaeus naiade raptus Hylas;
25   Addideratque iras, sed et has decuisse putares,
      Addideratque truces, nec sine felle minas.
      Et miser exemplo sapuisses tutius, inquit;
      Nunc mea quid possit dextera testis eris.
      Inter et expertos vires numerabere nostras,
30   Et faciam vero per tua damna fidem.
      Ipse ego si nescis strato Pythone superbum
      Edomui Phoebum, cessit et ille mihi;
      Et quoties meminit Peneidos, ipse fatetur
      Certius et gravius tela nocere mea.
35   Me nequit adductum curvare peritius arcum,
      Qui post terga solet vincere Parthus eques.
      Cydoniusque mihi cedit venator, et ille
      Inscius uxori qui necis author erat.
      Est etiam nobis ingens quoque victus Orion,
40   Herculeaeque manus, Herculeusque comes.
      Iupiter ipse licet sua fulmina torqueat in me,
      Haerebunt lateri spicula nostra Iovis.
      Caetera quae dubitas melius mea tela docebunt,
      Et tua non leviter corda petenda mihi.
45   Nec te stulte tuae poterunt defendere Musae,
      Nec tibi Phoebaeus porriget anguis opem.
      Dixit, et aurato quatiens mucrone sagittam,
      Evolat in tepidos Cypridos ille sinus.
      At mihi risuro tonuit ferus ore minaci,

21. iuvenis Sigeius: Ganymede, the Trojan boy
who served as Zeus's cupbearer.
24. Hylas: a youth loved by Hercules. Trying to
fetch water from a pool, he was pulled down by
amorous nymphs.
31. Apollo taunted Cupid for presuming to use the
bow. Cupid promptly shot him with a golden
arrow (love) and Daphne with a leaden one
(antipathy). See Ovid, *Met.* 1.452–567.
37. Crete was famous for its archers. ille/Inscius:
Cephalus, who heard a sound in the bushes,
threw his spear and killed his wife, Procris
(Ovid, *Met.* 7.835–62).
39. Orion pursued the seven daughters of Altas
(Pleiades).
40. Deianira, wife of Hercules, scolds him for his
submission to Omphale, who dressed him as a
maid and forced him to spin for her (Ovid, *Her.*
9.47).
47. See 31n.

that were worthy of a boy and of
Love. He was like the Sigean
youth[21] who mixes full cups for
his lover Jove on eternal Olym-
pus; or like Theodamas's son
Hylas,[24] abducted by a Naiad, he
who lured the beautiful nymphs
to his kisses—and he added
anger (but you would think it be-
came him), and he added bitter
threats, not without rancor. And
he said, "Unhappy man, it would
have been safer to have learned
from example; now you will be
witness to what my right hand
can do. You will be numbered
among those who have known
my power, and indeed I will
gain credibility through your
punishment. I myself, in case you
do not know, tamed proud Phoe-
bus after he had struck down
Python,[31] and he yielded to me;
and whenever he remembers the
daughter of Peneus, he himself
admits that my arrows hurt more
surely and more deeply. The
Parthian horseman, who is used
to winning behind his back, can-
not bend a taut bow more skill-
fully than I. And the Cydonian
hunter[37] yields to me, and he
who unknowingly was the author
of his wife's death. And even
huge Orion[39] was also outdone
by me, and the hands of Her-
cules, and the companion of Her-
cules.[40] Let Jupiter himself spin
his thunderbolts at me, our ar-
rows will stick in Jove's side. On
other things which you doubt,
my weapons will better convince
you, and your own heart, at
which I will aim with no lack of
seriousness. Fool, your muses
will not be able to defend you,
nor will Phoebus's serpent ex-
tend you any aid." He spoke, and
shaking a gold-tipped arrow,[47] he
flew away into the warm bosom
of Cypris. And when he thun-
dered fierce at me with his men-
acing speech, I laughed, and

50   Et mihi de puero non metus ullus erat.
      Et modo qua nostri spatiantur in urbe Quirites,
      Et modo villarum proxima rura placent.
      Turba frequens, facieque simillima turba
         dearum,
      Splendida per medias itque reditque vias.
55   Auctaque luce dies gemino fulgore coruscat,
      Fallor? an et radios hinc quoque Phoebus
         habet.
      Haec ego non fugi spectacula grata severus,
      Impetus et quo me fert iuvenilis agor.
      Lumina luminibus male providus obvia misi,
60   Neve oculos potui continuisse meos.
      Unam forte aliis supereminuisse notabam;
      Principium nostri lux erat illa mali.
      Sic Venus optaret mortalibus ipsa videri,
      Sic regina Deum conspicienda fuit.
65   Hanc memor obiecit nobis malus ille Cupido,
      Solus et hos nobis texuit ante dolos.
      Nec procul ipse vafer latuit, multaeque sagittae,
      Et facis a tergo grande pependit onus.
      Nec mora; nunc ciliis haesit, nunc virginis ori,
70   Insilit hinc labiis, insidet inde genis;
      Et quascunque agilis partes iaculator oberrat,
      Hei mihi, mille locis pectus inerme ferit.
      Protinus insoliti subierunt corda furores;
      Uror amans intus, flammaque totus eram.
75   Interea misero quae iam mihi sola placebat
      Ablata est, oculis non reditura meis.
      Ast ego progredior tacite querebundus, et
         excors,
      Et dubius volui saepe referre pedem.
      Findor; et haec remanet, sequitur pars altera
         votum;
80   Raptaque tam subito gaudia flere iuvat.

---

51. The favorite places to walk in London in the
seventeenth century were Gray's Inn Fields,
Lincoln's Inn Fields, Moorfields, and the Tem-
ple Garden.

there was no fear of the boy in me. And sometimes the places where our citizens stroll in the city[51] are pleasant, and sometimes the nearby countryside of the farmhouses. A dense crowd, much like a crowd of goddesses in their faces, goes to and fro, shining in the middle of the road. With its light enhanced, the day gleams with double splendor; am I wrong, or does Phoebus take his beams from them? I did not in sternness flee this welcome spectacle, and I was driven where youthful impulse carried me. With bad foresight I sent my eyes to meet theirs, nor could I hold back my sight. By chance I noticed one standing out above the others; that light was the beginning of my trouble. Such would Venus herself have hoped to appear to mortals; such the queen of the gods must have looked. That mindful, evil Cupid thrust her in our way, and he alone wove these plots for us ahead of time. The trickster himself hid not far away, and many arrows and a heavy load of torches hung on his back. No delay, now he clung to the eyelids, now to the virgin's mouth, from here he jumps to the lips, then he resides in the cheeks; and to whatever part the agile archer flits, alas for me, he strikes my unarmed heart in a thousand places. Unfamiliar furies immediately overran my heart, I burn inwardly in love, and I was all aflame. Meanwhile, she who was now the only one to please me in my misery was taken away, never to return to my sight. But I go about, silently complaining and out of my mind, and confused, I often wanted to retrace my steps. I am torn, and this part stays and the other part follows my hope, and it is sweet to weep for pleasure so suddenly taken back. In such a way did

Sic dolet amissum proles Iunonia coelum,
  Inter Lemniacos praecipitata focos.
Talis et abreptum solem respexit, ad Orcum
  Vectus ab attonitis Amphiaraus equis.
85 Quid faciam infelix, et luctu victus? Amores
  Nec licet inceptos ponere, neve sequi.
O utinam spectare semel mihi detur amatos
  Vultus, et coram tristia verba loqui!
Forsitan et duro non est adamante creata,
90 Forte nec ad nostras surdeat illa preces.
Crede mihi nullus sic infeliciter arsit;
  Ponar in exemplo primus et unus ego.
Parce precor teneri cum sis Deus ales amoris;
  Pugnent officio nec tua facta tuo.
95 Iam tuus O certe est mihi formidabilis arcus,
  Nate dea, iaculis nec minus igne potens:
Et tua fumabunt nostris altaria donis,
  Solus et in superis tu mihi summus eris.
Deme meos tandem, verum nec deme furores;
100 Nescio cur, miser est suaviter omnis amans:
Tu modo da facilis, posthaec mea siqua futura
  est,
  Cuspis amaturos figat ut una duos.

81. Vulcan (Hephaestus), the son of Juno (Hera), was hurled from heaven by Jove (Zeus) and fell for an entire day, landing on the island of Lemnos (*Il.* 1.590–93).

84. **Amphiaraus:** one of the seven against Thebes; he knew the cause was unjust and fled in shame when the attack failed. To save him from disgrace, Zeus opened the earth so that he and his chariot were dropped into Hades (Statius, *Thebaid* 7.690–823).

Jove's offspring[81] grieve for lost heaven after being hurled down among the Lemnian households; and so did Amphiaraus,[84] being carried off to Orcus by his crazed horses, look back at the sun that was being snatched away. What am I to do, unhappy, overcome with grief? It is not allowed either to put down the love that has begun or to follow it. Oh, would it be given to me to see that beloved face once, and to give my sad speech in private. And possibly she was not created out of hard adamant, and perhaps she would not be deaf to our prayers. Believe me, no one burned so unhappily; I may be put down as the first and only example. Spare me, I pray, since you are the winged god of tender love; do not let your deeds war against your office. Now your bow is surely terrifying to me, son of a goddess, powerful with your arrows and no less so with your fire; and your altars will smoke with my offerings, and you alone will be supreme to me among the gods. Please take away my ravings— But no, do not take them away. I do not know why, every lover is agreeably miserable. Just be kind enough to grant, if after this any female is to be mine, that one arrowhead transfix two loving hearts.

HAEC EGO MENTE

[A postscript to his elegies]

Haec ego mente olim laeva, studioque supino
   Nequitiae posui vana trophaea meae.
Scilicet abreptum sic me malus impulit error,
   Indocilisque aetas prava magistra fuit.
5   Donec Socraticos umbrosa Academia rivos
   Praebuit, admissum dedocuitque iugum.
Protinus extinctis ex illo tempore flammis,
   Cincta rigent multo pectora nostra gelu.
Unde suis frigus metuit puer ipse sagittis,
10   Et Diomedeam vim timet ipsa Venus.

These empty trophies to my wantonness I once made with a frivolous mind and perverse enthusiasm. Clearly malign error drove me when I was abducted this way, and untaught youth was my depraved teacher—until shady Academia offered its Socratic streams,[5] and made me unlearn the burden which I had taken up. With my flames quenched immediately from that time on, our heart stiffens, encased in thick ice. Whence the boy himself fears the cold on his arrows, and Venus herself dreads the strength of Diomedes.

5. Cp. *Apology* (*MLM* 851): "Thus from the laureate fraternity of poets, riper years, and the ceaseless round of study and reading led me to the shady spaces of philosophy, but chiefly to the divine volumes of Plato."

IN PRODITIONEM BOMBARDICAM

[On the Gunpowder Plot]

The four epigrams on the Gunpowder Plot, and the one on the inventor of gunpowder, were probably composed for the academic observance of Guy Fawkes Day. They were placed in the *Elegiarum Liber* in 1645 and 1673, as were the Leonora poems that follow them, because they were written in the elegiac meter.

Cum simul in regem nuper satrapasque
   Britannos
   Ausus es infandum perfide Fauxe nefas,
Fallor? an et mitis voluisti ex parte videri,
   Et pensare mala cum pietate scelus?
5   Scilicet hos alti missurus ad atria caeli,
   Sulphureo curru flammivolisque rotis.
Qualiter ille feris caput inviolabile Parcis
   Liquit Iordanios turbine raptus agros.

When, treacherous Fawkes, you once lately dared unspeakable evil against the king and satraps of Britain, am I wrong or did you wish to seem kind in part and to mitigate your crime with malign piety—planning, it would seem, to send them to the halls of highest heaven in a sulfureous chariot with wheels of spinning fire? Just so did that man[7] whose head could not be touched by the Fates leave the Jordanian fields, carried off in a whirlwind.

7. **ille:** Elijah, who was taken into Heaven without dying (2 Kings 2.7).

IN EANDEM
[On the same]

Siccine tentasti caelo donasse Iacobum
  Quae septemgemino Belua monte lates?
Ni meliora tuum poterit dare munera numen,
  Parce precor donis insidiosa tuis.
5 Ille quidem sine te consortia serus adivit
  Astra, nec inferni pulveris usus ope.
Sic potius foedos in caelum pelle cucullos,
  Et quot habet brutos Roma profana deos,
Namque hac aut alia nisi quemque adiuveris
    arte,
10 Crede mihi caeli vix bene scandet iter.

2. **Belua:** Protestants identified the beast of Rev.
13.1 with the Catholic Church.
6. James I died on March 27, 1625.
7. Cp. *PL* 3.473–94.

So you tried to give James to heaven, you beast[2] that hides in the seven hills? Unless your divinity can give better offerings, I pray spare us your gifts, traitor. He has indeed without you gone late to his kindred stars,[6] not using the aid of your infernal powder. Instead, blow foul monks to heaven that way,[7] and all the brutish gods that profane Rome holds! For believe me, unless you help them with this or another craft, scarcely any will climb the path to heaven.

IN EANDEM
[On the same]

Purgatorem animae derisit Iacobus ignem,
  Et sine quo superum non adeunda domus.
Frenduit hoc trina monstrum Latiale corona
  Movit et horrificum cornua dena minax.
5 Et nec inultus ait temnes mea sacra Britanne,
  Supplicium spreta relligione dabis.
Et si stelligeras unquam penetraveris arces,
  Non nisi per flammas triste patebit iter.
O quam funesto cecinisti proxima vero,
10 Verbaque ponderibus vix caritura suis!
Nam prope Tartareo sublime rotatus ab igni
  Ibat ad aethereas umbra perusta plagas.

1. James I condemned the idea of Purgatory
(McIlwain 125).
3. **Latiale:** Roman. The triple-crowned monster is
the pope.
4. **cornua dena:** See Rev. 13.1.
11. **Tartareo:** infernal, horrible.

James derided the soul's purgatorial fire,[1] without which the house of the gods cannot be approached. The triple-crowned monster of Latium[3] gnashed his teeth at this and, horrific and menacing, shook his ten horns.[4] And he said, "Briton, you will not scorn my sacred things unavenged; you will suffer punishment for spurning religion. And if you ever enter into the starry citadels, it will only be if a bitter path through flames opens up." Oh, how close you sang to the deadly truth, words barely failing to have weight! For he almost went on high, whirled by Tartarean fire, to the airy precincts as a charred ghost.

IN EANDEM
[*On the same*]

Quem modo Roma suis devoverat impia diris,
  Et Styge damnarat Taenarioque sinu,
Hunc vice mutata iam tollere gestit ad astra,
  Et cupit ad superos evehere usque deos.

Him whom impious Rome once denounced with curses and damned to Styx and the Taenarian gulf,[2] now with a different approach she works to lift up to the stars and wants to convey to the highest gods.

2. **Taenarioque sinu:** See *El* 5 66n. Baptized a Catholic, James was raised a Protestant. Catholics considered him excommunicate.

IN INVENTOREM BOMBARDAE
[*On the Inventor of Gunpowder*]

Iapetionidem laudavit caeca vetustas,
  Qui tulit aetheream solis ab axe facem;
At mihi maior erit, qui lurida creditur arma,
  Et trifidum fulmen surripuisse Iovi.

Blind antiquity praised the son of Iapetus,[1] who brought the heavenly torch from the sun's chariot; but to me he will be a greater man who is believed to have taken the lurid armaments and triple thunder of Jove.

1. **Iapetionidem:** Prometheus, who stole fire from heaven. In *PL* 6.470–506, Satan is the inventor of gunpowder.

AD LEONORAM ROMAE CANENTEM
[*To Leonora singing in Rome*]

Leonora Baroni was a well-known Italian singer. During his travels through Europe, Milton made two visits to Rome, in October–November 1638 and January–February 1639.

These three poems bring the *Elegiarum Liber* to a close.

Angelus unicuique suus (sic credite gentes)
  Obtigit aethereis ales ab ordinibus.
Quid mirum, Leonora tibi si gloria maior?
  Nam tua praesentem vox sonat ipsa Deum.
5 Aut Deus, aut vacui certe mens tertia coeli

A special winged angel—believe it so, peoples—has been allotted to each one from the heavenly orders. Why would it be surprising if your glory, Leonora, would be greater, for the sound of your voice makes God present. Either God or certainly a third mind[5]

5. **mens tertia:** perhaps the third person of the Trinity, perhaps the Neoplatonic World-Soul.

Per tua secreto guttura serpit agens;
Serpit agens, facilisque docet mortalia corda
Sensim immortali assuescere posse sono.
Quod si cuncta quidem Deus est, per cunctaque
    fusus,
10   In te una loquitur, caetera mutus habet.

from the empty sky glides affectingly in secret through your throat—glides affectingly, and with ease teaches mortal hearts to become accustomed bit by bit to immortal sound. For if God is indeed all things, and is suffused through all things, in you alone He speaks, and possesses other things in silence.

AD EANDEM

[*To the same*]

Altera Torquatum cepit Leonora poetam,
    Cuius ab insano cessit amore furens.
Ah miser ille tuo quanto felicius aevo
    Perditus, et propter te Leonora foret!
5   Et te Pieria sensisset voce canentem
    Aurea maternae fila movere lyrae,
Quamvis Dircaeo torsisset lumina Pentheo
    Saevior, aut totus desipuisset iners,
Tu tamen errantes caeca vertigine sensus
10   Voce eadem poteras composuisse tua;
Et poteras aegro spirans sub corde quietem
    Flexanimo cantu restituisse sibi.

Another Leonora captured the poet Torquato;[1] in his rage he surrendered to insane love for her. Ah, unhappy man, how much more blessedly he would have perished in your time, and because of you, Leonora! And he would have heard you, singing with your Pierian[5] voice, stroke the golden strings of your mother's[6] lyre. Even if he rolled his eyes more savagely than Dircaean Pentheus,[7] or became totally mindless and inert, you could still have calmed his senses with your voice as they wandered blindly whirling; and breathing peace into his sick heart, you could have restored him with a mind-bending song.

1. **Torquatum:** The poet Torquato Tasso (1544–95) suffered from insanity due, it was said, to his love for Leonora d'Este, the sister of his patron, the Duke of Ferrara.
5. **Pieria:** birthplace of the Muses.
6. Leonora's mother was a musician.
7. **Dircaeo:** Theban; **Pentheo:** Pentheus, an opponent of the Dionysian rites. The Bacchantes tore him to pieces.

AD EANDEM
[*To the same*]

Credula quid liquidam Sirena Neapoli iactas,
  Claraque Parthenopes fana Acheloiados,
Littoreamque tua defunctam naiada ripa
  Corpora Chalcidico sacra dedisse rogo?
5   Illa quidem vivitque, et amoena Tibridis unda
  Mutavit rauci murmura Pausilipi.
Illic Romulidum studiis ornata secundis,
  Atque homines cantu detinet atque deos.

2. **Parthenopes:** one of the Sirens. See *Masque* 879n.
4. **Chalcidico:** Neapolitan.
6. **Pausilipi:** Naples, which Leonora has left for Rome. There was a tunnel through Mount Posilipo famous for its noisy traffic.

Credulous Naples, why do you boast of the melodious siren and the famous shrine of Achelous's daughter Parthenope[2]—that when the Naiad of the coast died on your shore, you placed her sacred body on a Chalcidian[4] pyre? She is in fact alive, and changed the rumble of noisy Posilipo[6] for the pleasant waters of the Tiber. There, honored with the enthusiastic favor of the sons of Romulus, she entrances both men and gods with her song.

Sylvarum Liber
[Book of Miscellaneous Poems]

IN OBITUM PROCANCELLARII MEDICI
[On the Death of the Vice-Chancellor, a Physician]

John Gostlin, Master of Caius and Regius Professor of Physic, served as Vice-Chancellor in 1626 and died on October 21. Milton having been seventeen, not sixteen, at the time of his death, the Latin heading is in error.

◦━◦◦━◦

ANNO AETATIS 16

Parere fati discite legibus,
Manusque Parcae iam date supplices,
 Qui pendulum telluris orbem
  Iapeti colitis nepotes.
5 Vos si relicto mors vaga Taenaro
Semel vocarit flebilis, heu morae
 Tentantur incassum dolique;
  Per tenebras Stygis ire certum est.
Si destinatam pellere dextera
10 Mortem valeret, non ferus Hercules
 Nessi venenatus cruore
  Aemathia iacuisset Oeta.

AT AGE 16

Learn to obey the laws of fate, and now lift suppliant hands to Parca,[2] you sons of Iapetus[4] who inhabit earth's pendant globe. If wandering, mournful death, leaving Taenarus,[5] once calls you, alas delays and tricks are tried in vain; travel to the shades of Styx is certain. If a strong arm could repel destined death, fierce Hercules[10] would not have lain on Emathian Oeta, poisoned with the blood of Nessus; Ilium would not have seen Hector cut down by the shameful fraud of envious

---

2. **Parcae:** Milton alludes to one of the three Fates, but which one is unclear.

4. **Iapeti:** Iapetus was the father of Prometheus, who created man, and therefore a common ancestor of mankind.

5. **Taenaro:** There was supposed to be an entrance to Hades near this mountain.

10. The poison in Nessus's bloody shirt drove Hercules to suicide on *Oeta*, the mountain range between Aetolia and Thessaly.

Nec fraude turpi Palladis invidae
Vidisset occisum Ilion Hectora, aut
15 Quem larva Pelidis peremit
Ense Locro, Iove lacrimante.
Si triste fatum verba Hecateia
Fugare possint, Telegoni parens
Vixisset infamis, potentique
20   Aegiali soror usa virga.
Numenque trinum fallere si queant
Artes medentum, ignotaque gramina,
Non gnarus herbarum Machaon
Eurypyli cecidisset hasta.
25 Laesisset et nec te Philyrei
Sagitta echidnae perlita sanguine,
Nec tela te fulmenque avitum
Caese puer genitricis alvo.
Tuque O alumno maior Apolline,
30 Gentis togatae cui regimen datum,
Frondosa quem nunc Cirrha luget,
Et mediis Helicon in undis,
Iam praefuisses Palladio gregi
Laetus, superstes, nec sine gloria,
35 Nec puppe lustrasses Charontis
Horribiles barathri recessus.
At fila rupit Persephone tua
Irata, cum te viderit artibus
Succoque pollenti tot atris

Pallas,[13] nor he whom the phantom of Peleus's son killed[15] with a Locrian sword while Jove wept. If Hecate's words could drive away sad fate, the infamous parent of Telegonus[18] would have lived, and Aegialus's sister,[20] using her powerful wand. If doctors' arts and unknown plants could cheat the triune divinity, Machaon,[23] an expert with herbs, would not have fallen to Eurypylus's spear. Nor would an arrow smeared with the hydra's blood have wounded you, son of Philyra;[25] nor the weapons and thunder of your grandfather have wounded you, boy cut from the womb of your mother.[28] And you, O greater than your pupil Apollo, to whom was given the government of the betogaed society, whom leafy Cirrha[31] now mourns, and also Helicon amid its waters, you would still be leading Pallas's flock:[33] happy, a survivor, and not without glory—nor would you be traveling the horrid recesses of the underworld in Charon's[35] boat. But angry Persephone[37] cut your thread when she saw you had snatched so many from the dark

13. Disguised as Hector's brother Deiphobus, Pallas Athena persuaded Hector to fight Achilles. After Achilles missed him with his first cast, she retrieved his spear (*Il.* 22.226–404).
15. Sarpedon was killed by Patroclus, who wore the armor of Achilles. Zeus wept because Sarpedon was his son (*Il.* 16.458–505).
18. **Telegoni parens:** Circe. Telegonus was her child by Odysseus.
20. **Aegiali soror:** Medea, who murdered her brother Absyrtus or Aegialeus.
23. **Machaon:** Son of Asclepius, he tended the Greek army at Troy (*Il.* 2.732).
25. **Philyreie:** the centaur Chiron, who died when accidentally wounded by a poisoned arrow.
28. **puer:** Asclepius, whose skill as a physician was so great that he could revive the dead. To prevent that, Zeus killed him with a thunderbolt.
31. **Cirrha:** a town near Delphi sacred to Apollo.
33. **Palladio gregi:** the students of Cambridge University.
35. **Charontis:** Charon was the ferryman of the Styx.
37. **Persephone:** queen of Hades; her Latin name is Proserpina (see l. 46).

40   Faucibus eripuisse mortis.
     Colende praeses, membra precor tua
     Molli quiescant cespite, et ex tuo
        Crescant rosae, calthaeque busto,
        Purpureoque hyacinthus ore.
45   Sit mite de te iudicium Aeaci,
     Subrideatque Aetnaea Proserpina,
        Interque felices perennis
        Elysio spatiere campo.

jaws of death with your arts and powerful medicine. Reverend Governor, I pray that your limbs rest on soft turf, and that on your tomb roses flourish, and marigolds, and the hyacinth with its purple face. May Aeacus's[45] judgment on you be gentle, and may Etnaean[46] Proserpina smile, and may you walk forever among the blessed in the Elysian field.

45. **Aeaci:** Aeacus, one of the three judges of the dead in Hades.
46. **Aetnaea:** Sicilian (from Mount Etna).

IN QUINTUM NOVEMBRIS
[*On the Fifth of November*]

Like the four Latin epigrams on the Gunpowder Plot, *On the Fifth of November* was probably written for an academic celebration of the nation's deliverance from Catholic treachery on Guy Fawkes Day. As the young Milton's only epic work and only characterization of Satan, it has been scrutinized for anticipations of *Paradise Lost*.

ANNO AETATIS 17

Iam pius extrema veniens Iacobus ab arcto
Teucrigenas populos, lateque patentia regna
Albionum tenuit, iamque inviolabile foedus
Sceptra Caledoniis coniunxerat Anglica Scotis:
5   Pacificusque novo felix divesque sedebat
In solio, occultique doli securus et hostis:
Cum ferus ignifluo regnans Acheronte tyrannus,
Eumenidum pater, aethereo vagus exul Olympo,
Forte per immensum terrarum erraverat orbem,

AT AGE 17

Now, coming from the farthest north,[1] devout James took over the Troy-born people and the widely spread realms of Albion, and now an inviolable treaty brought the English scepter to the Caledonian Scots. The peacemaker sat happy and wealthy on his new throne, secure from hidden plot or enemy, while the fierce tyrant ruling over fiery Acheron,[7] the father of the Eumenides, a wandering exile from heavenly Olympus, happened to roam across the great globe of the earth, counting his allies in

1. James came from Scotland to rule England in 1603. The plotters finally decided to blow up Parliament on November 5, 1605.
7. Acheron, one of the rivers of Hades (not the burning one, which is Phlegethon), could stand for the region as a whole.

10 Dinumerans sceleris socios, vernasque fideles,
    Participes regni post funera moesta futuros;
    Hic tempestates medio ciet aere diras,
    Illic unanimes odium struit inter amicos,
    Armat et invictas in mutua viscera gentes;
15 Regnaque olivifera vertit florentia pace,
    Et quoscunque videt purae virtutis amantes,
    Hos cupit adiicere imperio, fraudumque
        magister
    Tentat inaccessum sceleri corrumpere pectus,
    Insidiasque locat tacitas, cassesque latentes
20 Tendit, ut incautos rapiat, ceu Caspia tigris
    Insequitur trepidam deserta per avia praedam
    Nocte sub illuni, et somno nictantibus astris.
    Talibus infestat populos Summanus et urbes
    Cinctus caeruleae fumanti turbine flammae.
25 Iamque fluentisonis albentia rupibus arva
    Apparent, et terra Deo dilecta marino,
    Cui nomen dederat quondam Neptunia proles
    Amphitryoniaden qui non dubitavit atrocem
    Aequore tranato furiali poscere bello,
30 Ante expugnatae crudelia saecula Troiae.
        At simul hanc opibusque et festa pace beatam
    Aspicit, et pingues donis Cerealibus agros,
    Quodque magis doluit, venerantem numina veri
    Sancta Dei populum, tandem suspiria rupit
35 Tartareos ignes et luridum olentia sulphur.
    Qualia Trinacria trux ab Iove clausus in Aetna
    Efflat tabifico monstrosus ab ore Tiphoeus.
    Ignescunt oculi, stridetque adamantinus ordo
    Dentis, ut armorum fragor, ictaque cuspide
        cuspis.
40 Atque pererrato solum hoc lacrimabile mundo
    Inveni, dixit, gens haec mihi sola rebellis,
    Contemtrixque iugi, nostraque potentior arte.

10. **vernas:** slaves by birth. The phrase *vernasque fideles* smacks of a predestination that the mature Milton would repudiate.
12. **medio . . . aere:** the middle region of the air, where devils reside throughout Milton's work.
23. **Summanus:** god of midnight storms.
27. **Neptunia proles:** Albion, the legendary king of Britain who named the island after himself. Hercules (*Amphitryoniaden*) killed him in Gaul.
37. For Typhoeus, see *PL* 1.198–99.

crime and his faithful slaves,[10] who would be sharers in his kingdom after their miserable funerals. Here he stirs up fearsome storms in the middle air,[12] there he creates hate between friends of a single mind, and arms unconquered peoples against one another's vitals, and overturns kingdoms that were flourishing in olive-bearing peace; and whatever lovers of pure virtue he sees, these he longs to add to his empire, and, a master of deceit, he tries to corrupt the heart closed off to sin and sets silent traps and spreads hidden nets to catch the unwary, just as the Caspian tigress tracks her trembling prey through the pathless deserts, on a moonless night while the stars wink with sleepiness. In such a way does Summanus,[23] wrapped in a smoking cloud of blue flame, assault nations and cities. And now white land with resounding cliffs appears, and territory dear to the god of the sea, to which long ago Neptune's offspring[27] gave his name—he who after crossing the sea did not hesitate to challenge the fierce son of Amphitryon to furious war before the cruel time of Troy's destruction.

But as soon as he sees this place blessed with wealth and festive peace, and the fields rich with the gifts of Ceres, and—what grieved him more—a people worshiping the sacred power of the true God, at length he broke into sighs smelling of Tartarean fire and yellow sulfur: such as savage, monstrous Typhoeus,[37] imprisoned by Jove in Trinacrian Etna, breathes forth from his corrosive mouth. His eyes flare, the adamantine array of his teeth grinds with a noise like that of arms and of spear struck by spear. "And after wandering over the entire world," he

Illa tamen, mea si quicquam tentamina possunt,
Non feret hoc impune diu, non ibit inulta.
45 Hactenus, et piceis liquido natat aere pennis;
Qua volat, adversi praecursant agmine venti,
Densantur nubes, et crebra tonitrua fulgent.
    Iamque pruinosas velox superaverat Alpes,
Et tenet Ausoniae fines, a parte sinistra
50 Nimbifer Appenninus erat, priscique Sabini,
Dextra veneficiis infamis Hetruria, nec non
Te furtiva Tibris Thetidi videt oscula dantem;
Hinc Mavortigenae consistit in arce Quirini.
Reddiderant dubiam iam sera crepuscula lucem,
55 Cum circumgreditur totam Tricoronifer urbem,
Panificosque deos portat, scapulisque virorum
Evehitur, praeeunt summisso poplite reges,
Et mendicantum series longissima fratrum;
Cereaque in manibus gestant funalia caeci,
60 Cimmeriis nati in tenebris, vitamque trahentes.
Templa dein multis subeunt lucentia taedis
(Vesper erat sacer iste Petro) fremitusque
    canentum
Saepe tholos implet vacuos, et inane locorum.
Qualiter exululat Bromius, Bromiique caterva,
65 Orgia cantantes in Echionio Aracyntho,
Dum tremit attonitus vitreis Asopus in undis,
Et procul ipse cava responsat rupe Cithaeron.
    His igitur tandem solenni more peractis,
Nox senis amplexus Erebi taciturna reliquit,
70 Praecipitesque impellit equos stimulante
    flagello,

52. **Thetidi:** Thetis (by synecdoche the sea itself).
60. The Cimmerians live on the edge of the world
in utter darkness (Homer, *Od.* 11.13–22).
64. **Bromius:** Bacchus, whose celebrations were
noisy.

said, "this is the only thing I have
found to make me weep; this na-
tion is the only one rebellious to
me, and scornful of my yoke, and
more powerful than our art. Still,
if my attempts have any effect, it
will not go unpunished long, it
will not go without retribution."
So much, and he swims through
the liquid air on wings of pitch;
where he flies, contrary winds
run before in a mass, clouds
thicken, and dense thunder
flashes.
    And now he speedily crossed
the frosty Alps and reaches Ital-
ian territory; on the left were the
cloud-bearing Apennines and the
ancient Sabines, on the right
Tuscany notorious for poisons,
nor does he fail to see you, run-
ning Tiber, giving kisses to
Thetis;[52] here he alights at the
citadel of Mars-born Quirinus.
Now late dusk had brought back
uncertain light, when the wearer
of the triple crown tours the en-
tire city and carries gods made of
bread, and is borne on men's
shoulders. Kings precede him
on bended knee, and a very
long line of begging friars, and
blindly they carry wax tapers in
their hands—born and dragging
out their life in Cimmerian dark-
ness.[60] Then they enter into tem-
ples lit with many torches (this
was the eve sacred to Peter), and
the roar often fills the empty
domes and the vacant spaces. In
such a way Bromius[64] wails, and
Bromius's company, singing or-
giastic songs on Echionian Ara-
cynthus, while stunned Asopus
trembles in his glassy waters, and
from far away Cithaeron itself
echoes from its hollow cliff.
    So when these things had fi-
nally been done according to
solemn rite, silent Night left
the embrace of aged Erebus
and drove her horses headlong
with her stinging whip: sightless

Captum oculis Typhlonta, Melanchaetemque
  ferocem,
Atque Acherontaeo prognatam patre Siopen
Torpidam, et hirsutis horrentem Phrica capillis.
Interea regum domitor, Phlegetontius haeres
75 Ingreditur thalamos (neque enim secretus
  adulter
Producit steriles molli sine pellice noctes);
At vix compositos somnus claudebat ocellos,
Cum niger umbrarum dominus, rectorque
  silentum,
Praedatorque hominum falsa sub imagine tectus
80 Astitit. Assumptis micuerunt tempora canis,
Barba sinus promissa tegit, cineracea longo
Syrmate verrit humum vestis, pendetque
  cucullus
Vertice de raso, et ne quicquam desit ad artes,
Cannabeo lumbos constrinxit fune salaces,
85 Tarda fenestratis figens vestigia calceis.
Talis uti fama est, vasta Franciscus eremo
Tetra vagabatur solus per lustra ferarum,
Silvestrique tulit genti pia verba salutis
Impius, atque lupos domuit, Libicosque leones.
90 Subdolus at tali Serpens velatus amictu
Solvit in has fallax ora execrantia voces;
Dormis nate? Etiamne tuos sopor opprimit
  artus?
Immemor O fidei, pecorumque oblite tuorum,
Dum cathedram venerande tuam, diademaque
  triplex
95 Ridet Hyperboreo gens barbara nata sub axe,
Dumque pharetrati spernunt tua iura Britanni:
Surge, age, surge piger, Latius quem Caesar
  adorat,
Cui reserata patet convexi ianua caeli,
Turgentes animos, et fastus frange procaces,
100 Sacrilegique sciant, tua quid maledictio possit,

80. Cp. Satan's disguise in *PR* 1.314–20, 497–98.

Typhlon and ferocious Melan-
chaetes and stolid Siope, sired by
an Acherontean father, and
bristling Phrix with his shaggy
hair. Meanwhile, the breaker of
kings, the heir of Phlegethon, en-
ters his bridal chamber (for the
secret adulterer does not spend
fruitless nights without a soft
whore), but sleep had scarcely
closed his composed eyes when
the black lord of the shadows, the
ruler of the silent, the predator of
men, stood there, dressed in a
false image: his temples gleam
with applied whiteness,[80] a
streaming beard covers his chest,
his ashen clothing sweeps the
ground with a long train, and his
cowl hangs from his shaved head,
and lest anything be lacking in
his artfulness, he bound his sala-
cious loins with a rope of hemp,
fitting his slow feet into latticed
shoes. So, the story goes, did
Francis in the vast desert travel
alone through the vile haunts of
animals and, unholy himself,
brought the holy words of salva-
tion to the people of the forest,
and tamed the wolves and the
Libyan lions.

Treacherous and veiled in
such clothing, the deceitful ser-
pent opened his accursed mouth
with these words: "Are you sleep-
ing, son? Does sleep still oppress
your limbs? O forgetful of your
faith, and oblivious of your flock,
while a barbarous nation born
under the Hyperborean sky
mocks your throne and triple
diadem—you who should be
worshiped—and while British
archers spurn your laws: arise,
act, arise, sluggard, whom Latin
Caesar adores, for whom the
locked gates of arched Heaven
stand open, break their swollen
spirits and their stubborn pride,
and let the sacrilegious know
what your curse can do, and what
the guardianship of the apostolic

Et quid Apostolicae possit custodia clavis;
Et memor Hesperiae disiectam ulciscere
    classem,
Mersaque Iberorum lato vexilla profundo,
Sanctorumque cruci tot corpora fixa probrosae,
105 Thermodoontea nuper regnante puella.
At tu si tenero mavis torpescere lecto
Crescentesque negas hosti contundere vires,
Tyrrhenum implebit numeroso milite Pontum,
Signaque Aventino ponet fulgentia colle:
110 Relliquias veterum franget, flammisque
    cremabit,
Sacraque calcabit pedibus tua colla profanis,
Cuius gaudebant soleïs dare basia reges.
Nec tamen hunc bellis et aperto Marte lacesses,
Irritus ille labor; tu callidus utere fraude,
115 Quaelibet haereticis disponere retia fas est;
Iamque ad consilium extremis rex magnus ab
    oris
Patricios vocat, et procerum de stirpe creatos,
Grandaevosque patres trabea, canisque
    verendos;
Hos tu membratim poteris conspergere in auras,
120 Atque dare in cineres, nitrati pulveris igne
Aedibus iniecto, qua convenere, sub imis.
Protinus ipse igitur quoscumque habet Anglia
    fidos
Propositi, factique mone, quisquamne tuorum
Audebit summi non iussa facessere Papae?
125 Perculsosque metu subito, casumque stupentes
Invadat vel Gallus atrox, vel saevus Iberus
Saecula sic illic tandem Mariana redibunt,
Tuque in belligeros iterum dominaberis Anglos.
Et nequid timeas, divos divasque secundas

key[101] can do; remember, and avenge Hesperia's[102] shattered fleet and the banners of the Iberians sunk in the wide ocean, and the bodies of so many saints fixed to the shameful cross[104] while the Thermodontean girl reigned of late. But if you prefer to languish in a soft bed and refuse to quell the enemy's growing strength, he will fill the Tyrrhenian Sea with a great army and plant his gleaming standards on the Aventine hill; he will smash your ancient relics and burn them in the flames, and tread with profane feet on your holy neck—you whose sandals kings rejoiced to kiss. Still, you shouldn't challenge him in battle and open war—that would be useless labor—but be clever and use trickery: it's lawful to spread any sort of net for heretics. And now the great king is summoning patricians from the farthest territories for counsel, and those born in the lineage of the great, and aged fathers venerated for their gown and white hair; these you could spatter piecemeal into the air and turn into ashes with the fire of nitrate powder injected into the depths of the buildings where they convene. Therefore you should yourself immediately alert whatever faithful England still has concerning this plan and action; who of your people would dare not carry out the orders of the supreme pope? Either the ferocious Gaul or the savage Iberian will invade them when they are overwhelmed with sudden fear, stunned at the event; so at last the Marian ages will return there, and you will again rule over the warlike English. And to keep you from being afraid, know that the gods and goddesses are favorable, all the divinities that are celebrated in your holidays." He spoke, and dropping his as-

101. **Apostolicae . . . clavis:** the Catholic doctrine by which each successive pope inherits the keys of the kingdom given originally to Peter (Matt. 16.19).
102. *Hesperiae* here refers to Spain. The passage alludes to the defeat of the Armada in 1588.
104. Omitting the Protestants burned by Mary, Satan remembers only the Catholics put to death under Elizabeth.

130   Accipe, quotque tuis celebrantur numina fastis.
      Dixit et adscitos ponens malefidus amictus
      Fugit ad infandam, regnum illaetabile, Lethen.
        Iam rosea Eoas pandens Tithonia portas
      Vestit inauratas redeunti lumine terras;
135   Maestaque adhuc nigri deplorans funera nati
      Irrigat ambrosiis montana cacumina guttis;
      Cum somnos pepulit stellatae ianitor aulae
      Nocturnos visus, et somnia grata revolvens.
        Est locus aeterna septus caligine noctis
140   Vasta ruinosi quondam fundamina tecti,
      Nunc torvi spelunca Phoni, Prodotaeque
          bilinguis
      Effera quos uno peperit Discordia partu.
      Hic inter caementa iacent praeruptaque saxa,
      Ossa inhumata virum, et traiecta cadavera ferro;
145   Hic Dolus intortis semper sedet ater ocellis,
      Iurgiaque, et stimulis armata Calumnia fauces,
      Et furor, atque viae moriendi mille videntur
      Et timor, exanguisque locum circumvolat
          Horror,
      Perpetuoque leves per muta silentia Manes,
150   Exululat tellus et sanguine conscia stagnat.
      Ipsi etiam pavidi latitant penetralibus antri
      Et Phonos, et Prodotes, nulloque sequente per
          antrum,
      Antrum horrens, scopulosum, atrum feralibus
          umbris,
      Diffugiunt sontes, et retro lumina vortunt;
155   Hos pugiles Romae per saecula longa fideles
      Evocat antistes Babylonius, atque ita fatur.
      Finibus occiduis circumfusum incolit aequor
      Gens exosa mihi, prudens Natura negavit
      Indignam penitus nostro coniungere mundo;

133. **Tithonia:** Aurora, wife of Tithonus.
143. **praeruptaque:** So 1673; 1645 had "semifractaque." Another change prompted by the metrical criticisms of Salmasius (see *El* 5.30n).
150. **Exululat:** So 1673; 1645 had "Exululant." The translation of 148–50 follows the errata sheet for 1673, discovered in 1695. See Hughes et al., 1:191–92.
156. **Babylonius:** In Protestant literature of this period, the Babylon of Rev. 14.8 and 17.5 is commonly identified with Rome.

sumed attire, the deceiver fled to unspeakable Lethe, his joyless kingdom.

Now rosy Tithonia,[133] opening the gates of dawn, clothes the gilded earth with returning light and, still mournfully weeping for the death of her black son, sprinkles the mountain peaks with ambrosial drops, when the gatekeeper of the starry palace has driven off sleep, rolling away nocturnal visions and welcome dreams.

There is a place enclosed within the eternal cloud of night, once the vast foundations of a ruined building, now the cave of grim Murder and double-tongued Treason, whom fierce Discord spawned in one birth. Here amid rubble and sharp rocks[143] lie the unburied bones of men and corpses pierced with iron; here dark Guile sits forever with his twisted eyes, and Quarrel, and Calumny, armed with a mouth of spikes, and Fury, and a thousand ways to die are seen, and Fear. Bloodless Horror and insubstantial ghosts fly perpetually around the place in the mute silence, and the conscience-stricken Earth wails[150] and is pooled with blood. Even Murder and Treason themselves hide in fear within the depths of the cavern, and though no one pursues them through that cavern— a horrid cavern, rocky, dark with deathly shadows—they flee guiltily, and turn to look behind. The Babylonian[156] priest summons these pugilists who have been faithful to Rome for long ages, and speaks so: "In the sea that flows around the western lands lives a nation hateful to me; prudent Nature refused to join it to our world for being utterly unworthy. This I order: hurry there with speedy step, and let the king and his satraps together, that

160   Illuc, sic iubeo, celeri contendite gressu,
Tartareoque leves difflentur pulvere in auras
Et rex et pariter satrapae, scelerata propago;
Et quotquot fidei caluere cupidine verae
Consilii socios adhibete, operisque ministros.
165   Finierat, rigidi cupide paruere gemelli.
   Interea longo flectens curvamine caelos
Despicit aetherea dominus qui fulgurat arce,
Vanaque perversae ridet conamina turbae,
Atque sui causam populi volet ipse tueri.
170   Esse ferunt spatium, qua distat ab Aside terra
Fertilis Europe, et spectat Mareotidas undas;
Hic turris posita est Titanidos ardua Famae
Aerea, lata, sonans, rutilis vicinior astris
Quam superimpositum vel Athos vel Pelion
    Ossae.
175   Mille fores aditusque patent, totidemque
    fenestrae,
Amplaque per tenues translucent atria muros;
Excitat hic varios plebs agglomerata susurros;
Qualiter instrepitant circum mulctralia bombis
Agmina muscarum, aut texto per ovilia iunco,
180   Dum Canis aestivum coeli petit ardua culmen.
Ipsa quidem summa sedet ultrix matris in arce,
Auribus innumeris cinctum caput eminet olli,
Queis sonitum exiguum trahit, atque levissima
    captat
Murmura, ab extremis patuli confinibus orbis.
185   Nec tot Aristoride servator inique iuvencae
Isidos, immiti volvebas lumina vultu,
Lumina non unquam tacito nutantia somno,
Lumina subiectas late spectantia terras.
Istis illa solet loca luce carentia saepe

---

172. The main classical sources for the description
of Fame and her tower are Ovid, *Met.* 12.39–63,
and Vergil, *Aen.* 4.173–88.
178. The simile of the flies buzzing about the milk
pail comes from Homer (*Il.* 2.469–73, 16.641–43).
Cp. *PR* 4.15–17.
185. Argus, sometimes said to be the son of Arestor,
was set to watch Io by the jealous Juno.

---

criminal brood, be scattered by Tartarean powder to the soft breezes. And call upon however many have been hot with desire for the true faith to be fellow conspirators and accomplices in the deed." He had finished, and the stern twins eagerly obeyed.

Meanwhile, the Lord who, bending the heavens in a wide arc, shoots lightning from his airy citadel, looks down and laughs at the vain efforts of that perverse mob, and he decides to defend his people's cause himself. There is said to be an area where fertile Europe is separated from the Asian land and looks toward the waters of Mareotis; here the steep tower of Fame,[172] child of Titans, is located: brazen, wide, resounding, reaching nearer to the ruddy stars than Athos or Pelion piled upon Ossa. A thousand doors and entrances stand open, and as many windows, and its large rooms gleam through the thin walls; the people crowded together here stir up variable murmurs, as when an army of flies makes a rumbling sound around the milk pails[178] or the sheepfolds of woven rushes, while the lofty Dog Star seeks the summertime peak of heaven. She herself sits, her mother's avenger, at the summit of the citadel; she holds her head high, covered with innumerable ears, with which she catches the slightest sound and gathers the lightest murmurs from the farthest confines of the wide world. Son of Arestor,[185] unjust guardian of the heifer Isis, you did not roll as many eyes in your unkind face, eyes never nodding in quiet sleep, eyes watching over the lands stretching widely below. With these she is accustomed to often scanning places empty of light, untouched even by the radiant sun. And talking with a

190 Perlustrare, etiam radianti impervia soli.
Millenisque loquax auditaque visaque linguis
Cuilibet effundit temeraria; veraque mendax
Nunc minuit, modo confictis sermonibus auget.
Sed tamen a nostro meruisti carmine laudes
195 Fama, bonum quo non aliud veracius ullum,
Nobis digna cani, nec te memorasse pigebit
Carmine tam longo; servati scilicet Angli
Officiis vaga diva tuis, tibi reddimus aequa.
Te Deus aeternos motu qui temperat ignes,
200 Fulmine praemisso alloquitur, terraque
    tremente:
Fama siles? an te latet impia Papistarum
Coniurata cohors in meque meosque Britannos,
Et nova sceptrigero caedes meditata Iacobo?
Nec plura, illa statim sensit mandata Tonantis,
205 Et satis ante fugax stridentes induit alas,
Induit et variis exilia corpora plumis;
Dextra tubam gestat Temesaeo ex aere
    sonoram.
Nec mora iam pennis cedentes remigat auras,
Atque parum est cursu celeres praevertere
    nubes,
210 Iam ventos, iam solis equos post terga reliquit:
Et primo Angliacas solito de more per urbes
Ambiguas voces, incertaque murmura spargit,
Mox arguta dolos, et detestabile vulgat
Proditionis opus, nec non facta horrida dictu,
215 Authoresque addit sceleris, nec garrula caecis
Insidiis loca structa silet; stupuere relatis,
Et pariter iuvenes, pariter tremuere puellae,
Effaetique senes pariter, tantaeque ruinae
Sensus ad aetatem subito penetraverat omnem.

194. The Gunpowder Plot was discovered when Lord Monteagle in October 1605 received an anonymous letter warning him to stay away from the opening of Parliament. Alerted, the government searched the cellar of the House of Lords, found the gunpowder, and arrested the custodian Guy Fawkes.

thousand tongues, she recklessly pours out to anyone what she has heard and seen; and being a liar, sometimes she shrinks the truth, and then augments it with fictitious reports. But still you have earned praise in our song,[194] Fame, a good thing than which none is more true—you are worthy to be sung by us, and there will never be cause to regret having remembered you in such a lengthy song; we English, surely saved through your offices, wandering goddess, give you your due. God, who guides the eternal fires in their motion, having sent down a thunderbolt, addressed you while the earth trembled: "Fame, are you silent? Is this unholy cohort of papists conspiring against me and my Britons, this innovative murder planned against scepter-bearing James hidden from you?" No more; she immediately sensed the commands of the Thunderer and, swift enough before this, put on whirring wings, and put varied feathers on her slender body; in her right hand she brings a loud trumpet of Temesaean brass. No delay, but she now rows with her wings through the yielding air; and it is not enough to outstrip the swift clouds in her course, she left now the winds, now the horses of the sun behind her back. And first, in her usual way, she scatters conflicting stories and uncertain murmurs throughout the cities of England; soon she clearly publicizes the plots and the detestable work of treason and actions horrible to speak of, and adds the crime's authors; nor as she talks away is she silent about the sites prepared for the blind ambush. People were stunned at these reports, young men and girls and weak old men trembled in equal measure, and the sense of great disaster suddenly struck all ages

220 Attamen interea populi miserescit ab alto
     Aethereus pater, et crudelibus obstitit ausis
     Papicolum; capti poenas raptantur ad acres;
     At pia thura Deo, et grati solvuntur honores;
     Compita laeta focis genialibus omnia fumant,
225 Turba choros iuvenilis agit: Quintoque
          Novembris
     Nulla dies toto occurrit celebratior anno.

221. **Aethereus pater:** a pagan phrase given a
Christian sense (Martial 9:35.10, 9.36.7; Claudian
22.26).

to the heart. But in the meantime the heavenly father[221] pities his people from on high, and stopped the papists' cruel venture. Captured, they are hurried off to harsh punishment; but holy incense is offered to God, and grateful honors. The happy crossroads all smoke with festive bonfires; a crowd of young people leads the dance: no day in the entire year comes with more celebration than the fifth of November.

IN OBITUM PRAESULIS ELIENSIS
[*On the Death of the Bishop of Ely*]

Nicholas Felton died in October 1626, less than a month after Lancelot Andrewes (see *Elegy 3* headnote), whom he had succeeded as Bishop of Ely. Felton and Andrewes were in fact close friends. Both men were scholars, fellows, and masters of Pembroke College, Cambridge, and both served as translators of the Authorized Version.

~~~~~~

ANNO AETATIS 17

    Adhuc madentes rore squalebant genae,
      Et sicca nondum lumina;
    Adhuc liquentis imbre turgebant salis,
      Quem nuper effudi pius,
5   Dum maesta charo iusta persolvi rogo
      Wintoniensis praesulis,
    Cum centilinguis Fama (proh semper mali
      Cladisque vera nuntia)
    Spargit per urbes divitis Britanniae,
10 Populosque Neptuno satos,
    Cessisse morti, et ferreis sororibus
      Te generis humani decus,
    Qui rex sacrorum illa fuisti in insula
    Quae nomen Anguillae tenet.

1. Milton is alluding to his grief for, and elegy for,
Lancelot Andrewes (*El 3*).
11. **sororibus:** the three Fates.
14. **Anguillae:** Ely means "eel-island."

AT AGE 17

My cheeks, still wet,[1] were caked with dew, and my eyes not yet dry; they were still swollen with the rain of salt water which in my reverence I had lately poured out while I performed my sad rites at the dear grave of the Bishop of Winchester, when hundred-tongued Fame (always, alas, a true messenger of evil and disaster) scattered it through the cities of wealthy Britain and the people descended from Neptune that you, the glory of the human race, who were king of the holy men in that island which has the name of Ely,[14] had succumbed to death and to the iron sisters.[11] Then straightway my troubled heart

15 Tunc inquietum pectus ira protinus
  Ebulliebat fervida,
  Tumulis potentem saepe devovens deam:
  Nec vota Naso in Ibida
  Concepit alto diriora pectore,
20 Graiusque vates parcius
  Turpem Lycambis execratus est dolum,
  Sponsamque Neobolen suam.
  At ecce diras ipse dum fundo graves,
  Et imprecor neci necem,
25 Audisse tales videor attonitus sonos
  Leni, sub aura, flamine:
  Caecos furores pone, pone vitream
  Bilemque et irritas minas.
  Quid temere violas non nocenda numina,
30 Subitoque ad iras percita?
  Non est, ut arbitraris elusus miser,
  Mors atra Noctis filia,
  Erebove patre creta, sive Erinnye,
  Vastove nata sub Chao:
35 Ast illa caelo missa stellato, Dei
  Messes ubique colligit;
  Animasque mole carnea reconditas
  In lucem et auras evocat:
  Ut cum fugaces excitant Horae diem
40 Themidos Iovisque filiae;
  Et sempiterni ducit ad vultus patris;
  At iusta raptat impios
  Sub regna furvi luctuosa Tartari,
  Sedesque subterraneas.
45 Hanc ut vocantem laetus audivi, cito
  Foedum reliqui carcerem,
  Volatilesque faustus inter milites
  Ad astra sublimis feror:
  Vates ut olim raptus ad coelum senex

seethed with fervent anger, cursing many times the goddess with power over tombs. Naso did not conceive with his deep heart more frightful curses against Ibis,[18] and the Greek bard[20] more sparingly execrated Lycambis's shameful deceit and his bride Neobole. But behold, while I pour out heavy imprecations and call down death upon Death, I seem, astonished, to hear, in a light breath under the breeze, sounds such as these: "Put away blind rage, put away glassy bile and useless threats. Why do you recklessly affront divinities that cannot be harmed and are quickly roused to anger? Death is not, as you think in your delusion and misery, the dark daughter of Night,[32] or sprung from her father Erebus, or from a Fury, or born under vast Chaos: but sent from the starry heaven, she everywhere gathers God's harvest; she summons souls buried in a mass of flesh up into the light and air—as when the fleeing Hours,[39] daughters of Themis and Jove, rouse the day—and she leads them before the face of the eternal Father; but being just, she hurries the impious down to the sorrowful kingdom of swarthy Tartarus and his subterranean habitations. Glad when I heard her call, I quickly left the foul prison, and was carried in happiness among flying soldiers to the stars on high, like the ancient prophet[49] hurried up to Heaven

18. Ovid in his exile wrote *Ibis,* an invective against an unidentified enemy.
20. **Graiusque vates:** Archilochus, a Greek poet of the seventh or eighth century B.C.E., avenged himself after an unsuccessful courtship with such scathing poems that both the father and the daughter hanged themselves (Horace, *Epist.* I.19.23–31).
32. Death is the daughter of Night in Hesiod, *Theog.* 758–59.
39. **Horae:** the Hours, goddesses of the seasons.
49. **Vates:** Elijah; see 2 Kings 2.11.

50   Auriga currus ignei.
      Non me Bootis terruere lucidi
        Sarraca tarda frigore, aut
      Formidolosi Scorpionis brachia,
        Non ensis Orion tuus.
55   Praetervolavi fulgidi solis globum,
        Longeque sub pedibus deam
      Vidi triformem, dum coercebat suos
        Fraenis dracones aureis.
      Erraticorum siderum per ordines,
60   Per lacteas vehor plagas,
      Velocitatem saepe miratus novam,
        Donec nitentes ad fores
      Ventum est Olympi, et regiam Chrystallinam, et
        Stratum smaragdis Atrium.
65   Sed hic tacebo, nam quis effari queat
        Oriundus humano patre
      Amœnitates illius loci? mihi
        Sat est in aeternum frui.

driving a chariot of fire. Bright Boötes's Wagon, slow from the cold, did not terrify me, nor did the arms of the formidable Scorpion, nor did your sword, Orion. I flew past the globe of the blazing sun, and far beneath my feet I saw the triform[57] goddess as she controlled her dragons with reins of gold. I am carried through the ranks of the wandering stars, through the Milky Way, often marveling at my new speed, until I have come to the shining gates of Olympus and the crystalline palace and the forecourt paved with emerald. But here I fall silent, for who born of a human father could speak the pleasures of that place? It is enough for me to enjoy them for eternity."

57. **triformem:** The moon has a triune divinity as Luna (in the heavens), Diana (on earth), and Hecate (in Hades).

NATURAM NON PATI SENIUM
[*That Nature does not suffer from old age*]

This work contributes to an important seventeenth-century debate. The idea that Nature is in a state of decay or corruption was proposed in England as early as 1580 but received a full exposition in Geoffrey Goodman's *The Fall of Man* (1616). Goodman was answered by George Hakewill's *Apology of the Power and Providence of God in the Government of the World. Or an Examination and Censure of the Common Error Touching Nature's Perpetual and Universal Decay* (1627). The issue did not bear exclusively on the natural world. When debaters came to consider whether or not human genius was in decline, they inevitably spawned another major controversy over the relative merits of the ancients and the moderns, and that debate, several times ignited in the Restoration and eighteenth century, eventually mutated into nineteenth- and twentieth-century disputes about the idea of progress (Jones 22–40).

The second edition of Hakewill's *Apology* in 1630 contained an account of a notable phlebotomy performed by Theodore Diodati, Charles's father. But Milton might have read the 1627 edition. Or the ideas might have been in the Cambridge air. Though it seems an academic exercise, this poem cannot be reliably dated.

Heu quam perpetuis erroribus acta fatiscit
Avia mens hominum, tenebrisque immersa
  profundis
Oedipodioniam volvit sub pectore noctem!
Quae vesana suis metiri facta deorum
5   Audet, et incisas leges adamante perenni
Assimilare suis, nulloque solubile saeclo
Consilium fati perituris alligat horis.
  Ergone marcescet sulcantibus obsita rugis
Naturae facies, et rerum publica mater
10 Omniparum contracta uterum sterilescet ab
  aevo?
Et se fassa senem male certis passibus ibit
Sidereum tremebunda caput? num tetra
  vetustas
Annorumque aeterna fames, squalorque
  situsque
Sidera vexabunt? An et insatiabile Tempus
15 Esuriet Caelum, rapietque in viscera patrem?
Heu, potuitne suas imprudens Iupiter arces
Hoc contra munisse nefas, et temporis isto
Exemisse malo, gyrosque dedisse perennes?
Ergo erit ut quandoque sono dilapsa tremendo
20 Convexi tabulata ruant, atque obvius ictu
Stridat uterque polus, superaque ut Olympius
  aula
Decidat, horribilisque retecta Gorgone Pallas.
Qualis in Aegaeam proles Iunonia Lemnon
Deturbata sacro cecidit de limine caeli.
25 Tu quoque Phoebe tui casus imitabere nati
Praecipiti curru, subitaque ferere ruina
Pronus, et extincta fumabit lampade Nereus,

Alas, driven by such enduring errors, the wayward mind of men grows weary and, immersed in deep shadows, revolves an Oedipodean night in the heart! Insanely it dares to measure the deeds of gods by its own, and to assimilate laws cut in eternal adamant to its own, and to bind fate's plan, unrevokable by any era, to the hours about to perish. Will therefore the face of Nature wither, covered with furrowing wrinkles, and the general mother[9] of things grow stale, shrunken from age in her all-parenting womb? And will she, showing that she is old, move badly with uncertain steps, shaking her starry head? Will foul old age and the years' eternal hunger and filth and rot trouble the stars? And will insatiable Time[14] devour Heaven, and thrust his father into his bowels? Alas, could improvident Jupiter not have fortified his own citadels against this outrage and exempted them from this evil of Time and given them eternal circuits? Therefore it will happen that the collapsed floor of the arched sky will fall with a great sound, and each pole, feeling the blow, will screech, and the Olympian will fall from his house above, and also Pallas,[22] horrifying with her Gorgon uncovered. In such a way did Juno's offspring,[23] hurled from the sacred threshold of heaven, fall to Aegean Lemnos. You too, Phoebus, will imitate the downfall of your son[25] in your headlong chariot, and you will be carried downward to sudden ruin, and Nereus will smoke from your quenched lamp and give out funereal hisses from the astonished sea. Then even the peak of lofty Haemus will shatter when its foundations are torn apart; and

9. **mater:** Ge, Earth, was the common ancestor of gods and men according to Hesiod, *Theog.* 117–63.

14. For centuries Chronos (Time) had been mistakenly identified with Cronos/Saturn, who devoured the children Rhea bore him (Panofsky 69–94).

22. Pallas Athena wears the Gorgon Medusa's head on her shield.

23. **proles Iunonia:** Vulcan, Juno's son; see *Elegy 7* 81–82n.

25. **tui . . . nati:** Phaethon. He lost control of his father's horses when driving the chariot of the sun; Zeus had to stop him with a thunderbolt.

Et dabit attonito feralia sibila ponto.
Tunc etiam aerei divulsis sedibus Haemi
30 Dissultabit apex, imoque allisa barathro
Terrebunt Stygium deiecta Ceraunia Ditem
In superos quibus usus erat, fraternaque bella.
　At Pater omnipotens fundatis fortius astris
Consuluit rerum summae, certoque peregit
35 Pondere fatorum lances, atque ordine summo
Singula perpetuum iussit servare tenorem.
Volvitur hinc lapsu mundi rota prima diurno,
Raptat et ambitos socia vertigine caelos.
Tardior haud solito Saturnus, et acer ut olim
40 Fulmineum rutilat cristata casside Mavors.
Floridus aeternum Phoebus iuvenile coruscat,
Nec fovet effoetas loca per declivia terras
Devexo temone Deus; sed semper amica
Luce potens eadem currit per signa rotarum,
45 Surgit odoratis pariter formosus ab Indis
Aethereum pecus albenti qui cogit Olympo
Mane vocans, et serus agens in pascua coeli;
Temporis et gemino dispertit regna colore.
Fulget, obitque vices alterno Delia cornu,
50 Caeruleumque ignem paribus complectitur
　　ulnis.
Nec variant elementa fidem, solitoque fragore
Lurida perculsas iaculantur fulmina rupes.
Nec per inane furit leviori murmure Corus,
Stringit et armiferos aequali horrore Gelonos
55 Trux Aquilo, spiratque hiemem, nimbosque
　　volutat.
Utque solet, Siculi diverberat ima Pelori
Rex maris, et rauca circumstrepit aequora concha
Oceani tubicen, nec vasta mole minorem

the uprooted Ceraunian moun-
tains, which had been used
against the gods, and fraternal
war, cast into the depths of the
underworld, will terrify Stygian
Dis. But the omnipotent father,
having set the stars more strongly
in their place,[33] took care con-
cerning the sum of things, and
poised fate's scales with a sure
weight, and commanded each
thing to keep a perpetual move-
ment within a supreme order.
Hence the first wheel of the uni-
verse turns on a daily cycle,[37]
and it speeds the heavenly sphere
with an allied rotation. Saturn is
no slower than his custom, and,
as fiercely as ever, Mars flashes
red lightning from his crested
helmet. Phoebus gleams in the
flower of eternal youth; the god
does not warm the exhausted
earth from a chariot steered
downward through the sloping
regions but, always powerful with
a friendly light, drives through
the same wheel tracks. He rises
just as beautiful from the per-
fumed Indies who, summoning
the dawn, gathers the eternal
herd into whitening Olympus
and, driving them out later into
the pastures of heaven, divides
Time's kingdom into two colors;
and Delia[49] shines and dies by
turns with alternating horns, and
embraces the blue fire in the
same arms. Nor do the elements
break faith; lurid lightning
smashes the stricken rocks with
its usual crash. Nor does Corus[53]
rage through the empty air with a
lighter roar, and fierce Aquilo[55]
confines the armed Gelonians
with the same shuddering, and
breathes forth winter, and tum-
bles the clouds. As he's used to,
the king of the sea batters the
base of Sicilian Pelorus, and
Ocean's trumpeter[58] surrounds
the sea with the sound of a rau-
cous conch shell, nor do the

33. The passage echoes Ovid, *Met.* 2.300, where
Earth begs Jove to kill Phaethon in order to
prevent the world from being destroyed.
37. Milton turns from myths of a violent end to the
enduring order of the cosmos as imaged by the
Ptolemaic spheres.
49. **Delia:** Diana, moon goddess, born on the is-
land of Delos.
53. **Corus:** the northwest wind.
55. **Aquilo:** the northeast wind.
58. **tubicen:** Triton, Neptune's herald.

Aegaeona ferunt dorso Balearica cete.
60   Sed neque Terra tibi saecli vigor ille vetusti
     Priscus abest; servatque suum Narcissus
          odorem,
     Et puer ille suum tenet et puer ille decorem
     Phoebe tuusque et Cypri tuus, nec ditior olim
     Terra datum sceleri celavit montibus aurum
65   Conscia, vel sub aquis gemmas. Sic denique in
          aevum
     Ibit cunctarum series iustissima rerum,
     Donec flamma orbem populabitur ultima, late
     Circumplexa polos, et vasti culmina caeli,
     Ingentique rogo flagrabit machina mundi.

Balearic whales carry on their backs an Aegaeon[59] any less vast in bulk. And you, Earth, are not lacking in that ancient vigor of the old days, and Narcissus keeps his odor; and that boy of yours,[62] Phoebus, and that boy of yours, Cypris, keep their attractiveness, nor was it a wealthier Earth that once, for conscience, hid gold dedicated to crime in the mountains, or jewels under the waters. So, then, the very just course of all things will continue forever, until the last fire[67] devastates the world, broadly enveloping the poles and the summits of vast heaven, and the fabric of the universe blazes on a huge pyre.

59. **Aegaeona:** a giant monster known to gods as Briareos (*Il.* 1.403–4). See *PL* 1.199–201.
62. On Apollo and Hyacinthus, see *Fair Infant* 23–27n; Ovid relates that Venus turned Adonis into an anemone after he was killed by a boar (*Met.* 10.728–39).
67. 2 Pet. 3.10 provides biblical sanction for the idea of a final conflagration.

DE IDEA PLATONICA QUEMADMODEM ARISTOTELES INTELLEXIT
[*Of the Platonic Idea as understood by Aristotle*]

In a letter to his friend Alexander Gill dated July 2, 1628, Milton discusses some verses he has been writing for another student to recite in the philosophical disputation at the Cambridge Commencement (held the day before the letter is dated). Milton describes the *leviculas . . . nugas* (trivial jokes) in these lines, and Carey plausibly suggests that *De Idea* fits this characterization better than *Naturam non pati senium*.

The poem adopts the role of literal-minded Aristotelian so uncompromisingly that it becomes a satire of Aristotle as much as of Plato. Aristotle's main criticisms of the doctrine of ideas are found in *Metaphysics* 1.9, 7.8.

Dicite sacrorum praesides nemorum deae,
Tuque O noveni perbeata numinis
Memoria mater, quaeque in immenso procul
Antro recumbis otiosa Aeternitas,
5   Monumenta servans, et ratas leges Iovis,
Caelique fastos atque ephemeridas deum,
Quis ille primus cuius ex imagine
Natura sollers finxit humanum genus,
Aeternus, incorruptus, aequaevus polo,
10 Unusque et universus, exemplar Dei?
Haud ille Palladis gemellus innubae
Interna proles insidet menti Iovis;
Sed quamlibet natura sit communior,
Tamen seorsus extat ad morem unius,
15 Et, mira, certo stringitur spatio loci;
Seu sempiternus ille siderum comes
Caeli pererrat ordines decemplicis,
Citimumve terris incolit lunae globum:
Sive inter animas corpus adituras sedens
20 Obliviosas torpet ad Lethes aquas:
Sive in remota forte terraum plaga
Incedit ingens hominis archetypus gigas,
Et diis tremendus erigit celsum caput
Atlante maior portitore siderum.
25 Non cui profundum caecitas lumen dedit
Dircaeus augur vidit hunc alto sinu;
Non hunc silenti nocte Pleiones nepos
Vatum sagaci praepes ostendit choro;
Non hunc sacerdos novit Assyrius, licet
30 Longos vetusti commemoret atavos Nini,

Speak, goddesses[1] who preside over the sacred groves, and you, Memory,[3] most blessed mother of the nine divinities, and Eternity,[4] you who recline unbusied far away in a great cavern, guarding the records and the established laws of Jove, the calendar of heaven and the logbook of the gods: Who was that first being from whose image skillful Nature fashioned the human race—eternal, uncorrupted, as old as the sky, unique and universal, the pattern for God? He does not reside as a child inside the mind of Jove, as twin brother to unmarried Pallas; but although his nature is more general, still he exists separately, in the manner of an individual, and, amazingly, is confined within definite boundaries of space. Perhaps, eternal companion of the stars, he wanders through the ranks of the tenfold heavens, or he inhabits the globe of the moon, the one nearest to Earth; or, sitting among the souls waiting for a body,[19] he dozes beside the forgetful waters of Lethe; or maybe in a remote tract of the world, man's archetype walks as an immense giant, and, bigger than Atlas, lifter of the stars, he raises his lofty head to frighten the gods. The Dircaean augur,[26] to whom blindness gave profound illumination, did not see him in his deep heart; Pleione's swift grandson[27] did not display him to the wise chorus of bards in the silent night; the Assyrian priest[29] did not know him, though he remembered the lengthy ancestry of Ninus,[30] and primordial

1. The goddesses might be Diana and her nymphs, who attend at births and are associated with groves, or more probably the nine Muses.
3. **Memoria:** Mnemosyne, mother of the Muses.
4. The idea of a mysterious old man controlling events from a remote cave can be found in Claudian 22.424–40 and Boccaccio (who calls him Eternity) in *De Genealogiis Deorum* 1.2.
19. The doctrine of metempsychosis is found in *Phaedo* 70–72 and Vergil, *Aen.* 6.713–51.
26. **Dircaeus augur:** Tiresias, the blind Theban prophet.
27. **Pleiones nepos:** Mercury, grandson of Atlas and Pleione.
29. It is uncertain which Assyrian sage Milton has in mind.
30. **Nini:** Ninus, founder of the Assyrian monarchy.

Priscumque Belon, inclitumque Osiridem.
Non ille trino gloriosus nomine
Ter magnus Hermes (ut sit arcani sciens)
Talem reliquit Isidis cultoribus.
35   At tu perenne ruris Academi decus
(Haec monstra si tu primus induxti scholis)
Iam iam poetas urbis exules tuae
Revocabis, ipse fabulator maximus,
Aut institutor ipse migrabis foras.

Belus,[31] and famous Osiris. Nor did that glorious one with the triple name, Thrice Great Hermes[33] (even if he was knowledgeable about secret things), bequeath such a one to the worshipers of Isis. But you, enduring glory of the rustic Academy[35] (if you were the first to bring such monsters into the schools), now, now you, the greatest storyteller, will call back the poets banished from your city, or else you, its founder, will depart.

31. **Belon:** The Assyrian god Bel was called Baal by the Hebrews.
33. **Ter magnus Hermes:** On the tradition of "Hermes Trismegistus" see Yates 1–156.
35. **Academi decus:** Plato, who excluded poets from his ideal state (*Rep.* 10.595–607).

AD PATREM
[*To His Father*]

This poem cannot be securely dated but probably belongs to the decade of the 1630s, and likely to the first half of it.

Only two of Milton's poems, *To His Father* and *Fair Infant,* deal directly with his birth family, and the English elegy does not expressly acknowledge that the dead child was Milton's niece or its mother his sister.

In his prose works, Milton left two grateful accounts of the "ceaseless diligence and care of my father" (*MLM* 839; also 1090) in providing him with a first-rate education. Sincere gratitude is surely among the emotions in *To His Father.* But here, uniquely, we have evidence of a rift between Milton and his father on the key matter of his poetic vocation. For however long a time, whether a month or years, in whatever manner, whether jokingly or solemnly or with some of each, John Milton, Sr., expressed a desire that his son abandon poetry as a central ambition and turn to something more worldly and practical. The poem is one of the earliest of many self-defenses in Milton's work.

Nunc mea Pierios cupiam per pectora fontes
Irriguas torquere vias, totumque per ora
Volvere laxatum gemino de vertice rivum;
Ut tenues oblita sonos audacibus alis
5   Surgat in officium venerandi Musa parentis.
Hoc utcunque tibi gratum pater optime carmen

Now I would wish the Pierian fountains[1] to divert their watery channels into my heart, and the entire stream loosed from the twin peaks to pour through my mouth, so that the Muse, forgetting trivial songs, may rise on bold wings to the duty of reverencing my parent. However wel-

1. **Pierios . . . fontes:** Pieria was the birthplace of the Muses.

Exiguum meditatur opus, nec novimus ipsi
Aptius a nobis quae possint munera donis
Respondere tuis, quamvis nec maxima possint
10 Respondere tuis, nedum ut par gratia donis
Esse queat, vacuis quae redditur arida verbis.
Sed tamen haec nostros ostendit pagina census,
Et quod habemus opum charta numeravimus
    ista,
Quae mihi sunt nullae, nisi quas dedit aurea
    Clio
15 Quas mihi semoto somni peperere sub antro,
Et nemoris laureta sacri Parnassides umbrae.
    Nec tu vatis opus divinum despice carmen,
Quo nihil aethereos ortus, et semina caeli,
Nil magis humanam commendat origine
    mentem,
20 Sancta Prometheae retinens vestigia flammae.
Carmen amant superi, tremebundaque Tartara
    carmen
Ima ciere valet, divosque ligare profundos,
Et triplici duros Manes adamante coercet.
Carmine sepositi retegunt arcana futuri
25 Phoebades, et tremulae pallentes ora Sibyllae;
Carmina sacrificus sollennes pangit ad aras,
Aurea seu sternit motantem cornua taurum;
Seu cum fata sagax fumantibus abdita fibris
Consulit, et tepidis Parcam scrutatur in extis.
30 Nos etiam patrium tunc cum repetemus
    Olympum,
Aeternaeque morae stabunt immobilis aevi,
Ibimus auratis per caeli templa coronis,
Dulcia suaviloquo sociantes carmina plectro,
Astra quibus, geminique poli convexa sonabunt.

come to you, best father, she is devising this song, a slight work, and we ourselves do not know a more suitable offering in payment for your gifts, although the greatest offering could not repay your gifts, still less could arid thanks which is given in vain words be equal to your gifts. But still, this page shows our account, and we have numbered on this paper what wealth we have: of which I have none except what golden Clio[14] has given, which my sleep has spawned in a remote cavern, and the laurel groves in the sacred wood, the shades of Parnassus. But do not look down on the poet's work, divine song; nothing more commends our celestial origins and heavenly seeds, nothing, because of its origin, more commends the human mind, keeping the sacred traces of Promethean fire.[20] The gods love song, song has power to stir the shuddering depths of Tartarus and bind the gods of the deep, and constricts the harsh shades with threefold adamant. With song the priestesses of Phoebus and the trembling, pale-mouthed Sibyls[25] uncover the secrets of the distant future; the sacrificing priest crafts songs at the solemn altar, whether he slays a bull tossing its golden horns, or when he skillfully reads the fates hidden in the smoking organs and seeks out Parca in the warm entrails. And when we return to our fatherland Olympus, and the eternal intervals of unmoving time stand still, we will go with golden crowns through the temples of heaven,[32] wedding sweet songs to the smooth-voiced lyre, with which the stars and the vaults of both poles will sound.

14. **Clio:** in Roman times the Muse of history.
20. Prometheus, who stole fire from heaven and gave it to man. "Prometheus clearly and expressly signifies Providence" (Bacon, *Wisdom of the Ancients,* "Prometheus").
25. **Phoebades:** priestesses of Apollo; **Sibyllae:** prophetesses, such as the Cumaean sibyl, who guides Aeneas through the underworld in *Aen. 6.*
32. The gold crowns come from Rev. 4.4, the harps from 5.8.

35 Spiritus et rapidos qui circinat igneus orbes
Nunc quoque sidereis intercinit ipse choreis
Immortale melos, et inenarrabile carmen;
Torrida dum rutilus compescit sibila Serpens,
Demissoque ferox gladio mansuescit Orion;
40 Stellarum nec sentit onus Maurusius Atlas.
Carmina regales epulas ornare solebant,
Cum nondum luxus, vastaeque immensa vorago
Nota gulae, et modico spumabat coena Lyaeo.
Tum de more sedens festa ad convivia vates,
45 Aesculea intonsos redimitus ab arbore crines,
Heroumque actus, imitandaque gesta canebat,
Et Chaos, et positi late fundamina mundi,
Reptantesque deos, et alentes numina glandes,
Et nondum Aetnaeo quaesitum fulmen ab antro.
50 Denique quid vocis modulamen inane iuvabit,
Verborum sensusque vacans, numerique
loquacis?
Silvestres decet iste choros, non Orphea, cantus,
Qui tenuit fluvios et quercubus addidit aures
Carmine, non cithara, simulachraque functa
canendo
55 Compulit in lacrimas: habet has a carmine
laudes.
Nec tu perge precor sacras contemnere Musas,
Nec vanas inopesque puta, quarum ipse peritus
Munere, mille sonos numeros componis ad
aptos,
Millibus et vocem modulis variare canoram
60 Doctus, Arionii merito sis nominis haeres.
Nunc tibi quid mirum, si me genuisse poetam
Contigerit, charo si tam prope sanguine iuncti
Cognatas artes, studiumque affine sequamur:
Ipse volens Phoebus se dispertire duobus,
65 Altera dona mihi, dedit altera dona parenti,

The fiery spirit[35] which circles the rapid spheres is itself now singing immortal music and indescribable song among the starry choirs, while the ruddy serpent[38] suppresses his scorching hisses, and fierce Orion, dropping his sword, grows calm, and Mauretanian Atlas does not feel the weight of the stars. Songs used to adorn regal banquets, when luxury and the huge maw of endless gluttony were not yet known and dinner foamed with Lyaeus in moderation. Then, by custom, the bard, sitting at the festive banquet, his uncut hair crowned with oak leaves, sang of the actions of heroes, deeds to be imitated, and of chaos and the broad foundations on which the universe is set, and of deities crawling and of acorns[48] feeding gods, and of the thunderbolt not yet sought from the cave of Etna. In the end, what good is an empty modulation of the voice, lacking words and sense and expressive meter? That is fitting for woodland choruses, not for Orpheus's music, which entranced streams and gave ears to oak trees with his song, not with his lyre, and brought dead phantoms to tears with his singing; he earned his praises from song. Do not, I pray, keep scorning the sacred Muses, and do not think them vain and useless, you who skilled in their gift set a thousand songs to fit rhythm, having learned to vary the melodious voice in a thousand tunes, so as to be a worthy heir of Arion's[60] name. Why should it surprise you if it happened I was begotten a poet—if, so closely joined to you by dear blood, we pursued related arts and kindred study? Phoebus,[64] wishing to distribute himself between two, gave one gift to me, the other to my parent, and we

35. Milton appears to be saying that his own *spiritus* leaves his body to join the high songs sung at the topmost rung of the universe. Carey 1964 cites Cicero's *Somnium Scipionis* and Macrobius's commentary on it.

38. **Serpens:** the constellation of the Serpent.

48. **glandes:** Ovid says that men in the Golden Age, before there was agriculture, ate acorns from Jove's tree (*Met.* 1.106).

60. **Arionii:** Arion charmed a dolphin with his lyre (Herodotus 1.23–24).

64. Apollo is the god of both music and poetry.

Dividuumque deum genitorque puerque
tenemus.
Tu tamen ut simules teneras odisse Camenas,
Non odisse reor, neque enim, pater, ire iubebas
Qua via lata patet, qua pronior area lucri,
70   Certaque condendi fulget spes aurea nummi;
Nec rapis ad leges, male custoditaque gentis
Iura, nec insulsis damnas clamoribus aures.
Sed magis excultam cupiens ditescere mentem,
Me procul urbano strepitu, secessibus altis
75   Abductum Aoniae iucunda per otia ripae,
Phoebaeo lateri comitem sinis ire beatum.
Officium chari taceo commune parentis,
Me poscunt maiora; tuo pater optime sumptu
Cum mihi Romuleae patuit facundia linguae,
80   Et Latii veneres, et quae Iovis ora decebant
Grandia magniloquis elata vocabula Graiis,
Addere suasisti quos iactat Gallia flores,
Et quam degeneri novus Italus ore loquelam
Fundit, Barbaricos testatus voce tumultus,
85   Quaeque Palaestinus loquitur mysteria vates.
Denique quicquid habet caelum, subiectaque
coelo
Terra parens, terraeque et coelo interfluus aer,
Quicquid et unda tegit, pontique agitabile
marmor,
Per te nosse licet, per te, si nosse libebit.
90   Dimotaque venit spectanda scientia nube,
Nudaque conspicuos inclinat ad oscula vultus,
Ni fugisse velim, ni sit libasse molestum.
   I nunc, confer opes quisquis malesanus avitas
Austriaci gazas, Peruanaque regna praeoptas.

75. **Aoniae . . . ripae:** The fountains of Aganippe
and Hippocrene near Mount Helicon in Aonia
(the Muses were termed Aonides) inspired
those who drank from them.
94. **Peruanaque regna:** Spain conquered gold-
rich Peru in the 1530s.

possess the divided god as father
and son. Though you pretend to
have hated the soft Muses, I do
not think you did, for you did
not, father, order me to go where
the broad way lies open, where
the field of wealth is more invit-
ing, and confident, golden hope
of making money shines out; nor
do you hurry me off to law and
the nation's badly kept statutes,
nor do you condemn my ears to
that ridiculous clamor. But, wish-
ing to enrich my cultivated mind,
you allow me, far removed from
the city's noise, in deep seclu-
sion, to pass through the joyful
leisure of the Aonian banks,[75] a
happy comrade by the side of
Phoebus. I say nothing about the
common office of a loving parent;
greater things summon me.
When, best father, at your ex-
pense the eloquence of the
tongue of Romulus was laid open
to me, the beauties of Latin and
the grand, exalted words of the
magniloquent Greeks, which
suited the mouth of Jove, you
persuaded me to add those flow-
ers of which France boasts, and
the speech that the new Italian
pours forth from a degenerate
mouth, attesting with his voice
the barbarian incursions, and the
mysteries that the Palestinian
prophet speaks. Finally, whatever
heaven holds, and parental earth
that lies under heaven, and the
air flowing between earth and
heaven, and whatever the waves
and the moving marble of the sea
cover, because of you I can learn,
because of you, if I want to learn
it. With the cloud moved away,
Science comes to be viewed, and
naked bends her illustrious face
to be kissed, unless I wish to flee,
unless it be unappealing to taste.
Go now, accumulate wealth,
whoever insanely prefers the
ancestral jewels of Austria and
the kingdoms of Peru.[94] What

95   Quae potuit maiora pater tribuisse, vel ipse
      Iupiter, excepto, donasset ut omnia, coelo?
      Non potiora dedit, quamvis et tuta fuissent,
      Publica qui iuveni commisit lumina nato
      Atque Hyperionios currus, et fraena diei,
100   Et circum undantem radiata luce tiaram.
      Ergo ego iam doctae pars quamlibet ima
         catervae
      Victrices hederas inter, laurosque sedebo;
      Iamque nec obscurus populo miscebor inerti,
      Vitabuntque oculos vestigia nostra profanos.
105   Este procul vigiles curae, procul este querelae,
      Invidiaeque acies transverso tortilis hirquo;
      Saeva nec anguiferos extende Calumnia rictus;
      In me triste nihil foedissima turba potestis,
      Nec vestri sum iuris ego; securaque tutus
110   Pectora, vipereo gradiar sublimis ab ictu.
        At tibi, care pater, postquam non aequa
         merenti
      Posse referre datur, nec dona rependere factis,
      Sit memorasse satis, repetitaque munera grato
      Percensere animo, fidaeque reponere menti.
115   Et vos, O nostri, iuvenilia carmina, lusus,
      Si modo perpetuos sperare audebitis annos,
      Et domini superesse rogo, lucemque tueri,
      Nec spisso rapient oblivia nigra sub Orco,
      Forsitan has laudes, decantatumque parentis
120   Nomen, ad exemplum, sero servabitis aevo.

99. **Hyperionios currus:** Hyperion, father of He-
lios, often stands for the sun itself.
118. **Orco:** Hades.

greater things could a father have bestowed, even if Jove himself had given all (with the exception of heaven)? He did not give more precious gifts, even if they had been given safely, who entrusted to his young son the common light and Hyperion's chariot[99] and the reins of day and the tiara billowing with radiant light. Therefore I, already part, though at the lowest rank, of the learned company, will sit among the triumphant ivies and laurels, and now I will no longer mingle in obscurity with the witless mob, and our footsteps will shun profane eyes. Be far away, wide-eyed worries, be far away, complaints and invidious looks twisted askance like a goat; do not reach your snake-bearing jaws toward me, savage Calumny. The foul gang of you can do nothing painful to me, nor am I under your law; safe in an untroubled heart, I shall walk above the viperous stroke. But for you, dear father, since I cannot repay you equally to your deserving or match gifts with deeds, let it be enough to have memorialized them, to count up your repeated favors with a grateful spirit, and to secure them in a faithful mind. And you, O our playthings, poems of our youth, if only you dare hope for endless years and to outlive your master's pyre and see the light, and black oblivion does not hurry you beneath crowded Orcus,[118] perhaps these praises and this singing of my father's name you will preserve as an example for a later age.

PSALM 114

In a 1634 letter to his friend Alexander Gill, who had himself published Latin and Greek poetry, Milton mentions his recent translation of a psalm into Greek heroic verse and notes that this was his first attempt to write Greek poetry since leaving school (Yale 1:321–22). This is almost certainly the work in question.

⸻

Ἰσραὴλ ὅτε παῖδες, ὅτ᾽ ἀγλαὰ φῦλ᾽ Ἰακώβου
Αἰγύπτιον λίπε δῆμον, ἀπεχθέα βαρβαρόφωνον,
Δὴ τότε μοῦνον ἔην ὅσιον γένος υἶες Ἰούδα.
Ἐν δὲ θεὸς λαοῖσι μέγα κρείων βασίλευεν.
5 Εἶδε καὶ ἐντροπάδην φύγαδ᾽ ἐρρώησε θάλασσα
Κύματι εἰλυμένη ῥοθίῳ, ὁ δ᾽ ἄρ᾽ ἐστυφελίχθη
Ἱρὸς Ἰορδάνης ποτὶ ἀργυροειδέα πηγήν.
Ἐκ δ᾽ ὄρεα σκαρθμοῖσιν ἀπειρέσια κλονέοντο,
Ὡς κριοὶ σφριγόωντες ἐϋτραφερῷ ἐν ἀλωῇ.
10 Βαιότεραι δ᾽ ἅμα πᾶσαι ἀνασκίρτησαν ἐρίπναι,
Οἷα παραὶ σύριγγι φίλη ὑπὸ μητέρι ἄρνες.
Τίπτε σύ γ᾽ αἰνὰ θάλασσα πέλωρ φυγάδ᾽ ἐρρώησας
Κύματι εἰλυμένη ῥοθίῳ; τί δ᾽ ἄρ᾽ ἐστυφελίχθης
Ἱρὸς Ἰορδάνη ποτὶ ἀργυροειδέα πηγήν;
15 Τίπτ᾽ ὄρεα σκαρθμοῖσιν ἀπειρέσια κλονέεσθε
Ὡς κριοὶ σφριγόωντες ἐϋτραφερῷ ἐν ἀλωῇ;
Βαιότεραι τί δ᾽ ἄρ᾽ ὕμμες ἀνασκιρτήσατ᾽ ἐρίπναι,
Οἷα παραὶ σύριγγι φίλη ὑπὸ μητέρι ἄρνες;
Σείεο γαῖα τρέουσα θεὸν μεγάλ᾽ ἐκτυπέοντα
20 Γαῖα θεὸν τρείουσ᾽ ὕπατον σέβας Ἰσσακίδαο
Ὅς τε καὶ ἐκ σπιλάδων ποταμοὺς χέε
    μορμύροντας,
Κρήνην τ᾽ ἀέναον πέτρης ἀπὸ δακρυοέσσης.

When the children of Israel, when the glorious tribes of Jacob left the hateful, barbarian-tongued country of Egypt, then indeed the sons of Judah were the only holy nation; God ruled the people with great power. The sea knew it and rushed headlong in flight, wrapped in a roaring wave, and sacred Jordan was thrust back to its silvery source. Limitless mountains ran bounding out, like lusty rams in a luxurious garden. At the same time, all the lower peaks skipped like lambs to the sound of a panpipe around their dear mother. Why, you dread monster sea, did you rush in flight, wrapped in a roaring wave? Why, you sacred Jordan, were you thrust back to your silvery source? Why, you limitless mountains, did you run bounding out like lusty rams in a luxurious garden? Why, you lower peaks, did you skip like lambs to the sound of a panpipe around their dear mother? Quake, earth, in fear of the great-thundering God—in fear, earth, of God, the highest majesty of the children of Isaac, who pours the raging rivers forth from the rocks and the everflowing spring from the weeping stone.

AD SALSILLUM POETAM ROMANUM
AEGROTANTEM. SCAZONTES

[*To Salzilli, the Roman poet, being ill. Scazons*]

Little is known of Giovanni Salzilli. Milton met him in Rome, probably during his first visit, in October–November 1638. Salzilli wrote a brief Latin poem in which he prefers Milton to Homer, Vergil, and Tasso. Milton printed the work, along with other commendatory pieces, as a preface to his Latin poems in 1645 and alludes to its flattery at the beginning of *To Salzilli.*

The poem is written in scazons, or "limping" iambic lines that end in a spondee or trochee.

O Musa gressum quae volens trahis claudum,
Vulcanioque tarda gaudes incessu,
Nec sentis illud in loco minus gratum,
Quam cum decentes flava Deiope suras
5   Alternat aureum ante Iunonis lectum,
Adesdum et haec s'is verba pauca Salsillo
Refer, camena nostra cui tantum est cordi,
Quamque ille magnis praetulit immerito divis.
Haec ergo alumnus ille Londini Milto,
10   Diebus hisce qui suum linquens nidum
Polique tractum (pessimus ubi ventorum,
Insanientis impotensque pulmonis
Pernix anhela sub Iove exercet flabra),
Venit feraces Itali soli ad glebas,
15   Visum superba cognitas urbes fama
Virosque doctaeque indolem iuventutis,
Tibi optat idem hic fausta multa Salsille,
Habitumque fesso corpori penitus sanum;
Cui nunc profunda bilis infestat renes,
20   Praecordiisque fixa damnosum spirat.
Nec id pepercit impia quod tu Romano
Tam cultus ore Lesbium condis melos.
O dulce divum munus, O Salus Hebes

O Muse who willingly drags a limping gait and enjoys moving slow with Vulcan's walk,[2] nor thinks this any less welcome in its place than when blond Dëiope[4] dances on her well-formed legs in front of Juno's golden bed: come and, if you are willing, take these few words to Salzilli, to whom our poetry is so dear that he undeservedly prefers it to the divine greats. This, therefore, from Milton, child of London, who lately leaving his nest and portion of the sky (where the worst of winds, unable to control its crazed lungs, blows breathless gusts around rapidly under Jove), comes to the fertile earth of Italy's soil, to see its renowned cities of proud fame, its men and the excellence of its learned youth: this same man wishes you much happiness, Salzilli, and good health throughout your wearied body—in which excessive bile now plagues the kidneys and, fixed in the chest, breathes forth poison; nor in its impiety has it spared you for composing with such cultivation Lesbian lyrics[22] for a Roman mouth. O sweet gift of the gods, O health, sister of Hebe![23] and you, Phoe-

2. Vulcan's fall from heaven left him lame. See *El 7* 81n.

4. Juno promised Aeolus the nymph Dëiope as a reward for sending a storm upon the Trojan fleet.

22. Alcaeus and Sappho were natives of Lesbos.

23. Hebe is the goddess of youth.

Germana! Tuque Phoebe morborum terror
25   Pythone caeso, sive tu magis Paean
Libenter audis, hic tuus sacerdos est.
Querceta Fauni, vosque rore vinoso
Colles benigni, mitis Evandri sedes,
Siquid salubre vallibus frondet vestris,
30   Levamen aegro ferte certatim vati.
Sic ille charis redditus rursum Musis
Vicina dulci prata mulcebit cantu.
Ipse inter atros emirabitur lucos
Numa, ubi beatum degit otium aeternum,
35   Suam reclivis semper Aegeriam spectans.
Tumidusque et ipse Tibris hinc delinitus
Spei favebit annuae colonorum:
Nec in sepulchris ibit obsessum reges
Nimium sinistro laxus irruens loro;
40   Sed frena melius temperabit undarum,
Adusque curvi salsa regna Portumni.

bus, the terror of diseases since the slaying of Python,[25] or if you prefer to be called Paean: this man is your priest. Oak forests of Faunus,[27] and hills rich with dew that smells of wine, gentle seat of Evander,[28] if anything medicinal flourishes in your valleys, bear that comfort quickly to the sick bard. Restored again thus to his dear muses, he will soothe the neighboring meadows with his sweet song. Numa[34] himself will wonder among the dark groves, where he spends his blessed eternal leisure, reclining and gazing forever on his Egeria. And charmed this way, even swollen Tiber[36] will be kind to the farmers' yearly hope; nor, running with the left rein too loose, will he go to besiege kings in their tombs, but will manage the waves' harness better, as far as the salty kingdom of curved Portumnus.

25. **Pythone caeso:** Python was a monstrous serpent slain by Apollo, who is the god of healing as well as of poetry and music.

27. **Fauni:** Faunus, Roman god of woods, identified with Pan.

28. **Evandri sedes:** Evander founded the city of Pallanteum on the banks of the Tiber where Rome was to stand.

34. **Numa:** Numa, the second of Rome's legendary kings, learned wisdom from the water nymph Egeria.

36. Horace describes how the Tiber flooded *monumenta regis* (*Odes* 1.2.15).

MANSO
[*Mansus*]

Giovanni Battista Manso (c. 1560–1645) was a patron of the arts who had befriended two notable Italian poets, Torquato Tasso and Giambattista Marino. His services to literature overshadowed his own work, which included poetry, philosophical dialogues, and a *Life of Tasso*. Milton met Manso in Naples in 1638 and later remembered him as "a man of high rank and influence, to whom the famous Italian poet, Torquato Tasso, dedicated his work on friendship. As long as I was there I found him a very true friend. He personally conducted me through the various quarters of the city and the Viceregal Court, and more than once came to my lodgings to call. When I was leaving he gravely apologized because even though he had especially wished to show me many more attentions, he could not do so in that city, since I was unwilling to be circumspect in regard to religion" (*MLM* 1092). Milton certainly means to establish in this passage that the future public opponent of Catholicism and apologist of the English Revolution was already on display in his reckless outspokenness in Italy, and one might expect a certain degree of exaggeration. But the Latin couplet by Manso that Milton printed in 1645 among the poems prefacing his Latin verse also calls attention to his Protestantism: "If your religious persuasions were equal to your mind, your handsome figure, your fame, your face, and your manners, then—good heavens!—you would be an angel, not an Englishman." When he invented the character of Abdiel in *Paradise Lost*, one might reply, Milton found a way to be both.

Manso has often been judged one of the best of Milton's Latin pieces.

Ioannes Baptista Mansus Marchio Villensis vir ingenii laude, tum literarum studio, nec non et bellica virtute apud Italos clarus in primis est. Ad quem Torquati Tassi dialogus extat de Amicitia scriptus; erat enim Tassi amicissimus; ab quo etiam inter Campaniae principes celebratur, in illo poemate cui titulus *Gerusalemme conquistata, lib. 20.*

> Fra cavalier magnanimi, è cortesi
> Risplende il Manso . . .

Is authorem Neapoli commorantem summa benevolentia prosecutus est, multaque ei detulit humanitatis officia. Ad hunc itaque hospes ille antequam ab ea urbe discederet, ut ne ingratum se ostenderet, hoc carmen misit.

Haec quoque Manse tuae meditantur carmina laudi
Pierides, tibi Manse choro notissime Phoebi,
Quandoquidem ille alium haud aequo est
    dignatus honore
Post Galli cineres, et Maecenatis Hetrusci.
5   Tu quoque si nostrae tantum valet aura
    Camenae,

Giovanni Battista Manso, Marquis of Villa, is among the most famous men in Italy because of his reputation for intelligence, as well as his devotion to literature and his courage in war. There is a dialogue of Torquato Tasso's, "On Friendship," written to him; for he was a very close friend of Tasso's, who celebrated him among the princes of Campania in his poem entitled "Jerusalem Conquered," Book 20: "Among the great-hearted and courtly knights Manso shines out . . ." He attended the author with great benevolence while he was staying in Naples, and did him many kind services. So, before he left that city, in order not to seem ungrateful as a guest, he sent him this poem.

Manso, the Pierians[2] also[1] rehearse this poem in your praise—for you, Manso, well known to Phoebus's choir, inasmuch as no one else is worthy of equal honor since the funerals of Gallus and Etruscan Maecenas.[4] You too, if the breath of our Muse has such power, will sit

1. **quoque:** Many other poems had been addressed to Manso.
2. **Pierides:** the Muses.
4. **Galli:** Cornelius Gallus, an elegiac poet and friend to Vergil; **Maecenatis:** Maecenas, patron of Vergil, Horace, and other poets.

Victrices hederas inter, laurosque sedebis.
Te pridem magno felix concordia Tasso
Iunxit, et aeternis inscripsit nomina chartis.
Mox tibi dulciloquum non inscia Musa
    Marinum
10 Tradidit; ille tuum dici se gaudet alumnum,
Dum canit Assyrios divum prolixus amores;
Mollis et Ausonias stupefecit carmine nymphas.
Ille itidem moriens tibi soli debita vates
Ossa, tibi soli supremaque vota reliquit.
15 Nec manes pietas tua chara fefellit amici;
Vidimus arridentem operoso ex aere poetam.
Nec satis hoc visum est in utrumque, et nec pia
    cessant
Officia in tumulo; cupis integros rapere Orco,
Qua potes, atque avidas Parcarum eludere leges:
20 Amborum genus, et varia sub sorte peractam
Describis vitam, moresque, et dona Minervae;
Aemulus illius Mycalen qui natus ad altam
Rettulit Aeolii vitam facundus Homeri.
Ergo ego te Clius et magni nomine Phoebi
25 Manse pater, iubeo longum salvere per aevum
Missus Hyperboreo iuvenis peregrinus ab axe.
Nec tu longinquam bonus aspernabere Musam,
Quae nuper gelida vix enutrita sub Arcto
Imprudens Italas ausa est volitare per urbes.
30 Nos etiam in nostro modulantes flumine cygnos
Credimus obscuras noctis sensisse per umbras,
Qua Thamesis late puris argenteus urnis
Oceani glaucos perfundit gurgite crines.
Quin et in has quondam pervenit Tityrus oras.

among the victorious ivy and laurels.[6] Happy concord once bound you to the great Tasso and wrote your names on eternal pages. Soon the knowing Muse entrusted sweet-voiced Marino[9] to you, and he rejoices to be called your student while he sings at length the Assyrian love story of the gods; and smoothly he struck the Italian nymphs dumb with his song. Accordingly, when he died he left his bones, as was fated, to you alone,[13] left his final wishes to you alone. Nor did your loving piety disappoint your friend's shade; we have seen the smiling poet in well-worked bronze. Nor did this seem enough for either, and your pious offices do not end at the grave; you long to snatch them intact away from Orcus, where you can, and escape the hungry laws of the Parcae; you are writing about their lineage, and life lived with mixed luck, and their habits, and the gifts of Minerva: emulating him who, born near lofty Mycale,[22] eloquently wrote the life of Aeolian Homer. Therefore, Father Manso, in the name of Clio and great Phoebus, I, a young man sent as a pilgrim from the Hyperborean[26] sky, order you to be healthy throughout a long life. Nor in your goodness will you spurn a distant Muse who, barely nourished of late under the frigid Bear, imprudently dares to fly through the cities of Italy. We also believe that we have heard swans[30] singing in our river in the dark shadows of night, where silver Thames pours forth her blue-gray hair broadly from pure urns in Ocean's stream. Why, Tityrus[34] once visited these

6. See *To His Father* 102. The ivy and laurel are emblematic of poetry or poetic distinction.

9. **Marinum:** The Italian poet Giambattista Marino (1569–1625), whose *L'Adone* (1623) tells of Venus and Adonis.

13. Milton suggests that Manso took charge of burying Marino and erecting his monument, but we have no corroborating evidence. Nor do we have Manso's biography of Marino.

22. The *Life of Homer* is no longer attributed to Herodotus.

26. **Hyperboreo:** Diodorus Siculus 2.47.1 placed the island of the Hyperboreans in the ocean beyond Gaul.

30. **cygnos:** swans (i.e., poets), as in Jonson calling Shakespeare the "Sweet Swan of Avon."

34. **Tityrus:** Spenser's name for Chaucer (*SC*, "February" 92).

35   Sed neque nos genus incultum, nec inutile
         Phoebo,
      Qua plaga septeno mundi sulcata Trione
      Brumalem patitur longa sub nocte Booten.
      Nos etiam colimus Phoebum, nos munera
         Phoebo
      Flaventes spicas, et lutea mala canistris,
40   Halantemque crocum (perhibet nisi vana
         vetustas)
      Misimus, et lectas Druidum de gente choreas.
      (Gens Druides antiqua sacris operata deorum
      Heroum laudes imitandaque gesta canebant.)
      Hinc quoties festo cingunt altaria cantu
45   Delo in herbosa Graiae de more puellae
      Carminibus laetis memorant Corineida Loxo,
      Fatidicamque Upin, cum flavicoma Hecaerge,
      Nuda Caledonio variatas pectora fuco.
      Fortunate senex, ergo quacunque per orbem
50   Torquati decus, et nomen celebrabitur ingens,
      Claraque perpetui succrescet fama Marini,
      Tu quoque in ora frequens venies plausumque
         virorum,
      Et parili carpes iter immortale volatu.
      Dicetur tum sponte tuos habitasse penates
55   Cynthius, et famulas venisse ad limina Musas:
      At non sponte domum tamen idem, et regis
         adivit
      Rura Pheretiadae caelo fugitivus Apollo;
      Ille licet magnum Alciden susceperat hospes;
      Tantum ubi clamosos placuit vitare bubulcos,
60   Nobile mansueti cessit Chironis in antrum,
      Irriguos inter saltus frondosaque tecta

---

36. Ursa Major has seven prominent stars and was
    often compared to oxen yoked to a wagon.
38. Callimachus relates that the Hyperborean
    maidens Loxo, Upis, and Hecaerge brought of-
    ferings of corn to Apollo and Artemis at Delos
    (*Hymn* 4.283–99).
42. See *Lyc* 53n on Druids and Bards.
46. **Corineida:** daughter of Corineus, who accom-
    panied the Trojan Brutus to Britain and came
    to govern Cornwall. See Geoffrey of Mon-
    mouth, *History of Britain* 1.12.
55. **Cynthius:** Apollo, born on Mount Cynthus.
58. See *Sonnet 23* 2n.
60. **Chironis:** Chiron the centaur, tutor of many
    heroes.

shores. But we are not an uncul-
tured nation, or useless to Phoe-
bus, who endure wintry Boötes in
the long night in that part of the
world furrowed by the sevenfold
Triones.[36] We also cultivate
Phoebus, we have sent Phoebus
offerings:[38] golden grain, and red
apples in baskets, and the fra-
grant crocus (unless tradition has
it wrong), and choice choirs from
the race of Druids. (The Druids,
an ancient race engaged in the
rituals of the gods,[42] sang the
praises and exemplary deeds of
heroes.) Hence whenever, ac-
cording to custom, Greek girls
surround the altars on grassy
Delos with festive singing, they
commemorate with happy songs
Corineus's daughter Loxo[46] and
prophetic Upis, along with
golden-haired Hecaerge, who
adorn their naked breasts with
Caledonian dye. Lucky old man,
since wherever throughout the
world the glory of Torquato and
his great name are celebrated,
and the bright fame of undying
Marino grows, you too will come
often to the lips and the applause
of men, and will take an immor-
tal journey with equal flight. It
will be said that Cynthius[55] of his
own free will dwelt with your
hearth gods, and the Muses came
as servants to your doors; but not
of his own free will did that same
Apollo, a fugitive from heaven,
visit the farm of the king who was
Pheres's son, even though that
man had as a host taken in great
Alcides.[58] Whenever it pleased
him to get away from the noisy
plowmen, he retired to the noble
cave of gentle Chiron,[60] amid the
moist glades and leafy shelters by

Peneium prope rivum: ibi saepe sub ilice nigra
Ad citharae strepitum blanda prece victus amici
Exilii duros lenibat voce labores.
65 Tum neque ripa suo, barathro nec fixa sub imo
Saxa stetere loco; nutat Trachinia rupes,
Nec sentit solitas, immania pondera, silvas;
Emotaeque suis properant de collibus orni,
Mulcenturque novo maculosi carmine lynces.
70 Diis dilecte senex, te Iupiter aequus oportet
Nascentem, et miti lustrarit lumine Phoebus,
Atlantisque nepos; neque enim nisi charus ab
   ortu
Diis superis poterit magno favisse poetae.
Hinc longaeva tibi lento sub flore senectus
75 Vernat, et Aesonios lucratur vivida fusos,
Nondum deciduos servans tibi frontis honores,
Ingeniumque vigens, et adultum mentis
   acumen.
O mihi si mea sors talem concedat amicum,
Phoebaeos decorasse viros qui tam bene norit,
80 Si quando indigenas revocabo in carmina reges,
Arturumque etiam sub terris bella moventem;
Aut dicam invictae sociali foedere mensae,
Magnanimos Heroas, et (O modo spiritus adsit)
Frangam Saxonicas Britonum sub Marte
   phalanges.
85 Tandem ubi non tacitae permensus tempora
   vitae,
Annorumque satur cineri sua iura relinquam,
Ille mihi lecto madidis astaret ocellis,
Astanti sat erit si dicam sim tibi curae;
Ille meos artus liventi morte solutos,

the banks of Peneus; there often, under a black oak, yielding to his friend's gentle prayer, he eased the harsh labors of exile with his voice to the sound of his lute. Then neither the riverbanks nor the boulders lodged in the bottom of the abyss stayed in their place; the Trachinian cliff nodded and did not feel the immense weight of its accustomed forest, and the ash trees were moved and hurried down from their hills, and the spotted lynxes were soothed by the novel song. Old man dear to the gods, Jupiter must have been favorable at your birth, and Phoebus looked at you with kind eyes, and also Atlas's grandson;[72] for unless dear to the heavenly gods from the start, one could not have befriended a great poet. That is why your long old age is a springtime of late-blooming flowers, and in its vigor gains Aesonian[75] spindles, still preserving the not yet decaying honors of your face,[76] lively in intellect and mature sharpness of mind. O, may my luck provide me with such a friend who knows well how to honor Phoebus's men, if ever I recall our native kings into song,[80] and Arthur, waging war even under the earth, or tell of the great-hearted heroes of the table made unconquerable by their joint oath, and (O may the spirit only be there) smash the Saxon phalanxes with British warfare. When at last I have measured out the time of a

72. **nepos:** Mercury, god of eloquence.
75. **Aesonios:** See *El 2* 7–8n.
76. There is evidence that Manso delighted his friends by removing his wig and displaying his baldness (Masson 1965, 1:813).
80–84. These lines are the earliest statement of Milton's interest in writing an Arthurian epic. See also *Damon* 162–71. Arthur does not appear in the list of twenty-eight subjects from British history that Milton set down in the *CMS* as possible material for an epic poem.

90 Curaret parva componi molliter urna.
Forsitan et nostros ducat de marmore vultus,
Nectens aut Paphia myrti aut Parnasside lauri
Fronde comas, at ego secura pace quiescam.
Tum quoque, si qua fides, si praemia certa
    bonorum,
95 Ipse ego caelicolum semotus in aethera divum,
Quo labor et mens pura vehunt, atque ignea
    virtus
Secreti haec aliqua mundi de parte videbo
(Quantum fata sinunt), et tota mente serenum
Ridens purpureo suffundar lumine vultus,
100 Et simul aethereo plaudam mihi laetus Olympo.

92. **Paphia:** Paphos, where there was a temple of
Venus, to whom the myrtle was sacred. After
Daphne was transformed into a laurel, Apollo
entwined laurel in his hair, bow, quiver, and
lyre.

life that has not been silent, and
full of years I leave to the ashes
their due, he would stand by my
bed with moist eyes, and it will be
enough if I say to him standing
there, "Let me be in your care."
My limbs, unstrung by livid
death, he would take care to
compose in a small urn; and per-
haps he might transpose my fea-
tures into marble, binding the
hair with a Paphian wreath[92] of
myrtle or a Parnassian one of
laurel, and I will rest in secure
peace. Then also, if any faith, if
any reward for good men is cer-
tain, I, far away in the ether of the
divine gods, where work and a
pure mind and fiery virtue lead,
will watch these things from
some part of the secret world (as
much as the Fates permit), and
laughing serenely with my whole
mind, I will be suffused in my
face with ruddy light and at the
same time applaud myself in
happiness on ethereal Olympus.

EPITAPH FOR DAMON

Milton's closest friend, Charles Diodati, died in England in August 1638 while
Milton was traveling in Italy. The poem itself (ll. 13–17) tells us that it was writ-
ten soon after his return to England in the summer of 1639. One copy survives
of a small private printing in 1640.

Epitaphium Damonis is in obvious ways a Latin *Lycidas.* Both are pastoral ele-
gies profoundly knowledgeable about the history of the form, both were occa-
sioned by the deaths of young men, and both rise to consoling visions of the
dead shepherds being welcomed into Heaven. But all the similarities point to
differences. Latin brings the *Epitaphium* closer to the pastoral tradition, as does
the refrain based on the final line of Vergil's final eclogue. Milton genuinely
loved Diodati, whereas he seems to have been at best a distant acquaintance of
Edward King. Finally, the vision of Heaven at the climax of *Lycidas* seems rather
sedate in comparison with the Christian bacchanalian at the end of *Epitaphium
Damonis,* all the more striking because of the absence of an epilogue.

Argumentum

Thyrsis et Damon eiusdem viciniae pastores, eadem studia sequuti a pueritia amici erant, ut qui plurimum. Thyrsis animi causa profectus peregre de obitu Damonis nuntium accepit. Domum postea reversus et rem ita esse comperto, se, suamque solitudinem hoc carmine deplorat. Damonis autem sub persona hic intelligitur Carolus Deodatus ex urbe Hetruriae Luca paterno genere oriundus, caetera Anglus; ingenio, doctrina, clarissimisque caeteris virtutibus, dum viveret, iuvenis egregius.

Himerides nymphae (nam vos et Daphnin et Hylan,
Et plorata diu meministis fata Bionis)
Dicite Sicelicum Thamesina per oppida carmen:
Quas miser effudit voces, quae murmura Thyrsis,
5   Et quibus assiduis exercuit antra querelis
Fluminaque, fontesque vagos, nemorumque recessus,
Dum sibi praereptum queritur Damona, neque altam
Luctibus exemit noctem loca sola pererrans.
Et iam bis viridi surgebat culmus arista,
10 Et totidem flavas numerabant horrea messes,
Ex quo summa dies tulerat Damona sub umbras,
Nec dum aderat Thyrsis; pastorem scilicet illum
Dulcis amor Musae Thusca retinebat in urbe.
Ast ubi mens expleta domum pecorisque relicti
15 Cura vocat, simul assueta seditque sub ulmo,
Tum vero amissum tum denique sentit amicum,
Coepit et immensum sic exonerare dolorem.

1. **Himerides:** pastoral Muses, after the two rivers named Himera in Sicily, home to Theocritus, Bion, and Moschus. The young shepherd Daphnis is mourned in Theocritus's first eclogue, which is the earliest pastoral elegy. On Hylas, see *El 7* 24n.
2. Bion is mourned in *Lament for Bion* (Moschus 3), the first pastoral elegy on the death of a poet.
4. **Thyrsis:** Milton adopts the name of the shepherd who mourns for Daphnis in Theocritus 1.

Thyrsis and Damon, shepherds of the same district, pursuing the same studies, were friends from boyhood, the closest possible. Thyrsis, traveling abroad for pleasure, received news of Damon's death. After returning home and on verifying that the report was true, he wept for himself and his loneliness in this song. By the name "Damon" here is meant Charles Diodati, descended from the Tuscan city of Lucca on his father's side, and otherwise an Englishman: while he lived, an extraordinary young man for talent, learning, and other most distinguished virtues.

Himeran nymphs[1] (for you memorialized Daphnis and Hylas and the long-lamented fate of Bion[2]), speak a Sicilian song through the villages of the Thames: the cries, the moans which Thyrsis[4] poured out in his misery, the unremitting complaints with which he troubled the caves and the rivers and the wandering fountains and the depths of the groves while he lamented that Damon was snatched from him, nor did he exempt dark night from his grieving as he wandered lonely sites. And already the stalk twice thrust upward with a green beard, and as many times the granaries counted the golden harvest since the last day took Damon into the shadows, and yet Thyrsis was not there; for sweet love of the Muse detained that shepherd in a Tuscan city. But when his full mind and care for the flock left behind called him home, and he sat down under his familiar elm, then truly, then at last he felt the loss of his friend,

Ite domum impasti, domino iam non vacat,
   agni.
Hei mihi! quae terris, quae dicam numina coelo,
20   Postquam te immiti rapuerunt funere, Damon;
Siccine nos linquis, tua sic sine nomine virtus
Ibit, et obscuris numero sociabitur umbris?
At non ille animas virga qui dividit aurea,
Ista velit, dignumque tui te ducat in agmen,
25   Ignavumque procul pecus arceat omne
   silentum.
   Ite domum impasti, domino iam non vacat,
   agni.
Quicquid erit, certe, nisi me lupus ante videbit,
Indeplorato non comminuere sepulcro,
Constabitque tuus tibi honos, longumque
   vigebit
30   Inter pastores: illi tibi vota secundo
   Solvere post Daphnin, post Daphnin dicere
      laudes
   Gaudebunt, dum rura Pales, dum Faunus
      amabit:
   Si quid id est, priscamque fidem coluisse,
      piumque,
   Palladiasque artes, sociumque habuisse
      canorum.
35   Ite domum impasti, domino iam non vacat,
   agni.
   Haec tibi certa manent, tibi erunt haec praemia
      Damon.
   At mihi quid tandem fiet modo? quis mihi fidus
   Haerebit lateri comes, ut tu saepe solebas
   Frigoribus duris, et per loca foeta pruinis,
40   Aut rapido sub sole, siti morientibus herbis?
   Sive opus in magnos fuit eminus ire leones,
   Aut avidos terrere lupos praesepibus altis?

and began to unburden himself of his immense grief:
"Go home unfed, lambs; your master has no time for you now.[18] Alas for me! what gods on earth, what gods in the sky will I call, now that they have taken you away from me, Damon, with a pitiless funeral? Is this how you leave us, will your virtue go this way without a name and join the number of the obscure shades? But may he[23] who divides the souls with his golden wand not want this, and may he lead you to a company worthy of you, and keep back all the ignoble herd of the silent.
"Go home unfed, lambs; your master has no time for you now. Whatever happens, surely, unless a wolf sees me first,[27] you will not wither in an unlamented tomb, and your honor will survive for you, and will long flourish among the shepherds. They will take pleasure in swearing oaths to you, second after Daphnis, and in speaking your praises, after Daphnis, as long as Pales, as long as Faunus[32] loves the country: if it counts for anything to have cultivated the ancient faith and piety and the arts of Pallas,[34] and to have had a singer for a companion.
"Go home unfed, lambs; your master has no time for you now. These things remain certain for you, these will be your rewards, Damon; but what then will become of me? What faithful companion will cling to my side, as you often used to do in the harsh cold, and in places teeming with frost, or under the scorching sun when the plants were dying of thirst? Whether our task was to track great lions from a distance or to frighten hungry wolves from the tall sheepfolds, who will

18. Milton's refrain reworks the last line of Vergil's last eclogue, *Ite domum saturae, venit Hesperus, ite capellae* (Go home, my full-fed goats, the evening star comes, go home).
23. **ille:** Mercury. According to Vergil, *Aen.* 4.242–44, Mercury uses his wand (*virga*) to summon ghosts.
27. An old superstition held that a man seen by a wolf before he saw it would be struck dumb.
32. **Pales:** Roman goddess of shepherds. For Faunus, see *To Salzilli* 27n.
34. Pallas Athena was goddess of wisdom; Diodati studied at Oxford and Geneva. The poetic friend is Milton.

Quis fando sopire diem cantuque solebit?
  Ite domum impasti, domino iam non vacat,
    agni.
45 Pectora cui credam? quis me lenire docebit
  Mordaces curas, quis longam fallere noctem
  Dulcibus alloquiis, grato cum sibilat igni
  Molle pyrum, et nucibus strepitat focus, at
    malus Auster
  Miscet cuncta foris, et desuper intonat ulmo?
50   Ite domum impasti, domino iam non vacat,
    agni.
  Aut aestate, dies medio dum vertitur axe,
  Cum Pan aesculea somnum capit abditus
    umbra,
  Et repetunt sub aquis sibi nota sedilia nymphae,
  Pastoresque latent, stertit sub sepe colonus,
55 Quis mihi blanditiasque tuas, quis tum mihi
    risus,
  Cecropiosque sales referet, cultosque lepores?
    Ite domum impasti, domino iam non vacat,
    agni.
  At iam solus agros, iam pascua solus oberro,
  Sicubi ramosae densantur vallibus umbrae,
60 Hic serum expecto; supra caput imber et Eurus
  Triste sonant, fractaeque agitata crepuscula
    silvae.
    Ite domum impasti, domino iam non vacat,
    agni.
  Heu quam culta mihi prius arva procacibus
    herbis
  Involvuntur, et ipsa situ seges alta fatiscit!
65 Innuba neglecto marcescit et uva racemo,
  Nec myrteta iuvant; ovium quoque taedet, at
    illae
  Moerent, inque suum convertunt ora
    magistrum.
    Ite domum impasti, domino iam non vacat,
    agni.
  Tityrus ad corylos vocat, Alphesiboeus ad
    ornos,
70 Ad salices Aegon, ad flumina pulcher Amyntas,

65. **Innuba:** The idea of the vine being "wedded"
  to the elm or poplar was a commonplace of
  Latin poetry; Horace calls trees without vines
  "celibate" or "widowed" (*Odes* 2.15.4, 4.5.30).

be easing the day with talk and song?

"Go home unfed, lambs; your master has no time for you now. To whom will I entrust my heart? Who will teach me to soften biting cares, who to cheat the long night with sweet conversation while a soft pear hisses before the welcome fire, and the hearth crackles with nuts, but outside evil Auster roils everything and thunders in the elm up above?

"Go home unfed, lambs; your master has no time for you now. Or in the summer, while the day turns to noontime, when Pan catches his sleep, concealed in the shade of oaks, and nymphs go back to their well-known stations beneath the water, and the shepherds are hidden, and the farmer snores under the hedge, who will bring back to me your flatteries, who will bring back to me your laughter and Athenian wit and cultivated charms?

"Go home unfed, lambs; your master has no time for you now. But now I wander alone through the fields, alone through the pastures; anywhere that the branched shadows are made thick by the valleys, there I wait for evening. Above my head the rain and Eurus make a sad sound, and the troubled twilight of the shattered frost.

"Go home unfed, lambs; your master has no time for you now. Alas, how my once cultivated fields are overrun with unrestrained weeds, and the tall grain itself droops from neglect! The unwed grapes[65] rot, their clusters untended, nor does the myrtle give pleasure; even the sheep are wearisome, and they grieve and turn their faces to their master.

"Go home unfed, lambs; your master has no time for you now. Tityrus calls to the hazels, Alphesiboeus to the ash trees, Aegon

Hic gelidi fontes, hic illita gramina musco,
Hic Zephyri, hic placidas interstrepit arbutus
   undas;
Ista canunt surdo, frutices ego nactus abibam.
   Ite domum impasti, domino iam non vacat,
   agni.
75 Mopsus ad haec, nam me redeuntem forte
   notarat
(Et callebat avium linguas, et sidera Mopsus)
Thyrsi, quid hoc? dixit, quae te coquit improba
   bilis?
Aut te perdit amor, aut te male fascinat astrum,
Saturni grave saepe fuit pastoribus astrum,
80 Intimaque obliquo figit praecordia plumbo.
   Ite domum impasti, domino iam non vacat,
   agni.
Mirantur nymphae, et quid te Thyrsi futurum
   est?
Quid tibi vis? aiunt, non haec solet esse iuventae
Nubila frons, oculique truces, vultusque severi;
85 Illa choros, lususque leves, et semper amorem
Iure petit; bis ille miser qui serus amavit.
   Ite domum impasti, domino iam non vacat,
   agni.
Venit Hyas, Dryopeque, et filia Baucidis Aegle,
Docta modos, citharaeque sciens, sed perdita
   fastu,
90 Venit Idumanii Chloris vicina fluenti;
Nil me blanditiae, nil me solantia verba,
Nil me, si quid adest, movet, aut spes ulla futuri.
   Ite domum impasti, domino iam non vacat,
   agni.
Hei mihi quam similes ludunt per prata iuvenci,
95 Omnes unanimi secum sibi lege sodales,
Nec magis hunc alio quisquam secernit amicum

88. **Hyas:** Hyas is killed by a lioness in Ovid, *Fasti*
5.169–82, though Milton may have a nymph in
mind. **Dryope:** appears in Ovid, *Met.* 9.331–93.
90. The river Chelmer in Essex flows into Black-
water Bay. Camden in his *Britannia* identified
the river with with Ptolemy's *Idumanius fluvius.*

to the willows, handsome Amyn-
tas to the streams: 'Here are cold
fountains, here grass spread with
moss, here zephyrs, here the ar-
butus mixes its noise with the
placid waves.' They sing to a deaf
person; reaching the bushes, I es-
caped.

"Go home unfed, lambs; your
master has no time for you now.
At this Mopsus, for he happened
to see me leaving (and Mopsus
knows the languages of the birds
and the stars), said, 'Thyrsis,
what is this? What unhealthy bile
troubles you? Either love slays
you, or an evil star bewitches
you; Saturn's star has often been
grim for shepherds, it pierces the
innermost heart with its slanting
lead.'

"Go home unfed, lambs; your
master has no time for you now.
The nymphs wonder, and say,
'What will become of you, Thyr-
sis? What do you want? The fore-
head of youth is not usually
cloudy like this, or the eyes
angry, or the looks severe; by
rights it seeks out dances and
easygoing games and, always,
love; he is twice as wretched who
loves too late.'

"Go home unfed, lambs; your
master has no time for you now.
Hyas[88] came, and Dryope, and
Aegle, the daughter of Baucis,
learned in music, knowledgeable
about the lyre, but undone by her
fastidiousness; Chloris, from near
the Idumanian river,[90] came.
Blandishments do not, comfort-
ing words do not move me, or
anything that is at hand, or any
hope of the future.

"Go home unfed, lambs; your
master has no time for you now.
Alas for me, how alike are the
young bulls playing in the
meadow, all comrades agreed
with each other in their law; none
singles out one friend more than
another from the herd. In the

De grege; sic densi veniunt ad pabula thoes,
Inque vicem hirsuti paribus iunguntur onagri;
Lex eadem pelagi, deserto in littore Proteus
100 Agmina phocarum numerat, vilisque volucrum
Passer habet semper quicum sit, et omnia
circum
Farra libens volitet, sero sua tecta revisens;
Quem si fors letho obiecit, seu milvus adunco
Fata tulit rostro, seu stravit arundine fossor,
105 Protinus ille alium socio petit inde volatu.
Nos durum genus, et diris exercita fatis
Gens homines aliena animis, et pectore discors;
Vix sibi quisque parem de millibus invenit
unum,
Aut si sors dederit tandem non aspera votis,
110 Illum inopina dies qua non speraveris hora
Surripit, aeternum linquens in saecula damnum.
Ite domum impasti, domino iam non vacat,
agni.
Heu quis me ignotas traxit vagus error in oras
Ire per aereas rupes, Alpemque nivosam!
115 Ecquid erat tanti Romam vidisse sepultam,
Quamvis illa foret, qualem dum viseret olim,
Tityrus ipse suas et oves et rura reliquit;
Ut te tam dulci possem caruisse sodale,
Possem tot maria alta, tot interponere montes,
120 Tot silvas, tot saxa tibi, fluviosque sonantes?
Ah certe extremum licuisset tangere dextram,
Et bene compositos placide morientis ocellos,
Et dixisse vale, nostri memor ibis ad astra.
Ite domum impasti, domino iam non vacat,
agni.

97. **thoes:** probably refers to a kind of weasel,
though Milton seems to have thought that it
means "wolves."
99. Proteus, the sea god, knew all things and could
change his shape to avoid answering questions
(see *Areop, MLM* 962).
117. *Tityrus* here means Vergil's Tityrus, who saw
Rome in its early days of splendor (*Ec.* 1.26), not
Chaucer, as in *Manso* 34.

same way wolves[97] go in packs for food, and shaggy asses are joined with their mates in turn. The law of the sea is the same: on the deserted shore Proteus[99] counts his company of seals. And the sparrow, the most insignificant of birds, always has someone to be with, to fly freely about all the grain, returning in the evening to his own home: whom if chance hurled to death, whether the kite bore its fate in a curved beak or a farmworker brought it down with his shaft, he then straightway seeks another as a companion in flight. We men are a hard race, a tribe drawn by a dire fate, unfriendly in spirit and troubled at heart; each finds scarcely one partner in a thousand, or if a fortune not hostile to our prayers finally gives us one, the unexpected day, the hour for which you had not hoped, snatches him away, leaving eternal loss for all time.

"Go home unfed, lambs; your master has no time for you now. Alas, what inconstant error dragged me to unknown shores, to go through the airy cliffs, the snowy Alps! Was it so important to have seen Rome in its tomb—even if it had been as it was when Tityrus[117] once left his sheep and fields to see it—that I should leave you, such a sweet companion, that I should interpose so many deep seas, so many mountains, so many forests, so many rocks, so many sounding rivers between us? Ah, surely it would have been permitted to touch his hand at the end, and the gently closed eyes of the peacefully dying man, and to have said, 'Farewell, you will go to the stars remembering us.'

"Go home unfed, lambs; your

125 Quamquam etiam vestri nunquam meminisse
        pigebit,
     Pastores Thusci, Musis operata iuventus,
     Hic charis, atque lepos; et Thuscus tu quoque
        Damon,
     Antiqua genus unde petis Lucumonis ab urbe.
     O ego quantus eram, gelidi cum stratus ad Arni
130 Murmura, populeumque nemus, qua mollier
        herba,
     Carpere nunc violas, nunc summas carpere
        myrtos,
     Et potui Lycidae certantem audire Menalcam.
     Ipse etiam tentare ausus sum, nec puto multum
     Displicui, nam sunt et apud me munera vestra
135 Fiscellae, calathique et cerea vincla cicutae;
     Quin et nostra suas docuerunt nomina fagos
     Et Datis, et Francinus, erant et vocibus ambo
     Et studiis noti, Lydorum sanguinis ambo.
        Ite domum impasti, domino iam non vacat,
        agni.
140 Haec mihi tum laeto dictabat roscida luna,
     Dum solus teneros claudebam cratibus hoedos.
     Ah quoties dixi, cum te cinis ater habebat,
     Nunc canit, aut lepori nunc tendit retia Damon,
     Vimina nunc texit, varios sibi quod sit in usus;
145 Et quae tum facile sperabam mente futura
     Arripui voto levis, et praesentia finxi,
     Heus bone numquid agis? nisi te quid forte
        retardat,
     Imus? et arguta paulum recubamus in umbra,
     Aut ad aquas Colni, aut ubi iugera Cassibelauni?

127. Diodati's forebears came from Lucca; see Do-
rian 5. *Lucumonis lucumo* (inspired person) was a
name given to Etruscan princes and priests.

132. Via the pastoral convention of the singing
match between shepherds, Milton alludes to
the poetry contests in the Florentine academies
(*MLM* 840).

134. **munera**: perhaps an allusion to the poetic en-
comia that Milton placed before his Latin verse
in the 1645 *Poems*.

137. Milton refers to two friends he made in Italy,
Carlo Dati and Antonio Francini, both of
whom wrote commendatory poems included in
the 1645 *Poems* (see previous note).

149. **Colni**: The river Colne flows near Horton.

master has no time for you now.
Yet still it will never trouble me
to remember you, shepherds of
Tuscany, young men devoted to
the Muses: Grace is here, and
Charm; and you also were a Tus-
can, Damon,[127] whence you take
your ancestry from the ancient
city of Lucca. O, how grand I felt,
stretched out by the murmurs of
the cold Arno and the poplar
grove, where the grass was softer,
to pluck now violets, now myrtle
sprays, and I could hear Menal-
cas in a contest[132] with Lycidas. I
even dared to compete, and I
don't think I greatly displeased,
for your gifts[134] are still with me:
baskets of twigs and baskets of
wicker and the wax fastenings of
a panpipe. And indeed Dati and
Francini[137] taught their beech
trees our name, and they were
both of them famous for voice
and learning, and both of Lydian
blood.

   "Go home unfed, lambs; your
master has no time for you now.
These things the dewy moon
used to say to me then when I was
happy, while in solitude I shut
the tender kids up in their pens.
Ah, how many times I said, when
dark ashes held you, 'Now
Damon is singing, or puts out
nets for the hare, now he weaves
wickerwork, for which he has
various uses.' And I lightly seized
with a wish future things which I
then readily hoped for in my
mind and pretended they were
present: 'Hello, good fellow, what
are you up to? Unless something
happens to hold you back, shall
we go and rest awhile in the
rustling shade, either by the wa-
ters of the Colne[149] or where the
acres of Cassivellaunus are? You

150 Tu mihi percurres medicos, tua gramina,
  succos,
Helleborumque, humilesque crocos, foliumque
  hyacinthi,
Quasque habet ista palus herbas, artesque
  medentum.
Ah pereant herbae, pereant artesque medentum
Gramina, postquam ipsi nil profecere magistro.
155 Ipse etiam, nam nescio quid mihi grande
  sonabat
Fistula, ab undecima iam lux est altera nocte,
Et tum forte novis admoram labra cicutis,
Dissiluere tamen rupta compage, nec ultra
Ferre graves potuere sonos; dubito quoque ne
  sim
160 Turgidulus, tamen et referam, vos cedite silvae.
  Ite domum impasti, domino iam non vacat,
  agni.
Ipse ego Dardanias Rutupina per aequora
  puppes
Dicam, et Pandrasidos regnum vetus Inogeniae,
Brennumque Arviragumque duces, priscumque
  Belinum,
165 Et tandem Armoricos Britonum sub lege
  colonos;

will run through your medi-
cines[150] for me, your plants and
juices: hellebore and the humble
crocus and the leaf of the hy-
acinth, whatever herbs and med-
ical arts this marsh holds.' Ah,
curse the herbs, curse the med-
ical arts, the plants, now that they
did no good for their own master.
And myself—for my pipe played
something grand, I know not what,
it is now the next day after the
eleventh night, and then by
chance I had placed my lips on
new reeds, but they fell apart,
their fastening broken, and they
could no longer carry serious
tunes, and I am unsure if I am
being grandiose, but still I will
recite; yield, you forests.[160]

"Go home unfed, lambs; your
master has no time for you now. I
myself will tell[162] of the Trojan
keels through the Rutupian sea,
and the ancient kingdom of Ino-
gene,[163] daughter of Pandrasus,
and the leaders Brennus and
Arviragus, and old Belinus,[164]
and Armorican settlers[165] at last

150. This passage is sometimes taken to suggest
  that the "certain shepherd lad" of *Masque*
  618–28 is Diodati.
160. **vos cedite silvae:** Vergil's Gallus turns away
  from pastoral with the words *concedite silvae* (*Ec.*
  10.63).
162. On Milton's plans for a British epic, see the
  less detailed account in *Manso* 80–84.
163. Pandrasus gave his daughter Inogene in mar-
  riage to the Trojan Brutus after Brutus de-
  feated him. See Milton's *History of Britain* (Yale
  5:11–13).
164. Brennus and Belinus were legendary British
  kings who conquered Rome (Geoffrey of Mon-
  mouth, *History of Britain* 3.1–10). Arviragus was
  King Cymbeline's son; Shakespeare rendered
  these characters in his *Cymbeline.*
165. British historians liked to believe that Con-
  stantine had founded a colony of veteran
  British soldiers in Gaul.

Tum gravidam Arturo fatali fraude Iogernen,
Mendaces vultus, assumptaque Gorlois arma,
Merlini dolus. O mihi tum si vita supersit,
Tu procul annosa pendebis fistula pinu
170 Multum oblita mihi, aut patriis mutata Camenis
Brittonicum strides, quid enim? omnia non licet
    uni
    Non sperasse uni licet omnia; mi satis ampla
    Merces, et mihi grande decus (sim ignotus in
      aevum
    Tum licet, externo penitusque inglorius orbi)
175 Si me flava comas legat Usa, et potor Alauni,
    Vorticibusque frequens Abra, et nemus omne
      Treantae,
    Et Thamesis meus ante omnes, et fusca metallis
    Tamara, et extremis me discant Orcades undis.
      Ite domum impasti, domino iam non vacat,
      agni.
180 Haec tibi servabam lenta sub cortice lauri,
    Haec, et plura simul, tum quae mihi pocula
      Mansus,
    Mansus Chalcidicae non ultima gloria ripae,
    Bina dedit, mirum artis opus, mirandus et ipse,
    Et circum gemino caelaverat argumento:

under British law; then Igraine,[166] heavy with Arthur through a fateful deception, the lying appearance, the putting on of Gorlois's armor—Merlin's trick. O, if life then is left to me, you, pipe,[169] will hang far off on an aged pine tree, all forgotten by me; or, changed to homeland muses, you will whistle a British theme. What then? All things are not allowed for one man, to hope for all things is not allowed for one man; it will be large enough reward for me, and great glory for me (let me be forever unknown and utterly without fame in the outside world) if yellow-haired Ouse[175] reads me, and the drinker of the Alne, and Humber, thick with eddies, and every grove of the Trent, and my Thames above all, and the Tamar,[178] dark with minerals, and the Orkneys in their distant waves study me.

"Go home unfed, lambs; your master has no time for you now. These things I was keeping for you under the rubbery bark of the laurel,[180] these and more as well, the twin cups which Manso[181]—Manso, not the least glory of the Chalcidian[182] shore—gave me, a wonderful work of art, and he himself a wonder, and he had engraved it about with a double theme: in the middle the water of the Red Sea and the perfumed spring, the long shores of Arabia and the forests exuding balsam; among

166. Uther Pendragon appeared to Igraine in the form of her dead husband, Gorlois, King of Cornwall, and fathered Arthur (Geoffrey of Monmouth, *History of Britain* 8.19).

169. **fistula:** the pastoral pipe. Commentators debate whether Milton is abandoning pastoral poetry or Latin poetry.

175. **Usa:** the river Ouse, initiating a catalog of English rivers; **potor Alauni:** Camden says that both the Alne in Northumberland and the united Stour and Avon in Hampshire bore the Latin name *Alaunus.*

178. **Tamara:** The Tamar flows between Cornwall and Devonshire; **Orcades:** the Orkney Islands.

180. Milton probably got the idea of verses carved or written on laurel bark from Vergil, *Ec.* 5.13-14.

181. **Mansus:** See the headnote to *Manso.* Some have taken the cups to be symbolic of other gifts from Manso—copies of his books, perhaps.

182. **Chalcidicae:** Neapolitan. Naples was settled by colonists from Chalcis.

185 In medio rubri maris unda, et odoriferum ver,
   Littora longa Arabum, et sudantes balsama
      silvae;
   Has inter Phoenix divina avis, unica terris,
   Caeruleum fulgens diversicoloribus alis,
   Auroram vitreis surgentem respicit undis.
190 Parte alia polus omnipatens, et magnus
      Olympus,
   Quis putet? hic quoque Amor, pictaeque in
      nube pharetrae,
   Arma corusca, faces, et spicula tincta pyropo;
   Nec tenues animas, pectusque ignobile vulgi
   Hinc ferit, at circum flammantia lumina
      torquens,
195 Semper in erectum spargit sua tela per orbes
   Impiger, et pronos nunquam collimat ad ictus;
   Hinc mentes ardere sacrae, formaeque deorum.
      Tu quoque in his, nec me fallit spes lubrica
      Damon,
      Tu quoque in his certe es, nam quo tua dulcis
      abiret
200 Sanctaque simplicitas, nam quo tua candida
      virtus?
   Nec te Lethaeo fas quaesivisse sub Orco,
   Nec tibi conveniunt lacrimae, nec flebimus
      ultra;
   Ite procul lacrimae, purum colit aethera
      Damon,
   Aethera purus habet, pluvium pede reppulit
      arcum;
205 Heroumque animas inter, divosque perennes,
   Aethereos haurit latices et gaudia potat
   Ore sacro. Quin tu coeli post iura recepta
   Dexter ades, placidusque fave quicunque
      vocaris,
   Seu tu noster eris Damon, sive aequior audis

these the phoenix,[187] the divine bird, unique in the world, gleaming blue with its multicolored wings, watches Aurora rising from the glassy waves. In another part, the unbounded sky and great Olympus—who would have thought?—here also Love,[191] and in a cloud his colorful quivers, his gleaming arms, his torches, and his arrows coated with golden bronze. From here he does not strike at frivolous souls or the ignoble heart of the mob, but turning his flaming eye about, he always, tirelessly, casts his weapons upward into the spheres, and never aims a downward blow. From this source sacred minds catch fire, and the forms of the gods.

"You too are among these—and slippery hope does not deceive me, Damon—you too are surely among these, for where would your sweet and holy simplicity go, or your pure white virtue? Nor is it lawful to have looked for you down in Lethaean Orcus,[201] nor are tears fitting for you, and we will weep no longer. Be gone far away, tears. Damon inhabits the pure heavens;[203] in his purity he possesses the heavens, he spurns the rainbow with his foot. Among the souls of heroes and the eternal gods he drinks heavenly liquid and downs its joys with his holy mouth. So now, after receiving your due in heaven, you are at my right hand; favor me also in your kindness, however you are called: whether you will be our Damon, or whether you prefer Diodati, by which divine

187. It has been suggested that Milton borrowed details from *De Ave Phoenice*, attributed to Lactantius, one of his favorite theologians, or from Tasso's *Le Fenice*.

191. Plato distinguished between the vulgar and the heavenly Aphrodite (*Symposium* 180–85). Ficino adapted the distinction to his Christian Neoplatonism in *Commentary on Plato's Symposium* 2.6.

201. See *El 7* 83n.

203. Daphnis is deified in Vergil, *Ec.* 5.56–59.

210   Diodatus, quo te divino nomine cuncti
      Coelicolae norint, silvisque vocabere Damon.
      Quod tibi purpureus pudor, et sine labe
          iuventus
      Grata fuit, quod nulla tori libata voluptas,
      En etiam tibi virginei servantur honores;
215   Ipse caput nitidum cinctus rutilante corona,
      Laetaque frondentis gestans umbracula palmae
      Aeternum perages immortales hymenaeos;
      Cantus ubi, choreisque furit lyra mista beatis,
      Festa Sionaeo bacchantur et Orgia thyrso.

210. **divino nomine:** probably an allusion to Dio-
dati's name, which means "God-given."
213. **tori:** Leonard, opposing the idea that Milton
was interested in chastity to the point of dis-
paraging marriage, translates *torus* as "bed"
rather than "marriage bed." Cp. Rev. 14.4: "These
are they which were not defiled with women."
215. **corona:** Cp. the "crown of glory" in 1 Pet. 5.4.
216. **palmae:** Cp. Rev. 7.9: "A great multitude,
which no man could number . . . stood before
the throne, and before the Lamb, clothed with
white robes, and palms in their hands."
217. **hymenaeos:** Cp. Rev. 19.7: "Let us be glad and
rejoice . . . for the marriage of the Lamb is come."
219. The thyrsus was a vine-leaved staff carried by
Bacchic celebrants.

name[210] all the gods know you, and you will be called Damon in the woodlands. Because blushing modesty and a youth without stain pleased you, because the joy of the marriage bed[213] was never tasted, lo, virginal honors are reserved for you. Girt about your shining head with a glowing crown,[215] and bearing the happy shade of a leafy palm,[216] you will partake forever in an immortal wedding,[217] where there is singing and the lyre rages in the midst of blessed dances, and orgiastic feasts have their bacchic celebration under the thyrsus[219] of Zion."

IN EFFIGIEI EIUS SCULPTOR

[On the Engraver of His Portrait]

Milton clearly felt that the frontispiece portrait to the 1645 *Poems*, engraved by the well-known artist William Marshall, did not do justice to his looks. He took his revenge by having the artist engrave these verses beneath the imperfect likeness. Marshall, having no Greek and expecting no attack, dutifully complied, thereby serving notice of his poor skill as an artist, his ignorance as a linguist, and his gullibility as a judge of men. The verses suggest that the engraving might better be regarded as Marshall's self-portrait.

~~~~~~~

Ἀμαθεῖ γεγράφθαι χειρὶ τήνδε μὲν εἰκόνα
Φαίης τάχ᾽ ἄν πρὸς εἶδος αὐτοφυὲς βλέπων.
Τὸν δ᾽ ἐκτυπωτὸν οὐκ ἐπιγνόντες φίλοι
Γελᾶτε φαύλου δυσμίμημα ζωγράφου.

You might readily say that this picture was drawn with an ignorant hand if you saw the real image; if you don't recognize the man being pictured, friends, laugh at this bad imitation of a worthless artist.

AD IOANNEM ROUSIUM,
OXONIENSIS ACADEMIAE BIBLIOTHECARIUM
[*To John Rouse, Librarian of Oxford University*]

Soon after the 1645 *Poems* appeared, Milton sent a copy to Rouse, along with the eleven prose pamphlets he had so far published, for deposit in the Bodleian Library. Somehow the *Poems* was lost in transit, and Rouse requested a second copy. Milton sent one, enclosing a manuscript of this poem. Both the manuscript and, apparently, the book are in the Bodleian to this day.

De libro Poematum amisso, quem ille sibi denuo mitti postulabat, ut cum aliis nostris in Bibliotheca publica reponeret, Ode

Ode on a lost book of poems, which he asked to have sent to him again, so that he could put it in the public library with our others

"... if you don't recognize the man being pictured, friends, laugh at this bad imitation of a worthless artist."

Strophe 1

Gemelle cultu simplici gaudens liber,
Fronde licet gemina,
Munditieque nitens non operosa,
Quam manus attulit
5   Iuvenilis olim,
Sedula tamen haud nimii poetae;
Dum vagus Ausonias nunc per umbras
Nunc Britannica per vireta lusit
Insons populi, barbitoque devius
10   Indulsit patrio, mox itidem pectine Daunio
Longinquum intonuit melos
Vicinis, et humum vix tetigit pede;

Antistrophe

Quis te, parve liber, quis te fratribus
Subduxit reliquis dolo,
15   Cum tu missus ab urbe,
Docto iugiter obsecrante amico,
Illustre tendebas iter
Thamesis ad incunabula
Caerulei patris,
20   Fontes ubi limpidi
Aonidum, thyasusque sacer
Orbi notus per immensos
Temporum lapsus redeunte coelo,
Celeberque futurus in aevum?

Twin-born book,[1] rejoicing in a single cover, though with a double leaf, and shining with unfussy neatness, which a youthful hand, earnest but not too much the poet, once bestowed while he amused himself wandering now through Italian shade and now through British greenery, unspoiled by people, and off by himself indulged his native lyre: soon in the same way with his Daunian[10] plectrum he sounded a far-off song for his neighbors, and scarcely touched the ground with his foot:

Who, little book, who stole you away by trickery from your brothers, when, sent from the city at the steady imploring of my learned friend, you were making the illustrious journey to the cradle of the Thames,[18] the blue father, where the clear fountains of the Aonides[21] are, and the sacred Bacchic dance known to the world across an immense lapse of time with the turning heavens, and to be renowned forever?

1. The English and Latin works in the 1645 *Poems* had separate title pages and pagination.
10. **Daunio:** Italian.
18. **Thamesis:** the upper reaches of the Thames. Oxford lies at the confluence of the Thames and the Cherwell.
21. **Aonidum:** the Muses.

Strophe 2

25 Modo quis deus, aut editus deo
    Pristinam gentis miseratus indolem
    (Si satis noxas luimus priores
    Mollique luxu degener otium)
    Tollat nefandos civium tumultus,
30 Almaque revocet studia sanctus
    Et relegatas sine sede Musas
    Iam pene totis finibus Angligenum;
    Immundasque volucres
    Unguibus imminentes
35 Figat Apollinea pharetra,
    Phineamque abigat pestem procul amne
        Pegaseo?

Antistrophe

    Quin tu, libelle, nuntii licet mala
    Fide, vel oscitantia
    Semel erraveris agmine fratrum,
40 Seu quis te teneat specus,
    Seu qua te latebra, forsan unde vili
    Callo tereris institoris insulsi,
    Laetare felix; en iterum tibi
    Spes nova fulget posse profundam
45 Fugere Lethen, vehique superam
    In Iovis aulam remige penna;

But what god or offspring of a god,[25] having pity for the ancient character of our nation (if we have sufficiently atoned for our earlier crimes and our laziness corrupted with womanish luxury), might take away the accursed upheaval of our citizens, and in holiness recall the nourishing studies[30] and the banished Muses now almost totally without a home within all the territory of England, and with Apollo's quiver transfix the loathsome birds[33] hovering with their claws and drive the Phinean plague beyond the river of Pegasus?

But you, little book, though by the bad faith or weariness of the messenger you have wandered this once from the company of your brothers, whether a ditch keeps you, or some hiding place whence you will be rubbed by the vile skin of a stupid shopkeeper: cheer up, lucky one; behold, new hope shines again for you to be able to avoid deep Lethe,[45] and be borne to the high hall of Jove with your wing as oarsman.

25. Cp. Horace's appeal to an unnamed hero in *Odes* 1.2.25–52.
30. From 1642 to 1646, when it surrendered to Fairfax, Oxford was the Royalists' headquarters, and the usual activities of the university were suspended.
33. The prophet Phineas was punished by Zeus with blindness and visits from the Harpies until delivered by the Argonauts (Apollonius of Rhodes 2.178–310).
45. **Lethen:** the river of oblivion in Hades.

Strophe 3

Nam te Rousius sui
Optat peculi, numeroque iusto
Sibi pollicitum queritur abesse,
50 Rogatque venias ille cuius inclyta
Sunt data virum monumenta curae:
Teque adytis etiam sacris
Voluit reponi quibus et ipse praesidet
Aeternorum operum custos fidelis,
55 Quaestorque gazae nobilioris
Quam cui praefuit Ion,
Clarus Erechtheides,
Opulenta dei per templa parentis
Fulvosque tripodas, donaque Delphica
60 Ion Actaea genitus Creusa.

Antistrophe

Ergo tu visere lucos
Musarum ibis amoenos,
Diamque Phoebi rursus ibis in domum
Oxonia quam valle colit
65 Delo posthabita,
Bifidoque Parnassi iugo:
Ibis honestus,
Postquam egregiam tu quoque sortem
Nactus abis, dextri prece sollicitatus amici.
70 Illic legeris inter alta nomina
Authorum, Graiae simul et Latinae
Antiqua gentis lumina, et verum decus.

Epodos

Vos tandem haud vacui mei labores,
Quicquid hoc sterile fudit ingenium;
75 Iam sero placidam sperare iubeo
Perfunctam invidia requiem, sedesque beatas

STROPHE 3

For Rouse wants you for his property and complains that, though you were promised to him, you are missing from the rightful list, and asks that you come—he into whose care have been given the famous monuments of men—and wished that you be placed in the sacred precincts over which he presides himself as the faithful guardian of eternal works, custodian of a nobler treasure[55] than that of which Ion, the famous descendant of Erechtheus, had charge in the opulent temples of his father the god, the yellow tripods and the Delphic gifts—Ion, born of Actaean[60] Creusa.

ANTISTROPHE

Therefore you will go to see the pleasant groves of the Muses, and you will go again to the divine house of Phoebus which he inhabits in the valley of Oxford, preferring it to Delos[65] and twin-peaked Parnassus; you will go in honor, since you also depart in possession of extraordinary luck, summoned by prayer of a beneficent friend. There you will be read among the greatest authorial names, the ancient lights and true glory of both the Greek race and the Latin.

EPODE

Then you are not in vain, my labors, whatever that sterile talent has poured forth; now at last I order you to look forward to a calm rest, done with envy, and the happy home which good

55. Milton is thinking of Euripides' *Ion*. The hero, son of Apollo, becomes guardian of his shrine and its treasures at Delphi.
60. **Actaea:** Attic (from Acte, an early name for Attica).
65. **Delo:** Delos, birthplace of Apollo.

Quas bonus Hermes
Et tutela dabit solers Rousi,
Quo neque lingua procax vulgi penetrabit,
      atque longe
80   Turba legentum prava facesset;
At ultimi nepotes,
Et cordatior aetas
Iudicia rebus aequiora forsitan
Adhibebit integro sinu.
85   Tum livore sepulto,
Si quid meremur sana posteritas sciet
Rousio favente.

Ode tribus constat Strophis totidemque Antistrophis una demum epodo clausis, quas, tametsi omnes nec versuum numero, nec certis ubique colis exacte respondeant, ita tamen secuimus, commode legendi potius, quam ad antiquos concinendi modos rationem spectantes. Alioquin hoc genus rectius fortasse dici monostrophicum debuerat. Metra partim sunt κατὰ σχέσιν, partim ἀπολελυμένα. Phaleucia quae sunt, spondaeum tertio loco bis admittunt, quod idem in secundo loco Catullus ad libitum fecit.

77. Hermes is the god of eloquence, roads, the lyre, and wisdom, and the conductor of shades.

Hermes[77] and the wise protection of Rouse will provide, where the unruly tongue of the mob will not penetrate, and the degenerate crowd of readers stays far away. But future descendants and a more sensible age will perhaps make fairer judgments with an unprejudiced heart. Then, with spite buried, a sane posterity will, thanks to Rouse, know if we have deserved anything.

The ode consists of three strophes and as many antistrophes, closed at the end with one epode: which, although they do not all correspond exactly in the number of verses or everywhere in precise metrical units, still we have divided up this way, more for the sake of convenience in reading than observing the rule of the ancient forms of prosody. In other regards this form should perhaps more accurately be called "monostrophic." The metrics are partly "responsive" and partly "irregular." The lines that are Phaleucian twice allow a spondee in the third foot, which Catullus did freely in the second foot.

EPIGRAM FROM *A DEFENSE OF THE ENGLISH PEOPLE*

Milton's *Defensio* was published in 1651, in answer to the *Defensio Regia Pro Carolo I* (1649) by the renowned classical scholar Claude de Saumaise, or Salmasius (1588–1653). Milton ridicules Salmasius' ignorance of English words and offers this epigram, an adaptation of Persius, *Prologue* 8–14, in which the imitated words are italicized.

Quis expedivit Salmasio suam Hundredam,
Picamque *docuit nostra verba conari?*
Magister artis venter, et Iacobei
Centum, exulantis viscera marsupii regis.
5   *Quod si dolosi spes refulserit nummi,*
Ipse Antichristi qui modo primatum Papae
Minatus uno est dissipare sufflatu,
Cantabit ultro Cardinalitium *melos.*

Who set Salmasius *loose* with his "hundreda,"[1] and *taught the magpie to try our vocabulary? His stomach is his schoolteacher,* and a hundred Jacobuses,[3] the innards of the exiled king's purse. *If hope of a dishonest penny glitters,* that man, who once threatened to blow away the supremacy of the papal antichrist[6] with one puff, will willingly *sing* the Cardinals' *tune.*

1. Saumaise mistakenly gave the plural of *hundred* as *hundreda* (*Defensio Regia* 204).
3. It was widely rumored that Charles I promised to reward Saumaise with a hundred Jacobuses (a gold coin valued at twenty-two shillings).
6. **primatum Papae:** Salmasius was also the author of *De Primatu Papae* (1645), which challenged papal authority.

EPIGRAMS FROM *A SECOND DEFENSE*

1. Salmasius died the year before Milton published his *Defensio Secunda* (1654). Milton explains that he wrote this epigram, centered on the old joke (Martial, *Epigrams* 3.2.1–5) that worthless books are good for wrapping fish, in the expectation that Salmasius would reply to his initial *Defensio* of 1652 (Yale 4:581).

Gaudete scombri, et quicquid est piscium salo,
Qui frigida hieme incolitis algentes freta;
Vestrum misertus ille Salmasius eques
Bonus amicire nuditatem cogitat;
5   Chartaeque largus apparat papyrinos
Vobis cucullos praeferentes Claudii
Insignia nomenque et decus Salmasii,
Gestetis ut per omne cetarium forum
Equitis clientes, scriniis mungentium
10   Cubito virorum, et capsulis gratissimos.

Rejoice, mackerels, and whatever fish there are in the sea[1] who, freezing, inhabit the frigid ocean in winter: out of pity for you, that good Sir Salmon[3] plans to clothe your nakedness and, generous with paper, is preparing papyrus hoods[6] for you, bearing the insignia, name, and honor of Claude Saumaise, so that as the knight's retainers you may bear them through the entire fish market, most welcome in the boxes and cartons of the men who wipe their noses on their elbows.[10]

1. This line parodies Catullus 31.13–14.
3. Milton puns on "Salmasius" and the Latin *salmo* (salmon).
6. **cucullos:** both "cowls" and "conical wrappers for merchandise," as also in Martial, *Epigrams* 3.2.5.
10. It was an ancient commonplace that fishmongers wiped their noses on their sleeves.

2. This adaptation of Juvenal 2.20–21 was directed against Alexander More, an opponent of the regicide whom Milton accused of having seduced Salmasius' maid.

de virtute loquutus
Clunem agitas: ego te ceventem, More, verebor?

having talked of virtue, you hunt for ass; shall I be in awe of you, More, when you grind your hips?

LATE MASTERPIECES

INTRODUCTION TO *PARADISE REGAINED*

An interesting anecdote about the composition of *Paradise Regained* comes from the memoirs of a Quaker named Thomas Ellwood. As a young man in 1662, he had arranged to meet the blind Milton in the hope of bettering his education and found the retired statesman willing. In exchange for reading to Milton, Ellwood was tutored in Latin. One day (perhaps in 1665) Milton loaned him a manuscript of *Paradise Lost*. Upon returning it, Ellwood remarked in a pleasant tone, "Thou hast said much here of Paradise lost, but what hast thou to say of Paradise found?" Milton, not answering, "sat some time in a muse" before changing the subject. Some while thereafter, date uncertain, Milton showed Ellwood a second manuscript, that of *Paradise Regained,* and told him, "This is owing to you; for you put it into my head by the question you put to me" (233–34).

One strongly suspects that Ellwood never achieved an understanding of his teacher on these occasions. It seems likely that Milton sat in a muse not because Ellwood had suddenly alerted him to a spiritual defect in *Paradise Lost* but because he was momentarily stunned that a reader of *Paradise Lost* (and Ellwood must have been one of the first) could be so simpleminded as to charge it with having little or nothing to say of "Paradise found": the poem names the "one greater man" who shall "restore us" in its first invocation, presents the invention of Christian salvation in the heavenly council of Book 3, emphasizes the Christian promise of the woman's seed bruising the serpent's head in the judgment scene of Book 10, and points biblical history in Books 11 and 12 toward the two comings of Christ. In handing Ellwood the manuscript of *Paradise Regained,* and thanking him for having inspired it, Milton passed on a friendly if impish fabrication, giving Ellwood the gift of a distinction that in his continuing simplemindedness he would accept and probably never forget, as in fact he did not. In a draft elegy for Milton, Ellwood celebrated him as the author of two complementary poems: "Th' one shows how man of Eden was bereft; / In t'other man doth Paradise regain" (Shawcross 2:86).

Further anecdotal information about *Paradise Regained* comes from Edward Phillips, the poet's nephew and former pupil. Having served at least for a while as Milton's amanuensis, he was as likely as anyone to know what the author was writing when, and therefore, despite numerous attempts by modern scholars to

suggest an earlier composition, we are strongly inclined to accept his clear asser-
tion that *Paradise Regained* was written after the publication of *Paradise Lost* in 1667,
and in a very short period of time. That Milton made, relatively speaking, quick
work of *Paradise Regained* is important for dating *Samson Agonistes*, since on that
basis it is reasonable to assume that he had time to compose both the new epic
and the drama between August 1667 and September 10, 1670, when the two works
were entered in the Stationer's Register (see introduction to *Samson Agonistes*).
They were published together in 1670 (see "A Note on the Text" in this volume).
The title of the epic appeared first on the title page, and in larger type, no doubt
in part because the publisher hoped to sell the volume to owners of *Paradise Lost.*

Phillips also reported that, despite the "sublimeness" of the work, "it is gen-
erally censured to be much inferior to the other [*Paradise Lost*]." Milton, how-
ever, "could not hear with patience any such thing when related to him."
Phillips wondered if the subject of the poem allowed for the "variety of inven-
tion" found in *Paradise Lost*. But even this difference was not in his view deci-
sive: "It is thought by the judicious to be little or nothing inferior to the other
for style and decorum" (Darbishire 75–76). The two works are connected by
their titles, their blank verse, their progression through Christian history, their
focus on temptation (the disobedient first Adam saved by the obedient second
Adam), and the shared characters of Satan and the Son. It may be this element
of connection that drove Milton to impatience when he heard that *Lost* was pre-
ferred to *Regained*: in his mind they were in some ways one work, not two. The
only invocation establishes that Milton's inspiration in the present poem con-
tinues the inspiration of *Paradise Lost.*

But as the author must have realized, there are differences as well. Far from
being inherent in the material or the result of declining artistic powers, they ap-
pear to be entirely deliberate. The style throughout aspires to a magnificent
plainness that is expressly justified in the work when Jesus prefers the Hebrew
Psalms to Greek poetry. Does this plain manner represent, as Shoulson argues, a
measured retreat from the inspired "enthusiasm" so often condemned by oppo-
nents of Puritan radicalism? If so, Milton's recoil from the poetic exuberance of
Paradise Lost could be linked to a gradual, deepening repudiation of the millenar-
ianism of his first pamphlets (Regina Schwartz 27–30; Revard 203; Guibbory). Yet as
early as 1642, Milton gave expression to this aesthetic conviction when explain-
ing in *The Reason of Church Government* that he had switched his literary ambitions
from Latin to "the adorning of my native tongue." Something he suspected or
did not like in the word *adorning* led to an immediate qualification: "not to make
verbal curiosities the end, that were a toilsome vanity, but to be an interpreter
and relater of the best and sagest things" (p. 840). The biblical "toilsome vanity"
rebukes an infatuation with "verbal curiosities" lurking in the treacherous
"adorning." There are quite a large number of verbal curiosities in *Paradise Lost.*
One could (and should!) argue that they are not "the end" but rather the means
by which meanings are generated in the large epic. One could (and should!)
argue that they are successes rather than failures. An appreciation for the opu-

lence of *Paradise Lost* dooms most of the world to prefer it to *Paradise Regained*. But the brief epic's "studied reserve of ornament," in the phrase of Charles Dunster (Shawcross 2:377), also doomed Milton to shake his head over our stubborn frivolity. For he believed in a higher style, a style suitable for "an interpreter and relater of the best and sagest things." The curtailing of simile and the simpler syntax in *Paradise Regained* are examples of what Phillips's judicious readers called "decorum," the adjustment of style to subject. Milton thought that Jesus exemplified a sublime plainness in both his life and his preaching. However audacious such a notion may seem to us, the opening lines of the work make it clear that, in the author's Christian mind, *Paradise Regained* is the epic *Aeneid* to *Paradise Lost's Eclogues* and *Georgics*. The flashy literariness of *Paradise Lost* yields in maturity to a studied reserve of ornament.

Elizabeth M. Pope's *Paradise Regained: The Tradition and the Poem* (1947) remains indispensable for acquiring a knowledge of how the temptations were understood in the traditions of biblical exegesis, theological commentary, and Christian art. Barbara K. Lewalski's *Milton's Brief Epic: The Genre, Meaning, and Art of Paradise Regained* (1966), the first of her notable studies of genre, argues that the poem is what Milton called a "brief" epic, citing the Book of Job as its model (Yale 1:813). But neither the Book of Job, nor the poems based on it, nor the other brief epics surveyed by Lewalski have quite the atmosphere of high-minded debate found in *Paradise Regained*. Milton had certainly experimented in *Paradise Lost* with poetic debates—the council of fallen angels in Book 2, the exchanges between Satan and the angelic guard in Book 4, the debate between Satan and Abdiel at the end of Book 6, the argument between Adam and Eve over working separately in Book 9, and the mutual accusations of the fallen pair at the end of Book 9. Indeed, his interest in the poetry of argument could be traced back to the temptation scene in *A Masque* or to *L'Allegro* and *Il Penseroso*. But in *Paradise Regained,* the whole poem is built on the conversing of absolute contraries. The main problem with Lewalski's study is that she makes the poem sound more traditional than it actually is. "Among numerous Italian and French Biblical poems of the sixteenth and seventeenth centuries, I have found none which even remotely resembles *Paradise Regained,*" MacKellar reported. "Milton, in short, displays a singular independence of traditional literary forms" (Hughes et al. 4:10).

Others have sought the genre of the poem not in the Book of Job but in Vergil's *Georgics* (Martz; Fowler 1984; Low 1985, 296–352). But this sort of classifying admits into one's sense of genre a rather alarming elasticity. The *Georgics* is didactic but not meditative, contains no action, and unlike *Paradise Regained* relies stylistically on profuse pictorial imagery and mythological allusion (Hughes et al. 4:15). Critics in search of English analogues have usually adduced Giles Fletcher's *Christ's Victory and Triumph* and Joseph Beaumont's *Psyche*. But Fletcher does not represent Mary, a significant presence in Milton. Neither work has the immense historical precision of Milton's temptation of the kingdoms, or the profoundly ironic recognition scene that he fashioned in the third temptation. As Northrop Frye observed, Milton's poem is "practically *sui generis.*

None of the ordinary literary categories apply to it; its poetic predecessors are nothing like it, and it has left no descendants" (1965, 235). *Paradise Regained* has nothing essential in common with the stiffly allegorical Fletcher or the diffuse Beaumont. However one may rank it vis-à-vis *Paradise Lost,* the fierce originality of the work ought to be appreciated.

A good deal of crucial material in *Paradise Regained* is left tacit and implicit. Milton does not expressly inform his readers, for example, exactly how much his protagonists know of each other. From Satan's "His first-begot we know, and sore have felt, / When his fierce thunder drove us to the deep; / Who this is we must learn" (1.89–91), we deduce that while Satan knows that Jesus is the woman's seed destined to bruise his head (1.64–65), he does not recognize in Jesus the Son of Book 6 of *Paradise Lost,* whose elevation prompted his envious rebellion and whose decisive appearance on the third day of the war drove him and his troops from Heaven. Jesus also indicates no knowledge of those cosmic events. He understands by searching the Scriptures that he is the prophesied Messiah, destined to redeem mankind and deliver a weakening blow to Satan (1.259–67), but he does not realize that defeating Satan belongs to his divinity as much as to his humanity. John Carey insists that Jesus in this poem never acts as more than a man, albeit a perfect one (1970, 124–30). But this reading blocks out the cosmic dimension in the climactic irony. Satan and Jesus move toward a showdown on the pinnacle. The Son manifests his divinity; Satan reels in amazement. The moment recapitulates the climax of *Paradise Lost*'s War in Heaven, as again Satan falls (or rather hurls himself, as before in *PL* 6.864–65), and again the victorious Son is hymned by angels. The intricate Christology of the work has been studied in its seventeenth-century context by Rogers and Stoll (231–63).

Phillips was surely wrong in supposing that Milton cut back on invention. The first temptation is rendered pretty much as in Luke 4.2–4, then expanded by the lavish demonic banquet. This enlargement by invention creates a pattern of expectation confirmed in the second temptation. The Bible's unspecified "kingdoms of the world" full of political and religious "power and glory" (Luke 4.5–6) first become incarnate in the kingdoms of Parthia and Rome. Thus far Milton's version is full of novelties but not exactly inventions, since he is filling in the Bible's unspecified kingdoms with plausible particulars. But the Athenian temptation, with its shift from political and religious power and glory to literary and intellectual power and glory, is a real addition.

Like the hero, we must be patient. Plots based on counting and repetition normally place their climax on the third time, third wish, third temptation. An alert reader of *Paradise Regained* comes to the third temptation eager to apprehend its novelty. And it awaits him there, the life of the work, the most extraordinary of Milton's inventions. As Rev. Calton noted in the Newton variorum of 1753: "All the poems that ever were written must yield, even *Paradise Lost* must yield, to the *Regained* in the grandeur of its close." An overstatement, surely. But one that today's readers, as they add *Paradise Regained* to their literary experience, may find inspiring.

PARADISE REGAINED

Book I

I who erewhile the happy garden sung,
By one man's disobedience lost, now sing
Recovered Paradise to all mankind,
By one man's firm obedience fully tried
5 Through all temptation, and the tempter foiled
In all his wiles, defeated and repulsed,
And Eden raised in the waste wilderness.
    Thou Spirit who led'st this glorious eremite
Into the desert, his victorious field
10 Against the spiritual foe, and brought'st him thence
By proof the undoubted Son of God, inspire,
As thou art wont, my prompted song else mute,
And bear through highth or depth of nature's bounds
With prosperous wing full summed to tell of deeds
15 Above heroic, though in secret done,
And unrecorded left through many an age,
Worthy t' have not remained so long unsung.

1–2. The opening lines allude to *Paradise Lost* via a four-line passage that appears at the beginning of the *Aeneid* in many Renaissance editions, where Vergil contrasts his rural pastoral songs with the martial subject of his epic; see Spenser, proem to *FQ.* Milton audaciously suggests that *PL*'s *happy garden* (not altogether so!) is a youthful pastoral in relation to the superlative epic heroism of *PR*.

2–4. "For as by one man's disobedience many were made sinners, so by the obedience of one shall many be made righteous" (Rom. 5.19).

8. **Spirit:** "Then was Jesus led up of the spirit into the wilderness" (Matt. 4.1). Conventionally, "spirit" in this verse was identified with the Holy Spirit, but Milton in *CD* 1.6, arguing against the idea of the Holy Spirit as a distinct person in the Godhead, concludes that the Holy Spirit "cannot be a God nor an object of invocation" (Yale 6:295); **eremite:** hermit, desert dweller.

12. **As thou art wont:** referring to the inspiration-aided creation of *PL*, and possibly other works.

14. **full summed:** in full plumage (falconry term).

16. **unrecorded:** But the Gospel accounts were recorded. Leonard would clear the problem away by supposing that *unrecorded* means "not rendered in song," yet what of poems such as Vida's *Christiad* (see *Passion* 26n)? According to Carey, the line implies that "Milton believed the events he adds to the gospel narrative really happened, and are revealed to him by the heavenly Muse." A similar difficulty arises with regard to *PL* 1.16.

Now had the great proclaimer with a voice
More awful than the sound of trumpet, cried
20   Repentance, and Heaven's Kingdom nigh at hand
To all baptized: to his great baptism flocked
With awe the regions round, and with them came
From Nazareth the son of Joseph deemed
To the flood Jordan, came as then obscure,
25   Unmarked, unknown; but him the Baptist soon
Descried, divinely warned, and witness bore
As to his worthier, and would have resigned
To him his heav'nly office, nor was long
His witness unconfirmed: on him baptized
30   Heaven opened, and in likeness of a dove
The Spirit descended, while the Father's voice
From Heav'n pronounced him his beloved Son.
That heard the Adversary, who roving still
About the world, at that assembly famed
35   Would not be last, and with the voice divine
Nigh thunderstruck, th' exalted man, to whom
Such high attest was giv'n, a while surveyed
With wonder, then with envy fraught and rage
Flies to his place, nor rests, but in mid-air
40   To council summons all his mighty peers,
Within thick clouds and dark tenfold involved,
A gloomy consistory; and them amidst
With looks aghast and sad he thus bespake.
    "O ancient powers of air and this wide world,
45   For much more willingly I mention air,
This our old conquest, than remember Hell
Our hated habitation; well ye know
How many ages, as the years of men,
This universe we have possessed, and ruled
50   In manner at our will th' affairs of earth,
Since Adam and his facile consort Eve
Lost Paradise deceived by me, though since

---

18. **great proclaimer:** John the Baptist.
20. Cp. Matt. 3.2.
23. **son of Joseph deemed:** Luke 3.23.
26. **divinely warned:** See John 1.33.
29–32. Milton mainly follows Matt. 3.16–17: "He saw the spirit of God descending like a dove: and lo a voice from heaven, saying, This is my beloved Son, in whom I am well pleased."
33. **the Adversary:** Satan; **still:** continually.

39. **place:** home; for the notion that devils rule the air, see Eph. 2.2.
42. **consistory:** council; the term was applied to the Catholic senate of the Pope and cardinals, and to the ecclesiastical court of the Anglican Church.
48. **as the years of men:** as men measure time.
51. **facile:** easily led.

With dread attending when that fatal wound
Shall be inflicted by the seed of Eve
55 Upon my head, long the decrees of Heav'n
Delay, for longest time to him is short;
And now too soon for us the circling hours
This dreaded time have compassed, wherein we
Must bide the stroke of that long threaten'd wound,
60 At least if so we can, and by the head
Broken be not intended all our power
To be infringed, our freedom and our being
In this fair empire won of earth and air;
For this ill news I bring, the woman's seed
65 Destined to this, is late of woman born;
His birth to our just fear gave no small cause,
But his growth now to youth's full flow'r, displaying
All virtue, grace and wisdom to achieve
Things highest, greatest, multiplies my fear.
70 Before him a great prophet, to proclaim
His coming, is sent harbinger, who all
Invites, and in the consecrated stream
Pretends to wash off sin, and fit them so
Purified to receive him pure, or rather
75 To do him honor as their king; all come,
And he himself among them was baptized,
Not thence to be more pure, but to receive
The testimony of Heav'n, that who he is
Thenceforth the nations may not doubt; I saw
80 The prophet do him reverence, on him rising
Out of the water, Heav'n above the clouds
Unfold her crystal doors, thence on his head
A perfect dove descend, whate'er it meant,
And out of Heav'n the sov'reign voice I heard,
85 'This is my Son beloved, in him am pleased.'

53. **attending:** awaiting.
53–55. **that fatal wound . . . head:** The protevangelium or "first gospel" of Gen. 3.15 is crucial to the design of both *PL* (see 10.175–81) and *PR*.
56. **longest time to him is short:** "A thousand years in thy sight art but as yesterday" (Ps. 90.4).
57. **too soon for us:** God has delayed the realization of his sentence with the grand nonchalance of an eternal being—but not long enough for the guilty devils. **circling hours:** See *PL* 6.3.
59. **bide:** endure.

60. **if so we can:** Whether devils may be mortal is a point of speculation in *PL* 2.94–101, 145–59.
62. **infringed:** broken (from Lat. *infrangere*).
66. Satan did not learn of Jesus at his baptism but has followed his life from infancy.
73. **Pretends:** claims.
83. **whate'er it meant:** Amazement in the face of divine action often characterizes the opponents of God in Milton's work; see *Areop* (*MLM* 960), *PL* 12.496–97, *SA* 1645, and the supreme instance of this motif, *PR* 4.562.

His mother then is mortal, but his sire,
He who obtains the monarchy of Heav'n,
And what will he not do to advance his Son?
His first-begot we know, and sore have felt,
90 When his fierce thunder drove us to the deep;
Who this is we must learn, for man he seems
In all his lineaments, though in his face
The glimpses of his Father's glory shine.
Ye see our danger on the utmost edge
95 Of hazard, which admits no long debate,
But must with something sudden be opposed,
Not force, but well-couched fraud, well-woven snares,
Ere in the head of nations he appear
Their king, their leader, and supreme on earth.
100 I, when no other durst, sole undertook
The dismal expedition to find out
And ruin Adam, and the exploit performed
Successfully; a calmer voyage now
Will waft me; and the way found prosperous once
105 Induces best to hope of like success."
　　　He ended, and his words impression left
Of much amazement to th' infernal crew,
Distracted and surprised with deep dismay
At these sad tidings; but no time was then
110 For long indulgence to their fears or grief:
Unanimous they all commit the care
And management of this main enterprise
To him their great dictator, whose attempt
At first against mankind so well had thrived
115 In Adam's overthrow, and led their march
From Hell's deep-vaulted den to dwell in light,
Regents and potentates, and kings, yea gods
Of many a pleasant realm and province wide.
So to the coast of Jordan he directs

---

87. **obtains:** holds.

89. **first-begot:** the Son; Satan then remembers *PL* 6.749–866.

91. **Who this is we must learn:** The high theological comedy of *PR* stems from this benighted quest. Satan already knows a great deal about Jesus: that he is the prophesied "woman's seed," that his fulfillment of the prophecy has been announced by John the Baptist, and that God himself has acknowledged Jesus as his Son. But Satan does not recognize in Jesus the thunder-

wielding conqueror of *PL* 6, in part because *His mother . . . is mortal,* whereas the Son in Heaven did not have a mother. See *PR* 4.500–540n.

94–95. **the utmost edge/Of hazard:** Cp. Shakespeare, *AWW* 3.3.6.

97. **well-couched:** well concealed.

100–102. **I . . . Adam:** See *PL* 2.430–66.

107. **amazement:** alarm.

113. **dictator:** Roman term for a person given extraordinary powers during a time of emergency.

120   His easy steps; girded with snaky wiles,
      Where he might likeliest find this new-declared,
      This man of men, attested Son of God,
      Temptation and all guile on him to try;
      So to subvert whom he suspected raised
125   To end his reign on earth so long enjoyed:
      But contrary unweeting he fulfilled
      The purposed council preordained and fixed
      Of the Most High, who in full frequence bright
      Of angels, thus to Gabriel smiling spake.
130   "Gabriel, this day by proof thou shalt behold,
      Thou and all angels conversant on earth
      With man or men's affairs, how I begin
      To verify that solemn message late,
      On which I sent thee to the virgin pure
135   In Galilee, that she should bear a son
      Great in renown, and called the Son of God;
      Then told'st her doubting how these things could be
      To her a virgin, that on her should come
      The Holy Ghost, and the power of the Highest
140   O'ershadow her: this man born and now upgrown,
      To show him worthy of his birth divine
      And high prediction, henceforth I expose
      To Satan; let him tempt and now assay
      His utmost subtlety, because he boasts
145   And vaunts of his great cunning to the throng
      Of his apostasy; he might have learnt
      Less overweening, since he failed in Job,
      Whose constant perseverance overcame
      Whate'er his cruel malice could invent.
150   He now shall know I can produce a man
      Of female seed, far abler to resist
      All his solicitations, and at length
      All his vast force, and drive him back to Hell,
      Winning by conquest what the first man lost
155   By fallacy surprised. But first I mean

126. A similar irony is found in *PL* 1.210–20.

128. **frequence:** assembly.

129. **Gabriel:** the angel of the Annunciation (Luke 1.26–38) and commander of the angels standing watch over Paradise in *PL* (4.549–50).

143. **assay:** practice by way of trial.

144. **His utmost subtlety:** probably Satan's utmost subtlety, though the phrase might refer to Jesus.

147. **overweening:** arrogance; **Job:** Milton believed that the Book of Job was the model for a "brief epic" (*MLM* 840). On the relationship between *PR* and Job, see Lewalski 1966, 10–36 and *passim*.

To exercise him in the wilderness,
There he shall first lay down the rudiments
Of his great warfare, ere I send him forth
To conquer Sin and Death the two grand foes,
160 By humiliation and strong sufferance:
His weakness shall o'ercome Satanic strength
And all the world, and mass of sinful flesh;
That all the angels and ethereal powers,
They now, and men hereafter may discern,
165 From what consummate virtue I have chose
This perfect man, by merit called my Son,
To earn salvation for the sons of men."
　　So spake the Eternal Father, and all Heav'n
Admiring stood a space, then into hymns
170 Burst forth, and in celestial measures moved,
Circling the throne and singing, while the hand
Sung with the voice, and this the argument.
　　"Victory and triumph to the Son of God
Now ent'ring his great duel, not of arms,
175 But to vanquish by wisdom hellish wiles.
The Father knows the Son; therefore secure
Ventures his filial virtue, though untried,
Against whate'er may tempt, whate'er seduce,
Allure, or terrify, or undermine.
180 Be frustrate all ye stratagems of Hell,
And devilish machinations come to naught."
　　So they in Heav'n their odes and vigils tuned:
Meanwhile the Son of God, who yet some days
Lodged in Bethabara where John baptized,
185 Musing and much revolving in his breast,
How best the mighty work he might begin
Of savior to mankind, and which way first
Publish his Godlike office now mature,

156. **exercise:** train by practice; prepare for a task by performing a similar but less difficult one.

159. **Sin and Death:** In *PL,* the offspring of Satan (2.648–73).

161. "God hath chosen the weak things of the world to confound the things which are mighty" (1 Cor. 1.27).

161–62. **Satanic . . . world . . . flesh:** See the renunciation of the world, the flesh, and the devil that precedes baptism in the Book of Common Prayer.

166. **This perfect man:** As Calton explains in the

1753 Newton variorum, "Not a word is here said of the Son of God, but what a Socinian would allow" (2:16), then argues that the overall plan of the work is *not* Socinian, in that Jesus shows a flash of his "God-like force" (4.602) at the end of the poem. See 4.561n.

171. **the hand:** musical instruments played by hand.

172. **argument:** subject matter.

182. **vigils:** night hymns.

188. **his Godlike office:** On the tripartite "office" or role of the Son—as Prophet, King, and Priest—see Lewalski 1966, 182–92.

One day forth walked alone, the Spirit leading,
190 And his deep thoughts, the better to converse
With solitude, till far from track of men,
Thought following thought, and step by step led on,
He entered now the bordering desert wild,
And with dark shades and rocks environed round,
195 His holy meditations thus pursued.
"O what a multitude of thoughts at once
Awakened in me swarm, while I consider
What from within I feel myself, and hear
What from without comes often to my ears,
200 Ill sorting with my present state compared.
When I was yet a child, no childish play
To me was pleasing, all my mind was set
Serious to learn and know, and thence to do
What might be public good; myself I thought
205 Born to that end, born to promote all truth,
All righteous things: therefore above my years,
The law of God I read, and found it sweet,
Made it my whole delight, and in it grew
To such perfection, that ere yet my age
210 Had measured twice six years, at our great feast
I went into the Temple, there to hear
The teachers of our Law, and to propose
What might improve my knowledge or their own;
And was admired by all, yet this not all
215 To which my Spirit aspired; victorious deeds
Flamed in my heart, heroic acts, one while
To rescue Israel from the Roman yoke,
Then to subdue and quell o'er all the earth
Brute violence and proud tyrannic power,
220 Till truth were freed, and equity restored:
Yet held it more humane, more heav'nly, first
By winning words to conquer willing hearts,
And make persuasion do the work of fear;
At least to try, and teach the erring soul

---

200. **sorting:** corresponding.

209–14. **To such perfection . . . by all:** Luke
2.46–50, to which Milton adds the idea that
Jesus came to the Temple to teach the doctors.

218. **subdue and quell:** The young Jesus already
considered, and rejected, a military conquest of
the kingdoms of the world, such as Satan will
offer him in 3.152–805.

220. **equity:** fairness; in law, an appeal to general
precepts of justice in order to correct or sup-
plement the normal provisions of the law (*OED*
2.3); see Hooker, *Of the Laws of Ecclesiastical
Polity*, 5.9.3.

223. **persuasion:** "Persuasion certainly is a more
winning, and more manlike way to keep men in
obedience than fear" (*RCG* in Yale 1:746).

225   Not wilfully misdoing, but unware
     Misled; the stubborn only to subdue.
     These growing thoughts my mother soon perceiving
     By words at times cast forth inly rejoiced,
     And said to me apart, 'High are thy thoughts
230   O son, but nourish them and let them soar
     To what highth sacred virtue and true worth
     Can raise them, though above example high;
     By matchless deeds express thy matchless sire.
     For know, thou art no son of mortal man,
235   Though men esteem thee low of parentage,
     Thy father is the Eternal King, who rules
     All Heav'n and Earth, angels and sons of men.
     A messenger from God foretold thy birth
     Conceived in me a virgin, he foretold
240   Thou shouldst be great and sit on David's throne,
     And of thy kingdom there should be no end.
     At thy nativity a glorious choir
     Of angels in the fields of Bethlehem sung
     To shepherds watching at their folds by night,
245   And told them the Messiah now was born,
     Where they might see him, and to thee they came;
     Directed to the manger where thou lay'st,
     For in the inn was left no better room:
     A star, not seen before in heav'n appearing
250   Guided the wise men thither from the east,
     To honor thee with incense, myrrh, and gold,
     By whose bright course led on they found the place,
     Affirming it thy star new-grav'n in heav'n,
     By which they knew thee King of Israel born.
255   Just Simeon and prophetic Anna, warned
     By vision, found thee in the temple, and spake
     Before the altar and the vested priest,
     Like things of thee to all that present stood.'
     This having heard, straight I again revolved
260   The law and prophets, searching what was writ
     Concerning the Messiah, to our scribes
     Known partly, and soon found of whom they spake
     I am; this chiefly, that my way must lie

---

226. **subdue:** 1671 reads "destroy," corrected in the errata to "subdue"; cp. *PL* 6.40–41.

233. **express:** manifest.

238. **messenger:** Gabriel; see Luke 1.26–33 and Matt. 1.20–23.

253. **grav'n:** fixed.

255. **Simeon:** See Luke 2.25–35; **Anna:** See Luke 2.36–38.

259. **revolved:** studied.

Through many a hard assay even to the death,
265 Ere I the promised kingdom can attain,
Or work redemption for mankind, whose sins'
Full weight must be transferred upon my head.
Yet neither thus disheartened or dismayed,
The time prefixed I waited, when behold
270 The Baptist (of whose birth I oft had heard,
Not knew by sight) now come, who was to come
Before Messiah and his way prepare.
I as all others to his baptism came,
Which I believed was from above; but he
275 Straight knew me, and with loudest voice proclaimed
Me him (for it was shown him so from Heav'n)
Me him whose harbinger he was; and first
Refused on me his baptism to confer,
As much his greater, and was hardly won;
280 But as I rose out of the laving stream,
Heaven opened her eternal doors, from whence
The Spirit descended on me like a dove,
And last the sum of all, my Father's voice,
Audibly heard from Heav'n, pronounced me his,
285 Me his beloved Son, in whom alone
He was well pleased; by which I knew the time
Now full, that I no more should live obscure,
But openly begin, as best becomes
The authority which I derived from Heav'n.
290 And now by some strong motion I am led
Into this wilderness, to what intent
I learn not yet, perhaps I need not know;
For what concerns my knowledge God reveals."
    So spake our morning star then in his rise,
295 And looking round on every side beheld
A pathless desert, dusk with horrid shades;
The way he came not having marked, return
Was difficult, by human steps untrod;
And he still on was led, but with such thoughts
300 Accompanied of things past and to come

---

279. **hardly won:** persuaded with difficulty.
286–87. **the time/Now full:** "When the fullness of time was come, God sent forth his Son" (Gal. 4.4).
290. **motion:** divine prompting in the soul.
292. **I learn not yet:** But he will; his doing of all things in a timely fashion, obedient to the prov-

idential scheme of the Father, lies at the center of his perfection. "Even the Son . . . does not know absolutely everything, for there are some secrets which the Father has kept to himself alone" (*CD* 1.5, Yale 6:265).
294. **morning star:** Rev. 22.16.
296. **horrid:** bristling, shaggy.

Lodged in his breast, as well might recommend
Such solitude before choicest society.
Full forty days he passed, whether on hill
Sometimes, anon in shady vale, each night
305 Under the covert of some ancient oak,
Or cedar, to defend him from the dew,
Or harbored in one cave, is not revealed;
Nor tasted human food, nor hunger felt
Till those days ended, hungered then at last
310 Among wild beasts: they at his sight grew mild,
Nor sleeping him nor waking harmed, his walk
The fiery serpent fled, and noxious worm,
The lion and fierce tiger glared aloof.
But now an aged man in rural weeds,
315 Following, as seemed, the quest of some stray ewe,
Or withered sticks to gather; which might serve
Against a winter's day when winds blow keen,
To warm him wet returned from field at eve,
He saw approach, who first with curious eye
320 Perused him, then with words thus uttered spake.
    "Sir, what ill chance hath brought thee to this place
So far from path or road of men, who pass
In troop or caravan? For single none
Durst ever, who returned, and dropped not here
325 His carcass, pined with hunger and with drought.
I ask thee rather, and the more admire,
For that to me thou seem'st the man, whom late
Our new baptizing prophet at the ford
Of Jordan honored so, and called thee Son
330 Of God; I saw and heard, for we sometimes
Who dwell this wild, constrained by want, come forth
To town or village nigh (nighest is far)
Where aught we hear, and curious are to hear,
What happens new; fame also finds us out."
335   To whom the Son of God. "Who brought me hither
Will bring me hence, no other guide I seek."
    "By miracle he may," replied the swain.
    "What other way I see not, for we here

302. **solitude before choicest society:** See *Masque* 375–80, *PL* 9.249, and Abraham Cowley's essay "Of Solitude."

303. **Full forty days:** Milton, like Matt. 4.2, puts the temptation at the end of forty days of fast-ing; Mark 1.13 and Luke 4.3 maintain that the temptation took forty days.

312. **noxious worm:** poisonous snake.

334. **fame:** rumor.

Live on tough roots and stubs, to thirst inured
340 More than the camel, and to drink go far,
Men to much misery and hardship born;
But if thou be the Son of God, command
That out of these hard stones be made thee bread;
So shalt thou save thyself and us relieve
345 With food, whereof we wretched seldom taste."
He ended, and the Son of God replied.
"Think'st thou such force in bread? Is it not written
(For I discern thee other than thou seem'st)
Man lives not by bread only, but each word
350 Proceeding from the mouth of God, who fed
Our fathers here with manna? In the mount
Moses was forty days, nor eat nor drank,
And forty days Eliah without food
Wandered this barren waste, the same I now.
355 Why dost thou then suggest to me distrust,
Knowing who I am, as I know who thou art?"
Whom thus answered th' Arch-Fiend now undisguised.
" 'Tis true, I am that spirit unfortunate,
Who leagued with millions more in rash revolt
360 Kept not my happy station, but was driv'n
With them from bliss to the bottomless deep,
Yet to that hideous place not so confined
By rigor unconniving, but that oft
Leaving my dolorous prison I enjoy
365 Large liberty to round this globe of earth,
Or range in th' air, nor from the Heav'n of Heav'ns
Hath he excluded my resort sometimes.
I came among the sons of God, when he

349–50. **Man . . . God:** It is written in Matt. 4.14 and Deut. 8.3.

352. **Moses:** See Exod. 24.18.

353. **Eliah:** Milton's idiosyncratic spelling of *Elijah*; for his forty-day fast, see 1 Kings 19.8.

354. **the same I now:** Commentators often identified the desert wilderness in which Jesus was tempted with the desert in which the Jews wandered for forty years and Moses and Elijah fasted (Pope 110–12). Milton earlier (1.193) places Jesus, more probably, in the desert between Jerusalem and Jericho. As Carey and Leonard suggest, Milton apparently chose typological elegance over realism.

355. **distrust:** The first temptation, especially for

Protestants, was an occasion to distrust God as provider.

356. **Knowing who I am:** Some read the line as proof that Satan, despite his earlier doubt (see 1.91), really knows who the Son is. But there is no evidence to suggest that either of them, at this point in the poem, recognizes each other from their previous encounter in the War in Heaven (*PL* 6). They have instead proportionate knowledge of each other: Satan knows that Jesus is the prophesied redeemer, entitled Son of God; Jesus knows that Satan is the tempter of Eve and head of the fallen angels.

363. **unconniving:** unwinking.

368. **I came among the sons of God:** "The sons

Gave up into my hands Uzzean Job
370 To prove him, and illustrate his high worth;
And when to all his angels he proposed
To draw the proud King Ahab into fraud
That he might fall in Ramoth, they demurring,
I undertook that office, and the tongues
375 Of all his flatt'ring prophets glibbed with lies
To his destruction, as I had in charge.
For what he bids I do; though I have lost
Much luster of my native brightness, lost
To be beloved of God, I have not lost
380 To love, at least contemplate and admire
What I see excellent in good, or fair,
Or virtuous; I should so have lost all sense.
What can be then less in me than desire
To see thee and approach thee, whom I know
385 Declared the Son of God, to hear attent
Thy wisdom, and behold thy Godlike deeds?
Men generally think me much a foe
To all mankind: why should I? They to me
Never did wrong or violence, by them
390 I lost not what I lost, rather by them
I gained what I have gained, and with them dwell
Copartner in these regions of the world,
If not disposer; lend them oft my aid,
Oft my advice by presages and signs,
395 And answers, oracles, portents and dreams,
Whereby they may direct their future life.
Envy they say excites me, thus to gain
Companions of my misery and woe.
At first it may be; but long since with woe
400 Nearer acquainted, now I feel by proof,
That fellowship in pain divides not smart,

---

of God came to present themselves before the
Lord, and Satan came also among them" (Job
1.6).
369. **Uzzean Job:** Job was from "the land of Uz"
(Job 1.1).
372. **Ahab:** See 1 Kings 22.19–35. The "lying spirit"
sent to destroy Ahab was identified with Satan.
fraud: the state of being deceived.
373. **they demurring:** while they hesitated.
375. **glibbed:** made smooth.
383. The snarled locution seems to mean that
Satan can feel no less than a desire to see and

approach Jesus, but it flirts with the opposite
sense: "This is the last thing I want to do."
385. **attent:** attentive.
393. **disposer:** both "giver" and "ruler."
394. **my advice:** Here Milton alludes to the idea
that the devils spoke through the pagan gods
and oracles; see *PL* 1.364–75.
397. **Envy:** malice.
400. **proof:** experience.
401. Satan repudiates an old maxim found espe-
cially in the friendship tradition. See Cicero,
Laelius: On Friendship 7.23; Seneca, *De Consola-*

Nor lightens aught each man's peculiar load.
Small consolation then, were man adjoined:
This wounds me most (what can it less) that man,
405 Man fall'n shall be restored, I never more."
    To whom our Savior sternly thus replied.
"Deservedly thou griev'st, composed of lies
From the beginning, and in lies wilt end;
Who boast'st release from Hell, and leave to come
410 Into the Heav'n of Heav'ns; thou com'st indeed,
As a poor miserable captive thrall
Comes to the place where he before had sat
Among the prime in splendor, now deposed,
Ejected, emptied, gazed, unpitied, shunned,
415 A spectacle of ruin or of scorn
To all the host of Heav'n; the happy place
Imparts to thee no happiness, no joy,
Rather inflames thy torment, representing
Lost bliss, to thee no more communicable,
420 So never more in Hell than when in Heav'n.
But thou art serviceable to Heaven's King.
Wilt thou impute to obedience what thy fear
Extorts, or pleasure to do ill excites?
What but thy malice moved thee to misdeem
425 Of righteous Job, then cruelly to afflict him
With all inflictions, but his patience won?
The other service was thy chosen task,
To be a liar in four hundred mouths;
For lying is thy sustenance, thy food.
430 Yet thou pretend'st to truth; all oracles
By thee are giv'n, and what confessed more true
Among the nations? That hath been thy craft,
By mixing somewhat true to vent more lies.
But what have been thy answers, what but dark
435 Ambiguous and with double sense deluding,
Which they who asked have seldom understood,
And not well understood as good not known?
Whoever by consulting at thy shrine

---

tione ad Polybium 12.2; Thomas Browne, *Christian Morals* 1.18.
414. **emptied:** devoid of merit.
420. A worthy addition to the line of new Heaven-and-Hell aphorisms strewn across *PL*. It is anticipated at *PL* 9.118–23 and might be viewed as

a dire reconfiguration of Satan's "To which the Hell I suffer seems a Heav'n" (*PL* 4.78).
435. **Ambiguous:** Their ambiguity was a familiar complaint against the pagan oracles, and not only among the church fathers; witness Cicero, *Of Divination* 2.56.

Returned the wiser, or the more instruct
440 To fly or follow what concerned him most,
And run not sooner to his fatal snare?
For God hath justly giv'n the nations up
To thy delusions; justly, since they fell
Idolatrous, but when his purpose is
445 Among them to declare his Providence
To thee not known, whence hast thou then thy truth,
But from him or his angels president
In every province, who themselves disdaining
To approach thy temples, give thee in command
450 What to the smallest tittle thou shalt say
To thy adorers; thou with trembling fear,
Or like a fawning parasite obey'st;
Then to thyself ascrib'st the truth foretold.
But this thy glory shall be soon retrenched;
455 No more shalt thou by oracling abuse
The Gentiles; henceforth oracles are ceased,
And thou no more with pomp and sacrifice
Shalt be inquired at Delphos or elsewhere,
At least in vain, for they shall find thee mute.
460 God hath now sent his living oracle
Into the world, to teach his final will,
And sends his Spirit of Truth henceforth to dwell
In pious hearts, an inward oracle
To all truth requisite for men to know."
465   So spake our Savior; but the subtle fiend,
Though inly stung with anger and disdain,
Dissembled, and this answer smooth returned.
    "Sharply thou hast insisted on rebuke,
And urged me hard with doings, which not will
470 But misery hath wrested from me; where
Easily canst thou find one miserable,
And not enforced ofttimes to part from truth,
If it may stand him more in stead to lie,
Say and unsay, feign, flatter, or abjure?
475 But thou art placed above me, thou art Lord;

---

447. **president:** presiding. Milton speculates in *CD* 1.9 that "angels are put in charge of nations, kingdoms and particular districts."

456. **oracles are ceased:** Christians believed that the prophecy of Micah 5.12 was confirmed by Plutarch's *The Obsolescence of Oracles*. The ora-cles became dumb at the birth of Jesus (as in *Nat Ode* 173–80).

462. **Spirit of Truth:** See John 16.13.

466. **disdain:** loathing.

474. **Say and unsay:** See Milton's contemptuous dismissal of such behavior in *PL* 4.947–49.

From thee I can and must submiss endure
Check or reproof, and glad to scape so quit.
Hard are the ways of truth, and rough to walk,
Smooth on the tongue discoursed, pleasing to th' ear,
480 And tunable as sylvan pipe or song;
What wonder then if I delight to hear
Her dictates from thy mouth? Most men admire
Virtue, who follow not her lore: permit me
To hear thee when I come (since no man comes)
485 And talk at least, though I despair to attain.
Thy Father, who is holy, wise and pure,
Suffers the hypocrite or atheous priest
To tread his sacred courts, and minister
About his altar, handling holy things,
490 Praying or vowing, and vouchsafed his voice
To Balaam reprobate, a prophet yet
Inspired; disdain not such access to me."
      To whom our Savior with unaltered brow.
"Thy coming hither, though I know thy scope,
495 I bid not or forbid; do as thou find'st
Permission from above; thou canst not more."
      He added not; and Satan bowing low
His gray dissimulation, disappeared
Into thin air diffused: for now began
500 Night with her sullen wing to double-shade
The desert, fowls in their clay nests were couched;
And now wild beasts came forth the woods to roam.

476. **submiss:** submissive (lit. "placed beneath").
477. **to scape so quit:** to escape with such a relatively mild reprisal.
487. **atheous:** impious.
491–92. **To Balaam . . ./Inspired:** When Balaam was ordered by his king to curse the Jews, he obeyed God and blessed them instead (Num. 23.20).
494. **scope:** purpose.
498. **gray dissimulation:** The phrase appears in Ford's *The Broken Heart* 4.2.101.
500. **double-shade:** Cp. *Masque* 335.

Book II

Meanwhile the new-baptized, who yet remained
At Jordan with the Baptist, and had seen
Him whom they heard so late expressly called
Jesus Messiah, Son of God declared,
5 And on that high authority had believed,
And with him talked, and with him lodged, I mean
Andrew and Simon, famous after known
With others though in Holy Writ not named,
Now missing him their joy so lately found,
10 So lately found, and so abruptly gone,
Began to doubt, and doubted many days,
And as the days increased, increased their doubt:
Sometimes they thought he might be only shown,
And for a time caught up to God, as once
15 Moses was in the mount, and missing long;
And the great Thisbite who on fiery wheels
Rode up to Heav'n, yet once again to come.
Therefore as those young prophets then with care
Sought lost Eliah, so in each place these
20 Nigh to Bethabara; in Jericho
The city of palms, Aenon, and Salem old,
Machaerus and each town or city walled
On this side the broad lake Genezaret,
Or in Perea, but returned in vain.
25 Then on the bank of Jordan, by a creek

14–15. **as once/Moses:** See Exod. 32.1.
16. **great Thisbite:** Elijah, born in the city of Thisbe; the story of his ascension appears in 2 Kings 2.11.
17. **yet once again to come:** as foretold in Mal. 4.5.
19. **Eliah:** Milton's way of spelling *Elijah*, though he uses the more familiar spelling in line 268.
21. **Aenon and Salem old:** cities where, as in Bethabara, John baptized (John 3.23).
22. **Machaerus:** a desert fortress, where John was believed to have been executed.
23. **lake Genezaret:** Sea of Galilee.
24. **Perea:** a land to the east of Jordan.

Where winds with reeds, and osiers whisp'ring play,
Plain fishermen, no greater men them call,
Close in a cottage low together got
Their unexpected loss and plaints outbreathed.
30   "Alas, from what high hope to what relapse
Unlooked for are we fall'n, our eyes beheld
Messiah certainly now come, so long
Expected of our fathers; we have heard
His words, his wisdom full of grace and truth,
35   Now, now, for sure, deliverance is at hand,
The kingdom shall to Israel be restored:
Thus we rejoiced, but soon our joy is turned
Into perplexity and new amaze:
For whither is he gone, what accident
40   Hath rapt him from us? Will he now retire
After appearance, and again prolong
Our expectation? God of Israel,
Send thy Messiah forth, the time is come;
Behold the kings of the earth, how they oppress
45   Thy chosen, to what highth their power unjust
They have exalted, and behind them cast
All fear of thee; arise and vindicate
Thy glory, free thy people from their yoke,
But let us wait; thus far he hath performed,
50   Sent his anointed, and to us revealed him,
By his great prophet, pointed at and shown,
In public, and with him we have conversed;
Let us be glad of this, and all our fears
Lay on his Providence; he will not fail
55   Nor will withdraw him now, nor will recall,
Mock us with his blest sight, then snatch him hence;
Soon we shall see our hope, our joy return."
        Thus they out of their plaints new hope resume
To find whom at the first they found unsought:
60   But to his mother Mary, when she saw
Others returned from baptism, not her son,
Nor left at Jordan, tidings of him none;
Within her breast, though calm, her breast though pure,
Motherly cares and fears got head, and raised
65   Some troubled thoughts, which she in sighs thus clad.

---

27. Imitating the opening line of Spenser's *SC*: "A   50. **his anointed:** *Messiah* means "the anointed
   shepherd's boy (no better do him call)."   one."
40. **rapt:** carried off.

"O what avails me now that honor high
To have conceived of God, or that salute
Hail highly favored, among women blest;
While I to sorrows am no less advanced,
70   And fears as eminent, above the lot
Of other women, by the birth I bore,
In such a season born when scarce a shed
Could be obtained to shelter him or me
From the bleak air; a stable was our warmth,
75   A manger his, yet soon enforced to fly
Thence into Egypt, till the murd'rous king
Were dead, who sought his life, and missing filled
With infant blood the streets of Bethlehem;
From Egypt home returned, in Nazareth
80   Hath been our dwelling many years, his life
Private, unactive, calm, contemplative,
Little suspicious to any king; but now
Full grown to man, acknowledged, as I hear,
By John the Baptist, and in public shown,
85   Son owned from Heaven by his Father's voice;
I looked for some great change; to honor? No,
But trouble, as old Simeon plain foretold,
That to the fall and rising he should be
Of many in Israel, and to a sign
90   Spoken against, that through my very soul
A sword shall pierce; this is my favored lot,
My exaltation to afflictions high;
Afflicted I may be, it seems, and blest;
I will not argue that, nor will repine.
95   But where delays he now? Some great intent
Conceals him: when twelve years he scarce had seen,
I lost him, but so found, as well I saw
He could not lose himself; but went about
His Father's business; what he meant I mused,
100 Since understand; much more his absence now
Thus long to some great purpose he obscures.
But I to wait with patience am inured;
My heart hath been a storehouse long of things

---

67. **that salute:** Gabriel's salutation at Luke 1.28.
76. **the murd'rous king:** Herod; see Matt. 2.16.
87. **Simeon plain foretold:** Luke 2.34–35.
96–99. **when . . . business:** Mary recalls the disputation in the Temple (see 1.209–14).

101. **obscures:** keeps secret.
103–4. Milton combines Luke 2.19 ("Mary kept all these things, and pondered them in her heart") and Luke 2.51 ("His mother kept all these sayings in her heart").

And sayings laid up, portending strange events."
105   Thus Mary pondering oft, and oft to mind
Recalling what remarkably had passed
Since first her salutation heard, with thoughts
Meekly composed awaited the fulfilling:
The while her son tracing the desert wild,
110   Sole but with holiest meditations fed,
Into himself descended, and at once
All his great work to come before him set;
How to begin, how to accomplish best
His end of being on Earth, and mission high:
115   For Satan with sly preface to return
Had left him vacant, and with speed was gone
Up to the middle region of thick air,
Where all his potentates in council sat;
There without sign of boast, or sign of joy,
120   Solicitous and blank he thus began.
           "Princes, Heaven's ancient sons, ethereal Thrones,
Demonian spirits now, from the element
Each of his reign allotted, rightlier called,
Powers of fire, air, water, and earth beneath,
125   So may we hold our place and these mild seats
Without new trouble; such an enemy
Is risen to invade us, who no less
Threatens than our expulsion down to Hell;
I, as I undertook, and with the vote
130   Consenting in full frequence was empowered,
Have found him, viewed him, tasted him, but find
Far other labor to be undergone
Than when I dealt with Adam first of men,
Though Adam by his wife's allurement fell,
135   However to this man inferior far,
If he be man by mother's side at least,
With more than human gifts from Heav'n adorned,
Perfections absolute, graces divine,
And amplitude of mind to greatest deeds.
140   Therefore I am returned, lest confidence
Of my success with Eve in Paradise

115. **preface:** earlier saying (Lat. *praefatio*); Satan
    said he would return (1.483–85).
116. **vacant:** at leisure.
120. **Solicitous:** anxious; **blank:** nonplussed.
122–24. Cp. *Il Pens* 93–96.

130. **frequence:** assembly.
131. **tasted:** examined, tested.
139. **amplitude of mind:** Cp. Cicero's "largeness of
    soul" (*amplitudinem animi*) in *Tusculan Disputa-
    tions* 2.26.

Deceive ye to persuasion oversure
Of like succeeding here; I summon all
Rather to be in readiness, with hand
145 Or counsel to assist; lest I who erst
Thought none my equal, now be overmatched."
  So spake the old serpent doubting, and from all
With clamor was assured their utmost aid
At his command; when from amidst them rose
150 Belial, the dissolutest spirit that fell,
The sensualest, and after Asmodai
The fleshliest incubus, and thus advised.
  "Set women in his eye and in his walk,
Among daughters of men the fairest found;
155 Many are in each region passing fair
As the noon sky; more like to goddesses
Than mortal creatures, graceful and discreet,
Expert in amorous arts, enchanting tongues
Persuasive, virgin majesty with mild
160 And sweet allayed, yet terrible to approach,
Skilled to retire, and in retiring draw
Hearts after them tangled in amorous nets.
Such object hath the power to soften and tame
Severest temper, smooth the rugged'st brow,
165 Enerve, and with voluptuous hope dissolve,
Draw out with credulous desire, and lead
At will the manliest, resolutest breast,
As the magnetic hardest iron draws.
Women, when nothing else, beguiled the heart
170 Of wisest Solomon, and made him build,
And made him bow to the gods of his wives."
  To whom quick answer Satan thus returned.
"Belial, in much uneven scale thou weigh'st
All others by thyself; because of old
175 Thou thyself dot'st on womankind, admiring
Their shape, their color, and attractive grace,
None are, thou think'st, but taken with such toys.

---

150. **the dissolutest spirit:** Belial is the lewdest of
 the devils, according to *PL* 1.490–91.
151. **Asmodai:** His lust for Sarah led him to destroy
 seven husbands (Tob. 3.8).
152. **incubus:** a demon that has intercourse with
 sleeping women (Augustine, *City of God* 15.23).
160. **terrible to approach:** Cp. *PL* 9.489–91.
164. **temper:** temperament.

165. **Enerve:** enervate, weaken.
166. **Draw out:** attract (continuing the idea of
 amorous nets in l. 162 and looking forward to the
 magnetic *draws* of l. 168).
169–71. On the amorous and religious faults of
 Solomon see, 1 Kings 11.4–8.
177. **toys:** unworthy trifles.

Before the Flood thou with thy lusty crew,
False titled Sons of God, roaming the earth
180 Cast wanton eyes on the daughters of men,
And coupled with them, and begot a race.
Have we not seen, or by relation heard,
In courts and regal chambers how thou lurk'st,
In wood or grove by mossy fountain-side,
185 In valley or green meadow to waylay
Some beauty rare, Calisto, Clymene,
Daphne, or Semele, Antiopa,
Or Amymone, Syrinx, many more
Too long, then lay'st thy scapes on names adored,
190 Apollo, Neptune, Jupiter, or Pan,
Satyr, or Faun, or Sylvan? But these haunts
Delight not all; among the sons of men,
How many have with a smile made small account
Of beauty and her lures, easily scorned
195 All her assaults, on worthier things intent?
Remember that Pellean conqueror,
A youth, how all the beauties of the east
He slightly viewed, and slightly overpassed;
How he surnamed of Africa dismissed
200 In his prime youth the fair Iberian maid.
For Solomon he lived at ease, and full
Of honor, wealth, high fare, aimed not beyond
Higher design than to enjoy his state;
Thence to the bait of women lay exposed;
205 But he whom we attempt is wiser far
Than Solomon, of more exalted mind,
Made and set wholly on the accomplishment
Of greatest things; what woman will you find,
Though of this age the wonder and the fame,
210 On whom his leisure will vouchsafe an eye
Of fond desire? Or should she confident,
As sitting queen adored on Beauty's throne,
Descend with all her winning charms begirt

178–81. Here Milton adopts a patristic tradition that the "sons of God" in Gen. 6.2–4 were fallen angels; but see *PL* 11.573–87, where he adopts the counterview that they were the sons of Seth.

186–88. A list of mortal women pursued by Greek and Roman gods, but actually pursued (as Satan here reveals) by lewd Belial.

189. **lay'st thy scapes:** blamed your escapades.

196. **Pellean conqueror:** Alexander the Great, born at Pella, treated female captives honorably (Plutarch, *Alexander* 21).

199. **he surnamed of Africa:** Scipio Africanus, who was presented with a comely Spanish captive after conquering Carthage and returned her to her betrothed (Livy 26.50).

To enamor, as the zone of Venus once
215 Wrought that effect on Jove, so fables tell;
How would one look from his majestic brow
Seated as on the top of Virtue's hill,
Discount'nance her despised, and put to rout
All her array; her female pride deject,
220 Or turn to reverent awe? For beauty stands
In the admiration only of weak minds
Led captive; cease to admire, and all her plumes
Fall flat and shrink into a trivial toy,
At every sudden slighting quite abashed:
225 Therefore with manlier objects we must try
His constancy, with such as have more show
Of worth, of honor, glory, and popular praise;
Rocks whereon greatest men have oftest wrecked;
Or that which only seems to satisfy
230 Lawful desires of nature, not beyond;
And now I know he hungers where no food
Is to be found, in the wide wilderness;
The rest commit to me, I shall let pass
No advantage, and his strength as oft assay."
235   He ceased, and heard their grant in loud acclaim;
Then forthwith to him takes a chosen band
Of spirits likest to himself in guile
To be at hand, and at his beck appear,
If cause were to unfold some active scene
240 Of various persons each to know his part;
Then to the desert takes with these his flight;
Where still from shade to shade the Son of God
After forty days fasting had remained,
Now hung'ring first, and to himself thus said.
245   "Where will this end? Four times ten days I have passed
Wand'ring this woody maze, and human food
Nor tasted, nor had appetite; that fast
To virtue I impute not, or count part
Of what I suffer here; if nature need not,

---

214. **zone of Venus:** Hera wore the girdle (*zone*) of Aphrodite when seducing Zeus (*Il.* 14.214–351).
220. **turn to:** turn into.
222–23. **plumes . . . shrink:** Ovid, discoursing on female love of praise in *The Art of Love* 1.627–28, adduces the example of "Juno's peacock," who spreads her plumes when complimented but hides them when confronted with male silence.

235. **grant:** assent.
242. **shade to shade:** shelter to shelter.
244. **Now hung'ring first:** Leonard, following Lewalski, thinks the passage contradicts 1.309. But this is overly scrupulous. Jesus, after forty days of fasting, observes in a general assessment of his situation that he is now hungry, precisely as the narrator has observed in 1.309.

250 Or God support nature without repast
Though needing, what praise is it to endure?
But now I feel I hunger, which declares,
Nature hath need of what she asks; yet God
Can satisfy that need some other way,
255 Though hunger still remain: so it remain
Without this body's wasting, I content me,
And from the sting of famine fear no harm,
Nor mind it, fed with better thoughts that feed
Me hung'ring more to do my Father's will."
260   It was the hour of night, when thus the Son
Communed in silent walk, then laid him down
Under the hospitable covert nigh
Of trees thick interwoven; there he slept,
And dreamed, as appetite is wont to dream,
265 Of meats and drinks, nature's refreshment sweet;
Him thought he by the brook of Cherith stood
And saw the ravens with their horny beaks
Food to Elijah bringing even and morn,
Though ravenous, taught to abstain from what they brought;
270 He saw the prophet also how he fled
Into the desert, and how there he slept
Under a juniper; then how awaked,
He found his supper on the coals prepared,
And by the angel was bid rise and eat,
275 And eat the second time after repose,
The strength whereof sufficed him forty days;
Sometimes that with Elijah he partook,
Or as a guest with Daniel at his pulse.
Thus wore out night, and now the herald lark
280 Left his ground-nest, high tow'ring to descry
The morn's approach, and greet her with his song:
As lightly from his grassy couch uprose
Our Savior, and found all was but a dream;
Fasting he went to sleep, and fasting waked.
285 Up to a hill anon his steps he reared,
From whose high top to ken the prospect round,
If cottage were in view, sheep-cote or herd;

259. Cp. John 4.34: "My meat is to do the will of him who sent me."
266. **brook of Cherith:** where ravens brought food to Elijah (1 Kings 17.5–6).
270. **the prophet:** Elijah, twice fed by an angel before his forty-day fast (1 Kings 19.4–8).
278. **Daniel at his pulse:** Daniel preferred *pulse* (lentils, beans, peas, et cetera) to the rich table of Nebuchadnezzar (Dan. 1.13–21); cp. *Masque* 721.

But cottage, herd or sheep-cote none he saw,
Only in a bottom saw a pleasant grove,
290   With chant of tuneful birds resounding loud;
Thither he bent his way, determined there
To rest at noon, and entered soon the shade
High-roofed and walks beneath, and alleys brown
That opened in the midst a woody scene,
295   Nature's own work it seemed (nature taught art)
And to a superstitious eye the haunt
Of wood-gods and wood-nymphs; he viewed it round,
When suddenly a man before him stood,
Not rustic as before, but seemlier clad,
300   As one in city, or court, or palace bred,
And with fair speech these words to him addressed.
    "With granted leave officious I return,
But much more wonder that the Son of God
In this wild solitude so long should bide
305   Of all things destitute, and well I know,
Not without hunger. Others of some note,
As story tells, have trod this wilderness;
The fugitive bond-woman with her son,
Outcast Nebaioth, yet found he relief
310   By a providing angel; all the race
Of Israel here had famished, had not God
Rained from Heav'n manna, and that prophet bold
Native of Thebez wand'ring here was fed
Twice by a voice inviting him to eat.
315   Of thee these forty days none hath regard,
Forty and more deserted here indeed."
    To whom thus Jesus, "What conclud'st thou hence?
They all had need, I as thou seest have none."
    "How hast thou hunger then?" Satan replied,
320   "Tell me if food were now before thee set,
Wouldst thou not eat?" "Thereafter as I like
The giver," answered Jesus. "Why should that

---

289. **bottom:** valley.

293. **brown:** shady, as in *PL* 4.246.

295. (**nature taught art**): In parenthetical short-hand, Milton addresses the old question of the relation of art to nature; for a similar perspective, see Shakespeare, *WT* 4.4.89–97.

302. **officious:** eager to please, obliging.

308. **fugitive bond-woman:** When Hagar and her son Ishmael were banished by Sarah, an angel

saved Ishmael's life by leading Hagar to a well (Gen. 21.9–21). Satan calls Ishmael *Nebaioth*, the name of his first son.

312. **manna:** See Exod. 16.35; **prophet bold:** Elijah; Milton has confused *Thebez*, a city mentioned in Judges 9.50, with Thisbe, where Elijah was born.

321–22. **Thereafter . . . giver:** Cp. *Masque* 702.

Cause thy refusal," said the subtle fiend,
"Hast thou not right to all created things,
325 Owe not all creatures by just right to thee
Duty and service, nor to stay till bid,
But tender all their power? Nor mention I
Meats by the law unclean, or offered first
To idols, those young Daniel could refuse;
330 Nor proffered by an enemy, though who
Would scruple that, with want oppressed? Behold
Nature ashamed, or better to express,
Troubled that thou shouldst hunger, hath purveyed
From all the elements her choicest store
335 To treat thee as beseems, and as her Lord
With honor; only deign to sit and eat."
      He spake no dream, for as his words had end,
Our Savior lifting up his eyes beheld
In ample space under the broadest shade
340 A table richly spread, in regal mode,
With dishes piled, and meats of noblest sort
And savor, beasts of chase, or fowl of game,
In pastry built, or from the spit, or boiled,
Grisamber-steamed; all fish from sea or shore,
345 Freshet, or purling brook, of shell or fin,
And exquisitest name, for which was drained
Pontus and Lucrine bay, and Afric coast.
Alas how simple, to these cates compared,
Was that crude apple that diverted Eve!
350 And at a stately sideboard by the wine
That fragrant smell diffused, in order stood
Tall stripling youths rich-clad, of fairer hue
Than Ganymede or Hylas; distant more
Under the trees now tripped, now solemn stood
355 Nymphs of Diana's train, and Naiades

---

324. **right to all created things:** See Heb. 1.2.
329. **young Daniel could refuse:** See Dan. 1.8.
340. **A table richly spread:** The banquet temptation, with no precedent either in the Bible or in tradition, is Milton's invention. Pope (70–79) argues that Milton wanted to strengthen the parallel between the temptations of Eve and Jesus, but the scene is in any case a great poetic setpiece with precedents in history (Lucan 10.115–16), romance (*Sir Gawain and the Green Knight* 884–94), and epic (Tasso, *GL* 10.64).
344. **Grisamber:** ambergris.

345. **shell:** Mosaic law forbids the consumption of shellfish, yet Satan has insisted that his banquet will not contain *Meats by the law unclean* (l. 328).
347. **Pontus:** the Black Sea; **Lucrine bay:** lagoon near Naples, famed for its oysters; **Afric coast:** the Nile, famed for its fish.
353. **Ganymede:** the handsome boy who served Zeus as his cupbearer; he was associated with homoerotic love. **Hylas:** the attractive boy who served Hercules.
354. **tripped:** stepped lightly.
355. **Naiades:** water nymphs.

With fruits and flowers from Amalthea's horn,
And ladies of th' Hesperides, that seemed
Fairer than feigned of old, or fabled since
Of fairy damsels met in forest wide
360 By knights of Logres, or of Lyonesse,
Lancelot or Pelleas, or Pellenore,
And all the while harmonious airs were heard
Of chiming strings, or charming pipes, and winds
Of gentlest gale Arabian odors fanned
365 From their soft wings, and Flora's earliest smells.
Such was the splendor, and the tempter now
His invitation earnestly renewed.
    "What doubts the Son of God to sit and eat?
These are not fruits forbidden; no interdict
370 Defends the touching of these viands pure;
Their taste no knowledge works, at least of evil,
But life preserves, destroys life's enemy,
Hunger, with sweet restorative delight.
All these are spirits of air, and woods, and springs,
375 Thy gentle ministers, who come to pay
Thee homage, and acknowledge thee their Lord:
What doubt'st thou Son of God? Sit down and eat."
    To whom thus Jesus temperately replied:
"Said'st thou not that to all things I had right?
380 And who withholds my power that right to use?
Shall I receive by gift what of my own,
When and where likes me best, I can command?
I can at will, doubt not, as soon as thou,
Command a table in this wilderness,
385 And call swift flights of angels ministrant
Arrayed in glory on my cup to attend:

356. **Amalthea's horn:** the cornucopia or horn of plenty with which Amalthea fed the infant Jupiter (Ovid, *Fasti* 5.115–28).

357. **Hesperides:** The Hesperides, the daughters of Hesperus, tended a garden containing golden apples; Milton calls the garden by their name.

360. **Logres:** the central area of Arthurian England; **Lyonesse:** the legendary land of Arthur's birth, now submerged.

361. A list of three Arthurian characters, all of whom appear in Malory's *Morte d'Arthur*. The adulterous and sometimes inebriated *Lancelot* is a major figure, but the ferociously combative *Pelleas* is a somewhat puzzling choice (though he pursues the Blatant Beast in Spenser's *FQ* 6.12); *Pellenore* was King of the Isles.

365. **Flora:** goddess of flowers.

368. **What doubts:** why hesitates.

369. **not fruits forbidden:** Satan ignores the shell-fish (see 344n).

370. **Defends:** forbids.

378. **temperately:** The adverb has almost an allegorical force, in that Jesus, as he speaks, *is* the ideal pattern of temperance.

382. **likes:** pleases.

384. See Ps. 78.19.

Why shouldst thou then obtrude this diligence,
In vain, where no acceptance it can find,
And with my hunger what has thou to do?
390 Thy pompous delicacies I contemn,
And count thy specious gifts no gifts but guiles."
　　　To whom thus answered Satan malcontent:
"That I have also power to give thou seest,
If of that power I bring thee voluntary
395 What I might have bestowed on whom I pleased,
And rather opportunely in this place
Chose to impart to thy apparent need,
Why shouldst thou not accept it? But I see
What I can do or offer is suspect;
400 Of these things others quickly will dispose
Whose pains have earned the far-fet spoil." With that
Both table and provision vanished quite
With sound of harpies' wings, and talons heard;
Only th' importune tempter still remained,
405 And with these words his temptation pursued.
　　　"By hunger, that each other creature tames,
Thou art not to be harmed, therefore not moved;
Thy temperance invincible besides,
For no allurement yields to appetite,
410 And all thy heart is set on high designs,
High actions; but wherewith to be achieved?
Great acts require great means of enterprise;
Thou art unknown, unfriended, low of birth,
A carpenter thy father known, thyself
415 Bred up in poverty and straits at home;
Lost in a desert here and hunger-bit:
Which way or from what hope dost thou aspire
To greatness? Whence authority deriv'st,
What followers, what retinue canst thou gain,
420 Or at thy heels the dizzy multitude,
Longer than thou canst feed them on thy cost?
Money brings honor, friends, conquest, and realms;
What raised Antipater the Edomite,

---

387. **diligence:** persistent effort to please.
401. **far-fet:** far-fetched.
403. **harpies' wings:** Harpies are large birds with female faces who snatch food and defile tables (Vergil, *Aen.* 3.225–28).
404. **importune:** persistent.

406. **that each other creature tames:** that tames every other creature.
420. "Or gain the dizzy multitude at your heels."
423. **Antipater:** Proconsul of Judea; Josephus, *Antiq.* 14.1, stresses his combination of wealth and seditiousness.

And his son Herod placed on Judah's throne
425 (Thy throne) but gold that got him puissant friends?
Therefore, if at great things thou wouldst arrive,
Get riches first, get wealth, and treasure heap,
Not difficult, if thou hearken to me,
Riches are mine, fortune is in my hand;
430 They whom I favor thrive in wealth amain,
While virtue, valor, wisdom sit in want."
To whom thus Jesus patiently replied;
"Yet wealth without these three is impotent,
To gain dominion or to keep it gained.
435 Witness those ancient empires of the earth,
In highth of all their flowing wealth dissolved:
But men endued with these have oft attained
In lowest poverty to highest deeds;
Gideon and Jephtha, and the shepherd lad,
440 Whose offspring on the throne of Judah sat
So many ages, and shall yet regain
That seat, and reign in Israel without end.
Among the heathen, (for throughout the world
To me is not unknown what hath been done
445 Worthy of memorial) canst thou not remember
Quintius, Fabricius, Curius, Regulus?
For I esteem those names of men so poor
Who could do mighty things, and could contemn
Riches though offered from the hand of kings.
450 And what in me seems wanting, but that I
May also in this poverty as soon
Accomplish what they did, perhaps and more?
Extol not riches then, the toil of fools,
The wise man's cumbrance if not snare, more apt
455 To slacken virtue, and abate her edge,
Than prompt her to do aught may merit praise.

432. **patiently:** again with virtually allegorical force (see 378n); the effect, at once simple and sublime, is repeated throughout the remainder of the poem.

439. **Gideon:** He stressed his impoverished background when commanded by God to lead Israel (Judg. 6.15); **Jephtha:** another champion of Israel with an impoverished youth (Judg. 11.1–3); **shepherd lad:** David, Jesus' ancestor who rose from shepherd to king and was promised that his seed would reign forever (Isa. 9.6–7).

446. A list, this time drawn from the Gentile world, of men who rose from poverty to power. **Quintius:** Lucius Quinctius Cincinnatus, b. c. 519 B.C.E., a Roman farmer who was briefly dictator; **Fabricius:** Gaius Fabricius Luscinus, d. after 275 B.C.E., a Roman war hero who resisted bribes; **Curius:** Manius Curius Dentatus, d. 270 B.C.E., another Roman war hero who refused to be bribed; **Regulus:** Marcus Atilius Regulus, d. c. 250 B.C.E., a captured Roman general who chose death rather than ransom.

What if with like aversion I reject
Riches and realms; yet not for that a crown,
Golden in show, is but a wreath of thorns,
460 Brings dangers, troubles, cares, and sleepless nights
To him who wears the regal diadem,
When on his shoulders each man's burden lies;
For therein stands the office of a king,
His honor, virtue, merit and chief praise,
465 That for the public all this weight he bears.
Yet he who reigns within himself, and rules
Passions, desires, and fears, is more a king;
Which every wise and virtuous man attains:
And who attains not, ill aspires to rule
470 Cities of men or head-strong multitudes,
Subject himself to anarchy within,
Or lawless passions in him which he serves.
But to guide nations in the way of truth
By saving doctrine, and from error lead
475 To know, and knowing worship God aright,
Is yet more kingly; this attracts the soul,
Governs the inner man, the nobler part,
That other o'er the body only reigns,
And oft by force, which to a generous mind
480 So reigning can be no sincere delight.
Besides to give a kingdom hath been thought
Greater and nobler done, and to lay down
Far more magnanimous, than to assume.
Riches are needless then, both for themselves,
485 And for thy reason why they should be sought,
To gain a scepter, oftest better missed.

458. **for that:** because. It is not the burdens of kingship that Jesus rejects.
459. **wreath of thorns:** anticipating the crown of thorns and the mocking "Hail, King of the Jews!" (Matt. 27.29).
476. **this:** ruling over oneself.

478. **That other:** political kingship; **o'er the body only reigns:** "Thoughts are no subjects" (Shakespeare, *MM* 5.1.451); see Tilley T244.
482–83. **to lay down . . . magnanimous:** Milton praised Cromwell for refusing kingship (*2Def* in *MLM* 1102).

Book III

So spake the Son of God, and Satan stood
A while as mute confounded what to say,
What to reply, confuted and convinced
Of his weak arguing, and fallacious drift;
5 At length collecting all his serpent wiles,
With soothing words renewed, him thus accosts.
    "I see thou know'st what is of use to know,
What best to say canst say, to do canst do;
Thy actions to thy words accord, thy words
10 To thy large heart give utterance due, thy heart
Contains of good, wise, just, the perfect shape.
Should kings and nations from thy mouth consult,
Thy counsel would be as the oracle
Urim and Thummim, those oraculous gems
15 On Aaron's breast: or tongue of seers old
Infallible; or wert thou sought to deeds
That might require th' array of war, thy skill
Of conduct would be such, that all the world
Could not sustain thy prowess, or subsist
20 In battle, though against thy few in arms.
These godlike virtues wherefore dost thou hide?
Affecting private life, or more obscure
In savage wilderness, wherefore deprive
All earth her wonder at thy acts, thyself
25 The fame and glory, glory the reward

---

2. **confounded:** a perplexity in defeat that will reappear, worsened, at the opening of Book 4, then become absolute in the *amazement* of 4.562.

14. **Urim and Thummim:** the gems in Aaron's breastplate, associated with divination (Num. 27.21).

16. **sought to:** called upon for.

25. **Fame and glory:** often assumed in classical culture to be the main motives for high achievement, as in Cicero, *On Duties* 1.8.26; the movement from the temptation of riches to the temptation of vainglory is mirrored in Spenser's *FQ* 2.

That sole excites to high attempts the flame
Of most erected spirits, most tempered pure
Ethereal, who all pleasures else despise,
All treasures and all gain esteem as dross,
30   And dignities and powers, all but the highest?
Thy years are ripe, and over-ripe; the son
Of Macedonian Philip had ere these
Won Asia and the throne of Cyrus held
At his dispose, young Scipio had brought down
35   The Carthaginian pride, young Pompey quelled
The Pontic king and in triumph had rode.
Yet years, and to ripe years judgment mature,
Quench not the thirst of glory, but augment.
Great Julius, whom now all the world admires,
40   The more he grew in years, the more inflamed
With glory, wept that he had lived so long
Inglorious: but thou yet art not too late."
    To whom our Savior calmly thus replied.
"Thou neither dost persuade me to seek wealth
45   For empire's sake, nor empire to affect
For glory's sake by all thy argument.
For what is glory but the blaze of fame,
The people's praise, if always praise unmixed?
And what the people but a herd confused,
50   A miscellaneous rabble, who extol
Things vulgar, and well weighed, scarce worth the praise?
They praise and they admire they know not what;
And know not whom, but as one leads the other;
And what delight to be by such extolled,
55   To live upon their tongues and be their talk,
Of whom to be dispraised were no small praise?
His lot who dares be singularly good.
Th' intelligent among them and the wise

---

27. **erected:** high-minded, exalted.
31. **Thy years:** According to Luke 3.23, Jesus at the time of his baptism was "about thirty years of age."
31–34. **the Son . . . dispose:** Alexander the Great had conquered the Persian Empire at twenty-five.
34–35. **young Scipio . . . pride:** Scipio at twenty-seven enjoyed victory over the Carthaginians in Spain.
35–36. **young Pompey . . . rode:** Actually, Pompey was in his forties when he defeated Mithridates,

the *Pontic king,* and celebrated his triumph in Rome.
39–42. Plutarch, *Life of Caesar* 11.3, tells how Caesar began to weep when reading a life of Alexander; asked why, he replied that he had just cause to weep, since Alexander at his age had conquered so many nations, whereas he (Caesar) had done nothing.
47–56. Contempt for popular acclaim in classical culture often went along with contempt for the *miscellaneous rabble* (l. 50): see Cicero, *Tusculan Disputations* 5.36.

Are few, and glory scarce of few is raised.
60 This is true glory and renown, when God
Looking on the earth, with approbation marks
The just man, and divulges him through Heav'n
To all his angels, who with true applause
Recount his praises; thus he did to Job,
65 When to extend his fame through Heav'n and Earth,
As thou to thy reproach may'st well remember,
He asked thee, 'Hast thou seen my servant Job?'
Famous he was in Heav'n, on Earth less known,
Where glory is false glory, attributed
70 To things not glorious, men not worthy of fame.
They err who count it glorious to subdue
By conquest far and wide, to overrun
Large countries, and in field great battles win,
Great cities by assault: what do these worthies,
75 But rob and spoil, burn, slaughter, and enslave
Peaceable nations, neighboring, or remote,
Made captive, yet deserving freedom more
Than those their conquerors, who leave behind
Nothing but ruin wheresoe'er they rove,
80 And all the flourishing works of peace destroy,
Then swell with pride, and must be titled gods,
Great benefactors of mankind, deliverers,
Worshipped with temple, priest and sacrifice;
One is the son of Jove, of Mars the other,
85 Till conqueror Death discover them scarce men,
Rolling in brutish vices, and deformed,
Violent or shameful death their due reward.
But if there be in glory aught of good,
It may by means far different be attained
90 Without ambition, war, or violence;
By deeds of peace, by wisdom eminent,
By patience, temperance; I mention still
Him whom thy wrongs with saintly patience borne,
Made famous in a land and times obscure;
95 Who names not now with honor patient Job?

59. **few:** It is precisely to "fit audience . . . though few" that *PL* is addressed (7.31).

60. **true glory and renown:** Cp. the distinction between earthly and heavenly fame in *Lyc* 70–84.

64. **thus he did to Job:** See Job 1.8.

81. **titled gods:** Kings and conquerors throughout the ancient world styled themselves gods; the Roman Senate bestowed divine titles on emperors.

82. **benefactors:** "The kings of the Gentiles . . . are called benefactors" (Luke 22.25).

86. **brutish vices:** Alexander drank heavily.

Poor Socrates (who next more memorable?)
By what he taught and suffered for so doing,
For truth's sake suffering death unjust, lives now
Equal in fame to proudest conquerors.
100 Yet if for fame and glory aught be done,
Aught suffered; if young African for fame
His wasted country freed from Punic rage,
The deed becomes unpraised, the man at least,
And loses, though but verbal, his reward.
105 Shall I seek glory then, as vain men seek
Oft not deserved? I seek not mine, but his
Who sent me, and thereby witness whence I am."
　　　To whom the tempter murmuring thus replied.
"Think not so slight of glory; therein least
110 Resembling thy great Father: he seeks glory,
And for his glory all things made, all things
Orders and governs, nor content in Heav'n
By all his angels glorified, requires
Glory from men, from all men good or bad,
115 Wise or unwise, no difference, no exemption;
Above all sacrifice, or hallowed gift
Glory he requires, and glory he receives
Promiscuous from all nations, Jew, or Greek,
Or barbarous, nor exception hath declared;
120 From us his foes pronounced glory he exacts."
　　　To whom our Savior fervently replied.
"And reason; since his word all things produced,
Though chiefly not for glory as prime end,
But to show forth his goodness, and impart
125 His good communicable to every soul
Freely; of whom what could he less expect
Than glory and benediction, that is thanks,
The slightest, easiest, readiest recompense
From them who could return him nothing else,
130 And not returning that would likeliest render
Contempt instead, dishonor, obloquy?
Hard recompense, unsuitable return

---

105. **seek glory:** "I seek not mine own glory" (John 8.50).
108. **murmuring:** complaining, accusing.
111. **for his glory:** See Rev. 4.11 and Milton, *CD* 1.7, where a number of biblical verses are cited.
119. **barbarous:** from the Greek, "foreign, non-Hellenic."

122. **And reason:** "And with good reason."
123–24. **chiefly … goodness:** That God's chief end in creation was to communicate his goodness, not just to achieve glory, was the opinion of Boethius, *Consolation of Philosophy* 3.9.4–9; Aquinas, *Summa Theologica* 1.44.4; and numerous other authorities.

For so much good, so much beneficence.
But why should man seek glory? Who of his own
135 Hath nothing, and to whom nothing belongs
But condemnation, ignominy, and shame?
Who for so many benefits received
Turned recreant to God, ingrate and false,
And so of all true good himself despoiled,
140 Yet, sacrilegious, to himself would take
That which to God alone of right belongs;
Yet so much bounty is in God, such grace,
That who advance his glory, not their own,
Them he himself to glory will advance."

145   So spake the Son of God; and here again
Satan had not to answer, but stood struck
With guilt of his own sin, for he himself
Insatiable of glory had lost all,
Yet of another plea bethought him soon.

150   "Of glory as thou wilt," said he, "so deem,
Worth or not worth the seeking, let it pass:
But to a kingdom thou art born, ordained
To sit upon thy father David's throne;
By mother's side thy father, though thy right
155 Be now in powerful hands, that will not part
Easily from possession won with arms;
Judaea now and all the promised land
Reduced a province under Roman yoke,
Obeys Tiberius; nor is always ruled
160 With temperate sway; oft have they violated
The temple, oft the law with foul affronts,
Abominations rather, as did once
Antiochus: and think'st thou to regain
Thy right by sitting still or thus retiring?
165 So did not Maccabeus: he indeed
Retired unto the desert, but with arms;

---

138. **recreant:** faithless, false.
140. **sacrilegious:** In *CD* 2.4, Milton defines *sacrilege* as "the appropriation of things vowed and dedicated to God."
154. **By mother's side thy father:** Matt. 1.1–16 and Luke 3.23–38 trace Jesus' genealogy back to David through Joseph; subsequent commentators assumed that Mary was also a descendant of David.

155. **in powerful hands:** in fact, in the hands of the Roman Empire.
160–61. **oft . . . temple:** Josephus, *Antiq.* 14, records outrages against the Temple and the law.
163. **Antiochus:** This Syrian emperor looted the Temple and forced the Jews to perform abominations (1 Macc. 1.20–2.61).
165. **Maccabeus:** Judas Maccabeus retired to Modin and rallied the Jews to defeat Antiochus (1 Macc. 3–5).

And o'er a mighty king so oft prevailed,
That by strong hand his family obtained,
Though priests, the crown, and David's throne usurped,
170 With Modin and her suburbs once content.
If kingdom move thee not, let move thee zeal,
And duty; zeal and duty are not slow;
But on Occasion's forelock watchful wait.
They themselves rather are occasion best,
175 Zeal of thy Father's house, duty to free
Thy country from her heathen servitude;
So shalt thou best fulfill, best verify
The prophets old, who sung thy endless reign,
The happier reign the sooner it begins;
180 Reign then; what canst thou better do the while?"
        To whom our Savior answer thus returned.
"All things are best fulfilled in their due time,
And time there is for all things, Truth hath said:
If of my reign prophetic writ hath told,
185 That it shall never end, so when begin
The Father in his purpose hath decreed,
He in whose hand all times and seasons roll.
What if he hath decreed that I shall first
Be tried in humble state, and things adverse,
190 By tribulations, injuries, insults,
Contempts, and scorns, and snares, and violence,
Suffering, abstaining, quietly expecting
Without distrust or doubt, that he may know
What I can suffer, how obey? Who best
195 Can suffer, best can do; best reign, who first
Well hath obeyed; just trial ere I merit
My exaltation without change or end.
But what concerns it thee when I begin
My everlasting kingdom, why art thou
200 Solicitous, what moves thy inquisition?
Know'st thou not that my rising is thy fall,
And my promotion will be thy destruction?"
        To whom the tempter inly racked replied.

---

171. **kingdom:** kingship.
173. **Occasion's forelock:** an allegorical common-place, in which Occasion (opportunity) has a forelock that must be grasped, since she is bald behind: an occasion must either be grasped quickly or lost forever.
174. **They:** zeal and duty.

183. **time there is for all things:** "To every thing there is a season, and a time to every purpose under the heaven" (Eccles. 3.1).
187. "It is not for you to know the times or the seasons, which the Father hath put in his own power" (Acts 1.7).
203. **inly racked:** as Satan was in *PL* 1.126.

"Let that come when it comes; all hope is lost
205 Of my reception into grace; what worse?
For where no hope is left, is left no fear;
If there be worse, the expectation more
Of worse torments me than the feeling can.
I would be at the worst; worst is my port,
210 My harbor and my ultimate repose,
The end I would attain, my final good.
My error was my error and my crime
My crime; whatever for itself condemned,
And will alike be punished; whether thou
215 Reign or reign not; though to that gentle brow
Willingly I could fly, and hope thy reign,
From that placid aspect and meek regard,
Rather than aggravate my evil state,
Would stand between me and thy Father's ire,
220 (Whose ire I dread more than the fire of Hell)
A shelter and a kind of shading cool
Interposition, as a summer's cloud.
If I then to the worst that can be haste,
Why move thy feet so slow to what is best,
225 Happiest both to thyself and all the world,
That thou who worthiest art shouldst be their king?
Perhaps thou linger'st in deep thoughts detained
Of the enterprise so hazardous and high;
No wonder, for though in thee be united
230 What of perfection can in man be found,
Or human nature can receive, consider
Thy life hath yet been private, most part spent
At home, scarce viewed the Galilean towns,
And once a year Jerusalem, few days'
235 Short sojourn; and what thence couldst thou observe?
The world thou hast not seen, much less her glory,
Empires, and monarchs, and their radiant courts,
Best school of best experience, quickest in sight
In all things that to greatest actions lead.
240 The wisest, unexperienced, will be ever

---

204. **Let that come when it comes:** proverbial courage; see Tilley C529.

206. **no hope . . . no fear:** See *PL* 4.108, spoken by Satan on Mount Niphates, where he is about to carry Jesus in *PR*. The following lines contain other reminiscences of Satan's soliloquy.

207–8. **the expectation . . . me:** "the expectation of worse torments me more."

222. **summer's cloud:** perhaps drawn from Isa. 25.5.

234. **once a year:** "His parents went to Jerusalem every year at the feast of the passover" (Luke 2.41).

Timorous and loth, with novice modesty,
(As he who seeking asses found a kingdom)
Irresolute, unhardy, unadvent'rous:
But I will bring thee where thou soon shalt quit
245 Those rudiments, and see before thine eyes
The monarchies of the earth, their pomp and state,
Sufficient introduction to inform
Thee, of thyself so apt, in regal arts,
And regal mysteries; that thou may'st know
250 How best their opposition to withstand."
    With that (such power was giv'n him then) he took
The Son of God up to a mountain high.
It was a mountain at whose verdant feet
A spacious plain outstretched in circuit wide
255 Lay pleasant; from his side two rivers flowed,
Th' one winding, the other straight, and left between
Fair champaign with less rivers interveined,
Then meeting joined their tribute to the sea:
Fertile of corn the glebe, of oil and wine,
260 With herds the pastures thronged, with flocks the hills;
Huge cities and high towered, that well might seem
The seats of mightiest monarchs, and so large
The prospect was, that here and there was room
For barren desert fountainless and dry.
265 To this high mountain top the tempter brought
Our Savior, and new train of words began.
    "Well have we speeded, and o'er hill and dale,
Forest and field, and flood, temples and towers
Cut shorter many a league; here thou behold'st
270 Assyria and her empire's ancient bounds,
Araxes and the Caspian lake, thence on
As far as Indus east, Euphrates west,

---

242. Saul, looking for his father's lost asses, found Samuel, who anointed him king (1 Sam. 9.3–10).

244. **But I will bring thee where:** Exactly the same locution appears in *PL* 4.470, where the context also involves a change from frustration to fulfillment.

249. **regal mysteries:** both "political skills" and "secrets of state."

252. **mountain high:** probably Niphates, as A. Gilbert (1919, 210) maintains.

255. **two rivers:** the Tigris (*straight*) and the Euphrates (*winding*), which after their confluence empty into the Persian Gulf.

259. **glebe:** cultivated land.

266. **new train of words:** The words that follow are in the ornate manner of the geographical and historical panoramas in *PL* 1.386–521 and 11.387–411, but here the poetic ornamentation expressly reflects a corrupt view of human aspiration.

270. **ancient bounds:** Satan describes the boundaries of the Assyrian Empire at its height between 722 and 626 B.C.E.

271. **Araxes:** a river (now the Aras) emptying into the Caspian Sea.

And oft beyond; to south the Persian Bay,
And inaccessible the Arabian drought:
275 Here Nineveh, of length within her wall
Several days' journey, built by Ninus old,
Of that first golden monarchy the seat,
And seat of Salmanassar, whose success
Israel in long captivity still mourns;
280 There Babylon the wonder of all tongues,
As ancient, but rebuilt by him who twice
Judah and all thy father David's house
Led captive, and Jerusalem laid waste,
Till Cyrus set them free; Persepolis
285 His city there thou seest, and Bactra there;
Ecbatana her structure vast there shows,
And Hecatompylos her hundred gates,
There Susa by Choaspes, amber stream,
The drink of none but kings; of later fame
290 Built by Emathian, or by Parthian hands,
The great Seleucia, Nisibis, and there
Artaxata, Teredon, Ctesiphon,
Turning with easy eye thou may'st behold.
All these the Parthian, now some ages past,
295 By great Arsaces led, who founded first
That empire, under his dominion holds,
From the luxurious kings of Antioch won.

274. **drought:** desert.
275. **Nineveh:** The sizable capital of Assyria, founded by Ninus.
278. **Salmanassar:** He captured the ten northern tribes of Israel (2 Kings 18.9–11).
280. **wonder of all tongues:** Editors, remembering the identification of Babel with Babylon in *PL* 12.342–43, hear a punning reference to the confusion of tongues here, but it is doubtful that Satan would find the joke amusing.
281. **rebuilt by him:** Nebuchadnezzer, who restored Babylon, captured Jerusalem and brought most of the Jews to his capital (2 Kings 25.1–22).
284. **Cyrus:** founder of the Persian Empire, who conquered Babylon and freed the Jews (Dan. 5); *Persepolis, Bactra, Ecbatana, Hecatompylos,* and *Susa* were key cities in his empire.
288. **Choaspes:** Herodotus 1.188 mentions that the kings of Persia drink only from the river Choaspes, but subsequent commentators, confused, maintained that only Persian kings drink

the waters of the Choaspes—hence Milton's *The drink of none but kings.*
290. **Emathian:** Macedonian (successors of Alexander).
291. **great Seleucia:** Seleucus Nicator, one of Alexander's generals, founded the Syrian monarchy of the Seleucidae in 301 B.C.E. and built a number of cities named after himself, including one on the river Tigris called *great. Nisibus,* modern Nisibin, is a city in northwestern Mesopotamia.
292. **Artaxata:** Armenian city on the river Araxes (now the Aras); **Teredon:** city at the junction of the Tigris and the Euphrates; **Ctesiphon**: city on the Tigris, near great Seleucus.
294–301. *Arsaces,* c. 250 B.C.E., invaded the Seleucid province of Parthia, which eventually won independence. Its ruler in the time of Christ was Artabanus III, who resisted Roman expansion as well as the barbarian Scythians.

And just in time thou com'st to have a view
Of his great power; for now the Parthian king
300 In Ctesiphon hath gathered all his host
Against the Scythian, whose incursions wild
Have wasted Sogdiana; to her aid
He marches now in haste; see, though from far,
His thousands, in what martial equipage
305 They issue forth, steel bows, and shafts their arms
Of equal dread in flight, or in pursuit;
All horsemen, in which fight they most excel;
See how in warlike muster they appear,
In rhombs and wedges, and half moons, and wings."
310   He looked and saw what numbers numberless
The city gates outpoured, light-armèd troops
In coats of mail and military pride;
In mail their horses clad, yet fleet and strong,
Prancing their riders bore, the flower and choice
315 Of many provinces from bound to bound;
From Arachosia, from Candaor east,
And Margiana to the Hyrcanian cliffs
Of Caucasus, and dark Iberian dales,
From Atropatia and the neighboring plains
320 Of Adiabene, Media, and the south
Of Susiana to Balsara's hav'n.
He saw them in their forms of battle ranged,
How quick they wheeled, and flying behind them shot
Sharp sleet of arrowy showers against the face
325 Of their pursuers, and overcame by flight;
The field all iron cast a gleaming brown,
Nor wanted clouds of foot, nor on each horn,
Cuirassiers all in steel for standing fight;
Chariots or elephants endorsed with towers

302. **Sogdiana:** the northernmost province of Alexander's empire.
309. **rhombs:** diamond-shaped formations; **wedges:** half rhombs; **half moons:** formations with the wings curved back, presenting an opponent with the army's main force; **wings:** divisions to the extreme right and left.
316. **Arachosia:** easternmost section of Parthia; **Candaor:** a province now part of Afghanistan.
317. **Margiana:** a region east of the Caspian Sea; **Hyrcanian:** Fertile Hyrcania lay to the south of Margiana.
318. **dark Iberian dales:** Iberia, modern Georgia, noted for its dense forests.
319. **Atropatia:** the northern portion of Media.
320. **Adiabene:** a plain near Nineveh.
321. **Susiana:** the southernmost province of Parthia; **Balsara's hav'n:** modern Basra, at the confluence of the Tigris and the Euphrates.
327. **clouds of foot:** translating the *nimbus peditum* of *Aen.* 7.793; **horn:** the wing of a formation (see 309n).
328. **Cuirassiers:** cavalry outfitted in cuirasses (plated body armor).
329. **endorsed:** fitted on their backs.

330 Of archers, nor of laboring pioneers
A multitude with spades and axes armed
To lay hills plain, fell woods, or valleys fill,
Or where plain was raise hill, or overlay
With bridges rivers proud, as with a yoke;
335 Mules after these, camels and dromedaries,
And wagons fraught with utensils of war.
Such forces met not, nor so wide a camp,
When Agrican with all his northern powers
Besieged Albracca, as romances tell;
340 The city of Gallaphrone, from thence to win
The fairest of her sex Angelica
His daughter, sought by many prowest knights,
Both paynim, and the peers of Charlemagne.
Such and so numerous was their chivalry;
345 At sight whereof the fiend yet more presumed,
And to our Savior thus his words renewed.
    "That thou may'st know I seek not to engage
Thy virtue, and not every way secure
On no slight grounds thy safety; hear, and mark
350 To what end I have brought thee hither and shown
All this fair sight; thy kingdom though foretold
By prophet or by angel, unless thou
Endeavor, as thy father David did,
Thou never shalt obtain; prediction still
355 In all things, and all men, supposes means;
Without means used, what it predicts revokes.
But say thou wert possessed of David's throne
By free consent of all, none opposite,
Samaritan or Jew; how couldst thou hope
360 Long to enjoy it quiet and secure,
Between two such enclosing enemies
Roman and Parthian? Therefore one of these
Thou must make sure thy own; the Parthian first
By my advice, as nearer and of late

337–44. Milton compares the *numbers numberless* (l. 310) of the Parthian army to the army of 2.2 million with which the Tartar king Agrican besieges Albracca in Boiardo's *Orlando Innamorato* 1.5–14.

347–49. **That . . . safety:** "So you may know that I do not intend to rouse your valor without making sure of your safety."

358. **opposite:** opposing.

359. **Samaritan or Jew:** By Christ's time, the Samaritans (whom the Jews despised as mongrels) occupied the northern territory where the ten tribes had lived. So Samaritans and Jews would have had to agree to accept Jesus as the king of David's old kingdom.

364–67. These events *of late* took place around 40 B.C.E. The Parthians invaded Syria and captured and eventually killed *Hyrcanus* II. But *Antigonus,*

365   Found able by invasion to annoy
Thy country, and captive lead away her kings
Antigonus, and old Hyrcanus bound,
Maugre the Roman: it shall be my task
To render thee the Parthian at dispose;
370   Choose which thou wilt by conquest or by league.
By him thou shalt regain, without him not,
That which alone can truly reinstall thee
In David's royal seat, his true successor,
Deliverance of thy brethren, those ten tribes
375   Whose offspring in his territory yet serve
In Habor, and among the Medes dispersed;
Ten sons of Jacob, two of Joseph lost
Thus long from Israel; serving as of old
Their fathers in the land of Egypt served,
380   This offer sets before thee to deliver.
These if from servitude thou shalt restore
To their inheritance, then, nor till then,
Thou on the throne of David in full glory,
From Egypt to Euphrates and beyond
385   Shalt reign, and Rome or Caesar not need fear."
      To whom our Savior answered thus unmoved.
"Much ostentation vain of fleshly arm,
And fragile arms, much instrument of war
Long in preparing, soon to nothing brought,
390   Before mine eyes thou hast set; and in my ear
Vented much policy, and projects deep
Of enemies, of aids, battles and leagues,
Plausible to the world, to me worth naught.
Means I must use thou say'st, prediction else
395   Will unpredict and fail me of the throne:
My time I told thee (and that time for thee
Were better farthest off) is not yet come;
When that comes think not thou to find me slack
On my part aught endeavoring, or to need

---

far from being captured, was installed as king of Judea. It is difficult to believe that Milton intended the inaccuracy.
368. Maugre: in spite of.
374. ten tribes: the tribes captured by Salmanassar (l. 278).
376. Habor: a tributary of the Euphrates.
377. Jacob: the patriarch of the ten lost tribes, two of which are also descended from his son *Joseph*.

384. Egypt to Euphrates: God told Abraham that the promised land stretched from "the river of Egypt unto … the river Euphrates" (Gen. 15.18).
387. fleshly arm: Cp. the "arm of flesh" that can do little without divine aid in 2 Chron. 32.8 and Jer. 17.5.
396–97. "My time is not yet come," Jesus tells his brothers in John 7.6.

400 Thy politic maxims, or that cumbersome
      Luggage of war there shown me, argument
      Of human weakness rather than of strength.
      My brethren, as thou call'st them, those ten tribes
      I must deliver, if I mean to reign
405 David's true heir, and his full scepter sway
      To just extent over all Israel's sons;
      But whence to thee this zeal, where was it then
      For Israel, or for David, or his throne,
      When thou stood'st up his tempter to the pride
410 Of numb'ring Israel, which cost the lives
      Of threescore and ten thousand Israelites
      By three days' pestilence? Such was thy zeal
      To Israel then, the same that now to me.
      As for those captive tribes, themselves were they
415 Who wrought their own captivity, fell off
      From God to worship calves, the deities
      Of Egypt, Baal next and Ashtaroth,
      And all the idolatries of Heathen round,
      Besides their other worse than heathenish crimes;
420 Nor in the land of their captivity
      Humbled themselves, or penitent besought
      The God of their forefathers; but so died
      Impenitent, and left a race behind
      Like to themselves, distinguishable scarce
425 From Gentiles, but by circumcision vain,
      And God with idols in their worship joined.
      Should I of these the liberty regard,
      Who freed, as to their ancient patrimony,
      Unhumbled, unrepentant, unreformed,
430 Headlong would follow, and to their gods perhaps
      Of Bethel and of Dan? No, let them serve
      Their enemies, who serve idols with God.
      Yet he at length, time to himself best known,
      Rememb'ring Abraham by some wond'rous call
435 May bring them back repentant and sincere,
      And at their passing cleave the Assyrian flood,

---

401. **Luggage:** encumbrance.
410. **num'bring Israel:** Displeased by this census, God sent a plague that killed 70,000 (1 Chron. 21.1–14).
415–16. **fell off/From God:** Jesus remembers the heathenish practices of the ten tribes in 1 Kings 12.25–33, 16.31–32, 17.7–18.

425. **circumcision vain:** See Rom. 2.25.
428. **patrimony:** heritage (of worshiping idols).
436. **Assyrian flood:** the Euphrates, which figures in Isaiah's prophecy about the return of the lost tribes (Isa. 11.15–16).

While to their native land with joy they haste,
As the Red Sea and Jordan once he cleft,
When to the promised land their fathers passed;
440 To his due time and providence I leave them."
So spake Israel's true King, and to the fiend
Made answer meet, that made void all his wiles.
So fares it when with truth falsehood contends.

438. God divided the Red Sea (Exod. 14.21–22) and
    the Jordan (Josh. 3.14–17).

Book IV

Perplexed and troubled at his bad success
The tempter stood, nor had what to reply,
Discovered in his fraud, thrown from his hope,
So oft, and the persuasive rhetoric
5   That sleeked his tongue, and won so much on Eve,
So little here, nay lost; but Eve was Eve,
This far his overmatch, who self-deceived
And rash, beforehand had no better weighed
The strength he was to cope with, or his own:
10   But as a man who had been matchless held
In cunning, over-reached where least he thought,
To salve his credit, and for very spite
Still will be tempting him who foils him still,
And never cease, though to his shame the more;
15   Or as a swarm of flies in vintage time,
About the wine-press where sweet must is poured,
Beat off, returns as oft with humming sound;
Or surging waves against a solid rock,
Though all to shivers dashed, the assault renew,
20   Vain battery, and in froth or bubbles end;
So Satan, whom repulse upon repulse
Met ever; and to shameful silence brought,
Yet gives not o'er though desperate of success,
And his vain importunity pursues.
25   He brought our Savior to the western side
Of that high mountain, whence he might behold
Another plain, long but in breadth not wide;
Washed by the southern sea, and on the north

---

5. **sleeked:** smoothed.
7. **This:** Jesus; **who:** Satan.

16. **must:** new wine.
19. **shivers:** fragments.

To equal length backed with a ridge of hills
30   That screened the fruits of the earth and seats of men
From cold Septentrion blasts, thence in the midst
Divided by a river, of whose banks
On each side an imperial city stood,
With towers and temples proudly elevate
35   On seven small hills, with palaces adorned,
Porches and theaters, baths, aqueducts,
Statues and trophies, and triumphal arcs,
Gardens and groves presented to his eyes,
Above the highth of mountains interposed.
40   By what strange parallax or optic skill
Of vision multiplied through air, or glass
Of telescope, were curious to inquire:
And now the tempter thus his silence broke.
     "The city which thou seest no other deem
45   Than great and glorious Rome, queen of the earth
So far renowned, and with the spoils enriched
Of nations; there the Capitol thou seest
Above the rest lifting his stately head
On the Tarpeian rock, her citadel
50   Impregnable, and there Mount Palatine
The imperial palace, compass huge, and high
The structure, skill of noblest architects,
With gilded battlements, conspicuous far,
Turrets and terraces, and glittering spires.
55   Many a fair edifice besides, more like
Houses of gods (so well I have disposed
My airy microscope) thou mayst behold
Outside and inside both, pillars and roofs
Carved work, the hand of famed artificers
60   In cedar, marble, ivory or gold.

29. **ridge of hills:** the Apennines.
31. **Septentrion blasts:** north winds; the Latin *septentrionalis*, "north," derives from the *septentriones* or "seven plow oxen" in the northern consellation Ursa Major.
32. **a river:** the Tiber.
36. **Porches:** covered colonnades.
37. **trophies:** spoils of war; **arcs:** arches.
40. **parallax:** apparent change in the location of an object.
40–41. **optic skill . . . air:** perhaps, as Svendsen (1949) suggests, linking this passage to the *airy microscope* of line 57, a fanciful device such as

the one described in Thomas Digges's *A Geometrical Practical Treatise Named Pantometria* (1591).
42. **curious:** excessively inquisitive.
49. **Tarpeian rock:** the cliffs of the Capitoline Hill.
51. **imperial palace:** probably, albeit anachronistically, the *Domus Aurea* or Golden House built by Nero after the fire of 64 C.E.
57. **airy microscope:** See 4.40–41n; by whatever trick of magnification he manages it, a desperate Satan hopes that views of the sumptuous exteriors and interiors of Roman buildings will weaken Jesus.

Thence to the gates cast round thine eye, and see
What conflux issuing forth, or ent'ring in,
Praetors, proconsuls to their provinces
Hasting or on return, in robes of state;
65   Lictors and rods the ensigns of their power,
Legions and cohorts, turms of horse and wings:
Or embassies from regions far remote
In various habits on the Appian road,
Or on the Aemilian, some from farthest south,
70   Syene, and where the shadow both way falls,
Meroe Nilotic isle, and more to west,
The realm of Bocchus to the Blackmoor sea;
From the Asian kings and Parthian among these,
From India and the golden Chersoness,
75   And utmost Indian isle Taprobane,
Dusk faces with white silken turbans wreathed:
From Gallia, Gades, and the British west,
Germans and Scythians, and Sarmatians north
Beyond Danubius to the Tauric pool.
80   All nations now to Rome obedience pay,
To Rome's great emperor, whose wide domain
In ample territory, wealth and power,
Civility of manners, arts, and arms,
And long renown thou justly mayst prefer
85   Before the Parthian; these two thrones except,
The rest are barbarous, and scarce worth the sight,
Shared among petty kings too far removed;
These having shown thee, I have shown thee all
The kingdoms of the world, and all their glory.
90   This Emperor hath no son, and now is old,

63. **Praetors:** judicial officers; **proconsuls:** governors of the Roman provinces.

65. **Lictors:** officials who executed the orders of Roman magistrates; **rods:** symbols of judicial power carried by lictors.

66. **Legion:** the largest unit of the Roman army; **cohorts:** a tenth part of a legion; **turms:** a tenth part of a wing; **wings:** cavalry deployed on either side of the infantry.

68–69. **Appian road . . . Aemilian:** The Via Appia and Via Aemilia were the chief roads to the south and north of Rome.

70. **Syene:** modern Aswan in Egypt.

70–71. Meroe, the Ethiopian capital on the Nile, thought by Roman authors to be an island, lies between the Equator and the Tropic of Cancer, so that shadows fall to the north in winter and to the south in summer.

72. **realm of Bocchus:** Mauretania, in Northern Africa; **Blackmoor sea:** the Mediterranean bordering Mauretania, home of moors or "blackamoors."

74. **golden Chersoness:** region to the east of India.

75. **Taprobane:** probably Sumatra.

77. **Gallia:** France; **Gades:** Cádiz; **the British west:** probably Brittany.

78. **Scythians:** See 3.294–301n; **Sarmatians:** barbarians to the north of the Scythians.

79. **Danubius:** the Danube, the northeastern boundary of the Roman Empire; **Tauric pool:** the Sea of Azov.

90. **This Emperor:** Tiberius, who left Rome in 26

Old, and lascivious, and from Rome retired
To Capreae, an island small but strong
On the Campanian shore, with purpose there
His horrid lusts in private to enjoy,
95 Committing to a wicked favorite
All public cares, and yet of him suspicious,
Hated of all, and hating; with what ease,
Endued with regal virtues as thou art,
Appearing, and beginning noble deeds,
100 Might'st thou expel this monster from his throne
Now made a sty, and in his place ascending,
A victor people free from servile yoke!
And with my help thou mayst; to me the power
Is giv'n, and by that right I give it thee.
105 Aim therefore at no less than all the world,
Aim at the highest, without the highest attained
Will be for thee no sitting, or not long
On David's throne, be prophesied what will."
    To whom the Son of God unmoved replied.
110 "Nor doth this grandeur and majestic show
Of luxury, though called magnificence,
More than of arms before, allure mine eye,
Much less my mind; though thou shouldst add to tell
Their sumptuous gluttonies, and gorgeous feasts
115 On citron tables or Atlantic stone;
(For I have also heard, perhaps have read)
Their wines of Setia, Cales, and Falerne,
Chios and Crete, and how they quaff in gold,
Crystal and myrrhine cups embossed with gems
120 And studs of pearl, to me should'st tell who thirst
And hunger still: then embassies thou show'st
From nations far and nigh; what honor that,
But tedious waste of time to sit and hear

C.E. and settled on Capri, where he indulged his lusts (Tacitus, *Annales* 4).

95. **wicked favorite:** Sejanus, executed in 31 C.E. after being denounced by Tiberius.

102. **servile yoke:** The oxen's yoke is a biblical symbol of slavery (Deut. 28.48, Gal. 5.1).

103–4. **to me the power / Is giv'n:** See Luke 4.6.

113. **thou should'st add to tell:** Jesus ironically intensifies Satan's tempting vision and shows that he too is a master of ornate description.

115. **citron:** made of citrus wood; **Atlantic stone:**

perhaps marble, perhaps another way of saying *citron tables.*

117–18. **Their wines . . . Crete:** Roman poets praised the Italian wines of *Setia, Cales,* and *Falerne,* and also prized Greek wines from the islands of *Chios* and *Crete.*

119. **myrrhine:** The meaning of the Latin *murra* is uncertain; it might refer to glass, onyx, or Chinese porcelain.

123–25. **But . . . flatteries?:** As Cromwell's Latin Secretary, Milton received embassies, and knew whereof Jesus speaks.

So many hollow compliments and lies,
125 Outlandish flatteries? Then proceed'st to talk
Of the emperor, how easily subdued,
How gloriously; I shall, thou say'st, expel
A brutish monster: what if I withal
Expel a devil who first made him such?
130 Let his tormenter conscience find him out;
For him I was not sent, nor yet to free
That people victor once, now vile and base,
Deservedly made vassal, who once just,
Frugal, and mild, and temperate, conquered well,
135 But govern ill the nations under yoke,
Peeling their provinces, exhausted all
By lust and rapine; first ambitious grown
Of triumph, that insulting vanity;
Then cruel, by their sports to blood inured
140 Of fighting beasts, and men to beasts exposed,
Luxurious by their wealth, and greedier still,
And from the daily scene effeminate.
What wise and valiant man would seek to free
These thus degenerate, by themselves enslaved,
145 Or could of inward slaves make outward free?
Know therefore when my season comes to sit
On David's throne, it shall be like a tree
Spreading and overshadowing all the earth,
Or as a stone that shall to pieces dash
150 All monarchies besides throughout the world,
And of my kingdom there shall be no end:
Means there shall be to this, but what the means,
Is not for thee to know, nor me to tell."
    To whom the Tempter impudent replied.
155 "I see all offers made by me how slight
Thou valu'st, because offered, and reject'st:
Nothing will please the difficult and nice,
Or nothing more than still to contradict:
On the other side know also thou, that I
160 On what I offer set as high esteem,
Nor what I part with mean to give for naught;

---

132. **That people:** the Romans.
138. **insulting:** Cp. *PL* 2.79.
139. **their sports:** Here Jesus echoes the condemnation of Tertullian, *De Spectaculis.*
147–51. Like Christian commentators to come, Jesus sees his reign as the fulfillment of the visions of the tree in Dan. 4.10–12 and the stone in Dan. 2.31–35.
151. "And of his kingdom there shall be no end" (Luke 1.33).
157. **nice:** choosy.
158. **still:** always.

All these which in a moment thou behold'st,
The kingdoms of the world to thee I give;
For giv'n to me, I give to whom I please,
165 No trifle; yet with this reserve, not else,
On this condition, if thou wilt fall down,
And worship me as thy superior lord,
Easily done, and hold them all of me;
For what can less so great a gift deserve?"
170   Whom thus our Savior answered with disdain.
"I never liked thy talk, thy offers less,
Now both abhor, since thou hast dared to utter
The abominable terms, impious condition;
But I endure the time, till which expired,
175 Thou hast permission on me. It is written
The first of all commandments, 'Thou shalt worship
The Lord thy God, and only him shalt serve;'
And dar'st thou to the Son of God propound
To worship thee accursed, now more accursed
180 For this attempt bolder than that on Eve,
And more blasphemous? Which expect to rue.
The kingdoms of the world to thee were giv'n,
Permitted rather, and by thee usurped,
Other donation none thou canst produce:
185 If giv'n, by whom but by the King of Kings,
God over all supreme? If giv'n to thee,
By thee how fairly is the giver now
Repaid? But gratitude in thee is lost
Long since. Wert thou so void of fear or shame,
190 As offer them to me the Son of God,
To me my own, on such abhorrèd pact,
That I fall down and worship thee as God?
Get thee behind me; plain thou now appear'st
That evil one, Satan forever damned."
195   To whom the fiend with fear abashed replied.
"Be not so sore offended, Son of God;

166–67. See Matt. 4.9.
174–76. **It . . . serve:** "Jesus . . . said unto him, Get thee behind me, Satan: for it is written, Thou shalt worship the Lord thy God, and him only shalt thou serve" (Luke 4.8); it is written in Deut. 6.13. Milton reverses the biblical order of these statements; *get thee behind me* does not appear until line 193.

184. **donation:** the bestowal of property or benefit on an inferior by a superior (Lat. *donatio*).
188. **gratitude in thee is lost:** See *PL* 4.51–53.
191. **To me my own:** ambiguous: "You offer to me kingdoms for my own" and "You offer to me my own kingdoms."

Though sons of God both angels are and men,
If I to try whether in higher sort
Than these thou bear'st that title, have proposed
200 What both from men and angels I receive,
Tetrarchs of fire, air, flood, and on the earth
Nations besides from all the quartered winds,
God of this world invoked and world beneath;
Who then thou art, whose coming is foretold
205 To me so fatal, me it most concerns.
The trial hath endamaged thee no way,
Rather more honor left and more esteem;
Me naught advantaged, missing what I aimed.
Therefore let pass, as they are transitory,
210 The kingdoms of this world; I shall no more
Advise thee, gain them as thou canst, or not.
And thou thyself seem'st otherwise inclined
Than to a worldly crown, addicted more
To contemplation and profound dispute,
215 As by that early action may be judged,
When slipping from thy mother's eye thou went'st
Alone into the temple; there wast found
Among the gravest Rabbis disputant
On points and questions fitting Moses' chair,
220 Teaching not taught; the childhood shows the man,
As morning shows the day. Be famous then
By wisdom; as thy empire must extend,
So let extend thy mind o'er all the world,
In knowledge, all things in it comprehend;
225 All knowledge is not couched in Moses' law,
The Pentateuch or what the prophets wrote;
The Gentiles also know, and write, and teach
To admiration, led by nature's light;

---

197. "For as many as are led by the Spirit of God, they are the sons of God" (Rom. 8.4); see also Hosea 1.10.

201. **Tetrarchs:** rulers of a fourth part, here referring to the rulers of the four elements.

215. **that early action:** See 1.209–14n.

219. **fitting Moses' chair:** befitting one sitting in Moses' chair (a scribe or Pharisee).

220–21. **childhood . . . day:** Mentioned alongside Wordsworth's "The child is father of the man" in *The Oxford Dictionary of English Proverbs,* ed. F. P. Wilson, and listed as a separate proverb in *A Dictionary of American Proverbs,* ed. Wolfgang Mieder.

221–22. **Be famous then/By wisdom:** Satan regards wisdom as another route to fame and glory (see 3.25n).

223. The idea of the mind as a kingdom was commonplace; see Dyer's "My mind to me a kingdom is," *HAM* 2.2.254–56, and *PL* 1.254–55.

226. **Pentateuch:** the first five books of the Old Testament.

228. **To admiration:** admirably; **nature's light:** a popular term in the theology of Milton's day, associated in particular with the Cambridge Platonists; see Nathanael Culverwel, *A Elegant and Learned Discourse of the Light of Nature* (1652).

And with the Gentiles much thou must converse,
230 Ruling them by persuasion as thou mean'st;
Without their learning how wilt thou with them,
Or they with thee hold conversation meet?
How wilt thou reason with them, how refute
Their idolisms, traditions, paradoxes?
235 Error by his own arms is best evinced.
Look once more ere we leave this specular mount
Westward, much nearer by southwest, behold
Where on the Aegean shore a city stands
Built nobly, pure the air, and light the soil,
240 Athens the eye of Greece, mother of arts
And eloquence, native to famous wits
Or hospitable, in her sweet recess,
City or suburban, studious walks and shades;
See there the olive grove of Academe,
245 Plato's retirement, where the Attic bird
Trills her thick-warbled notes the summer long;
There flowery hill Hymettus with the sound
Of bees' industrious murmur oft invites
To studious musing; there Ilissus rolls
250 His whispering stream; within the walls then view
The schools of ancient sages; his who bred
Great Alexander to subdue the world,
Lyceum there, and painted Stoa next:
There thou shalt hear and learn the secret power
255 Of harmony in tones and numbers hit
By voice or hand, and various-measured verse,
Aeolian charms and Dorian lyric odes,
And his who gave them breath, but higher sung,
Blind Melesigenes thence Homer called,

234. **idolisms:** idolatries; **paradoxes:** probably an allusion to moral maxims of the Stoic school, such as the ones Cicero discusses in *Paradoxa Stoicorum.*
235. **evinced:** conquered.
236. **specular:** affording an extensive view.
240. **eye of:** a classical idiom meaning "the seat of light or intelligence in."
244. **Academe:** the gymnasium west of Athens, planted with olive trees, where Plato taught.
245. **Attic bird:** the nightingale.
247. **Hymettus:** hills to the southeast of Athens, famous for their honey.
248. **industrious:** Vergil stressed the industry of

bees in *Georg.* 4.149–250; cp. "th' industrious bee" of Marvell's "The Garden."
249. **Ilissus:** small river to the south of Athens.
251. **his:** Aristotle, tutor to Alexander the Great.
253. **Lyceum:** the gymnasium where Aristotle taught; **painted Stoa:** a colonnade decorated with frescoes where philosophers congregated and argued; but particularly associated with Zeno, whose followers were therefore known as "Stoics."
257. **Aeolian charms:** Alcaeus and Sappho wrote songs (*charms*) in the Aeolian dialect; **Dorian lyric odes:** Pindar wrote odes in the Dorian dialect.
259. **Melesigenes:** a name sometimes given to

306 · Late Masterpieces

Whose poem Phoebus challenged for his own.
Thence what the lofty grave tragedians taught
In chorus or iambic, teachers best
Of moral prudence, with delight received
In brief sententious precepts, while they treat
265 Of fate, and chance, and change in human life;
High actions, and high passions best describing:
Thence to the famous orators repair,
Those ancient, whose resistless eloquence
Wielded at will that fierce democraty,
270 Shook the Arsenal and fulmined over Greece,
To Macedon, and Artaxerxes' throne;
To sage philosophy next lend thine ear,
From Heav'n descended to the low-roofed house
Of Socrates, see there his tenement,
275 Whom well inspired the oracle pronounced
Wisest of men; from whose mouth issued forth
Mellifluous streams that watered all the schools
Of Academics old and new, with those
Surnamed Peripatetics, and the sect
280 Epicurean, and the Stoic severe;
These here revolve, or, as thou lik'st, at home,
Till time mature thee to a kingdom's weight;
These rules will render thee a king complete
Within thyself, much more with empire joined."
285   To whom our Savior sagely thus replied.
"Think not but that I know these things, or think
I know them not; not therefore am I short

Homer, who was said to have been born on the banks of the river Meles; **thence Homer called:** so called because, by an ancient etymology, *Homer* derives from a Cumaean word meaning "blind."

260. Alluding to the *Greek Anthology* 9.455, where Apollo accuses Homer of plagiarizing him.

262. **In chorus or iambic:** Dialogue in Greek tragedy is written in the iambic meter, whereas the chorus has disparate meters.

269. **democraty:** democracy.

270. **Shook the Arsenal:** MacKellar cites E. C. Baldwin for the information that Demosthenes "shook" the *Arsenal* (dockyard) at Piraeus in that, on his advice, the building of it was suspended. **fulmined:** stormed in thunder and lightning.

271. **Artaxerxes' throne:** the Persian throne, hos-

tile to Greece and occupied by several kings named Artaxerxes.

273. **From Heav'n descended:** "Socrates was the first to call philosophy down from heaven" (Cicero, *Tusculan Disputations* 5.4.10).

275. **the oracle pronounced:** The Delphic oracle did indeed say that no man was wiser than Socrates (Plato, *Apology* 21), but Socrates himself interpreted this to mean that like all men he knew nothing, but unlike all men knew that he knew nothing. Jesus will allude to this point in lines 293–94.

279. **Peripatetics:** Aristotelians.

286. **Think not but:** "Think nothing but."

287–88. **not therefore . . . ought:** "I am not short of knowing what I ought in either case [knowing these Greek things, or not knowing them]."

Of knowing what I ought: he who receives
Light from above, from the fountain of light,
290 No other doctrine needs, though granted true;
But these are false, or little else but dreams,
Conjectures, fancies, built on nothing firm.
The first and wisest of them all professed
To know this only, that he nothing knew;
295 The next to fabling fell and smooth conceits,
A third sort doubted all things, though plain sense;
Others in virtue placed felicity,
But virtue joined with riches and long life,
In corporal pleasure he, and careless ease;
300 The Stoic last in philosophic pride,
By him called virtue; and his virtuous man,
Wise, perfect in himself, and all possessing
Equal to God, oft shames not to prefer,
As fearing God nor man, contemning all
305 Wealth, pleasure, pain or torment, death and life,
Which when he lists, he leaves, or boasts he can,
For all his tedious talk is but vain boast,
Or subtle shifts conviction to evade.
Alas what can they teach, and not mislead;
310 Ignorant of themselves, of God much more,
And how the world began, and how man fell
Degraded by himself, on grace depending?
Much of the soul they talk, but all awry,
And in themselves seek virtue, and to themselves
315 All glory arrogate, to God give none;
Rather accuse him under usual names,
Fortune and Fate, as one regardless quite
Of mortal things. Who therefore seeks in these
True wisdom, finds her not, or by delusion
320 Far worse, her false resemblance only meets,

---

295. **The next:** Plato.

296. **third sort:** the Skeptics.

297. **Others:** the Peripatetics, who argued that happiness demanded both virtue and material goods (Aristotle, *Nicomachean Ethics* I.11).

299. **he:** Epicurus; his teaching is more complex than Jesus allows.

302. **perfect in himself:** The Stoic ideal of autarchy (self-sufficiency) required the cultivation of *apatheia,* an utter indifference to all things outside the self.

306. **Which when he lists, he leaves:** Stoic self-sufficiency presupposed the possibility, should circumstances become intolerable, of committing suicide.

308. **subtle shifts:** the dialectical twists of Stoic argument.

317. **regardless quite:** The extremes in *regardless* deities in classical philosophy are the utterly indifferent gods of Lucretius, *On the Nature of Things,* 2.646–51.

An empty cloud. However, many books,
Wise men have said, are wearisome; who reads
Incessantly, and to his reading brings not
A spirit and judgment equal or superior,
325 (And what he brings, what needs he elsewhere seek)
Uncertain and unsettled still remains,
Deep-versed in books and shallow in himself,
Crude or intoxicate, collecting toys,
And trifles for choice matters, worth a sponge;
330 As children gathering pebbles on the shore.
Or if I would delight my private hours
With music or with poem, where so soon
As in our native language can I find
That solace? All our law and story strewed
335 With hymns, our psalms with artful terms inscribed,
Our Hebrew songs and harps in Babylon,
That pleased so well our victors' ear, declare
That rather Greece from us these arts derived;
Ill imitated, while they loudest sing
340 The vices of their deities, and their own
In fable, hymn, or song, so personating
Their gods ridiculous, and themselves past shame.
Remove their swelling epithets thick-laid
As varnish on a harlot's cheek, the rest,
345 Thin-sown with aught of profit or delight,
Will far be found unworthy to compare
With Sion's songs, to all true tastes excelling,
Where God is praised aright, and godlike men,
The Holiest of Holies, and his saints;

321. **empty cloud:** A likely allusion to the myth of Ixion, who embraced a cloud thinking it was Juno; the story often appears in indictments of erroneous intellectual pursuits.

321–22. **many books . . . wearisome:** "Of making many books there is no end; and much study is a weariness of the flesh" (Eccles. 12.12).

328. **Crude:** unable to digest.

329. **worth a sponge:** both "worth very little" and "worthy of being expunged" (sponges were used to wipe manuscripts clean so that the leaves could be overwritten).

336–37. Assyrian conquerors demand of captive Jews "songs of Zion" in Ps. 137.1–3.

338. **Greece from us these arts derived:** The Renaissance followed patristic sources in believing that the Jews invented the arts eventually

adopted by the Egyptians and Greeks. Poetry "had her original from heaven, received thence from the Hebrews, and had in prime estimation with the Greeks, transmitted to the Latins, and all nations that professed civility" (Jonson, *Timber*, in *Works*, ed. Herford and Simpson, 8:636).

341. **personating:** representing.

343. **swelling:** bombastic, pompous.

347. **to all true tastes excelling:** "All profane authors seem of the seed of the serpent that creeps; thou [God, inspirer of the Scriptures] art the dove that flies" (Donne, *Devotions* 19); **tastes:** according to the *OED* the first instance of the word meaning "the faculty of perceiving what is excellent in art or literature."

350 Such are from God inspired, not such from thee;
Unless where moral virtue is expressed
By light of nature not in all quite lost.
Their orators thou then extoll'st, as those
The top of eloquence, statists indeed,

355 And lovers of their country, as may seem;
But herein to our prophets far beneath,
As men divinely taught, and better teaching
The solid rules of civil government
In their majestic unaffected style

360 Than all the oratory of Greece and Rome.
In them is plainest taught, and easiest learnt,
What makes a nation happy, and keeps it so,
What ruins kingdoms, and lays cities flat;
These only with our law best form a king."

365   So spake the Son of God; but Satan now
Quite at a loss, for all his darts were spent,
Thus to our Savior with stern brow replied.
    "Since neither wealth, nor honor, arms nor arts,
Kingdom nor empire pleases thee, nor aught

370 By me proposed in life contemplative,
Or active, tended on by glory, or fame,
What dost thou in this world? The wilderness
For thee is fittest place, I found thee there,
And thither will return thee, yet remember

375 What I foretell thee, soon thou shalt have cause
To wish thou never hadst rejected thus
Nicely or cautiously my offered aid,
Which would have set thee in short time with ease
On David's throne; or throne of all the world,

380 Now at full age, fullness of time, thy season,
When prophecies of thee are best fulfilled.
Now contrary, if I read aught in heav'n,
Or heav'n write aught of fate, by what the stars
Voluminous, or single characters,

---

351. **Unless:** refers back to *unworthy to compare* in line 346.
352. **light of nature:** See 228n.
354. **statists:** statesmen.
377. **Nicely:** fastidiously.
380. **fullness of time:** "When the fullness of time was come, God sent forth his Son" (Gal. 4.4).
382. **Now contrary:** Satan sees an extraordinary difference between the *Now* of line 380 and this

Now. Jesus' moment is past, or so his forthcoming horoscope will suggest. Horoscopes of Christ had in fact been cast, and during Milton's lifetime a notorious one was published by Jerome Cardan (Shumaker 53–90).
384. **Voluminous:** the heavens regarded as a large volume or book; **or single characters:** "or considering the stars as individual letters in the text of the book."

385 In their conjunction met, give me to spell,
Sorrows, and labors, opposition, hate,
Attends thee, scorns, reproaches, injuries,
Violence and stripes, and lastly cruel death;
A kingdom they portend thee, but what kingdom,
390 Real or allegoric I discern not,
Nor when, eternal sure, as without end,
Without beginning; for no date prefixed
Directs me in the starry rubric set."
So saying he took (for still he knew his power
395 Not yet expired) and to the wilderness
Brought back the Son of God, and left him there,
Feigning to disappear. Darkness now rose,
As daylight sunk, and brought in louring Night,
Her shadowy offspring, unsubstantial both,
400 Privation mere of light and absent day.
Our Savior meek and with untroubled mind
After his airy jaunt, though hurried sore,
Hungry and cold betook him to his rest,
Wherever, under some concourse of shades
405 Whose branching arms thick intertwined might shield
From dews and damps of night his sheltered head,
But sheltered slept in vain, for at his head
The tempter watched, and soon with ugly dreams
Disturbed his sleep; and either tropic now
410 'Gan thunder, and both ends of heav'n, the clouds
From many a horrid rift abortive poured
Fierce rain with lightning mixed, water with fire
In ruin reconciled: nor slept the winds
Within their stony caves, but rush'd abroad
415 From the four hinges of the world, and fell
On the vexed wilderness, whose tallest pines,

---

385. **conjunction:** when two stars or planets occupy the same sign of the zodiac; **spell:** read; cp. *Il Pens* 170–71.

390. It is, of course, both *real* and *allegoric.*

391–92. **as without end/Without beginning:** Satan speaks mockingly here. Christ's kingdom, being eternal, has the attribute of being endless, but it also has that other eternal attribute of being without beginning, and is therefore never to be established.

393. **starry rubric:** the heavens metaphorically considered as a *rubric,* or handbook of rules.

402. **jaunt:** tiring journey.

408. **ugly dreams:** Satan uses a similar tactic when inspiring Eve's "uncouth dream" in *PL* 5.27–128.

But that dream was seductive; this dream aims at producing fear, ultimately (4.465–83) the fear that Jesus is tardy in seizing his destiny.

409. **either tropic:** north and south (Cancer and Capricorn).

410. **ends of heav'n:** east and west.

411. **horrid rift abortive:** "The clouds are imagined to be wombs that miscarry the elements of fire and water" (Leonard).

413. **ruin:** both "destruction" and "falling."

414. **caves:** where Aeolus imprisons the winds (*Aen.* 1.52–54).

415. **four hinges:** the four cardinal (Lat. *cardo,* "hinge") points of the compass.

Though rooted deep as high, and sturdiest oaks
Bowed their stiff necks, loaden with stormy blasts,
Or torn up sheer: ill wast thou shrouded then,
420 O patient Son of God, yet only stood'st
Unshaken; nor yet stayed the terror there;
Infernal ghosts, and hellish furies, round
Environed thee, some howled, some yelled, some shrieked,
Some bent at thee their fiery darts, while thou
425 Sat'st unappalled in calm and sinless peace.
Thus passed the night so foul till Morning fair
Came forth with pilgrim steps in amice gray;
Who with her radiant finger stilled the roar
Of thunder, chased the clouds, and laid the winds,
430 And grisly specters, which the fiend had raised
To tempt the Son of God with terrors dire.
And now the sun with more effectual beams
Had cheered the face of earth, and dried the wet
From drooping plant, or dropping tree; the birds
435 Who all things now behold more fresh and green,
After a night of storm so ruinous,
Cleared up their choicest notes in bush and spray
To gratulate the sweet return of morn;
Nor yet amidst this joy and brightest morn
440 Was absent, after all his mischief done,
The Prince of Darkness, glad would also seem
Of this fair change, and to our Savior came,
Yet with no new device, they all were spent,
Rather by this his last affront resolved,
445 Desperate of better course, to vent his rage
And mad despite to be so oft repelled.
Him walking on a sunny hill he found,
Backed on the north and west by a thick wood;
Out of the wood he starts in wonted shape;
450 And in a careless mood thus to him said.
    "Fair morning yet betides thee Son of God,
After a dismal night; I heard the rack
As earth and sky would mingle; but myself

419. **shrouded:** sheltered.
420. **only:** uniquely.
421. **nor yet stayed the terror there:** "nor yet did the terror [the *ugly dreams* of l. 408] cease."
422–23. Cp. Shakespeare *R3* 1.4.58–59.
427. **amice:** hood.
437. **Cleared up:** brightened, polished.

438. **gratulate:** welcome, give thanks for.
446. **despite:** hatred, resentment.
449. **wonted shape:** It is unclear whether this means "in his customary disguise (an old man)" or "as Satan, the fallen angel."
452. **rack:** storm; crashing sound.

Was distant; and these flaws, though mortals fear them
455 As dang'rous to the pillared frame of heav'n,
Or to the Earth's dark basis underneath,
Are to the main as inconsiderable,
And harmless, if not wholesome, as a sneeze
To man's less universe, and soon are gone;
460 Yet as being ofttimes noxious where they light
On man, beast, plant, wasteful and turbulent,
Like turbulencies in th' affairs of men,
Over whose heads they roar, and seem to point,
They oft fore-signify and threaten ill:
465 This tempest at this desert most was bent;
Of men at thee, for only thou here dwell'st.
Did I not tell thee, if thou didst reject
The perfect season offered with my aid
To win thy destined seat, but wilt prolong
470 All to the push of fate, pursue thy way
Of gaining David's throne no man knows when,
For both the when and how is nowhere told,
Thou shalt be what thou art ordained, no doubt;
For angels have proclaimed it, but concealing
475 The time and means: each act is rightliest done,
Not when it must, but when it may be best.
If thou observe not this, be sure to find,
What I foretold thee, many a hard assay
Of dangers, and adversities and pains,
480 Ere thou of Israel's scepter get fast hold;
Whereof this ominous night that closed thee round,
So many terrors, voices, prodigies
May warn thee, as a sure foregoing sign."
So talked he, while the Son of God went on
485 And stayed not, but in brief him answered thus.
"Me worse than wet thou find'st not; other harm
Those terrors which thou speak'st of, did me none;
I never feared they could, though noising loud
And threat'ning nigh; what they can do as signs
490 Betok'ning, or ill-boding, I contemn
As false portents, not sent from God, but thee;
Who knowing I shall reign past thy preventing,

454. **flaws:** squalls.
455. **pillared frame of heav'n:** See Job 26.11, and the "pillared firmament" of *Masque* 598.
457. **the main:** the world at large, the macrocosm.

470. **push:** critical juncture.
475–76. **each act ... best:** See Jonson, "To the Immortal Memory and Friendship of . . . Sir. Lucius Cary and Sir. H. Morison," 59–62.

Obtrud'st thy offered aid, that I accepting
At least might seem to hold all power of thee,
495 Ambitious spirit, and wouldst be thought my God,
And storm'st refused, thinking to terrify
Me to thy will; desist, thou art discerned
And toil'st in vain, nor me in vain molest."
        To whom the fiend now swoll'n with rage replied:
500 "Then hear, O son of David, virgin-born,
For Son of God to me is yet in doubt,
Of the Messiah I have heard foretold
By all the prophets; of thy birth at length
Announced by Gabriel with the first I knew,
505 And of th' angelic song in Bethlehem field,
On thy birth-night, that sung thee Savior born.
From that time seldom have I ceased to eye
Thy infancy, thy childhood, and thy youth,
Thy manhood last, though yet in private bred;
510 Till at the ford of Jordan whither all
Flocked to the Baptist, I among the rest,
Though not to be baptized, by voice from Heav'n
Heard thee pronounced the Son of God beloved.
Thenceforth I thought thee worth my nearer view
515 And narrower scrutiny, that I might learn
In what degree or meaning thou art called
The Son of God, which bears no single sense;
The son of God I also am, or was,
And if I was, I am; relation stands;
520 All men are sons of God; yet thee I thought
In some respect far higher so declared.
Therefore I watched thy footsteps from that hour,
And followed thee still on to this waste wild;
Where by all best conjectures I collect
525 Thou art to be my fatal enemy.
        Good reason then, if I beforehand seek

496. **storm'st:** both "gets angry" and "raises a storm"; **refused:** when refused.

500–40. This angry (hence not primarily cunning) speech bears directly on the much-debated question of what Satan knows of Jesus. Personal observation, though it prompted the temptation to vainglorious learning (ll. 214–22), has supplied no proofs of divinity. Satan's knowledge of "Son of God" is largely scriptural; the baptismal theophany, though impressive, was just more words. Moreover, since Satan became

Satan in resisting the divine elevation of the Son of God in Heaven (*PL* 5.600–907), he is prone to regard the whole subject of "Son of God" with doubt, faith's opposite.

515. **that I might learn:** Cp. 1.91 and note. Milton transforms the third temptation into a test of Christ's identity, the meaning of "Son of God." See 552n.

520. **All men are Sons of God:** "All of you are children of the most High" (Ps. 82.6–7).

524. **collect:** infer.

To understand my adversary, who
And what he is; his wisdom, power, intent,
By parle, or composition, truce, or league
530   To win him, or win from him what I can.
And opportunity I here have had
To try thee, sift thee, and confess have found thee
Proof against all temptation as a rock
Of adamant, and as a center, firm
535   To the utmost of mere man both wise and good,
Not more; for honors, riches, kingdoms, glory
Have been before contemned, and may again:
Therefore to know what more thou art than man,
Worth naming Son of God by voice from Heav'n,
540   Another method I must now begin."
            So saying he caught him up, and without wing
Of hippogrif bore through the air sublime
Over the wilderness and o'er the plain;
Till underneath them fair Jerusalem,
545   The holy city, lifted high her towers,
And higher yet the glorious temple reared
Her pile, far off appearing like a mount
Of alabaster, topped with golden spires:
There on the highest pinnacle he set
550   The Son of God; and added thus in scorn:
            "There stand, if thou wilt stand; to stand upright
Will ask thee skill; I to thy Father's house
Have brought thee, and highest placed; highest is best;
Now show thy progeny; if not to stand,
555   Cast thyself down; safely if Son of God:

529. **parle:** parley; **composition:** treaty.
532. **sift:** make trial of, scrutinize narrowly.
534. **adamant:** a mythical rock of impregnable hardness, with perhaps a play on *Adam.*
542. **hippogrif:** a fabulous creature, half griffin, half horse, that carries the heroes of Ariosto's *Orlando Furioso* on various wonderful journeys; **sublime:** raised aloft.
547–48. **far off . . . spires:** Josephus says that the front of the Temple, white marble covered with plates of gold, appeared at a distance "like a mountain covered with snow" (*Wars of the Jews,* 5.5.6)—thus Milton's *like a mount/Of alabaster.* This is not the Temple of Solomon but the one built on its site by Herod.
549. **highest pinnacle:** Both Matt. 4.6 and Luke 4.10 have Satan placing Christ on a "pinnacle," but the Greek word translated *pinnaculum* in the

Vulgate is uncertain of meaning, particularly in view of the fact that the roof of the Temple was apparently flat. Milton seems to identify his pinnacle with one of the *golden spires* in line 548.
552. **Will ask thee skill:** Satan, speaking scornfully, does not believe that a man can stand on this pinnacle. A miracle is required, and in this regard Milton deviates from most commentators, who interpreted the third temptation (following the order in Luke) as one of presumption—that God would provide for someone who deliberately puts himself in danger.
555. **Cast thyself down:** In the Bible (Matt. 4.6, Luke 4.10) this injunction implies a choice: Jesus can either stand or presumptively cast himself down. Milton's Satan supposes that Jesus will either fall and die, proving himself no more than a

For it is written, 'He will give command
Concerning thee to his angels, in their hands
They shall uplift thee, lest at any time
Thou chance to dash thy foot against a stone.' "
560   To whom thus Jesus: "Also it is written,
'Tempt not the Lord thy God,' " he said and stood.
But Satan smitten with amazement fell
As when Earth's son Antaeus (to compare
Small things with greatest) in Irassa strove
565 With Jove's Alcides, and oft foiled still rose,
Receiving from his mother Earth new strength,
Fresh from his fall, and fiercer grapple joined,
Throttled at length in the air, expired and fell;
So after many a foil the tempter proud,
570 Renewing fresh assaults, amidst his pride
Fell whence he stood to see his victor fall.
And as that Theban monster that proposed
Her riddle, and him who solved it not devoured;
That once found out and solved, for grief and spite
575 Cast herself headlong from th' Ismenian steep,
So struck with dread and anguish fell the fiend,
And to his crew, that sat consulting, brought
Joyless triumphals of his hoped success,

perfect man, or fall and be saved by angels, proving himself something beyond that.
556. **For it is written:** Like the Satan of Luke 4.10–11, Milton's Satan quotes Ps. 91.11–12. But the Son is the stone—the *adamant* of line 534, the *solid rock* of line 18—against which Satan is dashed.
560–61. **Also . . . thy God:** quoting, as in Luke 4.12, Deut. 6.16: "Ye shall not tempt [make trial of] the Lord your God." Christ announces that he is God, then enacts, by standing, his words.
560. **smitten with amazement:** All of Satan's bafflements come to a head. Eve during the course of her temptation is progressively amazed (*PL* 9.552, 614, 640): the fate of the tempted in *Paradise Lost* now becomes the fate of the tempter. Satan, receiving the head bruise promised him by the protevangelium (see 1.53–55n), realizes that Jesus is both a man and the divine Son of God who drove him from Heaven in *PL* 6.856–66.
561. **and stood:** "Here is what we may call after Aristotle the *anagnorisis*, or the discovery. Christ declares himself to be the God and Lord of the Tempter; and to prove it, stands upon the pinnacle" (Calton in Newton 2:194).

563–71. The giant *Antaeus* was the son of Ge (*Earth*). Wrestling Hercules (*Jove's Alcides*), he arose strengthened from each contact with mother Earth, until Hercules strangled him in the air (Lucan, *Pharsalia* 4.593–660). But Christ defeats Satan, "Prince of the power of the air" (Eph. 2.2), in his native element.
563–64. **to compare . . . greatest:** Milton adds the superlative *greatest* to Vergil's formula for comparing great (epic or urban) things with small (pastoral or rustic) things (*Ec.* 1.23; *Georg.* 4.176); Vergil's great things are Milton's small ones. Cp. *PL* 2.921–22, 6.310, 10.306.
571. Another confirmation that Satan expected Jesus to fall. Satan's fall, though known in visual representations, is not mentioned in the Bible or the commentary tradition.
572–75. The Sphinx leapt to her death from the acropolis at Thebes (*Ismenian steep*) when Oedipus answered her riddle: What creature goes first on four, then on two, and finally on three legs? "Man" was the answer. Satan, as it were, posed the riddle "Who is the Son of God?"—and "man" was only half the answer.
578. **triumphals:** tokens of success.

Ruin, and desperation, and dismay,
580 Who durst so proudly tempt the Son of God.
So Satan fell and straight a fiery globe
Of angels on full sail of wing flew nigh,
Who on their plumy vans received him soft
From his uneasy station, and upbore
585 As on a floating couch through the blithe air,
Then in a flow'ry valley set him down
On a green bank, and set before him spread
A table of celestial food, divine,
Ambrosial, fruits fetched from the Tree of Life,
590 And from the Fount of Life ambrosial drink,
That soon refreshed him wearied, and repaired
What hunger, if aught hunger had impaired,
Or thirst; and as he fed, angelic choirs
Sung Heav'nly anthems of his victory
595 Over temptation, and the tempter proud.
    "True image of the Father whether throned
In the bosom of bliss, and light of light
Conceiving, or remote from Heav'n, enshrined
In fleshly tabernacle, and human form,
600 Wand'ring the wilderness, whatever place,
Habit, or state, or motion, still expressing
The Son of God, with Godlike force endued
Against th' attempter of thy Father's throne,
And thief of Paradise; him long of old
605 Thou didst debel, and down from Heaven cast
With all his army; now thou hast avenged

---

582. **angels:** "Angels came and ministered to him" (Matt. 4.11).

583. **vans:** wings; **him:** meaning Christ, but seeming momentarily to refer to *Satan* in line 581; see Kerrigan 1983, 90–92.

584. **his uneasy station:** This phrase, Carey (1970) argued, proves his feat was human: an uneasy Jesus stands. MacCallum replied that the station, not the standing, is uneasy. Carey (1997) countered that *station* meant "manner of standing" (*OED* 1) as well as "place to stand" (*OED* 7a), but angels would not receive Jesus from a "manner of standing." MacCallum was right, and Carey recklessly mocked the consequences: "It would be curious if this meant 'uneasy for anyone else except the person here being discussed.'" Curious? The "person here being discussed" is the Son of God, whose deeds are the *greatest* (563–64n).

585. **blithe air:** glad air. The air is happy that Christ is being borne on it, rather than (like Satan) falling through it. Air, the traditional domain of Satan's kingdom, is converted at the poem's climax.

587. **and set before him:** Christ also has a banquet laid before him in Giles Fletcher's poem on the temptation, *Christ's Victory and Triumph*, 2.61.

589. **the Tree of Life:** a human food, native to Eden, which balances the celestial food of line 588 and signifies that the Son has regained our lost Paradise.

590. **Fount of Life:** See Rev. 21.6.

598. **Conceiving:** receiving (perhaps an indication of Milton's heterodox views on the Son of God; see MacKellar).

605. **debel:** vanquish.

Supplanted Adam, and by vanquishing
Temptation, hast regained lost Paradise,
And frustrated the conquest fraudulent:
610 He never more henceforth will dare set foot
In Paradise to tempt; his snares are broke:
For though that seat of earthly bliss be failed,
A fairer Paradise is founded now
For Adam and his chosen sons, whom thou
615 A savior art come down to reinstall.
Where they shall dwell secure, when time shall be
Of tempter and temptation without fear.
But thou, infernal serpent, shalt not long
Rule in the clouds; like an autumnal star
620 Or lightning thou shalt fall from heav'n trod down
Under his feet: for proof, ere this thou feel'st
Thy wound, yet not thy last and deadliest wound
By this repulse received, and hold'st in Hell
No triumph; in all her gates Abaddon rues
625 Thy bold attempt; hereafter learn with awe
To dread the Son of God: he all unarmed
Shall chase thee with the terror of his voice
From thy demoniac holds, possession foul,
Thee and thy legions; yelling they shall fly,
630 And beg to hide them in a herd of swine,
Lest he command them down into the deep
Bound, and to torment sent before their time.
Hail Son of the Most High, heir of both worlds,
Queller of Satan, on thy glorious work
635 Now enter, and begin to save mankind."
      Thus they the Son of God our Savior meek
Sung victor, and from Heav'nly feast refreshed
Brought on his way with joy; he unobserved
Home to his mother's house private returned.

---

612. **be failed:** be extinguished; see *PL* 11.829–34.

613. **A fairer Paradise:** reminiscent of the "paradise within thee, happier far" in *PL* 12.587.

619. **autumnal star:** a comet or meteor; cp. the "ev'ning dragon" in *SA* 1692.

620. **Or lightning:** "I beheld Satan as lightning fall from heaven" (Luke 10.18); cp. *PL* 10.183–85.

621. **ere this:** before the fuller defeats to come.

622. **Thy wound:** the wound promised him by the protevangelium or "first gospel" woven into the first judgment of Gen. 3.15 (see 1.53–55n). This

passage (ll. 618–32) concerns its typological unfolding. For the *last and deadliest wound,* see Rev. 20.10.

624. **Abaddon:** Hell (see Job 26.6).

628. **holds:** strongholds; **possession:** Satan's military positions (*holds*), and therefore "demonic possessions" as well.

630. See Matt. 8.28–34, Mark 5.1–13, Luke 8.26–33.

636. **Son of God our Savior meek:** "I am meek and lowly in heart" (Matt. 11.29).

INTRODUCTION TO *SAMSON AGONISTES*[1]

Samson Agonistes was first published in 1671, in the same volume as *Paradise Regained* but with its own supplementary title page and separate pagination. Through the first half of the twentieth century, it was almost always thought to have been composed soon after *Paradise Regained* in 1667–70, but in 1949 W. R. Parker's suggestion of an earlier date opened the way to decades of speculation about the beginning and finishing of *Samson Agonistes*. As is the case with *Paradise Lost*, the germ of *Samson* first appeared in a list of possible subjects for a tragic drama found in the Trinity College manuscript and usually dated 1640–41. Some authorities have pushed the composition back to the 1640s, before the advent of the author's full blindness in 1652, to a time when, so far as we know, Milton had no real hint of the affliction awaiting him. The early dating removes any personal element in the work's representation of blindness. Similarly, by placing the drama before the Restoration of 1660, the early dating removes any personal element from its political denunciation of the backsliding, self-enslaved Israelites. A work long savored for its autobiographical power becomes, if written in the 1640s, merely prescient.

But in the absence of compelling evidence, the traditional dating should be retained. With the exception of Samson's anger with Dalila, which may in some fashion tap Milton's resentment of his Royalist first wife, the emotions of the drama do not favor the 1640s. It is highly unlikely that Milton wrote an ambitious poem in the 1650s, a decade consumed by his secretaryship for the Cromwell government, his political pamphleteering, his adjustment to blindness, his efforts to forestall the Restoration, and in the end by his narrow survival of that turnaround. He might have begun the epic in 1658, as his nephew Edward Phillips seems to have reported to John Aubrey (p. xxii), but one must agree with Jonathan Richardson that, given the tumultuous events of

---

1. The title, like the work, embodies the meeting of Hebrew (*Samson*) and Greek (*Agonistes*). The Greek epithet means "struggling" or "contending" or "agonizing" (see Sellin 1964). It was familiarly applied to athletes and champions, or to spiritual heroes who were metaphorically athletes and champions. Hale reminds us that *agonistes* also means "actor," and that it can be transferred to the character acted, as in our "antagonist" and "protagonist" (181); with this added meaning, the title glances at Samson playing a part in the Hebrew-Greek-Christian tragic drama Milton discerned in Judges.

those two years, "it seems probable he set not about the work in good earnest till after the Restoration" (Darbishire 288). In the first half of the 1660s, Milton wrote *Paradise Lost*. Let us assume that Ellwood was handed the manuscript of the large epic in 1665 and of its sequel in 1667 (see introduction to *Paradise Regained*). In this case, Milton would have had ample time to write *Samson* before the two works were licensed in June 1670 and entered in the Stationer's Register on September 10 of the same year. If he averaged twelve lines a day, which is about the pace at which *Paradise Lost* was composed, he would have needed around 143 working days for the drama. It is true, as William Parker emphasized (1949), that our best guide to matters of dating, Edward Phillips, declared that *Samson*'s time of composition "cannot certainly be concluded" (Darbishire 75), but Parker may have been wrong to weigh this uncertainty so heavily. During 1667–70, Phillips was tutor to the Earl of Pembroke's son and was no doubt often separated from his uncle. Modern scholars have explored numerous affiliations between Puritan nonconformism in the early Restoration and the politics of *Samson Agonistes* (Worden; Mueller; Achinstein 115–53).

When all the arguments about its dating have been examined, *Samson* still feels more like the end of something than a midcareer experiment. "And calm of mind, all passion spent." Could there be a better line on which to end a poetic career? A great ode, a great masque, two great pastoral elegies, a great epic, and a brief epic had been written. One last major genre remained to be conquered. Milton completed a career in heroic Christian poetry with *Paradise Lost*. He then published in one volume *Paradise Regained*, which recounts the beginning of a career that is the very pattern of Christian heroism, and *Samson Agonistes*, which deals with the end of a heroic career—an imperfectly human, not altogether exemplary or Christian one, into which a blind, politically disappointed Milton could pour a lifetime of "true experience" (l. 1756).

It was reading *Samson Agonistes*, in 1830, not *Paradise Lost*, that convinced Johann Wolfgang Goethe of Milton's greatness: "I have lately read his Samson," he told Eckermann, "which has more of the antique spirit than any other production of any other modern poet. He is very great, and his own blindness enabled him to describe with so much truth the situation of Samson. Milton was really a poet, to whom we owe all possible respect" (346–47). This high estimate rests on two accomplishments. The first may be termed romantic: his Samson is at once an objective character and an act of self-expression. The second is neoclassical: though many European dramatists tried to write a modern Greek tragedy, Milton alone succeeded. Samuel Taylor Coleridge also felt that *Samson* was "the finest imitation of the ancient Greek drama that ever had been, or ever would be written" (*Lectures* 14). Aside from Judges, the work has no sources other than Greek drama. Scholars have made claims for the Dutchman Joost van den Vondel's 1660 *Samson, of Heilige Wraeck, Treurspel* (translated in Kirkconnell), but they have been convincingly dismissed by Verity (1897, 158–68). From Judges itself, Milton takes only the catastrophe. The Danite companions, the visit of Dalila, the notion that she was Samson's wife, the entire character of Harapha, Manoa's attempt to ransom Samson, the idea that the building toppled was a partially roofed theater—these and many other details are the poet's inventions.

Even the unpatterned rhymes, lawlessly shifting line lengths, and other prosodic peculiarities of the work, though critics have related them to Italian (Prince 145–69, 178–83), Greek, and Hebrew (Kermode) models, are essentially without precedent. In key letters to Robert Bridges (August 21, 1877) and R.W. Dixon (October 5, 1878), Gerard Manley Hopkins described the choruses of *Samson Agonistes* as unique instances of "counterpointed" rhythm, able simultaneously to support two mutually inconsistent scansions. One was conventional. The other was a revolutionary "sprung rhythm," free from the arithmetical regularities of standard accentual-syllabic verse.

Milton's finest poems are to a certain extent about their genres. Here the tragic form is clearly Greek. After an introductory soliloquy and an exchange between Samson and the Chorus, the drama proceeds through a series of episodes, each of them a dialogue between two people and all of them divided by choric interludes. The catastrophe takes place offstage and, as was conventional in Greek tragedy, is reported by a messenger. There is a great deal of Sophoclean irony, in which what is said takes on a second and ironic meaning in relation to the full plot. For a time in the early twentieth century, critics such as Richard Jebb wondered whether the work might be Greek in form but Hebraic or Christian in spirit. W. R. Parker laid this tradition to rest, at least for a couple of decades, by asserting that Greek drama is in spirit grave, elevated, thoughtful, didactic, and religious, all of which are characteristics of *Samson* (1937, 189–210). Like Coleridge and Goethe before him, A. W. Verity was right to suppose that "*Samson Agonistes* is unique because here the genius of Greek tragedy does live—really live. So oft invoked in vain, it wakes at last from the long sleep of centuries" (1897).

Samuel Johnson presented a fecund issue to the formal study of Milton's tragedy by observing that the play is defective in Aristotelian terms. For its middle scenes do not bring about the catastrophe: "The poem, therefore, has a beginning and end which Aristotle himself could not have disapproved; but it must be allowed to want a middle, since nothing passes between the first act and the last that either hastens or delays the death of Samson" (*Works* 4:376). Samson discusses with the Chorus and Manoa his wretched condition in relation to divine justice and his own responsibility. He denounces Dalila's claim to have acted out of high-minded religious and patriotic motives, or out of love, and threatens to tear her apart if she as much as touches him. He punctures the boastfulness of Harapha and dares the giant to close with him. The catastrophe approaches. But how has it been brought on by these events? Moreover, when the Philistine Officer relays the lords' command that Samson perform feats of strength at the festival of Dagon, Samson refuses (1319–21, 1332, 1342, 1345). He does not change his mind until "I begin to feel/Some rousing motions in me which dispose/To something extraordinary my thoughts" (1381–83). It is, apparently, the entrance of the will of God into dramatic time that points the play's inconsequential middle toward its catastrophe.

Johnson no doubt overstated the case. There is a causal middle of a sort in *Samson*. A frustrated Harapha stomps offstage, vowing that Samson will regret his insults "in irons loaden on thee" (1243). The Chorus remarks that "He will directly to the lords, I fear,/And with malicious counsel stir them up/Some way or other yet further to afflict thee" (1250–52). When, a few lines later, the Officer appears with the summons from "our lords" (l. 1310), it seems reasonable to infer that Harapha has indeed convinced them further to break and humiliate Samson. But this thin thread of causality does not constitute a solid Aristotelian middle, and nothing is here for tears. Johnson's criticism has actually had the effect of making the form of the drama seem mysterious and challenging rather than defective. Richard Cumberland addressed Johnson's strictures in 1785 (Shawcross 2:333–38). His answer animates many later discussions. Milton was not a determinist. The motions of divine guidance must be accepted by a freely willed act. In the course of the play we behold, alongside his terrible self-condemnation, the revival of Samson's fighting spirit. Accepting the blame and defending divine justice, denouncing Dalila, deflating Harapha, the disgraced and remorseful giant has again become able to see himself as God's champion. So he gropes his way toward an act that can be at once his revenge and his death, open as ever to the guidance of God. The revelation of his character, therefore, which is the main burden of the middle of the play, does in fact motivate or at least render comprehensible the tragic climax.

The question of the work's Christian spirit temporarily closed by Parker reemerged when a new generation of Miltonists, aware of the long and pervasive history of Christian typology, wanted to discuss how Milton modified Greek tragic structure to accommodate biblical figuralism. F. Michael Krouse demonstrated that commentaries on Judges identified Samson as a type of Christ. William Madsen cautioned that *type* did not mean "equivalent," and suggested that Milton was measuring the moral difference between Samson and Christ even as he connected them. Albert Cirillo found the Christological elements of the poem concentrated in the climactic appearance of the Phoenix (1971, 227–29).

Perhaps the structural soundness appropriate to a Christian Greek tragedy was not a middle, a causal paving making step after step into a linear road from the beginning to the end, but a pervasive irony that moves us back and forth from particular temporal moments to the full revelation at the conclusion. Anthony Low carefully categorized the kinds of irony in the work, ranging from simple reversals, in which characters do not in the end receive what they currently expect, to a unique "irony of alternatives" in which either-or disjunctions become both-and propositions from the perspective of the end (1974, 62–89). When Samson says, "This day will be remarkable in my life/By some great act, or of my days the last" (1388–89), the play ultimately collapses the pillars of his alternatives, revealing this day to be *both* remarkable by a great act *and* his last. Versions of this ironic effect appear throughout the work. Just a few lines later, Samson, leaving with the Officer, confesses that he does not know whether his life draws to an end: "The last of me or no I cannot warrant" (1426). Is it the last of him? He dies, but "though her body die, her fame survives" (1706), as the Chorus declares of the Samson-Phoenix. And does this ongoing fame contain the typological promise of the greater man to come, the beginning of whose career was in 1671 bound into the same volume containing Samson's ironically open end? Maintaining that the entire tragedy was adumbrated in the "guiding hand" of its opening passage, and repeatedly thereafter, even in the details of the imagery, Edward Tayler spoke of the work's "proleptic form": "We . . . find ourselves in the presence of a very considerable work of art, perhaps the unique example of specifically Christian tragedy; for Samson guided solely by God is not 'tragic,' as Samson guided solely by himself is not 'Christian.' " Downing the pillars of disjunctive logic, Milton invested Sophoclean irony with providential force (1979, 105–22).

A new chapter in Samson criticism was opened in 1986 with the publication of Joseph Wittreich's *Interpreting Samson Agonistes.* The catastrophe does not foreshadow Christ. The point of the 1671 volume is to manifest the ethical chasm between a sublime Christ and a barbarian Samson. His destruction of the temple is no better than vengeful mass murder. When Samson informs the Philistine assembly that he means to show them a feat of strength "of my own accord" (1643), he is telling them that he now acts on his own, without the sanction of God, despite the fact that in context he is distinguishing between his earlier commanded feats and his next uncommanded feat, and despite the fact that it is hard to fathom what his motive would be for so indirectly broaching this bit of theological news to uncomprehending Philistines. Wittreich claimed to find precedents for his view in the commentary tradition. His handling of historical evidence was called into question by Philip Gallagher (1987, 108–17) and Anthony Low (1987, 415–18); the books cited in *Interpreting Samson Agonistes* often fail to bear out the author's representation of them. But Wittreich's sense of the drama gained adherents. Galbraith Crump, Jacqueline DiSalvo, and others have accepted at least its general drift: Samson is a bad man. Aristotle thought the tragic hero should be somewhat better than ourselves (*Poetics* 13), since only in that case could real catharsis occur. The old idea of the work's Attic purity was quietly routed to oblivion along with recent discussions of the play's Christian form.

In 1994 a participant at the International Milton Seminar termed Samson a "terrorist." The practice has since become commonplace. "Could Milton have been celebrating the glory of an isolated terrorist?" Roy Flannagan asks, steering students toward the Wittreich interpretation. John Carey, in a piece written to commemorate the first anniversary of the 9/11 Al Qaeda attacks on the United

States, refers to the (in his mind) similar terrorist act at the climax of Milton's poem and announces that we are now once and for all beyond the old view of Samson acting with divine accord: "September 11 has changed *Samson Agonistes,* because it has changed the readings we can derive from it while still celebrating it as an achievement of the human imagination" (2002, 16; see also, among the many essays spawned by this piece, Mohamed 2005, 2006; Loewenstein; Fish; Rajan; Gregory). This alarming statement would not allow us to discuss whether it should be taken at face value, as an odd but genuine expression of shock at the existence of violence in the world, or might instead be an instance of crass moral opportunism, allowing a critic to entertain the monstrously grandiose idea that his opponents have been smitten by history as profoundly as the Holocaust smote anti-Semites.

If Milton condemned Samson, might he have harbored goodwill toward Samson's opponents? William Empson, pre-Wittreich, wrote in defense of Dalila's worldliness, which he found attractive in contrast to the self-righteous fanaticism of her husband (1960). Empson declared himself to be alone in this endeavor, but admiring accounts of Dalila are now legion. John Ulreich observes of Dalila asking to touch Samson's hand, "Beneath all her elegant finery, Dalila is a woman desperately seeking love, struggling to find means by which to communicate her feelings to the man who hates her" (189). Any hint that Dalila might want to use sex to dominate and imprison Samson has been rigorously excluded from this airbrushed recitation of the episode. Roy Flannagan confesses that "Milton's Dalila is perhaps a more fascinating character than her male counterpart" (788). One cannot be quite sure what *counterpart* means here, since Dalila is not a giant, not a Philistine military hero, not a slayer of Israelites, not separate to Dagon, et cetera. Irene Samuel might have been in another world when she wrote, in an essay otherwise foreshadowing Wittreich's reading of the drama, "Dalila is surely the most bird-brained woman ever to have gotten herself involved in major tragedy" (248).

The Wittreich interpretation runs together a moral revulsion at the idea of God sanctioning the Philistine deaths with a corrective reading purporting to show that this revulsion is the play's intended sense. We should be clearer than we sometimes are about exactly what is at issue in assessing such claims. First of all, the judgment of this reading must not itself be driven by moral urgency. Wittreich's *Samson* should stand or fall as all readings do, by its support from the meanings of words and the formal designs of the work, by how plausibly it sorts with the author's other works and the works of his contemporaries. Were it to fail these tests, and the partnership of Samson and God celebrated in the choral victory ode (1660–1707) be deemed the work's probable intended meaning, any moral revulsion that readers feel at this sense would, of course, remain in place. This revulsion cannot be expected to disappear or conceal itself because the work could not legitimately be remade in its image. Like *Paradise Lost, Samson* is saturated with theodicy (Rumrich 2002). Disapproving readers should argue with Milton's God, or Milton, or the Western tradition's misuse of biblical folk-tales. Although one hears otherwise in the tense climate of current academic controversies, the defeat of an interpretation does not at all mean that a particular moral point of view will be "silenced." Times change. Interpretations come and go. The vast preponderance of them turn out to be wrong. But moral debates continue so long as there are proponents to be heard.

SAMSON AGONISTES

Of that Sort of Dramatic Poem which is Called Tragedy

Tragedy, as it was anciently composed, hath been ever held the gravest, moralest, and most profitable of all other poems: therefore said by Aristotle[1] to be of power by raising pity and fear, or terror, to purge the mind of those and such-like passions, that is to temper and reduce them to just measure with a kind of delight, stirred up by reading or seeing those passions well imitated. Nor is nature wanting in her own effects to make good his assertion: for so in physic things of melancholic hue and quality are used against melancholy, sour against sour, salt to remove salt humors.[2] Hence philosophers and other gravest writers, as Cicero, Plutarch, and others, frequently cite out of tragic poets, both to adorn and illustrate their discourse. The Apostle Paul himself thought it not unworthy to insert a verse of Euripides into the text of Holy Scripture, I Cor. 15.33, and Paraeus[3] commenting on the Revelation, divides the whole book as a tragedy, into acts distinguished each by a chorus of heavenly harpings and song between. Heretofore men in highest dignity have labored not a little to be thought able to compose a tragedy. Of that honor Dionysius the elder[4] was no less ambitious than before of his attaining to the tyranny. Augustus Caesar also had begun his *Ajax*,[5] but unable to please his own judgment with what he had begun, left it unfinished. Seneca the philosopher[6] is by some thought the author of those tragedies (at least the best of them) that go under that name. Gregory Nazianzen,[7] a Father of the Church, thought it not unbeseeming the sanctity of

---

1. **said by Aristotle:** Aristotle thought that "pity" was caused by the spectacle of a great man in distress, while "fear" resulted from our realization that a power higher than any human power determines events.
2. The analogy between tragic catharsis and homeopathic cures can be found in Minturno's *De Poeta* (1563) and Guarini's *Il Compendio della Poesia Tragicomica* (1601). See Sellin 1961.
3. **Paraeus:** David Paraeus, a German Calvinist, whose work on Revelation was translated into English as *On the Divine Apocalypse* (1644) by Elias Arnold.
4. **Dionysius the elder:** The Tyrant of Syracuse (431–367 B.C.E), who devoted much time to his poetry. He died while celebrating the news that one of his plays had at last won first prize at Athens.
5. **Augustus Caesar . . . Ajax:** Suetonius 2.85 says that Emperor Augustus, dissatisfied with his play *Ajax*, erased it.
6. **Seneca the philosopher:** Lucius Annaeus Seneca (55 B.C.E.–39 C.E.) wrote both philosophy and tragic drama, though there was some doubt over this fact in Milton's day.
7. **Gregory Nazianzen:** Fourth-century Bishop of Constantinople, and possible author of the play *Christus Patiens*, which contains passages from Euripides.

his person to write a tragedy, which he entitled *Christ Suffering*. This is mentioned to vindicate tragedy from the small esteem, or rather infamy, which in the account of many it undergoes at this day with other common interludes;[8] happening through the poet's error of intermixing comic stuff[9] with tragic sadness and gravity; or introducing trivial and vulgar persons, which by all judicious hath been counted absurd; and brought in without discretion, corruptly to gratify the people. And though ancient tragedy use no prologue,[10] yet using sometimes, in case of self-defense, or explanation, that which Martial[11] calls an epistle, in behalf of this tragedy coming forth after the ancient manner, much different from what among us passes for best, thus much beforehand may be epistled: that chorus is here introduced after the Greek manner, not ancient only, but modern, and still in use among the Italians.[12] In the modeling therefore of this poem, with good reason, the ancients and Italians are rather followed, as of much more authority and fame. The measure of verse used in the chorus is of all sorts, called by the Greeks monostrophic, or rather apolelymenon,[13] without regard had to strophe, antistrophe, or epode, which were a kind of stanzas framed only for the music, then used with the chorus that sung; not essential to the poem, and therefore not material; or being divided into stanzas or pauses, they may be called allaeostropha. Division into act and scene referring chiefly to the stage (to which this work never was intended) is here omitted.

It suffices if the whole drama be found not produced beyond the fifth act.[14] Of the style and uniformity, and that commonly called the plot, whether intricate or explicit,[15] which is nothing indeed but such economy, or disposition of the fable as may stand best with verisimilitude and decorum, they only will best judge who are not unacquainted with Aeschylus,[16] Sophocles, and Euripides, the three tragic poets unequaled yet by any, and the best rule to all who endeavor to write tragedy. The circumscription of time wherein the whole drama begins

8. **interludes:** comic plays.

9. **intermixing comic stuff:** Milton condemns the practice of mingling comic and tragic elements on the Elizabethan stage.

10. **prologue:** an initial speech in which a figure representing the author addresses the audience. In Greek drama, the "prologue" was the part of the play before the appearance of the Chorus. Samson's first speech (1–114) is, in the Greek sense, a prologue.

11. **Martial:** In the epistle to Book 2 of his *Epigrams*, Martial noted that plays, since they cannot speak for themselves, might need epistles. Dedicatory epistles were common features of Restoration plays in particular.

12. **among the Italians:** In part because of the influence of Seneca, the Chorus was a familiar feature of Italian Renaissance drama.

13. **monostrophic:** of only one stanza; **apolelymenon:** "freed" (from the restriction of a stanza pattern). In Greek drama the *strophe* was a stanza sung as the Chorus moved from right to left, while the *antistrophe* was a stanza sung during the opposite movement. The final *epode* was sung standing still. Milton suggests that if his choruses have stanzas, they are *allaeostropha*, or "irregular in strophes."

14. **not produced beyond the fifth act:** Horace maintained that a play should have five acts (*A.P.* 189). Dryden considered the matter in *An Essay of Dramatic Poesy* (*Essays* 1.45).

15. **intricate or explicit:** See Aristotle's *Poetics* 6, where plots are divided into complex and simple.

16. **Aeschylus:** At this time he was not commonly ranked with *Sophocles* and *Euripides*, but see Jonson, "To the Memory of . . . Shakespeare," 33–34.

and ends is according to ancient rule,[17] and best example, within the space of twenty-four hours.

THE ARGUMENT

Samson made captive, blind, and now in the prison at Gaza, there to labor as in a common work-house, on a festival day, in the general cessation from labor, comes forth into the open air, to a place nigh, somewhat retired there to sit a while and bemoan his condition. Where he happens at length to be visited by certain friends and equals of his tribe, which make the Chorus, who seek to comfort him what they can; then by his old father Manoa, who endeavors the like, and withal tells him his purpose to procure his liberty by ransom; lastly, that this feast was proclaimed by the Philistines as a day of thanksgiving for their deliverance from the hands of Samson, which yet more troubles him. Manoa then departs to prosecute his endeavor with the Philistian lords for Samson's redemption; who in the meanwhile is visited by other persons; and lastly by a public officer to require his coming to the feast before the lords and people, to play or show his strength in their presence; he at first refuses, dismissing the public officer with absolute denial to come; at length persuaded inwardly that this was from God, he yields to go along with him, who came now the second time with great threatenings to fetch him; the Chorus yet remaining on the place, Manoa returns full of joyful hope, to procure ere long his son's deliverance: in the midst of which discourse an Hebrew comes in haste confusedly at first; and afterward more distinctly relating the catastrophe, what Samson had done to the Philistines, and by accident to himself; wherewith the tragedy ends.

THE PERSONS

Samson
Manoa, the father of Samson
Dalila his wife
Harapha of Gath
Public Officer
Messenger
Chorus of Danites

The scene before the prison in Gaza

---

17. **ancient rule:** There was no ancient rule about circumscription of time except in the minds of Renaissance neoclassicists.

Samson. A little onward lend thy guiding hand
To these dark steps, a little further on;
For yonder bank hath choice of sun or shade,
There I am wont to sit, when any chance
5   Relieves me from my task of servile toil,
Daily in the common prison else enjoined me,
Where I a prisoner chained, scarce freely draw
The air imprisoned also, close and damp,
Unwholesome draft: but here I feel amends,
10   The breath of heav'n fresh-blowing, pure and sweet,
With day-spring born; here leave me to respire.
This day a solemn feast the people hold
To Dagon their sea-idol, and forbid
Laborious works; unwillingly this rest
15   Their superstition yields me; hence with leave
Retiring from the popular noise, I seek
This unfrequented place to find some ease,
Ease to the body some, none to the mind
From restless thoughts, that like a deadly swarm
20   Of hornets armed, no sooner found alone,
But rush upon me thronging, and present
Times past, what once I was, and what am now.
O wherefore was my birth from Heaven foretold
Twice by an angel, who at last in sight
25   Of both my parents all in flames ascended
From off the altar, where an off'ring burned,
As in a fiery column charioting
His godlike presence, and from some great act
Or benefit revealed to Abraham's race?
30   Why was my breeding ordered and prescribed

1–2. Milton imitates Greek models. Sophocles' *Oedipus at Colonus* opens with the blind Oedipus led by his daughter Antigone, and the blind Tiresias is likewise led by his daughter in Euripides' *Phoenician Women* 834–35.

3. **choice of sun or shade:** Cp. 1605–11, where the choice becomes a matter of life and death for Philistines attending the festival of Dagon.

5. **servile:** Grinding was a task given to slaves of the lowest class (Exod. 11.5, 12.29).

6. **else:** at other times.

11. **day-spring:** daybreak.

13. **Dagon their sea-idol:** Dagon, a Phoenician god particularly associated with Gaza and Ashdod, appears in *Paradise Lost* as a "sea monster, / upward man/And downward fish" (1.462–63).

15–22. Cp. *PR* 1.196–200. In the first of many parallels with the companion poem, Samson like the Son of God retires to a place of solitude and is subject to swarming thoughts. The parallels also throw into relief fundamental differences between the heroes of the two poems.

22. **what once . . . am now:** Cp. *PL* 4.24–25.

23–24. **foretold / Twice by an angel:** Judg. 13.3–5 and 10–13. This double foretelling is recounted three times; see lines 361 and 635.

27. **charioting:** Samson is probably thinking of Elijah's translation to Heaven (2 Kings 3.11; also Ezek. 1 and 10).

28. **from some great act:** as from some great act.

As of a person separate to God,
Designed for great exploits, if I must die
Betrayed, captived, and both my eyes put out,
Made of my enemies the scorn and gaze,
35 To grind in brazen fetters under task
With this Heav'n-gifted strength? O glorious strength
Put to the labor of a beast, debased
Lower than bondslave! Promise was that I
Should Israel from Philistian yoke deliver;
40 Ask for this great deliverer now, and find him
Eyeless in Gaza at the mill with slaves,
Himself in bonds under Philistian yoke;
Yet stay, let me not rashly call in doubt
Divine prediction; what if all foretold
45 Had been fulfilled but through mine own default,
Whom have I to complain of but myself?
Who this high gift of strength committed to me,
In what part lodged, how easily bereft me,
Under the seal of silence could not keep,
50 But weakly to a woman must reveal it,
O'ercome with importunity and tears.
O impotence of mind, in body strong!
But what is strength without a double share
Of wisdom? Vast, unwieldly, burdensome,
55 Proudly secure, yet liable to fall
By weakest subtleties; not made to rule,
But to subserve where wisdom bears command.
God, when he gave me strength, to show withal
How slight the gift was, hung it in my hair.
60 But peace, I must not quarrel with the will
Of highest dispensation, which herein
Haply had ends above my reach to know:
Suffices that to me strength is my bane,
And proves the source of all my miseries;
65 So many, and so huge, that each apart

31. **separate:** Samson is a Nazarite, one set apart to serve God. The term derives from the Hebrew *nazar,* "to separate." See Num. 6.2–8.
34. **gaze:** display, spectacle.
37. **labor of a beast:** Asses were employed in mills; see line 1162.
38. **Promise was:** it was promised; see Judg. 13.5.
43–44. **Yet stay . . . prediction:** Like *A Masque* and *Paradise Lost, Samson Agonistes* is concerned with theodicy. See 60–62, 210, 1745–58.
50. **woman:** The implication is that it would have been bad enough to tell his secret to a man but worse to tell it to a woman.
55. **secure:** heedless, overconfident (from Lat. *securus*).
63. **suffices:** I.e., "it is enough that I realize."

Would ask a life to wail, but chief of all,
O loss of sight, of thee I most complain!
Blind among enemies, O worse than chains,
Dungeon, or beggary, or decrepit age!
70   Light, the prime work of God, to me is extinct,
And all her various objects of delight
Annulled, which might in part my grief have eased,
Inferior to the vilest now become
Of man or worm; the vilest here excel me,
75   They creep, yet see; I dark in light exposed
To daily fraud, contempt, abuse and wrong,
Within doors, or without, still as a fool,
In power of others, never in my own;
Scarce half I seem to live, dead more than half.
80   O dark, dark, dark, amid the blaze of noon,
Irrecoverably dark, total eclipse
Without all hope of day!
O first-created beam, and thou great word,
"Let there be light, and light was over all,"
85   Why am I thus bereaved thy prime decree?
The sun to me is dark
And silent as the moon,
When she deserts the night
Hid in her vacant interlunar cave.
90   Since light so necessary is to life,
And almost life itself, if it be true
That light is in the soul,
She all in every part, why was the sight
To such a tender ball as th' eye confined?
95   So obvious and so easy to be quenched,
And not as feeling through all parts diffused,
That she might look at will through every pore?
Then had I not been thus exiled from light;

---

66. **ask:** require, need.

68–79. This catalog of mutually aggravating evils is anticipated in the letter to Henry Oldenburg, July 6, 1654, where the blind Milton promises continued labors for liberty "if illness allow and this blindness, which is more oppressive than the whole of old age, and finally the cries of such brawlers" (Yale 4, pt. 2, 866).

70. **prime work:** first creation (after Heaven and Earth); see Gen. 1.3.

77. **still:** always.

83. **Without all:** without any.

85. **bereaved:** robbed of.

87. **silent:** "of the moon: not shining" (*OED* 5a); see Pliny, *Natural History* 16.74.

89. **vacant:** "empty" and "at leisure"; **interlunar cave:** Following an ancient conception, Samson thinks of the moon as resting in a cave between the old and new moons.

93. **She all in every part:** Milton thought, with Augustine and others, that the soul is entire in every part of the body; see *CD* 1.7.

95. **obvious:** exposed, vulnerable.

96. **as feeling:** as feeling is.

As in the land of darkness yet in light,
100 To live a life half dead, a living death,
And buried; but O yet more miserable!
Myself my sepulcher, a moving grave,
Buried, yet not exempt
By privilege of death and burial
105 From worst of other evils, pains and wrongs,
But made hereby obnoxious more
To all the miseries of life,
Life in captivity
Among inhuman foes.
110 But who are these? For with joint pace I hear
The tread of many feet steering this way;
Perhaps my enemies who come to stare
At my affliction, and perhaps to insult,
Their daily practice to afflict me more.
115   *Chorus.* This, this is he; softly a while,
Let us not break in upon him;
O change beyond report, thought, or belief!
See how he lies at random, carelessly diffused,
With languished head unpropped,
120 As one past hope, abandoned,
And by himself given over;
In slavish habit, ill-fitted weeds
O'er-worn and soiled;
Or do my eyes misrepresent? Can this be he,
125 That heroic, that renowned,
Irresistible Samson? Whom unarmed
No strength of man, or fiercest wild beast could withstand;
Who tore the lion, as the lion tears the kid,
Ran on embattled armies clad in iron,
130 And weaponless himself,
Made arms ridiculous, useless the forgery
Of brazen shield and spear, the hammered cuirass,
Chalybean tempered steel, and frock of mail
Adamantean proof;

---

100. **a living death:** a fate feared by Adam (*PL* 10.788).
106. **obnoxious:** exposed (to injury).
118. **at random:** without care; **diffused:** spread out.
119. **languished:** drooping.
128. **tore the lion:** Samson tears a lion in Judg. 14.5–6.
129. **embattled:** armed for battle and arranged in battle formations.

131. **forgery:** forging.
132. **cuirass:** breastplate.
133. **Chalybean:** The Chalybes, of Pontus on the Black Sea, were known for their work in iron and steel. **frock of mail:** coat of mail.
134. **Adamantean proof:** capable of withstanding adamant, the hardest substance.

135 But safest he who stood aloof,
When insupportably his foot advanced,
In scorn of their proud arms and warlike tools,
Spurned them to death by troops. The bold Ascalonite
Fled from his lion ramp, old warriors turned
140 Their plated backs under his heel;
Or grov'ling soiled their crested helmets in the dust.
Then with what trivial weapon came to hand,
The jaw of a dead ass, his sword of bone,
A thousand foreskins fell, the flower of Palestine
145 In Ramath-lechi famous to this day:
Then by main force pulled up, and on his shoulders bore
The gates of Azza, post, and massy bar
Up to the hill by Hebron, seat of giants old,
No journey of a Sabbath day, and loaded so;
150 Like whom the Gentiles feign to bear up heav'n.
Which shall I first bewail,
Thy bondage or lost sight,
Prison within prison
Inseparably dark?
155 Thou art become (O worst imprisonment!)
The dungeon of thyself; thy soul
(Which men enjoying sight oft without cause complain)
Imprisoned now indeed,
In real darkness of the body dwells,
160 Shut up from outward light
To incorporate with gloomy night;
For inward light alas
Puts forth no visual beam.

136. **insupportably:** irresistibly.

137. **tools:** weapons.

138. **Spurned:** trampled; **Ascalonite:** Ascalon was a Philistine city near Gaza.

139. **lion ramp:** a lion reared on its hind legs, familiar in heraldry.

142–43. See Judg. 15.15–16 for Samson's feats with the jawbone of an ass.

144. **foreskins:** uncircumcised Philistines.

145. **Ramath-lechi:** Samson in Judg. 15.17 discards the jawbone in Ramath-lechi, which took its name from the Hebrew for "lifting up or casting away of a jawbone."

147. **Azza:** variant form of Gaza. Samson's exploit with the gate is taken from Judg. 16.3.

148. **Hebron:** Hebron was the home of giants, the sons of Anak (Num. 13.22–33).

149. **No journey of a Sabbath day:** Jewish law restricted travel on the Sabbath, depending on one's computation, to between a half mile and a mile and a half. Hebron is roughly forty miles from Gaza.

150. **whom . . . heav'n:** Atlas, one of the Titans, who was supposed to support the heavens on his head and shoulders.

156–63. **thy soul . . . visual beam:** The Neoplatonist commonplace that the soul is imprisoned in the body is mistaken (and therefore *without cause*) because, in Milton's materialist perspective, the soul and body are continuous. But because of Samson's blindness, with its blocking of the *visual beam* usually thought in Milton's time to travel from the perceiver to the perceived object, he is in a different and true sense trapped inside the dark walls of his body. His soul now *incorporates* (161), or becomes one body with, night and darkness.

O mirror of our fickle state,
165 Since man on earth unparalleled!
The rarer thy example stands,
By how much from the top of wondrous glory,
Strongest of mortal men,
To lowest pitch of abject fortune thou art fall'n.
170 For him I reckon not in high estate
Whom long descent of birth
Or the sphere of fortune raises;
But thee whose strength, while virtue was her mate,
Might have subdued the earth,
175 Universally crowned with highest praises.
     Samson. I hear the sound of words, their sense the air
Dissolves unjointed ere it reach my ear.
     Chorus. He speaks, let us draw nigh. Matchless in might,
The glory late of Israel, now the grief,
180 We come thy friends and neighbors not unknown
From Eshtaol and Zora's fruitful vale
To visit or bewail thee, or if better,
Counsel or consolation we may bring,
Salve to thy sores; apt words have power to 'suage
185 The tumors of a troubled mind,
And are as balm to festered wounds.
     Samson. Your coming, friends, revives me, for I learn
Now of my own experience, not by talk,
How counterfeit a coin they are who friends
190 Bear in their superscription (of the most
I would be understood); in prosperous days
They swarm, but in adverse withdraw their head
Not to be found, though sought. Ye see, O friends,
How many evils have enclosed me round;
195 Yet that which was the worst now least afflicts me,
Blindness, for had I sight, confused with shame,
How could I once look up, or heave the head,

---

164. **mirror:** reflector; pattern, exemplar.
165. "Unparalleled since the creation of man."
169. **pitch:** Though *pitch* usually refers to height, here it clearly means depth.
172. **sphere of fortune:** the familiar metaphor of the "wheel of fortune" figured as a spinning globe.
173. **visual beam:** in one Renaissance theory of vision, the eye must emit a ray of light.
178–86. On the advice and counsel offered by the Chorus in this work, see Horace, *Ars Poetica*, ll.

193ff. (in Ben Jonson's translation, ll. 276–86).
181. **Eshtaol and Zora:** Manoa and his wife lived in Zora; Samson was first moved by the Spirit between Zora and nearby Eshtaol, and he was buried between the two cities (Judg. 13.2, 13.25, and 16.31).
185. **tumors:** the swelling of passion in the mind.
190. **superscription:** inscription on a coin.
190–91. **of the most/I would be understood:** "I am speaking of most people."

Who like a foolish pilot have shipwrecked
My vessel trusted to me from above,
200 Gloriously rigged; and for a word, a tear,
Fool, have divulged the secret gift of God
To a deceitful woman: tell me, friends,
Am I not sung and proverbed for a fool
In every street, do they not say, "How well
205 Are come upon him his deserts?" Yet why?
Immeasurable strength they might behold
In me, of wisdom nothing more than mean;
This with the other should, at least, have paired,
These two proportioned ill drove me transverse.
210   *Chorus.* Tax not divine disposal; wisest men
Have erred, and by bad women been deceived;
And shall again, pretend they ne'er so wise.
Deject not then so overmuch thyself,
Who hast of sorrow thy full load besides;
215 Yet truth to say, I oft have heard men wonder
Why thou shouldst wed Philistian women rather
Than of thine own tribe fairer, or as fair,
At least of thy own nation, and as noble.
   Samson. The first I saw at Timna, and she pleased
220 Me, not my parents, that I sought to wed,
The daughter of an infidel: they knew not
That what I motioned was of God; I knew
From intimate impulse, and therefore urged
The marriage on; that by occasion hence
225 I might begin Israel's deliverance,

---

197. **heave:** lift, as in *Masque* 885; *L'All* 145.

198–200. **Who ... rigged:** The first of several nautical metaphors in the poem; see also lines 710–19, 1044–45, 1061–63, and 1070.

200. **for:** because of.

207. **mean:** middling, average.

208. "His wisdom should have been equal to (*paired with*) his strength." Samson returns to an argument made in his first speech (52–57).

209. **transverse:** off course (continuing the ship metaphor).

210. **Tax not divine disposal:** "Do not blame God's direction of events."

210–11. **wisest men . . . been deceived:** Here as elsewhere Samson gives voice to Milton's preoccupations. He wrote in the *Doctrine and Discipline of Divorce* of the susceptibility of the best and wisest men to poor marriage choices: "It may yet befall a discreet man to be mistaken in

his [marriage] choice, and we have plenty of examples. The soberest and best governed men are least practiced in these affairs" (*MLM* 873). See also *Tetrachordon* (*MLM* 999).

212. **pretend they ne'er so wise:** "however wise they claim to be" or "however wise their intentions may be" (*pretend* = intend).

216–18. In Judges, Samson marries only the woman of Timna; Dalila may or may not have been Philistian. Milton supposes her to be a Philistine and to be Samson's wife.

219–27. For Samson's marriage to the woman of Timna, see Judg. 14.1–20. Timna, modern Tibneh, is a town south of Gath.

222. **motioned:** proposed.

223. **intimate:** inward.

224. **by occasion hence:** by the chance or opportunity the marriage afforded.

The work to which I was divinely called;
She proving false, the next I took to wife
(O that I never had! Fond wish too late)
Was in the vale of Sorec, Dalila,
230 That specious monster, my accomplished snare.
I thought it lawful from my former act,
And the same end; still watching to oppress
Israel's oppressors: of what now I suffer
She was not the prime cause, but I myself,
235 Who, vanquished with a peal of words (O weakness!),
Gave up my fort of silence to a woman.
    Chorus. In seeking just occasion to provoke
The Philistine, thy country's enemy,
Thou never wast remiss, I bear thee witness:
240 Yet Israel still serves with all his sons.
    Samson. That fault I take not on me, but transfer
On Israel's governors and heads of tribes,
Who, seeing those great acts which God had done
Singly by me against their conquerors,
245 Acknowledged not, or not at all considered
Deliverance offered: I on th' other side
Used no ambition to commend my deeds;
The deeds themselves, though mute, spoke loud the doer;
But they persisted deaf, and would not seem
250 To count them things worth notice, till at length
Their lords, the Philistines, with gathered powers
Entered Judea seeking me, who then
Safe to the rock of Etham was retired,

---

228. **Fond:** foolish.

229. **in the vale of Sorec, Dalila:** See Judg. 16.4; the meter here and elsewhere tells us that Milton pronounced the name with stresses on the first and last syllables, "Dá li lá."

230. **specious:** fair-seeming but deceptive; **accomplished:** "complete," in that Samson has indeed been snared, and also a rueful reference to Dalila's many accomplishments (such as cunning, persuasiveness, ability to wound and humiliate).

231–32. **from my former act/And the same end:** Samson had done the same thing before (marry a Philistine), and for the same reason (to oppress the Philistines).

235. **peal:** The word was used of any loud noise. Given *fort* in the next line, Milton probably has in mind an artillery barrage.

241–76. While recounting events recorded in Judges 15, Milton almost certainly alludes to the Restoration and rebukes the English for rejecting their deliverers (among whom Milton claimed for himself a prominent place) and embracing servitude under a corrupt monarch. "I wonder how the licensers of those days let it pass," Jortin remarked in the Newton variorum (1:228).

247. **ambition:** active canvassing for public support and recognition.

251. **powers:** armed forces.

253. **rock of Etham:** Judg. 15.8. Note that Milton elides in his account what immediately precedes Samson's retirement to the rock of Etham, his firing of the grain fields of Timna by releasing foxes with burning tails, an episode that Milton once listed as a potential subject for a tragedy (Yale 8.556); in Milton's account, overtones of private grudge and vandalism are replaced by an emphasis on principled political action.

Not flying, but forecasting in what place
255   To set upon them, what advantaged best;
Meanwhile the men of Judah to prevent
The harrass of their land, beset me round;
I willingly on some conditions came
Into their hands, and they as gladly yield me
260   To the uncircumcised a welcome prey,
Bound with two cords; but cords to me were threads
Touched with the flame: on their whole host I flew
Unarmed, and with a trivial weapon felled
Their choicest youth; they only lived who fled.
265   Had Judah that day joined, or one whole tribe,
They had by this possessed the towers of Gath,
And lorded over them whom now they serve;
But what more oft in nations grown corrupt,
And by their vices brought to servitude,
270   Than to love bondage more than liberty,
Bondage with ease than strenuous liberty;
And to despise, or envy, or suspect
Whom God hath of his special favor raised
As their deliverer; if he aught begin,
275   How frequent to desert him, and at last
To heap ingratitude on worthiest deeds?
      Chorus. Thy words to my remembrance bring
How Succoth and the fort of Penuel
Their great deliverer contemned,
280   The matchless Gideon in pursuit
Of Madian and her vanquished kings:
And how ingrateful Ephraim

---

254. **forecasting:** planning.

258. **on some conditions:** i.e., that the Israelites would not themselves attack Samson (Judg. 15.12).

261–62. **cords . . . flame:** Judg. 15.13–14.

263. See lines 142–45.

266. **by this:** by this time; **Gath:** Philistine city, home of Harapha (1068), here standing in for all of Philistia.

270–71. **to love bondage . . . strenuous liberty:** Samson here speaks in the accents of Milton's polemical prose. The same sentiment is placed, ironically, in the mouth of Mammon in *PL:* "preferring / Hard liberty before the easy yoke / Of servile pomp" (2.255–57).

272–76. As Masson suggested, Milton in these lines may well have had himself in mind. In his prose he often referred to himself as God's spokesperson and agent of liberty. After the Restoration, he found himself "fall'n on evil days, / . . . and evil tongues; / In darkness, and with dangers compassed round, / And solitude" (*PL* 7.25–28).

278–81. In Judg. 8.4–9, the Israelites in *Succoth* and *Penuel* refuse to help Gideon's army as it pursues Zebah and Zalmunna, the vanquished Midian kings.

282–89. Another example from Judges (11.12–33, 12.1–6). The Ephraimite Israelites, having refused to help *Jephtha* and the Gileadites against the *Ammonites*, threatened Jephtha after his victory. At the fords of the Jordan, Jephtha slaughtered the defeated Ephraimites, who were betrayed by their inability to pronounce "Shibboleth."

Had dealt with Jephtha, who by argument,
Not worse than by his shield and spear
285 Defended Israel from the Ammonite,
Had not his prowess quelled their pride
In that sore battle when so many died
Without reprieve adjudged to death,
For want of well pronouncing "Shibboleth."
290   *Samson.* Of such examples add me to the roll;
Me easily indeed mine may neglect,
But God's proposed deliverance not so.
        Chorus. Just are the ways of God,
And justifiable to men,
295 Unless there be who think not God at all;
If any be, they walk obscure,
For of such doctrine never was there school
But the heart of the fool,
And no man therein doctor but himself.
300   Yet more there be who doubt his ways not just,
As to his own edicts, found contradicting,
Then give the reins to wand'ring thought,
Regardless of his glory's diminution;
Till by their own perplexities involved
305 They ravel more, still less resolved,
But never find self-satisfying solution.
        As if they would confine th' interminable,
And tie him to his own prescript,
Who made our laws to bind us, not himself,
310 And hath full right to exempt
Whom so it pleases him by choice
From national obstriction, without taint
Of sin, or legal debt;

---

283. **Had dealt:** would have dealt.

291. **mine:** my compatriot Hebrews.

294. "Just and true are thy ways" (Ps. 145.17, Rev. 15.3). Theodicy is never far from Milton's mind; his main intention in *PL* is to "justify the ways of God to men" (1.26). See 43–44n.

295. **think not God:** do not think that God exists.

297. **such doctrine . . . school:** Atheism never became a sect professing a systematic philosophy.

298. **the heart of the fool:** "The fool hath said in his heart, There is no God" (Ps. 14.1). Milton quotes this verse at the beginning of *CD* 1.2, and goes on to remark: "But he [God] has left so many signs of himself in the human mind, so many traces of his presence through the whole

of nature, that no sane person can fail to realize that he exists" (p. 1145).

299. **doctor:** learned man, teacher.

302. **wand'ring thought:** compare the devils' aimless and godless thinking, "in wand'ring mazes lost," and Belial's "thoughts that wander through eternity" in *PL* 2.561 and 2.148. Wandering thought in Milton is opposed to thought directed by apprehension of the divine plan.

305. **ravel:** become entangled; **still less resolved:** ever in greater doubt and perplexity.

312. **national obstriction:** legal obligation not to marry a Gentile (Deut. 7.3); the Chorus suggests that God can *dispense* with (abrogate, cancel) this law and move an Israelite to marry a

For with his own laws he can best dispense.
315   He would not else who never wanted means,
Nor, in respect of the enemy just cause
To set his people free,
Have prompted this heroic Nazarite,
Against his vow of strictest purity,
320   To seek in marriage that fallacious bride,
Unclean, unchaste.
        Down Reason then, at least vain reasonings down,
Though Reason here aver
That moral verdict quits her of unclean:
325   Unchaste was subsequent, her stain not his.
        But see here comes thy reverend sire
With careful step, locks white as down,
Old Manoa: advise
Forthwith how thou ought'st to receive him.
330   *Samson.* Ay me, another inward grief awaked,
With mention of that name renews th' assault.
        Manoa. Brethren and men of Dan, for such ye seem,
Though in this uncouth place; if old respect,
As I suppose, towards your once gloried friend,
335   My son now captive, hither hath informed
Your younger feet, while mine cast back with age
Came lagging after; say if he be here.
        Chorus. As signal now in low dejected state,
As erst in highest, behold him where he lies.
340   *Manoa.* O miserable change! Is this the man,
That invincible Samson, far renowned,
The dread of Israel's foes, who with a strength
Equivalent to angels walked their streets,
None offering fight; who single combatant
345   Dueled their armies ranked in proud array,
Himself an army, now unequal match
To save himself against a coward armed
At one spear's length? O ever-failing trust
In mortal strength! And O what not in man

Gentile; *strictest purity* (319) refers to avoidance
of mixed marriages, not to celibacy, which was
not required of Nazarites.
321. **Unclean:** according to Mosaic Law.
324. **quits:** acquits.
325. **Unchaste was subsequent:** The woman of
Timna, having been rejected by Samson, was
given to Samson's companion (Judg. 14.20), and

thus the unchastity was subsequent to their
wedding.
327. **careful:** full of care.
328. **advise:** consider.
332. **Dan:** the territory of Samson's tribe.
333. **uncouth:** unfamiliar.
335. **informed:** directed, guided.
338. **signal:** conspicuous.

350 Deceivable and vain! Nay what thing good
    Prayed for, but often proves our woe, our bane?
    I prayed for children, and thought barrenness
    In wedlock a reproach; I gained a son,
    And such a son as all men hailed me happy;
355 Who would be now a father in my stead?
    O wherefore did God grant me my request,
    And as a blessing with such pomp adorned?
    Why are his gifts desirable, to tempt
    Our earnest prayers, then, giv'n with solemn hand
360 As graces, draw a scorpion's tail behind?
    For this did the angel twice descend? For this
    Ordained thy nurture holy, as of a plant;
    Select, and sacred, glorious for a while,
    The miracle of men: then in an hour
365 Ensnared, assaulted, overcome, led bound,
    Thy foes' derision, captive, poor, and blind,
    Into a dungeon thrust, to work with slaves?
    Alas methinks whom God hath chosen once
    To worthiest deeds, if he through frailty err,
370 He should not so o'erwhelm, and as a thrall
    Subject him to so foul indignities,
    Be it but for honor's sake of former deeds.
        Samson. Appoint not Heavenly disposition, father,
    Nothing of all these evils hath befall'n me
375 But justly; I myself have brought them on,
    Sole author I, sole cause: if aught seem vile,
    As vile hath been my folly, who have profaned
    The mystery of God giv'n me under pledge
    Of vow, and have betrayed it to a woman
380 A Canaanite, my faithless enemy.
    This well I knew, nor was at all surprised
    But warned by oft experience: did not she
    Of Timna first betray me, and reveal
    The secret wrested from me in her highth
385 Of nuptial love professed, carrying it straight

354. **as:** that.
363. **Select:** set aside.
373. **Appoint:** both "assign blame to" and "fix, or place a limit on."
377. **profaned:** disclosed a sacred secret (Lat. *profanum*, "outside the temple").
380. **Canaanite:** the Philistines had occupied Canaan.

384. **secret:** the solution to Samson's riddle (Judg. 14). Samson had posed a riddle to the thirty Philistine groomsmen at his first wedding; they prevailed upon the woman of Timna to draw the answer from Samson, who slew the thirty in a rage. The treachery of the woman of Timna foreshadows Dalila's, and thus adds to the *experience* (382) that makes Samson more culpable.

To them who had corrupted her, my spies,
And rivals? In this other was there found
More faith? Who also in her prime of love,
Spousal embraces, vitiated with gold,
390 Though offered only, by the scent conceived
Her spurious first-born, Treason against me?
Thrice she assayed with flattering prayers and sighs,
And amorous reproaches to win from me
My capital secret, in what part my strength
395 Lay stored, in what part summed, that she might know:
Thrice I deluded her, and turned to sport
Her importunity, each time perceiving
How openly, and with what impudence
She purposed to betray me, and (which was worse
400 Than undissembled hate) with what contempt
She sought to make me traitor to myself;
Yet the fourth time, when must'ring all her wiles,
With blandished parleys, feminine assaults,
Tongue-batteries, she surceased not day nor night
405 To storm me over-watched, and wearied out.
At times when men seek most repose and rest,
I yielded, and unlocked her all my heart,
Who with a grain of manhood well resolved
Might easily have shook off all her snares:
410 But foul effeminacy held me yoked
Her bond-slave. O indignity, O blot
To honor and religion! Servile mind
Rewarded well with servile punishment!
The base degree to which I now am fall'n,
415 These rags, this grinding, is not yet so base
As was my former servitude, ignoble,
Unmanly, ignominious, infamous,
True slavery, and that blindness worse than this,
That saw not how degenerately I served.
420   *Manoa.* I cannot praise thy marriage choices, son,

389–91. The mere offer, or *scent,* of gold is enough to impregnate Dalila with treason, her illegitimate, or *spurious,* child. **vitiated:** corrupted.
392–409. Judg. 16.6–22.
394. **capital:** both "lethal" and "pertaining to the head."
403. **blandished parleys:** flattering conversations.
405. **over-watched:** tired from being on alert.
414. **degree:** rank.

420. The line is sometimes said to be an example of bathetic understatement. But our desire for a humorous moment should not blind us to the disciplined plain speaking here, given that Manoa is but a man and cannot understand if or why God would lead his son to such women. Cp. the plainness of Jesus in *PR* 4.171: "I never liked thy talk, thy offers less."

Rather approved them not; but thou didst plead
Divine impulsion prompting how thou might'st
Find some occasion to infest our foes.
I state not that; this I am sure, our foes
425   Found soon occasion thereby to make thee
Their captive, and their triumph; thou the sooner
Temptation found'st, or over-potent charms
To violate the sacred trust of silence
Deposited within thee; which to have kept
430   Tacit was in thy power; true; and thou bear'st
Enough, and more the burden of that fault;
Bitterly hast thou paid, and still art paying
That rigid score. A worse thing yet remains:
This day the Philistines a popular feast
435   Here celebrate in Gaza, and proclaim
Great pomp, and sacrifice, and praises loud
To Dagon, as their god who hath delivered
Thee Samson bound and blind into their hands,
Them out of thine, who slew'st them many a slain.
440   So Dagon shall be magnified, and God,
Besides whom is no God, compared with idols,
Disglorified, blasphemed, and had in scorn
By th' idolatrous rout amidst their wine;
Which to have come to pass by means of thee,
445   Samson, of all thy sufferings think the heaviest,
Of all reproach the most with shame that ever
Could have befall'n thee and thy father's house.
       Samson. Father, I do acknowledge and confess
That I this honor, I this pomp have brought
450   To Dagon, and advanced his praises high
Among the heathen round; to God have brought
Dishonor, obloquy, and oped the mouths
Of idolists and atheists; have brought scandal
To Israel, diffidence of God, and doubt

---

422. **prompting:** suggesting.

423. **infest:** annoy, plague.

424. **state not:** do not comment upon. Manoa will not discuss whether Samson's marriages were both divinely prompted but will instead pass on to the subject about which he is certain.

433. **rigid score:** stiff debt.

434–38. With Samson blinded and captive, the Philistine lords resolved "to offer a great sacrifice unto Dagon their god, and to rejoice: for they said, Our god hath delivered Samson our enemy into our hand" (Judg. 16.23).

439. **Them out of thine:** the Philistines out of Samson's hands; **slew'st them many a slain:** slew many of them, to their loss; an imitation of the Latin dative of disadvantage.

442. **Disglorified:** deprived of glory.

443. **rout:** multitude; the word is frequent in Milton, and always derogatory.

450. **advanced:** raised aloft.

454. **diffidence:** distrust.

455 In feeble hearts, propense enough before
     To waver, or fall off and join with idols;
     Which is my chief affliction, shame and sorrow,
     The anguish of my soul, that suffers not
     Mine eye to harbor sleep, or thoughts to rest.
460 This only hope relieves me, that the strife
     With me hath end; all the contest is now
     'Twixt God and Dagon; Dagon hath presumed,
     Me overthrown, to enter lists with God,
     His deity comparing and preferring
465 Before the God of Abraham. He, be sure,
     Will not connive, or linger, thus provoked,
     But will arise and his great name assert:
     Dagon must stoop, and shall ere long receive
     Such a discomfit, as shall quite despoil him
470 Of all these boasted trophies won on me,
     And with confusion blank his worshippers.
          Manoa. With cause this hope relieves thee, and these words
     I as a prophecy receive: for God,
     Nothing more certain, will not long defer
475 To vindicate the glory of his name
     Against all competition, nor will long
     Endure it, doubtful whether God be Lord,
     Or Dagon. But for thee what shall be done?
     Thou must not in the meanwhile here forgot
480 Lie in this miserable loathsome plight
     Neglected. I already have made way
     To some Philistian lords, with whom to treat
     About thy ransom: well they may by this
     Have satisfied their utmost of revenge
485 By pains and slaveries, worse than death inflicted
     On thee, who now no more canst do them harm.
          Samson. Spare that proposal, father, spare the trouble
     Of that solicitation; let me here,
     As I deserve, pay on my punishment;
490 And expiate, if possible, my crime,
     Shameful garrulity. To have revealed

---

455. **propense:** ready, inclined.
456. **fall off:** break away from allegiance.
460. **only:** one, sole.
466. **connive:** tolerate; carries the Latin sense of "shut the eyes."
467. **assert:** champion.
469. **discomfit:** defeat.

470. **won on:** won over.
471. **confusion:** ruin, overthrow; **blank:** confound.
481–83. **I . . . ransom:** Milton adds Manoa's attempt to ransom Samson to the biblical account.
481–82. **made way/To:** approached.
483. **by this:** by this time.

Secrets of men, the secrets of a friend,
How heinous had the fact been, how deserving
Contempt, and scorn of all, to be excluded
495 All friendship, and avoided as a blab,
The mark of fool set on his front?
But I God's counsel have not kept, his holy secret
Presumptuously have published, impiously,
Weakly at least, and shamefully: a sin
500 That Gentiles in their parables condemn
To their abyss and horrid pains confined.
    Manoa. Be penitent and for thy fault contrite,
But act not in thy own affliction, son,
Repent the sin, but if the punishment
505 Thou canst avoid, self-preservation bids;
Or th' execution leave to high disposal,
And let another hand, not thine, exact
Thy penal forfeit from thyself; perhaps
God will relent, and quit thee all his debt;
510 Who evermore approves and more accepts
(Best pleased with humble and filial submission)
Him who imploring mercy sues for life,
Than who self-rigorous chooses death as due;
Which argues over-just, and self-displeased
515 For self-offense, more than for God offended.
Reject not then what offered means, who knows
But God hath set before us, to return thee
Home to thy country and his sacred house,
Where thou may'st bring thy off'rings, to avert
520 His further ire, with prayers and vows renewed.
    Samson. His pardon I implore; but as for life,
To what end should I seek it? When in strength
All mortals I excelled, and great in hopes
With youthful courage and magnanimous thoughts
525 Of birth from Heav'n foretold and high exploits,

---

493. **fact:** deed.
496. **front:** forehead.
499–501. **a sin . . . confined:** Tantalus was punished for revealing the gods' secrets (Euripides, *Orestes* 10). Ovid emphasizes his garrulity (*Ars Amatoria* 2.603–7). Another example is the suffering Zeus imposed on Prometheus for giving heaven's fire to mankind.
503–15. In *CD* 2.8, Milton relates suicide to "a perverse hatred of oneself" (Yale 6:719). Manoa cautions Samson against suicide, advising his

son to leave judgment and punishment to God. Samson often sounds suicidal (595–98, 647–52, 1262–67), and readers argue over whether his final act is a divinely authorized attack on the enemies of Israel or a blamable act of suicide or both (see 1584–86).
509. **quit thee all his debt:** cancel all your debt to him.
514. **argues over-just:** shows one to be overly scrupulous.

Full of divine instinct, after some proof
Of acts indeed heroic, far beyond
The sons of Anak, famous now and blazed,
Fearless of danger, like a petty god
530 I walked about admired of all and dreaded
On hostile ground, none daring my affront.
Then swoll'n with pride into the snare I fell
Of fair fallacious looks, venereal trains,
Softened with pleasure and voluptuous life;
535 At length to lay my head and hallowed pledge
Of all my strength in the lascivious lap
Of a deceitful concubine who shore me
Like a tame wether, all my precious fleece,
Then turned me out ridiculous, despoiled,
540 Shav'n, and disarmed among my enemies.
        Chorus. Desire of wine and all delicious drinks,
Which many a famous warrior overturns,
Thou couldst repress, nor did the dancing ruby
Sparkling, out-poured, the flavor, or the smell,
545 Or taste that cheers the heart of gods and men,
Allure thee from the cool crystalline stream.
        Samson. Wherever fountain or fresh current flowed
Against the eastern ray, translucent, pure,
With touch ethereal of Heav'n's fiery rod
550 I drank, from the clear milky juice allaying
Thirst, and refreshed; nor envied them the grape
Whose heads that turbulent liquor fills with fumes.
        Chorus. O madness, to think use of strongest wines
And strongest drinks our chief support of health,
555 When God with these forbidd'n made choice to rear
His mighty champion, strong above compare,
Whose drink was only from the liquid brook.
        Samson. But what availed this temperance, not complete
Against another object more enticing?

526. **instinct:** impulse; cp. lines 223 and 1382.
528. **sons of Anak:** giants; **blazed:** much spoken of.
531. **my affront:** to meet me face to face.
533. **fallacious:** deceptive, perhaps with a pun on *phallic*; **venereal trains:** sexual traps.
535. **At length to lay:** at length so softened as to lay (see Judg. 26.19); **pledge:** his hair, the source of his strength and mark of divine favor.
537. **concubine:** Here Samson for once does not own Dalila as his wife.

538. **wether:** castrated ram.
541–46. As a Nazarite, Samson took a vow to abstain from alcohol (Judg. 13.4).
543. **dancing ruby:** flashing red wine.
549. **fiery rod:** sunbeam.
550. **milky juice:** pure, clear water; cp. *PL* 5.306.
552. **fumes:** undigested effluvia of wine, which cloud and befuddle the mind. Milton traced his own blindness to incompletely digested food.
557. **liquid:** clear, transparent.

560 What boots it at one gate to make defense,
      And at another to let in the foe,
      Effeminately vanquished? By which means,
      Now blind, disheartened, shamed, dishonored, quelled,
      To what can I be useful, wherein serve
565 My nation, and the work from Heav'n imposed,
      But to sit idle on the household hearth,
      A burdenous drone; to visitants a gaze,
      Or pitied object, these redundant locks
      Robustious to no purpose clust'ring down,
570 Vain monument of strength; till length of years
      And sedentary numbness craze my limbs
      To a contemptible old age obscure.
      Here rather let me drudge and earn my bread,
      Till vermin or the draff of servile food
575 Consume me, and oft-invocated death
      Hasten the welcome end of all my pains.
            Manoa. Wilt thou then serve the Philistines with that gift
      Which was expressly given thee to annoy them?
      Better at home lie bed-rid, not only idle,
580 Inglorious, unemployed, with age outworn.
      But God who caused a fountain at thy prayer
      From the dry ground to spring, thy thirst to allay
      After the brunt of battle, can as easy
      Cause light again within thy eyes to spring,
585 Wherewith to serve him better than thou hast;
      And I persuade me so; why else this strength
      Miraculous yet remaining in those locks?
      His might continues in thee not for naught,
      Nor shall his wondrous gifts be frustrate thus.
590   *Samson.* All otherwise to me my thoughts portend,
      That these dark orbs no more shall treat with light,
      Nor th' other light of life continue long,
      But yield to double darkness nigh at hand:
      So much I feel my genial spirits droop,
595 My hopes all flat, nature within me seems
      In all her functions weary of herself;

560. **What boots it:** what good does it do.
568. **redundant:** abundant to fullness or even excess (*OED* 2.a).
569. **Robustious:** robust.
571. **craze:** impair.
574. **draff:** refuse, dregs; wash or swill given to pigs.
581–83. **But God . . . battle:** Judges 15.18–19. In the

AV, the water comes from the jawbone itself. Milton follows another possibility in the ambiguous Hebrew version, and has water flowing at a rock named after the jawbone.
594. **genial:** arising from one's "genius" or natural character.
595. **flat:** overthrown.

My race of glory run, and race of shame,
And I shall shortly be with them that rest.
    Manoa. Believe not these suggestions which proceed
600 From anguish of the mind and humors black,
That mingle with thy fancy. I however
Must not omit a father's timely care
To prosecute the means of thy deliverance
By ransom or how else: meanwhile be calm,
605 And healing words from these thy friends admit.
    Samson. O that Torment should not be confined
To the body's wounds and sores
With maladies innumerable
In heart, head, breast, and reins;
610 But must secret passage find
To th' inmost mind,
There exercise all his fierce accidents,
And on her purest spirits prey,
As on entrails, joints, and limbs,
615 With answerable pains, but more intense,
Though void of corporal sense.
    My griefs not only pain me
As a ling'ring disease,
But finding no redress, ferment and rage,
620 Nor less than wounds immedicable
Rankle, and fester, and gangrene,
To black mortification.
Thoughts my tormentors armed with deadly stings
Mangle my apprehensive tenderest parts,
625 Exasperate, exulcerate, and raise
Dire inflammation which no cooling herb
Or med'cinal liquor can assuage,
Nor breath of vernal air from snowy alp.
Sleep hath forsook and giv'n me o'er
630 To death's benumbing opium as my only cure.
Thence faintings, swoonings of despair,
And sense of Heav'ns desertion.
    I was his nursling once and choice delight,

---

600. **humors black:** black bile, which when pre-dominant causes melancholy. See the induction to Ben Jonson's *Every Man out of his Humour.*
603. **prosecute:** pursue, persist in.
609. **reins:** kidneys, thought to be the seat of feelings or affections.
612. **accidents:** unfavorable symptoms.

613. **purest spirits:** most refined corporal sub-stance; cp. the "intellectual" spirits of *PL* 5.485.
615. **answerable:** corresponding.
622. **mortification:** gangrene.
624. **apprehensive:** receptive, sensitive.
625. **exulcerate:** cause ulcers.
628. **alp:** any high, snowcapped mountain.

His destined from the womb,
635 Promised by Heavenly message twice descending.
Under his special eye
Abstemious I grew up and thrived amain;
He led me on to mightiest deeds
Above the nerve of mortal arm
640 Against the uncircumcised, our enemies.
But now hath cast me off as never known,
And to those cruel enemies,
Whom I by his appointment had provoked,
Left me all helpless with th' irreparable loss
645 Of sight, reserved alive to be repeated
The subject of their cruelty, or scorn.
Nor am I in the list of them that hope;
Hopeless are all my evils, all remediless;
This one prayer yet remains, might I be heard,
650 No long petition, speedy death,
The close of all my miseries, and the balm.
        Chorus. Many are the sayings of the wise
In ancient and in modern books enrolled,
Extolling patience as the truest fortitude,
655 And to the bearing well of all calamities,
All chances incident to man's frail life,
Consolatories writ
With studied argument, and much persuasion sought
Lenient of grief and anxious thought;
660 But with th' afflicted in his pangs their sound
Little prevails, or rather seems a tune,
Harsh, and of dissonant mood from his complaint,
Unless he feel within
Some source of consolation from above;
665 Secret refreshings, that repair his strength,
And fainting spirits uphold.
        God of our fathers, what is man!
That thou towards him with hand so various,
Or might I say contrarious,

635. **message:** messenger.
637. **Abstemious:** abstaining from wine; **amain:** greatly, exceedingly.
639. **nerve:** muscle.
643. **appointment:** command.
645. **repeated:** repeatedly.
656. **incident:** likely to befall.
657. **Consolatories:** writings on the topic of consolation.

659. **Lenient:** soothing, softening.
662. **mood:** not only an emotional state but also a musical mode, picking up on *tune* in the previous line.
667. **what is man:** The question recalls, but reverses the emphasis of, the question in Job 7.17, "What is man, that thou shouldest magnify him?" (See also Ps. 8.4 and Heb. 2.6).
669. **contrarious:** both contradictory and hostile.

670 Temper'st thy providence through his short course,
    Not evenly, as thou rul'st
    The angelic orders and inferior creatures mute,
    Irrational and brute.
    Nor do I name of men the common rout,
675 That wand'ring loose about
    Grow up and perish, as the summer fly,
    Heads without name no more remembered;
    But such as thou hast solemnly elected,
    With gifts and graces eminently adorned
680 To some great work, thy glory,
    And people's safety, which in part they effect:
    Yet toward these thus dignified, thou oft,
    Amidst their highth of noon,
    Changest thy countenance, and thy hand with no regard
685 Of highest favors past
    From thee on them, or them to thee of service.
        Nor only dost degrade them, or remit
    To life obscured, which were a fair dismission,
    But throw'st them lower than thou didst exalt them high,
690 Unseemly falls in human eye,
    Too grievous for the trespass or omission,
    Oft leav'st them to the hostile sword
    Of heathen and profane, their carcasses
    To dogs and fowls a prey, or else captíved:
695 Or to th' unjust tribunals, under change of times,
    And condemnation of the ingrateful multitude.
    If these they scape, perhaps in poverty
    With sickness and disease thou bow'st them down,

---

676. **the summer fly:** Summer flies typified short life; see Shakespeare, *LLL* 5.2.408, and George Herbert, "Complaining."

677. **Heads without name:** persons unknown to fame. Thomas Browne thought that most human beings were in fact destined to be *heads without name:* "The greater part must be content to be as though they had not been, to be found in the Register of God, not in the record of man" (*Urn Burial 5*).

678. **solemnly elected:** The sense of being specially elect by God for great service links Samson with Milton himself. Here the Chorus testifies to Samson's status.

687. **remit:** send back.

694. **To dogs and fowls a prey:** The image recalls

the degrading exposure of Greek bodies in the first lines of the *Iliad.*

695. **unjust tribunals, under change of times:** As Thomas Newton noted in 1749, this passage evokes prosecution of Milton's party at the Restoration. Buried Parliamentary leaders and regicides were exhumed and their *carcasses* (693) displayed (Leonard notes that Cromwell's skull was not reinterred until 1960); living ones were imprisoned, and Sir Henry Vane was hanged, drawn, and quartered, a grisly punishment that Milton came close to suffering. The reference to the *ingrateful multitude* (696) echoes Milton's frequent condemnation of the backsliding English. See the image of the "misguided and abused multitude" that closes *REW* (*MLM* 1136).

Painful diseases and deformed,
700 In crude old age;
Though not disordinate, yet causeless suff'ring
The punishment of dissolute days: in fine,
Just or unjust, alike seem miserable,
For oft alike, both come to evil end.
705   So deal not with this once thy glorious champion,
The image of thy strength, and mighty minister.
What do I beg? How hast thou dealt already?
Behold him in this state calamitous, and turn
His labors, for thou canst, to peaceful end.
710   But who is this, what thing of sea or land?
Female of sex it seems,
That so bedecked, ornate, and gay,
Comes this way sailing
Like a stately ship
715 Of Tarsus, bound for th' isles
Of Javan or Gadier
With all her bravery on, and tackle trim,
Sails filled, and streamers waving,
Courted by all the winds that hold them play,
720 And amber scent of odorous perfume
Her harbinger, a damsel train behind;
Some rich Philistian matron she may seem,
And now at nearer view, no other certain
Than Dalila thy wife.
725   *Samson.* My wife, my traitress, let her not come near me.
    Chorus. Yet on she moves, now stands and eyes thee fixed,
About t' have spoke, but now, with head declined
Like a fair flower surcharged with dew, she weeps
And words addressed seem into tears dissolved,

699. **deformed:** disfiguring.
700. **crude:** premature.
701–2. **Though not disordinate . . . days:** Although they have not led dissolute lives, they receive the punishment appropriate to the dissolute.
702. **in fine:** in conclusion.
706. **minister:** servant.
711–13. Reflecting literary practice, Milton has the Chorus compare Dalila to a ship.
714–15. **ship/Of Tarsus:** In the Old Testament, the ships of Tarshish are symbols of pride and objects of divine anger (Ps. 48.7, 2 Chron. 9.21).

Milton identified *Tarsus* in Cilicia with Tarshish in Spain.
716. **Javan:** the Greek islands; Javan, Noah's grandson, was thought to be the ancestor of the Greeks. **Gadier:** modern Cádiz on the coast of Spain.
717. **bravery:** finery; **tackle trim:** rigging in good order. *Trim* could also allude to a woman's toilette, meaning "nicely arrayed" or "got up."
719. **hold them play:** hold them in play, keep them occupied.
720. **amber scent:** fragrance, as of ambergris.
729. **addressed:** prepared.

730 Wetting the borders of her silken veil:
But now again she makes address to speak.
     Dalila. With doubtful feet and wavering resolution
I came, still dreading thy displeasure, Samson,
Which to have merited, without excuse,
735 I cannot but acknowledge; yet if tears
May expiate (though the fact more evil drew
In the perverse event than I foresaw)
My penance hath not slack'ned, though my pardon
No way assured. But conjugal affection,
740 Prevailing over fear and timorous doubt,
Hath led me on desirous to behold
Once more thy face, and know of thy estate.
If aught in my ability may serve
To lighten what thou suffer'st, and appease
745 Thy mind with what amends is in my power,
Though late, yet in some part to recompense
My rash but more unfortunate misdeed.
     Samson. Out, out hyena; these are thy wonted arts,
And arts of every woman false like thee,
750 To break all faith, all vows, deceive, betray,
Then as repentant to submit, beseech,
And reconcilement move with feigned remorse,
Confess, and promise wonders in her change,
Not truly penitent, but chief to try
755 Her husband, how far urged his patience bears,
His virtue or weakness which way to assail:
Then with more cautious and instructed skill
Again transgresses, and again submits;
That wisest and best men full oft beguiled,
760 With goodness principled not to reject
The penitent, but ever to forgive,
Are drawn to wear out miserable days,
Entangled with a pois'nous bosom snake,
If not by quick destruction soon cut off
765 As I by thee, to ages an example.

---

731. **makes address:** prepares.
736. **fact:** deed.
737. **event:** outcome.
739. **No way assured:** a Latinate construction, meaning "be no way assured."
748. **hyena:** The hyena was associated with deception and treachery. See Gosson's *School of Abuse:*

"*Hyena* speaks like a friend, and devours like a foe" (1587, 3).
752. **move:** propose.
755. **bears:** endures.
759. **That:** so that.
760. **principled:** instructed.

> *Dalila.* Yet hear me Samson; not that I endeavor
> To lessen or extenuate my offence,
> But that on th' other side, if it be weighed
> By itself, with aggravations not surcharged,
> 770 Or else with just allowance counterpoised,
> I may, if possible, thy pardon find
> The easier towards me, or thy hatred less.
> First granting, as I do, it was a weakness
> In me, but incident to all our sex,
> 775 Curiosity, inquisitive, importune
> Of secrets, then with like infirmity
> To publish them, both common female faults:
> Was it not weakness also to make known
> For importunity, that is for naught,
> 780 Wherein consisted all thy strength and safety?
> To what I did thou show'dst me first the way.
> But I to enemies revealed, and should not.
> Nor shouldst thou have trusted that to woman's frailty:
> Ere I to thee, thou to thyself wast cruel.
> 785 Let weakness then with weakness come to parle,
> So near related, or the same of kind;
> Thine forgive mine, that men may censure thine
> The gentler, if severely thou exact not
> More strength from me, than in thyself was found.
> 790 And what if love, which thou interpret'st hate,
> The jealousy of love, powerful of sway
> In human hearts, nor less in mine towards thee,
> Caused what I did? I saw thee mutable
> Of fancy, feared lest one day thou wouldst leave me
> 795 As her at Timna, sought by all means therefore
> How to endear, and hold thee to me firmest:
> No better way I saw than by importuning
> To learn thy secrets, get into my power
> Thy key of strength and safety: thou wilt say,
> 800 Why then revealed? I was assured by those
> Who tempted me, that nothing was designed
> Against thee but safe custody, and hold:

---

769. **with aggravations not surcharged:** not weighted or made heavier with extrinsic circumstances.
775–76. **importune/Of:** persistent in uncovering.
782. **But:** but you will say.
785. **come to parle:** confer in order to settle disputed points.

786. **kind:** nature, quality.
794. **fancy:** love.
795. **her at Timna:** ironic, since the woman at Timna lost Samson's love, as did Dalila, by revealing her husband's secret.
800–802. In the *AV*, the Philistines want Samson's secret so that they may "afflict" him (Judges

That made for me; I knew that liberty
Would draw thee forth to perilous enterprises,
805 While I at home sat full of cares and fears
Wailing thy absence in my widowed bed;
Here I should still enjoy thee day and night
Mine and love's prisoner, not the Philistines',
Whole to myself, unhazarded abroad,
810 Fearless at home of partners in my love.
These reasons in love's law have passed for good,
Though fond and reasonless to some perhaps;
And love hath oft, well meaning, wrought much woe,
Yet always pity or pardon hath obtained.
815 Be not unlike all others, not austere
As thou art strong, inflexible as steel.
If thou in strength all mortals dost exceed,
In uncompassionate anger do not so.
    Samson. How cunningly the sorceress displays
820 Her own transgressions, to upbraid me mine!
That malice not repentance brought thee hither,
By this appears: I gave, thou say'st, th' example,
I led the way; bitter reproach, but true,
I to myself was false ere thou to me;
825 Such pardon therefore as I give my folly,
Take to thy wicked deed: which when thou seest
Impartial, self-severe, inexorable,
Thou wilt renounce thy seeking, and much rather
Confess it feigned. Weakness is thy excuse,
830 And I believe it, weakness to resist
Philistian gold: if weakness may excuse,
What murderer, what traitor, parricide,
Incestuous, sacrilegious, but may plead it?
All wickedness is weakness: that plea therefore
835 With God or man will gain thee no remission.
But love constrained thee; call it furious rage
To satisfy thy lust: love seeks to have love;
My love how couldst thou hope, who took'st the way
To raise in me inexpiable hate,
840 Knowing, as needs I must, by thee betrayed?

16.5); Leonard notes that in the Greek of the
Septuagint, the word is "humiliate," which may
not give the lie to Dalila's claim here; in either
reading, however, the hostile intent of the
Philistines is clear.

803. **That made for me:** that influenced me, or
that worked to my advantage.
812. **fond:** foolish.
826. **which:** referring to *pardon* in the previous line.
838. **hope:** hope for.

In vain thou striv'st to cover shame with shame,
Or by evasions thy crime uncover'st more.
    Dalila. Since thou determin'st weakness for no plea
In man or woman, though to thy own condemning,
845 Hear what assaults I had, what snares besides,
What sieges girt me round, ere I consented;
Which might have awed the best resolved of men,
The constantest to have yielded without blame.
It was not gold, as to my charge thou lay'st,
850 That wrought with me: thou know'st the magistrates
And princes of my country came in person,
Solicited, commanded, threatened, urged,
Adjured by all the bonds of civil duty
And of religion, pressed how just it was,
855 How honorable, how glorious to entrap
A common enemy, who had destroyed
Such numbers of our nation: and the priest
Was not behind, but ever at my ear,
Preaching how meritorious with the gods
860 It would be to ensnare an irreligious
Dishonorer of Dagon: what had I
To oppose against such powerful arguments?
Only my love of thee held long debate,
And combated in silence all these reasons
865 With hard contest: at length that grounded maxim
So rife and celebrated in the mouths
Of wisest men, that to the public good
Private respects must yield, with grave authority
Took full possession of me and prevailed;
870 Virtue, as I thought, truth, duty so enjoining.
    Samson. I thought where all thy circling wiles would end;
In feigned religion, smooth hypocrisy.
But had thy love, still odiously pretended,
Been, as it ought, sincere, it would have taught thee
875 Far other reasonings, brought forth other deeds.
I before all the daughters of my tribe
And of my nation chose thee from among
My enemies, loved thee, as too well thou knew'st,

841–42. **to cover . . . uncover'st more:** Leonard notes the likeness to *PL* 9.1057–61, when Adam and Eve are "naked left/To guilty Shame: he covered, but his robe/Uncovered more. So rose the Danite strong/Herculean Samson, from the harlot-lap/Of Philistean Dalila."

866. **rife:** widespread, often heard.
868. **respects:** considerations.
876–78. Samson's claims here and at lines 1192–93 ignore his earlier admission (227–33) that he married Dalila in order to find occasion to "oppress/Israel's oppressors."

Too well, unbosomed all my secrets to thee,
880 Not out of levity, but overpow'red
By thy request, who could deny thee nothing;
Yet now am judged an enemy. Why then
Didst thou at first receive me for thy husband?
Then, as since then, thy country's foe professed:
885 Being once a wife, for me thou wast to leave
Parents and country; nor was I their subject,
Nor under their protection but my own,
Thou mine, not theirs: if aught against my life
Thy country sought of thee, it sought unjustly,
890 Against the law of nature, law of nations,
No more thy country, but an impious crew
Of men conspiring to uphold their state
By worse than hostile deeds, violating the ends
For which our country is a name so dear;
895 Not therefore to be obeyed. But zeal moved thee;
To please thy gods thou didst it; gods unable
To acquit themselves and prosecute their foes
But by ungodly deeds, the contradiction
Of their own deity, gods cannot be:
900 Less therefore to be pleased, obeyed, or feared.
These false pretexts and varnished colors failing,
Bare in thy guilt how foul must thou appear?
    Dalila. In argument with men a woman ever
Goes by the worse, whatever be her cause.
905   *Samson.* For want of words no doubt, or lack of breath,
Witness when I was worried with thy peals.
    Dalila. I was a fool, too rash, and quite mistaken
In what I thought would have succeeded best.
Let me obtain forgiveness of thee, Samson,
910 Afford me place to show what recompense
Towards thee I intend for what I have misdone,
Misguided; only what remains past cure
Bear not too sensibly, nor still insist
To afflict thyself in vain: though sight be lost,
915 Life yet hath many solaces, enjoyed
Where other senses want not their delights

---

880. **levity:** "Gravity entails careful moderation of words and actions. . . . Opposed to this is levity" (*CD* 2.13).

897. **acquit themselves:** perform their offices.

901. **varnished colors:** false displays; in *Animad.*, Milton attacks the hypocrite for "painting his lewd and deceitfull principles with a smooth, and glossy varnish . . . to bring about his wickedest purposes" (Yale 1:720).

904. **Goes by:** gets.

913. **sensibly:** sensitively.

916. **want:** lack.

At home in leisure and domestic ease,
Exempt from many a care and chance to which
Eyesight exposes daily men abroad.
920 I to the lords will intercede, not doubting
Their favorable ear, that I may fetch thee
From forth this loathsome prison-house to abide
With me, where my redoubled love and care
With nursing diligence, to me glad office,
925 May ever tend about thee to old age
With all things grateful cheered, and so supplied,
That what by me thou hast lost thou least shalt miss.
    Samson. No, no, of my condition take no care;
It fits not; thou and I long since are twain;
930 Nor think me so unwary or accursed
To bring my feet again into the snare
Where once I have been caught; I know thy trains
Though dearly to my cost, thy gins, and toils;
Thy fair enchanted cup, and warbling charms
935 No more on me have power, their force is nulled,
So much of adder's wisdom I have learned
To fence my ear against thy sorceries.
If in my flower of youth and strength, when all men
Loved, honored, feared me, thou alone could hate me
940 Thy husband, slight me, sell me, and forgo me;
How wouldst thou use me now, blind, and thereby
Deceiveable, in most things as a child
Helpless, thence easily contemned, and scorned,
And last neglected? How wouldst thou insult
945 When I must live uxorious to thy will
In perfect thraldom, how again betray me,
Bearing my words and doings to the lords
To gloss upon, and censuring, frown or smile?
This jail I count the house of liberty
950 To thine whose doors my feet shall never enter.
    Dalila. Let me approach at least, and touch thy hand.

---

919. **abroad:** outdoors.
926. **grateful:** pleasing
929. **thou and I long since are twain:** Samson here exercises the Hebrew right of divorce that Milton argued for in the 1640s.
932–33. **trains . . . gins . . . toils:** various traps.
934. The *cup* and *charms* relate Dalila to Homer's Circe and to Milton's own Comus (*Masque 51, 150*).

935. **nulled:** annulled, canceled.
936–37. referring to the belief that adders are deaf (Ps. 58.4–5).
942. **Deceiveable:** likely to be deceived.
948. **gloss upon:** comment upon; **censuring:** judging.
950. **To:** compared to.

Samson. Not for thy life, lest fierce remembrance wake
My sudden rage to tear thee joint by joint.
At distance I forgive thee, go with that;
955   Bewail thy falsehood, and the pious works
It hath brought forth to make thee memorable
Among illustrious women, faithful wives:
Cherish thy hastened widowhood with the gold
Of matrimonial treason: so farewell.

960   *Dalila.* I see thou art implacable, more deaf
To prayers, than winds and seas, yet winds to seas
Are reconciled at length, and sea to shore:
Thy anger, unappeasable, still rages,
Eternal tempest never to be calmed.

965   Why do I humble thus myself, and suing
For peace, reap nothing but repulse and hate?
Bid go with evil omen and the brand
Of infamy upon my name denounced?
To mix with thy concernments I desist

970   Henceforth, nor too much disapprove my own.
Fame if not double-faced is double-mouthed,
And with contrary blast proclaims most deeds;
On both his wings, one black, th' other white,
Bears greatest names in his wild airy flight.

975   My name perhaps among the circumcised
In Dan, in Judah, and the bordering tribes,
To all posterity may stand defamed,
With malediction mentioned, and the blot
Of falsehood most unconjugal traduced.

980   But in my country where I most desire,
In Ecron, Gaza, Asdod, and in Gath
I shall be named among the famousest
Of women, sung at solemn festivals,
Living and dead recorded, who to save

985   Her country from a fierce destroyer, chose

---

953. **tear thee joint by joint:** Samson has torn apart a lion (128). In Euripides' *Hecuba,* Polymestor threatens to tear apart Hecuba, who has blinded him. See Lieb 252–53.

954. **go with that:** leave content with that (my forgiveness at a distance).

958–59. **gold/Of:** gold gained by.

968. **denounced:** pronounced.

969. **concernments:** affairs.

971–73. For Milton's Fame, see *Aen.* 4.173ff. Milton is unusual in the tradition for making Fame male. By contrast, see *On the Fifth of November* 172–216.

971. **double-mouthed:** Chaucer describes Fame as attended by the trumpeter Aeolus, who bears two trumpets—a black one to announce infamous deeds and a golden one for good deeds (*House of Fame* 3.485–92, 582–98).

975. **the circumcised:** the Jews.

981. **Ecron . . . Gath:** major Philistine cities.

Above the faith of wedlock-bands, my tomb
With odors visited and annual flowers.
Not less renowned than in Mount Ephraim
Jael, who with inhospitable guile
990 Smote Sisera sleeping through the temples nailed.
Nor shall I count it heinous to enjoy
The public marks of honor and reward
Conferred upon me for the piety
Which to my country I was judged to have shown.
995 At this whoever envies or repines
I leave him to his lot, and like my own.
    Chorus. She's gone, a manifest serpent by her sting
Discovered in the end, till now concealed.
    Samson. So let her go; God sent her to debase me,
1000 And aggravate my folly who committed
To such a viper his most sacred trust
Of secrecy, my safety, and my life.
    Chorus. Yet beauty, though injurious, hath strange power,
After offense returning, to regain
1005 Love once possessed, nor can be easily
Repulsed, without much inward passion felt
And secret sting of amorous remorse.
    Samson. Love-quarrels oft in pleasing concord end,
Not wedlock-treachery endangering life.
1010   *Chorus.* It is not virtue, wisdom, valor, wit,
Strength, comeliness of shape, or amplest merit
That woman's love can win or long inherit;
But what it is, hard is to say,
Harder to hit,
1015 (Which way soever men refer it)
Much like thy riddle, Samson, in one day
Or seven, though one should musing sit;
    If any of these or all, the Timnian bride
Had not so soon preferred
1020 Thy paranymph, worthless to thee compared,
Successor in thy bed,
Nor both so loosely disallied

---

987. **odors:** incense.
988–90. The Israelite *Jael,* wife of Heber, lured the Canaanite leader Sisera to take refuge with her after his defeat by the Hebrews, and slew him (Judg. 4.17–24; 5.24–31).
1000. **aggravate:** The Latin sense, from *gravitas,* is "add to the weight of."

1008. See Terence, *Andria* 3.23.
1010–17. An elaborately rhymed passage in the middle of a mostly unrhymed poem. The rhyming continues, though less insistently, in lines 1018–33.
1020. **paranymph:** groomsman (see 384n).
1022. **both:** both wives.

Their nuptials, nor this last so treacherously
Had shorn the fatal harvest of thy head.
1025 Is it for that such outward ornament
Was lavished on their sex, that inward gifts
Were left for haste unfinished, judgment scant,
Capacity not raised to apprehend
Or value what is best
1030 In choice, but oftest to affect the wrong?
Or was too much of self-love mixed,
Of constancy no root infixed,
That either they love nothing, or not long?
Whate'er it be, to wisest men and best
1035 Seeming at first all heavenly under virgin veil,
Soft, modest, meek, demure,
Once joined, the contrary she proves, a thorn
Intestine, far within defensive arms
A cleaving mischief, in his way to virtue
1040 Adverse and turbulent, or by her charms
Draws him awry enslaved
With dotage, and his sense depraved
To folly and shameful deeds which ruin ends.
What pilot so expert but needs must wreck
1045 Embarked with such a steers-mate at the helm?
Favored of Heav'n who finds
One virtuous, rarely found,
That in domestic good combines:
Happy that house! His way to peace is smooth:
1050 But virtue which breaks through all opposition,
And all temptation can remove,
Most shines and most is acceptable above.
Therefore God's universal law
Gave to the man despotic power
1055 Over his female in due awe,
Nor from that right to part an hour,

1025. **for that:** because.

1030. **affect:** prefer.

1034. **wisest men and best:** See 759n.

1035–36. Cf. Milton's *DDD:* "who knows not that the bashful muteness of a virgin may oft-times hide all the unliveliness and natural sloth which is really unfit for conversation" (*MLM* 873).

1037. **joined:** married.

1038. **Intestine:** domestic, internal.

1039. **cleaving:** both "clinging" and "dividing."

1039–40. **in his way ... turbulent:** "Women were born to mar the lives of men / Ever, unto their surer overthrow" (Euripides, *Orestes* 605–6).

1048. "Who joins with her spouse in domestic happiness"; see Prov. 31.10ff for the praises of a virtuous wife.

1053–60. On the doctrine of male superiority, see *DDD* 15 and *PL* 4.295–99, 635–38; 9.1182–86; 10.145–56, 888–95.

Smile she or lour:
So shall he least confusion draw
On his whole life, not swayed
1060 By female usurpation, or dismayed.
   But had we best retire? I see a storm.
  Samson. Fair days have oft contracted wind and rain.
  Chorus. But this another kind of tempest brings.
  Samson. Be less abstruse, my riddling days are past.
1065 *Chorus.* Look now for no enchanting voice, nor fear
  The bait of honeyed words; a rougher tongue
  Draws hitherward, I know him by his stride,
  The giant Harapha of Gath, his look
  Haughty as is his pile high-built and proud.
1070 Comes he in peace? What wind hath blown him hither
  I less conjecture than when first I saw
  The sumptuous Dalila floating this way:
  His habit carries peace, his brow defiance.
  Samson. Or peace or not, alike to me he comes.
1075 *Chorus.* His fraught we soon shall know, he now arrives.
  Harapha. I come not Samson, to condole thy chance,
  As these perhaps, yet wish it had not been,
  Though for no friendly intent. I am of Gath,
  Men call me Harapha, of stock renowned
1080 As Og or Anak and the Emims old
  That Kiriathaim held, thou know'st me now
  If thou at all art known. Much I have heard
  Of thy prodigious might and feats performed
  Incredible to me; in this displeased,
1085 That I was never present on the place
  Of those encounters, where we might have tried
  Each other's force in camp or listed field:
  And now am come to see of whom such noise
  Hath walked about, and each limb to survey,
1090 If thy appearance answer loud report.

1068. **Harapha:** Milton adds him to the biblical account; his name derives from the Hebrew *ha-raphah*, or "the giant." Like *Dalila*, the name is stressed on first and third syllables.

1069. **pile:** a lofty mass of buildings, here figurative of Harapha's huge body.

1073. **habit:** clothing.

1075. **fraught:** freight (his news or commands).

1076. **condole thy chance:** lament your fate.

1080. **Og . . . Anak . . . Emims:** biblical giants (see Num. 13.33, 21.33–35; Deut. 2.10–11, 3.11).

1081. **Kiriathaim:** home of the Emims (Gen. 14.5).

1081–82. **thou know'st . . . known:** Harapha echoes Milton's Satan, who tells Ithuriel and Zephon, "Not to know me argues yourselves unknown" (*PL* 4.830).

1087. **camp:** battlefield; **listed field:** field prepared for jousting.

1088. **noise:** fame, report.

Samson. The way to know were not to see but taste.
Harapha. Dost thou already single me; I thought
Gyves and the mill had tamed thee? O that fortune
Had brought me to the field where thou art famed
1095 To have wrought such wonders with an ass's jaw;
I should have forced thee soon wish other arms,
Or left thy carcass where the ass lay thrown:
So had the glory of prowess been recovered
To Palestine, won by a Philistine
1100 From the unforeskinned race, of whom thou bear'st
The highest name for valiant acts; that honor
Certain to have won by mortal duel from thee,
I lose, prevented by thy eyes put out.
  Samson. Boast not of what thou wouldst have done, but do
1105 What then thou wouldst; thou seest it in thy hand.
  Harapha. To combat with a blind man I disdain,
And thou hast need much washing to be touched.
  Samson. Such usage as your honorable lords
Afford me assassinated and betrayed,
1110 Who durst not with their whole united powers
In fight withstand me single and unarmed,
Nor in the house with chamber ambushes
Close-banded durst attack me, no not sleeping,
Till they had hired a woman with their gold,
1115 Breaking her marriage faith to circumvent me.
Therefore without feigned shifts let be assigned
Some narrow place enclosed, where sight may give thee,
Or rather flight, no great advantage on me;
Then put on all thy gorgeous arms, thy helmet
1120 And brigandine of brass, thy broad habergeon,
Vantbrace and greaves, and gauntlet, add thy spear
A weaver's beam, and seven-times-folded shield,
I only with an oaken staff will meet thee,
And raise such outcries on thy clattered iron,
1125 Which long shall not withhold me from thy head,

1091. **taste:** try, examine by touch.
1092. **single:** challenge to single combat.
1093. **Gyves:** chains, shackles.
1102. **mortal duel:** fight to the death.
1109. **Afford:** allow; **assassinated:** treacherously attacked.
1113. **Close-banded:** secretly combining.
1116. **feigned shifts:** deluding tricks.
1120–21. **brigandine:** body armor; **habergeon:**
sleeveless coat of mail. **Vantbrace and greaves:** arm and leg armor; **gauntlet:** mailed glove.
1121–22. **spear / A weaver's beam:** a spear as large as a loom's heavy roller, like Goliath's spear (1 Sam. 17.7).
1122. **seven-times-folded shield:** made from a bull's hide folded seven times like the shields of Ajax (*Il.* 7.200) and Turnus (*Aen.* 12.925).

That in a little time while breath remains thee,
Thou oft shalt wish thyself at Gath to boast
Again in safety what thou wouldst have done
To Samson, but shalt never see Gath more.

1130   *Harapha.* Thou durst not thus disparage glorious arms
Which greatest heroes have in battle worn,
Their ornament and safety, had not spells
And black enchantments, some magician's art,
Armed thee or charmed the strong, which thou from Heaven

1135 Feign'dst at thy birth was giv'n thee in thy hair,
Where strength can least abide, though all thy hairs
Were bristles ranged like those that ridge the back
Of chafed wild boars, or ruffled porcupines.
    Samson. I know no spells, use no forbidden arts;

1140 My trust is in the living God who gave me
At my nativity this strength, diffused
No less through all my sinews, joints and bones,
Than thine, while I preserved these locks unshorn,
The pledge of my unviolated vow.

1145 For proof hereof, if Dagon be thy god,
Go to his temple, invocate his aid
With solemnest devotion, spread before him
How highly it concerns his glory now
To frustrate and dissolve these magic spells,

1150 Which I to be the power of Israel's God
Avow, and challenge Dagon to the test,
Offering to combat thee, his champion bold,
With th' utmost of his godhead seconded:
Then thou shalt see, or rather to thy sorrow

1155 Soon feel, whose god is strongest, thine or mine.
    Harapha. Presume not on thy god, whate'er he be,
Thee he regards not, owns not, hath cut off
Quite from his people, and delivered up
Into thy enemies' hand, permitted them

1160 To put out both thine eyes, and fettered send thee
Into the common prison, there to grind
Among the slaves and asses thy comrades,
As good for nothing else, no better service

1132–40. Todd notes that Harapha's challenge and Samson's response echo the oath taken by knights engaged in trial by combat: "I do swear, that I have not upon me, nor on any of the *arms* I shall use, words, *charms*, or *enchantments*, to which I trust for help to conquer my enemy, but that *I do only trust in God,* in my right, and in the strength of my body and arms."

1138. **chafed:** enraged.
1146. **invocate:** pray for.
1147. **spread:** lay out.

With those thy boist'rous locks, no worthy match
1165 For valor to assail, nor by the sword
Of noble warrior, so to stain his honor,
But by the barber's razor best subdued.
    Samson. All these indignities, for such they are
From thine, these evils I deserve and more,
1170 Acknowledge them from God inflicted on me
Justly, yet despair not of his final pardon
Whose ear is ever open; and his eye
Gracious to readmit the suppliant;
In confidence whereof I once again
1175 Defy thee to the trial of mortal fight,
By combat to decide whose god is God,
Thine or whom I with Israel's sons adore.
    Harapha. Fair honor that thou dost thy god, in trusting
He will accept thee to defend his cause,
1180 A murderer, a revolter, and a robber.
    Samson. Tongue-doughty giant, how dost thou prove me these?
    Harapha. Is not thy nation subject to our lords?
Their magistrates confessed it, when they took thee
As a league-breaker and delivered bound
1185 Into our hands: for hadst thou not committed
Notorious murder on those thirty men
At Ascalon, who never did thee harm,
Then like a robber stripp'dst them of their robes?
The Philistines, when thou hadst broke the league,
1190 Went up with armèd powers thee only seeking,
To others did no violence nor spoil.
    Samson. Among the daughters of the Philistines
I chose a wife, which argued me no foe;
And in your city held my nuptial feast:
1195 But your ill-meaning politician lords,
Under pretense of bridal friends and guests,
Appointed to await me thirty spies,
Who, threat'ning cruel death, constrained the bride

1164. **boist'rous:** coarse, violent.
1169. **thine:** your people (the Philistines).
1181. **Tongue-doughty:** brave of tongue; **prove me these:** prove me to be these (murderer, revolter, robber).
1183–91. **Their magistrates . . . spoil:** The Israelites handed Samson over to the Philistines (Judg. 15.11–13) after he had killed thirty Askalonites, taking their robes to pay his debt to the thirty Philistines who had suborned the

woman of Timna to discover and reveal the secret of Samson's riddle (Judg. 14.12 and 19). These events are recorded in lines 250–61 and 382–87.
1195. **politician:** scheming.
1197. **await:** wait upon; Milton borrows from Josephus (*Antiq.* 5.8) the idea that the thirty Philistines were guards posing as companions.

To wring from me and tell to them my secret,
1200 That solved the riddle which I had proposed.
When I perceived all set on enmity,
As on my enemies, wherever chanced,
I used hostility, and took their spoil
To pay my underminers in their coin.
1205 My nation was subjected to your lords.
It was the force of conquest; force with force
Is well ejected when the conquered can.
But I a private person, whom my country
As a league-breaker gave up bound, presumed
1210 Single rebellion and did hostile acts.
I was no private but a person raised
With strength sufficient and command from Heav'n
To free my country; if their servile minds
Me their Deliverer sent would not receive,
1215 But to their masters gave me up for naught,
Th' unworthier they; whence to this day they serve.
I was to do my part from Heav'n assigned,
And had performed it if my known offense
Had not disabled me, not all your force:
1220 These shifts refuted, answer thy appellant
Though by his blindness maimed for high attempts,
Who now defies thee thrice to single fight,
As a petty enterprise of small enforce.
    Harapha. With thee a man condemned, a slave enrolled,
1225 Due by the law to capital punishment?
To fight with thee no man of arms will deign.
    Samson. Cam'st thou for this, vain boaster, to survey me,
To descant on my strength, and give thy verdict?
Come nearer, part not hence so slight informed;
1230 But take good heed my hand survey not thee.
    Harapha. O Baäl-zebub! Can my ears unused
Hear these dishonors, and not render death?
    Samson. No man withholds thee, nothing from thy hand
Fear I incurable; bring up thy van,

1201–3. **When I perceived . . . enemies:** When I
saw all Philistines set on hatred, I treated all of
them as enemies.
1208. **I a private person:** Samson, as line 1211 makes
clear, is not conceding this point but simply
characterizing Harapha's description of him.
1220. **appellant:** challenger.
1221. **maimed for:** made incapable of.
1222. **defies thee thrice:** By custom, a military or

dueling challenge was repeated three times.
See *I.R* 5.7.108–16.
1223. **of small enforce:** of small difficulty, easy to do.
1228. **descant:** comment at length.
1231. **Baäl-zebub:** literally "god of the flies," a form
of Baal, the Philistine sun god; **unused:** i.e., un-
used to hearing dishonors.
1234. **van:** first line of battle; i.e., begin to fight.

1235 My heels are fettered, but my fist is free.
    Harapha. This insolence other kind of answer fits.
    Samson. Go baffled coward, lest I run upon thee,
    Though in these chains, bulk without spirit vast
    And with one buffet lay thy structure low,
1240 Or swing thee in the air, then dash thee down
    To the hazard of thy brains and shattered sides.
    Harapha. By Astaroth, ere long thou shalt lament
    These braveries in irons loaden on thee.
    Chorus. His giantship is gone somewhat crestfall'n,
1245 Stalking with less unconscionable strides,
    And lower looks, but in a sultry chafe.
    Samson. I dread him not, nor all his giant-brood,
    Though fame divulge him father of five sons
    All of gigantic size, Goliah chief.
1250   *Chorus.* He will directly to the lords, I fear,
    And with malicious counsel stir them up
    Some way or other yet further to afflict thee.
    Samson. He must allege some cause, and offered fight
    Will not dare mention, lest a question rise
1255 Whether he durst accept the offer or not,
    And that he durst not plain enough appeared.
    Much more affliction than already felt
    They cannot well impose, nor I sustain,
    If they intend advantage of my labors,
1260 The work of many hands, which earns my keeping
    With no small profit daily to my owners.
    But come what will, my deadliest foe will prove
    My speediest friend, by death to rid me hence,
    The worst that he can give, to me the best.
1265 Yet so it may fall out, because their end
    Is hate, not help to me, it may with mine
    Draw their own ruin who attempt the deed.
    Chorus. Oh how comely it is, and how reviving
    To the spirits of just men long oppressed!
1270 When God into the hands of their deliverer
    Puts invincible might

1237. **baffled:** publicly disgraced.

1242. **Astaroth:** a collective noun for manifestations of the Canaanite fertility goddess, Baal's counterpart. See *PL* 1.422–38.

1243. **braveries:** boasts.

1244. **His giantship:** mocking title.

1245. **unconscionable:** excessive.

1246. **sultry chafe:** angry rage.

1249. **Goliah:** Goliath; for the sons of the giant (*haraphah*) of Gath, see 2 Sam. 21.22.

1250–52. It is implied that the summons soon to be brought Samson by the officer (1310–18) was due to Harapha. In this sense, the visit of Harapha advances the drama toward its catastrophe.

To quell the mighty of the Earth, th' oppressor,
The brute and boist'rous force of violent men
Hardy and industrious to support
1275 Tyrannic power, but raging to pursue
The righteous and all such as honor truth;
He all their ammunition
And feats of war defeats
With plain heroic magnitude of mind
1280 And celestial vigor armed,
Their armories and magazines contemns,
Renders them useless, while
With wingèd expedition
Swift as the lightning glance he executes
1285 His errand on the wicked, who surprised
Lose their defense, distracted and amazed.
    But patience is more oft the exercise
Of saints, the trial of their fortitude,
Making them each his own deliverer,
1290 And victor over all
That tyranny or fortune can inflict.
Either of these is in thy lot,
Samson, with might endued
Above the sons of men; but sight bereaved
1295 May chance to number thee with those
Whom patience finally must crown.
This idol's day hath been to thee no day of rest,
    Laboring thy mind
More than the working day thy hands.
1300 And yet perhaps more trouble is behind,
For I descry this way
Some other tending, in his hand
A scepter or quaint staff he bears,
Comes on amain, speed in his look.
1305 By his habit I discern him now
A public officer, and now at hand.
His message will be short and voluble.

1283. **expedition:** speed.
1286. **amazed:** confounded; stronger than the modern *astonished*.
1287. **patience:** The primary meaning is "suffering"; in *Paradise Lost*, Milton redefines heroism in terms of "patience and heroic martyrdom" (9.32).
1288. **saints:** the faithful and therefore blessed; the term from Protestant discourse is applied anachronistically here; Dunster, cited by Todd, faults Milton for using the "fanatical language of the republican party."
1300. **behind:** yet to come.
1303. **quaint:** curiously wrought.
1305. **habit:** clothing.
1307. **voluble:** quickly delivered.

Officer. Hebrews, the pris'ner Samson here I seek.
Chorus. His manacles remark him, there he sits.
1310 *Officer.* Samson, to thee our lords thus bid me say;
This day to Dagon is a solemn feast,
With sacrifices, triumph, pomp, and games;
Thy strength they know surpassing human rate,
And now some public proof thereof require
1315 To honor this great feast, and great assembly;
Rise therefore with all speed and come along,
Where I will see thee heartened and fresh clad
To appear as fits before th' illustrious lords.
Samson. Thou know'st I am an Hebrew, therefore tell them,
1320 Our law forbids at their religious rites
My presence; for that cause I cannot come.
Officer. This answer, be assured, will not content them.
Samson. Have they not sword-players, and ev'ry sort
Of gymnic artists, wrestlers, riders, runners,
1325 Jugglers and dancers, antics, mummers, mimics,
But they must pick me out with shackles tired,
And over-labored at their public mill,
To make them sport with blind activity?
Do they not seek occasion of new quarrels
1330 On my refusal to distress me more,
Or make a game of my calamities?
Return the way thou cam'st, I will not come.
Officer. Regard thyself, this will offend them highly.
Samson. Myself? My conscience and internal peace.
1335 Can they think me so broken, so debased
With corporal servitude, that my mind ever
Will condescend to such absurd commands?
Although their drudge, to be their fool or jester,
And in my midst of sorrow and heart-grief
1340 To show them feats, and play before their god,
The worst of all indignities, yet on me
Joined with extreme contempt? I will not come.

1309. **remark:** distinguish, mark out.
1312. **triumph:** a procession celebrating a victory.
1313. **rate:** The 1671 edition's "race" was corrected by the Errata to "rate." The word means "degree."
1317. **heartened:** refreshed.
1320. **Our law forbids:** The Second Commandment forbids idol worship or service to other gods.

1325. **antics:** clowns; **mummers, mimics:** mimes.
1333. **Regard thyself:** look to your own interest.
1342. **Joined:** enjoined, imposed; **I will not come:** Samson repeats his refusal, by an ancient narrative and ritual formula, for the third time (see 1321 and 1332); for the significance of the repetition and the reversal at line 1384, see Kerrigan 1986.

    Officer. My message was imposed on me with speed,
    Brooks no delay: is this thy resolution?
1345   *Samson.* So take it with what speed thy message needs.
    Officer. I am sorry what this stoutness will produce.
    Samson. Perhaps thou shalt have cause to sorrow indeed.
    Chorus. Consider, Samson; matters now are strained
    Up to the highth, whether to hold or break;
1350 He's gone, and who knows how he may report
    Thy words by adding fuel to the flame?
    Expect another message more imperious,
    More lordly thund'ring than thou well wilt bear.
    Samson. Shall I abuse this consecrated gift
1355 Of strength, again returning with my hair
    After my great transgression, so requite
    Favor renewed, and add a greater sin
    By prostituting holy things to idols;
    A Nazarite in place abominable
1360 Vaunting my strength in honor to their Dagon?
    Besides, how vile, contemptible, ridiculous,
    What act more execrably unclean, profane?
    Chorus. Yet with this strength thou serv'st the Philistines,
    Idolatrous, uncircumcised, unclean.
1365   *Samson.* Not in their idol-worship, but by labor
    Honest and lawful to deserve my food
    Of those who have me in their civil power.
    Chorus. Where the heart joins not, outward acts defile not.
    Samson. Where outward force constrains, the sentence holds,
1370 But who constrains me to the temple of Dagon,
    Not dragging? The Philistian Lords command.
    Commands are no constraints. If I obey them,
    I do it freely; venturing to displease
    God for the fear of man, and man prefer,
1375 Set God behind: which in his jealousy
    Shall never, unrepented, find forgiveness.
    Yet that he may dispense with me or thee

1344. **Brooks:** suffers.

1346. **I am sorry:** I am sorry to think; **stoutness:** defiance, courage.

1355. **again returning:** echoing Manoa at lines 586–87, and anticipating Manoa at 1496–99. Samson for the first time expresses an awareness of renewed strength.

1369. **sentence holds:** maxim holds true.

1375. **jealousy:** In promulgating the Second Com-

mandment, God says, "I the Lord thy God am a jealous God" (Exod. 20:5).

1377. **Yet:** This word locates the *peripeteia* or "turning point," which Frye terms "the most precisely marked in the whole range of drama" (1973, 156).

1377–78. **may dispense . . . Present:** can grant a dispensation for you or me to be present.

Present in temples at idolatrous rites
For some important cause, thou need'st not doubt.
1380   *Chorus.* How thou wilt here come off surmounts my reach.
      Samson. Be of good courage, I begin to feel
Some rousing motions in me which dispose
To something extraordinary my thoughts.
I with this messenger will go along,
1385 Nothing to do, be sure, that may dishonor
Our law, or stain my vow of Nazarite.
If there be aught of presage in the mind,
This day will be remarkable in my life
By some great act, or of my days the last.
1390   *Chorus.* In time thou hast resolved, the man returns.
      Officer. Samson, this second message from our lords
To thee I am bid say. Art thou our slave,
Our captive, at the public mill our drudge,
And dar'st thou at our sending and command
1395 Dispute thy coming? Come without delay;
Or we shall find such engines to assail
And hamper thee, as thou shalt come of force,
Though thou wert firmlier fastened than a rock.
      Samson. I could be well content to try their art,
1400 Which to no few of them would prove pernicious.
Yet knowing their advantages too many,
Because they shall not trail me through their streets
Like a wild beast, I am content to go.
Masters' commands come with a power resistless
1405 To such as owe them absolute subjection;
And for a life who will not change his purpose?
(So mutable are all the ways of men.)
Yet this be sure, in nothing to comply
Scandalous or forbidden in our Law.
1410   *Officer.* I praise thy resolution; doff these links:
By this compliance thou wilt win the lords
To favor, and perhaps to set thee free.

1380. **come off:** escape.

1382. **motions:** workings of God in the soul. Recent readers vary on whether the motions are divine in origin or generated/imagined by Samson. The Argument declares that Samson was "persuaded inwardly that this was from God." See line 1426.

1389. **or:** By the end of the drama, we realize that the alternatives are simultaneously true, as Samson performs a great act on the last day of his life. This ironical play with the word *or* oc-

curs often in the work. It was first noticed by Summers (158–59), termed "the irony of alternatives" by Low (1974, 79–83), and related to the effect of eternity on dramatic plot by Tayler (1979, 118–22).

1400. **pernicious:** deadly.

1402. **Because:** so that.

1410. **praise thy resolution:** the Philistine praises the resolution to go, but not the resolution to obey Hebrew law.

      Samson. Brethren farewell, your company along
      I will not wish, lest it perhaps offend them
1415 To see me girt with friends; and how the sight
      Of me as of a common enemy,
      So dreaded once, may now exasperate them
      I know not. Lords are lordliest in their wine;
      And the well-feasted priest then soonest fired
1420 With zeal, if aught religion seem concerned:
      No less the people on their holy-days
      Impetuous, insolent, unquenchable;
      Happen what may, of me expect to hear
      Nothing dishonorable, impure, unworthy
1425 Our God, our law, my nation, or myself,
      The last of me or no I cannot warrant.
          Chorus. Go, and the Holy One
      Of Israel be thy guide
      To what may serve his glory best, and spread his name
1430 Great among the heathen round:
      Send thee the angel of thy birth, to stand
      Fast by thy side, who from thy father's field
      Rode up in flames after his message told
      Of thy conception, and be now a shield
1435 Of fire; that spirit that first rushed on thee
      In the camp of Dan
      Be efficacious in thee now at need.
      For never was from Heaven imparted
      Measure of strength so great to mortal seed,
1440 As in thy wond'rous actions hath been seen.
      But wherefore comes old Manoa in such haste
      With youthful steps? Much livelier than erewhile
      He seems: supposing here to find his son,
      Or of him bringing to us some glad news?
1445   *Manoa.* Peace with you brethren; my inducement hither
      Was not at present here to find my son,
      By order of the lords new parted hence
      To come and play before them at their feast.
      I heard all as I came, the city rings,

1420. **if aught:** if in any way.
1426. "I cannot be confident whether or not this is my last day."
1431–35. See lines 23–29.
1435–36. Samson first learned of his power when

"the Spirit of the Lord began to move him at times in the camp of Dan" (Judg. 13.25).
1442. **Much livelier than erewhile:** See lines 336–37.
1445. **Peace with you:** a common salutation in the Bible (Judg. 6.23, 19.20).

1450 And numbers thither flock; I had no will,
    Lest I should see him forced to things unseemly.
    But that which moved my coming now, was chiefly
    To give ye part with me what hope I have
    With good success to work his liberty.
1455   *Chorus.* That hope would much rejoice us to partake
    With thee; say reverend sire, we thirst to hear.
        Manoa. I have attempted one by one the lords
    Either at home, or through the high street passing,
    With supplication prone and father's tears
1460 To accept of ransom for my son their pris'ner.
    Some much averse I found and wondrous harsh,
    Contemptuous, proud, set on revenge and spite;
    That part most reverenced Dagon and his priests:
    Others more moderate seeming, but their aim
1465 Private reward, for which both god and state
    They easily would set to sale; a third
    More generous far and civil, who confessed
    They had enough revenged, having reduced
    Their foe to misery beneath their fears,
1470 The rest was magnanimity to remit,
    If some convenient ransom were proposed.
    What noise or shout was that? It tore the sky.
        Chorus. Doubtless the people shouting to behold
    Their once great dread, captive, and blind before them,
1475 Or at some proof of strength before them shown.
        Manoa. His ransom, if my whole inheritance
    May compass it, shall willingly be paid
    And numbered down: much rather I shall choose
    To live the poorest in my tribe, than richest,
1480 And he in that calamitous prison left.
    No, I am fixed not to part hence without him.
    For his redemption all my patrimony,
    If need be, I am ready to forego

1450. **I had no will:** I had no desire to go to the feast.

1453. **give ye part:** let you share.

1454. **success:** outcome.

1457. **attempted:** entreated.

1459. **prone:** either prostrate or bending forward.

1461–66. **Some . . . to sale:** Early readers quoted by Todd recognized topical allusions here. According to Thyer, in describing the first group, that *reverenced Dagon and his priests,* Milton "in-

dulges that inveterate spleen, which he always had against public and established religion." Dunster saw in the second, *more moderate seeming* group, the "Presbyterian party."

1470. They thought it magnanimous to give up the rest of their revenge.

1478. **numbered down:** counted out.

1481. **not to part hence without him:** Nor does he, albeit with Samson's dead body. This speech brims with ironies.

And quit: not wanting him, I shall want nothing.

1485   *Chorus.* Fathers are wont to lay up for their sons,
Thou for thy son are bent to lay out all;
Sons wont to nurse their parents in old age,
Thou in old age car'st how to nurse thy son,
Made older than thy age through eyesight lost.

1490   *Manoa.* It shall be my delight to tend his eyes,
And view him sitting in the house, ennobled
With all those high exploits by him achieved,
And on his shoulders waving down those locks,
That of a nation armed the strength contained:

1495 And I persuade me God had not permitted
His strength again to grow up with his hair
Garrisoned round about him like a camp
Of faithful soldiery, were not his purpose
To use him further yet in some great service,

1500 Not to sit idle with so great a gift
Useless, and thence ridiculous about him.
And since his strength with eyesight was not lost,
God will restore him eyesight to his strength.

    Chorus. Thy hopes are not ill founded, nor seem vain,

1505 Of his delivery, and thy joy thereon
Conceived, agreeable to a father's love,
In both which we, as next, participate.

    Manoa. I know your friendly minds—O what noise!
Mercy of Heav'n what hideous noise was that?

1510 Horribly loud unlike the former shout.

    Chorus. Noise call you it or universal groan
As if the whole inhabitation perished,
Blood, death, and deathful deeds are in that noise,
Ruin, destruction at the utmost point.

1515   *Manoa.* Of ruin indeed methought I heard the noise,
O it continues, they have slain my son.

    Chorus. Thy son is rather slaying them, that outcry
From slaughter of one foe could not ascend.

    Manoa. Some dismal accident it needs must be;

1484. **wanting:** lacking.
1485. **wont:** accustomed to.
1495. **had not:** would not have.
1503. **to:** in addition to.
1504–5. **Thy hopes . . . delivery:** I.e., "Your hope of freeing Samson, as opposed to your hope for his recovered eyesight, is neither baseless nor

foolish"; the Chorus, however, will in a moment join in that hope (1527–28).
1506. **agreeable to:** suitable to.
1507. **next:** next of kin (the Chorus are Danites).
1515. **ruin:** with its literal Latin meaning of "fall" or "collapse"; a favorite word of Milton's, e.g., Satan's fall from Heaven in "hideous ruin" (*PL* 1.46).

1520 What shall we do, stay here or run and see?
      Chorus. Best keep together here, lest running thither
  We unawares run into danger's mouth.
  This evil on the Philistines is fall'n,
  From whom could else a general cry be heard?
1525 The sufferers then will scarce molest us here,
  From other hands we need not much to fear.
  What if his eyesight (for to Israel's God
  Nothing is hard) by miracle restored,
  He now be dealing dole among his foes,
1530 And over heaps of slaughtered walk his way?
      Manoa. That were a joy presumptuous to be thought.
      Chorus. Yet God hath wrought things as incredible
  For his people of old; what hinders now?
      Manoa. He can, I know, but doubt to think he will;
1535 Yet hope would fain subscribe, and tempts belief.
  A little stay will bring some notice hither.
      Chorus. Of good or bad so great, of bad the sooner;
  For evil news rides post, while good news baits.
  And to our wish I see one hither speeding,
1540 An Hebrew, as I guess, and of our tribe.
      Messenger. O whither shall I run, or which way fly
  The sight of this so horrid spectacle
  Which erst my eyes beheld and yet behold;
  For dire imagination still pursues me.
1545 But providence or instinct of nature seems,
  Or reason though disturbed, and scarce consulted,
  To have guided me aright, I know not how,
  To thee first reverend Manoa, and to these
  My countrymen, whom here I knew remaining,
1550 As at some distance from the place of horror,
  So in the sad event too much concerned.
      Manoa. The accident was loud, and here before thee
  With rueful cry, yet what it was we hear not:
  No preface needs, thou seest we long to know.

1527–37. In the 1671 edition, lines 1527–35 and 1537 were missing, but printed in the Omissa, and line 1536 was given to the Chorus, not Manoa. We print the passage as it appeared in the second edition of 1680.

1529. **dole:** dealing of blows, death, and the grief those deaths will cause.

1535. **fain subscribe:** assent willingly.

1538. **rides post:** travels quickly; **baits:** rests (and therefore travels slowly).

1539. **to:** according to.

1543. **erst:** just now.

1552. **accident:** as yet unexplained occurrence; the word has its root in the Latin *cadere*, "to fall," as does *Occasions* at line 1596.

1555   *Messenger.* It would burst forth, but I recover breath
And sense distract, to know well what I utter.
     Manoa. Tell us the sum, the circumstance defer.
     Messenger. Gaza yet stands, but all her sons are fall'n,
All in a moment overwhelmed and fall'n.
1560   *Manoa.* Sad, but thou know'st to Israelites not saddest
The desolation of a hostile city.
     Messenger. Feed on that first, there may in grief be surfeit.
     Manoa. Relate by whom.
     Messenger.   By Samson.
     Manoa.   That still less'ns
The sorrow, and converts it nigh to joy.
1565   *Messenger.* Ah Manoa I refrain, too suddenly
To utter what will come at last too soon;
Lest evil tidings with too rude irruption
Hitting thy agèd ear should pierce too deep.
     Manoa. Suspense in news is torture, speak them out.
1570   *Messenger.* Then take the worst in brief, Samson is dead.
     Manoa. The worst indeed, O all my hope's defeated
To free him hence! But death who sets all free
Hath paid his ransom now and full discharge.
What windy joy this day had I conceived
1575 Hopeful of his delivery, which now proves
Abortive as the first-born bloom of spring
Nipped with the lagging rear of winter's frost.
Yet ere I give the reins to grief, say first,
How died he? Death to life is crown or shame.
1580 All by him fell thou say'st, by whom fell he,
What glorious hand gave Samson his death's wound?
     Messenger. Unwounded of his enemies he fell.
     Manoa. Wearied with slaughter then or how? Explain.
     Messenger. By his own hands.
     Manoa.   Self-violence? What cause
1585 Brought him so soon at variance with himself
Among his foes?
     Messenger.   Inevitable cause
At once both to destroy and be destroyed;
The edifice where all were met to see him
Upon their heads and on his own he pulled.
1590   *Manoa.* O lastly over-strong against thyself!

1567. **irruption:** breaking in.
1574. **windy:** vain, empty.
1574–75. **conceived . . . delivery:** imagined . . . emancipation, with an implied metaphor of conception and birth.

A dreadful way thou took'st to thy revenge.
More than enough we know; but while things yet
Are in confusion, give us if thou canst,
Eye-witness of what first or last was done,
1595 Relation more particular and distinct.
    Messenger. Occasions drew me early to this city,
And as the gates I entered with sunrise,
The morning trumpets festival proclaimed
Through each high street: little I had dispatched
1600 When all abroad was rumored that this day
Samson should be brought forth to show the people
Proof of his mighty strength in feats and games;
I sorrowed at his captive state, but minded
Not to be absent at that spectacle.
1605 The building was a spacious theater
Half round on two main pillars vaulted high,
With seats where all the lords and each degree
Of sort, might sit in order to behold;
The other side was open, where the throng
1610 On banks and scaffolds under sky might stand;
I among these aloof obscurely stood.
The feast and noon grew high, and sacrifice
Had filled their hearts with mirth, high cheer, and wine,
When to their sports they turned. Immediately
1615 Was Samson as a public servant brought,
In their state livery clad; before him pipes
And timbrels, on each side went armèd guards,
Both horse and foot before him and behind
Archers, and slingers, cataphracts and spears.
1620 At sight of him the people with a shout
Rifted the air, clamoring their god with praise,
Who had made their dreadful enemy their thrall.
He patient but undaunted where they led him,
Came to the place, and what was set before him
1625 Which without help of eye might be assayed,
To heave, pull, draw, or break, he still performed

1595. **relation:** report.
1596. **Occasions:** business affairs.
1599. **little I had dispatched:** I had not completed much business.
1603. **minded:** decided.
1605–10. For the temple of Dagon, see Judg. 16.25–29; for the significance of Milton's modifications, see 1659n. The choice of sun or shade

from the opening of the poem becomes, at the temple of Dagon, life or death.
1610. **banks:** benches; **scaffolds:** stands.
1616. **livery:** uniform. Cf. the officer's words at lines 1317–18.
1617. **timbrels:** tambourines.
1619. **cataphracts:** mounted and armored soldiers; **spears:** spearsmen.

All with incredible, stupendious force,
None daring to appear antagonist.
At length for intermission sake they led him
1630 Between the pillars; he his guide requested
(For so from such as nearer stood we heard)
As overtired to let him lean a while
With both his arms on those two massy pillars
That to the archèd roof gave main support.
1635 He unsuspicious led him; which when Samson
Felt in his arms, with head a while inclined,
And eyes fast fixed he stood, as one who prayed,
Or some great matter in his mind revolved.
At last with head erect thus cried aloud,
1640 "Hitherto, lords, what your commands imposed
I have performed, as reason was, obeying,
Not without wonder or delight beheld.
Now of my own accord such other trial
I mean to show you of my strength, yet greater;
1645 As with amaze shall strike all who behold."
This uttered, straining all his nerves he bowed,
As with the force of winds and waters pent,
When mountains tremble, those two massy pillars
With horrible convulsion to and fro
1650 He tugged, he shook, till down they came and drew
The whole roof after them, with burst of thunder
Upon the heads of all who sat beneath,
Lords, ladies, captains, counsellors, or priests,
Their choice nobility and flower, not only
1655 Of this but each Philistian city round
Met from all parts to solemnize this feast.
Samson with these immixed, inevitably
Pulled down the same destruction on himself;
The vulgar only scaped who stood without.

1630. **his guide:** the "lad" of Judg. 16.26; for the episode of the destruction of the Temple, see Judg. 16.23–30.
1637. **as one who prayed:** Milton is more ambiguous than his source. In Judg. 16.28–30, Samson clearly prays, and in doing so asks to die with the Philistines; see Allen 83f. In the poem, Samson appears to pray, and although he has wished to die throughout the work, we don't know definitely whether he does so at the end. See 1664–66n.
1645. **amaze:** confusion; see 1286n.

1647–48. Volcanoes and earthquakes were traced to subterranean motions of wind and water, as in *PL* 1.230–37 and 6.195–98. The winds of the earth were also thought to play a part in various meterological phenomena, such as comets and meteors.
1659. **vulgar:** common people; Milton changes Judges, in which three thousand watching from the roof perish in addition to the Philistine nobility, in order to save the common people. See 3n. Those who abhor the climactic violence often speak of it as an indiscriminate ethnic

1660   *Chorus.* O dearly-bought revenge, yet glorious!
      Living or dying thou hast fulfilled
      The work for which thou wast foretold
      To Israel, and now li'st victorious
      Among thy slain self-killed
1665 Not willingly, but tangled in the fold
      Of dire necessity, whose law in death conjoined
      Thee with thy slaughtered foes in number more
      Than all thy life had slain before.
          Semichorus. While their hearts were jocund and sublime,
1670 Drunk with idolatry, drunk with wine,
      And fat regorged of bulls and goats,
      Chanting their idol, and preferring
      Before our Living Dread who dwells
      In Silo his bright sanctuary:
1675 Among them he a spirit of frenzy sent,
      Who hurt their minds,
      And urged them on with mad desire
      To call in haste for their destroyer;
      They only set on sport and play
1680 Unwittingly importuned
      Their own destruction to come speedy upon them.
      So fond are mortal men
      Fall'n into wrath divine,
      As their own ruin on themselves to invite,
1685 Insensate left, or to sense reprobate,
      And with blindness internal struck.
          Semichorus. But he though blind of sight,
      Despised and thought extinguished quite,
      With inward eyes illuminated
1690 His fiery virtue roused
      From under ashes into sudden flame,

---

cleansing. But it is more precisely a slaughter of the Philistine aristocracy.

1660–1707. Hale discusses the way Pindaric elements appear in this passage and ultimately dominate the choral victory hymn, lifting the work into an epic realm (189–92).

1661. **Living or dying:** in your life and death alike.

1664–66. The Chorus agrees with St. Augustine and most annotators of Judges that Samson, because he acts on divine prompting, is not guilty of suicide; Hughes (1957) illustrates the contrary position from Donne's *Biathanatos* (3.5.4).

The Argument speaks of "what Samson had done to the Philistines, and by accident to himself." It seems likely that the Chorus speaks for Milton, though the point cannot be proven.

1669. **sublime:** uplifted, elated.

1671. **fat:** Leonard notes that the eating of fat is prohibited in Lev. 3.17.

1674. **Silo:** Shiloh, then the location of the Ark of the Covenant.

1682. **fond:** foolish.

1685. "Left senseless or with godless (and therefore disordered) sense."

And as an ev'ning dragon came,
Assailant on the perchèd roosts,
And nests in order ranged
1695 Of tame villatic fowl; but as an eagle
His cloudless thunder bolted on their heads.
So virtue giv'n for lost,
Depressed, and overthrown, as seemed,
Like that self-begott'n bird
1700 In the Arabian woods embossed,
That no second knows nor third,
And lay erewhile a holocaust,
From out her ashy womb now teemed,
Revives, reflourishes, then vigorous most
1705 When most unactive deemed,
And though her body die, her fame survives
A secular bird ages of lives.
    Manoa. Come, come, no time for lamentation now,
Nor much more cause; Samson hath quit himself
1710 Like Samson, and heroic'ly hath finished
A life heroic, on his enemies
Fully revenged, hath left them years of mourning,
And lamentation to the sons of Caphtor

1692. **dragon:** serpent. Readers have traditionally pictured a large snake and been perplexed by the adjective *evening*. See Dobranski, 454–57. Tayler (1972) suggested the *draco volans,* or fire-drake, a comet Londoners occasionally saw at evening over the Thames (Winny, 167–68). This identification makes better sense of *fiery virtue* and *sudden flame,* and also links with the *winds* of line 1647. Comets were thought to begin as windy exhalations from the earth.

1695. **villatic:** barnyard (Italian *villa* means "farm-house"). **but as an eagle:** The second meta-phorical bird, the eagle, traditionally delivered the thunderbolts of Jove and was immune to their power. Carey (1997) accuses Tayler of missing the "contrastive force" of *but* in identi-fying the evening dragon with a comet (see pre-vious note). The word indicates that the eagle attacks suddenly from above while the evening dragon comes slowly and attacks from below, and cannot therefore be a comet. But it may be that the conjunction simply contrasts two omi-nous "birds" seen in the sky.

1696. **cloudless thunder:** Horace, *Odes* 1.34.5, at-tests to the extraordinary effect of hearing thunder on a clear day. See also Browne, *Pseu-dodoxia Epidemica* 2.5.

1697. **giv'n for:** considered.

1699. **self-begott'n bird:** The third and climactic bird, the mythical phoenix, was reborn from its ashes every five hundred or one thousand years.

1700. **embossed:** imbosked, sheltered by the woods.

1701. Only one phoenix exists at a time.

1702. **holocaust:** sacrifice consumed by fire.

1703. **teemed:** brought forth, born.

1706–7. Most editors print a comma at the end of l. 1706, which derives from the Errata to the first printing in 1671. Calton and Newton (1753) sug-gest deleting the comma. See Dobranski, 462–63, on the controversy. With a comma, the lines mean that the fame of virtue lasts, as the Phoenix lasts, ages of lives. Without it, the lines mean that the fame of virtue outlives any par-ticular life of the Phoenix by ages of lives. Leaning toward the variorum's reading, we have dropped the comma.

1707. **secular:** lasting for *saecula,* ages or centuries.

1709. **quit:** acquitted.

1713. **sons of Caphtor:** Philistines.

Through all Philistian bounds. To Israel
1715 Honor hath left, and freedom, let but them
Find courage to lay hold on this occasion;
To himself and father's house eternal fame;
And which is best and happiest yet, all this
With God not parted from him, as was feared,
1720 But favoring and assisting to the end.
Nothing is here for tears, nothing to wail
Or knock the breast, no weakness, no contempt,
Dispraise, or blame, nothing but well and fair,
And what may quiet us in a death so noble.
1725 Let us go find the body where it lies
Soaked in his enemies' blood, and from the stream
With lavers pure and cleansing herbs wash off
The clotted gore. I with what speed the while
(Gaza is not in plight to say us nay)
1730 Will send for all my kindred, all my friends
To fetch him hence and solemnly attend
With silent obsequy and funeral train
Home to his father's house: there will I build him
A monument, and plant it round with shade
1735 Of laurel ever green, and branching palm,
With all his trophies hung, and acts enrolled
In copious legend, or sweet lyric song.
Thither shall all the valiant youth resort,
And from his memory inflame their breasts
1740 To matchless valor, and adventures high:
The virgins also shall on feastful days
Visit his tomb with flowers, only bewailing
His lot unfortunate in nuptial choice,
From whence captivity and loss of eyes.
1745 *Chorus.* All is best, though we oft doubt,
What th' unsearchable dispose
Of highest wisdom brings about,

1715. **hath:** he has.

1723. **nothing but well:** nothing but what is well.

1727. **lavers:** washbasins.

1728. **with what speed:** as quickly as I can.

1729. **not in plight:** not in a condition to.

1732. **obsequy:** funeral ceremony.

1736–37. **enrolled . . . legend:** written out in a detailed inscription.

1741–42. **The virgins . . . flowers:** This is the honor Dalila promised herself (986–87).

1745–48. These lines resemble the typical closing choruses of Euripides, which emphasize the unpredictable nature of divine intervention in human affairs.

1745–58. The Chorus's final speech, although mixing tetrameter and pentameter lines and including two trochaic lines, is modeled on the English or Shakespearean sonnet.

1746. **dispose:** disposition, dispensation.

And ever best found in the close.
Oft he seems to hide his face,
1750 But unexpectedly returns
And to his faithful champion hath in place
Bore witness gloriously; whence Gaza mourns
And all that band them to resist
His uncontrollable intent;
1755 His servants he with new acquist
Of true experience from this great event
With peace and consolation hath dismissed,
And calm of mind, all passion spent.

1749. **hide his face:** God is figured as hiding his
face in anger in Ps. 27.9 and 30.7.
1755. **His servants:** Manoa, the Chorus, and Mil-
ton's sympathetic readers; **acquist:** acquisition.

1758. A perfect definition of regained faith and
cathartic cure, and a perfect line on which to
end a poetic career.

WORKS CITED

I. EDITIONS OF MILTON

Browne, R. C. *English Poems by John Milton.* 2 vols. Clarendon Press, 1894.

Carey, John. *Complete Shorter Poems.* 2nd ed. Longman, 1997.

Cowper, William. *Latin and Italian Poems of John Milton: Translated into English Verse, and a Fragment of a Commentary on Paradise Lost.* J. Johnson, 1808.

Flannagan, Roy. *The Riverside Milton.* Houghton Mifflin, 1998.

Honigmann, E. A. J. *Milton's Sonnets.* St. Martin's Press, 1966.

Hughes, Merritt Y. *Complete Poems and Major Prose.* Odyssey Press, 1957.

Leonard, John. *John Milton: The Complete Poems.* Penguin, 1998.

Masson, David. *The Poetical Works of John Milton.* 3 vols. Macmillan, 1882.

Newton, Thomas. *Paradise Regained . . . Samson Agonistes . . . and Poems upon Several Occasions.* 2 vols. Tonson, 1753.

Ricks, Christopher. *John Milton: "Paradise Lost" and "Paradise Regained."* Signet Classics, 1968.

Smart, John S. *The Sonnets of Milton.* Maclehose, 1923.

Todd, H. J. *The Poetical Works of John Milton.* 6 vols. R. Gilpert, 1826.

Verity, A. W. *Milton's Ode on the Morning of Christ's Nativity, L'Allegro, Il Penseroso and Lycidas.* Cambridge Univ. Press, 1891.

———. *Milton's Samson Agonistes.* Cambridge Univ. Press, 1897.

———. *Comus.* Cambridge Univ. Press, 1909.

Warton, Thomas. *Poems upon Several Occasions . . . by John Milton.* James Dodsley, 1785.

Wolfe, Don M., et al. *The Complete Prose Works of John Milton.* 8 vols. Yale Univ. Press, 1953–82.

Wright, B. A. *Shorter Poems of John Milton.* Macmillan, 1938.

II. CRITICAL AND HISTORICAL WORKS

Achinstein, Sharon. *Literature and Dissent in Milton's England.* Cambridge Univ. Press, 2003.

Allen, D.C. *The Harmonious Vision: Studies in Milton's Poetry.* Johns Hopkins Univ. Press, 1954.

Aubrey, John. *Aubrey's Brief Lives,* ed. Oliver Lawson Dick. Secker and Warburg, 1950.

Bacon, Francis. *Of the Proficiencie and Advancement of Learning.* Henrie Tomes, 1605.

Baldwin, Edward C. "Shook the Arsenal: A Note on *Paradise Regained*," *Philological Quarterly* 18 (1939): 218–22.

Barker, Arthur. "The Pattern of Milton's *Nativity Ode*," *University of Toronto Quarterly* 10 (1940–41): 167–81.

Berryman, John. *The Freedom of the Poet.* Farrar, Straus & Giroux, 1976.

Binyon, Lawrence. "A Note on Milton's Imagery and Rhythm." In John Dover Wilson, ed., *Seventeenth-Century Studies Presented to Sir Herbert Grierson,* pp. 184–92. Clarendon Press, 1938.

Boddy, Margaret. "Milton's Translation of Psalms 80–88," *Modern Philology* 64 (1966): 1–9.

Boesky, Amy. "The Maternal Shape of Mourning: A Reconsideration of *Lycidas*," *Modern Philology* 95 (1998): 463–83.

Breasted, Barbara. "*Comus* and the Castlehaven Scandal," *Milton Studies* 3 (1971): 201–24.

Brooks, Cleanth, and John Hardy. *Poems of Mr. John Milton.* Harcourt, Brace, 1951.

Browne, Sir Thomas. *Religio Medici.* Andrew Crooke, 1642.

———. *Pseudodoxia Epidemica.* Ed. Robin Robbins. 2 vols. Oxford Univ. Press, 1981.

Burton, Robert. *The Anatomy of Melancholy.* Ed. Floyd Dell and Paul Jordan-Smith. Tudor Publishing, 1927.

Calvin, John. *Institutes of the Christian Religion.* 2 vols. Trans. Ford Lewis Battles. Eerdmans, 1986.

Campbell, Gordon. *A Milton Chronology.* Macmillan, 1997.

Carey, John. "Milton's *Ad Patrem*, 35–37," *Review of English Studies* 15 (1964): 180–84.

———. *Milton.* Arco, 1970.

———. "A Work in Praise of Terrorism?" *TLS,* 6 Sept. 2002: 15–16.

Cirillo, Albert R. "Time, Light, and the Phoenix: The Design of *Samson Agonistes*." In Joseph A. Wittreich, ed., *Calm of Mind: Tercentenary Essays on Paradise Regained and Samson Agonistes,* pp. 209–33. Press of Case Western Reserve Univ., 1971.

Clark, Andrew, ed. *Aubrey's Brief Lives.* 2 vols. Clarendon Press, 1898.

Coleridge, S. T. *Table Talk.* Ed. Henry Morley. Routledge and Sons, 1886.

———. *Lectures and Notes on Shakespeare and Other English Poets.* Ed. T. Ashe. G. Bell & Sons, 1902.

Conti, Natale. *Mythologiae.* Ed. Stephen Orgel. New York, 1979.

Cowley, Abraham. *Poems.* Ed. A. R. Waller. Cambridge Univ. Press, 1905.

Creaser, John. "Editorial Problems in Milton," *Review of English Studies* XXXV, No. 135 (1983): 279–303.

————. "Editorial Problems in Milton" (Concluded), *Review of English Studies* XXXV, No. 137 (1984): 44–60.

————. "Editing *Lycidas*: The Authority of Minutiae," *Milton Quarterly* 44, No. 2 (2010): 73–121.

Crick, Julia C. *Historia Regum Britannie of Geoffrey of Monmouth.* Woodbridge, 1989.

Crump, Galbraith. "Milton: Generic Dualist," *Sewanee Review* 95 (1987): 648–56.

Darbishire, Helen. *Early Lives of Milton.* Oxford Univ. Press, 1932.

Dobranski, Stephen B. *A Variorum Commentary on the Poems of John Milton.* Ed. Paul J. Klemp. Vol. 3: *Samson Agonistes.* Duquesne Univ. Press, 2009.

Dorian, Donald C. *The English Diodatis: A History of Charles Diodati's Family and of His Friendship with Milton.* Rutgers Univ. Press, 1950.

Eliot, T. S. *On Poetry and Poets.* Faber, 1957.

———. *Selected Essays.* Harcourt, Brace & World, 1964.

Elledge, Scott, ed. *Milton's "Lycidas": Edited to Serve as an Introduction to Criticism.* Harper & Row, 1966.

Ellwood, Thomas. *The History of the Life of Thomas Ellwood.* J. Sowle, 1714.

Emerson, Ralph Waldo. *The Early Lectures of Ralph Waldo Emerson.* Ed. Stephen E. Whicher and Robert E. Spiller. 3 vols. Harvard Univ. Press, 1959.

Empson, William. "A Defense of Dalila," *Sewanee Review* 68 (1960): 240–55.

Fallon, Stephen M. *Milton Among the Philosophers: Poetry and Materialism in Seventeenth-Century England.* Cornell Univ. Press, 1991.

Felltham, Owen. *Resolves.* George Purslowe, 1628.

Ficino, Marsilio. *Commentary on Plato's Symposium on Love.* Trans. Sears Jayne. Spring Publications, 1985.

Fish, Stanley. " 'There Is Nothing He Cannot Ask': Milton, Liberalism, and Terrorism," in Michael Lieb, Albert C. Labriola, eds., *Milton in the Age of Fish: Essays on Authorship, Text, and Terrorism,* pp. 243–64. Duquesne Univ. Press, 2006.

Fixler, Michael. *Milton and the Kingdoms of God.* Faber, 1964.

Flosdorf, J. W. " 'Gums of Glutinous Heat': A Query," *Milton Quarterly* 7 (1973): 4–5.

Fowler, Alastair. *"Paradise Regained:* Some Problems of Style." In Piero Boitano, Anna Torli, eds., *Medieval and Pseudo-Medieval Literature,* pp. 181–89. Cambridge Univ. Press, 1984.

Frye, Northrop. "The Typology of *Paradise Regained,*" *Modern Philology* 53 (1956): 227–38.

———. *The Return to Eden: Five Essays on Milton's Epics.* Univ. of Toronto Press, 1965.

———. "Agon and Logos: Revolution and Revelation." In Balachandra Rajan, ed., *The Prison and the Pinnacle,* pp. 135–36. Univ. of Toronto Press, 1973.

Gaskell, Phillip. *From Writer to Reader: Studies in Editorial Method.* Clarendon Press, 1978.

Gilbert, Allan H. *A Geographical Dictionary of Milton.* Yale Univ. Press, 1919.

Goethe, Johann Wolfgang. *Conversations of Goethe with Eckermann.* Trans. John Oxenford. J. M. Dent, 1930.

Goldberg, Jonathan. *James I and the Politics of Literature.* Johns Hopkins Univ. Press, 1983.

Gregory, Tobias. "The Political Messages of *Samson Agonistes,*" *Studies in English Literature,* 50, 1 (Winter 2010): 175–203.

Grossman, Marshall. "The Fruit of One's Labor in Miltonic Practice and Marxian Theory," *English Literary History* 59 (1992): 77–105.

Guibbory, Achsah. "Rethinking Millenarianism, Messianism, and Deliverance in *Paradise Regained,*" *Milton Studies* 48 (2008): 135–59.

Hale, John. *Milton's Languages: The Impact of Multilingualism on Style.* Cambridge Univ. Press, 1997.

Hammond, Gerald. *Fleeting Things: English Poets and Poems, 1616–1660.* Harvard Univ. Press, 1990.

Hanford, James Holly. "The Chronology of Milton's Private Studies," *PMLA* 36 (1921): 251–314.

Harding, Davis P. *The Club of Hercules: Studies in the Classical Background of Paradise Lost.* Illinois Studies in Language and Literature, vol. 50. Univ. of Illinois Press, 1962.

Haskin, Dayton. *Milton's Burden of Interpretation.* Univ. of Pennsylvania Press, 1994.

Havens, Raymond Dexter. *The Influence of Milton on English Poetry.* Russell & Russell, 1961.

Heninger, S. K. *Touches of Sweet Harmony: Pythagorean Cosmology and Renaissance Poetics.* Huntington Library, 1974.

Herford, C. H., Percy Simpson, Evelyn Simpson, eds. *Ben Jonson.* 11 vols. Clarendon Press, 1935–47.

Hill, Christopher. *The English Bible and the Seventeenth-Century Revolution.* Penguin, 1993.

Hiltner, Ken. *What Else Is Pastoral?: Renaissance Literature and the Environment.* Cornell Univ. Press, 2011.

Hooker, Richard. *Of the Laws of Ecclesiastical Polity.* John Windet, 1593.

Hoxby, Blair. *Mammon's Music: Literature and Economics in the Age of Milton.* Yale Univ. Press, 2002.

Hughes, Merritt Y. " 'Lydian Airs,' " *Modern Language Notes* 40 (1925): 129–37.

Hughes, Merritt Y., et al. *A Variorum Commentary on the Poems of John Milton.* 4 vols. Columbia Univ. Press, 1970–75.

Hunter, William B. "Milton Translates the Psalms," *Philological Quarterly* 40 (1961): 485–97.

Hunter, William B., gen. ed. *A Milton Encyclopedia.* 10 vols. Bucknell Univ. Press, 1978.

Huntley, Frank Livingstone. *Bishop Joseph Hall and Protestant Meditation in Seventeenth-Century England.* Medieval and Renaissance Texts and Studies, 1981.

Huttar, Charles A. "The Passion of Christ in *Paradise Regained,*" *English Literary Notes* 19 (1982): 236–60.

Jebb, Richard. "*Samson Agonistes* and the Hellenic Drama," *Proceedings of the British Academy* 3 (1907–8): 341–48.

Johnson, Samuel. *Lives of the English Poets.* Ed. George Birkbeck Hill. 3 vols. Clarendon Press, 1905.

———. *The Yale Edition of the Works of Samuel Johnson.* Ed. W. J. Bate and Albrecht B. Strauss. Yale Univ. Press, 1958.

Jones, Richard Foster. *Ancients and Moderns: A Study of the Rise of the Scientific Movement in Seventeenth-Century England.* Univ. of California Press, 1961.

Josephus, Flavius. *Works.* Trans. William Whiston. Armstrong and Plaskitt, 1832.

Kelly, James, and Catherine Bray. "The Keys to Milton's 'Two-Handed Engine' in *Lycidas* (1637)," *Milton Quarterly* 44 (2010): 122–42.

Kermode, Frank. "*Samson Agonistes* and Hebrew Prosody," *Durham Univer. Journal* 14 (1953): 59–63.

Kerrigan, William. "The Heretical Milton: From Assumption to Mortalism," *English Literary Renaissance* 5 (1975): 125–166.

———. *The Sacred Complex: On the Psychogenesis of Paradise Lost.* Harvard Univ. Press, 1983.

———. "The Irrational Coherence of *Samson Agonistes,*" *Milton Studies* 22 (1986): 217–32.

———. "The Politically Correct *Comus*: A Reply to John Leonard," *Milton Quarterly* 27 (1993): 150–54.

Kirkconnell, Watson. *That Invincible Samson: The Theme of Samson Agonistes in World Literature with Translations of the Major Analogues.* Univ. of Toronto Press, 1964.

Klein, Robert. *Form and Meaning: Writings on the Renaissance and Modern Art.* Viking, 1979.

Klibansky, Raymond, Erwin Panofsky, and Fritz Saxl. *Saturn and Melancholy.* Nelson, 1964.

Knoppers, Laura Lunger, ed. *The Complete Works of John Milton.* Vol. 2. Oxford Univ. Press, 2009.

Krouse, F. Michael. *Milton's Samson and the Christian Tradition.* Princeton Univ. Press, 1949.

Leavis, F. R. *Revaluation: Tradition and Development in English Poetry.* George W. Stewart, 1947.

LeComte, Edward. *Milton's Unchanging Mind: Three Essays.* Kennikat Press, 1973.

Lee, Sidney, and C. T. Onions, eds. *Shakespeare's England: An Account of the Life and Manners of His Age.* 2 vols. Clarendon Press, 1916.

Leishman, J. B. *Translating Horace.* B. Cassirer, 1956.

Lewalski, Barbara Kiefer. *Milton's Brief Epic: The Genre, Meaning, and Art of Paradise Regained.* Brown Univ. Press, 1966.

Lieb, Michael. *Milton and the Culture of Violence.* Cornell Univ. Press, 1994.

Loewenstein, David. "*Samson Agonistes* and the Culture of Religious Terror." In Michael Lieb and Albert C. Labriola, eds., *Milton in the Age of Fish: Essays on Text, Authority, and Terrorism,* pp. 203–28. Duquesne University Press, 2006.

Low, Anthony. *The Blaze of Noon: A Reading of Samson Agonistes.* Columbia Univ. Press, 1974.

———. *The Georgic Revolution.* Princeton Univ. Press, 1985.

———. Review of Joseph Wittreich, *Interpreting Samson Agonistes, Journal of English and Germanic Philology* 86 (1987): 415–18.

MacCallum, Hugh. *Milton and the Sons of God: The Divine Image in Milton's Epic Poetry.* Univ. of Toronto Press, 1986.

MacKellar, Walter. *A Variorum Commentary on the Poems of John Milton,* Vol. 4: *Paradise Regained.* Columbia Univ. Press, 1975.

Madsen, William. "From Shadowy Types to Truth." In Joseph H. Summers, ed., *The Lyric and Dramatic Milton,* pp. 94–114. Columbia Univ. Press, 1965.

Mahomed, Feisal G. "Confronting Religious Violence: Milton's *Samson Agonistes," PMLA* 120 (2005): 327–40.

———. "Reading *Samson* in the New American Century," *Milton Studies* 46 (2006): 243–63.

Marcus, Leah. "The Milieu of Milton's *Comus*: Judicial Reform at Ludlow and the Problem of Sexual Assault," *Criticism* 25 (1983): 293–327.

———. *The Politics of Mirth: Jonson, Herrick, Milton, Marvell, and the Defense of Old Holiday Pastimes.* Univ. of Chicago Press, 1986.

Martz, Louis. "*Paradise Regained*: The Meditative Combat," *English Literary History* 27 (1960): 223–47.

Masson, David. *The Life of John Milton.* 6 vols. Peter Smith, 1965.

Mieder, Wolfgang, ed. *A Dictionary of American Proverbs.* Oxford Univ. Press, 1992.

Milgate, Wesley, ed. *The Satires, Epigrams and Verse Letters of John Donne.* Clarendon Press, 1992.

Miller, Leo. "John Milton's 'Lost' Sonnet to Mary Powell," *Milton Quarterly* 25 (1991): 102–7.

Morse, C. J. "The Dating of Milton's Sonnet XIX," *TLS,* 15 Sept. 1961: 620.

Moseley, C. W. R. D. *The Poetic Birth: Milton's Poems of 1645.* Scolar Press, 1991.

Mueller, Janel. "The Figure and the Ground: Samson as a Hero of London Nonconformity, 1662–1667." In Graham Parry, Joad Raymond, eds., *Milton and the Terms of Liberty,* pp. 137–62. Cambridge University Press, 2002.

Multhauf, Robert P. "Van Helmont's Reformation of the Galenic Doctrine of Digestion," *Bulletin of the History of Medicine* 29 (1955): 154–63.

Mundhenk, Rosemary K. "Dark Scandal and the Sun-Clad Power of Chastity: The His-
torical Milieu of Milton's *Comus*," *Studies in English Literature* 15 (1975): 141–52.

Nelson, Jr., Lowry. *Baroque Lyric Poetry.* Yale Univ. Press, 1961.

Nicolson, Marjorie Hope. *The Breaking of the Circle: Studies in the Effect of the "New Science"
on Seventeenth-Century Poetry.* Columbia Univ. Press, 1960.

O'Reilly, Mary Oates. "A New Song: Singing Space in Milton's Nativity Ode." In Eu-
gene Hill, William Kerrigan, eds., *The Wit to Know: Essays on English Renaissance Liter-
ature for Edward Tayler,* pp. 95–116. George Herbert Journal Monographs, 2000.

Orgel, Stephen. *The Illusion of Power: Political Theater in the English Renaissance.* Univ. of
California Press, 1975.

Panofsky, Erwin. *Studies in Iconology.* Harper & Row, 1967.

Parker, William R. *Milton's Debt to Greek Tragedy in Samson Agonistes.* Johns Hopkins Univ.
Press, 1937.

———. "Milton's Last Sonnet," *Review of English Studies* 21 (1945): 235–38.

———. "The Date of *Samson Agonistes*," *Philological Quarterly* 18 (1949): 145–66.

———. *Milton: A Biography.* 2 vols. Clarendon Press, 1968.

———. *Milton's Contemporary Reputation.* Haskell House, 1971.

Parry, Graham. *The Golden Age Restor'd: The Culture of the Stuart Court, 1603–42.* St. Martin's
Press, 1981.

Patrides, C. A. *Milton's Lycidas: The Tradition and the Poem.* Univ. of Missouri Press, 1983.

Pope, Elizabeth M. *Paradise Regained: The Tradition and the Poem.* Johns Hopkins Univ.
Press, 1947.

Prince, F. T. *The Italian Element in Milton's Verse.* Clarendon Press, 1954.

Quint, David. "Expectation and Prematurity in Milton's Nativity Ode," *Modern Philol-
ogy* 97 (1999): 195–219.

Rajan, Balachandra. "Samson Hath Quit Himself/Like Samson," *Milton Quarterly* 41,
No. 1 (2007): 1–11.

Revard, Stella. "Milton and Millenarianism: From the Nativity Ode to *Paradise Re-
gained*." In Juliet Cummins, ed., *Milton and the Ends of Time,* pp. 42–81. Cambridge
University Press, 2003.

Richardson, Robert D. *Emerson: The Mind on Fire.* Univ. of California Press, 1995.

Rogers, John. "*Paradise Regained* and the Memory of *Paradise Lost*." In Nicholas McDow-
ell, Nigel Smith, eds., *The Oxford Handbook of Milton,* pp. 589–612. Oxford Univ. Press,
2009.

Rohr-Sauer, Philipp von. *English Metrical Psalms from 1600 to 1660.* Poppen & Ortmann,
1938.

Rumrich, John Peter. "*Samson* and the Excluded Middle." In Mark R. Kelley, Joseph A.
Wittreich, eds., *Altering Eyes: New Perspectives on Samson Agonistes,* pp. 307–32. Univ. of
Delaware Press, 2002.

———. "Milton's *Theanthropos*: The Body of Christ in *Paradise Regained*," *Milton Studies*
42 (2003): 50–67.

Rust, George. *A Letter of Resolution Concerning Origen and the Chief of His Opinions.* Colum-
bia Univ. Press, 1933.

Salmasius, Claudius. *Defensio Regia, pro Carolo I* [*Defense of Kingship, on behalf of Charles I*].
Sumptibus Regiis, 1650.

Samuel, Irene. "*Samson Agonistes* as Tragedy." In Joseph A. Wittreich, ed., *Calm of Mind,*
pp. 335–58. Press of Case Western Reserve Univ., 1971.

Schwartz, Louis. *Milton and Maternal Mortality.* Cambridge Univ. Press, 2009.

Schwartz, Regina M. "Redemption and *Paradise Regained,*" *Milton Studies* 42 (2003): 26–49.

Sellin, Paul R. "Sources of Milton's Catharsis: A Reconsideration," *Journal of English and Germanic Philology* 60 (1961): 712–20.

———. "Milton's Epithet *Agonistes,*" *Studies in English Literature* 4 (1964): 137–62.

Shakespeare, William. *The First Folio of Shakespeare: The Norton Facsimile,* ed. Charlton Hinman. W. W. Norton, 1968.

Shawcross, John T. *Milton: The Critical Heritage.* 2 vols. Routledge, 1970–72.

Shoulson, Jeffrey S. "Milton and Enthusiasm: Radical Religion and the Poetics of *Paradise Regained,*" *Milton Studies* 47 (2008): 219–57.

Shumaker, Wayne. *Renaissance Curiosa.* Center for Medieval and Early Renaissance Studies, 1982.

Smith, G. C. Moore. "Milton and Randolph," *TLS,* 19 Jan. 1922: 44.

Spitzer, Leo. *Classical and Christian Ideas of World Harmony,* ed. A. G. Hatcher. Johns Hopkins Univ. Press, 1963.

Sprott, S. E. *John Milton: "A Maske," the Earlier Versions.* Univ. of Toronto Press, 1973.

Stoll, Abraham. *Milton and Monotheism.* Duquesne Univ. Press, 2009.

Studley, Marian H. "Milton and the Paraphrases of the Psalms," *Philological Quarterly* 4 (1925): 364–72.

Summers, Joseph, ed. *The Lyric and Dramatic Milton.* Columbia Univ. Press, 1965.

Svendsen, Kester. "Milton's Aery Microscope," *Modern Language Notes* 64 (1949): 525–27.

———. *Milton and Science.* Greenwood Press, 1969.

Tayler, Edward W. "Milton's Firedrake," *Milton Quarterly* 6 (1972): 7–10.

———. *Milton's Poetry: Its Development in Time.* Duquesne Univ. Press, 1979.

Teskey, Gordon. "Introduction" to David R. Slavitt, trans., *Milton's Latin Poems.* Johns Hopkins Univ. Press, 2011.

Tilley, Morris Palmer. *A Dictionary of the Proverbs in England in the Sixteenth and Seventeenth Centuries.* Univ. of Michigan Press, 1966.

Tuve, Rosemond. *Images and Themes in Five Poems by Milton.* Harvard Univ. Press, 1957.

Ulreich, John C. " 'Incident of All Our Sex': The Tragedy of Dalila." In Julia M. Walker, ed., *Milton and the Idea of Woman,* pp. 185–210. Univ. of Illinois Press, 1988.

Welsford, Enid. *The Court Masque.* Cambridge Univ. Press, 1927.

Williams, R. F., ed. *The Court and Times of Charles the First.* 2 vols. H. Colburn, 1848.

Wilson, F. P. *The Plague in Shakespeare's London.* 2nd ed. Oxford Univ. Press, 1963.

Wilson, F. P., ed. *The Oxford Dictionary of English Proverbs.* Clarendon Press, 1970.

Wittkower, Rudolf, and Margot Wittkower. *Born Under Saturn.* Norton, 1963.

Wittreich, Joseph A. *Interpreting Samson Agonistes.* Princeton Univ. Press, 1986.

Worden, Blair. "Milton, *Samson Agonistes,* and the Restoration." In Gerald MacLean, ed., *Culture and Society in the Stuart Restoration,* pp. 111–36. Cambridge Univ. Press, 1995.

Wright, George. "Hendiadys and *Hamlet,*" *PMLA* 96 (1981): 168–93.

Yates, Frances A. *Giordano Bruno and the Hermetic Tradition.* Vintage, 1969.

INDEX

This index includes names of historical persons and authors to whom Milton refers, or who are mentioned in the accompanying text and footnotes. Names of biblical and mythological characters are omitted. Milton's name and the titles of his works are not indexed; however, his Milton and Phillips relatives are included.

ABOUT THE EDITORS

WILLIAM KERRIGAN is the author of many books, including *The Sacred Complex: On the Psychogenesis of Paradise Lost,* for which he won the James Holly Hanford Award of the Milton Society of America. A former president of the Milton Society, he has also earned numerous honors and distinctions from that group, including its award for lifetime achievement. He is professor emeritus at the University of Massachusetts.

JOHN RUMRICH is the author of *Matter of Glory: A New Preface to Paradise Lost* and *Milton Unbound: Controversy and Reinterpretation.* An award-winning editor and writer, he is A. J. and W. D. Thaman Professor of English at the University of Texas at Austin, where he teaches early modern British literature.

STEPHEN M. FALLON is the author of *Milton's Peculiar Grace: Self-Representation and Authority* and *Milton among the Philosophers: Poetry and Materialism in Seventeenth-Century England,* winner of the Milton Society's Hanford Award. He is professor of liberal studies and English at the University of Notre Dame.

A NOTE ON THE TYPE

The principal text of this Modern Library edition
was set in a digitized version of Janson, a typeface that
dates from about 1690 and was cut by Nicholas Kis,
a Hungarian working in Amsterdam. The original matrices have
survived and are held by the Stempel foundry in Germany.
Hermann Zapf redesigned some of the weights and sizes for
Stempel, basing his revisions on the original design.

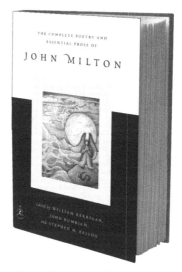

MODERN LIBRARY IS ONLINE AT
WWW.MODERNLIBRARY.COM

MODERN LIBRARY ONLINE IS YOUR GUIDE
TO CLASSIC LITERATURE ON THE WEB

THE MODERN LIBRARY E-NEWSLETTER

Our free e-mail newsletter is sent to subscribers, and features sample chapters, interviews with and essays by our authors, upcoming books, special promotions, announcements, and news. To subscribe to the Modern Library e-newsletter, visit **www.modernlibrary.com**

THE MODERN LIBRARY WEBSITE

Check out the Modern Library website at
www.modernlibrary.com for:

- The Modern Library e-newsletter
- A list of our current and upcoming titles and series
- Reading Group Guides and exclusive author spotlights
- Special features with information on the classics and other paperback series
- Excerpts from new releases and other titles
- A list of our e-books and information on where to buy them
- The Modern Library Editorial Board's 100 Best Novels and 100 Best Nonfiction Books of the Twentieth Century written in the English language
- News and announcements

Questions? E-mail us at **modernlibrary@randomhouse.com**.
For questions about examination or desk copies, please visit
the Random House Academic Resources site at
www.randomhouse.com/academic.

Printed in the United States
by Baker & Taylor Publisher Services